"You don't want to stay down here steaming like a clam. We can clear out, go up to Saratoga for the races. That's where I'm heading for. I wouldn't be here this long if it wasn't for you. You got me roped and tied, seems like."

"Saratoga? Is that a nice place?"

"July and August there's nothing like it in the whole country. Races every day, gambling, millionaires and pickpockets and sporting people and respectable family folks and politicians and famous theater actors and actresses, you'll find them all at Saratoga."

EDNA FERBER
Saratoga Trunk

PRAISE FOR STEPHEN DOBYNS'S
CHARLIE BRADSHAW MYSTERIES

"A cross between Graham Greene and Raymond Chandler"

—*The Washington Post*

"The Bradshaw series is unusually well done. Mr. Dobyns is a superb stylist and never is there a false note in his characterizations or dialogue."

—*The New York Times Book Review*

"Dobyns is a poet who also writes detective novels and this lends his fiction a glow uncommon in the genre."

—*The New Yorker*

"Stephen Dobyns is one of the most imaginative creators of fiction on the current scene."

—*San Francisco Chronicle*

"I look forward to any and all of Stephen Dobyns's Charlie Bradshaw novels. . . . This is a first-rate series, and it appears only to be getting better."

—*Minneapolis Star-Tribune*

"Dick Francis . . . had better look to his laurels. An American long shot, appropriately named Dobyns, is coming up fast on the outside."

—*The Houston Post*

PENGUIN CRIME FICTION

SARATOGA TRIFECTA

Stephen Dobyns is a professor of English at Syracuse University who also teaches in the MFA program at Warren Wilson College. He is the author of fifteen novels and eight volumes of poetry. He has written eight Charlie Bradshaw mysteries.

Books by Stephen Dobyns

NOVELS

Saratoga Backtalk
The Wrestler's Cruel Study
Saratoga Haunting
After Shocks/Near Escapes
Saratoga Hexameter
The House on Alexandrine
Saratoga Bestiary
The Two Deaths of Señora Puccini
A Boat Off the Coast
Saratoga Snapper
Cold Dog Soup
Saratoga Headhunter
Dancer with One Leg
Saratoga Swimmer
Saratoga Longshot
A Man of Little Evils

POETRY

Velocities: New and Selected Poems, 1966–1992
Body Traffic
Cemetery Nights
Black Dog, Red Dog
The Balthus Poems
Heat Death
Griffon
Concurring Beasts

Stephen Dobyns

SARATOGA TRIFECTA

▼▼▼

SARATOGA LONGSHOT

SARATOGA SWIMMER

SARATOGA HEADHUNTER

PENGUIN BOOKS

PENGUIN BOOKS
Published by the Penguin Group
Penguin Books USA Inc., 375 Hudson Street,
New York, New York 10014, U.S.A.
Penguin Books Ltd, 27 Wrights Lane,
London W8 5TZ, England
Penguin Books Australia Ltd, Ringwood,
Victoria, Australia
Penguin Books Canada Ltd, 10 Alcorn Avenue,
Toronto, Ontario, Canada M4V 3B2
Penguin Books (N.Z.) Ltd, 182–190 Wairau Road,
Auckland 10, New Zealand

Penguin Books Ltd, Registered Offices:
Harmondsworth, Middlesex, England

This volume first published in Penguin Books 1995

1 3 5 7 9 10 8 6 4 2

Saratoga Longshot first published in the United States of America by Atheneum Publishers 1976
Slightly revised edition published in Penguin Books 1987
Copyright © Stephen Dobyns, 1976, 1987
All rights reserved

Saratoga Swimmer first published in the United States of America by Atheneum Publishers 1981
Published in Penguin Books 1983
Copyright © Stephen Dobyns, 1981
All rights reserved

Saratoga Headhunter first published in the United States of America by
Viking Penguin Inc. 1985
Published in Penguin Books 1986
Copyright © Stephen Dobyns, 1985
All rights reserved

LIBRARY OF CONGRESS CATALOGING-IN-PUBLICATION DATA
Dobyns, Stephen, 1941–
Saratoga trifecta / Stephen Dobyns.
p.   cm.
Contents: Saratoga longshot—Saratoga swimmer—Saratoga
headhunter.
ISBN 0 14 02.5196 0
1. Bradshaw, Charlie (Fictitious character)—Fiction. 2. Private
investigators—New York (State)—Saratoga—Fiction. 3. Saratoga
Springs (N.Y.)—Fiction. I. Title.
PS3554.O2A6 1995
813'.54—dc20   95–10380

Printed in the United States of America
Set in Sabon

CONTENTS

SARATOGA
LONGSHOT

▼▼▼

FOR DON AND MINNIE MAE

1

▼▼▼

C HARLIE BRADSHAW WAS LEAVING Saratoga. It was his
birthday and he was going to New York City. Charlie
was forty-one years old.

The Adirondack Trailways bus pulled away from the Spa
City Diner, turned right onto South Broadway and headed out
of town, gathering speed past the Washington, then the Lincoln
Baths. Trying to get comfortable, Charlie shifted in his seat
and banged his knee against the ashtray attached to the seat
in front of him.

The fact of his birthday and the trip to New York were
coincidental. His birthday, however, made the trip seem momentous, as if it were a present he was giving himself: something he had deserved a long time and at last decided to take.

He hoped it would be spring in New York. In Saratoga, 180
miles north, it was still winter. There had been flurries earlier
that morning and it had snowed over the weekend: mostly wet
snow which had melted, but Charlie could still see patches of
white between the small pines of the Saratoga Tree Nursery.

It was 9:15 Monday morning, April 7. Charlie hadn't been
in New York since the summer of 1960. His memory of the
city was a memory of warmth.

Shifting again, Charlie bumped the man in the aisle seat.
The man had refused to move when Charlie got on, forcing
Charlie to climb over him. He was about forty-five and had
large pink jowls that looked like the intermediate point between a silk purse and a sow's ear. A gray golfing cap was
pulled down over his forehead and a gray raincoat was buttoned up to his neck. Charlie imagined he wore no shirt.

Accepting the bump as a kind of introduction, the man
asked, "You live in Saratoga?" And continuing before Charlie

could answer: "You know, I must of come through from War-rensburg a hundred times. Always meant to stop at one of those big hotels. Put my feet up and buy a cigar. They must be torn down now."

"There're some left," said Charlie. His mother had worked as a maid at the Grand Union Hotel until it closed in 1952.

"Should of kept them open, you know, as a kind of monu-ment to the past. Always regretted I never stopped. Of course I saw the movie several times."

"Pardon me?" Charlie's attention had drifted to the country-side and its architecture, which, along Route 9, consisted of motels, trailer parks and a few split-levels: the seedlings of a suburbia moving up from Albany.

"*Saratoga Trunk,* there's greatness for you. I remember sit-ting through it time and again one Saturday afternoon as a kid until the usher came along and kicked me out. They should of kept the hotel just because of the movie. Show the world the very rooms where Clint Maroon and Clio Dulaine slept."

The man from Warrensburg inserted an index finger between his neck and the collar of his raincoat, pulled, then puffed out his large pink cheeks. They looked so soft that Charlie wanted to touch them.

The war finished the hotels. There was no racing between 1942 and 1946, and the United States Hotel was seized by the city for back taxes. The Grand Union dragged along, opening only for the races each August. Then Senator Kefauver's inves-tigation of organized crime led to the shutdown of the gam-bling casinos in 1951. The Grand Union closed the following year, and Charlie's mother returned to full-time waitressing.

She had been his waitress that morning. Either he didn't know or had forgotten she was working at the Spa City Diner. He should have brought a Thermos. It always embarrassed him to be waited on by his mother.

Mabel Bradshaw was a thin woman who kept her short, gray hair in tight, immaculate curls. Over the years her memory of being a maid had become distorted so that in talking to her one would think she had been a guest.

The man from Warrensburg nudged Charlie. "There's a

girls' school too, right?" And again he didn't wait for an answer: "Must of been a great place to grow up. Saratoga, I mean. Think of the broads."

Charlie ignored him. He preferred to think about New York, not Saratoga Springs. He saw himself embarking upon a new part of his life and wanted to keep his mind on the future. Despite this, he found himself thinking of Gladys Cheney. Not the Gladys he had seen on Saturday when she had begged him to go to New York—an overweight, potato-like woman with no teeth. He saw her as he had seen her first in tenth grade: blond with frizzy hair like Little Orphan Annie, and large soft breasts that made it hard for her to play baseball.

It had been Mrs. Cavendish, his English teacher, who had first brought his attention to the girl by saying, "Someday a gentleman will come along and draw the lady out of Gladys."

Charlie had missed the pun, but at the age of fifteen he still hoped to be a gentleman. As he thought about it, he recalled that Gladys had been toothless when she returned to Saratoga in 1960 with her ten-year-old son Sammy.

He considered asking his companion if he had known a Gladys Cheney in Warrensburg in the 50's, but saw that the man had tilted back his seat and drawn his golf cap over his eyes.

The bus was three quarters full and smelled of cleaning fluid. People were dozing or talking quietly. A few were reading the *New York Times*, as if to prepare themselves. There was a general hawking and coughing. Signs over the front window told him that his "operator" was J. Stone and that the bus's number was 62606.

Charlie looked fondly at these people. He was a kind, inquisitive man who liked children. He was happy to be going to New York. Deciding to read for a while, he took a book from his pocket. Its full title was *The Authentic Life of Billy, the Kid, the Noted Desperado of the Southwest, Whose Deeds of Daring and Blood Made His Name a Terror in New Mexico, Arizona & Northern Mexico, a Faithful and Interesting Narrative by Pat F. Garrett, Sheriff of Lincoln Co., N.M., by Whom He Was Finally Hunted Down & Captured by Killing Him.*

Charlie knew the book well, but instead of opening it he left it in his lap and looked out the window.

The bus was approaching the bridge over the Mohawk River, which formed the boundary between Saratoga and Albany counties. Less than ten miles to Albany now. It wasn't much of a bridge, just a rise in the highway over 150 yards of water. For Charlie those people who lived south of the river were southerners, people who lived a little differently.

Charlie hoped he would have time for sightseeing in New York. He wanted to visit Water Street and see where Sportsmen's Hall had stood over 100 years before. Kit Burns had entertained his customers with battles between rats and terriers, while a man called Jack the Rat would bite off the heads of mice for a dime and live rats for a quarter. The Slaughter Housers had hung out at Sportsmen's Hall, as had the Swamp Angels, the Border Gang, the Daybreak Boys and others.

As he named these gangs to himself, Charlie looked out at the rows of tract houses which formed the northern boundary of the capitol district. In the front yard of one, he saw a small boy urging a dog to pull a red wagon by pointing a gun at it: a green water pistol.

Charlie raised his book again and shifted in his seat, still trying to get comfortable. Turning, he bumped the armrest, then winced as the butt of his own gun, a Smith & Wesson .38 Special, dug into his hip.

2

▼▼▼

ALTHOUGH CHARLIE HAD BEEN in the Port Authority Bus Terminal before, it seemed unfamiliar. His bus had arrived at 12:35 and disgorged him onto the sloping floor of the lower concourse. He was now twisting through the crowd trying to find his way out while avoiding a thin man in yellow robes who wanted to talk to him. Charlie's only comfort came from the Hoffritz cutlery store. At least he had seen their ads.

When he emerged onto Eighth Avenue, he was pleased to discover that it was fifteen degrees warmer than Saratoga; and even the sky, while not quite blue, was certainly trying. Springish. Fifteen years ago, when Charlie had come to New York for what he thought of as a last fling before his marriage, he had stayed at the YMCA's Sloane House on 34th Street. He saw no reason not to go there again.

Pleased with the weather and excited about being in New York, Charlie turned into the crowd of pedestrians and headed south. He walked slowly and was constantly jostled by people who hurried past him the way water divides around a rock. In his right hand he carried a small, green plaid canvas suitcase that he had bought at the Big N on Sunday.

Charlie Bradshaw was not a noticeable man. At least four inches under six feet, he was becoming stout: cherubic, his wife said, a woman who did not like cherubs. His light brown hair had begun to recede. Not wishing to be accused of hiding it, he brushed it straight back. At the moment, it was hidden by a tan porkpie hat with a red tartan band.

His face in profile was a series of forward curves; from the front it was round and thoughtful with large blue eyes. It was a smooth face that easily turned pink from cold weather, physical exertion or simple embarrassment. It was neither youthful nor handsome. "Presentable" was the word Charlie used.

His clothes were permanent press: gray slacks, an olive green raincoat over a dark gray sport coat and white shirt. His tie had wide red, yellow and orange stripes. Both it and the hat had been chosen especially for the trip, as had the brown wing-tipped shoes which he thought of as his wedding-funeral-and-court-appearance shoes.

As he passed cheap clothing stores and pizza counters, Charlie thought he hadn't seen this many people in all the time since his last visit to New York. It was like being caught in the crowd leaving the races, except that the crowd didn't disperse but stayed with him block after block. He knew if he adapted his pace to the people around him, he would have fewer collisions, and his bag wouldn't beleaguer the knees of the passersby. He continued to amble.

Charlie sometimes thought that his most important faculty was memory, that much of his pleasure came from recollecting the past, his own and others'. Occasionally he would even accuse himself of doing something only to translate it into the more durable and controllable state of memory. And he knew that might be one of the reasons he had come to New York; that beyond the problems of Gladys Cheney and her son, he had felt the need on the summit of his forty-first birthday to feed and refurbish a memory grown tired of Saratoga Springs.

Walking down Eighth Avenue, he could feel his mind drawing in sensations like a plant responding to light. He saw that the New Yorker Hotel was closed and gawked at the New Madison Square Garden. He found himself expecting to see Sam Cheney, had even felt some surprise at not seeing him at the bus station. Not that Sam knew he was coming or would meet him if he did; but since he was the cause of his trip, it seemed that Sam had increased in stature or that there were more of him.

He had last seen Sam Cheney on a summer afternoon in 1972. Charlie had just turned onto Caroline Street from Broadway, and saw Sam emerging from the Tin and Lint: a basement bar on the corner that catered to the young dog about town.

Charlie had honked and Sam ignored him. Charlie had honked again. This time Sam walked slowly over to the car. At twenty-two he was tall and thin with long black curly hair. He had on blue denim cutoffs nearly hidden by a long white Indian shirt. His feet were bare and he stepped gingerly to avoid broken glass.

"Get in."

"I don't want to be seen with you."

"Get in!"

They had driven over to a lot by Congress Park. Charlie had learned that the police were preparing to make a series of arrests for narcotics violations, mostly marijuana. Sam was known to be a minor pusher.

Charlie had not intended to tell Sam about the impending arrests, thinking it a kind of betrayal; but when he saw Sam that day he changed his mind, deciding it was more of a betrayal to keep silent.

"I'm sure you'll be picked up with the others," Charlie had told him. "I'm not telling you what to do, but if you're smart . . ."

"Don't do me any favors."

"I'm doing it for Gladys."

Sam left town. The police made a dozen arrests. A warrant had been issued for Sam but never served.

Charlie still felt guilty about telling him. Sam was the sort of uncommunicative young man whose silence seemed a general condemnation of life. This often led Charlie to go out of his way to be friendly as if to prove that things weren't so bad. He knew quite well, however, that ever since Gladys had brought Sam to Saratoga in 1960, he had been jeopardizing his own security and well-being by getting Sam out of trouble, which in fact was why he was in New York City.

Turning up 34th Street, Charlie thought of Pat Garrett's partial justification of Billy the Kid. "The fact that he lied, swore, gambled, and broke the Sabbath in his childhood, only proved that youth and exuberant humanity were rife in the child."

The same could never be said of Sam who had as much exuberance as a turtle. Sullen was how he was usually described.

In the lobby of the YMCA was a sign saying "Welcome" in six languages. Behind the sign was an office for job referrals. It was closed. A dark purple runner extended from the main entrance to the row of five elevators. Apart from the purple, most of the colors were dark tans and browns, making the lobby dim and noncommittal.

At the registration desk, a thin man handed Charlie a membership card. When Charlie had filled it out, the man said, "Eight or nine bucks?"

"Pardon me?"

"Television or no television?"

"No television."

"That'll be nine bucks."

"I don't understand."

"You get the buck back when you return your key. Let's see some identification."

"Identification?"

"Some ID. How do I know you are who you say you are, that you're ..." he raised Charlie's card and squinted at it, "that you're Charles F. Bradshaw from Saratoga Springs? What kind of name's that? You could be anybody."

Charlie drew out his wallet. He wanted to tell the clerk that he was a policeman, that he had been a policeman for twenty years. Instead he showed him his driver's license.

The clerk barely glanced at it. "See the cashier."

The cashier's cage was a few feet along the counter. To get to it, however, Charlie had to walk an extra fourteen feet out around a red velvet rope.

Behind the bars of the cage sat a heavy woman with a crooked silver fang hanging from a thin chain around her neck. Charlie gave her a ten. As he waited, he looked around the lobby. There were about twenty people: young dapper blacks, old down and out whites and foreign tourists, mostly orientals. The young blacks and tourists hurried back and forth; the old whites just poked along.

The cashier was speaking to him. "Take these and go to the last window." She gave him two receipts.

At the last window a tall black man told him to sign one of the receipts. When Charlie handed it back to him, the man gave him a key, holding it out as if it were a morsel being given to a quick animal that could snap up his fingers. He didn't speak.

Charlie assumed he was done. Picking up his bag, he walked to the elevator. The number on his key was 931. Charlie pushed the button for the ninth floor. As the doors began to close, two orientals with cameras dove through them. They laughed about it all the way up.

The elderly whites, thought Charlie, were not actually down and out. They were one step above and had all the dignity of people who saw themselves as coping rather than drifting. Some reminded him of old drunks he had known during his early days as a patrolman: feisty, isolated men whose lives usually centered around the race tracks. Invariably they would remember his father and claim his friendship.

"That man," one had told him, "he would bet on anything, just anything." And Charlie had imagined money wagered on ants crossing sidewalks and which sparrow would land first.

Charlie's pleasant mood disappeared when he opened the door of Room 931. It was about six by ten feet with dark mustard walls and a white ceiling. The cracked paint was smudged with words he couldn't read, and he imagined a depressed tourist writing "help" and "despair" on the walls in Burmese.

The only decoration was a color reproduction over the bed showing the Maine coast with rocks and seagulls and a man pulling a red rowboat out of the water. The narrow bed with its green spread, the tiny desk and chair—all looked like they had been pilfered from a nursery school. Charlie sat down on the chair and it swayed.

He was surprised at being in the room, at coming to New York. He had decided to come less than twenty-four hours before and that too surprised him. He was the sort of man who made careful decisions and didn't trust people who acted on impulse.

Charlie thought again of Gladys Cheney; not as he had seen her on Saturday, blowzy and crying about Sam, but as he had known her in high school. There had been a warm Saturday evening in October. He had never touched a girl's breasts before, had hardly kissed a girl except at parties where it was expected. They had lain on a blue blanket under a row of tall pines: part of the rose garden of an estate at the edge of Saratoga. She had told him that Skidmore girls came there, and spoke knowledgeably of "petting parties."

Even at fifteen Charlie was aware of doing something partly in order to recollect it later when he would tell his older and more experienced cousins. The buttons on his fly had nearly finished him. He had had an orgasm a scant three seconds after entry while Gladys was still craning her neck for shooting stars.

On the back of the door of Room 931 was a sheet of instructions. Charlie read: "It is expected that the residents at all times will conduct themselves in harmony with the ideals of the Association. Gambling, profane or obscene language, disorderly, immoral or unlawful conduct or the possession or use of alcohol or illegal drugs will be sufficient cause for immediate cancellation of all privileges."

3
▼▼▼

CHARLIE SAT IN A GRAY metal chair next to a gray metal desk. Around him in neat rows were about twenty more gray metal desks at which men sat in their shirt sleeves, mostly white shirts. Like Charlie, they wore .38's. It was a quiet room. A secretary was typing. There was the hum of fluorescent lights. There was an occasional guffaw from two men talking by the drinking fountain.

The man who went with the desk next to Charlie was across the room in a small office. Charlie could see him through the glass door laughing and joking with an older man. Charlie felt his face grow red. He could guess what they were joking about.

The desk belonged to Sergeant Ralph Benedetto. Charlie had been introduced to him in such a way as to assume that "Sergeant" was part of his baptized name. He was a square, muscular man with curly brown hair who chewed constantly on a yellow pencil. Benedetto was a few years younger than Charlie and his shirt was a very light blue.

Charlie sat twisting a piece of cardboard with the number 37 printed on it. The card allowed him to move freely within police headquarters. It was about four o'clock, later than he had intended. Mistakenly he had taken the Broadway local instead of the Seventh Avenue express, forcing him to walk an extra seven blocks up Chambers. Then he had felt shy about barging into police headquarters, and had moped around City Hall Park trying to summon up interest in a statue of Horace Greeley.

Sergeant Benedetto came back across the room and sat down in his gray swivel chair as if there were no one two feet away staring at him expectantly. Leaning back, he cupped his hands and pressed them against his nose and mouth. He looked down at a row of seven pencils on the left side of his desk.

"Tell me," he said through his fingers, "let's talk straight. You got some chippy here in town and you took the week off to come down and see her. But so you could ball her without complications, you told your old lady you were coming down on business. And now you've come over to see us just to lower the bullshit level. Right?"

For a moment, Charlie couldn't think. Then it occurred to him to feel angry. He had come to police headquarters hoping to be accepted as a comrade from the north, not as some clown. But apart from a certain disappointment, he didn't feel much of anything.

"You can check the hospitals and . . ."

"Sure, sure." Benedetto glanced at Charlie, then looked away. He picked up a yellow pencil, put it back down and folded his arms across his chest. "This guy, this Sam Cheney, he's been gone two weeks. Right? He's about twenty-five. He lives in the East Village. He's got a history of being involved with drugs. . . ."

"Marijuana."

"Drugs is drugs. Two weeks ago Saturday his mother calls him from Saratoga. A strange man answers and says Sam Cheney hasn't been home all night. The strange man says he's worried or it's odd or some fuckin' thing like that, though I don't see what's odd about a twenty-five-year-old man being out all night unless he wears an iron lung. Anyway they hang up. For the next two weeks the mother keeps calling, but nobody answers. She can't even get the strange man anymore.

Right? Okay, so she goes to you, her local cop." Benedetto stopped and recupped his hands over his mouth. He stared at Charlie over his knuckles.

"Now here comes the part I don't understand. Instead of telephoning or just forwarding a request for assistance, you hop on a bus and come down here, spend your own good money for a room at the Y of all places. Tell me, what's your relationship with these people?"

"A friend of the family." Charlie tried to smile.

"You got a big department up there? This a slack season? How many men?"

"Fifty-four." Charlie considered adding that it went up to about eighty in the summer when they hired the temporaries.

"That's not much more than we have in missing persons. Look, you know the routine. Two weeks is nothing. A guy like that, what reason do you have to think anything's wrong? You're in the juvenile division up there? A sergeant?"

"Community and Youth Relations Bureau."

"I don't care what the fuck you call it. Kids is kids. You must get paid a helluva lot to make little trips like this. Don't tell me, I don't want to know."

Benedetto picked up a color snapshot of Sam Cheney that lay on his desk. It showed a young man with long black hair standing next to a large red motorcycle. A thin face with large brown eyes and full lips, a satyrish face.

Watching him, Charlie found himself remembering the poem that Black Bart had left for the posse after holding up the Wells Fargo Stage from Fort Ross, California.

> I've labored long and hard for bread,
> For honor and for riches
> But on my corns too long you've tred,
> You fine-haired sons-of-bitches.

Benedetto tossed the picture back on his desk. "What a punk. And all you've got is his address and the name of the place he works, a men's store on Eighth Street. Jesus, we've had this guy in here a thousand times."

"Sam?"

"No, punks like him." Benedetto picked up a yellow pencil and stuck it in the side of his mouth. "Okay, okay, we'll do the hospital routine. But look, talk straight, what'd you really come down here for? You got a chippy, right?"

4

▼▼▼

FORTY MINUTES LATER, as Charlie walked up Fourth Avenue from Astor Place, absorbing the sunlight and looking forward to summer, he thought that his wife Marge was probably in New York at that moment, although she might have left early to avoid rush hour traffic. She and her sister Lucy ran a dress shop that catered to Skidmore girls. Marge had spent the weekend in New York investigating fall fashions and Indian blouses.

Charlie's wife liked to think of herself as a strong, nononsense woman. They had an affable, childless marriage. Lucy, his sister-in-law, had married his middle cousin Robert. Charlie sometimes thought that Marge too had wanted to marry one of his three cousins, but since they had been taken she had married him as a way of getting into the family.

Marge liked the fact that he was a policeman. She saw herself as a woman of some power and having a policeman for a husband seemed proof of it. She had urged him to be active in the Lions, Rotary, the American Legion. When he had been elected treasurer of the Protective and Benevolent Association, she had bought him an expensive chocolate cake.

Charlie felt kindly toward his wife. A shy man, he felt grateful to Marge for taking the trouble to penetrate his shyness. He knew he occasionally confused gratitude with love, but he was basically comfortable and Marge allowed him his own life, enclosing him like a fence around forty acres.

Charlie suspected that Marge was part of the reason he was in New York. No more than five percent of the total motivation, but still a reason. It was unlike him to pack up and leave, and it had jolted Marge when he had talked to her on the phone the night before.

"But why go down yourself? Can't you call?"

"It's a delicate situation."

"I don't see what's so delicate about Sam Cheney. You've been wasting your time on him ever since they moved to Saratoga."

Charlie could picture her sitting on the edge of the bed in some immaculate hotel room, looking angrily into the phone as if trying to catch his eye. She was a tall, severe woman who wore outfits rather than clothes.

"I feel it's something I have to do."

"Tomorrow's your birthday."

"That doesn't matter." And he had thought she would be gone for most of his birthday even if he stayed at home.

Charlie tried to imagine telling Sergeant Benedetto that he thought it a good idea to give his wife an occasional surprise. As he crossed to 13th Street, he considered his meeting with the policeman. He knew that part of the problem was that he neither looked nor acted like an officer of the law. Instead, he might be a vacuum cleaner salesman or a clerk for an insurance company: someone who rode buses and kept a canary, who put off buying a new pair of shoes. Although Charlie had spent years trying to achieve this effect, there was still the regret. Maybe he should have given Benedetto a karate chop or eaten a light bulb.

When he had accepted the fact that Benedetto wouldn't treat him as an equal, Charlie had begun to hold back information. He would find Sam by himself. Sam was his special task, had been his task ever since Sam had been picked up for shoplifting at the age of twelve. Sergeant Benedetto wouldn't have understood that either.

Gladys had given Charlie two other pieces of information. She had told him the name of a bar where Sam often went: The Lamplighter on First Avenue near 10th Street. And she had given him the name and address of Sam's girlfriend: Anastasia Doyle who lived on 13th Street between Fifth and Sixth avenues.

Charlie was on his way to see her now and would have been there already if he had had a better knowledge of the subway system. Fortunately the day had become increasingly spring-like, and Charlie enjoyed looking at buildings, which along here were mostly small shops and five and six story red, yellow or gray brick apartment buildings with black metal railings on their front stoops. Several smaller buildings reminded him of the building that Herman Mudgett, alias Dr. Harry Holmes, had built in Chicago in the early 1890's. It had been named Murder Castle after the police had discovered within it the bodies of more than 200 women.

Mudgett had once been a medical student at the University of Michigan, but had been expelled after he was caught stealing the corpse of a young woman from the lab. When the watch-man asked what he was doing, Mudgett replied, "Taking my girl for a walk, you idiot."

The address that Gladys had given him turned out to be a seven-story red brick apartment building with shrubbery out in front. It looked expensive and not a bit like Mudgett's Mur-der Castle. Charlie pushed open the glass door.

On the wall to his left were two columns of fifteen buttons with numbers but no names. Beneath the two columns was another button next to the word "Super." The buttons were purple and protruded from a polished brass plate. Written above in scarlet spray paint were the words, *Eat shit* and *Slash '77*. Charlie pressed the button marked "Super."

He was standing in a small lobby between two sets of glass doors. Beyond the second set was a larger lobby with an eleva-tor, a bank of mail boxes and a green door marked "Private." The door opened and through it came a heavy-set middle-aged man followed by the oldest and biggest German shepherd Charlie had ever seen. The man held the door open and the dog lumbered through it. Then both man and dog lumbered toward Charlie, who felt he had unleashed some global threat.

Reaching the door, the man mouthed a word which Charlie took to be, "Yeah?"

"Does Anastasia Doyle live here?"

The super rolled his eyes and opened the door three inches. He had on a green work shirt and green work pants. The dog collapsed behind him and appeared to go to sleep.

"Who?"

"Anastasia Doyle?"

"Who wants to know?"

"I do."

The super again rolled his eyes and closed the door an inch. "So who are you?"

Charlie showed him a badge which identified him as a Saratoga Springs police sergeant.

The super had short gray hair that grew in patches, hair alternating with pink areas of scalp like spots on a Dalmatian. He scratched his chin.

"Fake ID? What if you stole it? I bet I could prove I'm the King of Siam."

Charlie brought out a series of cards: driver's license, Lions Club, social security, Little League Booster Club. He moved his right foot so he could quickly shove it in the crack.

"Maybe you stole the whole thing. Who's to say?"

Charlie tried to look inoffensive. "Does Anastasia Doyle live here? That seems simple enough."

"She don't like the name Anastasia. Call her Stacy, she says. You sure don't know her very well."

"I don't know her at all; I just want to talk to her."

"You and a hundred other fellas." The man opened the door. "Don't try any funny stuff or I'll put the dog on you, cop or no cop."

Charlie glanced down at the dog which lay sprawled as if doped. A long pink tongue just touched the floor.

"What are you going to do," he asked, "throw it at me?"

Unexpectedly, the super laughed, a single laugh: "Hah!" He bent down and patted the dog's head. The dog didn't wake.

"This dog, she killed a guy once. I keep her just for that, must prey on her conscience. Some kid, a burglar, took too long getting through that door and Queenie was all over him. She was fast then. Throw her at you. Hah. Yeah, Stacy Doyle lives here but she don't get back before 5:30. You can wait here in the lobby. You can't miss her. She's your height, long black hair. A looker, you know? She'll be carrying books."

The super turned and lumbered back toward the green door.

Charlie noticed he wore purple velveteen slippers which matched the purple of the buttons on the brass plate. Queenie remained prostrate at Charlie's feet.

When he reached the door, the super glanced back. "Come on, Queenie, get your ass up."

The dog groaned and hauled itself to its feet. Looking dourly at Charlie, it licked its chops and shambled off.

The super was right about not missing Stacy Doyle. She was nearly beautiful: black hair that hung loose past her waist, a thin face with a long straight nose and slightly slanted green eyes.

She wore a bright yellow spring jacket and a short blue denim skirt. A green Indian cloth bag hung from her shoulder and in her arms were five large books. The top one was in German: The Something Hill. Charlie had spent his two years in the army stationed in northern Germany.

Stacy Doyle reminded Charlie of many Skidmore students, the sort of woman who looks well groomed even in a paper hat. The slanted eyes reminded him of Gladys Cheney.

"I haven't seen Sam in over two weeks." She stood by the elevator and looked wary.

"Do you know where he went?"

"Why do you want to know?"

"I'm trying to find him."

"That's rather obvious, isn't it? Does he owe you money?"

A strand of black hair fell across her right eye and she tossed her head, flicking it away. Charlie guessed she combed her hair so it would fall like that, allowing her to toss her head in a way she had probably seen in a Joan Crawford movie. Under her jacket she wore a white Indian blouse and around her neck was a yellow and green striped Moroccan bead on a leather thong.

"His mother's worried," said Charlie. "She hasn't been able to reach him. I was coming down anyway and . . ."

"You're a policeman?"

"A friend of the family."

Her lips, too, were like Gladys', soft and well formed, but her manner was completely different. Stacy was impatient and businesslike, while Gladys, even at forty-one, was a large, soft child.

"I thought Sam told his mother."

"Told her what?"

"About his trip, that he was going out west."

"Where?"

"San Diego. He left two weeks ago. He was going to call her or write."

"She hasn't heard a word."

Watching her, Charlie thought she was lying. She seemed one of those tense people who force themselves to appear relaxed only when not telling the truth.

"That's just like him, he never remembers a thing. But I don't see why his mother should freak."

"Freak?"

"Send a cop all the way down just to look for him."

"She didn't send me."

Stacy tossed her head again, then glanced at her watch. It had a wide red plastic band.

"Is there anything else? I've got French at 6:30 and I'm famished."

"Not right now. Maybe I'll see you later or something."

"Later?"

"You know a bar called The Lamplighter?" He saw the wary expression return. It was like being looked at sideways.

"It's over on First, isn't it?"

"That's right, maybe I'll see you there later."

Charlie went through the double set of glass doors and out onto the street. The sun was still shining. He felt pleased with himself.

5

▼▼▼

THERE WERE SMALL RIPS in the arms of the brown Naugahyde chair and cotton mushrooms of light gray padding were pushing up through the holes. Charlie picked at the padding while watching a man across the living room in a similar chair, although his was green. Between them against one green cement black wall was a gray Naugahyde couch. The furniture looked as if it had grown old in the office of a local doctor. A stomach specialist, thought Charlie.

Across from the couch was a thirty-gallon fish tank with a fluorescent light. Charlie could see about fifteen fish, plus a couple of snails. At the bottom of the tank was a plastic figure in an orange diver's suit. A stream of bubbles rose up from it to the surface.

Both Charlie and his companion held Budweiser beer cans. Charlie had been squeezing his and it was dented. In a day of minor frustrations, this was the first man he wanted to hit.

"Look," said the man, whose name was Victor Plotz, "so I'm a bastard. What else is new? You know, I lost two fish today. Something's eating them. I mean another fish. I think it's the fucking angelfish. Angel. That's a laugh. Those fish are children to me. Okay, so maybe I been too sharp with my tongue."

Victor Plotz was caretaker of the tenement building where Sam Cheney rented an apartment. He was in his early fifties and had a round red face with gray bushy eyebrows and gray bushy sideburns and gray bushy hair, giving his head a soft mushroom shape.

Plotz's hair reminded Charlie of the dust balls that accumulated under his bed at home. Plotz had a large bulbous nose criss-crossed with tiny red capillaries. Charlie thought these were veins and came from drinking. He could also see them on Plotz's round cheeks. They looked like delicate nets meant to keep the skin in place.

"What d'you know about fish?"

"Tartar sauce."

"Fuck you."

On the floor in front of Charlie was a large gray cat whose fur so matched Plotz's gray bushy hair that it seemed that one was furred or haired with the sheddings of the other. The cat was crouched, twitching its rear end and staring at Charlie, who, although he didn't exactly dislike cats, was allergic to them to the extend that his nose ran and eyes watered whenever one got too close. Cats seemed to know this and searched him out. This cat was missing its left eye, and as it stared at Charlie, preparing to leap, its empty socket twitched gently.

"I call the cat Moshe because of the eye," Plotz had told him. "She was in a fight. I don't know who won. Who the fuck cares? Whenever some fish gives me grief, I toss it to Moshe. Moshe the Enforcer. I been telling those angelfish, 'Watch out, you fuck with me and it's Moshe the Enforcer for you. Understand?' "

It was shortly after seven o'clock. Sam's building was a yellow tenement on 6th Street at First Avenue across from a complex of new high-rises. Charlie had arrived nearly an hour before and was now trying to keep himself from shouting.

"All I want," said Charlie, subtly trying to kick the cat so it wouldn't jump on him, "all I want is a quick look around. Just give me the key and I'll have it back in five minutes. There might have been trouble."

The cat sprang up over Charlie's shoe and landed in his lap. He gingerly pried its claws from his trousers and dropped it to the floor.

"Long as the rent's been paid, there's been no trouble. If my boss even knew I was talking to you, he'd put my ass in a sling."

"I'm a cop."

"He wouldn't care if you were Mighty Joe Young."

"How would he know?"

Moshe gave another leap, this time landing on Charlie's chest, fastening its claws in his gray sport coat. Charlie pried the claws loose and tossed the cat on the floor, first giving it a quick squeeze to show he meant business. He began brushing gray fur off his red, yellow and orange striped tie.

"I've already let you go up and bother the neighbors. Look, my hands are tied. Want another beer?"

"Sure."

Sam's neighbors hadn't been helpful. He had talked to two: an old man who was nearly deaf and a girl about fourteen who stood in her doorway nursing a baby that looked like a small badger. Charlie had tried to keep himself from staring at her bare breast while she told him she hadn't heard any noise from Sam's apartment for a couple of weeks.

"Here." Plotz gave him another Budweiser.

"Maybe he's dead in there."

"He'd smell."

"Maybe they wrapped him in plastic."

Charlie drew his billfold from his breast pocket and took out a twenty. He held it up.

Plotz looked disgusted. "What do you think I am?"

Charlie put back the twenty. The cat was sitting as close to his feet as it could without actually touching them. It stared at Charlie as it might stare at a little bird. The eyelid twitched over the empty socket. Charlie's eyes began to water.

"Did he have any visitors?" he asked.

"Not that I saw."

Plotz stood up and walked over to the fish tank. Although only slightly taller than Charlie, he probably outweighed him by twenty-five pounds. He wore an old gray cardigan that was baggy from keeping his hands pushed down in the pockets. He looked suspiciously into the water.

"You think this diver thing's been killing the fish? Supposed to aerate the water or something. Just got it the other day. Lifelike, don't you think? Reminded me of John Paine in *Captain China*. Now there was a movie. Remember at the end when he doesn't come up? And Gail Russell. When I heard she killed herself, I don't know, I wasn't myself for a week."

Plotz crossed his arms on his stomach and began scratching his elbows. "I can just see that little diver thingy beginning to creep along the bottom the moment I flick off the light. Nah, Sam Cheney didn't have any visitors except for his girlfriend and that new roommate of his."

Charlie picked a bit of cat fur from his lower lip. "I thought he lived alone."

"He did mostly. This guy just moved in."

"Is he up there now?"

"Nope, he hasn't been around either. Don't give me that plastic bag shit. Matter of fact, I had to look in last week to see about a pipe. Believe me, no bodies, just dust and roaches."

Charlie still wanted to see for himself. "Who was this roommate?"

"Just a guy. About Sam's age. He moved in almost a month ago, maybe less. Said he came from California."

Charlie's nose began to run. Moshe continued to sit at his feet. "What's his name?"

Plotz walked over to a small metal desk by the door. He leafed through some papers. "Bonenfant, Peter Bonenfant. Comes from San Diego." He put away the papers and went back to scratching his elbows. "Been getting some mail too."

Charlie finished his beer and put the can on the floor. He imagined grabbing the cat, plunging it into the fish tank and holding it down on the orange plastic diver. He tried to think about Sam Cheney. He assumed it was Bonenfant who had talked to Gladys. But Charlie still wanted to see Sam's apartment if only to count the toothbrushes.

"You won't change your mind?"

"No way. Jobs is hard enough without losing one. Want another beer?"

Charlie got up. It occurred to him that Gail Russell had been his favorite actress all through high school. "Some other time," he said.

Victor Plotz followed him to the door. "Don't think me a shit or anything. I mean, you've got your job and I've got mine. What the fuck, it's a living."

"That's okay, maybe I'll be back."

Before leaving the building, Charlie again went up to Sam's apartment on the third floor. The corridor smelled of cooked food: cauliflower or broccoli, he wasn't sure which. Sam's door was brown metal and had two shiny brass locks. Charlie tried the knob and shook it. The door wouldn't budge.

6

▼▼▼

THE SKIN OF THE WOMAN'S ASS was the color of heavy cream. A blue rhinestone chain seemed embedded in the crack. Moving slowly back and forth, the ass swung about seven feet from Charlie's face. What Charlie minded was paying $2 for a bottle of Schlitz. There weren't even any stools.

The bar was long, about fifty feet, and above it a narrow stage ran its full length. On the wall behind the stage was a floor-to-ceiling mirror that continued around two sides of the room, transforming the two dancers into hundreds.

The dancer in front of Charlie was blond, heavy and Germanic. She reminded him of girls whose heifers won prizes at the Washington County Fair. Along with the blue rhinestone G-string, she wore matching pasties, three-inch silver platform shoes and black net stockings. She danced facing the mirror, smiling at herself and gently pinching her nipples. Now and then she would lean forward and kiss her reflection.

The second dancer off to Charlie's right was doing a subtle dance with a red velvet chaise longue. She lay on her back and moved as much as a sound sleeper might move on a rough train ride between New York and Montreal. She was young and dark haired, and her rhinestones were red and silver. Occasionally she would lift a leg and point a toe at the ceiling.

The nine other men at the bar appeared bored and hardly watched the dancers. Charlie watched but was disappointed. The only music came from the jukebox: *Rock Your Baby* by George MacRae. Charlie had come expecting to hear Cozy Cole. The Metropole Cafe had changed a lot in fifteen years. He doubted they even served coffee.

He had begun to think he had waited too long in coming to New York. He had planned to have dinner, his birthday dinner, at Jack Dempsey's Restaurant, only to find it closed. Instead, he had gone to a place next to the Metropole named,

27

apparently, Tab Pizza Custard. Eating his two slices of pizza, Charlie had looked suspiciously at the Metropole's marquee with its sign advertising *Topless Go-Go*.

The music ended and the blond dancer turned toward the bar. She stood with her legs apart, puffing her cheeks and fanning her face with her hands.

"Don't call me fat," she half-shouted to a man near Charlie. "I'm not fat, don't call me fat." The she grinned.

The dancer on the chaise longue spread a thin smile over the ten men at the bar as one might spread a single pat of butter over several pieces of toast. The music began again. Something called *Shame, Shame, Shame*. She slowly raised her leg.

Although not usually sentimental about birthdays and anniversaries, Charlie missed the usual congratulations. He was sorry he hadn't told Victor Plotz. At least his mother had wished him a happy birthday that morning at the Spa City Diner. She had even given him a birthday doughnut filled with a jelly mixture which he suspected was rhubarb.

Mabel Bradshaw had been cheerful, telling him it was only ten days until the start of harness racing at Saratoga Raceway, and offering to lend him her copy of *Racing Form* while he waited for the bus.

Even at sixty, Mabel still hoped to make her fortune from the tracks. Often Charlie would be sitting in some restaurant when suddenly his mother would appear beside him wanting to discuss horses. She would pull out a paper, point to a trotter that had come in last at Batavia Downs and say:

"See that horse? I got a $200 piece of it. When I'm in the money, don't think I'll forget my boy."

Unfortunately, her horses too often turned out to be afraid of robins, dandelions and other horses. Not that it stopped her. A winner was always a few days in the future, while in the present she half-starved herself in order to buy fractions of animals that could be out-distanced by toddlers on scooters. During the past few years even these fractions had diminished as inflation had tripled the annual cost of maintaining a trotter to about $3,000. If one of her horses accidentally happened to win a $5,000 purse, Mabel's share would hardly amount to $100.

At least she managed to support herself. Charlie's father, as he appeared in Mabel's stories, had left the track broke unless he won on the last race. Charlie understood this, which was why he avoided gambling. He knew that given the chance he, too, would bet on ants crossing sidewalks and sparrows preparing to land. Sometimes it frightened him how easily he could enter into the role of gambler, which, for him, was half ritual and half play.

Whenever he went to the flat track in August, he was always careful to enter by the same gate and made sure to tip the Salvation Army lassie fifty cents for luck. But it was between races that Charlie practiced the major part of his ritual. Armed with his program and *Racing Form* opened to the past performance page, he would watch the horses being saddled under the elms, watch the horses and jockeys enter the walking ring, then watch the parade to the track. Charlie thought of it as studying rather than watching. Often he would then run inside to see how his favorites walked, trotted, cantered or galloped to the gate. Naturally he had field glasses.

Reviewing his information, Charlie would seek a logical conclusion. It was rarely correct. His indecision about two horses might be based on their colors, while a jockey with a pleasant face could lead Charlie from one defeat to another. He was impressed by the brisk efficiency of Ron Turcotte and charmed by the angelic smile of Jorge Velasquez.

Charlie approached gambling as a romantic. He wasn't betting two dollars, he was pledging his troth, and if, in the course of his wanderings, a horse sneezed, coughed or nodded in his direction, he would back it even if it were bandaged up to its stifles.

His three older cousins, The Cousins, as his wife called them, went casually to the races half a dozen times a year, and their winnings or losses rarely exceeded $10. It was just as well that Charlie and his mother had moved in with Uncle Frank, a respectable plumber, after the death of his father.

The blond dancer still faced the bar. Actually, her dancing

was a form of jogging. She had large, heavy breasts that lunged up and down in time to the music. Grinning and pinching her nipples, she called again to a man near Charlie: "See, I'm not fat."

The blond dancer reminded him sightly of Gladys, as had many women he had seen that day. In high school she had been considered fast, dating seniors and boys who had quit school. Charlie, on the other hand, had collected stamps and was secretary of the chess club. He had enjoyed the way people looked at him when it became known that he was going around with Gladys Cheney. In those days she had worn tight skirts and Charleston beads, pink frilly see-through blouses over large white bras.

Charlie thought again of Sam. If Billy the Kid was as "open-handed, generous-hearted, frank and manly" as Pat Garrett claimed then Sam's only similarity to the outlaw was in his love for his mother, for Billy loved and honored his mother "more than anything else on earth." The same could be said of Sam, and it had always struck Charlie as unhealthy.

But where Billy was gregarious, Sam was solitary. Even stealing cars had been a private act. Charlie had difficulty seeing him with a roommate. Possibly Stacy had been telling the truth. Maybe Sam really had gone to California, taking his new roommate with him. Peter Bonenfant, the good child.

Charlie finished his beer. It was after nine. He had been avoiding going to The Lamplighter. In his mind he saw it as a smoky den where customers lay stretched on benches with opium pipes.

That, however, wasn't the main reason for avoiding the place. He was afraid of being disappointed. Originally he had thought finding Sam would be easy. He had seen himself as coming into the city, poking around and there would be Sam, perhaps under a rock. It had been as simple as something in a daydream.

The dancer's body was like Gladys', or rather as Gladys had been in 1950. The music stopped and the dancer returned to fanning her face. She had thick, well-formed legs. It seemed to Charlie that Gladys had had legs like that; not that he had ever seen her naked but there had been a class picnic out at Lake Saratoga and everyone had gone swimming.

Uncle Frank had been a quiet man, but when he learned that Gladys was pregnant he had nearly broken Charlie's jaw.

7

▼▼▼

N O PLACE COULD HAVE been more usual than The Lamplighter, despite its various pretensions, as if its owner couldn't decide between a bar for swinging singles, the thirsty proletariat, East Village intellectuals or simply turning it into a cocktail lounge. While the owner made up his mind, the bar grew shabbier and shabbier.

It was a large, dark, square room with the bar itself, a narrow horseshoe, taking up most of the center. Along the side walls were red vinyl booths and above each booth hung a black plastic pot with red plastic geraniums.

The walls were papered with the large sort of theater poster found in suburban railway stations: *Pajama Game, West Side Story.* Above the bar hung a dozen red, blue and yellow lights which rotated slowly, coloring the faces of the customers beneath. The bar itself was padded with more red vinyl. At the back on the left side was a Foos Ball game, and at the back on the right was a jukebox. There were fifteen people in the bar, and not one had an opium pipe.

Charlie sat at the bottom of the U, drinking draft beer. He had already talked to the bartender, a thin, bald man in a white shirt and black suspenders whom people called Luke. At first he hadn't recognized Sam's name, then, when he saw the picture: "Oh, yeah, Sam, no, haven't seen him for, jeez, can't say how long."

"How long do you think?"

"Maybe three weeks, maybe a month, maybe less. You know how it is. What're you drinking?"

It struck Charlie that Sam and Peter Bonenfant were probably off on some perfectly innocent journey. With embarrassment he realized he had come to New York hoping for the worst, at least to find death or disfigurement, something to justify his trip. He was not, after all, wearing his revolver just to visit places like the Metropole Cafe.

"Do you know where he might have gone?"

Luke shook his head. "Not me, I don't believe in asking questions."

There were nine other people sitting at the bar, all close enough to hear anything Charlie said. They could have been store clerks, students or factory hands. With one exception, they seemed indifferent to his presence.

Ever since he had come in, Charlie had been aware of a man watching him from the left side of the bar. Charlie thought he was about fifty. He had a large square head with gray hair brushed straight back and blue eyes that were too far apart. He wore a dark green blazer, light green shirt and a yellow tie. Theatrical, thought Charlie.

Whenever Charlie had looked at him, the man turned away, but each time he turned a little less, as if trying to overcome a certain disinclination or shyness. Now when Charlie glanced at him, the man looked back and smiled. Then it was Charlie's turn to look away as it occurred to him that the man might have nothing to do with Sam Cheney, but rather thought Charlie was trying to pick him up.

It was too late. The man got up and walked toward him, bringing his drink and still smiling. He looked like an elderly but still handsome frog. Sitting down next to Charlie, he put his drink on the bar. From this distance, Charlie thought the smile was a little forced.

"So you're looking for Sam, are you?"

Charlie nodded. The man gave him a card which identified him as Lawrence A. Driscoll. In the top left-hand corner was the word "consultant."

Charlie handed back the card. "What do you consult about?"

"Consumer relations, free lance. I'm also looking for Sam."

When Driscoll spoke, he opened his mouth more than necessary as if he thought his words so important that they needed more space than the words of lesser men.

"How come?"

Charlie wondered if Sam was involved in shoplifting again. But whatever Driscoll did, Charlie doubted he was a store detective. He had grown aware of a strong lilac scent that came from his new acquaintance.

"He owes me twenty bucks. Why're you looking for him?"

"He owes me twenty bucks too."

"Oh." There was a pause. Driscoll looked at his drink which was a Black Russian. "You acted more like a cop."

"I am a cop. Have you seen Sam recently?"

"Not for a couple of weeks. You a New York cop?"

"Saratoga Springs."

Driscoll seemed relieved. "Ingrid Bergman, right? Gary Cooper?"

"Pardon me?"

"The movie, *Saratoga Trunk*. You come all the way down here just to collect twenty bucks?" Driscoll had thick, gray eyebrows which he kept raising either in emphasis or nervousness.

"His mother wants to get in touch with him. I'm a friend of the family."

"Maybe he left town."

"Maybe."

"You come down all this way just because of his mother?"

"No, I had to get a new silver whistle."

Driscoll raised hie eyebrows.

"Once I get a whistle," continued Charlie, "I'll have to get a whole new uniform. The chief wants us to look sharp what with the bicentennial and all. What do you mean, free-lance consumer relations?"

Driscoll gave a little jump. He had the unsettled air of someone who meant to ask a favor.

"Oh, you know, public relations, keeping people happy. Macy's, Korvettes, I've had a lot of experience. I'm semi-retired now, just help out my friends."

"That so. You know anything about locks?"

"Locks? What kind?"

"Cylinder locks, I guess."

"Well, you've got a plug or cylinder with about five holes in it and five pin tumblers down in the holes to keep the cylinder from turning, and when you use the right key the pins are pushed out of the cylinder which can then rotate and move the bolt so the door can be opened. Is that what you mean?"

But Charlie was no longer paying attention. Stacy Doyle had sat down on the other side of him.

8
▼▼▼

"I'M SORRY I was rude to you earlier. I knew there would be a quiz in French and, well, shall we sit in a booth?" She looked past Charlie to Driscoll who was finishing his Black Russian and ordering another. Stacy's black hair was pinned in a bun. It made her look older.

As he followed her toward a booth by the jukebox, Charlie asked, "Did Sam give you an address in San Diego? Someplace you could reach him?" He tried to keep himself from staring at her legs. She was still wearing the short denim skirt, Indian blouse and yellow jacket.

Stacy sat down, turned and put her feet up on the seat so her bare knees showed above the edge of the table. There was a red candle stuck in a wax-covered wine bottle. After digging around in her Indian bag for some matches, Stacy lit the candle.

"No, Sam said he'd call or write. He only meant to be gone three weeks. I've been sort of expecting him."

"Maybe he's staying with Bonenfant's parents. I take it Bonenfant went with him."

There was the smallest pause. "No, Peter doesn't get along with his parents. I don't know where they're staying. What should I call you? I can't just say Mr. Bradshaw."

Charlie had always preferred Chuck as a nickname. In Saratoga, however, he had always been known as Charlie. It seemed a name for cartoon characters and clowns.

"Chuck, you can call me Chuck. Did Sam say why he was going to San Diego?"

But Stacy had taken out a small pad and pencil and was writing down numbers. The turning lights above the bar brushed red, blue and yellow over her thin face, giving her three slightly different faces and making Charlie even more aware of the original.

Stacy looked up. "Chuck Bradshaw, that makes you a seven."

"Pardon me?"

"Numerology."

"I don't understand." Charlie found himself afraid that the difference of age, place and society were too great to be bridged.

"Every letter has its numerical equivalent. I use the Hebrew system with some help from the Greek. The letters of your name add up to forty-three. Then you add the four and three to get seven."

Charlie nodded. "How did Sam happen to know this Peter Bonenfant?"

"They met once when Sam was out west. UCLA, I think. Peter was a student there."

"What does Bonenfant look like?"

"Oh, you know, thin, long hair, jeans. Just about like anyone. You're lucky to be a seven. It's one of the best numbers." She still held her pad and seemed to be consulting it.

"What does it mean?"

Stacy put the pad on the table. "It's a number of completeness and the number of the moon. Seven controls the cycles of life. The body renews itself every seven years; each phase of the moon has seven days. There are seven colors in the spectrum, seven notes in the scale, seven days in the week, seven orifices in a man's body."

"What's that have to do with me?"

"It makes you who you are. Sevens are very serious, even

scholarly. They stay by themselves, think and meditate a lot. You know, unworldly. They're very dignified and self-controlled. All sevens are smart and imaginative. With many people you know their number right off, but sevens are more hidden; you always think they're something else. They're aloof and don't care about money."

When Stacy spoke, she stared directly into his face, neither blinking nor turning away. The bar had become crowded, and the noise and people surrounded them like a small room, almost adding to their privacy. Charlie couldn't decide why she was telling him about numbers.

He began to ask another question about Bonenfant, then said, "Why don't you use the whole name? I mean, my name's Charles Fletcher Bradshaw."

Turning in her seat, Stacy leaned toward Charlie until her face shone in the light of the candle.

"You use the name the person is known by or how he sees himself. Numerologists believe the name of something contains the essence of its being. Your name is a miniature image of you. So to find out what a person's like, you study his name. The whole thing goes back to Pythagoras and has to do with the cycle of vibration. I'm still learning about that. Did you know the medieval Jews believed you could cure a sick man, save his life, just by changing his name?"

"No," said Charlie, "I didn't." He watched as Stacy began to write something else on her pad. Her earrings were small golden stars and reflected the candlelight. Glancing through the people toward the bar, Charlie saw Driscoll staring at him. Driscoll raised his eyebrows.

"You also have two other numbers," said Stacy. "Do you want to know about them?"

"Why did Bonenfant come to New York?"

"I don't know. He just showed up."

"Okay, tell me about the numbers."

"Well, there's your heart number and your personality number. You get your heart number by adding up the vowels in your name. You've only got three and they come out to eight.

To get your personality number, you add up the consonants. Those come out to eight, too. That's rare, usually you have different numbers."

"What's an eight?" asked Charlie.

"It stands for worldly involvement and either material success or failure. Eight is twice four, and four is the number of earth and matter. Four is also the number of defeat, so eight can be a spectacular defeat. But in Christian symbolism, eight is the number of life after death, so it can be success or failure, you know, heaven or hell. Eight is the number of eternity or infinity. That's why the mathematical symbol for infinity is an eight lying on its side. Eight also means new life. A woman's body has one more orifice than a man's, and that eighth hole is the child's entrance to the world. In churches the baptismal font traditionally has eight sides, meaning that baptism is the beginning of new life. And it used to be that Jews would only name a baby boy on its eighth day."

Charlie finished his beer. "What's any of that have to do with my heart and personality?"

"It all applies to who you are. Most eights are businessmen or politicians, even policemen. They're hard workers, but they can be unimaginative and selfish. Sometimes they get mean and push people around. Often they don't like themselves. They're sure they'll fail or that other people don't like them. They can also be rebellious. You know, spend half their lives doing something, then turn around and do something else or just screw it up. But the main thing is that they will either succeed tremendously or fail tremendously. There's no in between."

"How long have you been telling fortunes?"

Stacy looked at him seriously. "I'm not predicting anything. I'm just telling you what already exists."

Charlie nodded and looked away. "What if my name was Charlie?"

Stacy wrote down some numbers. "Charlie Bradshaw comes out to eight. Great success or failure."

"How about Charles F. Bradshaw?"

After a moment Stacy said, "That makes you a nine. They've

really got class. Three times three, the number of brilliance. Both Lincoln and Kennedy were nines. Tremendous mental and spiritual achievement."

"What about Sam? What's his number?"

Stacy answered without hesitation. "Sam's a five."

"What's that?"

"It stands for sexuality. Fives make the best lovers. Sensuality too because there are five senses. It's the number of Don Juan. Fives are gamblers, always moving around, taking new chances. But mostly it's sexuality."

"What's your number?"

Stacy glanced up at him. "I'm also a five." She reached out and touched Charlie's wrist with one finger. "Sevens are good lovers, too."

Charlie tried not to jump. "What do you do when you're not talking about numbers?"

Stacy laughed and leaned back in the booth. "I'm a graduate student in modern languages at NYU."

Charlie knew he was being seduced but he didn't know why. Although not ugly, neither was he particularly dashing. And even accepting the sexuality of sevens, he didn't think eights were known for much. Great success or failure. Charlie could count his sexual conquests on one maimed hand. Most had come when he was stationed in Germany.

He didn't count his wife a sexual conquest. He was a solidly married solid citizen of Saratoga Springs. Whatever his inclinations, Charlie lacked the opportunity. Even if the chance arose, his shyness would defeat him.

But Stacy seemed indifferent to his shyness. Why should she seduce him? He guessed it had something to do with Sam and he wanted to know more about that. The question was whether to agree, but even the asking of it caused him to breathe faster. Again he found himself thinking of his birthday. Stacy sat back watching him. Being an eminently polite man, Charlie wasn't sure how to say he was willing to be seduced.

Stacy solved that problem for him. Picking up her pad, she said, "Let's go back to my apartment."

TUESDAY

9

▼▼▼

WHEN CHARLIE WOKE at seven the next morning, he at first didn't know where he was. Fully clothed except for his shoes, he lay on a blue couch, the springs of which were so broken that the pillowed surface could be converted into a roller coaster for braver mice. Charlie's back was killing him. His mouth felt dry and he thought that wherever he was, he must have been drunk when he arrived.

Then, looking across the room, he saw a double bed with white sheets and a white bedspread. Long black hair was spread out on the pillows.

Charlie sat up and pulled off the army blanket that had covered him. Wishing to be gone before Stacy woke, he began hunting for his shoes and found them side by side next to the couch. His tan porkpie hat was on top of his shoes and his striped tie was carefully folded on top of his hat.

The room was full of sunlight. Apart from the couch and bed, the only furniture was a white wooden table with several straight chairs and a small white bureau. The walls were white and bare. Along the wall by the door were ten cardboard boxes full of books.

Charlie finished tying his shoes and stood up. He looked at Stacy, half-covered by the white bedspread. She was naked and lay on her side with her knees drawn up. Her hair was like a black fan on the pillows.

They had only talked the night before. Talked. Charlie had done most of the talking with an animation intended to make sure there were no long pauses during which she might ask him why he was sitting on the couch. At last she had gone to sleep.

He told himself he did not want to act in a way which he

would disapprove of in others. He told himself he had to be careful in New York, that he wasn't taking a vacation and couldn't allow himself to let down his guard. He had also been shy, afraid of appearing a fool with a woman young enough to be his daughter. He had been afraid that he wouldn't be able to maintain or even achieve an erection. So he had talked.

He had talked about himself and Saratoga Springs as if the town were a tree and he were one of its branches. Saratoga Springs: home of Charlie Bradshaw, parimutuel betting and the potato chip. He told her how in 1830 Dr. John Clarke was shipping out 1,200 bottles of mineral water a day for such complaints as scorbutic ulcers and depraved appetite. He talked about his father's wedding present to his mother: a balding parrot named Kentucky after the first winner of the Travers Stakes. If Stacy hadn't been naked, Charlie would have shown her the scar on the back of his left hand where Kentucky had bit out a chunk when Charlie was six.

Unsure of where he was or what to do, Charlie comforted himself by describing where he had been and what he had done. He told her how he had spent the previous year's vacation driving around central New York following the trail of the Loomis gang who had raided farms from the 1840's until nearly 1900, and had sold thousands of stolen horses to the U.S. Army during the Civil War. And he was sorry he hadn't brought the photographs of the farm house in Nine Mile Swamp where George Washington Loomis, Jr., leader of the gang, had been beaten to death by vigilantes in 1865, and his brother, Plumb, had been beaten and thrown into a bonfire.

Stacy hadn't said much. She had taken off her clothes and gotten in bed. Charlie had looked away, while realizing she wouldn't have cared if he had circled her with a camera. Then she had sat in bed watching him, presumably waiting for him to join her while he talked faster and faster. When he finished telling about the Loomis gang, he saw she was asleep. He had taken the army blanket from the foot of the bed and covered himself on the couch. Since entering her apartment, he hadn't mentioned Sam Cheney.

Now Charlie wanted to escape. He had no experience with

young women and was afraid of appearing even more ridiculous. He walked quietly to the door.

"Are you leaving?"

Turning, he saw Stacy up on one elbow watching him. He was more aware of her bare breasts than her face.

"There's some stuff I've got to do."

"I mean, are you going back up to Saratoga?"

"Not today."

He stopped as Stacy got out of bed and walked to the white bureau. She made no attempt to cover herself. The loveliness of her body was like an eraser on Charlie's mind. She drew a pair of white panties and faded blue jeans from the bureau and put them on. Charlie looked away again. He felt bullied in a way he wasn't used to.

"Tell me more about Peter Bonenfant."

Stacy had been slipping a rope belt through the loops on her jeans. She stopped and looked at Charlie in surprise. She had small firm breasts with small nipples.

"I told you, he's a friend of Sam's. They met at UCLA."

"Was he a student there?"

"I think so."

"What was he studying?" Charlie carefully kept his eyes on her face.

"I don't know, sociology or psychology. Is it important?"

"It might be. Why'd he come to New York?"

Stacy finished putting on her belt. "I don't know, maybe he just felt like it."

Charlie kept pushing. "Didn't Sam know he was coming?"

"I don't think so."

"Are you sure?"

Stacy glanced at him angrily and walked over to the kitchenette. Putting some water in a tea kettle, she lit the stove and put the kettle on the front burner.

"Do you want some coffee?"

"No, thanks." Charlie didn't move from the door. "Are you sure Sam didn't know he was coming?"

Stacy turned quickly, her black hair fell across her right shoulder partly hiding her breast.

"I don't know much about it. He seemed to just show up, you know, on the spur of the moment. At least Sam didn't say anything."

"So then Sam decided to go out west?"

"That's right. He's been meaning to take a vacation so he decided to go back with Peter."

"And they drove?"

Stacy nodded. Opening a small refrigerator next to the sink, she took out a bottle of orange juice. "Would you like a glass?"

"No, thanks. Where did Sam get a car?"

Stacy took a glass from the cupboard above the sink and poured herself some orange juice. She kept her bare back to Charlie. "He borrowed one."

"Borrowed?"

"That's right."

"Are you sure?"

Stacy turned and some of the juice slopped over the rim of the glass. "What the hell is this? You want to twist my arm?"

She put down the juice, walked to a closet near Charlie and took a yellow sweater from a hook. As she put it on, Charlie could have reached out and touched one of her breasts. He moved back a step.

"And you say there's absolutely no way I can get in touch with Sam?"

"I've told you, I don't know where he is. It's that simple."

Charlie found himself thinking that he very rarely saw his own wife naked. Marge changed her clothes in the bathroom, and at night she always wore men's pajamas.

"Okay," said Charlie, "I'll probably see you later."

He opened the door, paused and added over his shoulder, "I'm sorry if I kept you up last night."

10

▼▼▼

C HARLIE GOT BACK to the YMCA at 9:30. He had stopped
for breakfast and at a printers on Seventh Avenue to
order some business cards:

CHARLES F. BRADSHAW

SERGEANT

COMMUNITY AND YOUTH RELATIONS BUREAU

SARATOGA SPRINGS, N.Y.

The man at the counter had said he could pick them up that
afternoon. Charlie thought the cards would be useful in solicit-
ing funds for Little League Baseball.

After paying for another night, Charlie went upstairs to
change his clothes and wash. The mustard yellow halls were
crowded with Puerto Rican maids pushing linen carts and
shouting in Spanish.

Unlocking the door of Room 931, Charlie entered, then
stopped as abruptly as if he had bumped into a second door
a few feet beyond the first. A large, thick man in a gray overcoat and gray fedora sat on the small chair by the desk. He was
holding Charlie's book: *The Authentic Life of Billy, the Kid.*

"You reading this?"

"Sort of, I mean, I've read it before."

The man tossed the book on the desk. "What'd you do,
get laid?"

"What . . . ?"

"Bet your fucking A. you did. Sam Cheney, he's going to
love you."

Charlie started to reach for his revolver. The big man casually stuck out his hand, palm forward.

"Don't do it. Jesus, Benedetto said you were a stooge. He
didn't know the half of it. Big fucking cop you are."

He took out his wallet and showed Charlie his identification which said he was Conrad Zack, a lieutenant with the New York Police Department.

Charlie took no pleasure in seeing him. "How'd you get in here?"

"Through the window, you prick. You really take the cake. Why're you looking for this Sam Cheney anyway? Or have you quit now that you're balling his old lady?"

Charlie began to get angry, then thought better of it. He took off his hat and raincoat, and sat down on the bed. What bothered him most was that Zack could get into his room, while he couldn't get into Sam Cheney's. He looked at Zack, still restraining himself. The New York lieutenant was about forty-five with a square head, square chin and sagging brown eyes like a hound's. He returned Charlie's stare with a mixture of boredom and disgust.

"His mother's worried about him," said Charlie at last.

"Jesus, you fuck her too? I better cross my legs."

"You got anything special to say or are you just going to sit there and insult me?"

"I'm gonna insult you awhile longer, you dumb fuck. I want you to check out of here and go back to Saratoga Springs."

Charlie leaned back against the wall. "Is there anyone I can report you to for breaking into my room?"

"I told you I want you to go home."

"I'm looking for Sam Cheney."

Zack shook his head. Then, taking off his fedora, he looked inside it as if it were the place where he kept clever remarks. His gray hair was in a crew cut. Charlie guessed it had been in a crew cut ever since Zack had gone into the Marines or army or whatever he had gone into twenty-five years before.

"Look, don't think I'm a bastard. We got something all arranged down here. If you hang around, you're going to mess it up."

"What sort of thing?"

"That's none of your business. You just believe me, that's all. If you keep poking around and asking questions, you're going to screw it up for the rest of us." He had a low nasal voice, devoid of any emotion except anger and boredom.

"What about Sam?"

Zack got to his feet. He was about six inches taller than Charlie. "You think you're Pat Garrett? You think this Sam Cheney's some Billy the Kid? What kind of game are you playing?"

Charlie kept his voice calm. "I've got to call Benedetto."

"Why? I talked to Benedetto yesterday, I talked to him today. Believe me, Sam Cheney isn't in any hospital, though it would be better for him if he was. You go home, okay?"

"What kind of trouble is he in?" asked Charlie.

"I don't want to talk about it."

"Drugs?"

"I said I don't want to talk about it."

"What if I don't go back?"

Zack held out his right hand, then slowly closed his fingers, making a fist. "What do they teach you in Saratoga? How to be a fast prick? I'm being a nice guy, okay? We'll find your punk for you. If you stay down here and step on our toes, well, there's nothing to say I gotta keep being a nice guy."

Charlie tried to think of something insulting; something that would leave Zack crushed. Instead he said, "Sure."

Zack stared down at him. Disdain, boredom, it wasn't a pleasant expression. Then he left.

Charlie shut the door after him, kept himself from slamming it. He was a thoughtful man and he disliked anger because it interfered with thought. It made him angry not to be taken seriously.

Opening his suitcase, he rummaged around for his toothbrush and shaving gear. He found it interesting that Zack had known he had been with Stacy Doyle. Either he was having her followed or The Lamplighter was under surveillance or both. Taking out a clean shirt, Charlie grabbed a towel from the shelf and walked to the door.

As with Benedetto, Charlie would have preferred to be accepted as a fellow policeman. Indeed, it was unfortunate that

Zack hadn't been more friendly. Charlie told himself that if Zack had been halfway polite, he would have gone back to Saratoga Springs.

As it was, he didn't see why he should allow Zack to influence him. He knew he was being stubborn, but as he walked to the washroom, Charlie told himself that Zack's problems were no concern of his.

11
▼▼▼

A T ONE O'CLOCK Charlie Bradshaw was strolling up Fifth Avenue toward the Plaza, staring into store windows and gawking as much as any tourist from Kansas. He was particularly interested in a fifty-story building on 57th Street with glass walls that widened near the bottom forming a ten-story slide. He was curious to know what would happen to someone who jumped from the top. Would he strike the street or land in the lap of a terrified secretary on the fourth floor? Although he watched for nearly ten minutes, no one jumped.

It was a bright, sunny day, and while the air was cool, not much more than forty degrees, it had the feel of air that had blown from some spring-like place. Many people on the crowded sidewalk had their coats open, and no one had that huddled look of someone enduring the chill of winter. Charlie had walked from the YMCA to the Empire State Building and had then turned up Fifth in an attempt to improve his mood which had gotten better by the time he reached the library.

He hadn't done much washing at the Y. In the toilet stalls were such messages as: *Sex in Room 943, Come to the showers for a big one, Sex in the showers anytime,* and *Bobo, be in the showers at one.*

Charlie felt some concern for the present occupant of Room 943. None of the messages were dated. Perhaps Room 943 now contained an asthmatic old man with a weak heart. Did he complain about people tapping on his door at 3 a.m.? Did he wonder about the sly looks of his neighbors?

Pausing by the Pulitzer Fountain, Charlie glanced around for an empty bench but all seemed occupied. He was enjoying the crowds of people who on a day like this seemed friendly and less withdrawn. He watched an attractive young woman get into a light gray Rolls Royce in front of the Plaza Hotel, and he thought she might be a celebrity. She was bound to be someone. He considered telling his friends in Saratoga that he had seen—who had he seen? The women who had once excited him in films were no longer young. Princess Grace? Jane Russell? Charlie continued up Fifth Avenue toward the statue of General Sherman.

When he had left the Y that morning, he had found a message to call Stacy. Surprisingly, she had apologized for being rude.

"I'm never friendly in the morning," she had said. "Maybe we can get together later unless you're going back. Please don't think I was bored last night."

Despite his better judgment, Charlie had been flattered. "I'll be over at The Lamplighter this evening."

"What time? I'll meet you."

"Around nine." Charlie paused. "You know, when I got back to the Y this morning, I found a cop waiting for me."

"Oh?"

"Yeah, he was waiting in my room. Must have had someone open it up for him. Sort of irritated me." He waited to see what she would say. For a moment she didn't say anything. The room with the phones was a long narrow room off the main lobby. It was empty except for Charlie.

"I should think it would. Who was it?"

"A lieutenant by the name of Conrad Zack."

"He's a narc." That was said quickly.

"How do you know?"

"It's common knowledge. I mean, he's a lieutenant, isn't he? What did he want?"

Charlie had ignored this. "Has Sam been in any trouble with drugs in New York?"

"No, well, one time he was picked up at a place where some guys were sniffing coke. The police said he was loitering in the presence of a controlled drug or something like that. They let him go after a while. What did Zack want?"

"Just to say hello. Did you know Sam was almost arrested in Saratoga for selling grass?"

"I didn't know he was selling it."

"Well, he was. A warrant was issued but Sam left town before it could be served."

"I knew you had helped him."

Charlie was surprised. "Sam told you about me?" His first thought was that he had told Stacy to call him Chuck, while Sam would have referred to him as Charlie.

"Look, I've got to run. I'll try and meet you at The Lamplighter. Okay?" She had hung up without waiting for an answer.

Although Zack was a lieutenant, Charlie knew there were between 500 and 600 men in the narcotics division of the New York Police Department. He told himself that Stacy had probably seen the policeman's name in the newspaper, but he didn't really believe it.

Charlie stood near the statue of General Sherman and watched several horse-drawn carriages waiting for customers on Central Park South. He considered what it would be like to ride down Fifth Avenue in a carriage, leaning back and looking up at skyscrapers and blue sky, while next to it drove a police car with Zack staring from the back seat. It would do nothing to change Zack's opinion that Charlie was a punk cop, a goof.

Actually, thought Charlie, wandering into the park, I've had all sorts of training.

Over the years Charlie's chief had enrolled him in a variety of courses, ranging from new weapons to the feasibility of mounting television cameras on street corners. Since these courses were paid for by the government, Chief Peterson had thought it foolish not to take advantage of them and somehow it had been Charlie who was always sent.

Most memorable had been several weeks at the Civil Defense

Agency school in Battle Creek. He had learned how to control food riots and had qualified as a fallout shelter manager. One day in class a police detective from Saginaw had nudged him and said, "You know, a shelter manager, he's got the pick of the broads."

Sometimes, late at night, Charlie would think of this police-man, waiting for the Bomb in Saginaw so he could at last attain sexual fulfillment.

Charlie again thought of Stacy with regret. He was sure, however, that if the moment were repeated he would still refuse to get into her bed. It remained surprising that he had even gone to her apartment. Partly it was because of his birthday, and partly because she reminded him of Gladys. But if Stacy were Gladys, that would put Zack into the role of his uncle who was the gentlest of men, always excepting the day when he heard Gladys was pregnant.

Uncle Frank had accused Charlie of being just like his father, a cheap Don Juan who never cared about the consequences. That had been more painful than the blow for which Uncle Frank had later apologized.

Each day in school, Gladys had teased Charlie about getting her pregnant and passed him notes accusing him of being the father of a child she was already calling Little Leroy. Charlie had been humiliated.

At the time he had no idea that Gladys was also teasing four other boys, any one of whom could have been the father of Little Leroy. Of the five, one had left town, two had coughed up money, one had proposed and one had kept very quiet. Charlie had been the last. Uncle Frank had been certain it would end in court, although he was more afraid of scandal than legal retribution.

Then, unaccountably, Gladys' mother had taken her up to Warrensburg. When Gladys had returned, Sam had been ten years old. At least she hadn't named the child Leroy.

By now Charlie had reached the zoo. Even the animals seemed invigorated by the warmer weather. Monkeys cavorted and tropical birds made noises like nails being drawn from wood. But it was the zebras that attracted Charlie the most.

As he stood before their pen, he realized that without his knowing it the zebra had always been his favorite animal. They were so tidy, not clean but tidy in their stripes. So contained and suitcase-like. He remembered reading that they couldn't be trained for riding, and he felt it must be because no one had ever properly tried or had had enough sympathy. Charlie asked himself if, given the chance, he would rather domesticate the zebra or find Sam Cheney. The question depressed him and he moved away from the pen. He would find Sam Cheney.

12

▼▼▼

A T FIVE O'CLOCK Charlie sat on a stool at The Lamplighter drinking his first beer of the day. He had no definite plans but he knew his presence was an irritant and he hoped something might come of that. If nothing else, it would irritate Conrad Zack.

Earlier, after picking up his business cards, he had gone down to the men's store on Eighth Street where Sam worked. It was the sort of place that calls its merchandise "trend-setters." One such trend-setter in the window was a three-piece, double-breasted suit of pink velveteen.

Talking to the manager, Charlie had learned that Sam hadn't been seen since Friday, March 21st. He hadn't even picked up his paycheck. It was unlike Sam to leave money lying around.

As he left the store, Charlie had been stopped by one of the clerks: a thin, emaciated young man with dyed blond hair. Perched on the tip of his nose were a pair of glasses with octagonal wire rims. At first Charlie had thought they were very clean, then he realized they had no lenses.

"I don't know if you know this," the clerk had said, "but Sam was trying to raise a lot of money before he . . . left."

"How much money?"

"Oh, I don't know, maybe thousands. I mean, that's why it's funny about his paycheck. You know what they say . . ."

"A fool and his money are soon parted?"

The clerk tugged at his yellow bow tie. "I was thinking of 'every little bit counts.' "

Later, sitting in The Lamplighter, Charlie was trying to arrange his pieces of knowledge. 1—Sam's Disappearance. 2—Sam's need of money. 3—Sam's involvement with drugs. 4—Conrad Zack. It seemed that either Sam was going to buy drugs or he owed money to some drug-related person. In the past, Sam's involvement had been with marijuana. Charlie would have suspected that he was again mixed up with marijuana if it weren't for Zack. He didn't think a police lieutenant would directly involve himself for a few kilos of grass.

As he considered this, Charlie wondered about Peter Bonenfant. He couldn't decide about the level of his involvement. Also, if Sam's disappearance had some perfectly natural explanation, why hadn't he contacted the clothing store about his check? It could easily have been forwarded to California.

Charlie went over these questions with growing irritation. It seemed that just as he was about to reach some new plateau of speculation, he would have a mental picture of Stacy Doyle lying naked on her white bed. Charlie disliked these intrusions: such erotic fragments made him mistrust his judgment.

Charlie was also fearful that he might be growing infatuated with a twenty-three-year-old woman. He thought it undignified. It wasn't that he believed being forty-one limited him to certain prescribed courses of action. Rather he wanted to remain the master of his actions, whatever they were.

A cautious man, he distrusted people who were not in control of themselves: people driven by love, anger, drunkenness or a desire to bet all their money on tenth-rate horses. He told himself he didn't want his life disrupted. But even as he thought that, he knew it wasn't entirely true. He knew that by coming to New York he had chosen a kind of disruption. He had chosen to leave the orderly path of his life in Saratoga.

Charlie called Luke over and ordered another beer. There were eight other customers in the bar, and most of the noise came from four men playing Foos Ball, slamming the metal rods and shouting whenever the ball shot past the miniature goalie. As Charlie received his beer, Lawrence A. Driscoll climbed onto the stool to his left.

"I thought you might be gone."

"No, not yet."

"Don't you get bored doing this kind of thing?"

As on the previous evening, there was condescension in Driscoll's voice; and although Charlie believed it might come from Driscoll's own insecurity, he was tired of assuming the role of bumpkin. Driscoll still wore his green blazer. Under it he had on a tight green turtleneck which made his large stomach look like half a green apple.

"Actually," said Charlie, lengthening his vowels, "actually I been sightseeing. I'll bet dollars to doughnuts you didn't know this was the northern stamping ground of The Dead Rabbits."

Driscoll's slightly indifferent expression turned to concern.

"Don't worry," said Charlie, patting his shoulder, "all The Dead Rabbits been dead for some time. They were a gang of toughs who robbed, mugged and worked for Tammany Hall in the 1850's. Their battle flag was a dead rabbit stuck up on a spear. The reason I'm interested is that for a while their leader was Old Smoke Morrissey."

"Oh?"

"You see, it was Morrissey who brought big time gambling to Saratoga Springs. Morrissey's Club House later became the Canfield Casino. Old Smoke used to tell people, 'No man can say that I ever turned a dishonest card or struck a foul blow.'

"And it was Morrissey, not Travers, who made horse racing fashionable. 'Course, once Travers saw there was money in it, he started his own racing association and pushed Morrissey out. Old Smoke's track was called Horse Haven and they keep it on as a training track."

"Is that so." Mild concern had subsided back to indifference.

It was clear to Charlie that Driscoll had not joined him by choice. He wanted to ask, Are you a policeman? An undercover host of the city? Watching him, Charlie was reminded of a fat boy, nicknamed Salt Pork, whom he had known in grade school. Salt Pork was a lethargic child whose only enthusiasm came from opening the paper bag containing his lunch. This was a ritual that could last fifteen minutes as Salt Pork prodded, squeezed, sniffed and finally unpacked the bag as one might open a Christmas present from a favorite aunt. The eating was always done quickly. Weak and pimply, Salt Pork was a constant target for bullies; and Charlie felt guiltily grateful for this, thinking that if Salt Pork hadn't been the class victim, he might have been chosen himself.

Charlie put his hand on Driscoll's green sleeve. "Now you're a cultured man. I'd think you'd be interested in a story like Old Smoke's. Did you know he was heavyweight boxing champion of the United States? Whipped Yankee Sullivan bare-fisted in thirty-eight rounds. And did you know he spent four years in the House of Representatives? One time Old Smoke offered to fight any ten Congressmen but no one took him up on it."

"Pity." Driscoll ordered a Black Russian and sipped it slowly.

"Sad thing is that none of it made any difference. Old Smoke spent his whole life trying to break into society and he never made it. People saw him as low class. Then he made the mistake of falling in with Cornelius Vanderbilt. He got Old Smoke to invest in railroads and Old Smoke lost a million dollars, dropped $800,000 on Black Friday alone. He died at forty-seven of a broken heart."

Driscoll stared silently into his glass.

"Bet you're curious why they called him Old Smoke."

"Ummm."

"Once when he was leading The Dead Rabbits, Old Smoke and another guy fought it out over a woman named Kate who ran a whorehouse. They did their fighting in a saloon. The other guy knocked Old Smoke into the fire, then sat on him until he started to burn. Well, Morrissey threw the other guy off, but after that people always called him Old Smoke."

"So you aren't interested in Sam Cheney anymore?"

Charlie glanced at Driscoll. "Sure, but I heard he'd gone out west."

"I don't know anything about that, but I was talking to a young man who said he'd seen him." Driscoll went back to sipping his Black Russian.

"He saw Sam? When?"

"Recently."

"Who is this guy?"

"He's just someone who hangs around here sometimes."

"What's his name?"

Twisting uncomfortably on his stool, Driscoll said, "Tateo. He said he'd give me a call. You want to talk to him?"

"Sure."

They sat for a while without talking. Charlie didn't much like Driscoll and what he mostly didn't like was the way Driscoll looked: the long gray hair, the eyes too far apart, the way he dressed. Disliking these things, however, made Charlie friendlier than he might have been. He even went so far as to buy Driscoll another Black Russian. Driscoll accepted the drink without comment, and Charlie returned to his own thoughts which were mostly about Stacy.

At forty-one, Charlie still believed he could pick up any new work and, depending on his effort, be successful. What depressed him about Stacy was that no amount of effort could make up for the differences between them. The fact that she was with Sam meant nothing. Even if she were unattached, it could never work.

Driscoll was called to the telephone shortly after six o'clock. Charlie watched him talk for a few minutes, then nod, write something down and hang up.

When he came back, he said, "He wants you to go over and see him. It's only a couple of blocks."

"I thought I was supposed to talk to him on the phone."

Driscoll shook his head, then touched his hair to make sure he hadn't disturbed anything. "Some people don't like phones. He's at a hotel on Third Avenue. You know Hudsons? An army-navy store on Third and 13th? It's just north of there. Here, I'll draw you a map."

Charlie's feet hurt. He was certain he had walked twenty miles since coming to the city. But it was partly because he believe his feet shouldn't hurt, and partly because he didn't want Driscoll to think he disliked him, that he left The Lamplighter.

As Charlie was about to cross Second Avenue at 11th Street, a white Chevrolet pulled up beside him. Conrad Zack stuck his head out the side window.

"Don't say I didn't warn you," he said.

13

▼▼▼

WHEN CHARLIE SAW the hotel on Third Avenue, he guessed it did most of its business by the hour. It was called The Olympia and its narrow entrance was tucked between a pizza counter and a discount record store that blared music out onto the street.

Charlie went up a flight of stairs to a small lobby on the second floor. There was no one at the desk. The walls were a dirty pink and the pigeonholes above the desk were empty. Driscoll had told Charlie to look for Room 38 on the third floor. After waiting a little, Charlie continued up the stairs. There was no sound in the hotel.

Room 38 was down a short hall to the left of the stairs. Charlie knocked.

"Come on in."

Charlie opened the door, stepped forward and hesitated. It was a small room with green walls, a battered brown bureau and a double bed in a brown metal frame. The mattress was covered with a yellow bedspread. A lanky young man in blue jeans and a jean jacket was sitting on the bed. He had on dark glasses in thick black plastic frames. His brown hair was curly and clipped close to his head. Charlie thought he was about thirty, but it was difficult to tell because of the glasses.

"You Tateo?"

"That's right."

Charlie took another step into the room. The someone gave him a slight push and the door shut behind him. Recovering his balance, Charlie turned quickly and saw a second young man who had been standing behind the door.

"Hi," the man said, and grinned.

He, too, was thin and wore jeans, along with a brown T-shirt. He had a small red stone in his right ear. It was more like a tie-tack than an earring. Charlie was mostly struck by his hair which was yellowish-orange. It was short and brushed back flat against his head, probably stuck down with something. It looked like cat's fur, an unhealthy cat.

"Nice of you to come," said the man.

Charlie guessed he was several years younger than the man on the bed.

"Why're you looking for Sammy?" asked Tateo.

"Because I want to find him."

Although Charlie now faced the bed, the second man remained behind him, so close that Charlie could feel his breath on the back of his neck. There were no windows in the small room.

"Yeah, but how come?"

"You know where he is?"

"He left town," said the man behind him. Charlie didn't turn.

"That's right," said Tateo. "He left town. How come you're looking for him?" The lenses of his dark glasses were moon-shaped, making Tateo's face look thinner and more delicate. He had almost no lips, just a horizontal line below his nose.

"Do you know where he went?" asked Charlie.

"Out west. He had to make a run."

"Run?"

"Hey, you a cop? We heard you're a cop."

"Saratoga Springs." Charlie considered giving Tateo one of his new calling cards.

"Shit, they got cops up there? Where's your horse?"

The man behind Charlie laughed; it was more of a giggle, an explosion of breath that tickled the back of Charlie's neck. He tried to ignore it.

"What d'you mean, he had to make a run?" Charlie asked.

"Just what I said. Sammy deals grass. He gets it in L.A. from a dude who brings it up the coast from Baja. So he goes out to L.A. coupla times a year, picks up a coupla kilos. No big thing."

"Why tell me? Why not tell Zack?"

"Zack?"

Charlie disliked talking to people who wore dark glasses. He also disliked men who wore earrings and dyed their hair. He disliked being breathed on, especially in a small, stuffy, windowless room.

"Zack's a narcotics lieutenant. He knows Sam. I saw him just this morning."

Tateo drew up his right leg and began picking at something on the heel of his boot. "If you're really down here because his mother's looking for him, why talk to Zack?"

"We're old chums."

Tateo stopped picking at his heel and slowly folded his arms. His jeans and blue denim jacket looked brand new. "You been talking to a lotta cops about Sammy?"

"Missing persons, and Zack of course. Did you see Sam leave for California?"

"That's what I been telling you, isn't it?"

"Did he drive, fly or take a bus?"

Tateo raised his voice. "How the fuck should I know. What d'you think, I followed him? Maybe he flew. He didn't say."

"You want him to get busted?" asked Charlie.

There was another giggle from the man behind him. Tateo leaned back on the bed, supporting himself on his elbows.

"Sammy owes us some bread. I'm not worrying about that. If he gets busted, then this dude in L.A., he'll need someone else for his New York dealing. Right?"

"Sure."

"You going back to your horses?" asked Tateo, sitting up.

"I expect so."

"Let him out, Jukes."

The man behind Charlie moved so that Charlie could open the door.

Once out on the street, Charlie decided not to go back to The Lamplighter. He would see if Stacy was home. He also wanted to think about Tateo and Jukes. He wasn't sure if he would mention them to Stacy.

14

▼▼▼

T HE HEAT WENT ON in Room 931 shortly before six. By six-thirty it had climbed to over 100 and Charlie had been forced to open the window. The Puerto Rican maids began shouting at eight, and at 8:05 one of them simultaneously knocked on and opened Charlie's door. He slammed it shut. There were shouts of apology or at least he assumed it was apology.

Down the hall he could hear someone yelling, "Eight bucks, I pay eight bucks so I can sleep. What's this, a fuckin' jail?"

And a maid was yelling over and over: "No spika anglis!"

Unable to return to sleep, Charlie lay on his back looking at the dirty white ceiling. He considered his dreams. A solitary man with many acquaintances, Charlie's dreams were filled with friends: people who didn't exist in a real world. Sleeping, he was always in a crowd, surrounded by men and women who felt kindly toward him. There were no celebrations or momentous events. His dreams had a pastoral quality, and whole nights might be spent picnicking or visiting friends or playing baseball. There was always lots of baseball, and once there had been a team of black bears in blue caps embroidered with the letter "B."

Occasionally, Charlie's wife would tell him her dreams and they would deal with fires and rapes, random violence, sexual frustration and insecurity—what Charlie thought of as working dreams. He felt himself lucky that his own dreams seemed to exist only to amuse him while he slept. That particular night he had dreamt of playing golf: as if his subconscious were attempting to deal with his sore legs.

It was later, during breakfast in the cafeteria, that the frustrations of the day began. The cashier had been unable to give change for a twenty, and Charlie had had to wait until money could be brought from New Jersey or Connecticut, he wasn't sure which. The silverware, if it could be called that, was white plastic, and the knife snapped as he smeared grape jelly on his toast.

The cafeteria was a large room and each wall was painted a different color: red, blue, yellow and green. A sign on the blue wall said that occupancy by more than 201 persons was illegal. Although the cafeteria was half full, few people were eating. Again there was the split between young blacks and older whites down on their luck. These last sat together in small groups arguing passionately about tax rebates, subway fare hikes and the past. Two old men were ready to come to blows over whether Harry Truman had had a dog in the White House.

As he sat in the cafeteria, Charlie began thinking of Stacy. They had had dinner at an Italian restaurant a few blocks from her apartment. Although the food was expensive, customers were invited to take as much wine and antipasto as they wished. Consequently Charlie had gotten slightly drunk and gorged himself on greens in an attempt to bring down the general cost of the meal.

Stacy had talked about graduate school and how she hoped to work as a translator at the UN or some embassy. Her life was so different from Charlie's that he thought it like something he might read in a book. She was full of plans, the plans of someone embarking on her adult life, seemingly surrounded by alternatives.

Because of his growing infatuation, Charlie tried to find what Stacy said fresh and fascinating, but he could remember his own aspirations, and as a youth officer he had talked to many young people. In truth, he was slightly bored, and he began to take his interest not from her words, but from her beauty and youth. She had on a light green dress that looked expensive and her black hair was piled up on her head. The wine, the waiters speaking Italian, the flowers and dim light— all were romantic to the extent that Stacy became like an actress in a movie from Charlie's youth or some advertisement for expensive perfume or champagne. What was missing in Stacy's words was replaced by Charlie's memory.

Charlie didn't mention Tateo or Jukes, nor did he talk about Sam. It was as if he were separating her from Sam's world, pretending she wasn't involved. She didn't talk about Sam either, and her only reference to Charlie's presence in New York came when he walked her back to her apartment at nine so she could study.

They stood in front of her building and she took his hand. In the light from the streetlamp, Charlie couldn't help recalling similar occasions twenty years before when he had taken a girl home after a date. Stacy wore a long green and white striped scarf looped over her head and around her neck.

"I think you should go back to Saratoga," she said.

"Why?"

"It won't be good for either of us if you stay here."

"I don't plan to stay long. Will I see you tomorrow?"

"You should go back tomorrow."

At the time he had been flattered to think she was afraid of becoming emotionally involved. But sitting in the cafeteria of the YMCA, Charlie again saw her as part of Sam's world. After all, she had said they were both fives, and while Charlie didn't understand what that meant, it indicated where her loyalties lay.

At best their dinner had been a time-out period. More likely she had been looking for weak spots. As he thought that, he grew angry at himself for a cynicism that belittled the strength of his feelings. But he had been a policeman for nearly twenty years. He knew the danger of letting down his guard, of thinking he was on vacation, of accepting the week as an extended birthday present.

Charlie didn't believe that Sam and Peter Bonenfant had gone to California. Alive or dead, he thought they were in New York, and he might had suspected dead if Stacy weren't so casual. He believed she was hiding something, but he doubted it was the death of her lover.

As for Bonenfant, Charlie wondered if Tateo and Jukes knew about him or if that mattered. He was aware their accusation that Sam was selling marijuana could easily be true. But again, Charlie didn't believe that Conrad Zack would involve himself over a few kilos of marijuana. Presumably he had perfectly competent subordinates to do that. He came back again to Peter Bonenfant. Charlie decided he wanted to know more about him.

Leaving the cafeteria, he checked at the desk and found a message to call Chief Peterson in Saratoga. This startled him. Although Peterson had okayed a week's leave, he hadn't known that Charlie was going to New York. His first impulse was not to call. Then he shrugged and walked toward the telephone room.

Charlie had worked with Peterson for over ten years. They weren't close but they respected each other. Charlie was a good youth officer, particularly skilled at handling runaways. Often he knew the kids from his contact with local organizations: Boy Scouts, YMCA, an orphanage, a variety of baseball teams.

Charlie's only complaint about his chief stemmed from Peterson's desire "to run a tight ship," which caused paranoia within the department. Peterson had spent ten years in the military police and often spoke of them as the happiest years of his life. Charlie called him collect.

"Why didn't you tell me you were going down to New York?"

"I didn't see that it mattered."

"We've received a complaint. Doesn't that matter?" Peterson spoke in a gravelly voice which Charlie suspected he had copied from a policeman on television.

"Lieutenant Zack?"

"That's right. He says you're getting in his way. You know as well as I do, Charlie, we gotta keep up relations with New York. Why're you looking for Sam Cheney anyhow?"

"His mother thinks something's happened to him."

"So what else is new? Coupla years in jail, it's just what he needs."

Charlie doubted that anyone would be better for a couple of years in jail. "I think something may have happened to him too."

"Look, Charlie, it's none of your business. Why the fuck didn't you just call? This Zack, he said he'd keep an eye out. What the hell can you do? No offense, Charlie, but you don't want to buck the NYPD. Do me a favor, come on back, will you? Zack said he'd call the moment he knew anything. You don't want to pick quarrels with cops."

Charlie found himself getting mad. Not at Peterson, who was caught in the middle, but at Zack. He saw Zack as behaving unfairly, of sneaking around behind his back.

"Chief, I really think I'm on to something."

"Forget it, Charlie, it's none of your business. If you know anything just tell it to Zack and come on home. Okay?"

There was no point in angering Peterson. "Okay, there won't be any trouble."

"You coming back today?"

"Maybe not today. I've got some other stuff to do. Don't worry, I'll probably spend the whole day in a bar."

15

▼▼▼

SOMEWHAT SENTIMENTALLY Charlie liked to tell himself that his earliest memory was his father's suicide. This wasn't quite true. What he remembered was that one day the house was full of large kindly men in blue uniforms who took care of him. He thought he remembered a gunshot, but he didn't. It was just that a shot was necessary before he could get to the more pleasant memory of the policemen.

Of his father he remembered nothing. His mother had had a snapshot, taken at a party, that Charlie had carried for years. It showed a room full of people eating, drinking and laughing while off to one side a small dark man was looking out the window. That was his father. He had wanted to be a jockey but he wasn't small enough for flat track racing. He had tried steeple chasing but lost his nerve after breaking an arm. He disliked harness racing except for betting. "I should spend the exciting moments of my life looking into a horse's ass?" he had asked his wife. "It's too much like that already."

One day in early September when Charlie was four his father had come home and barricaded himself in an upstairs bedroom with a bottle of whiskey and an old Colt .45 automatic. Then, when the whiskey was gone and the police were forcing the door, he had shot himself. He left no note except for his IOU's. He owed the bookmakers about $25,000.

When Charlie got depressed, he would think of his father's suicide and remember the snapshot of the party and the man staring out of the window. But to cheer himself he would think of the kindly men in their blue uniforms.

Usually this led to a progression of memories: moving in with Uncle Frank, tagging along after his older cousins: James, Robert and Jack. Charlie had lived in his uncle's house off and on until he joined the army, although at least once a year his mother had rented a cheap apartment where they would stay until her money ran out. Mabel always did well in the summer and could count on steady work until Christmas. But by February or March, at a time when many waitresses went south, Mabel moved in again with her brother.

That morning at The Lamplighter Charlie was still brooding about his father's suicide when Lawrence A. Driscoll climbed onto the stool to his left. Driscoll sat without acknowledging Charlie, raising and lowering his eyebrows as if signaling to someone on the other side of the room. He still wore his green blazer, this time with a yellow shirt, and a tie with green and yellow flowers.

"How's the free-lance consulting business going?" asked Charlie.

"I thought you might have returned to Saratoga."

Charlie tried to assume a jovial expression. "Not me. I've taken a lease on the stool. I've always had a soft spot for red vinyl. Those friends of yours, Tateo and Jukes, how'd you happen to meet?"

"I never told you they were friends," said Driscoll. There was a small gravy stain on the right lapel of his green blazer.

"Acquaintances then, what the hell. Buddies is buddies,

right? Tateo and Jukes. What kind of names are those? Sounds like a vaudeville routine. 'I say, Jukes, I admire your guts.' 'Good heavens, Tateo, are they showing?' Then they do a little dance. Bet Tateo got called Potato as a kid. You know them long?"

"Only a few weeks." Driscoll abruptly closed his mouth.

"That's what amazes me about this fast-paced world. You know a man a few weeks and it seems you've known him your whole life. How'd you happen to meet?"

Driscoll glanced suspiciously at Charlie who was fiddling with an empty beer bottle.

"I don't know. They were in here one day and we just started talking."

"Where'd they come from?"

"Uptown, I think."

"Uptown? Oh, you mean in the city."

Charlie disliked being obnoxious. Like most people, he preferred to be thought well of. He decided to return the conversation to a friendlier level.

"You got a wife and family?" he asked.

Driscoll seemed slightly dismayed. "What do you mean?" He began patting and smoothing back his hair.

"Just a friendly question. Lotta men have a wife and family, but, on the other hand, a lotta men don't, I guess."

"I was married once as a matter of fact," said Driscoll, giving Charlie a quick look. "It only lasted a couple of years. She wanted to go back to Philadelphia."

"Kids?"

"No."

"Me neither. Always regretted that. I even wanted to adopt one but the wife said no. Told me she didn't believe in taking care of someone else's mistakes."

Charlie paused. He decided to change the subject.

"So you're from Philadelphia, are you? Is that where you learned so much about locks?"

Driscoll quickly finished his drink as if preparing to leave. "I was brought up in Philadelphia, went to college there, then worked at Wanamakers. They transferred me to New York."

"What college?"

"Penn."

"Graduate?"

"Well, there was the war and . . . Why are you asking me these questions? What business is it of yours?" Driscoll's ears began to grow red.

"Friendly questions, that's all, just friendly questions. I mean, it was Wanamakers in New York that used to be Stewart's department store, and it was Alexander T. Stewart who once owned the Grand Union Hotel in Saratoga where my mother worked. See how it fits together?"

As Charlie spoke, Driscoll got off his stool. His arms were pressed to his sides, but his hands jerked and fluttered.

"I'm sick to death of Saratoga," he said.

"Then can I buy you another drink?"

But Driscoll was intent on leaving. "I'm sick to death of the whole business!" He turned and left the bar with more speed than Charlie would have thought possible.

Stacy appeared at three. If she was surprised to see Charlie, she didn't show it. She wore a short khaki skirt, a green sweater and her yellow jacket. As on the first time he had seen her, she was carrying books. Charlie couldn't make out the titles.

"I didn't know if you'd be here or not," she said. Her voice was friendly.

"What the hell, I've got the week off. No point in going back before I have to."

She smiled but didn't say anything. Charlie wanted her to like him, and couldn't bring himself to play the fool as he had done with Driscoll.

"Can I buy you a beer?" he asked.

"No, thanks, I've got a class soon. I just wanted to see if you were still around. Have you seen Zack again?"

"No, he just stopped by to say hello. Old chums. He likes the races in August."

"You don't plan to go back right away?"

"No, I'll stick around until Saturday. Take in a show or two. You want to have dinner tonight?"

"I can't. Perhaps I could meet you later."

"Here?"

"Sure. . . ." She began to say something else, and hesitated; balanced, it seemed, between several alternatives. Then she shifted the books in her arms, holding them tightly against her breast. "Well, I'll see you later."

As he watched her go, Charlie tried to guess what she had been about to say. He hoped she had been about to refer to their dinner the previous evening: some memory that would have indicated the warmth of her feelings.

He thought again about the slight similarity between Stacy and Gladys, and wondered if that said something psychologically significant about Sam or merely about himself. He considered calling Gladys. It wouldn't have surprised him if she had heard from Sam. Charlie could see Sam frantically calling his mother, begging her to get that cop out of his hair.

It was fortunate that Gladys had lost all sexual attraction for him. After her return to Saratoga, Gladys had continued her hints that Charlie was Sam's father. It was only later Charlie realized that these had begun at the same time as Sam's criminal career. They had even been effective. There were four or five occasions when Sam had avoided jail only because of Charlie.

Not that Sam was grateful. In fact he had told Charlie to mind his own business. Nor had he responded to Charlie's attempts to get him interested in the Boy Scouts or baseball. Charlie had gone so far as to enroll Sam in a team composed entirely of boys rejected elsewhere, organized by some Rotarians who believed that every kid deserved the chance to play ball. One boy had been missing an arm, while another played from his wheelchair. Sam's only talent consisted of getting hit in the head by perfectly respectable pitches. At last one of the Rotarians called Charlie, beginning him to urge Sam to quit the team. Sam had needed no urging.

In his most logical moments, Charlie knew that his early affair with Gladys had been founded on hypocrisy. She hadn't really been interested in him. Rather she had been after his cousin, Jack, who was a year older and star tackle of the football team. But not only did Jack have clean tastes, he could get any girl he wanted.

Gladys would come over to the house, wait around for some sign from Jack and then go off with Charlie, maybe hoping to make Jack jealous. Jack never noticed. When Gladys finally accepted this, she dropped Charlie who was the team's assistant equipment manager.

Charlie had been crushed. For nearly a month he had hung around under Gladys' window at night, hoping she would see him and take him back. Then she had begun to tease him about being pregnant.

16
▼▼▼

"WHATCHA COME BACK here for? Still think I'll show you that apartment? Fat fucking chance." Victor Plotz stood in his doorway, shading his eyes from the glare of the 200-watt bulb in the basement ceiling.

"Thought I'd come back for that other beer. How're the fish?"

"Those fuckers." Plotz turned and walked back into the room, leaving Charlie to close the door. "Got rid of the angelfish yesterday and today I find two dwarf gourami floating on the surface. Either the swordtail zapped them or they got flukes. Personally, I think they're suiciding. Bring 'em home, put 'em in a nice tank and zckzckzck," Plotz drew a finger across his throat, "they die. Never pick a fish for a friend. Fuckin' roaches are smarter. Beer's in the fridge, help yourself. Don't take the Heineken, I'm saving it for my birthday."

Charlie walked toward the kitchen. The cat, Moshe, jumped from the couch and followed him. "Did you give the angelfish to the cat?"

"I was going to, but I've had that fish five years. Was old enough to be the cat's mother, know what I mean? I told

Moshe, I said, 'What d'you think, good fish grow on trees? Go chummy up to the Purina.' Nah, I gave it to a broad upstairs. She's got a tank and said she'd let me visit it. Maybe it'll remember me. Who knows."

Charlie opened the refrigerator and took out a Rheingold. On the top shelf was a large blue bowl containing enough spaghetti for twenty people. Next to it was an old can of tomato juice with a cockroach perched on the rim. When it saw Charlie, it ran down the far side of the can.

"You know you got roaches in your refrigerator?"

"The bastards, as long as they don't touch the Heinekens, I don't care."

Charlie returned to the living room and sat down in the brown Naugahyde chair. Plotz stood in front of the aquarium scratching his elbows. His gray cardigan looked like a stray kindergarten class had been fighting over it. Along with the sweater, he wore wrinkled gray work pants and a white shirt. These were several sizes too large, as if Plotz had once been a much bigger man who had become smaller through some shock or loss.

The cat had followed Charlie back from the kitchen and was sitting by his feet. Charlie nudged it with his shoe. "I once knew a man who had mice in his refrigerator."

"Yeah?"

"Maybe just one mouse. It ate through a milk container, a full gallon, and all the milk poured down to the bottom of the refrigerator. Then the mouse fell in it and drowned. When the man opened the refrigerator, there was a great wave of milk with the dead mouse surfing on the crest of it."

"Guess I'm lucky, hunh?"

"Could be worse."

Victor sat down in the green chair. "Tell me, why'd you come back? Still hoping to see that apartment?"

"Will you let me in?"

"No can do."

Charlie looked down at the cat. It was motionless except for the slight twitch of the eyelid over the empty socket.

"What I want," said Charlie, "is an address on that other guy, Peter Bonenfant. You said he'd been getting mail."

"Yeah, and he got a package today." Plotz leaned back and rubbed his scalp. He was pleased with himself. "Suppose you want to see the return address?"

"I'd appreciate it."

"They could get me for tampering with the mail."

"Look, Victor . . ."

"Call me Vic."

"Okay, Vic, do me a favor before I kick in your fish tank, will you?"

"No need to get nasty. I'm just a fella, right? Gotta make a living same as the next man. You know I used to sell clothes? What I don't know about tweed suits you could put into a thimble. Wanna nother beer? I'll get it for you."

"Sure. Can I see the return address?"

"Sure, just hold your horses, will you? What's the fuckin' hurry?" Vic went out to the kitchen.

Moshe chose that moment to spring. Charlie caught the cat in mid-air. His eyes were watering. "I hate you," he whispered. Then he tossed Moshe toward the couch eight feet away. The cat landed on all fours and began washing itself.

The refrigerator door slammed shut. "Those fuckin' roaches, they want that tomato juice, they can have it. It's gone bad anyhow. You know you can kill roaches by putting out baking soda?"

Victor Plotz came back into the room carrying a Rheingold and a Heineken. He gave the Heineken to Charlie who appreciated the honor but accepted it without comment.

Victor returned to his chair. "The roaches eat the soda, see? Then they gotta belch, just like anyone else. Trouble is, they're physically unequipped to belch. The roach don't have a belcher. So instead of belching, he just gets bigger and bigger until Bang. He explodes. You put out a plate of soda and you hear this pop-popping all night long. 'Course after a while they stop eating it. I mean, roaches aren't dumb. They see their buddies turning to shrapnel before their eyes and after a while they wise up.

"So you try something else, like, for instance, Parmesan cheese. Roaches are crazy for Parmesan cheese. It's like whiskey, and they eat it until it kills them. You put out a little plate of Parmesan cheese before you go to bed and the next morning it's gone. But you know what? All around the plate will be a ring of fat little dead roaches all reeking of Parmesan cheese. Betcha could grind 'em up put 'em right on the spaghetti. Practically the same thing except for the color.

"Now me, I don't kill the roaches. 'Course if one's so stupid to fall into the tomato juice and drown, that's his tough luck. The owner, he has a guy come in and spray each month. That don't do much except piss 'em off. Betcha think I get so lonely that I keep roaches around to talk to. Them and the fish and Moshe. You wouldn't be half wrong. Sometimes it gets so bad I go out and talk to the street light. It's the only fuckin' thing that won't walk away. You wanna nother beer?"

"Sure," said Charlie.

17
▼▼▼

CHARLIE WAS A LITTLE DRUNK when he left Victor Plotz's apartment at eight o'clock, but in his pocket he had the name John Bonenfant and an address in San Diego. He guessed this was Peter Bonenfant's father. Charlie then went back to the Y to change his clothes, which were covered with cat fur, use the telephone and look for a place to eat. At the desk, he found a message to call his wife.

Charlie stared at it unhappily as he waited for the elevator. Marge, he was certain, meant to give him her good advice.

When Charlie unlocked his door he half-expected to find Zack on the other side of it. His room was empty. He hoped Zack had forgotten about him but knew that was unlikely. He felt like a mouse trying to make a cat disappear by wishing very hard.

Since he planned to meet Stacy, Charlie dressed carefully,

putting on a pair of blue slacks and his last fresh shirt: a white Oxford cloth with thin blue stripes. Then he spent five minutes trying to decide on one of his three ties. He regretted only bringing three and wondered what color tie he would have brought if he had known he was going to fall in love.

At last he decided on the blue one with horses' heads. He combed his hair, rubbed his shoes with a towel and took extra traveler's checks from his suitcase. He removed his .38, put it in a desk drawer, then changed his mind and put it on again, telling himself he felt uncomfortable without it. Having prepared himself for a possible lover, he went downstairs to call his wife.

Charlie had hoped Marge wouldn't be home, but she must have been waiting by the phone because she answered on the first ring. She went right to the point. "Charlie, Chief Peterson came by the store today. He said he'd received a complaint about you from the New York Police Department. What are you doing down there?" Her voice was like the high rat-tat of a child's drum.

Charlie made a face at the ceiling. "I told you, trying to help Sam Cheney out of another jam." He was irritated to discover that he was slurring his words. "How was your trip to New York? See some nice things?"

Marge ignored this. "Listen, Charlie, if I had a dime for every hour you've wasted on Sam Cheney. . . . Chief Peterson said your being in New York could make trouble for the department."

Their phone was in what Marge called "the television room," and in the background Charlie could hear the bright chatter and audience laughter of a variety show. "You know Peterson, he worries too much. I'll come home when I find Sam."

After hanging up, Charlie called San Diego information for John Bonenfant's number. When he dialed it, however, there was no answer.

By 9:30, Charlie had eaten and was on his way back to The Lamplighter. Afraid that he didn't have much time, he wanted to make as big a display of himself as possible.

Charlie found ten people at the bar and eight more in booths. Driscoll sat at the bottom of the U with an empty stool on either side of him. Charlie climbed onto the stool to his left.

"So how you been?" he asked.

Driscoll began to cough. The moving lights over the bar tinged his face red, blue and yellow, looking like emotions he was trying to repress.

"Sinus," said Charlie. "People always bothered by sinus this time of year. It's the pollen count. On the other hand, I once knew a man who choked to death on a piece of $10 steak. Want me to slap you on the back?"

"No, I'm all right now." There was a cringing look about Driscoll.

"You had me worried," said Charlie. He spoke loudly and saw people glancing at him. He nudged Driscoll in the ribs. "I been celebrating. What the hell, you're only forty-one once. Hard life being a cop."

At the word "cop" Charlie saw Driscoll flinch. Several people at the bar turned toward him. Luke took some change and went over to the jukebox. Staring off to his right, Driscoll tried to pretend that Charlie was a drunk who had just stumbled in.

Charlie glanced at the other nine people at the bar. Eight were men and any of them might be working for Zack. Mostly middle-aged, they were talking quietly or staring at nothing in particular. Sitting at the bar to Charlie's left was a woman about forty-five wearing an orange dress and thick orange lipstick. On the bar in front of her were at least fifty colored beads which she was trying to string on a white thread. Her hand shook, however, and, as far as Charlie could tell, she was still on the first bead: a blue one that she held tightly between her left thumb and index finger. Even she, thought Charlie, might be working for Zack.

Driscoll was still trying to ignore him. Charlie nudged him again in the ribs. "So when was the last time you were in Philly?"

Driscoll caught himself on the edge of the bar as the jukebox began booming out the Beach Boys' *Good Vibrations*. "I wish you wouldn't do that," he said.

"You ever play any ball?" Charlie asked, trying simple conversation.

"Ball?"

"You know, you take a bat and a ball and maybe a good mitt . . ."

"As a matter of fact," said Driscoll, "I used to want to be a good first baseman more than anything, but they said I had flabby hands." He looked down at his hands as if they had tricked him.

"Oh, did you," said Charlie. He thought again of Salt Pork as Driscoll fussed with his tie, sipped his drink and appeared to regret the momentary confidence.

"By the way," said Driscoll, "that girl was in here earlier looking for you. What's her name?"

"Oh, her. Yeah, she's an old chum. The city's full of old chums. What time did she come in?"

"About an hour ago. Isn't she a friend of Sam's?"

"Well, sure, she couldn't know me without knowing Sam."

Charlie distrusted Driscoll's interest in Stacy. "By the way," he asked, "have you seen your friends again?"

"Who do you mean?"

"Potato and Jukes: Five-foot-two-eyes-a-blue-kootchy-kootchy . . ."

"I told you, they're not friends of mine."

"When did you last see them?"

"Not for some time."

Driscoll's resistance seemed firm on that level. Charlie decided to try another tack. "You know, what I wouldn't give for a big glass of mineral water."

Driscoll raised his eyebrows. "Mineral water?"

"That's right," said Charlie. "Did you know that the first white man to take advantage of the springs in Saratoga was Sir William Johnson? He was suffering from the gout and rich living and some of his Indian buddies took him up for a cure."

Driscoll climbed off his stool. "Excuse me," he said, "I have another appointment."

Stacy appeared five minutes later. Seeing her, Charlie rediscovered a kind of erotic shyness that he hadn't felt for twenty years. In her yellow jacket, she looked like a brighter light come to compete with the ones over the bar.

"There you are," she said. "I stopped by earlier but you weren't here. I'm afraid I've got to do something right now. Will you wait? I'll be back by eleven."

She put her hand on his bare wrist. Charlie felt himself start. He disliked such Pavlovian reactions.

"I'll be here."

"You're sweet." She turned and left.

Sweetness and light, thought Charlie. He ordered another beer, and as he moved he became aware of the gun on his hip. It was now 10:15. To Charlie it seemed impossible that he could last out the hour with any semblance of calm. Perhaps he could name the banks robbed by Jesse James or the twenty-one men shot down by John Wesley Hardin. One of Hardin's victims had been a black policeman by the name of Green Paramoor. Charlie thought that was one of the most beautiful names he knew.

Maybe it would have been better three summers ago to let Sam go to jail, instead of giving him the chance to leave town. But it was years too late. Gladys should have put Sam up for adoption. She had always treated him more like a toy than a child. She and her sisters had the sort of relationship with their mother where she was only kind to them when they were pregnant or nursing. Gladys once told Charlie that she had nursed Sam, "till he'd just run up and grab it." She felt cheated that she only had one child, and envious of her two sisters who had seven illegitimate children between them.

Now, slatternly at forty-one, she specialized in obscure pains and fundamentalist religion, while worrying about her only son alone in New York.

She had not raised him well. Sam's most attractive trait was a childlike egoism that unfortunately kept his interest entirely on himself. An explorer within the boundaries of his skin, he was constantly searching for new ways to give himself pleasure. Charlie remembered a time when he had tried to teach Sam civic pride by taking him on a tour of Saratoga's mansions. Sam's interest had come from learning about the wealth of the original owners; his excitement from telling Charlie what he would do with an equal amount of money.

Sam had been arrested for stealing cars in 1965 and again in 1966. The second time he had been put on probation. He would have gone to jail if it weren't for Charlie. After he had told Sam what the juvenile home was like, Sam had stopped stealing cars.

Stacy reappeared exactly at eleven. She ordered a whiskey sour, which Charlie paid for, and they went over to a booth.

"Have you been having a nice vacation?" she asked. "What have you been doing?"

"Just wandering around." He wanted to tell her about Victor Plotz and his fish, but was afraid she would make fun of him.

"Wandering around where?"

"Times Square, Fifth Avenue, Central Park. My legs are killing me, but I enjoy it. I enjoy looking at things. You know they used to keep pigs and goats on 42nd Street? Used to be a real shanty town."

Stacy smiled. Her wide mouth reminded him of one of the star ballerinas who came to Saratoga each summer.

"It hasn't changed much," she said. She leaned forward with her elbows on the table. Her hair hung in a single black braid down her back.

"No? Maybe not."

"What kind of things do you look at?"

"Just things, little things. Like there was the window of a bookstore near Times Square. One of those pornography places? It was jammed with sex magazines and books. Lots of whips and rubber goods. But off to one side was a book of photographs called *Natural Childbirth Before Your Eyes*. Now that surprised me. Who would have thought it?"

Stacy reached out and took his hand. "Come back to my apartment," she said.

18

▼▼▼

THE WEATHER had turned colder. Charlie buttoned his raincoat and pulled his hat firmly down to his ears. "I should have driven down here," he told Stacy as they walked up 11th Street. "If I was training for soccer, I couldn't do any more."

"It's just a few blocks," said Stacy.

"That's just the trouble, everything's a few blocks. It makes you feel foolish taking a bus."

They were alone on the street. Stacy walked a little ahead and Charlie had to hurry to stay with her. Their footsteps echoed off the buildings. Each time Stacy passed a gap between two parked cars, her stockings shone in the light from the street lamp: small explosions of light.

"Bet there're rats around here," said Charlie. "Nice street like this, see 'em troop by carrying a baby or something."

While not drunk, neither was he sober. It felt like someone had spent the day stuffing cotton in his ears. Stacy continued to remain ahead of him. Apartment buildings and small shops on one side, parked cars on the other: Charlie felt as if he were being pulled along a narrow slide.

"What's the rush . . . ?"

As he hurried forward, Charlie heard a noise behind him. He started to turn, but someone grabbed him, wrapping an arm around his neck and pulling him back. Then a second person stepped out from behind a Ford van. He wore a red ski mask.

Charlie twisted, trying to break away. The man in the red ski mask moved quickly toward Charlie and kicked out, his foot hitting Charlie's thigh and glancing into his groin. As Charlie retched, the man stepped forward and hit him in the stomach while the second man let go of his neck. Charlie fell to his knees, vomiting beer onto the sidewalk. For a second he remained resting on his knees and elbows, his forehead pressed against the cold vomit-smeared concrete. He was aware of a man on either side of him. He was aware of shoes: tennis shoes and boots. He couldn't get his breath and kept gagging.

One of the boots moved out of Charlie's sight, then he felt a tremendous blow in his ribs. He rolled over, curling himself up. Before covering his head, he saw the other man, also in a ski mask: black with white vertical stripes that seemed to divide his face into slices. The man in the red ski mask raised a boot and kicked Charlie again. Charlie rolled in his vomit, trying to make himself smaller, guard his head with his hands.

As the two men started to kick him together, a horn began honking down the street. At first Charlie didn't hear it. Each kick made a small flash in his mind, blotting out all other sensations. But after a moment, the men stopped and Charlie heard the horn: quick, short blasts, over and over.

"Come on," said one man. "Get his wallet."

Charlie was aware of someone touching him. It was almost soothing. "He's got a gun."

"Take that too. Let's go."

The honking had stopped. Charlie heard their footsteps running down the empty street. He lay motionless, feeling that if he moved he would shatter like a china cup.

He heard footsteps approaching. Afraid that the men were coming back, he tried to move but it was too awful.

Someone touched his shoulder. "Chuck. Charlie."

Charlie didn't say anything.

"Charlie, I thought I could get help," said Stacy. "I was afraid. Can you get up?" Her voice was soft and concerned.

Charlie still didn't move.

Stacy knelt down next to him, stroking his hair. "Charlie, I'm sorry. Please say something. Should I get a doctor?"

Cautiously, Charlie tried moving. It hurt so he stopped. He could remember no time in his life when he hurt so much. He tried to speak but there was only a sound that cattle might make or a squeaky door. He could hear Stacy crying.

"Please, Charlie, say something. Are you all right? Please try to get up." She kept stroking his head.

He uncurled his legs and rolled over on his back. There was a sharp pain in his left side and he guessed there was at least one broken rib, maybe more. He opened his eyes and saw Stacy in her yellow jacket kneeling beside him. There were tears on her cheek. Beyond her he saw a fire hydrant and a white Ford van parked at the curb. Light from the street lamp reflected dimly off an apartment building and fire escape. He could see the sky; there were no stars. He felt briefly that the sky was beneath him and he was about to fall.

"How badly are you hurt? Can you sit up? Let me help you."

There was more pain as he sat up. His hands slipped in the vomit and he fell back. Stacy took his arm and he got to his knees, then to his feet. He stood leaning against the Ford van, bent over with his hands on his knees. Slowly he straightened up. There was again the sharp pain in his left side. Stacy handed him his hat. It was crumpled but he put it on, half hoping it would help him think. He had never believed much in coincidences.

Stacy held his arm. "Can you walk? It's only a few blocks."

Charlie pulled away and nearly fell, slid along the cold metal of the van. "Leave me alone."

"Charlie, I . . ."

"Just leave me alone."

Whenever he spoke or breathed, there was another stab of pain. He was lucky they had stopped kicking when they did, that the horn had started honking.

Stacy moved back toward the apartment building. In the shadow, she became like a person disguised. "Charlie, you need help. Come back with me. It's not far."

Charlie shook his head. "I don't want to see you."

Stacy began to walk off, then turned back and took several steps toward Charlie, reaching out her hand so he could touch it if he wanted.

"Get away from me!"

Stacy turned sharply. Charlie watched her go, the yellow of

her jacket beginning to blend with the dark. He leaned against the van, holding his sides.

"Stacy!"

She stopped about thirty feet away and stood with her back toward him. She looked small.

"Stacy, they took my wallet. I've no money to get back to the Y."

Slowly, she walked back to him, fumbling with her green Indian cloth bag and taking out her wallet. She gave Charlie a five-dollar bill. It was impossible to tell what she thought. Without a word or even glancing at him, she turned and walked away.

19
▼▼▼

I T WAS PAST ONE when Charlie got back to the YMCA. He had stopped at an all-night restaurant and attempted to clean himself up in the men's room. His olive-green raincoat was torn up the back and smeared with vomit, reeked of vomit and beer. His blue slacks were torn at the knees. His shirt was torn and his blue tie had flecks of vomit between the white horses' heads. At his waist there was an uncomfortable feeling where his gun had been. The only identification he had left were the business cards he had bought on Tuesday.

If Charlie moved cautiously, his pains would subside into a series of aches, all except the pain in his left side. Entering the Y, he walked toward the elevators, careful not to look at the night clerk or the few people hanging around. He imagined the night clerk taking out his card and putting a small check by his name.

It was when the elevator opened that Charlie remembered John Bonenfant in San Diego. At first he was tempted to forget about him. He didn't want to talk to anyone. But as he thought of his beating, he began to feel stubborn. The elevator door closed with Charlie still standing in the lobby. Certainly he would call.

A woman answered. Charlie asked to speak to John Bonenfant. Despite his bruises, he felt a slight thrill to be talking with someone who might be within sight of the Pacific Ocean.

"Hello? This is John Bonenfant." It was an older voice: educated and sure of itself.

"My name is Charles Bradshaw, and I'm with the Saratoga police department, Saratoga Springs, New York? And I'm calling . . ."

"Has anything happened to Peter?" The voice lost its sureness.

"Not that I know of."

"You startled me." He sounded relieved. "You see, we haven't been able to reach our son. Is there something I can help you with? I don't think I've ever been in Saratoga Springs."

Charlie wanted to hang up. He saw no way of not frightening this man in California. "Actually, I'm trying to find Sam Cheney."

"Then it is about Peter. I mean, Peter was staying with Sam. You say he's missing?"

"Not technically missing." Charlie tried to sound soothing. "We just don't know exactly where he is. Sam and your son probably went off someplace. You know kids. Probably decided to go trout fishing or something like that."

"Why are you looking for Sam?"

"Just wanted to ask him some questions. How did your son happen to come to New York?"

There was a pause. "Sam invited him. I thought it was foolish and that he should wait until August as he had planned . . ."

"Maybe you should tell me more about it. How did they happen to know each other?"

There was a crackling on the line. Charlie held tightly to the black receiver as if that pressure alone were holding up the wire to California.

"What sort of questions did you want to ask Sam?"

"Some of his friends are dealing marijuana," Charlie lied. "There may be trouble from outsiders."

"Trouble?"

"I don't want to talk about it on the phone, but anything you can tell me might be useful." There was a longer pause. Charlie pressed his head against the cool green wall. When he shut his eyes, he saw a figure in a red ski mask. "Are you still there?" he asked.

"I'm sorry. Peter was at UCLA and that's where he met Sam. I don't know the exact circumstances. Peter planned to go to graduate school in New York. NYU. He'd been accepted in psychology. But he meant to work this year and save some money. He was going to stay here until August, then move in with Sam until he found a place."

"What changed his mind?"

"Sam called around the beginning of March and told Peter that he'd found him a job. It was at the clothing store where Sam worked. He told Peter to come now and he'd lend him the plane fare. Peter had a construction job. He didn't like it much. So he decided to quit and go to New York. I thought he should stay. I mean once you start something . . . but, well, he quit anyway."

"Did Sam ask him to do anything? Pick up anything for him? Go on any kind of errand?"

"As a matter of fact, he did. Sam asked him to pick up an envelope from a man in Los Angeles. How did you know?"

"Did Peter do it?"

"Yes, he picked it up the day he flew to New York. March 13. He really should have waited because it turned out the job at the clothing store fell through. I talked to him. He was having a good time, you know, sightseeing, but he said he'd have to start looking for a job right away. Since then we haven't been able to reach him. My wife keeps saying I should call the police. I was going to tomorrow. Don't you know anything?"

"No." Charlie felt afraid for this man. "As I say, I only

wanted to ask Sam some questions. His girlfriend told me he had gone out west."

"With Peter? But then he would have called. You think something's happened?"

"No, no, I'm sure they're fine. Kids is kids." There was nothing he could do to help John Bonenfant. Feeling like a coward, he put the receiver back on the hook.

20

▼▼▼

CHARLIE FOUND ZACK lying on his bed reading *The Authentic Life of Billy, the Kid*. His black size-twelve wingtips were up on the green bedspread.

"Can't you be arrested for breaking in here?"

"Nope. How you feelin'?"

"How do you think?"

Zack put down the book. "Honking was all I could do. Anything else would have interfered too much."

"You could have driven down the street and made an arrest." Charlie took off his hat and torn raincoat. The smell of vomit sickened him. He sat down on the small chair by the desk and it creaked. "Get your feet off my bed."

Zack sat up and swung his feet around to the floor. He wore a gray overcoat, although the room was warm. "This is a delicate situation. You got no business . . ."

"Who were they?"

"Beats me."

"You're a liar. They got my revolver, you know that?"

"You shouldn't of been wearing it. Someday it'll be used to kill a cop and wind up on my desk."

"Break my heart."

Zack sat looking at him, elbows on his knees, holding his fedora in his large pale hands. His gray crew cut was ragged, as if some large animal had been chewing on it. His face showed nothing except boredom. "They hurt you much?"

"Broken rib."

"You sure?"

" 'Course I'm sure. What'd you come down here for anyway? To gloat?"

It was difficult for Charlie to think that Conrad Zack had people who loved him. He imagined a yellow dog cowering in a cellar, waiting for its master's size-twelve footsteps. But presumably Zack had a more human side. Presumably there was a wife and children. He might be the kind of man whose eyes misted over at the thought of stray dogs and orphans, who enjoyed sitting around telling jokes with his pals who would know him by some affectionate nickname. After all, Jesse James was called Dingus by his closest friends and even Alvin Karpis who had robbed banks with Ma Barker and her boys was called Old Creepy by Freddie Barker. Perhaps Zack was known by some name like Old Creepy.

Zack stood up and put on his hat. "If I catch you going back to that bar again, I'll charge you with obstruction."

"Why?"

"Because you're getting in my way."

Charlie slapped his hand down on the desk, making his toothbrush jump and overturning a can of shaving cream. "You think I came to New York for a stupid reason? What right do you have to judge me? You go tiptoeing around, afraid I'm going to screw up some narcotics deal of yours. I don't owe you a damn thing."

"How'd you know it's narcotics?"

"Since when's a narc been doing anything else?"

"How do you know I'm in narcotics?"

"Common knowledge."

"Stubborn prick, aren't you?"

Charlie didn't answer him. Zack tossed his hat onto the bed and sat back down.

"Two weeks ago we got a call from the San Francisco police. They had a woman in the hospital there. Two guys had broke into her apartment and beat her up, really took her apart. The police found some dope in her apartment, marijuana. They got a warrant and found almost a pound of it. That was on Thursday, March 20. The woman didn't want to talk at first, didn't want to get anybody mad. Then the police charged her with possession and she changed her mind. She said her boyfriend had a coupla kilos of pretty pure cocaine and that he was coming to New York to sell it. She said he was going to make the sale this Friday."

"Who beat her up?" asked Charlie.

"Dunno. But apparently the boyfriend was doing the run for someone else. Then he got greedy and decided to keep the whole thing for himself. These two guys, they're probably working for the other guy, the one that owns the dope."

"And it's coming to The Lamplighter?"

"Not necessarily, although the woman in California knew the name of the place. Actually, the boyfriend had set up a mailbox in New York where he'd pick up any last-minute information. We got the mailbox staked out. But The Lamplighter's involved and if you keep hanging around the whole deal might be canceled. We can probably get all kinds of information from this guy, but we can't do anything unless we bust him with the dope."

"You think Sam Cheney's going to buy it?"

"Beats me."

"What if I don't go back?"

Instead of answering, Zack reached over and picked up the book on Billy the Kid. He began leafing through it. "You know this book of yours, there's a sentence here that made me think of you. 'His misfortune was, he could not and would not stay whipped.' Ring any bells? I'm not kidding about that obstruction charge. You hang around that bar and I'll throw your ass in jail."

Zack put on his hat and stood up. "Come on, I know a man who'll tape up those ribs."

"Don't do me any favors."

"Come on, come on, don't be a twerp."

Charlie got to his feet.

THURSDAY

21

▼▼▼

T HE NEXT MORNING Charlie awoke before the arrival of the Puerto Rican maids. His bruises and the pain in his side made sleeping impossible. He lay on his back and stared at the picture over his bed showing the Maine coast and the man pulling the red rowboat out of the water. It occurred to Charlie that he knew nothing of the criminal history of Maine.

Along with his discomfort, he felt keenly frustrated. What had begun as an attempt to make his life more interesting had gotten out of control. Charlie had seen himself as coming to New York City, finding Sam Cheney and returning to Saratoga a modest but definite hero. Because of Zack, however, he must return having failed.

At least Zack had begun to treat him more as an equal. Not that they were friendly, but Zack seemed to accept Charlie's silence about his beating as a kind of stoicism. That was fortunate because Charlie was angry enough to ignore Zack's warnings if he felt he weren't being taken seriously. Perhaps Zack had seen that. Stubbornness is a form of passivity, and like many quiet people Charlie could be extremely stubborn.

They hadn't talked much when Zack had driven him to a police doctor. Charlie could see that Zack was being kind, as far as he was able, and felt guilty at not having done more to stop Charlie's attackers.

The police doctor had found three cracked ribs. He had taped him up and told him to avoid physical activity.

"Cracked?" said Zack. "Shit, you said they were broken."

By the time the Puerto Rican maids began their shouting, Charlie had decided to return to Saratoga. That was a pity. For years he had believed himself content, but after three days in New York he found himself questioning the fabric of his life: his job, his wife, his three cousins.

He was not yet discontented. He was still interested in his life. But he was surprised at how willing he was to shed those things he thought he valued. As he got out of bed, he wondered what it would matter if he never went back to Saratoga. He thought of his friends and acquaintances. Despite the little he knew of Victor Plotz, there was no one in Saratoga he would set above him. As for his wife, Charlie only had to review his willingness to get involved with Stacy to make him question the value of his marriage.

When he went downstairs, Charlie found a message to call Chief Peterson in Saratoga Springs. As he read it, he told himself he should rip it up. There was nothing Peterson could say which would encourage Charlie to leave now that he had reached that decision for himself. Therefore it was almost out of perversity that he went into the telephone room.

He got through to Peterson right away.

"Charlie, that New York lieutenant called me again yesterday afternoon. What the fuck you doing down there? He said if you don't leave, he'll pick you up for obstruction. Charlie, this can only mean trouble for one person."

There were six phones in the phone room and three others were occupied by men calling about jobs. Charlie cupped his hand over the mouthpiece. "What do you mean?"

"Charlie, if you got arrested in New York, what d'you think we'd look like? Are you trying to ruin us? Twenty years or no twenty years, if you're not up here today I'll have to suspend you. This Zack, he even said you'd found yourself a little chippy. What about Marge? You gotta good woman there, Charlie. You musta gone right round the bend."

Charlie had the sense that Peterson was a stranger, someone he was talking to for the first time. "I want to find Sam Cheney. He's in trouble."

"Look, Charlie, you're the one in trouble. I mean, I don't care if a dozen chinks are feeding him ground glass. If you're not in my office this afternoon, you're out. There'd have to be a hearing, but I'd hope you'd have the decency to resign. You know as well as I do, Charlie, these things can be a can of worms."

What bothered Charlie most was Peterson's assumption that he had no reason for being in New York. He imagined Peterson sitting in his office with its paneling and black leather. Peterson raised show dogs: Irish setters. On the walls of his office were framed color photographs of his three champions seen from a variety of angles, plus citations, awards and bits of parchment commending him for raising the quality of the breed.

"I don't mind telling you, Charlie, this Zack, he scared me. We talked some. He almost went so far to say that if you didn't get back up here, he'd cut us off. Look, Charlie, you know what that means. This year we're going to have the biggest fair in the whole state. Two fucking weeks. And the trots start next Thursday. We depend on New York. There are times if they hadn't tipped us, we'd of looked like fools. Drugs, pickpockets, you know that as well as I do. Where would we be if they didn't call us? Even one summer? Some smart crook come up here, we'd look like clowns. So tell me, what are you going to do?"

"You'd really suspend me?"

Peterson snorted. "What fuckin' choice do I have? They pick you up and the reporters get it and the wire services, the fuckin' papers up here would be fighting for it. Television, radio, it'd be a zoo, Charlie. One of my men arrested for obstruction? A sergeant? My hands would be tied. At best, I'd have to say you were sick, that you'd gone off your fuckin' rocker and I'd had to let you go. What else could I do? What the fuck, Charlie, you know what life's like. You gonna be in my office today?"

Charlie put his hand against the wall and pushed slightly. "Sure," he said, "I'll be there."

"That's a promise, right?"

"There's a bus at eleven."

"Hey, Charlie, check in with me. Okay? We'll have a coupla laughs over a beer."

"Sure. Sure thing."

Charlie went upstairs to pack his bag.

22

▼▼▼

CHARLIE WAS A MAN who liked eating and enjoyed cooking. As he walked up Ninth Avenue toward Port Authority Bus Terminal, it was an indication of his frame of mind that he could pass so many stores dedicated to food with such apparent lack of interest.

Although his mind seemed blank, he was aware that some part of it was thinking and would not be distracted by stores specializing in nuts, spices, tea and coffee, fruits and vegetables. The only exception was a butcher shop. Hanging in a row in its window was a white rabbit, a black rabbit, a gray rabbit and a small pink pig. Charlie had never eaten rabbit. His sensibilities would not allow him to eat an animal that, deep down, he still referred to as "bunny." But, pausing before the shop window, he wondered if there was any difference in taste between white, black and gray rabbit.

He hurried on. Although this Thursday was the most spring-like day of his visit, Charlie was freezing. He had left his olive-green raincoat wadded up in a ball in a YMCA wastebasket. Torn and smelling of beer and vomit, the coat would only make people stare. His gray sport coat, however, although wool, was too thin to be effective. It seemed unfair to Charlie that along with his bruises and disappointments, he should be cold as well.

He reached the bus station shortly before ten. Learning that an Adirondack Trailways bus left from Gate 27 at eleven o'clock, he went down to the lower concourse to wait. The terminal was crowded, and Charlie moved slowly because of his ribs, trying to avoid being bumped. Across from Gate 27 was a row of plastic seats. He lowered himself into the nearest.

He felt dissatisfied with himself and betrayed by the people around him. It seemed he had spent his whole life following the instructions of others, and that even now he was leaving his self-appointed task because that was what other people wanted.

Charlie knew if he stayed in New York, he faced arrest and the loss of his whole life in Saratoga Springs. But what now bothered him was the feeling that his life in Saratoga wasn't very important. Indeed, one of his reasons for returning was to convince himself that he was wrong, that he was perfectly happy with his life as policeman, husband, cousin and all-around good guy. And he would have gone readily if there weren't such pressure on him to go.

Charlie felt increasingly defiant. The more he was pushed, the more he wanted to find Sam Cheney. He also felt that if he found Sam, then he would be free of him, as if Sam were an irksome spirit who had inhabited him for twenty-five years. To find him would be to exorcise him.

From the moment he had learned Gladys was pregnant, Charlie had thought of the child as his. It wasn't until fifteen years later that he discovered that was impossible. He was sterile. After five childless years of marriage, he had forced himself to see a doctor, submitted to tests and learned he could never father a child.

Sam Cheney was not his son. But after thinking him his son for fifteen years, and listening to Gladys' coy hints that he was Sam's father, it was difficult not to feel fatherly. Sam might be no good, but he was as close to a son as Charlie would ever have.

Perhaps that was why Gladys found him so easy to manipulate. Charlie had always wanted a large family. He had seen himself as living in a large Victorian house surrounded by children of all sizes.

Childless, Charlie tried to content himself with orphanages, the children's wards of hospitals, various baseball organizations. He became known as an easy touch by the more enterprising children of Saratoga. Young salesmen of greeting cards, candy, magazines would put Charlie at the top of their list, while children with seeds would walk across town to sell him the parsnip and turnip seeds that no one else wanted, even though Charlie planted nothing but a few tomatoes.

Charlie was a man of fatherly feelings and many of them had been directed toward Sam. But along with these feelings, he had a very clear idea of what Sam was like. Charlie hadn't come to New York with any thought of rescuing an innocent child from a den of vipers. More likely it would be the vipers that needed rescuing. But he still wanted to find Sam.

He assumed that Sam and Peter Bonenfant were hiding in the city, waiting for the cocaine. Jukes and Tateo were also waiting for the cocaine. The sale was to take place on Friday. What was one day? Charlie told himself he was leaving too soon.

Sitting in the bus station, he knew his life had reached a place of major choices. He could stay in New York or he could return to Saratoga and continue his life as a youth officer. But, although that was what he was best at, there would be no surprises. He could anticipate almost everything that would happen until he retired.

Charlie guessed that another factor pressing him to leave was his own fear. He was frightened of Zack. He was frightened of being beaten again. He was frightened of losing what he had achieved in Saratoga. But his fear embarrassed him. His decision to go or stay seemed a matter of morality, and it seemed wrong to be influenced by physical fear and economics.

Charlie found himself thinking of Black-Face Charley Bryant, a member of the Dalton Gang, who had once boasted, "I want to get killed in one hell-firing minute of smoking action." He had had his wish, dying in a gunfight with a U.S. Marshal whom he mortally wounded.

Even better were the last words of Billie Clanton as he lay in the dust of Fremont Street near the O.K. Corral. Wounded five times and with Wyatt Earp standing over him, Clanton had raised his empty pistol and said, "God, God, won't somebody give me some cartridges for a last shot."

As further encouragement, there were the words of Wyatt Earp himself as he raised his guns at the beginning of that shoot-out: "You sons-of-bitches, you have been looking for a fight and now you can have it."

It was 10:40. Gate 27 was about fifteen feet away. The lower concourse was actually a sloping corridor, about thirty-five feet across and 100 yards long. One end was about twenty feet higher than the other, so that a bowling ball released at the top to Charlie's left would create havoc when it reached the coffee shop called—Charlie craned his neck—*Post and Coach Snacks* thirty yards to his right. Next to the coffee shop was a flight of stairs leading to the main concourse and the Eighth Avenue Subway.

Charlie wondered why Tateo had told him that Sam had flown to California. And he wondered why he hadn't mentioned Peter Bonenfant. Perhaps he didn't know about him. Altogether, Charlie found Bonenfant's involvement curious. He had brought an envelope from Los Angeles to New York which presumably contained part of the money for the cocaine. But although Bonenfant might have been an innocent courier, Charlie couldn't imagine him hiding with Sam, waiting for the sale on Friday.

It then occurred to him that Sam and Peter Bonenfant might not be together. It was plausible they were together but not necessarily true. But if they were apart, where was Peter Bonenfant? As he thought this, Charlie had a great desire to see Sam's apartment.

A speaker in the ceiling announced that the Adirondack Trailways bus to Albany, Saratoga Springs, Glens Falls, Lake George and Warrensburg was now receiving passengers. Charlie picked up his bag, walked toward the gate and joined the few people who were gathered in line. He glanced around the lower concourse for someone who looked like a plainclothesman. He could see about 100 people and any one of them might be working for Zack.

At the head of the line, the Trailways driver was stamping tickets. Charlie recognized him as the same man who had driven him down three days before. That time seemed long enough to be measured in years. The driver took his ticket; he didn't recognize Charlie. The door gave on to an open area where the buses were parked; beyond them were lanes by which they entered and left the building.

As he passed through the door, Charlie very calmly told himself that he wasn't going back to Saratoga. He walked toward the bus until its bulk hid him from the windows of the lower concourse, then he ducked down and moved toward the exit lane. Turning left, he jogged up the ramp, staying close to the darkness of the far wall. With each running step, there was a spurt of pain from his side. He still carried his suitcase and it banged against his knee. A few drivers and porters stared, but made no move to stop him.

When he got outside, Charlie paused to catch his breath and reaccustom his eyes to the sunlight. He thought of Black-Face Charley Bryant. Walking toward Eighth Avenue, he began looking for a bank where he could cash his traveler's checks and a liquor store where he could buy a large bottle of Jack Daniels.

23

▼▼▼

"YOU'RE BACK, ARE YOU? Didn't figure to see you again."
Victor Plotz held open his door. His dust-kitty hair was mussed and Charlie guessed he had been sleeping. Hibernation would be more like it. With his size and shambling gait, he seemed related to a Walt Disney bear.

"Brought you a present." Charlie handed Victor a brown paper bag.

Victor drew out the bottle of Jack Daniels. "You must wanta see that room pretty bad."

Putting down his suitcase, Charlie passed through the living room into the kitchen. Moshe jumped off the couch and followed him, weaving in between Charlie's legs. Charlie took a tray of ice from the refrigerator and knocked it into a blue bowl. Then he found a couple of glasses and returned to the living room, still followed by the cat.

Victor stood by the suitcase with his hands pushed down in the pockets of his gray cardigan. He had opened the whiskey and put it on the table by the fish tank.

"You want the glass that says, *Peanut Butter Can Be Fun*," asked Charlie, "or the one with Bozo the Clown?"

"Long as it holds whiskey, what's the diff? How come you brought a suitcase? You a slow drinker?"

"I was going back to Saratoga, then changed my mind. Can I leave it here for a while?"

Victor took the Bozo the Clown glass, put in two ice cubes and filled it half full of Jack Daniels. "Sure, sleep on the couch if you want. What the hell. You okay? You look a little peaked."

Charlie sat down on the brown Naugahyde chair. The question made his bruises ache. "Some guys beat me up last night, trying to get me to leave. They took my wallet and revolver. I lost all my ID. There wasn't much money in the wallet, but the revolver, that's embarrassing. You're not supposed to lose your revolver. Also, I'll have to pay for a new one."

It occurred to Charlie that he wouldn't be needing a revolver if he were fired, nor would he be needing his new business cards.

"The bastards. They hurt you much?"

"Not much," said Charlie. "How're the fish?" Looking toward the tank, he noticed some new vegetation and that the orange diver was gone.

Holding Moshe, Victor sat down in the other Naugahyde chair and began scratching the cat under its chin. "I finally discovered the guilty party. It wasn't the angelfish after all. It was the fuckin' swordtail, the red one. I caught him bustin' a guppy. Too bad, the swordtails were always Moshe's favorite. Sometimes they'd get excited and jump out of the tank. I'd find 'em lying between Moshe's paws. Moshe didn't hurt 'em or anything, just licked 'em very, very gently. Fuckin' fish practically had a stroke. Didn't jump out of the tank for a while, I can tell you. But bustin' guppies, that's something else again."

"What'd you do?" asked Charlie.

"Had a regular trial. Put the swordtail in a glass in front of the tank, put Moshe up on the table, then put the last surviving guppy in a glass on the other side of him. You know, the grieving widow. No question that the swordtail was guilty. I mean, I saw him with my own eyes. Had a regular execution, just like Sing Sing. Zap. Gave the swordtail to Moshe right in front of the tank as a warning to the other fish. No licking this time. Coupla quick bites and he was gone.

"Anyway, I been making some changes. Got rid of the diver which I figured was riling them up. Bought some more green veg, Ludwigia it's called. And from now on I'm raising nothin' but mollies: nice peaceful fish that don't eat their kids and don't mind dirty water. Just toss in some salt and you're all set. The molly is God's gift to the lazy man. They'll even eat lettuce in a pinch."

Charlie glanced around the room. There was an old portable television on a table by the couch. On top of the television was a stack of crossword puzzle magazines.

"How long have you lived here?" Charlie asked.

Victor finished his whiskey. "Seven years last February. Had a place in Brooklyn but when Matt, he's my son, when Matt moved to Chicago I said, what the fuck I need five rooms for? And I heard about this job and, well, everything worked out." He looked around the room and his eyes settled on the fish tank. "It's good for the fish. Basements are naturally damp."

"What happened to your wife?"

"She died thirteen years ago. Cancer."

"I'm sorry." Charlie thought with self-dislike that his idea of conversation had always been to ask questions. Out of shyness and a fear of silence, he was constantly prying into other people's lives.

"Not your fault, nor mine either. That's one good thing about cancer. You can't blame me for it." Victor got up, put several more ice cubes in his glass and filled it half full.

"You're not drinking enough," he told Charlie. "How you going to get me drunk if you're not going to drink yourself? Sarah, that was my wife, she never appreciated good drinking. And Herbie Schultz, he didn't either. They would have made a fine couple. Schultz owned the clothing store where I worked. He was always kissing ass. You know, an Italian to the Italians, a Jew to the Jews. He never even voted 'cause he was afraid of being caught picking a side. Stores like that, they're like mastodons. It specialized in middle-aged Jewish men. The dumb fuck. Times change, that's all. That's what pissed me off about that friend of yours, Sam Cheney. Works in a clothing store, does he? He don't know the first fucking thing. He'd make jokes about us being in the same business. Ah, what the hell, it's a living, right? What's it matter what a man does as long as he washes his hands. Take you, for instance, a cop. You musta seen a lot of stuff. Does it show? You got the face of a baby. I'm not making fun, don't get me wrong. You always been a cop?"

By two o'clock the Jack Daniels was nearly gone. Charlie had been trying to hold back, but he had drunk almost a third. The conversation had continued to be about their own lives, bringing up one event after another as if they were mathematicians going over columns of figures to discover how certain sums had been reached.

At one point Charlie found himself saying: "My mother, she's always had this idea that she's about to become rich. Either she's going to marry a Vanderbilt or one of her trotters is going to turn out to be Secretariat or something. And you know what she's going to do with the money? I remember as a kid, we'd be living with my uncle; and my mother, she'd always be talking about opening a tourist home. Over the years I got to know that imaginary house better'n any place in Saratoga. It was going to be a big three-story white frame house with a screened-in porch on three sides and two wineglass elms in the front yard. And there'd be a green sign with the word *Guests* painted in white, and the name of the house: Happy Haven or Wayfarers Arms, she could never decide which. But she'd talk about that house until you could hear the creak of the glider on the front porch.

"It'd cater to people who came for the races: gentlemen of the turf, she'd call them. Flats by day, trots by night. And each year the same ones would come back and she'd always have free ice and papers.

"Then the elms died and motels got big, and she started thinking of having a motel instead, something small, no more'n twenty units, and she'd call it Shady Nook or Bidawee and again the same gentlemen would come back year after year and think it was good luck to stay there, and there'd be free ice and papers."

"You know those people?" asked Victor. "Like the Vanderbilts?"

"Sure, I mean they come up in the summer. And the Whitneys. They come up too. That always sort of irritates me. People call Saratoga a one-month town. I live there all year round." Charlie paused as Victor poured the last of the Jack Daniels into his Bozo the Clown glass. "Say, Victor . . ."

"Vic."

"Okay, Vic, say you walk into the john and find $50 on the floor, and then, say, I walk into the john and find a key lying on the floor and say this key just happens to be the one to Sam Cheney's apartment. Then say I go out for a little walk and I come back and you just happen to go back to the john and, what the hell, you must have dropped your keys because there they are lying right on the floor and you pick 'em up and put 'em in your pocket and nobody knows a thing. What d'you think about that?"

Victor got up and walked to his desk. As he bent over, rummaging through the belly drawer, he looked like half an arch made of soft gray stone. After a brief search, he took out a ring with two keys. He tossed the keys to Charlie who caught them in his right hand.

"You want those keys so much, then you can have them. I'm not takin' money from a buddy. But if the landlord hears about it and I lose my job, then I'm coming up to Saratoga with Moshe and the fish and pester you 'til you find me another. Okay?"

Charlie put the keys in his pocket. "Sure. I even know of an opening on the police force."

"I don't know about that," said Victor, "it doesn't need to be anything special. Just talk to those Vanderbilts of yours. But since you have all that money and since we're out of Jack Daniels, you might consider contributing ten bucks toward another bottle. What d'you say?"

"Sure," said Charlie, drawing out the money.

24

▼▼▼

T HE 9 x 12 LIGHT GRAY RUG was filthy and spotted with crumbs, cigarette butts and three empty Genessee bottles, but between the two windows that looked out onto 6th Street was a lighter patch that had been recently cleaned. Charlie knelt down beside it.

It was an area shaped like a horse's head, about four square feet and next to the yellow linoleum between the rug and the wall. Part of the linoleum had also been cleaned. Lifting the edge of the rug, Charlie saw that the clean linoleum extended beneath it, following the general shape of the horse's head. On the underside of the rug, however, was a brown stain.

Taking out his pen knife, he scraped the stain, then looked at the brown flecks that had come off on the blade. He wiped the blade on the rug, and inserted it between the floor and molding. Scraping it back and forth several times, he saw there were new brown flecks on the blade. Charlie stood up and inspected the knife in the sunlight. The brown flecks took on a reddish tinge.

Putting his knife away, Charlie crossed to a green couch along the opposite wall and sat down. The apartment reminded him of Sam: pale, shabby and secretive. It was a studio apartment: one room, 15 x 20, and a kitchenette closed off by a plastic shower curtain. Charlie had earlier made the mistake of looking behind it. The dishes in the sink had been spotted with mold and cockroaches. Grease and tomato sauce had been caked on the white enamel of the two-burner stove.

Sam's room was furnished with a Murphy bed, a green couch, a bureau and a seemingly brand-new pink formica table and four metal chairs with padded seats and pink vinyl backs. Charlie couldn't imagine Sam buying them.

The two windows had venetian blinds but no curtains. Between them was a poster for a New York Dolls concert. On the wall above the couch was an Escher print of a bunch of geese turning into a bunch of fish or vice versa.

As he looked around the apartment, Charlie wondered how much he would care if Sam were dead. He knew he would regret it. His second thought was that he would hate to break the news to Gladys. There was a photograph of Gladys on the bureau next to a small pile of *Mad* magazines and *Playboy*. The photograph was a grainy 8 x 10 enlargement of the sort of snapshot taken by machines in dime stores. It showed Gladys at age twenty laughing and looking up to her left, probably toward the young man who was paying. Her forehead was hidden by bangs and her blond hair curled just past her shoulders. Even at that age she had begun to look seedy: bad teeth, poor complexion. Her lipstick was crooked and smeared.

It occurred to Charlie that Sam's father was probably Louie Farelli who now sold cars in Glens Falls. Louie had about a dozen illegitimate children scattered across Saratoga, Washington and Warren counties. He had been two years ahead of Charlie in school. When Gladys had begun to publicize her pregnancy, Louie had left town, returning only after Gladys had gone to Warrensburg.

Charlie had last seen Louie Farelli at a veterans meeting in the fall. He had gained forty pounds and lost his curly black hair. During the evening, he had told Charlie three times that his doctor had made him give up Scotch and Vichy.

Charlie began to search the apartment leisurely, pulling down the Murphy bed, going through the drawers of the bureau, looking in the closet. He had hoped to find a picture of Stacy but there wasn't one. Although he inspected all the clothes, he didn't think there were enough for two people.

The bathroom was filthy. There was a stall shower with a torn green curtain. The mirror over the sink was flecked with toothpaste. Around the rim of the white toilet seat someone had written, "Dis is de place," in black ink. There were no towels and only one toothbrush.

Charlie wanted to talk to Driscoll and Stacy. He knew they had lied to him, but he wasn't sure of the importance of what they had concealed. He decided to see Stacy first. Perhaps he could learn more about Bonenfant. As he went downstairs to return the keys, he wondered what would happen when Zack discovered that Sam had had a roommate.

Charlie found Victor stretched out on the couch with his eyes closed, and singing, *I'll give you a daisy a day*. The cat had disappeared and the fish were behind the Ludwigia. On the floor next to Victor was another bottle of Jack Daniels about two-thirds full. Charlie put the keys on the desk and left quietly.

25

▼▼▼

EITHER STACY WASN'T AT HOME or she refused to answer the bell. It was 3:30 so she could easily be at NYU. As he walked away from her building toward the Bon Marché store on the corner, it occurred to Charlie that Zack might be having her building watched.

He knew he should be paying more attention to Zack, but, having decided to ignore him, he was making the mistake of forgetting about him as well. Zack would certainly arrest him if he had known Charlie was going to The Lamplighter. But the policeman probably assumed Charlie was on his way back to Saratoga. Not that he had any evidence of that. Zack, however, was used to being obeyed and might substitute an assumption of obedience for proof.

The sky was cloudless, although hazy, and the day had become warmer. Charlie was almost comfortable in his sport coat. When he neared Astor Place, he began looking for a cab. He knew if he approached The Lamplighter on foot, he would most likely be stopped; but if he appeared in a cab and went directly inside, he might be safe.

In any case, his desire to talk to Driscoll was greater than his fear of Zack. Charlie now saw himself as searching for Bonenfant rather than Sam. Driscoll had never mentioned Bonenfant. Either he didn't know about him or he was hiding something. But it seemed unlikely that the Driscoll-Tateo-Jukes faction knew nothing of Bonenfant, especially since it was Bonenfant who had picked up the money in California. If possible, Charlie wanted to get Driscoll away from the bar, take him someplace where he could exert more pressure. Maybe he could rent an uncomfortable wooden chair, a gooseneck lamp and a 200-watt bulb.

There were five customers in The Lamplighter and Driscoll wasn't one of them. They didn't look up when Charlie entered. He imagined they were all plain-clothesmen. Taking a cup of coffee, five Slim Jims and a bag of chips over to a booth, Charlie sat down to wait. He asked himself if he would be acting this extravagantly if he hadn't drunk so much Jack Daniels.

Charlie's tangible threat from Zack came ten minutes later. He had gone to the restroom and was standing at the urinal. As Charlie unzipped his fly, a man entered and went up to the urinal beside him.

"Want some good advice?" said the man.

Charlie disliked conversations at urinals, especially with strangers. "What?" he asked. He didn't look at the man but at a graffito which warned him that if he was reading this message, he must be pissing in his shoe.

"You get out of here right now and maybe you'll only get yelled at. You hang around here and you'll go to jail. Zack, he's ready to kill you."

As he zipped up his fly, Charlie tried to think of some cutting answer. The man was Charlie's age and wore greasy blue coveralls. Charlie had seen him before and had assumed he repaired Jaguars. There were even spots of grease on his face.

"You must really want to go to jail," said the man. "You self-destructive types, what d'you get out of it?"

Driscoll appeared at 4:45. He tried to show no surprise at seeing Charlie. He still wore his green blazer, this time with a yellow shirt and plain purple tie. Charlie realized that Driscoll wore it not out of fondness but poverty, and he guessed that free-lance consulting was not one of nature's money-makers.

Seeing that Driscoll intended to avoid him, Charlie called him over.

"Say, Mr. Driscoll, I believe I owe you an apology. Sometimes when I been drinking a little, I let my tongue run away with me, and, well, you know how it is. Can I buy you a drink?"

At first Driscoll looked suspicious, but Charlie's apology required acknowledgment. Charlie saw several more food stains on Driscoll's blazer, and thinking of Salt Pork he imagined this quiet man experiencing his only passion when confronted with a plate of spaghetti.

"Perhaps a very small one."

"What'll it be?"

"Perhaps a Black Russian." He lowered himself slowly onto the seat across from Charlie. On the wall above the two men was a theater poster advertising Lauren Bacall in *Applause*.

When Charlie returned with the Black Russian, he found Driscoll more composed. "Have you been sight-seeing?" asked Driscoll.

Charlie sat down across from him. "More or less. Did you know that Bowery is from a Dutch word meaning farm?"

"You don't say." Driscoll sipped his drink.

"Actually," continued Charlie, "I'm in a lot of trouble. Never rains but it pours. Right?"

"How do you mean?"

"The police are looking for me."

Driscoll leaned forward as if he hadn't heard correctly. "What on earth for?"

"Well, you see, I let myself get carried away when I was looking for Sam. I broke into his apartment. The super there, a guy named Plotz, he called the police this morning."

"What are you going to do?" Driscoll's composure had disappeared.

"Get out of town, I guess. Trouble is I'll probably be picked up at the bus station. If I could get over to Paramus, I'd be all set. The bus to Saratoga stops there after it leaves New York. I don't know, whatever happens I'll be in hot water. The cops will probably bust in here and arrest me."

"In here?"

"Why not?"

Driscoll leaned back in the booth and looked at his watch. It was five o'clock. With his head and thick gray hair combed back, his face became a series of rectangles. Charlie imagined his photograph under the caption: *Can you draw this man? A career in commercial art can be yours.* He tried to decide if a student could capture the worried expression and slight trace of fear.

"But you're a policeman," said Driscoll at last.

Charlie laughed. "That doesn't mean anything. Sure, the New York cops will call Saratoga, but my chief doesn't even know I'm down here. I told him I was sick. When he learns I'm here, he'll be furious. He'll probably tell the New York cops to keep me. You know, throw away the key?"

Driscoll nodded in a depressed sort of way. Charlie glanced toward the bar and saw the pretend mechanic in his greasy coveralls staring at him. He decided to give Driscoll another push.

"I got a plan though," said Charlie. "When the cops pick me up, I'll tell them that I think something happened to Sam. Maybe he got killed."

"But that wouldn't be true. What would you do that for?"

"Law of the jungle. Dog eat dog. Can I buy you another drink?"

Driscoll shook his head. He fidgeted with his empty glass, rattling the ice cubes. "What if I drove you to Paramus? I can get a car. At least I think I can."

"That's be swell," said Charlie. "You're a good buddy."

Driscoll winced as he got out of the booth. "Let me make a call."

26

▼▼▼

D RISCOLL HAD GONE to get a car. The plan was for him
to drive up to the back door of The Lamplighter at
exactly six o'clock. Charlie would jump into the back
seat and be driven away. He didn't entirely like the plan, but
every time he tried to think of another he noticed the pretend
mechanic watching him from the bar. At least it would thwart
Zack. Looking at his watch, Charlie saw he had twenty minutes to wait.

There were now about thirty people in the bar. Most had
come in since five and about half were retired men allowing
themselves their first drink of the day. At the back of the room,
four young men were doing their best to break the Foos Ball
game. Occasionally a ball would go skittering across the floor
and the smallest of the four men would chase it, followed by
shouts of "There goes Joe" and "Go get 'em, Joe." The jukebox blared out the Pointer Sisters. Charlie continued to drink
coffee.

Driscoll had told him to expect a gray Valiant. Charlie was
to get into the back and lie down on the floor. Driscoll would
then drive to Paramus, or at least that was the plan. But Charlie
meant to find out more about Peter Bonenfant, and he meant
to find out more about Tateo and Jukes, who were certainly
the ones that had beaten up the woman in San Francisco. It
seemed he could get that information without the extreme step
of going to New Jersey.

Charlie disliked waiting. Twice he had called Stacy but there
had been no answer. Sitting in the booth, it was too easy to
doubt the wisdom of his plans; and he worried that he might
have fallen into a losers' syndrome he had experienced at the
track: that the more you lose, the more you bet in hope of
making up your losses.

What was he throwing away and for what reason? As Charlie waited, it seemed that his main reason was pride, that having decided to find Sam Cheney he would do it no matter what the cost. With mild astonishment, Charlie wondered at the series of events that had led him to jeopardize all that he thought important; but with that astonishment was some pleasure that he refused to be controlled by the circumstances of his life.

The Cousins would never understand that. Charlie tried to guess what they would say when they learned he had been suspended. Or worse: that he was in jail in New York City. He could see them shaking their heads and offering to lend him a little money. They wouldn't be terribly surprised. James, five years older than Charlie, was a carpenter and owned a small construction company. Robert, three years older than Charlie, sold insurance and real estate. Jack, a year older, managed a hardware store.

The Cousins were men who never felt temptation. Their lives were as orderly as a bus trip. Apparently content, they couldn't understand Charlie's mild restlessness.

For years, they had told him he was the luckiest man alive: good job, lovely wife, lots of friends. What more could he ask for? And Charlie, although he didn't want more, felt guilty that he wasn't happier, that he would daydream about sneaking off to, say, Elkhart, Indiana, where he would get a job with the fire department and live a life almost exactly the same as his life in Saratoga Springs. He found it frightening that as he got older there seemed fewer opportunities, that he could anticipate a future without surprises.

At one minute to six, Charlie left the booth and walked slowly toward the back door of The Lamplighter, just past the rest rooms. His hat was still on the table, and he was careful not to look at the pretend mechanic. At six exactly, he opened the door. There was the gray Valiant. The engine was running and its rear door was open. Charlie half-dove and half-fell through it, trying not to bang his ribs. The Valiant started forward and the door slammed shut. The sudden motion made it hard to keep his balance as he knelt on the floor. The car turned quickly out of the alley onto 10th Street, and Charlie was pushed down onto his left shoulder. He was surprised by the smell of perfume, then he felt something cold brush his cheek. Managing to turn over, he looked up into an automatic pistol less than an inch from his eye.

"Didn't expect to see me, did you?"

Charlie caught a glimpse of yellow-orange hair before the gun was shoved against his eyelid, forcing him back down to the floor.

"You know," said Jukes, "you shoot a guy in the eye like this and it hardly makes any noise at all. The dude's whole head acts like a kind of silencer. I heard once that you can do the same thing by cramming an apple onto the barrel. Trouble is, I don't have any apples."

"You're not going to kill him?" asked Driscoll. He sounded terrified.

"No, you dumb fuck, I'm just going to put out his eye. Why don't you watch out where you're driving. Hate to have an accident with me half over the seat like this."

27

▼▼▼

I N JOHN WESLEY HARDIN'S account of his capture by Texas Ranger Lieutenant John B. Armstrong on the train in Pensacola in 1877, Hardin said that when Armstrong placed his pistol against his forehead, he told the lieutenant, "Blow away! You will never blow a more innocent man's brains out, or one that will care less!"

Charlie tried to draw comfort from this as he was forced up the stairs to Driscoll's apartment. Jukes had one hand on his collar while shoving his pistol into Charlie's right ear. The pistol hurt. Driscoll led the way, but kept turning around as if to make sure Charlie was still alive.

Unfortunately, Armstrong's own account differed too much to allow Charlie to take solace from Hardin's. Armstrong said that as he walked down the aisle, Hardin recognized him as a Texas Ranger and attempted to stand up and draw his guns at the same time. He moved too quickly, however, and his guns caught on his suspenders. As Armstrong described it: "He almost pulled his breeches over his head." Armstrong then stepped forward and cold-cocked him.

Tateo was waiting in Driscoll's apartment. He wore dark glasses even though the shades were drawn. He had on new blue jeans and a jean jacket.

"Have any trouble?"

"Clockwork."

"Did he have a gun?"

Jukes shook his head. "Some cop he is, right? Maybe up in Saratoga the cops carry cattle prods or something." He slapped Charlie on the back, making him stumble forward.

It was a shabby apartment, and Charlie doubted that Driscoll had changed anything since first coming to New York. There was a dark-paneled hall, then the large living room with a purple rug and purple drapes obscuring the windows. The two armchairs and couch were Germanic and rectangular. A design of dark flowers and ivy ran in vertical stripes on the graying wallpaper.

Tateo sat in a low purple armchair, facing Charlie with his feet stretched out in front of him. His brown cowboy boots had high heels and pointed toes. Above him was a black metal birdcage on a black metal stand. The cage was empty.

"What are you going to do with him?" asked Driscoll. He stood back in the hallway, holding his hands crossed in front of him. It made him look like someone come to inquire about a job. He was careful not to look at Charlie.

Jukes grinned at him. "Don't worry. Whatever we do, we'll do someplace else."

He and Charlie stood in the center of the room, his gun resting lightly on Charlie's ear. It acted like something electric on Charlie's mind, kept him from concentrating.

Tateo raised his right hand and pointed a finger at Driscoll. "Go get a necktie." He spoke quietly, almost in a whisper.

"Will I get it back?"

"No."

Driscoll moved out of the hallway toward a door on the left

side of the room. He walked quickly as if barely keeping himself from running.

Jukes tapped Charlie's ear with his gun. "Lie down on the floor. Face down."

Charlie got down slowly. He had bumped his ribs in the car and it was painful to move. The purple rug smelled musty. He watched Driscoll return, or rather he watched his brown shoes. Beyond him, in the other room, he saw a brown wooden bedstead.

"This tie all right?"

"S'long as it ties, what the fuck?" Jukes prodded Charlie with his shoe. "Okay, Saratoga, put your hands behind your back."

Charlie did as he was told. He felt the tie wrapped around his wrists, and winced as it was pulled tight.

"There," said Jukes, "I wasn't in the fuckin' Boy scouts for nothing." He walked over to a dark green couch and sat down. Driscoll continued to stand at the bedroom door, as if he thought he'd be less at fault if he remained partly out of the room.

For a moment, Charlie lay quietly, then he rolled over. He would have sat up but he couldn't because of his ribs.

"Hey, Saratoga, I didn't say you could do that."

"Leave him alone," said Tateo. He hadn't moved since Charlie had been brought in. Charlie guessed he was staring at him, but he couldn't be certain because of the dark glasses. With their thick plastic frames and moon-shaped lenses, they seemed to cover half of his thin face.

"What'd you tell the cops about us?" asked Tateo.

"Nothing."

Tateo turned toward Jukes who got up again and walked over to Charlie. "I asked you a question," said Tateo. He was still almost whispering.

"I told you, I didn't tell them anything."

Jukes raised his foot. Charlie tried to twist away but he wasn't fast enough. Jukes kicked him in the shoulder, and Charlie rolled over groaning.

"I mean it," said Charlie, "I didn't tell them anything."

Jukes followed him, kicking him lightly in the back. "Hey, Driscoll, you want to kick him this time?"

"Of course not."

"Don't be a lily-ass, kick him in the face."

Driscoll stayed in the bedroom doorway. "No, please, you said I didn't have to do anything."

"Sit down, Jukes."

Jukes grinned and walked back to the couch. He wore jeans, tennis shoes and a black sweatshirt with the sleeves cut off at the shoulders. In his right hand, he carried a small black automatic. Charlie didn't recognize the make. Turning quickly, Jukes tried to spin it in a border roll but the pistol was too small. He raised it, grabbing his wrist with his left hand, and swept the room in a wide arc. "Bepbepbepbepbepbepbepbep." He laughed, then sat back down on the couch. "So what we going to do?"

"I already told you." Tateo still faced Charlie.

"All that way? I thought you were joking."

"No."

"That's a fuckin' stupid idea."

Half sitting up, Tateo turned toward Jukes. He didn't say anything, just stared until Jukes began to grin.

"We're taking him to see Sammy," said Tateo at last. "That's the way I want to do it."

Jukes shrugged, then raised his pistol and again swept the room in an arc. "Bepbepbepbepbep. You like my gun?" he asked Charlie. "Tateo gave it to me. Iron. That's what they say. 'He's packing iron.' " He grinned.

Charlie was struck by how much his yellowish-orange hair looked like fur: dyed rat or weasel, short and plastered back on his head.

"Tateo collects guns," continued Jukes. "This one's Italian. A Beretta 9mm automatic pistol Model 1934. Right, Tateo? Takes a .38 shell. They used 'em in the Italian army. It's got RE stamped on the grip. I don't know what that means. Maybe *real effective*. Is that what it means, Tateo? Bepbepbep-bepbepbep."

Charlie lay on his side watching Jukes. He felt sick in his

stomach but he didn't intend to give them the pleasure of seeing his fear.

"Did you two beat me up last night?" he asked.

Jukes lowered the Beretta. "Us? When?"

"Last night about 11:30. I'd been at The Lamplighter. Some guys beat me up and took my wallet."

"No fooling. Wasn't us, Saratoga. I don't approve of beating guys up. It's a good way to fuck up your hands. I mean, if you want to get a guy, why not just shoot him? You might as well go whole hog. Don't get me wrong, I know guys that swear by it. But to my way of thinking, nothin' beats a pill in the eye."

Charlie thought of the girl who had been beaten up in San Francisco.

"They hurt you much?" asked Jukes, as he again tried to do the border roll with the Beretta.

"Cracked some ribs."

"No fooling. First that happens and now this, right? Guy never knows when he's well off. Who do you think they were?"

"Junkies."

"Wouldn't be surprised. What a way to fuck up your life."

Charlie didn't answer. He lay quietly, trying to keep his fear from overwhelming his mind. Jukes kept playing with his pistol; Driscoll fidgeted in the doorway. Only Tateo seemed motionless. He still faced Charlie with his sharp-toed boots stretched out in front of him. He could have been made out of wax. Charlie imagined the eyes moving behind the dark glasses.

"Let's go," said Tateo. "It's dark enough."

Along with his fear, Charlie felt hopeless. He thought of the bodies he had seen as a policeman: homicides, accident victims, suicides. He thought of his own body, lying in the careless manner of the dead, surrounded by a small ring of officials who shuffled their feet, spoke quietly and had seen it before. He strained to pull his wrists apart but the necktie wouldn't give.

Jukes stood above him. "Okay, Saratoga, get up."

Charlie rolled over on his stomach, got to his knees, then to his feet. "Where we going?"

"Tateo's got his plan to take you over to New Jersey."

"Shut up."

"It's a fucking stupid plan, Tateo!" shouted Jukes.

Tateo stood up and took a step toward Jukes.

"Okay, okay," said Jukes, "but why take him so far?"

Tateo spoke softly. "Because that's what I want to do."

"But why?"

"I just told you." He turned away.

Jukes grabbed Charlie's arm and pulled him toward the door. "What can you do with a guy like that?"

There was a noise from Driscoll. He started to move toward Charlie, then stopped. His face became wrinkled. "I . . ." He didn't say anything else."

"You lily-ass," said Jukes. Letting go of Charlie, he stepped forward and hit Driscoll in the stomach. It was like a dancing exercise. Driscoll twisted away and fell back against the wall, holding on to his stomach as if it had broken in his hands. He slid down the wall to the floor.

"There," said Jukes. "If you hit a guy, hit him where he's soft. Just watch out for his belt buckle, that's all."

"Come on," said Tateo. "Stop fucking around."

As Charlie was taken down to the car he searched his mind for some comforting recollection. But the only person he could think of was Cherokee Bill who was hanged in Oklahoma Territory in 1896 at the age of twenty for killing thirteen men. As he was led to the gallows, he looked up at the sun and blue sky, and said, "This is about as good a day as any to die."

When the guard asked him if he had anything else to say, Cherokee Bill answered, "No. I came here to die, not make a speech."

28

▼▼▼

T HEY WERE GOING THROUGH the Lincoln Tunnel. Tateo drove. Charlie sat beside him, twisted uncomfortably to the left because of his tied hands. Jukes, perched on the edge of the back seat, rested the muzzle of his Beretta lightly against Charlie's jaw. Gray sponge rubber dice with pink spots hung from the rear view mirror. Attached to the top of the steering wheel was a clear plastic knob containing a small yellow rose.

"How'd you know Sammy was going to deal cocaine?" asked Jukes, giving the pistol a slight push.

Charlie tried to raise his head away from it. "He told me. He was trying to raise the money to buy it. He said it was an investment. Whatever I put in, he'd double."

"Did you do it?"

"I didn't have the money right then."

"Jeez, fine fucking cop you are."

"The stuff belong to you?"

"Belongs to a man we work for."

It was hard for Charlie to believe that he was being taken someplace to be shot. Jukes seemed perfectly calm, was simply indulging in a little light conversation with a fellow passenger. Tateo, on the other hand, ignored them completely. He had removed his dark glasses, but Charlie still couldn't see his eyes.

"Why bother about me?" he asked Jukes. Charlie couldn't bring himself to say the words "kill" or "murder" or "shoot."

Jukes kept his pistol against Charlie's jaw. "It's easier, that's all. You shouldn't of been hanging around that bar. I mean, it's not as if we don't like you or anything. You're not a bad guy."

"Thanks," said Charlie.

"Now me, I wanted to do it in the city, but Tateo thinks different. He likes everything neat and orderly. What the hell, we go a little out of our way, who's going to regret it?"

They had left the Lincoln Tunnel and were driving west on Route 3. "Where are going?" asked Charlie.

"Tateo once worked out here, driving a truck. What's the name of the place? Secaucus, that's it, Secaucus. Sounds like a bird, don't it?"

"Why don't you shut up, Jukes." Tateo spoke without turning his head.

"What the fuck, who's he going to tell? Sammy?" Jukes gave a high laugh, then leaned forward and whispered in Tateo's ear. Charlie couldn't hear what he said.

Jukes sat back again, giving Charlie's head a slight tap with his pistol. "To my way of thinking, any delay is another chance taken. A bird in the hand, you know? This is my first visit to the City and so far I like it a lot better than L.A., although we haven't exactly been sightseeing. But I'll come back, you don't have to worry about that. When I see a place I like, I always come back. Like Mexico City. Remember that, Tateo? Shit, did we have one fuckin' time."

Tateo didn't say anything. He had turned south off Route 3. There wasn't much traffic, but occasionally another car would pass in the opposite direction, lighting up their faces and making the sponge rubber dice glitter. On Tateo's face, the light looked like a mask, stressing the sharp angles of the nose and jaw. On either side of the road were chain link fences and corrugated metal warehouses. The land seemed swampy and wet.

"It don't look like much," said Jukes, "but where we're going you can even see the Empire State Building."

Tateo slowed down and turned right on a narrow paved road. With each turn, Charlie became more afraid. He knew his main hope depended on appearing calm, of convincing Jukes that he wouldn't cause trouble. It seemed that he and Jukes were acting out some dangerous hypocrisy in which both pretended that nothing of any importance was about to happen. Charlie decided to carry his bravado a little further.

"Look, guys, I wonder if I could ask you a favor, for my wife's sake."

Jukes gave the pistol a shove. "What's on your mind?"

"My wife, she's squeamish, so I wonder, you know, when you shoot me maybe you won't do it in the face. It's going to be bad enough on her just to do the ID." Charlie felt some satisfaction at the control he had over his voice.

Jukes was silent for a moment. "You're a hard little fucker, Saratoga, I gotta say that for you. Sure, you give us no trouble and we'll keep you pretty. Promise?"

The gray Valiant crossed a single railway line, then Tateo turned right onto a narrow dirt road that followed the tracks. The headlights swept across high reeds. Charlie thought it was about ten o'clock. He didn't answer Jukes. After driving about 100 yards, Tateo stopped and turned out the lights.

"Get out of the car."

Jukes quickly opened his door and get out while keeping his gun against Charlie's head. He unlocked Charlie's door and opened it. "Come on," he said.

Charlie got out of the car. He was embarrassed to discover that his legs felt weak. Tateo came around the front holding a small flashlight. He shone the light briefly in Charlie's face, then turned it toward a path. "Let's go."

Jukes didn't move. "Tateo, what's the point of taking all these chances? Let's do it here."

Tateo took a few steps along the path, then stopped. He didn't turn around. "I'm going to let him see Sammy."

"What the fuck's it matter? I mean, in ten minutes it'll be all the same. If some watchman calls the cops, Jesus, Tateo, it's not worth it."

Moving quickly, Tateo came back to Jukes, stopping a few inches from him. He didn't speak or touch him, but just stood facing him for about fifteen seconds. Then Tateo turned and walked up the path, shining his light a little behind him so Charlie could follow.

Jukes grabbed Charlie's arm and shoved him along the path. "You ever seen someone with a cut throat, Saratoga? A big double grin? Your wife, she sees that and she'll puke. Believe me. You just walk along behind Tateo and keep quiet."

Charlie followed Tateo along the path. He felt almost grateful to him for keeping him alive, and he was relieved to discover they were afraid of making noise. The path was muddy and at places it was covered by an inch or so of water. Tateo's boots left bullet-shaped tracks in the mud. Although the night was clear, there was no moon. Charlie could hear Jukes cursing behind him. It was the first time Charlie had seen stars since coming to New York.

Tateo stopped at a chain link fence that stretched off to the right and left across the path. Jukes pushed Charlie up against it.

"This is close enough," he said. "Come, Tateo. Please."

Ignoring him, Tateo turned right along the fence. The ground was soft and overgrown with reeds. Jukes grabbed Charlie's arm and pushed him after Tateo.

"You better be fucking grateful," said Jukes, "that's all I can say."

Charlie's feet were wet and he was cold. His bruises ached. He was even aware that he was hungry. But all these were distant feelings that required conscious notice, otherwise he was hardly aware of them. Mostly he was aware of Jukes' pistol. Secondly, he was aware of Tateo's small flashlight that snaked a trail through the reeds. Thirdly, there was the imminence of his own death. He could hardly believe that, despite his fear. Beyond those feelings, Charlie was aware of a kind of indignation that Tateo and Jukes thought they could get rid of him so simply. He wanted to hurt them and felt frustrated by his powerlessness. Ever since leaving Manhattan, he had been straining against the necktie that bound his hands, but, although he had loosened it, he still couldn't pull his hands free.

Tateo had stopped and Charlie almost bumped up against him. He flashed his light on a hole in the fence. "I'll go through first."

Beyond the fence was a pile of steel drums, lying on their sides and lined up in a row, layer upon layer. The three men climbed through the hole. Tateo led the way around to the left of the drums, then paused at the edge of a small field littered with rusting containers, lids, pieces of wood and cardboard, rubber tires. Thirty feet away was another pile of drums, perhaps eight layers high and forty feet long. Several hundred yards beyond it was a large corrugated metal warehouse lit by half a dozen yellow lights. A row of semitrailers was lined up to the left of the warehouse. There were also more piles of steel drums, some rusted, some new and painted black. A junked Corvair was lying on its roof near a pile of lumber, wooden crates, sheets of plywood scattered like large playing cards.

"Pretty isn't it," said Jukes. "This is where I'm coming on my honeymoon."

Quietly, Tateo began to cross the small field toward the nearest pile of drums. Jukes gave Charlie a shove. They had to keep walking around rusted containers and avoid tripping on lids, old two-by-fours, tires. The ground was covered with cinders. Looking back at Jukes, Charlie saw the top of the Empire State Building with its red light off in the distance. It was almost comforting.

Tateo had reached the pile of steel drums and appeared to be counting. In his left hand, he held an iron bar and used it to point at the drums.

"That's it. The tenth one."

"We'll put you in adjoining barrels," whispered Jukes. "Just like the fuckin' Ritz."

While Jukes held the flashlight, Tateo pried the lid off the drum with the iron bar. With his other hand, Jukes kept his pistol pointed at Charlie who stood slightly to their left, about fifteen feet from the end of the row.

The lid came off all of a sudden, clattering to the ground. Tateo stumbled back. The smell of decomposing flesh seemed to surge out of the barrel. It was like a hand slapped over their noses. Very slowly, as the light shown on the open drum, a head and shoulders toppled back onto the ground.

"Smells like 'Nam," said Jukes. "There's Sammy. Take a look at him." He shone the light on the dead man's face.

Charlie was reminded of moldy bread. The face was gray and puffy, as if the person had been holding his breath day after day, waiting for this moment. A watchdog began to bark by the warehouse. As he looked at the blond hair, the empty blue eyes staring up at the sky, Charlie felt sadder than he would have believed possible. He thought of the man he had talked to in California.

"That's not Sam Cheney," he said. "It's Peter Bonenfant, his roommate."

29

▼▼▼

THE BARKING GREW LOUDER. Charlie knew that after this moment he would have no further chances. As Jukes and Tateo stared down at the body, he stepped forward and kicked Jukes' knee, knocking him off balance. Jukes swore and stumbled against Tateo. Aiming high, Charlie kicked him again, trying for his groin. Jukes fell back, dropping the flashlight and grabbing at Tateo. Both men were stumbling, attempting to keep themselves from falling onto the body of Peter Bonenfant. Charlie turned and ran.

As he reached the end of the row of barrels, he saw some blurred movement to his left. Tateo shouted, "The dog! Get the dog!"

There was a shot and a yelp, then a second shot. Charlie didn't pause; bent over, scurrying more than running, he crossed a small, open yard toward another pile of barrels. Several spotlights went on near the warehouse, lighting up the whole area. Charlie twisted and turned to avoid tripping over the pieces of metal and wood littering the ground.

Reaching the barrels, he ducked behind them, looking for a temporary hiding place. He saw a small tarpaper shack about ten yards to his right. Scattered around it were square bales of paper or cardboard. Crouching down, he ran for the shed.

They were rags. Charlie squeezed himself between a damp, smelly bundle and the corner of the shed. The tarpaper was rough and studded with nails. Hoping to cut Driscoll's necktie, Charlie began to rub it against the building. He kept looking to his left but it was darker on this side of the barrels and he could see nothing, nor hear any sound.

The tie broke. Charlie stayed where he was, rubbing his wrists. There was still no sign of Tateo and Jukes. Ten yards in front of him the row of barrels rose up like a high wall about forty feet long. Above the barrels was the glow of the lights. Charlie began to look for a weapon. He felt around on the ground, picking up and discarding about a dozen rocks before settling on two that were the comfortable size of baseballs.

He felt exhilarated, as if his body were stronger, his senses keener. Although afraid, he felt himself capable of outwitting his enemies. It didn't occur to him that he was submitting to a new fantasy. Already he was searching for the words with which to describe his adventure to his friends in Saratoga.

There was a noise of metal against metal. Looking to his left, Charlie saw someone standing at the end of the row of barrels about thirty feet away. It was hardly a person at all, just a black shape against the darkness. It began to move forward, very slowly, as if waiting for the slightest sound. Charlie couldn't tell if it was Tateo or Jukes, but his fear made him think of Tateo. He wanted to run, but forced himself to stay motionless. As the figure came closer, Charlie could hear the crunch of cinders.

He didn't trust himself not to betray his position. The sound of his pulse, his heart and breathing—he was certain these would give him away. The figure had stopped and appeared to be listening.

Balancing one of the rocks in his hand, Charlie drew back his arm and hurled the rock over the pile of barrels. There was a clang as it hit some metal object in the farther yard. The figure remained motionless, then, as Charlie began to think he had been found out, it turned silently and hurried back the way it had come.

When Charlie was sure the person was gone, he crept back behind the tarpaper shed. Beyond the shed was a field littered with broken barrels and lids. In the center of the field was a burned-out car. Charlie made his way toward it. He had emerged from his fantasy and wanted to get away as fast as possible.

The car was little more than a rusted shell. Charlie crouched down, watching the end of the barrels where the figure had disappeared. From his new position, he could also see the warehouse, the lawn in front of it and a driveway leading to a high gate. There were lights in several windows, and a pickup truck was parked by the side entrance.

As he began to relax and feel less frightened, Charlie became aware of the cold and the pains in his body. They were not small, located pains, but whole areas; and Charlie imagined black and blue marks like continents against the white of his skin. He knew he had to get away, but he was afraid of going back to the hole in the fence.

Looking behind him, Charlie could just make out the chain link fence and see where it turned left toward the gate. Near the gate was a small flood-lit sign: *Freeman Container Company*, surrounded by low shrubbery. Beyond the gate was a road, and on the other side of it was another warehouse and a line of semitrailers.

Not wishing to go directly to the gate. Charlie crouched down and ran toward the fence. He hoped to find another hole. As he moved along, he kept thinking he saw Tateo creeping up behind him. The thought brought him near panic and he forced himself to empty his mind.

The fence was eight feet high and topped with barbed wire. There were no holes and no way he could crawl under. Charlie told himself that if it weren't for his cracked ribs, he might be able to climb over, but he knew that was a lie. Even as a young man in the army, he would not have been able to climb the fence.

He had expected the gate to be locked before he reached it, so that was only a minor disappointment, but he was surprised by the loneliness of being on the wrong side of a locked gate. Deciding that to climb was his only hope, Charlie had just begun to look for a handhold when he saw headlights coming down the road. He turned and ran back to the sign, *Freeman*

Container Company, and lay down between it and the shrubbery.

A police car drew up to the fence. After a moment, a man hurried out of the warehouse and unlocked the gate. The police car drove through it slowly with its lights off. Charlie could hear the watchman talking but he couldn't make out the words.

Lying under the bushes, Charlie saw the watchman climb into the back seat of the police car. After a few seconds, the car drove slowly around the side of the warehouse. Almost before it was out of sight, Charlie was up and running for the gate. He passed through it and turned down the road. His exhilaration returned. He wanted to tell someone about his adventure. He hurried down the center of the road, half running, half jogging.

He thought of the time that Butch Cassidy kept Kid Curry from shooting Woodcock, the express car guard on the Union Pacific's Overland Flyer. Woodcock had refused to open the car door and had to be blasted out with dynamite. The explosion had stunned him. When Kid Curry rode forward to finish him off, Butch Cassidy stood in his way and said, "Leave him be, Kid. A man with nerve deserves not to be shot."

Jogging along the dark road somewhere in Secaucus, Charlie repeated to himself, "A man with nerve deserves not to be shot."

30

▼▼▼

I T WAS PAST ONE when Charlie got back to Manhattan. After walking for several miles, he had been picked up by four teenagers in a dark purple 1949 Mercury. It was the kind of car that Charlie had once coveted, with tinted blue glass and a roof which had been lowered so the windshield was no more than a foot high. The seats were covered with blond tuck-and-roll upholstery.

Drunk and jovial, the kids had driven him directly to Victor's apartment, refusing to take any money except for gas and tolls. A frizzy-haired girl in the back seat had told him he looked like her father. Given his present condition, Charlie felt sorry for her.

Victor came up and let him in. "I hope you had a good time making yourself look like that."

"If anyone asks, just say you haven't seen me."

"Mister, the way you look, I wouldn't want to admit it."

Victor led the way back to his apartment. He had on a dark green robe of some shiny material with wide, black lapels. The cord at his waist was tipped with yellow tassels. Charlie saw there were blankets and sheets on the couch.

Going into the kitchen, Victor said, "I didn't know if you'd come back, but I figured if you did then you'd want a place to sleep."

He reappeared with the bottle of Jack Daniels and two glasses. The cat jumped from the couch, made a small leap for the yellow tassels, missed and began washing itself.

"Moshe's been sleeping on the blankets but I didn't figure you'd mind." Victor handed Charlie a glass half full of whiskey. "Bet you're surprised to see any of this stuff left. Well, I'd of finished it if it weren't for the cops."

"Cops?" Charlie had sat down on the couch and was—as his mother used to say—resting his eyes.

"That's right." Victor filled his glass three quarters full, then went back to the brown chair. Moshe made another unsuccessful snatch for the yellow tassels. Victor didn't seem to notice.

"What about the cops?" asked Charlie.

Victor shook his head. "I'm not supposed to have anything to do with you."

Charlie sipped his whiskey and waited. He thought again of kicking Jukes' knee and hiding by the tarpaper shed.

"Why didn't you say you'd been talking to the cops?" asked Victor after a minute. "At least you might of warned me."

"What happened?"

"They came bombing in here with a search warrant. Wanted

to see Sam Cheney's apartment. So I let 'em in and they poked around."

"Who was it?"

"Cops, that's all."

Charlie rubbed his chin with his fist. He needed a shave and wished he could spend several hours in a bathtub. "Someone must have been in charge."

"Yeah, a big guy. Name like a sneeze."

"Zack."

Victor nodded. "He asked me all kinds of questions about Sam Cheney and Peter Bonenfant. What the fuck could I tell him? Then he asked if I knew you and if I'd let anyone into Cheney's apartment. I said you'd been around but was I going to break the law? Not on your ass. Good thing I put your suitcase in the closet.

Charlie guessed that Peter Bonenfant's father had called the police. "Did he believe you?"

"Sure, why not? He's still going to nail me, though. Those cops showed up around eight. Then an hour later a whole new set showed up with cameras and stuff like I seen 'em do on TV. I don't suppose you wore gloves this afternoon."

"Maybe they won't know the prints are mine."

Victor rolled his eyes. "Sure. We'll cut off your fingers and feed 'em to the fish, and when the cops come back to take your prints we'll say, 'Tough luck, copper, I'm outta prints right now.' Believe-you-me, I lose my job over this and I'm coming up to Saratoga and you can talk to those rich friends of yours and find me another. I'm not particular what it is."

Charlie couldn't tell if Victor was serious. "I don't have any rich friends in Saratoga."

"Don't give me that, you were even talking about them. Vanderbilts, Whitneys, Markeys, Phipps. I read the papers; I know their names. Just give them a call."

"To tell the truth," said Charlie, "I wouldn't know a Vanderbilt if he came up and punched me in the eye."

Victor seemed indignant. He put his glass on the floor as if he couldn't drink and argue at the same time. "You live right there with 'em. What the hell you been doing all your life?"

"That's not how it works," said Charlie patiently, "I know their summer houses and we get told when they come into town. I may even recognize their cars or know how much some Whitney paid for a horse at the auction. I even went to the auction once, coupla years ago. They sell more'n sixty yearlings a day for four days, make over $8 million. You see these guys buying a $100,000 horse by raising a little finger. You can't get inside without a ticket and you can't get a ticket unless your credit's good. Me and a crowd of other people looked in through the big windows. One cheap horse, it was $7,000. I told myself I could afford that. Mortgage my house, sell my car. I'd have my own race horse, except that for $7,000 it's bound to be a loser, and training and unkeep costs about $20 a day. So there I'd be with an untrained horse in my garage which the bank wants to repossess. Maybe I could take the horse out on Sundays, you know, walk it around the block, because I couldn't ride it. Anyway at this auction there was a bar and I went to the bar. I mean, I can't buy a horse but I can still afford Molsons. Money, jewels, you're almost blinded. I found myself thinking like a communist or something. I didn't go back."

Victor leaned forward and put his elbows on his knees. "So I get fired, you can't get me a new job."

"Maybe I could. Did you know that Wyatt Earp only got paid $2.50 a month for being marshal of Dodge City?"

"What's that got to do with anything?"

Charlie stood up. "Not much. It makes me happy. Where's my bag? I've got to change my clothes and go out again. And can you let me have a key so I can get back in?"

Victor waved his arm behind him. "Your bag's in the closet. If I'd known you were going to be this much trouble, I'd never of let you in. Baby face or no baby face."

Charlie's pants were torn and so were the pair he had worn the previous night. The light gray pair he had worn down on Monday were simply dirty. He put them on along with a soiled white shirt.

Victor poured himself some more whiskey. He was grinning and appeared to take pleasure in Charlie's discomforts. "Way you're going you should of brought down a Saratoga trunk. You think Sam Cheney's dead?"

In his mind, Charlie again saw the lid fall off the metal drum, and the head and shoulders of Peter Bonenfant flop back to the ground. He could almost smell the stench. "No, he's probably as healthy as you are. Can I borrow a jacket?"

"Help yourself. Where you going this time of night?"

Charlie put on a blue, waist-length, wool jacket. He thought it looked a little like the kind baseball managers wore. That made him feel better even though the jacket was several sizes too large. "I'm going over to see Sam's girlfriend."

Victor tossed him a key and Charlie caught it. "Business or pleasure?"

Charlie fastened the snaps on the jacket. "You're a rude son-of-a-bitch, you know that?"

"Everyone needs a hobby."

31

▼▼▼

Assuming that Stacy was still watched by the police, Charlie took a cab to her building. It was 2:30 by the time he got there. The driver didn't want to wait. Charlie gave him $10 and one of the cards identifying him as a Saratoga Springs police sergeant.

"That's okay, buddy, my brother-in-law he gave me some cards for Christmas, said I was the Queen of Sheba."

Inside the foyer, Charlie pressed the purple button for Stacy's apartment, and kept pressing it for nearly a minute. There was a crackling noise as Stacy's voice came through the small speaker.

"Who is it?"

"Charlie. I want to talk."

"We have nothing to talk about."

"If you don't let me in, I'll go to the police."

There was a pause. Charlie made star-shaped patterns with his thumb print on the polished brass.

"What for?" asked Stacy.

"I'll tell them where to find Peter Bonenfant's body." Charlie was fairly certain that Tateo and Jukes had moved the body, but he doubted they had taken it far.

"I'm coming down."

Charlie waited. Apart from his cab, the street seemed empty. Zack probably had a man in one of the surrounding buildings. Charlie imagined him picking up the phone.

Stacy appeared at the door in jeans, a blue sweater and brown terrycloth slippers. Charlie found himself staring at her thin face, looking for the lines that would turn into wrinkles then creases as she got older. Her black hair hung loosely down her back.

"Let's go upstairs," she said.

They stood in the lobby by the bank of mailboxes. "We can talk here."

"It's more private upstairs."

They took the elevator and waited for it to arrive at the third floor like two strangers, even though the elevator was the size of a large bathtub. Charlie didn't want to go into her apartment and suspected a trap. He knew, however, that given his present state of mind, he would suspect a trap in a Salvation Army meeting hall.

He wasn't comfortable until he had looked in her closet, bathroom and kitchenette. Then he stayed by the front door. He had felt foolish in Victor's dark blue jacket, thinking that Baseball Coach was not the image he cared to project.

"Do you want to look under the bed?" asked Stacy.

Charlie stayed where he was. "When I got beat up last night," he said, "you led me right into it. You knew Sam was out there waiting with some other guy. At first I thought it was Peter Bonenfant, but he's dead. Even when it happened, I knew you'd set me up, but I was such a fool I wouldn't let myself believe it."

The combination of a high ceiling and not much furniture

made Charlie's voice echo against the bare walls. Stacy sat in the middle of the couch with her legs curled up under her.

"Did Sam tell you to seduce me as well?" Charlie asked. "All that junk about numbers. You must have really thought I was an idiot when I told you my name was Chuck. . . ."

It depressed him that he couldn't speak to her coldly, that he wanted to ask her to run away with him to the Yukon where they would build a log cabin and live on bear meat and salmon. He told himself that it was the idea of a young woman he loved, not Stacy. He had fallen victim to her interest and flattery. Charlie tried to work up some anger, but continued to feel sad. He carefully stayed by the door.

"I know about the cocaine and where it's coming from," he said. "I know that Sam used Bonenfant to bring money from California and as a decoy. I know the names of the guys that killed him and will kill Sam if they get the chance. I know that Sam plans to pick up the cocaine tomorrow."

"So? Go to the police."

Charlie shook his head. "I came down here to find Sam and that's what I mean to do. I've been bothering about him for his whole life, a stupid sort of bothering that hasn't led anywhere. Now I'm done with it. He wants to get himself killed or thrown in jail, that's his business. But I want to see him, just talk to him, person to person."

Stacy hadn't moved. "You think he's your son, don't you?"

"No. His mother used to tell me that Sam was my son, but she was lying. I don't have any children."

"I don't know where Sam is."

Charlie looked at her sadly. "Yes you do. You're going to set up a meeting for early this morning. I'll call you at seven. If you refuse or if he refuses to see me, I'll go to the police. If he does see me and tries any funny stuff, I'll make sure the police still find out about it. All I want is to talk to him. It'll take five minutes, then I'll go back to Saratoga."

Stacy was silent for a while. In her jeans and blue sweater, she looked like part of the blue couch: something soft and comfortable. She seemed to be looking at a blank spot on the wall.

"I'll call him," she said at last.

"Good."

"What are you going to do now?"

"Go back and get a few hours' sleep."

"Do you want to stay here?"

"I've got a cab outside."

"Send it away."

Charlie was startled by the amount of desire she could cause in him. It made him feel like his body's puppet. He told himself that nothing that had happened made any difference. He could sleep with her, spend the night with her, and it would be a gift: a free period in which there would be no fault or responsibility. Tomorrow he would go back to Saratoga, get some job as a Pinkerton guard and pursue his next forty-one years. He argued that she was something he owed himself. They would have one night without any words.

"I'd like to stay," said Charlie, "but I don't know who you are. Goodnight, Stacy. I'll call you at seven. I'm sorry things didn't work out."

32

▼▼▼

CHARLIE HAD THE CAB drop him off at Cooper Union, then walked the last three blocks. Not only would Zack learn of his visit to Stacy's, he would learn the number of his cab as well. There was no point in leading him to Victor.

As Charlie unlocked the door, he heard Victor snoring. It was a mellow rumble like the '49 Mercury which had brought him back to Manhattan. Charlie saw a note on the couch and went to pick it up.

"There's Heinekens and sliced ham in the fridge. Make yourself at home. Sorry I finished the Jack Daniels. Vic."

Charlie made himself a ham and cheese sandwich, then came back and ate it on the couch. He hadn't noticed the ham earlier and suspected Victor had bought it with him in mind. The light was off in the aquarium. As he ate, Charlie considered the sleeping habits of fish to keep from thinking about Stacy. It was a partial success.

Although tired, he knew he wouldn't sleep. He kept thinking of Saratoga and the people who would call him a fool for staying in New York. He could imagine the boredom he would feel when listening to them, and then felt bored with himself for worrying about what other people thought. There were more important losses to consider.

Along with the loss of his job, Charlie would have to resign from The Protective and Benevolent Association. That meant quitting as assistant coach of the Pony League team which the association sponsored. He regretted that. It seemed a pity that his trip to New York had coincided with the beginning of baseball season.

Not that Charlie had ever been much of a player. In school he had never made the team despite the hours he had practiced fielding fake flies from the roof of his uncle's two-story house. During his senior year, he had been promoted equipment manager.

But neither was he a terrible player. Of the twenty kids that used to meet on Saturdays at the diamond across from St. Clements, Charlie would be picked about sixth by the captains choosing up sides. A reliable right fielder, he would wait patiently all afternoon, grabbing a few bouncing grounders while the aggressive center fielder shagged the pop flies. At bat he could be counted on for a base hit, depending on the skill of the opposing shortstop.

Charlie went out to the kitchen for another beer. As he moved, he was again aware of the pains in his body. He had not been surprised that Sam had beaten him up. Sam was a person of few loyalties, and Charlie had never pretended to believe that Sam was grateful for any of the help he had given him. Indeed, it was this outlaw quality, this chosen isolation, that Charlie almost admired.

Charlie returned to the couch. Despite his regret at losing his job and the respect of his acquaintances, Charlie knew that part of him felt pleased. He too, if only for a short time, had chosen isolation, had shared this outlaw quality. He had overthrown his established life.

Charlie also felt pleased at the way he had handled himself. Never before had he been in a situation where his life was in such danger. In his fantasies, he might see himself as capturing Tateo and Jukes single-handed, but that would have been impossible without a gun and improbable with one. It had been enough to escape, while the memory of that escape would be a source of pleasure for a long time.

Already he felt pride. In his years as a policeman, he had rarely felt afraid. Not much had happened. There had been men who resisted arrest, mostly drunks, with whom he might briefly struggle. Once a sixteen-year-old boy had threatened him with a gun when Charlie had come to arrest him for robbing a gas station. Once a woman had attacked him with a knife during a family trouble run.

His inexperience with fear always led Charlie to wonder how he would handle himself, and worry that he might not behave with dignity. In his reading of criminal history, Charlie would pay particular attention to how some outlaw met his death, and admire his bravery while deploring his crime. For instance, there was Francis "Two-Gun" Crowley who sauntered up to the electric chair in Sing Sing smoking a cigar. As the straps were adjusted, he flicked the cigar at the reporters, and hit one in the forehead. "Give my love to mother," he said. Then the current was turned on.

Against this, Charlie would remember the story of a man he had once met in Saratoga whose squad of fifteen men had been captured by the Germans at the end of the war. The Germans were retreating and had no time for prisoners. They had started to machine gun them, and killed eight soldiers before being stopped by their captain. Charlie's acquaintance had lost control of his bowels and fouled himself.

"Walked ten miles with shit in my pants. Fuckin' krauts knew what I'd done. Laugh, they thought it was a fuckin' joke."

Charlie had always been afraid he might do that. But now, although he might lose his job and be criticized by people in Saratoga, he could recall his escape from Tateo and Jukes and know he had behaved with dignity. Foolishly perhaps, but with dignity.

FRIDAY

33
▼▼▼

C HARLIE AND STACY walked along the north side of Fulton Street toward the Fulton Fish Market and Pier 16 where they would meet Sam Cheney. Charlie carried his canvas suitcase. It was 8:45 and the morning was bright, and chilly enough to make Charlie regret that he had turned down Victor's offer of a sweater. He was freezing in his sport coat.

Charlie had said good-bye to Victor at 7:30. Victor promised to visit, maybe right away if he lost his job, or in August during the races when he could search out a real Vanderbilt or Whitney. Charlie promised to get back down to New York. Both men knew they probably wouldn't see each other again.

When he had called Stacy, she told him to be in front of St. Paul's Chapel on Broadway at Fulton Street at 8:30. He found her dressed in jeans and a brown quilted jacket. She wore dark glasses and her hair was hidden by a brown and white scarf.

Seeing her, Charlie was grateful that she had obscured her face. She could have been almost anybody. As he thought that, he realized his feelings for Gladys had been transferred to Stacy, as if he had scraped together a remembered emotion, revitalized it and presented it to Stacy as something new and original.

This morning, however, she wanted none of it. She was cool, businesslike and, after nodding to him, had turned down Fulton Street expecting him to follow. Charlie looked regretfully at her back. He had never been in this part of the city and would have liked to glance in at the Chapel and its small graveyard. There was no telling who might be buried there.

The sidewalks and streets were crowded with people hurrying to work, rush hour traffic, produce and delivery trucks. Charlie had to walk quickly to keep up with Stacy. He kept asking himself what he would say to Sam. It was almost as if there were two of them: the one in Charlie's imagination and the flesh and blood Sam Cheney who he would see that morning. Charlie knew that although the real Sam might beat him up, it was the imaginary one that did the most damage. Hadn't he brought him to New York? By meeting him, Charlie hoped the two Sams would be brought together.

They crossed Water Street and entered the area known as South Street Seaport Museum. A row of four-story Federal-style buildings with red paint flaking off their bricks stretched off to the right. There were several small fish markets, restaurants, a book and chart store and a store selling marine supplies and foul weather gear. Charlie sniffed the smell of fish. They had left the rush hour crowd at Water Street and here the sidewalks were almost empty. Stacy remained a few feet ahead of him. He called after her.

"Stacy, if you don't leave New York, you'll probably go to jail."

She kept walking, gave no sign of hearing what he had said.

"Sam's in a lot of trouble," he continued. "The best thing you can do is stay out of it."

She neither turned nor slowed down. Charlie started to say that he was warning her for her own good, then he stopped himself, afraid that he was only protecting his conscience from whatever might happen.

They stopped at South Street to wait for a gap in the traffic. Above them rose the elevated East River drive. After a minute, they made a dash to the other side. The cars honked but didn't slow down. A small bald man in a red Pinto gave Charlie the finger. Closer to the market the smell of fish was much stronger.

They threaded their way between about thirty parked cars to the gate of Pier 16. As they passed through the gate, Charlie noticed a young man standing off to his right by a small information booth. He was about twenty-three and wore jeans, a brown leather jacket and cowboy boots. The man looked at Charlie, then looked away.

Charlie touched Stacy's shoulder. "Is that Sam's buddy over there? He's the other guy that beat me up, right?"

Stacy ignored him and continued quickly along the pier. To their left was a one-story, pre-fab restaurant. Orange life preservers hung in its windows. Moored to the pier beyond the restaurant, were a number of old ships. To their right was the *Wavetree*, a huge, iron-hulled, square-rigged cargo ship. Rows of blue metal chairs were lined up around the restaurant and along the edge of the pier. On the far side was moored a large ferry boat, *The Robert Fulton*, painted white with red trim. Beyond it, at the end of the pier, was the lightship *Ambrose*. Charlie looked ahead at the East River and the massive sweep of the Brooklyn Bridge against the blue sky. There was no one else in sight.

Stacy led the way toward the lightship. The bright red of its hull was interrupted only by the white letters of its name: *Ambrose*. The rest of the ship was white except for the two masts and funnel which were yellowish brown. Charlie thought the ship was about 100 feet long.

Stacy went up the gangplank at the stern. As Charlie followed her, he saw a young man in a brown corduroy jacket leaning over the rail. Across the river was Brooklyn, and directly across were docks and a large yellow building with the word *Watchtower* on its roof in red letters. Above the letters was a lighted sign indicating that the time was 8:58 and the temperature 39 degrees.

The man at the rail was thin with long, black, curly hair that fell past his neck and came to a point like the point of a shovel. He had on light brown corduroy pants and black tennis shoes. Although he must have heard their footsteps, he didn't move until Charlie said his name: "Sam Cheney."

Sam turned. Without seeing his face, it had been possible to give him all sorts of qualities, but looking at him now Charlie thought he saw proof of the faults he had hoped to find. The narrow chin, the brown eyes slanted like his mother's, the thinness of his face, even his pallor: these for Charlie became evidence of Sam's greed and small-mindedness, a smug and undeserved self-confidence. He had full lips and a mouth too small for his teeth. Under his jacket, he wore a white Indian shirt and a turquoise and silver necklace.

For nearly half a minute, Sam stared at Charlie without speaking. Charlie knew he was meant to feel intimidated. He smiled slightly.

"You know, you've killed me," said Sam. "You couldn't of killed me any better if you'd shot me yourself." He spoke softly.

Charlie shook his head. It was colder on the river and he crossed his arms, tucking his hands under his elbows.

"Those two guys, they won't leave town until I'm dead. What the fuck you come down here for anyway? It was none of your business."

Charlie began to say that Gladys had been worried. It sounded silly. He wondered if it were even true. "You're responsible for whatever's happened, Sam." He winced at the paternal tone. It was unfortunate that Sam was such a difficult young man to love. If Sam had ever responded to his fatherly affection, Charlie would have done anything for him.

Sam grew angrier. "My whole fucking life you been butting in, and just when I think I'm free of you, shit, here you come again. What'd you tell those guys anyway?"

"They know they killed Peter Bonenfant."

"And the cops, what do they know?"

While Charlie had no wish to help Zack, neither did he wish to interfere. "They're expecting you to meet a man at The Lamplighter later today."

Sam appeared relived. In his anger, however, he looked like a possum or weasel. It made his crowded teeth seem pointer.

"That's something at least," he said. "Jesus, I can't believe how you've fucked things up. I'll bet you'll be really happy when those guys kill me."

Charlie didn't want to talk anymore. Having seen Sam and spoken to him, he wanted to leave. He thought himself freed of the illusions he had once had, and to stay any longer would only stress the mistakes he had made about Sam during the past fifteen years. Seeing him, he was free of him. He would return to Saratoga.

"Where's my wallet?" he asked.

"What d'you mean?"

"My wallet, you stole it the other night when you beat me up, you and that guy at the end of the pier."

"I don't know what you're talking about."

Charlie looked away at the blue sky, the Brooklyn Bridge, the river leading out to the ocean beyond. It seemed too nice a day for this. He was aware of Stacy standing behind him to his left.

"Early last month," Charlie began, "you learned you could buy some cocaine cheap. You learned it from a guy in Los Angeles who supplies you with marijuana that you sell here in New York. You started getting some money together and called your friend Peter Bonenfant in San Diego, telling him you had a job for him at the clothing store where you worked. That was a lie. You had no job, but you wanted him here in case there was trouble from the real owners of the cocaine, and you wanted him to pick up an envelope of money from your partner in Los Angeles. Peter Bonenfant was looking forward to coming to New York. What was he here, nine days, before he got killed?

"You could have prevented that. Your mother talked to Bonenfant on Saturday, March 22. That's the day he was murdered. He was worried about you, said you hadn't been home all night. What I think is that you heard these guys were looking for you so you hid, leaving Bonenfant in your apartment. You didn't even warn him. Maybe they had seen him in California, and maybe that's why you had him pick up the money. In any case, he never had a chance. They came to your apartment and killed him, thinking he was you. Nice friend you are.

"When I arrived, you were afraid I'd mess up your cocaine deal. You got Stacy to pump me for information and when I didn't leave you a buddy beat me up and took my wallet and gun. Did you tell Stacy to fuck me too?"

As Charlie said that, Sam lunged at him. Charlie stepped aside. What had worked once would work again. Charlie kicked Sam in the left knee. Sam yelled, fell back against the railing, then dropped to the deck. Charlie glanced guiltily at Stacy, but she stood against the cabin watching Sam as if he were an experiment.

Turning back toward Sam, Charlie saw him reach for something under his jacket. He guessed what it was. He moved forward and when Sam drew a revolver, Charlie kicked his wrist, sending the gun in a high arc over the railing and into the East River. It was only when he saw the splash that Charlie realized it was his own revolver. He raised his foot again.

"Don't hurt me!" Sam tried to shield his head with his arm.

"Where's my wallet?"

"I don't know. I took the money, then dumped it. Tossed it into a trash can."

"You owe me thirty bucks, give it to me."

"I don't have it."

"Give it to me before I kick you to pieces."

Sam got to his feet, holding his wrist where Charlie had kicked it. He took out his wallet and gave Charlie $30. Charlie was tempted to throw the wallet into the river but decided that was too petty. He didn't really care about the $30, but he wanted something. His badge had been in his wallet, and Sam had taken it more easily than Chief Peterson could have done. For a moment it seemed he had traded his badge for his business cards only because of Stacy's flattery: *Charles F. Bradshaw, Sergeant.*

Sam leaned against the railing, trying to rub his wrist and knee at the same time. Charlie wanted to take Stacy's arm and say, "Can't you see how cheap he is? How could you have betrayed me for someone like that?" It was hard to stop thinking about it.

"Are you going to the police?" said Sam.

"I told you I wasn't."

"What're you going to do?"

"Go back to Saratoga."

"You going to see my mother?"

"Not if I can help it. I just wanted to find you, that's all."

"Thanks a fuckin' lot."

Charlie began to turn away, then stopped. "Sam, you might

just forget about the cocaine. Leave the city. The police were in your apartment last night and found bloodstains. They'll match it with Peter Bonenfant as soon as they have his blood type."

Sam shook his head. "It's too good a chance. Look, Charlie, you help me with the cops and I'll let you in on this. It could means $5,000."

The only responses open to Charlie were physical and violent. Ignoring Sam, he turned toward Stacy. She had taken off her dark glasses and looked back at him with her green eyes. Her cheeks were pink from the cold. He wanted to touch her but was afraid to.

"If you come with me now," he told her, "you'll be all right."

"Is that a bribe?" There was no expression on her face.

"You just walk away with me now, and I'll give you money to get out of the city. I mean no more than that."

She lowered her head. "I'm staying with Sam."

"Because of those numbers? What's he done for you?"

Stacy reached out, touched Charlie's arm, then moved back. "You're a nice man. I'm sorry you were hurt." Her face was still expressionless. She stuck her hands in the pockets of her brown coat and turned away toward the Brooklyn Bridge.

Without saying anything else, he walked away from her and down the gangplank of the *Ambrose*. When Charlie reached the pier, Sam called after him, "You sure you're not going to the cops?"

"You're a punk, Sam Cheney," said Charlie without looking back. As he left the pier, he saw the young man in boots still playing lookout by the information booth. Charlie called to him, "You're a punk too!"

34
▼▼▼

CHARLIE AGAIN SAT ACROSS from Gate 27 in the lower concourse of Port Authority Bus Terminal. It was 10:15 and he was waiting for the eleven o'clock bus to Saratoga Springs. His green plaid canvas suitcase was wedged between his feet so he wouldn't forget it. Crowds of people streamed by in either direction. Charlie tried to calculate how many he could count in ten minutes. Certainly over a thousand. Upstairs a kindly information clerk had told him that nearly 7,500 buses used the terminal each day.

Charlie was attempting to avoid thinking about New York and Saratoga. It depressed him that his imagined quest so closely resembled a Shirley Temple movie. Had he really seen himself as rescuing little Sam Cheney and carrying him back to his mother? Nor could he say that the experience had made him any wiser. Next week, next year: he might again be tempted to submit himself to some story drawn from a 1930's film. It saddened him that he could set aside the rational portion of his mind and throw over the quiet routine of his life with such pleasure.

In any case it was over, or at least his part of it was over. Sam's pursuit of the cocaine, Tateo's pursuit of Sam, the machinery of the police—all that could work itself out without him. Zack would win; he was strongest. Charlie had no desire to observe the details. To stay any longer would be the same as having been driven back to Saratoga earlier: it would mean submitting to the rules and definitions of other people.

Charlie did not regret any of his actions. He was excited by the memory of his bravery in New Jersey. He was pleased with the memory of Victor Plotz and his fish and Moshe the Enforcer. And although saddened by the memory of Stacy, it was something to know he was capable of such strong emotion.

He knew these memories would comfort him when he was back in Saratoga as Charlie Bradshaw: ex-youth officer, present stable guard, hardware-store salesman, museum guard, whatever. His cousins would find him a new job. He would take it. That might be weakness, but whenever he thought he was too weak, he would remember kicking Jukes in the knee.

It was now 10:30. Charlie would be boarding soon. He sat watching the stream of people. Perhaps it was like a movie where the crowd of 1,000 is actually 100 extras, each seen in ten different hats. As Charlie idly tried to penetrate the diguises of people he had seen before, he saw the two plainclothesmen.

Since they were walking directly toward him, they weren't difficult to spot. They were both six feet, between thirty-five and fifty and wore dark raincoats. They had the faces of men who might be foolish, but never silly.

Charlie considered running through Gate 27, leaping onto the bus and claiming sanctuary. But it was too late to do anything but look expectant.

"Charles Bradshaw?" They showed their badges.

Charlie nodded. He again thought of his business cards. They would probably think he was reaching for a weapon.

"You're to come with us."

"My bus is about to leave."

"We can't help that."

"Can't you tell Zack I've already left?"

"Want us to use cuffs?"

35

▼▼▼

THE TWO PLAINCLOTHESMEN drove Charlie to a precinct station on 35th between Eighth and Ninth avenues. They neither spoke nor acknowledged his presence. The lobby of the precinct station was full of efficient-looking men, both in and out of uniform. No one looked at Charlie. He didn't suppose they were any different from Saratoga Springs policemen; but as he was led across the lobby to the stairs, he felt like a creature from another species, a smaller species.

Charlie was taken upstairs and led to an open doorway. Then, giving him a push, one of the the plainclothesmen said, "Here he is," and left him.

Stumbling slightly, Charlie entered a large conference room with light blue walls and a map of the city of New York. Zack stood by a long table talking to three men who were sorting through a small pile of 8 x 10 photographs. He had on a brown suit, a tan shirt and a brown tie. His short gray hair was brushed up so it was perfectly flat on top. When he saw

Charlie, he turned and began walking toward him. Charlie thought he looked like an angry bus conductor. He didn't feel like being yelled at. Zack stopped a foot away, close enough for Charlie to see a tiny patch of gray bristles under his nose which Zack had presumably missed while shaving.

The police lieutenant tapped Charlie on the chest with a thick index finger. "What'd you tell him?"

"Tell who?"

"Don't fuck with me. What'd you tell Sam Cheney?"

Charlie was angry with himself for feeling frightened. He stared up at the pink roof of Zack's mouth.

"I didn't tell him anything."

"Don't lie to me. What did you tell him?"

"Nothing."

Zack reached out and grabbed Charlie's jacket. "You little turd, you want to go to jail?"

Charlie didn't say anything. He didn't trust himself to speak calmly. What he wanted to do most was knee the policeman in the groin. At last he said, "Did you ever hear of Sam Bass?"

"Who?"

"He was a train robber and bank robber who got shot up in Round Tree, Texas, when one of his gang betrayed him to the Rangers. That was maybe in 1878."

Zack let him go. "Are you crazy?"

"Sam Bass was wounded but he managed to ride out of town. A little later Texas Ranger Major John B. Jones found him sitting on a farmer's front porch dying with a bullet in his stomach. Jones asked him what had happened to his gang. Sam Bass didn't answer. Jones asked him again and you know what Sam Bass said?"

Zack stood with his head tilted a little to the right. "What did he say, you crazy son-of-a-bitch?"

"He said, 'It's agin my trade to blow on my pals. If a man knows anything, he ought to die with it in him.' Then he said, 'The world is bobbing around.' Then he died."

Zack looked at Charlie, arms crossed, head still tilted to one side. Then he turned abruptly and took a few steps toward the table. He stopped and turned back. "You know, I heard you were dead. That's what the story was last night. You'd got yourself killed. You think I looked forward to calling Saratoga Springs and breaking the news? Lotta questions. Lotta bad publicity. Then one of my men saw you leave that broad's building. You fuck her again? Jesus, you're just like a rabbit. You'd gotten yourself killed, this whole fuckin' thing would get blown up in the papers. I'd wind up in a precinct in Brooklyn. Brooklyn, shit. Mobile, Alabama. Why didn't you tell me about this Peter Bonenfant?"

Charlie shrugged and put down his suitcase. He looked at the map of New York City on the wall, trying to see where he had been. It made his legs ache. The three men at the table continued to sort through the photographs. They hadn't even glanced at Charlie. Maybe they thought he was delivering shirts. Charlie saw that the photographs were of Sam: Sam on the street, Sam in a park, Sam walking, running, standing still.

After a moment, he said, "I didn't owe you anything. I mean, I don't want to make it sound like you've hurt my feelings, but I don't owe you a darn thing. Why should I tell you about Peter Bonenfant?"

Zack stood with his hands in his back pockets. "You're a prick."

"I take it you've talked to Bonenfant's father."

"Look, prick, I could have you put in jail. You'd never get out."

"And you talked to Driscoll. Did you arrest him?"

"It's too bad, prick, that you're not a cop in New York. It'd give me pleasure to bust you. Bonenfant's dead, right?"

Charlie thought of saying that thanks to Zack he was no longer a cop anywhere. "He's been dead for nearly three weeks. I saw his body last night. It was crammed into a steel container someplace over in New Jersey. It's probably gone now."

"Tateo and Jukes?"

"That's right. Tateo's from New York. Apparently he used to drive a truck for this container place. The other guy, Jukes, he's from Los Angeles. Driscoll talked to you about them?"

Zack nodded. "Do me a favor and tell me what happened."

At first he didn't intend to, then he found himself talking

about Driscoll and how he had been tricked, tied up and driven
to New Jersey. About what had happened at the container
company, Charlie only said, "When they looked at the body,
I was able to get away. There was a watchdog and Jukes shot
it. The watchman heard the noise. When the police came, I
slipped out through the front gate." He was surprised at how
simple it sounded.

Zack listened silently. With his jowls and square chin, he
looked like a man in an advertisement for tires that Charlie
used to see in *The Saturday Evening Post*. When Charlie had
finished, Zack went to use the telephone on the table near the
three men.

The three men had stopped talking and were looking at their
fingernails or the ceiling or the floor or their shoes or their
watches. All three were in their mid-forties. They had short
and neatly combed brown or gray hair. They wore dark suits.
One wore glasses. Another had a small moustache. The third
sucked on an empty pipe. Otherwise they could have had inter-
changeable parts. Charlie imagined they composed a Yugoslavian fact-finding team that had been sent to New York for two
weeks by the Yugoslavian government. Now they were waiting
to be taken someplace and shown something. On the other
hand, Charlie thought, perhaps I am being shown to them. He
wondered what they were doing with the photographs of Sam.

Zack hung up the phone and walked back toward Charlie.
"What did you tell Sam? Don't fuck with me now, it's
important."

"I told him you were watching The Lamplighter. I said if
he didn't leave town, he'd be arrested."

"Will he leave?"

"No. He's greedy and vain and he thinks he can outsmart
you. He set Bonenfant up. It's Sam's fault he got killed."

For a second, Charlie saw the red lightship, the blue sky
and the darker blue of the river, the Brooklyn Bridge with
the Manhattan Bridge beyond it, Brooklyn itself like a city of
mushrooms, the shipping yards, the blue river trailing out to a
bluer sea, and Sam in his brown corduroy jacket leaning

against the rail of the *Ambrose,* greedy, small-minded and spitting out words.

"I gave Sam a tremendous chance," continued Charlie, "Stacy too. I've done a lot of favors for Sam, but none as big as that one. How much does he figure to make?"

"He's buying for twenty; he could sell for at least sixty. I don't know what kind of deal he's got with his partner."

Charlie started to speak, call Sam names; he was sorry he hadn't kicked him again. Mostly he was sorry that he couldn't stop thinking about him. "What about Driscoll?" he asked.

"He's working for us now. Thinks it'll keep him out of jail."

"Will it?"

"Might."

"Can I get out of here now? I want to get back to Saratoga."

"We need you here for a bit. You're a witness. We'll have to get a statement. You know the routine. I want to keep an eye on you."

"What the hell for?" But Charlie already knew. It seemed unfair that he should be made to watch the details of Sam's arrest. He had finished his discoveries; there was nothing else he wanted to learn.

The phone rang before Zack could answer. While he waited, Charlie studied the map of New York. He noticed a park at the very bottom of the city: Battery Park. He imagined it full of pencils, pennies, lipstick containers, Kleenex, keys—objects that had fallen from the pockets of New Yorkers and rolled to the foot of the city. He was sorry he hadn't visited the park. He noticed it contained a statue of Verrazano, the Florentine merchant who had "found" Manhattan. Charlie seemed to remember that Verrazano had later found a tribe of cannibals in the Caribbean and they had eaten him.

36
▼▼▼

"**D**OG WAS HIT TWICE. Once in the shoulder, once in the head. Not bad for quick shooting. Jersey police couldn't find Bonenfant's body, but there's a hole in the fence and a lotta footprints. Also tire tracks. It's a fucking swamp over there. They're dragging for the body. I wish 'em luck." Zack carefully reached in his shirt pocket and drew out a wrinkled Lucky Strike. Breaking it in two, he stuck one half in his mouth and put the other back in his pocket. "Trying to cut down," he told Charlie.

They were in an unmarked white Chevrolet driving south on West Street under the West Side Elevated Highway. Charlie didn't know their exact location, but several blocks back they had passed the entrance to the Holland Tunnel. The uneven paving stones made the car bounce like a worn-out carnival ride. Charlie was wedged in the front seat between Zack and the driver. In the back seat were three plainclothesmen looking exactly, Charlie thought, like See No Evil, Hear No Evil, Speak No Evil. It was 11:30. Occasionally Charlie caught a glimpse of the World Trade Center about a mile ahead.

"The way you were talking to Driscoll," Zack continued, "I knew he had to be involved. That's the only fuckin' thing you've done for us. I had him picked up after you disappeared, grabbed him right off the street. I mean, finding that blood in Cheney's apartment made this a whole new ball game. Hand me that lighter, will you?"

Charlie gingerly gave Zack the hot lighter. Zack used it and gave it back. "Anyway, Driscoll told us you were dead. Scared? He was petrified. Even more scared of Jukes and Tateo. They'd been paying him to watch the bar, but they didn't trust him. He claims he doesn't know where they're staying. Tateo always telephones him, either at The Lamplighter or his apartment."

Zack rolled down the window and threw out the cigarette butt. "Hardly worth the time, was it?"

The Chevrolet had turned east on Hubert, then north on Hudson. Now it turned west on Laight: a one-way street lined with gray and reddish-brown warehouses from five to ten stories high. Most of the buildings had ornate cornices, black metal fire escapes and rounded brick arches over the windows. Several semitrailers were pushed up to loading docks with high overhead doors and metal roofs or awnings. They crossed Collister. The paving stones were littered with cardboard and bits of wood.

At Greenwich and Laight a tractor-trailer had been pulled half across the intersection. And at the other end of the block, at Washington, Charlie saw another truck. Both trucks had red cabs and silver trailers with the name *Townsend* printed across their entire length in fat black letters. Between the two trucks the street was empty, except for several parked cars.

The Chevrolet turned left and stopped in front of a pair of green folding doors. The doors opened. They drove into a garage large enough for about ten vehicles and parked beside three other cars. A policeman stood by one of them, neatly arranging half a dozen small two-way radios on its hood.

"Best we could do on short notice," said Zack, opening his door.

Charlie followed him up some steps and into an office with a large picture window from which they could see most of the street. Two plainclothesmen stood by the window, while a third sat on a long work-table talking into a telephone. He had a red puffy face and red hair. When he saw Zack, he put a hand over the mouthpiece and said, "Driscoll gave them the address three minutes ago. I got two men in each truck."

The office was dark with dark oak paneling. On the walls were rows of old photographs showing wagons drawn by teams of six horses. About ten men sat or stood on each wagon. At the bottom of each picture was written the date and the names of the men in white ink. Against the far wall was a rolltop desk.

Charlie saw a second white Chevrolet pull into the garage. "What do you plan to do?" he asked.

Zack had taken a pink fingernail brush out of his coat pocket and was steadily brushing back his short gray hair. He stood near the two plainclothesmen by the window.

"When Tateo called, Driscoll told him that Sam Cheney had come into the bar and left an envelope with the bartender. Driscoll said he got hold of the envelope and that it contained an address. This address."

"Did he believe him?"

Zack put away the nail brush. "We'll see. The main thing in favor is that Driscoll isn't supposed to know that Sam Cheney's alive."

The three members of the Yugoslavian fact-finding team entered the room. They carried suitcases, and at first Charlie thought they had chosen this moment to return to their native land. But the suitcases were too thin, no more than four inches deep; and too long, about four feet by one foot. They were covered with brown, leather-like plastic and each had three brass locks. The three men put the cases on the table and unlocked them. Snapping open, the locks made a half-musical pinging noise.

The insides of the cases were lined with blue convoluted foam rubber. It made the rifles with their telescopic sights look like thin men in their coffins.

Charlie joined Zack by the window. "What about the guy with the cocaine?" he asked.

"No trouble there. We spotted him when he opened his mailbox and followed him back to a midtown hotel. When he and Cheney get together, we'll grab 'em."

As he spoke, Zack watched the three members of the SWAT team, special weapons and tactics. "Things used to be a lot simpler," he told Charlie. Then he walked over to the red-haired man on the telephone. "Any word yet?"

"No. We'll pick 'em up when they cross Canal Street or West Broadway. How many gray Valiants are there?"

"Millions. Shit, we don't even know which way they're coming from. Tell those guys to start their trucks."

"Will do."

Despite the pressure, Charlie was aware of a certain calm. He wondered if Texas Ranger John B. Jones had been this businesslike as he waited for Sam Bass's gang in Roundtree, Texas, or what Ranger Frank Hamer had thought about while waiting in ambush for Bonnie and Clyde near Gibland, Louisiana.

Behind him, Charlie could hear the three snipers quietly discussing the merits of a Sako-Finnbear four-shot 7mm magnum with a Redfield 4x–12x variable scope.

"Strongest bolt action rifle around," said the one with the small moustache. "Handmade French walnut stock. Just look at that checkering."

"Hollow points?" asked the sniper with the glasses.

"Banana peels."

"Ever try wasp-waisted sonics?" asked the one with the pipe. "One-eighties?"

"One-fifties are good enough in a .308."

"Give me banana peels every time," said the sniper with the moustache. "See this Monte Carlo cheek piece? Class, that's what I like."

"Come on, you guys," said Zack, "pick up your radios and get upstairs. You, Harris, take your banana peels across the street. Schmidt will let you in. We got about five minutes."

The snipers picked up their rifles and left the room. Charlie was sorry they weren't Yugoslavs.

"Where's Sam and Stacy?" he asked.

Zack had just lit the other half of his Lucky Strike, nearly burning his lips and fingers. He rubbed his mouth with the back of his hand. "If I make it dangerous enough, maybe I'll quit. Cheney's over on East 32nd. His buddy's got an apartment there. The girl's down in the Village. NYU. Been going around talkin' to the eggheads. Think she'll stay?"

"I don't know," said Charlie. But he began to consider what would happen if Sam were arrested and Stacy remained free. The thought took his breath.

The red-haired man began talking excitedly into the telephone. "Okay, okay. Great. Hey, Lieutenant, that gray Valiant's on West Broadway."

Zack walked to the door and called to someone in the garage. "Tell Harris to wait till they've had a chance to surrender. Those guys upstairs too. They got those trucks running? Okay, tell 'em to get ready."

Coming back into the room, he unbuttoned the top button of his tan shirt and loosened his tie. "The more complicated something gets," he told Charlie, "the more there is to fuck up. It's a fact of life. I'd feel better if they hadn't done such a neat job of shooting that dog."

Charlie, Zack and the man on the telephone were the only ones left in the office. "You still have someone at The Lamplighter?" Charlie asked.

Zack shook his head. "No need."

"Here they come," said the red-haired man.

Charlie and Zack ducked down by the picture window. Charlie was mildly irritated with himself for feeling grateful to Zack, as if the lieutenant's decision to bring him along was based on a new-found sense of comradeship rather than the suspicion that he might contact Sam or Stacy.

It was shortly after noon and the street was brightly sunlit. There were no shadows except along the edge of the opposite warehouses and under the roofs of the loading docks. Harris had crawled to the edge of the roof directly across from them. Charlie could just make him out next to one of the support cables which ran from the loading dock roof up to the fourth story of the warehouse.

Bits of paper and excelsior blew down the street in the spring breeze. Two Styrofoam cups appeared to be chasing each other and six sparrows quarreled over a slice of bread. At the top of the fire escape of a warehouse across the street, someone had set out a number of green plants. There was a false pastoral quality to the scene. Charlie was certain that every other street in the area was crowded with workers eating their lunches, drinking coffee or beer. Whatever Tateo's faults, Charlie didn't think he was stupid. Then he saw the gray Valiant.

It had just passed the red cab of the first semi and drove slowly down the center of the street. Charlie saw the rubber dice swinging from the rearview mirror, but beyond the dice he could only make out two thin shapes, almost silhouettes. He imagined Tateo in his sunglasses and jeans jacket, Jukes with his yellowish-orange hair and red tie-tack earring. The Valiant slowed until Charlie guessed it was going no more than five miles per hour. It had come a dozen yards past the semi. Now it edged forward ten more feet and stopped. There was no movement inside. From where he crouched, Charlie could barely hear the sounds of traffic from the West Side Elevated Highway. The Valiant sat in the middle of the street, sunlight shimmering off its hood.

"Too fucking suspicious," said Zack.

There was a roar as the semi at Washington and Laight surged forward. Then there was a second roar as the semi nearest the Valiant began to pull across the intersection at Greenwich. But instead of one smooth motion, it lunged, then stopped, lunged and stopped. Then it stalled.

With a screech of its tires, the Valiant shot backward, aiming for the gap between the semi and the opposite brick wall. Sunlight reflected off its windshield, making it impossible to see inside. Then Charlie saw a hand holding a black gun reach out of the side window and point back toward the red cab of the semi. A steady whirring noise came from the truck as the driver tried to start the stalled engine. This was interrupted by the high crack of a pistol, then again, and a third time.

"You dumb son-of-a-bitch!" shouted Zack.

The lieutenant ran out of the office. As Charlie followed him, he heard explosions from upstairs and across the street which drowned out the noise of the pistol. The rifle shots echoed and reverberated between the warehouses, making an almost continuous roar.

When Charlie next saw the Valiant, he thought its windshield was covered with giant dandelion clocks. Then there was another explosion and the windshield disappeared; another explosion and the hood slammed up, hiding the windshield altogether.

The whirring noise was still coming from the truck. There was a sputtering cough, then a whirring noise again. Charlie couldn't see the driver. Presumably he had ducked down to avoid being hit, although the pistol had stopped firing. The rifle shots continued and clang-crashed through the hood of the Valiant or ricocheted off its top with a whine.

Again there was a sputtering cough, then another which developed into a roar. The semi lunged forward. But the Valiant was too close. It swerved briefly as its front tire exploded, then it straightened only a few feet short of the gap and weaved through it. Seconds too late, the truck surged across the opening and slammed into the brick wall of the warehouse bringing a small cascade of bricks and mortar clanging down on its red hood. The explosions stopped. Dropping to one knee, Charlie looked under the trailer and saw the Valiant weaving backward up the next block. He ran after Zack.

The driver of the truck climbed down from his cab. He had blood on his face and more blood dripped from his left arm. He was a young man about Sam's age with blond hair and frightened brown eyes. The truck's windshield was smashed but whether from bullets or falling bricks Charlie didn't know. The young man began apologizing to Zack, apparently thinking that Zack meant to punish him. Zack ignored him and ducked under the trailer.

As Charlie went under the trailer, he heard a honking and screech of brakes, then a crash farther up the block. At first he worried about Zack, but coming out from under the truck he saw the policeman still running. Beyond him, however, a green Volkswagen had spun around in a half circle and crashed against a loading dock. Across from it, on the north side of the street, the Valiant was tilted halfway up a set of wide stone steps. Above it the top of a streetlight swung in slow circles.

Zack ran with his gun in his right hand. His brown suit coat flapped behind him and his left arm was outstretched for balance. A horn was blaring; it had a high despairing sound. Charlie saw men staring from windows and standing in the doorways of loading platforms. He began to feel vulnerable and slowed down behind Zack.

"Stay back!" shouted the police lieutenant. "Stay back, they've got guns!"

The warning was unnecessary. Tateo had disappeared. Jukes

sat in the front seat, covered with glass from the broken wind-shield. His hands lay in his lap, fingers curled upward. His face was completely gone.

Staring at him through the empty windshield, Charlie thought of the hole in the head of a needle. Blood was mixed with the yellowish-orange hair, and the red tie-tack earring seemed like just another drop of it. Charlie backed away. Steam rose from the radiator of the Valiant. The horn was still blowing.

"What a fuck-up," said Zack. "Look at those clowns."

Looking back, Charlie saw the three snipers jogging toward them, holding their rifles across their chests. Their neck ties flapped back over their shoulders. They were laughing and jok-ing among each other.

"You dump son-a-bitches, where'd you learn to shoot?"

Charlie touched Zack's arm. "You better do something about Driscoll."

37
▼▼▼

BUT WHEN THEY REACHED The Lamplighter, they found a small crowd gathered outside. Two patrol cars were parked diagonally at the curb, their lights still flashing. A young patrolman was urging people to go home. No one paid any attention.

Neither Zack nor Charlie said anything as they got out of the white Chevrolet. They walked quickly toward the bar. Charlie could hear sirens in the distance. Above the door was a picture of an old man in a cocked hat lighting a street lamp with a long taper.

As Charlie entered behind Zack, he noticed a broken glass on the floor near the foot of the U-shaped bar. The glass was mixed with a chocolate-colored liquid, and Charlie knew it was a Black Russian.

Four customers, all retired or middle-aged men he had seen

before, were gathered in a booth to his right trying to tell another young patrolman what had happened. A third patrolman spoke with Luke, the bartender, while a fourth stood nervously by Driscoll's body at the rear left of the room. The red, blue and yellow rotating lights along with the theater posters of *Damn Yankees* and *Pajama Game* made the policemen seem particularly obtrusive.

"What'd I tell you," said Zack. "A fuck-up."

A siren died away into a whine as another police car pulled up outside. Three plainclothesmen entered the bar.

"Homicide," said Zack.

The officer in charge was a stocky middle-aged man in a dark blue raincoat and dapper Irish tweed hat.

"This your baby?" he asked Zack.

"Not if I can help it."

"What's the story?"

Zack shook his head. "Just got here myself."

The policemen spent about five minutes poking around and talking to the patrolmen, then they took Luke back to the rear of the bar. Thin, bald, white shirt and apron, black pants: he looked like he was aspiring to a better place. By now he had realized this was an important moment in his life: his name would be in the papers, business would improve. He didn't appear to recognize Charlie, and spoke directly to Zack and the homicide detective whom Zack called Jonesy.

Luke began by raising his hands and pressing them against his chest. "Who'd want to hurt him? He was one of the nicest men you'd ever want to meet. Been coming in here ten-twelve years. Quiet, never any trouble. Now and then he'd have one too many, who doesn't? And I'd say, Mr. Driscoll, time to go home, sir. And he'd smile and say, Thanks Luke, you're a pal. Then he'd go home. Maybe he'd even leave a tip if he remembered or had anything left."

"What is this," said Jonesy, "memory lane? Save it for the papers."

Luke held out his palms to the policemen. His gold cufflinks were in the shape of tiny locomotives. "You asked me what happened, I'm telling you. We got a respectable place here.

Never even had a hold-up." He raised his hands higher as Jonesy began to interrupt. "Okay, okay. Mr. Driscoll, he was sitting at the end of the bar, just where he always sits. Been there two-three hours, drinking more than's usual. Did it relax him, you ask? No it didn't. He was jumpy as two peas in a pod.

"Then this young guy comes into the bar, wearing sunglasses and dressed up like a cowboy. 42nd Street, right? Guy never opened his mouth, but Mr. Driscoll heard the door and turned around. He knew him right off. When he saw this young guy, he screamed. I kid you not. He screamed and half fell, half jumped off his stool and ran toward the back of the bar. This guy that came in, this cowboy, he takes off his dark glasses very slowly and pulls a gun from his belt . . ."

"What kind?" asked Jonesy.

"Beats me. A little black jobby. Anyway, he aims it, still moving slowly, and shoots. I guess he hit Driscoll in the leg because he fell against the Foos Ball table. Mr. Driscoll never stopped screaming. Just sounds, know what I mean?" Luke wiped his hands on his white apron as if he hoped the memory were like so much spilled beer.

"Then this young guy walked up to him. Still slow, like he had all the time in the world. Mr. Driscoll kept making that screaming sound, kept trying to climb back up on the Foos Ball table. He didn't have a chance. The young guy shot him three times in the stomach. Then he stuck his gun in his belt, put on his dark glasses and kept going out the back door. Never looked at the rest of us, which was all right by me. Poor Mr. Driscoll though, he was still screaming, but it was quieter, like he was in some other room. Then it got quieter still, like he was right out of the building. Then it stopped. That was all, it just stopped."

After a moment, Charlie walked around the bar toward the Foos Ball table. A patrolman stood near the body, trying not to look at it, but unable to turn completely away. Driscoll lay on his back on the table, his right hand cast backward, his left on his chest. His feet just touched the floor while his head hung over the other side. Strands of gray hair dangled down like wisps of ribbon.

Driscoll's body had bent the bars on the table and had broken off several miniature red and blue soccer players that lay in his blood like additional victims. Moving closer, Charlie saw that the blood had divided into two streams that disappeared into the holes by the two miniature goalies.

Driscoll wore his dark green blazer and light green turtleneck. With his back bent over the table, his large stomach was thrust upward like the curve of a rubber ball. There were three bullet holes in his stomach, each surrounded by a dark powder burn.

Driscoll's whole face expressed pain. His eyes were open and his eyebrows were raised as if doubting the fact of his death. There was the smell of excrement and urine. Charlie reached forward and closed Driscoll's eyelids.

He was aware of Zack standing behind him. "The guy with the cocaine," said Zack, "he just left his hotel."

38
▼▼▼

"MUST OF DUCKED THROUGH the warehouse and picked up the Eighth Avenue at Canal Street, then transferred uptown at Fulton. I put a man on it, but it's a dead horse. Probably have better luck at Port Authority." Zack reached out for the padded dash as the white Chevrolet skidded to a halt before a laundry truck which had cut in front of them at 25th Street. Bellevue Hospital was on their right.

The driver revved the siren and the laundry truck moved slowly out of their path. With a screech of its tires, the Chevrolet accelerated up First Avenue.

The man with the cocaine had gone to an apartment house across from Central Park where he was apparently waiting for Sam. Zack had taken over a vacant apartment in the same building. They were going there now from The Lamplighter.

Charlie was in the back seat between two plainclothesmen. Zack was in front with the driver. It was 1:45.

"Won't he go after Sam?" asked Charlie.

Zack kept his hands on the dashboard. "How's he know where he is? He thought he was dead until last night."

Charlie was still dissatisfied, but he attributed his doubts to his guilt at having exposed Sam to Tateo. He thought of the eleven o'clock bus, which by now was more than halfway to Saratoga.

The Chevrolet was going as fast as it could without using its siren. The driver kept one hand on the horn, and grinned happily, as if his whole life had been a preparation for this movement. The road dipped slightly at intersections and the Chevrolet swooped into them, making it feel more like a boat than an automobile.

Trying not to look at the road, Charlie asked, "Sam's still on East 32nd?"

"Yeah, but he should be leaving soon. When he makes his buy, we'll have as clean a bust as you'd ever hope to see. You feel bad about his going to jail?"

Charlie felt worse about seeing him trapped and arrested. "Where's Stacy?" he asked.

"Still at NYU."

"If she stays down there, will you leave her alone?"

"Can't tell yet. That apartment where the guy's waiting is rented by someone named Doyle. He and his family have been in Europe for a month, and they're not expected back until the first. Your girlfriend must of had a key. I figure we got enough for a conspiracy charge. Probably pull her in and let the lawyers fight over it."

The white Chevrolet was now going north on Madison Avenue, swerving from lane to lane. Charlie kept bumping against the policemen on either side of him. The man on his left didn't seem to mind. He stared out his window and yawned. The plainclothesman on his right, however, winced each time the driver blew the horn.

Seeing Charlie had noticed, he became apologetic. "I've always hated these rides. Must have a weak stomach or some-thing. Some fuckin' delivery truck will squeeze a light and then where are you? Right after lunch, too."

The driver slowed as a yellow taxi cut him off, then he moved up behind the taxi's back bumper and blew his horn. Although Charlie liked Madison Avenue, he found it difficult to play the role of tourist in a speeding car. Just as he was trying to get a better look of the back of St. Patrick's Cathedral, the Chevrolet weaved around a bus, braked for a bicycle, changed lanes and surged forward again, sending Charlie against the shoulder of the plainclothesman on his right.

The man grunted. He had a round, smooth face and a shaggy gunfighter moustache of the sort affected by the three Earp brothers.

"You been around here long?" he asked. "Haven't seen you before."

"I'm just visiting."

Zack turned around in his seat. "Visiting, hell, he's under arrest, practically. Thinks he's Pat Garrett."

"Who?"

"Pat Garrett," said Zack.

"I knew a Garrett in the army," said the plainclothesman after a moment. "Everyone called him Smitty. Never did know why." He began to say something else, then turned and looked out his window instead.

"You going to let the lawyers fight over me too?" asked Charlie. He tried to make a joke of it.

"We'll just see how everything works out," said Zack.

"Did you call Saratoga again?"

Zack grinned. There was no humor in it. "I told you, we'll see how everything works out."

Several minutes later, the Chevrolet turned west on 67th Street. "Park anywhere," said Zack. "They should have cleared a place."

The driver pulled up next to a fire hydrant. The five men got out, and Zack led the way toward Fifth Avenue. The plain-clothesman with the moustache tried to put as much distance as possible between himself and Charlie. As he followed him,

Charlie decided that his moustache was much shorter than the ones worn by the Earps, unless perhaps Virgil's. It was more like Tom Horn's moustache. Horn was a one-time lawman and Pinkerton operative who had realized there was better money to be made as a hired killer and switched sides. He was accused of killing several dozen men before being brought to trial in Cheyenne. In jail, he wrote his memoirs (*Life of Tom Horn, Government Scout and Interpreter, Written by Himself: A Vindication*), wove the rope that would hang him and finally shaved off his gunfighter moustache. Charlie considered telling the plainclothesman about Tom Horn but thought better of it.

On the corner was a fourteen-story apartment building with a red awning over its entrance on 67th Street. Zack opened the large glass door. Charlie and the moustached plainclothesman followed him, while the two others continued toward Fifth Avenue. There was no doorman in sight. They passed through a highly polished lobby to a waiting elevator.

Getting off at the third floor, Zack turned left down a short hallway and knocked on a door that was opened by a uniformed patrolman. He stood back to let them pass.

Charlie found himself in a large living room which smelled of paint. The floor and furniture were covered with white dropcloths. The walls were being painted light blue, covering a light yellow which, Charlie thought, looked quite new.

"Beggars can't be choosers," said the man with the Tom Horn moustache.

The only uncovered furniture consisted of three paint-spotted step ladders and two wooden kitchen chairs. The red-haired plainclothesman from the warehouse sat on one of the step ladders talking into a pink princess phone. He nodded to Charlie. Two more plainclothesmen stood by a row of three windows which overlooked Fifth Avenue. To their right was a door to a small balcony. Another row of five windows overlooked 67th Street to Charlie's left. The smell of paint began to give him a headache.

The red-haired man was saying, "He just got here, I told you, hold your fuckin' horses." He handed the phone to Zack. "Max," he said.

Charlie wandered over to the window. Across the street was a larger-than-life bronze statue of seven doughboys charging with fixed bayonets. Actually only three were charging. Two or three others had been shot and the last was supporting one of the wounded. The sun shone on it, emphasizing the dark green of the bronze. In the park behind the statue was a children's playground the size and shape of a hockey rink with red, blue and yellow swings and slides and red, blue and yellow benches for mothers. To his left Charlie could see the line of buildings on Central Park South beginning with the Plaza Hotel.

"Hey, Bradshaw," said Zack, still holding the telephone, "I've got some bad news for you."

"What is it?" Charlie moved away from the window.

"The girl just joined Sam Cheney on 32rd Street."

Although he had been expecting it, Charlie was startled by the strength of his disappointment. He realized that some part of him had still hoped to run away with Stacy, whether to the Yukon or Far Rockaway, it didn't matter. He felt grief, and it occurred to him that what had died was his own hope of ever experiencing a youthful emotion: whether love or infatuation, that didn't matter either.

Then another thought occurred to him. "Did she stop by her apartment?"

"What's it matter?"

"Tateo knew she was Sam's girlfriend. He might have been watching her building."

Zack began talking quickly into the phone. Charlie returned to the window and stood looking down at the children's playground. A fat child in a blue parka was swinging back and forth by himself, opening and closing his mouth as if singing some grand song.

"Charlie," said Zack, "the girl left her building at 1:20, carrying a small red suitcase."

Charlie walked back to the center of the room. He thought of Sam on the lightship *Ambrose*, and Sam's statement that Tateo would kill him and that it would be Charlie's fault. "I don't want to tell you your business," said Charlie, "but you'd better check and see if any cars have been stolen near her apartment or The Lamplighter."

"I've already done it."

"Hurry up and wait," said the man with the Tom Horn moustache. "Story of my life."

"Shut the fuck up," said Zack.

39

▼▼▼

THE THREE SNIPERS were unhappy. As they entered the apartment carrying their thin rifle cases, they criticized Zack for what they considered his lack of professionalism.

"First he badmouths us and says we're done," said Harris, the sniper with the Sako-Finnbear, "then he grabs us just as we're about to go eat and says he needs us again."

"No respect," said the one with the glasses.

The sniper with the pipe put his case down on the white dropcloth covering the floor, and removed his rifle: a Mossberg .308. "Never trust a man who don't know his own mind," he said.

"Does he want us on the roof?" asked Harris. He, too, had taken out his rifle and began to load it.

"Too high," said the one with the glasses. "We're to shoot from the windows."

The sniper with the pipe rubbed his Mossberg with a clean white cloth. "Get a nice shot from the balcony there."

"Too public," said Harris. "Somebody might bitch."

The snipers didn't acknowledge Charlie or the plainclothes-man on the phone or the plainclothesman Charlie had embarrassed in the car. Zack had gone down to the street to tell his men not to look like "sore thumbs."

Charlie realized that no matter who else was nearby, the snipers always gave the sense of being alone. Even when Zack spoke to them, they barely paid attention. He imagined them as not speaking to anyone who scored less than 495 out of 500 bull's-eyes. Once Charlie had seen a man with a Marlin .22 hit the edge of a playing card, cutting it in half, ten times out of ten from a distance of thirty feet. He wondered if such skill with instruments of death kept the snipers from seeing lesser men as among the living.

Zack reentered the room. He had lost the businesslike calm that he had had at the warehouse, and his movements had become quick and abrupt. "That fuckhead upstairs, he's just sitting there watching the TV. Maybe he plans to move in. Harris, get by that side window. You two stick to the front. You're looking for the guy you missed earlier. Remember that? Nobody else. Keep those fucking guns out of the window or you'll be doing your shooting at Coney Island from now on. Hey, Bradshaw, your buddy Sam Cheney have a gun?"

"No," said Charlie.

"I thought he swiped yours."

"I got it back." Charlie didn't care to say that it was at the bottom of the East River.

The phone rang and the red-haired man answered it. After a moment he told Zack, "They just left 32nd Street in a blue, 1967 four-door Plymouth."

"Is Stacy with them?" Charlie tried to keep his voice calm.

"The girl? I'll check." He relayed the question, then paused and said, "Yeah, the girl's with them."

"Let me talk to him." Zack took the phone. "Carter? Is there any chance they're being followed by another car?" Zack looked at Charlie and shrugged. "What do you mean, you can't be positive?" Charlie joined Zack by the phone. "What d'you mean 'reasonably positive'?" Zack said. "What the hell am I to do with that? Okay, okay, just make sure, that's all." He gave the phone back to the red-haired man. "Dumb fuck."

"Arrest them now," said Charlie, "don't wait for them to get here."

"I want to get him making his buy."

"You're risking his life."

"He's doing that all by himself," said Zack.

Charlie started to reach out and take Zack's arm, then he stopped himself. "Did you learn anything about stolen cars?"

Zack moved away from him. "There are two from that general area, but that doesn't mean anything. Even if he stole a car, we probably wouldn't get a report on it until after five. Personally, I don't think this Tateo guy is after them."

"Keep hoping," said Charlie.

The three snipers had opened their windows and pulled down the shades, leaving about six inches of space. Through the windows Charlie could hear the traffic on Fifth Avenue: cars and buses stopping for the light, then pulling away. Occasionally he could hear the shouts of children from the playground. He walked over to the window between the two snipers.

Looking down, he could see about twenty kids, none more than six or seven, on the swings and teeter-totters, scrambling over the red and blue jungle jim, playing in the sandbox. It was about 2:45 and the temperature had reached the midfifties. Charlie thought he could even see buds on the trees. The child in the blue parka now stood on the pedestal of the statue of the charging doughboys, maintaining his balance by holding on to a bronze bayonet.

The snipers had knelt down by their windows. Across the room by the side windows, Harris was quietly whistling *Get Me to the Church on Time.*

"Fuckin' trees," said the sniper with the pipe. "Hey, Zack, couldn't you pick a better place. Your guy runs into the park and those trees will give us real grief."

Zack ignored him.

"Get the mayor to cut them down," said the sniper with glasses.

"Lieutenant," said the man on the phone, "that blue Plymouth just crossed 62nd on Madison."

Charlie began to pay particular attention to four or five men spread out over 100 yards near the low stone wall separating the sidewalk and the park. Although he was certain they were policemen and thought he recognized the driver of the white

Chevrolet he didn't believe they would do any good. He kept seeing Driscoll's body draped across the Foos Ball table with three bullet holes in his stomach. Then he imagined Sam dead, or Stacy.

As he crouched by the window, Charlie marveled at the bungle of events that had begun with his coming to New York to rescue Sam and might conceivably end with getting him killed.

But although he was concerned for Sam, he was frightened for Stacy. Charlie had begun to see her as an innocent victim, and while he knew this was foolish, he couldn't stop thinking of her and kept seeing her thin face and the curve of her body in his mind. He regretted a world where there was no place for romantic action, and at times felt lost in that empty area between the films of his childhood and the business of the Saratoga Springs police department.

"Hey, Lieutenant," said the man on the phone, "the blue Plymouth went up and turned on 69th Street. Should be seeing it any minute now."

Going to the window, Zack raised and lowered the shade several times. "What about another car?" he asked.

"Still no sign," said the man on the phone.

Zack joined Charlie between the two snipers. "We only got one car following them. Two or three, we might know something, but there's not much we can do with one."

Charlie stared up Fifth Avenue looking for the blue Plymouth. There was a lot of traffic, while on the sidewalk about twenty people were walking dogs, pushing baby carriages or just strolling along in the spring weather.

"Too bad we can't arrange these things for rainy days," said Zack.

"You just better hope your snipers are accurate." Charlie was still angry at Zack for refusing to arrest Sam earlier.

"Nah, I'll bet you ten bucks we get him at Port Authority."

Charlie didn't answer. He had just seen the blue Plymouth. It was behind a bus on the far side of Fifth, closer to 68th than 67th. Dented and repainted, it looked like one of those cars that had grown old as a yellow cab before being sold with

200,000 miles on its rebuilt engine. The driver was carefully obeying all the laws. He drew up to the curb by the light and stopped. After a moment, Sam and Stacy got out. The Plymouth pulled away. Charlie told himself that if he could only get across Fifth and into the building, they would be safe.

Sam and Stacy stood waiting for the light to change. Sam held a brown attaché case. The wind blowing across the park blew his black hair into his eyes. He wore a brown corduroy jacket and corduroy jeans. Charlie could just make out his turquoise and silver necklace. He guessed that the brown corduroy had some political significance, that somebody in a bar had once told Sam about people wearing brown corduroy in Portugal or Cambodia or Hanoi.

"Okay," said Zack to the man on the phone, "tell 'em to get the guy in the Plymouth. He should be circling the block." The red-haired man relayed his instructions. "Jesus, what are they waiting for?"

The wind flicked Stacy's hair around her face in a small black cloud. She had on jeans and a yellow sweater. Charlie tried to read some emotion into the way she was standing—fear or excitement—but she simply looked like someone waiting to cross the street. Neither she nor Sam made any attempt to cross against the light even though the traffic had cleared.

Glancing up Fifth, Charlie noticed a green Econoline van weaving across the three lanes of traffic toward the park, cutting off a taxi that began honking indignantly. The van was rusty and dust-covered. At one time someone had taken off its front bumper and replaced it with several black two-by-six boards. Through the van's front window, Charlie could see a young man in a jeans jacket. The cab driver kept honking his horn.

"That's him!" said Charlie.

"Son-of-a-bitch!"

"Lieutenant," said the man on the phone, "they think maybe a green . . ."

Charlie ran to the door of the balcony, pulled it open and stepped to the edge where there was a black metal fence. "Run!" he shouted. "Run!"

But Sam and Stacy were already running toward the park. Reaching the intersection, the van crashed up over the curb, barely passing between a tree and a lightpole. There was a rasping noise as its tailpipe scraped along the concrete. It braked, screeching to a halt. Its rear end slewed around to the left and smashed into a litter barrel, knocking it into Fifth Avenue and sending paper and trash up into the wind.

Tateo was out of the truck before it had come to a complete stop. He ran toward the park, holding a small black gun in his right hand.

Charlie could hear Zack shouting. "Bust the guy upstairs! Don't hurt him. No, nobody's buying a fuckin' thing!"

The sniper with the pipe suddenly appeared on the balcony. He fell to his stomach and shoved his rifle through the bars of the railing.

"Too many trees and civilians. Can't get a fuckin' aim."

Sam and Stacy were already past the entrance to the playground. Charlie could see Stacy's yellow sweater moving jerkily through the trees. Tateo had vaulted the low stone wall and was weaving and twisting between the bushes and shrubbery toward the park sidewalk. His jean jacket flapped open behind him and he held his pistol up over his head, more like a torch than a weapon. Now other men were running toward the van or the park entrance.

"Still can't get a bead," said the sniper.

Charlie stood gripping the railing. There was an explosion from inside the apartment and a small evergreen blew apart to the right of Tateo.

"Make fucking sure!" shouted Zack.

Sam and Stacy had cut across the grass up a small rise topped with several large rocks. Beyond them to their left was a slight decline and a sidewalk leading to a tunnel under one of the roads crossing the park. The tunnel emerged by the children's zoo. Ten more feet and they would be on the other side of the rise. San was a few feet ahead of Stacy. He still held the brown attaché case.

Tateo had dropped to one knee on the far side of a line of green benches just past the entrance to the playground. He raised the pistol, holding it with both hands. Sam and Stacy were at the top of the rise.

"Now the fuckin' bench's in the way," said the sniper.

There was another explosion from inside the apartment and a large chunk of wood flew up from the bench behind Tateo.

Charlie saw the pistol jerk in Tateo's hand, then he heard a slight crack, small and insubstantial, almost hidden by the sounds of traffic and shouting that came from the park. He couldn't believe it would cause any harm, something that small.

Stacy had stopped and stood swaying at the top of the rise. Her arms were outstretched toward Sam who had disappeared over the other side. She took a small step, then another, like a child learning to walk. Then, without bending her knees, she slowly fell forward onto the grass.

Sam reappeared at the top of the rise and ran back toward Stacy. He seemed small, the size of someone on a television screen. He held his left hand out in front of him as if to protect himself or warn someone away or simply give up. His mouth was open but Charlie couldn't hear any sound.

Zack appeared at the door of the balcony. "What the fuck you doing?" he shouted.

"I think I got a bead on him now," said the sniper.

There was another thin cracking noise. Charlie saw Sam twist, swinging the attaché case in a wide arc, and stumble backward toward the rocks. The pistol shot was immediately followed by an explosion at Charlie's feet. Tateo was flung up and sent sprawling as if he had been kicked.

"Nice," said the sniper.

40
▼▼▼

B Y THE TIME Charlie reached the park, uniformed police-men had appeared and were already pushing away the crowd. The green Econoline van half blocked the side-walk, its engine still running. Two little girls with blond hair and matching red jackets stood on tiptoe to see in its front window.

Charlie ran through the entrance of the park and past a green sign reading, "This is your park *please* help us keep it clean." Low shrubbery bordered the sidewalk. A plainclothesman hurried by in the opposite direction. To his right Charlie noticed about ten children watching from behind the black iron bars of the playground, while beyond them several mothers were herding more children back toward the swings.

Charlie stopped by a blue wooden box containing trashcans. There was a sign on a lamp post warning people to keep their dogs on leashes. Near the benches ahead of him a group of five men surrounded something on the ground.

Moving forward, Charlie approached the men. Then one of them stepped aside and Charlie saw Tateo lying with his arms and legs apart: a blue X-shape on the leaves and brown grass. A black automatic lay a few inches beyond the reach of his right hand.

There was no question that he was dead. The top of his head was completely gone, making it seem as if he had dyed his brown hair red to match the hair on his dead friend. He had been thrown forward with such force that one of his cowboy boots had been pulled half off and lay twisted upward, as if his ankle had been broken as well.

Charlie hurried past Tateo's body and up the rise toward Stacy. She lay on her back with two policemen bending over her. She kept turning her head back and forth, back and forth, and as she turned her black hair was tossed up and around her face, half hiding it. Her eyes were open and she seemed to stare at the trees or sky. Her mouth was open but she made no noise. There was a red, widening stain on her yellow sweater.

Charlie looked for Sam and saw him about fifteen feet away farther along the rise. He was alone, although a policeman was walking toward him. Sam was on all fours and crawling very slowly. His head hung down and his black hair brushed the ground. He wasn't crawling toward Stacy or the attaché case, but in some new third direction as if he had chosen this moment to change his life.

Two, three, four more people were walking toward him. They didn't stop him, but watched him crawl across the brown grass toward the tunnel under the road. Then a uniformed policeman reached out and gently touched Sam's shoulder. Sam collapsed, toppling forward onto his right side. His legs kept moving, how ever, pumping slowly up and down, like a turtle that's been turned over on its back and is still trying to walk. His face was pinched and cringing. He, too, had a widening red stain on his white Indian shirt.

Looking at him, Charlie thought of a photograph he had once seen of Bob and Grat Dalton after they had been caught robbing the bank in Coffeyville, Kansas, and had been shot down with their gang in Death Alley. The photograph showed six men trying to hold up the bodies of the two outlaws: knees collapsing, hands against their stomachs, eyes crinkled shut.

Bob Dalton's last words had been to his brother Emmett, who was trying to save him: "Don't mind me, boy. I'm done for. Don't surrender! Die game!"

The plainclothesman with the Tom Horn moustache took off his sport coat, folded it and put it under Sam's head.

Charlie went back to where Stacy lay surrounded now by about half a dozen people. She was still turning her head back and forth. Charlie sat down on the ground beside her and began stroking her forehead, pushing her hair out of her face. Although her eyes were open, she didn't appear to see him. Slowly, however, she stopped moving her head. Charlie stayed beside her, looking down at her and stroking her head. The sky was warm and blue. A small black child ran in circles shouting, "Bang, bang, bang!" There were sirens on Fifth Avenue.

Zack joined the small crowd of people around Charlie and Stacy. "What'd I tell you?" he said. "A fuck-up."

41

▼▼▼

T HE BUS THAT TOOK Charlie back to Saratoga Springs was a Greyhound and continued on to Montreal. For nearly four hours he had been half aware of passengers speaking quietly in French. It seemed a civilized and peaceful language. As the bus pulled into the Spa City Diner, Charlie began to think of going on to Montreal.

He had talked to Marge on the phone the previous evening. She had been worried and urged him to come home. She had not heard again from Chief Peterson and knew nothing about Charlie's future with the police department. Whatever happened, she told him, they could count on his cousins for help. That had not pleased him, but he had been moved by her concern.

Nor had he been pleased by Zack who had said he would call Chief Peterson as long as Charlie promised not to talk to reporters. It would never have occurred to Charlie to talk to reporters, but he was angry at Zack's bungling of events and even angrier at Zack's insistence that he be a witness to it. Charlie had told the police lieutenant not to do him any favors.

Tateo, Jukes and Driscoll were dead. Sam and Stacy were in the hospital. They would recover but go to jail. The driver of the Plymouth had been arrested, as had the man with the cocaine. When the police had burst into the apartment, he had said only, "I didn't think this would work."

And now Charlie was thinking about Montreal. He imagined sitting back and continuing north. He could find a job; it wouldn't matter what. Maybe he could learn French. In any case, he wouldn't return to Saratoga.

People began to get off the bus. Looking out into the parking lot, Charlie expected to see police cars with flashing lights or at least his three cousins. The only person he recognized was a frail white-haired old man known generally as Old Mac Davis who spent his life meeting buses, still waiting for someone who should have arrived during the war.

A young couple behind him continued to speak French. Although Charlie had no knowledge of the language, it sounded welcoming. He knew if he went to Montreal, no one would be terribly upset. People would miss him but they would get over it. Even his wife would get over it.

As for himself, he would miss kids' baseball and being a youth officer. He would miss poking around and finding out about things. Maybe he could be a policeman in Montreal. But as he thought this, the stronger memory passed through his mind of Stacy in her yellow sweater lying wounded on the ground. He couldn't stand the idea of her being hurt. He didn't know how he would endure not seeing her again.

The bus driver walked back along the aisle. He nodded to Charlie. "Saratoga Springs," he said. "You getting off?"

The young couple behind him stopped talking. Charlie glanced out the window at Old Mac Davis waiting for someone who would never arrive. The sun was shining. Charlie shrugged and got to his feet, reached up and pulled his green plaid canvas bag from the overhead rack. Then he walked toward the front of the bus.

Descending the steps to the parking lot, Charlie was pleased to discover that it was a warm spring day. He paused to look around at the parked cars, the motels and rooming houses across the street. Then he turned toward the diner. He had, after all, found Sam Cheney.

SARATOGA SWIMMER

▾▾▾

The good old times of Saratoga, I believe, as of the world in general, are rapidly passing away. The time was when it was the chosen resort of none but 'nice people.' At the present day, I hear it constantly affirmed, 'the company is dreadfully mixed.' What society may have been at Saratoga when its elements were thus simple and severe, I can only vaguely and mournfully conjecture. I confine myself to the dense, democratic, vulgar Saratoga of the current year.

HENRY JAMES
"Saratoga" (1870)

1

▼▼▼

I T WAS A COLD EVENING for July, not quite 55°, and it had
been raining since noon, but the man climbing out of the
gray Mercedes parked in front of the Saratoga Springs
YMCA intended to go swimming. His name was Lew Ackerman and in his left hand he held a brown leather attaché case,
which contained a green Speedo suit, goggles, shampoo, and a
large yellow bath towel.

Behind him, Ackerman's bodyguard and chauffeur, Jack
Krause, grabbed a copy of the *Racing Form* off the front seat
and locked the car doors. He didn't know how to swim and
found even baths suspect. In his twenty years as a boxer, swimming had never been part of his physical routine and now,
despite his devotion to Ackerman, he couldn't help but regret
his employer's nightly visits to the pool.

Ackerman passed through the double glass doors and Krause
hurried after him. The clock above the security desk said 9:30.
Ackerman checked it against his digital watch and decided the
clock was two minutes slow.

The young man at the desk glanced up. "Good evening, Mr.
Ackerman." He had been reading a magazine on jogging.

Ackerman slowed slightly. "How you doin, Bobby? How's
the knee?"

"Better. I'm keeping it taped."

"That's the way." Ackerman turned right and passed
through the door to the men's locker room with Krause behind
him. In the game room to the left of the desk, two small boys
who had paused to watch Ackerman walk through the lobby
resumed their sword fight with broken pool cues.

Ackerman pulled off his tie and began unbuttoning his pale
blue shirt as he passed through the locker room door. Remov-

ing the jacket of his tan three-piece suit, he handed it to Krause who shook it slightly and hung it in a locker. As Ackerman undressed, leaving his clothes on a bench, Krause folded the vest and shirt, gathered the shoes and socks and put them away.

Ackerman's body was well-tanned except for the white area at the hips normally covered by his bathing suit. As he pulled on the green suit, the white area disappeared. He was a tall, muscular man in his late forties, with wavy, blond hair and a square jaw. His nose had once been broken in a brawl and improperly reset so that it formed a vertical ripple in the middle of his face. In the fleshy part of his left arm above the elbow was the craterlike scar of an old bullet wound.

Ackerman went to the toilet, then returned tying the string of his suit. "That tomorrow's *Form*?" Ackerman nodded at the newspaper on the bench.

"Just came in."

"Red Fox is running at Belmont tomorrow. That'll be his last race before we bring him back up."

Krause picked up the paper and put it under his arm. "I've already put down my ten bucks," he said. "I just want to look over the competition."

Ackerman shook his head. "He's not ready. Just don't forget about him opening day, that's all. You sure you want to watch me swim? You know how you hate it."

Krause looked embarrassed. He was a heavyset man in his early fifties, nearly bald and with a round ragged face that seemed to bear a souvenir from each of his one hundred fights. He wore a dark brown suit and shiny black wing-tip shoes. "I don't mind," he said. "Anyway, you said I should keep an eye out."

"Go on. A night like this, it's warmer in here. Sit down and read your paper."

"Maybe I'll lift some weights," said Krause.

"Maybe you will." Ackerman walked to the shower room on the balls of his feet, turned on the water and remained under long enough to wet his hair, which he pushed back out of his face with one hand. Then he walked to the door of the pool on the far side of the showers. "See you later," he called.

The pool was twenty-five yards long and eight lanes wide. Ackerman entered by a door near the shallow end. To his right on the deck beyond the deep end sets of collapsible bleachers were pushed up against the wall. The air was thick and humid, smelling of chlorine. Sitting Indian-fashion on the diving board, the lifeguard, a high school girl in a blue tank suit, was reading a copy of *Cosmopolitan*.

Ackerman waved and walked toward her. "That's not going to help your swimming," he said.

The girl glanced up and smiled. "You take care of your stroke and I'll take care of mine. How many you going to do tonight?" Their voices echoed in the great empty space.

"Maybe I'll try a mile. I feel pretty good." Ackerman slapped his belly.

"Remember to keep your feet up."

Nodding, Ackerman spat into his goggles, then smeared the saliva around with one finger until there was a squeaking noise. He walked to the edge of the pool, rinsed off the goggles, and began to put them on. Two other men were swimming and Ackerman knew them both: Philip Nathan, a blind swimmer, was slowly swimming laps in the far lane near where Ackerman had come in, while Jim Connor, a young man who tended bar and worked on a novel about racing, swam in the middle. As Connor approached the deep end of the pool, he waved at Ackerman without breaking stroke, did a flip turn and headed back the other way.

Ackerman chose a lane between Nathan and Connor. "Hey, Nathan," he called, "when're we going to race?"

"That you, Lew? Anytime, fella, anytime." Nathan's stroke was more of a slow dog paddle and he usually did one lap to four of Ackerman's or six of Connor's.

Ackerman put on his goggles, pushed his toes over the edge of the pool, and dove into the lane, keeping his head down so the goggles wouldn't be forced off. He had a long smooth stroke and he liked how the evenness of his stroke made his body feel like a machine. He arched his back slightly to keep his legs near the surface. Beneath him through the clear turquoise water was the black line he would follow back and forth. On either side of him he could occasionally see those parts of Nathan and Connor that were underwater: Nathan rough and angular, seeming to go against the water, Connor smooth and rhythmic like himself.

As the black line beneath him ended in a T, Ackerman dunked his head and swung up his legs in a flip turn. He didn't, however, blow enough air out through his nose and consequently took in water. He wrinkled his nose, trying to ignore the pain and maintain his smooth stroke, as he swam back toward the deep end. He was just learning the flip turn and still couldn't blow out properly.

For the next ten minutes, the swimmers continued without pause. The only noise was the sound of splashing, the whirr of the pumps circulating the water and the slight sound of the rain on the roof twenty-five feet above the pool. The whirr of the pumps, however, was loud enough to obscure other noises, and when the back door, marked Fire Exit, opened about six inches, the lifeguard, Judy Dunn, didn't look up from her magazine.

The fire exit door was at the bottom of five steps at the left hand corner of the shallow end of the pool. It let out on a narrow walkway between the south side of the YMCA and Sharri Tefila, the Jewish Community Center next door. The door was now open about a foot, letting in a cold draft of air. Because of the five steps, the shoulders of anyone outside were at the same level as the deck of the pool.

Philip Nathan stopped at the shallow end and stood up. He felt the draft from the open door, cocked his head, but didn't hear anything. He assumed someone was coming or going and thought no more of it. Then he began flicking both hands rapidly above the water, because he enjoyed the cool touch of the air on his wet skin.

When Nathan stood up, the door closed a few inches. Now it slowly opened again, although not wide enough for anyone to be seen. Ackerman was swimming toward the shallow end and had reached the middle of the pool. He had become comfortable with his stroke and was engaged in what he called violent meditation, making his mind go blank or simply remembering old poker hands. Connor was just negotiating another flip turn and was also swimming toward the shallow end.

When Ackerman was about twenty feet from the end, the fire exit door opened wide and a figure in a white raincoat and rain hat swiftly climbed the stairs and walked toward the edge of the pool. Disguising and mutilating his face under the white hat was a nylon stocking. As Ackerman approached the shallow end, the figure took a pistol from under his coat. Attached to the barrel was a long black tube. Sighting down the tube, the person fired. The bullet struck Ackerman in the middle of the back, catching him in mid-stroke with his left arm raised above his head and bringing him to a complete stop in the water. The next two bullets blew off the top of his head. The sound made by the pistol was no more than three loud puffing noises, which was heard by nobody but Nathan who lifted his head and stared blankly at the killer.

The first Jim Connor knew that anything was wrong was when the clear turquoise water turned pink, then red all around him: a great red cloud which grew thicker and thicker until he burst gasping from the water in time to see a person in a white raincoat and rain hat hurrying down the stairs to the fire exit. This hardly registered, however, as all his attention became fixed on Ackerman sinking below the surface a few feet away.

From her spot on the diving board, Judy Dunn could tell something awful had happened and she jumped to her feet. Seeing the far end of the pool slowly becoming red and Ackerman sinking into the water, she began to scream, dropping her magazine into the pool and pressing her fists to her face. She had not seen the person in the white raincoat or noticed the closing of the back door.

"What's wrong?" shouted Nathan. "Tell me what's wrong!"

The door to the locker room slammed open and Jack Krause came barreling through holding an upraised .38 revolver in his right hand.

2
▼▼▼

PERHAPS THE TERRIBLE Harpe brothers as they swam out to plunder and slaughter the settlers drifting on flatboats down the Ohio River; perhaps any number of pirates, such as Captain George Wall who robbed and sank fishing boats off the Isles of Shoals after they had responded to his distress flag; or perhaps the Indians who swam out to kill Joshua Slocum as he rode at anchor for the night near the opening of the Straight of Magellan—perhaps these men had swum through blood. But Charlie Bradshaw thought it improbable. More likely it was the victims themselves who swam through blood, unfortunately their own, as they made their futile attempts at escape. True, Slocum's Indians, driven off by tacks spread on deck, must have swum back to shore with bloody feet, but the amount of blood must have been negligible.

Jim Connor stirred the ice cubes in his Vichy with one finger. "Does this mean you'll be out of a job?" he asked.

"It depends what Field does with the stable."

"What if they arrest Field?"

Charlie shook his head. "I can't believe he murdered Ackerman. He's not that kind of guy."

Charlie and Jim Connor sat in a corner booth at the Backstretch, a bar on the west side of Saratoga Springs. Ackerman had been murdered the previous Friday, and this Tuesday afternoon he had been buried in Green Ridge Cemetery. Charlie had gone to the funeral, partly because Ackerman was his friend, partly because he was Charlie's employer.

"It's common knowledge they weren't getting along," said Connor. "Even Peterson asked me if the guy in the raincoat could have been Field." Connor scratched the back of his head. Although only in his mid-twenties, his blond hair had begun to recede radically. When teased about it, he said it made him look like Lenin. It did, sort of. Connor wore a tight green alligator shirt which showed off his swimmer's shoulders. When he wasn't fiddling with his drink or his matches, he was picking at the alligator on his shirt.

"Could it have been Field?" asked Charlie.

He disapproved of Peterson giving Connor leading questions. Peterson was police chief of Saratoga Springs and had been Charlie's boss for ten of his twenty years on the force. However, two years ago, after returning to Saratoga after a mistaken adventure in New York City, Charlie had quit the police department. Most people assumed Charlie had been fired: an assumption Peterson never tried to contradict. Lew Ackerman, when he offered Charlie the job of head guard at Lorelei Stables, hadn't cared if Charlie had been fired or quit. He never asked about it. He knew Charlie would be first-rate and the rest didn't count.

"I couldn't see who it was," said Connor. "Maybe I saw a white blur. You know how it is. You don't really see anything in front of you." Connor's round, placid face seemed to tighten as the memory of Ackerman's death in the pool again took shape in his mind.

"You know, it didn't strike me until later," he continued, "I mean all that shit I was swimming through, the blood and brain tissue and, whatever it was, it didn't strike me until later that that was Ackerman. I took a long shower at the pool, then at home, thinking about the whole thing, I took another, really scrubbed myself. I haven't gone back yet. You been there?"

"No. They drained the pool. It's supposed to open tomorrow." Charlie had been swimming regularly for the past year and now swam half a mile to a mile three days a week. Vaguely, he hoped that his improved physical condition would allow him to move through middle age with as much of his personal vanity intact as possible.

Charlie had meant to go to the pool the night Ackerman was killed, but it had been cold and rainy and Charlie hadn't felt like driving in from his small house on the lake. Since then, he had felt a little guilty, thinking he might have been able to do something had he been there. That was unlikely. But perhaps, he told himself, he might have seen the man in the white raincoat. Field was small and thin and would look so even in a heavy raincoat. Still, Charlie didn't believe Field would have murdered his partner, no matter how badly they were getting along.

"Were there a lot of hoods at the funeral?" asked Connor.

"I don't know. They didn't wear buttons."

"I liked Ackerman," said Connor, "but they say he knew a lot of crooks, you know, organized crime. He could have been killed for all sorts of reasons we'll never know about. Some mechanic could fly in here from the West Coast, waste Ackerman in the pool, and buzz back to L.A. the same night."

"Mechanic?"

"That's what they call them on TV. You know, hired killers."

Charlie nodded uncertainly. What Connor had said again made him question the theatrical nature of the murder. It was more like a murder on television than one in real life. He wondered if there was a reason for that. Then he gave it up and looked around for the waitress. The one he particularly wanted hadn't come in yet, so he ordered a beer from the bartender.

Despite the name of the Backstretch, the four walls of the long narrow room displayed eight-by-ten framed photographs of boxers. There must have been over a hundred and each bore a different inscription: "To Berney, a great guy, Jake LaMotta;" "To Berney, one in a million, Willie Pep." Berney McQuilkin was the owner of the Backstretch. Charlie had once studied these photographs with some care only to realize that the handwriting on each picture was the same. Tonight the bar was nearly empty. In the back room, which was a Chinese restaurant during the day and early evening, the topless dancer was lazily gyrating to "Sympathy for the Devil." In her right hand, she held a ham sandwich. Her audience consisted of a boy shooting pool and four poets from a nearby artists' colony who sat as close as possible to the miniature stage. At the bar, Berney McQuilkin was playing dollar poker with a wizened ex-jockey who had given up the track to become a TV repairman. The jockey's chin just reached the level of the bar, and whenever he won or lost he would slap the counter with a diminutive hand and shout, "Ha!"

"I heard Field didn't go to the funeral," said Connor.

Charlie nodded and drank some beer.

"Don't you consider that suspicious?"

"Maybe, I mean, perhaps he hated Ackerman, but that doesn't mean he shot him. Field didn't seem friendly with Lew, but then he isn't friendly with anyone. He's an accountant and he's got a lot of investments and he handles a lot of people's money, but he doesn't like people much. He stays out at that house on the lake and all the paperwork gets brought to him." Charlie paused to think of Field alone in his big house and how little he knew about him. "Maybe I've spoken ten words to the man in two years," he continued. "He isn't particularly friendly, but he doesn't necessarily seem mean-hearted. He just seems blank."

"Weren't you surprised he wasn't at the funeral?"

"I didn't even realize it until later. It was huge. I mean, people came in from all over the country: a lot of big owners, rich people. . . ."

"And hoods. . . ."

"Sure, I guess there were hoods. Lew had all kinds of friends."

That morning, before the funeral, Charlie had thought it too bad that the day was clear and warm, one of the best days of summer. He felt the weather should be bleak and the sky overcast to match his feelings. But then at the funeral someone had called it a fast track sort of day, and Charlie had realized that was what Ackerman would have preferred.

The service at the funeral home was so crowded that many people were forced to stand out on the porch. Nearly a hundred and fifty cars were in the procession to the cemetery. Charlie had recognized a congressman and a federal judge, numerous sports writers, besides the shadier mourners who interested Connor. There had also been people from every aspect of the racing world from the wealthiest owner to the guy that shoveled out the stalls: trainers, groups of jockeys, grooms, exercise boys, track officials, even some Pinkerton guards. And what struck Charlie was they all appeared to grieve. He wondered what Ackerman's three children had thought of it. They had flown in from San Francisco where they lived with their mother; they hadn't seen their father for several years. Even Chief Peterson had been there with about half the police department. Although he glowered at Charlie, he hadn't spoken.

At the cemetery a eulogy was delivered by Robert Dwyer, another stable owner in town who, like Ackerman, was part owner, part trainer, and part landlord for horses being trained away from the track or stabled temporarily. But while Ackerman had been still a relatively young man, Dwyer was silver headed and confined to a wheelchair, and it struck Charlie as ironic that the eulogy for someone so strong and healthy should be delivered by someone frail and infirm.

Dwyer had been pushed forward by his son-in-law, Wayne Curry, who stood behind the older man as Dwyer talked about Ackerman's service to the community and to racing: words which Charlie found overly conventional but which were made moving by the sounds and smells carried by an east wind from the stables surrounding Saratoga Raceway, the harness track, two blocks away.

"I heard Krause was pretty upset," said Connor. He had gotten some beer nuts from the bar and was ripping open the bag.

"I'd say that. For a moment it looked like he was going to jump down into the grave."

"Like in *Hamlet*." Connor offered some nuts to Charlie who shook his head.

"Maybe so. Personally, I don't think he was going to jump, but he ran to the edge when they lowered the coffin and he was crying. Somebody grabbed his arm." Charlie remembered the look on Krause's face as he stood at the side of the grave, staring down, as if all his wrinkles and badly healed boxing bruises had doubled in number, as if he were a man who now had nothing.

"I guess he feels pretty guilty," said Connor.

"How could he have known? There was no reason to think that Ackerman was going to get shot."

"It was his job," said Connor.

Charlie was going to argue this, when he saw the waitress, Doris Bailes, come into the bar. She was the only reason Charlie ever came to the Backstretch. Seeing Charlie and Connor, she walked over to their booth. Doris had short dark hair and an oval face so smooth and free from wrinkles that she looked more like 28 than the 38 she actually was. Even so, she was six years younger than Charlie and sometimes he worried that she rejected his advances because of his age, even though she had told him she wasn't going to get involved with anyone until divorce proceedings against her present husband were over and done with. She was a woman of medium height, slightly stocky and muscular in a way that Charlie found comforting. She wore Levi's, a blue blouse, and jogging shoes. Pinned to the blouse was a large white button with a picture of a whale.

Reaching Charlie, she touched his shoulder. "How was the funeral?"

"Five cars full of flowers and several hundred people. Everything Lew would have hated."

"Jack Bishop told me that the bodyguard tried to throw himself into the grave."

Bishop, a local realtor, hadn't even been there, to Charlie's recollection. "He just got too close to the edge and people got excited." Charlie considered for a moment, then turned to Connor. "What did Krause do that night at the pool. Did he go after the guy in the raincoat?"

Connor shook his head and swallowed a mouthful of nuts. "He came running in and when he saw Ackerman in the water, he didn't even pause. Jumped right in after him. Dumb guy couldn't even swim. He grabbed Ackerman, then began thrashing around. I had to drag him out." Connor looked away and began rubbing his chin with his thumb. "Then he took a swing at me and went in again. He kept doing that until I had to drag Ackerman in too. It was a real mess. I mean, half of Ackerman's head was gone."

3

▼▼▼

J UDGED BY ITSELF, the car parked along the road by Charlie's house meant nothing. But when he saw his house was dark as well, he kept on driving. The electric timer should have switched on the living room lamp at eight and shut it off at midnight. But now, at eleven o'clock, the house was dark and a strange car was parked on the road nearby.

Charlie drove another hundred yards and stopped. He had an old yellow Volkswagen Beetle and he pulled it onto the sand by the lake. Charlie had moved out to this small house, actually a cottage, on Saratoga Lake two years before when he left his wife and quit his job with the police department. What with well-meaning friends and his three interfering cousins, he wanted to be away from Saratoga during that change in his life. However, after friends and cousins alike heard he had been arrested in New York, and taken up with a girl young enough to be his daughter, and had been fired from his job with the Saratoga police department, they gave him all the privacy he could possibly want. He hadn't minded that privacy, but as he sat in his Volkswagen wondering what to do next he wished for a few people to call on. At last he took a deep breath and got out of the car.

Although Charlie had a pistol, it was tucked between some dish towels in a drawer in his kitchen; and although, what with swimming and general care, he was in better physical shape than at any other time of his life apart from basic training, the prospect of physical violence made him somewhat gloomy.

He was not a large man. Although stocky and even muscular, he was a good four inches under six feet. His round face was smooth and pink like a baby's, and he had large, blue, contemplative eyes that always seemed to be resting thoughtfully on something. His thinning hair was light brown and he brushed it straight back so people wouldn't think he was trying to hide his increasing baldness. He presented, he thought, an innocuous, anonymous figure, and he liked that. Other people would describe him as attentive, and Ackerman once told him he looked like a robin listening for a worm. That night Charlie had on a brown short-sleeve shirt and new khaki pants, and he was sorry at the prospect of a bit of roughhousing, as he called it, which would lead him to mess up his clothes.

It was a clear night and a three-quarter moon shone over the lake, making a silver moon path that shimmered across the water. Charlie's cottage was on Route 9p, a quarter of a mile past Snake Hill. While most of the cottages on the lake were packed together and nearly touched the pavement, Charlie had been able to buy one with a little space around it and set back from the road. It had originally been white, but Charlie had always disliked white houses and so the day after the closing he painted it dark blue with bright yellow trim around the windows and doors. Charlie had heard it said he bought the cottage with money made from various cocaine deals in New York City. Actually, the money came from savings and a five percent loan, which Ackerman had given him.

Charlie reached the strange car. It was a fairly new, maroon Oldsmobile with Saratoga plates. There was nothing inside except for a couple of white styrofoam cups and a pair of tan driving gloves. Taking a deep breath, Charlie moved on toward the driveway, keeping close to the bushes and tall maples that bordered the road.

Entering the driveway, he ducked down, trying to see through his windows thirty feet away. His cottage had a large living room with a fireplace, a bedroom, kitchen, and bathroom. The living room had windows on three sides and with the moon on the other side of the house, he hoped he could look through to see if anyone was waiting. Up until this moment, he still believed his house must be empty and kept chiding himself for being melodramatic. But then, as he got closer, he thought he saw someone, and as he moved to within fifteen feet of the house he made out the dark outline of a man standing in the middle of his living room. Charlie stepped back toward a big evergreen at the edge of his property. There were cicadas and he could hear frogs along the lake.

What Charlie wanted most was to tiptoe back to his car, drive to the nearest phone, and call the police. But as he thought of it he saw Chief Peterson's face as he had seen him that afternoon at the funeral: fat, rude, and diminishing. The face of someone who thought him a fool. A week ago Charlie might have called Ackerman or even now he might call one or more of the guards who worked for him at the stable. At this time of year, he had five men working under him. He could even go to the stable to borrow a gun. But as these alternatives flipped through his mind, he grew gloomier and gloomier, until at last he found himself ducking down and crossing the driveway toward his kitchen door. If he could open it quietly enough perhaps he could get to his pistol. He tried to remember if it was loaded. As he neared the woodpile, he picked up a thin, four-foot length of wood. A car passed on the road. From a cottage further down the lake, Charlie could hear laughter and rock 'n' roll music. He tried to think how many beers he had drunk at the Backstretch and wondered if he would be creeping toward his own house in the dark armed with a club if, like Connor, he had drunk only Saratoga Vichy.

Again, all his historical precedents were reversed. Although Charlie could name a hundred burglars and sneak thieves who had graduated from Marm Mandlebaum's burglar school at 79 Clinton Street in New York during the 1870s, he couldn't think of anyone, outside of a character in a P. G. Wodehouse novel, who had burgled his own house.

When Charlie reached his kitchen door, he opened the screen and tried the knob. It was unlocked. Gently, he turned the knob and pushed open the door. He was both surprised and pleased by how completely silent it was. He slipped through the door, shut the screen, then moved quietly across the tile floor of the kitchen, trying to remember loose floorboards and where the floor squeaked. The drawer with the gun was on the right side of the sink. As he slid it open, he began to think how simple it all was.

Then someone laid a hand on his shoulder. "What the fuck

you pussyfooting through the back door for? You're lucky I'm not a nervous man."

Charlie gently pushed the drawer closed and tried to slow his breathing. It was Victor Plotz, another guard at the stable and someone Charlie thought of as his best friend.

"Was that you in the living room?" Charlie whispered.

"Nah, I was on the can."

"Then there's someone in the living room."

"Yeah, that's Krause. Whyn't you tell me you can't run the blender, the toaster, and the TV without bustin a fuse? Where do you keep'm anyway?"

"I ran out."

"Is that so. Whatcha carryin a cane for?"

Fifteen minutes later Charlie and Victor sat at the round dining room table watching Krause eat a huge plate of scrambled eggs by candlelight. It turned out that the body-guard had hardly eaten anything since Ackerman's death four days before. Krause was wearing a brown suit which looked rumpled and slept in. He kept putting down his fork and pushing back his chair as he argued with Charlie.

"I tell you, Ackerman left me ten grand. I'll let you have the whole thing."

"I still can't do it," said Charlie.

"That's a lotta moolah, Charlie," said Plotz. "Think of the good times."

"Keep out of this, Victor."

"Vic."

Charlie ignored him and drank some beer. Across the table Krause was staring at his eggs which seemed to flicker in the shadows thrown by the candles.

"You mean it's not enough?" asked Krause.

Charlie sighed. "It's not the money. It's just that there's no point. The police are investigating and even if they were doing nothing you still couldn't hire me. I mean, I'm nobody. I'm not a cop. I'm not a private detective. I've got no credentials. I'm a stable guard."

"Yeah, but you were a cop," said Krause. In the candlelight, Krause's round face appeared pock-marked and cratered like the surface of the moon. It was a sullen, unhappy face and Charlie wished he could do something for it.

"Look. Leave it to Peterson," said Charlie at last. "He's got to be working hard on this. A prominent citizen gunned down in the YMCA pool. It's as much as his job's worth to catch the guy."

Krause again pushed away his plate. "Peterson's nothing. He's looking in all the wrong places."

"How d'you mean?"

"He thinks either Lew was killed by Field or he was killed by hoods. Sure he knew a lotta hoods. Who don't? But that doesn't mean some hood killed him. Lew had a lotta friends. He was always on the up and up. Hoods don't shoot their buddies."

"What about Field?"

"What for? Maybe sometimes they quarreled, but Lew never spoke badly of him. No, there was something else on his mind."

Victor tapped Charlie's arm. "You listen to him, Charlie. I wouldn't of brought him over if I thought he was a screwball." Victor was drinking his beer in a large, 24-ounce stein with the name Munich written across it in black Germanic print and pictures of crenelated towers. He had brought it to Charlie's some weeks before so, as he said, he would have something decent to drink out of.

"So what was on his mind?" asked Charlie.

Krause had decided to eat some more eggs. After a moment, he delicately wiped his mouth on a bit of paper towel and resumed talking. "Something was bothering him. Most of the time I don't carry a gun. What's the point? Down in New York, maybe, but not in Saratoga. Anyway, two days before he's killed, he asks me if I'm carrying and I say no I'm not and he says maybe I'd better for a while."

"Did he seem frightened?" asked Charlie.

"No, I wouldn't say frightened. He seemed angry, like something had happened to make him angry."

Victor poked Charlie again. "See what I mean?"

"You have any idea what made him angry?"

"No, except it had been growing on him for about a week.

Then, Tuesday night, he went off by himself after swimming. I asked him if he wanted me to drive him, but he said no, he wanted to go someplace on his own. So I told him to take the car, but he said he didn't need it."

"He went swimming at 9:30?"

"No, 7:30. He went at 9:30 Monday, Wednesday, and Friday, and he went at 7:30 on Tuesday and Thursday. So it was about 8:30 that I left him."

"Did he walk or was he picked up?"

"I don't know. Later, when he came in around 10:30, he said he'd gotten a ride back."

"You let him go even though he'd told you to start carrying a gun?" asked Victor.

"No, it was that night after he got back that he told me to start carrying it." Krause paused and glanced out the windows at the lake. One window was open and white curtains billowed slightly into the room.

Ackerman had lived in one of the Victorian mansions on North Broadway near the new Skidmore College campus. Krause lived there as well, while trainers, favorite jockeys, owners might stop in to stay as long as a month. All were looked after by an elderly Ukrainian woman who for years had kept a hotdog stand at the track until she retired to become Ackerman's housekeeper.

"And you have no idea where he went that night?" asked Charlie.

"None. He never said a word about it."

Charlie had seen Ackerman every day and they talked about horses or something to do with Charlie's job or just shot the breeze. For the week before Ackerman's death, Charlie had seen less of him, but that was because Charlie had been working nights. During spring and summer, when the stable was the busiest, Charlie had to hire three extra men, beginning in early April before the harness track opened. That's when he had offered Victor Plotz a job after Victor had called to say he no longer wanted to live in New York City.

The last time Charlie saw Ackerman alive had been Friday afternoon. For the hundredth time Charlie wondered if Ackerman had seemed any different, but he'd seemed the same as ever: relaxed and comfortable with his world. Ackerman had told him what horses would be coming in that weekend, then teased him about his nonblooming romance with the waitress at the Backstretch. Thinking about it, Charlie could still see him standing at the rail of the training track, wearing his white Western shirt and jeans and with his sunglasses pushed up on his forehead, like he always did whenever he stopped to talk to somebody. As they had parted, they agreed to meet out at Lake Lonely at 6:30 Saturday evening, where they would rent a boat and fish for bass. They had done this several times before, and Saturday evening, even though he knew Ackerman was dead, Charlie made the mistake of keeping the date himself. Once out on the lake, he hadn't even bothered to bait his hook but just rowed around and felt miserable.

It seemed to Charlie that the fact Ackerman had said nothing to him about being more watchful suggested that if Ackerman was worried, his concern had little or nothing to do with the stable. Since Ackerman had few interests apart from horses, Charlie couldn't imagine what else might have bothered him.

"Did you tell Peterson about Ackerman going off?"

Krause turned back to Charlie and shrugged. "Yeah, but he didn't pay much attention to it. He figured Lew had a hot date. Sure Lew went out with a number of women, but he was never quiet about it. I'm not saying he bragged, but he liked women and, you know he'd talk about it."

"Maybe some husband was after him," suggested Victor. "I've had that happen myself and believe me it can be ticklish."

Charlie looked at his friend who was in his mid-fifties, nearly bald apart from the puffs of gray hair that rose from his scalp like dust kitties found under a bed, and had a nose big enough and red enough to light a ship safely to harbor. The fact that Victor had many girlfriends always gave Charlie hope about his own dim prospects.

"No," said Krause, "Lew made sure his girlfriends were unattached. I told that to Peterson and he just grinned. If he hadn't been a cop, well, he don't know shit from Shinola, that's why I think you could do a better job."

Charlie poured himself some more beer. "I'm not a cop and my reputation's so bad that nobody would talk to me even if I was."

"What if you just looked around a little bit? Ackerman thought you were pretty good, you know, the best. He was your friend, too, right?" Krause mopped up the last of his eggs with a piece of bread. Even though he was overweight and now had food in his stomach, he still looked undernourished somehow.

"Maybe," said Charlie, "I could talk to people at the stable." Even as he said it he knew he was committing himself to something he ought not be doing. But sure Ackerman had been his friend, and if he had gone swimming that night maybe he could have done something.

"What if Charlie catches the guy?" asked Victor. "You tell him what you want when he does that. Listen to this, Charlie."

Krause put his hands together on the table in front of his plate. They were big hands and in the dim light with the fingers entwined they looked like a great pale chrysanthemum.

"I want you to let me kill him," Krause said.

4

▼▼▼

RED FOX, A TALL, two-year-old, chestnut colt, was being led along the shed rows toward the hot-walker by Petey Gomez when Charlie came around the corner of the barn and nearly bumped into them. Charlie was mostly suspicious of horses. More than once a horse had pushed its head out of its stall when he passed to make a grab for his guard's cap. But Red Fox was an exception. For a while, Ackerman had also been involved in breeding horses and still had a small interest in a farm in Kentucky. The colt had been born there shortly after Charlie started working for Ackerman, and Ackerman had given Charlie the honor of naming it.

Red Fox had been the name of Jesse James's horse during the three years after the terrible Northfield Raid when Jesse was laying low and running a small farm near Nashville. Going by the last name of Howard, Jesse had entered Red Fox in a number of Nashville races, riding him himself and winning several. Charlie couldn't imagine naming the horse anything else and Ackerman hadn't minded.

Charlie reached out and gently touched the horse's shoulder. Red Fox flicked his tail and shivered, the panniculus muscle quivering beneath the skin.

"Maybe he recognizes you," said Petey. He was a small, black-haired man who had been slightly too big and too undisciplined an eater to be a jockey. He wore jeans, a ragged black T-shirt and a red Boston Red Sox cap. "You wanna wash him down?" he asked hopefully.

"Can't right now. When did he come in?"

"Brought him up from Belmont last night. Warner's got him scheduled to run opening day. Times were pretty good this morning."

Frank Warner was the trainer who worked with Ackerman. He was a few years older than Charlie, had been born and raised in Saratoga, and was a friend of Charlie's three older cousins. This, unfortunately, put him in the camp of those prominent citizens who thought of Charlie as shiftless. Although Warner had never seen Charlie behave in any way which could be considered shiftless, he was always careful to let Charlie know he had his eye on him and, what particularly irritated Charlie, to let it be known that if for some strange reason Charlie was not behaving irresponsibly at Lorelei Stables it was only because he, Frank Warner, was watching.

"You seen Frank this morning?" asked Charlie.

"Yeah, he's rushing around like he's got a tack up his ass. In fact, if he sees me standing here jawing, he'll probably bite my head off. Catch you later."

Gomez led Red Fox on toward the hot-walker, which already had three horses attached to its four horizontal arms. At the sight of the horses circling docilely between the training track and the row of stalls with their white paint and green trim shadowed by tall maples and oaks, Charlie felt nearly overcome with nostalgia and memories of forty Saratoga summers. And although the tourism and crowds often irritated him and, like the Chamber of Commerce, he often heard himself arguing that Saratoga was more than a one-month town, still, it was that one month he cared most about: four weeks of thoroughbred racing. Even as he thought about it Charlie could almost hear that noise which was a mixture of the sound of the sea and an approaching express train: the increasing roar as the horses circled the track, the swelling vocal crescendo as they reached the finish line, the mass shout of thirty thousand people which could be heard all over the east side of Saratoga. And Charlie, whether just walking along or directing traffic or trimming a hedge, would find himself lifting his head and holding his breath as if something immensely important were about to be settled in his life.

Now as opening day approached and more horses were being brought into town and the last bit of painting and cleaning and beautifying was being done to the race track, Charlie felt his body and mind quickening, his senses growing more alert. With this realization came a wave of anger that Ackerman wasn't here as well, that despite the time Ackerman spent at Belmont or at the Florida and California tracks, this coming month of August was the month he had liked best.

Charlie continued along the shed row toward Ackerman's office, past other horses, grooms, men and women rubbing down horses, a tack salesman, trainers, a jockey's agent. Most he knew and spoke to, and as he walked Charlie felt himself growing more and more angry at whoever had taken it upon himself to kill Ackerman and deny him this life. At the moment, the stables seemed subdued. No music or shouting or fooling around—everyone had a sense of Ackerman's absence, while beyond that was the question of what was going to happen next. Field might be arrested; Field might sell the stable; Field might hire a general manager who would run everything differently.

Ackerman's office was a small, white cottage with green trim about the same size as Charlie's cottage on the lake. It was located near the training track between two large white and green barns. One of the area's few remaining wineglass elms stood nearby, planted, as Charlie knew, for the Centennial of 1876. Ackerman's office was locked and Charlie opened it with his passkey.

The room was musty and smelled of leather. Charlie opened a window that looked out on the track. The cottage consisted of one large room with fourteen windows looking out on all sides, making the room wonderfully bright but freezing in the winter. A red enamel Swedish wood stove stood on one side of the room, while across from it stood Ackerman's large Victorian desk. Charlie walked to the desk, sat down in the oak and red leather swivel chair, and looked around. On all four walls were photographs of every horse Ackerman had ever owned or trained. There was even a picture of Charlie standing next to Red Fox. Looking at it, Charlie remembered when Ackerman had taken it in early spring, how Ackerman had tried to convince Charlie to sit on the horse wearing a jockey's cap and how Charlie had refused, claiming it was beneath his dignity, not wanting Ackerman to know that he was a little afraid of horses.

The top of the desk was clean except for a black telephone with five lines, a Condition Book telling the eligibility requirements for the coming meet at Saratoga, and a gray metal box containing six-by-eight cards for all the horses that Ackerman owned or trained, showing where they were running, how well they were training, what their workout speeds had been and other pertinent information: taped legs, blinkers, doses of phenylbutazone and so on. Charlie glanced in the box, saw that it seemed to be in order and closed it.

The desk was covered with a new gray blotter. Ackerman was a compulsive doodler and usually went through four or five blotters a year. On this blotter was a telephone number, a drawing of a fire engine, a drawing of a horse, and the number 730. Charlie picked up the phone and dialed the telephone number only to discover it belonged to a pizza and sub shop in Saratoga.

Hanging up, Charlie opened the belly drawer. Along with pens in five colors, paper clips, and note pads, it contained a yellow plastic rose, a pair of swimming goggles and a snub-nosed .38. Charlie took out the rose, goggles, and revolver.

Holding up the revolver, he saw it was empty. The goggles were resting on the blotter just over the number 730. They were Speedo goggles and rose tinted. Charlie was about to look through the other drawers when the door slammed open and Frank Warner stormed in.

"What're you doing in here?" he demanded.

The question took Charlie by surprise, because, thinking about it, he really didn't know what he was doing. He had told himself he wanted to look at Ackerman's office, but he didn't think he was looking or anything in particular, nor did he expect to find anything.

"I asked you a question, Bradshaw." Warner was about fifty and had the thin, wiry shape of a steeplechase jockey. He wore jeans and a red, yellow, and blue striped shirt.

Charlie leaned back in the chair. "Just thinking about Lew, I guess. Something upsetting you?" While Charlie didn't actually dislike Warner, he found him generally tiresome.

"Yeah, I got enough to do around here without checking up on your snooping." After storming into the office, Warner had stopped near the door. His glance kept shifting from Charlie to the gun on the gray blotter.

"I'm chief of security for Lorelei Stables and Lew was a friend of mine. I have a key to every building and every office, including your own. Why should I snoop? Come on, Frank, tell me what's on your mind."

Warner stayed where he was. He had a long, narrow face like a garden spade. "Where'd that gun come from?" he asked.

"It was in the top drawer of the desk. It's empty. I didn't know Lew kept one around."

"Neither did I. Least it wasn't there two weeks ago."

Charlie restrained himself from asking Warner if he had been snooping. "How do you know?"

"I was looking for some stamps."

"What's upsetting you today?"

Warner's narrow shoulders sagged a little and he turned away. "I'm busy, that's all. Nobody knows what's going on. Field won't say anything. Meanwhile, more horses are arriving every day and I'm shorthanded."

"You mean because of Lew?"

"One of the grooms is sick, least his wife says he is."

"Who is it?"

"Neal Claremon."

"I don't recognize the name."

"He's a new guy. Lew hired him himself. Worked five days and now he's been sick five days. Not that I believe for two seconds that he's sick, mind you."

"Why not?"

"I keep calling and telling his wife to put him on the phone. She says he's too sick to talk on the phone. I figure a man too sick to talk on the phone should be in the hospital." As he spoke, Warner began cracking his fingers one by one, tugging at each finger like someone might pull at a ring he couldn't get off. "What I think is he's drinking, that's all. Also, the wife's a little rude. Now, if you're trying to protect your husband's job, you're not going to be rude to his boss."

"Have the police been talking to you?"

"Yeah, what of it?"

"You tell them about this Claremon?"

"No, why should they care if I got a groom who's a drunk? They were around here asking questions and interfering. Just like you're asking questions. Look, Bradshaw, I don't have the time. . . ."

"Just wait a second," said Charlie. "You have any ideas about why Lew might have been shot?"

Warner shoved his hands into his back pockets and began to look angry again. "Bradshaw, I train horses. Far as I could see Lew had nothing but friends. But he used to be a kinda wild guy. Who knows, maybe somebody he used to know just got out of jail. You got anything else to say?"

"When was this blotter replaced?"

"Jesus, Bradshaw. . . ."

"It's a serious question."

"A week, two weeks ago. Yeah, about two weeks ago."

"You had pizza around then? You were working late and Lew called out?"

"That's right, Sherlock. You going to solve this case for the cops? You and your team of stable guards? You'd better be careful or Field will hear you're being a nuisance and fire your ass. You have any more dumb questions? If not, I got work to do." Turning on his heel, Warner slammed out of the office as abruptly as he had entered.

Actually, Charlie had wanted to ask him about the number 730, but he shrugged it off. Then he quickly looked through the rest of the desk. There seemed nothing out of the ordinary. He looked again at the revolver and wondered why Ackerman had decided to keep it around. At last he put it back in the desk along with the goggles and yellow plastic rose. For several minutes, Charlie sat with his elbows on the desk and his chin in his hands, then he decided to walk over to his office on the other side of the stable.

As he walked back along the shed row, he saw Petey Gomez coming from the hot-walker with Red Fox.

Gomez called to him, "Hey, Charlie, whyn't you tell me you was going to find Lew's killer?"

"Who told you that?"

Petey pushed his Red Sox cap back on his head. "That guard, Plotz, he said you were going to teach the cops how to do it. Give 'em a few lessons in efficiency."

"Plotz has been pulling your leg."

"You mean you're not? Damn, Charlie, why not?"

Once as a policeman five years before Charlie had arrested Petey Gomez for passing a bad check. Petey had made the check out to himself and signed it John Whitney, of one of the big Saratoga racing families. It had been a check for $1,000 and Petey had tried to cash it in a small clothing store in payment for a three-piece suit of blue plush and a pair of red patent leather platform shoes. The store had called the police and Charlie had been sent over. On the way back to the station, Charlie had told Petey all the terrible things he would find in prison, how he wouldn't be able to protect himself, how he wouldn't be able to work for a stable again when he got out. Then, when they had nearly reached the police station, Charlie had let him go. Not only had Petey never again tried to pass a bad check, but he decided that Charlie was far smarter than any cop on television, presumably because he'd been smart enough to see through Petey's forgery.

"Because the cops can take care of it themselves," said Charlie.

Red Fox tried to rear up and Petey pulled him back down. "They couldn't find their way around the track," he said, patting the horse's neck.

"By the way," said Charlie, "did you get to know that new guy, Neal Claremon?"

"That guy that's out sick? I talked to him a little."

"What's he like?"

"I don't know, jumpy somehow. Like he expected a brick to fall on him."

"Ever see him with a bottle?"

"Never."

"Did he say anything about himself?"

"No, but he knew a lot about horses. Ackerman hired him instead of Warner and I saw him going into Ackerman's office a couple of times."

"Why'd Ackerman hire him?"

"Beats me. Guess he thought he needed another groom."

"What's he look like?"

"He's a real thin guy. You know the jockey Braulio Baeza? He's thin like Baeza was, but taller."

"Was anybody particularly friendly with Claremon?"

"Not that I could see. Stayed by himself a lot. I tried to talk to him a couple of times, but he'd just say yes or no or I dunno. Not much to build on. He wasn't rude or anything, just not too chummy."

Charlie left Gomez and headed toward Warner's office. He decided to get Claremon's address and go talk to him. If Claremon had been out the past five days, that meant the first day he had called in sick was the day after Ackerman had been murdered.

5

▼▼▼

NEAL CLAREMON LIVED out on the north end of Maple Avenue at the edge of Saratoga. As he drove across Saratoga that Wednesday morning, Charlie was struck by the increasing numbers of track people he saw downtown, the number of horse trucks and milling tourists. If he had still been with the police department, this was the week when he would be receiving the names of pickpockets, gamblers, confidence men, and common thugs which various police departments around the country believed to be heading toward Saratoga Springs.

Actually, Charlie's mother had lived on this part of Maple Avenue before leaving Saratoga about a year before. His mother had worked for the huge tourist hotels, the United States and the Grand Union, during the thirties and forties; had worked for the Grand Union until its final season in 1952, although during those last years work had been spotty. Afterward, she had worked as a waitress until just a year ago. That too had been seasonal, and as a child Charlie and his mother moved several times a year, always ending up with his prosperous and successful uncle, a plumber, and his three sons who were still the bane of Charlie's existence. When he was little, Charlie had dreaded these moves which landed him each spring at his uncle's house where his interests and accomplishments became decidedly second-rate and even questionable when compared to the successes of his cousins.

Despite this economically precarious existence, Hazel's ambition in life was to open a motel which would cater to the racing crowd: an ambition which had seemed pure fantasy until about a year ago when she had almost accidentally claimed a race horse which was turning out to be a winner.

Charlie stopped his Volkswagen across the street from Claremon's house, or rather the refinished garage that passed as a house. Charlie doubted it was any bigger than his own house, and although it had a second floor, it seemed no more than a small room made smaller by a sloping roof. Nearly touching the house was a slightly bigger but even more dilapidated two-story white house—the original possessor of the fixed-up garage which Claremon was presumably renting. In front of the house, a small dirty boy of about three on a rusty tricycle, wearing only a yellow T-shirt, was pursuing a spotted dog.

On one side of the house was a Gulf station and on the other was a motel called The Shady Nook. Charlie was surprised at that since Shady Nook was one of the names his mother had considered using for her own motel. The last time Charlie had been down this street, the motel had been called the Calvin Coolidge, and if Charlie hadn't received a postcard from his mother two days before, he would have suspected the motel of belonging to her. Since it didn't, she would be disappointed to scratch that name from her list of possibilities.

Hazel's card said only that Ever Ready was still winning and she urged him to make up his quarrel with his cousins because she would need their help when she returned to Saratoga. The card had come from Louisville, Kentucky. As always Charlie was irritated with his mother's assumption that he had quarreled with his cousins, rather than admitting, as she well knew, that they had dropped him after his return from New York. In their minds, he was following in the footsteps of his hard-gambling, alcoholic father who had committed suicide when Charlie was four as a way of skipping out on $25,000 worth of IOU's. Actually, Charlie didn't mind being free from his cousins' everlasting advice. All that he minded about his current bad reputation was that he could no longer coach Little League baseball, which for Charlie, standing by third base on a warm summer evening and urging some little kid to slide, was what life was all about.

Charlie crossed the street to Claremon's house. As he reached the sidewalk, he noticed a white curtain with huge yellow flowers quiver slightly in a downstairs window. He was forced to redirect his attention immediately, however, by a high-pitched scream at knee level followed by a sharp pain in his left foot as the dirty boy in the dirty yellow T-shirt ran his tricycle into his leg.

"Gotcha," the boy said. He had bright red hair with a glob of what appeared to be tar stuck on top.

Charlie extricated himself from the tricycle and patted the boy on the shoulder. Then he continued toward Claremon's door. He knocked. There was no answer. He knocked again.

"You're an old fart," shouted the boy.

Charlie knocked a third time. Since he had seen the curtain move, he was prepared to knock all afternoon. He was just lifting his hand to knock again when the door opened and a small thin woman of about his age stood before him.

"What do you want?"

"I'd like to speak to Neal Claremon."

"He's sick."

"It's important."

"He's sleeping right now and I don't want to disturb him." The woman wore a blue checked gingham dress and stood with her arms crossed. Her bare elbows were so sharp and pointed that Charlie thought she could dig holes with them.

"I'm afraid I have to ask you to wake him up," said Charlie.

"Who are you anyway?"

"Chief of security, Lorelei Stables." Charlie straightened his back a little. Now that he was thinner, he hoped his bearing was somewhat more military. As a chubby policeman, he knew he had looked like a penguin in uniform.

The woman glanced down at her feet and shook her head. "I don't want to wake him up. Maybe you can try later or maybe I can help you in some way."

He found something familiar about her which he couldn't place. Perhaps he had seen her around Saratoga. She had large brown eyes and a sharp angular face that must have been quite pretty twenty years before. He tried to imagine it a little softer and less lined and again there was that nagging sense of familiarity.

"It has to do with his job at the stable and the death of his employer," said Charlie, lowering his voice a little. "If you don't let me see him, I'll go over to the motel, call the police, and wait until they arrive. I'm sorry to bother you, but I told you it was important."

The woman again looked down at her feet. "I was lying to you. He's not here." She looked ready to flinch, as if she had taken a lot of abuse in her life.

Charlie tried to speak gently. "Why should I believe you now?"

"Come in and see for yourself." She backed away from the door and after a moment's hesitation Charlie followed her into a shabby living room with motel-modern furniture and cheap pine panelling on the walls.

"Where is he?" asked Charlie, glancing around.

"I've no idea." The woman walked back to the kitchen and Charlie followed. The kitchen was clean, white, and small with New England scenes from *Yankee* magazine thumbtacked above the sink.

In his mind, Charlie was sorting through his life year by year, trying to determine where he had known her. Turning away from a picture of a white steeple rising above a snow-covered village, Charlie saw the woman was climbing the stairs. He followed her up to the bedroom, but stood only in the doorway out of what he thought of as a rather stupid shyness, as if he thought this tired woman would seduce him or was afraid she might think he wanted to attack her. In any case, the bedroom was empty and the bed made and covered with a white chenille spread. Not only was Neal Claremon nowhere in evidence, but the room was so neat and tidy that it seemed completely unused. On the pine bureau were some cheaply framed photographs and looking at a wedding picture of a smiling young woman, who through disappointment and hard times had evolved into the woman standing in front of him, Charlie remembered where he had known her before. He was so taken back by this and felt such a wave of sympathy that he turned and descended the stairs. Mrs. Claremon followed him.

When he reached the bottom, he said, "I expect you do know where your husband is, and I'd appreciate it if you'd tell me. I don't mean to make trouble for him, but he might know something about Ackerman's murder and so I'd like to talk to him."

"I already told you, I don't know where he is." The woman went to the sink and tried to shut off a dripping faucet. Watching her, Charlie felt he was deceiving her by remembering who she was, while she, apparently, didn't recall him.

"If you don't tell me, then, as I say, I'll have to call the police and they'll ask you these questions."

The woman didn't answer but kept pushing at the handle of the dripping faucet. She had short gray hair and Charlie remembered when it had been brown and silky.

"Aren't you Janet Macomb?" he asked.

She turned quickly and stared at him, trying to place him, but not succeeding.

"I'm Charlie Bradshaw. Remember?"

She obviously didn't, although she still watched him intently. Charlie wondered if he had looked so different twenty-five years ago.

"We were in typing class together in high school," he said. "You were a year behind me. But I sat next to you, remember?"

This time Janet Macomb gave an abrupt laugh, then clapped her hand over her mouth, then folded her arms again. "We traded tests," she said at last.

Charlie nodded. "That's right."

Charlie had taken typing because his cousins had told him it would be useful in his future career. At that time they had planned for him to become a bookkeeper. Actually, it had been quite useful to him as a policeman since it speeded up the writing of endless reports. By some fluke Charlie had been an extremely fast and accurate typist, while Janet Macomb, who sat beside him, was the class dummy. Even when she managed forty words per minute, her endless mistakes often awarded her a minus score. Apart from typing class, Janet was successful and sought after: a cheerleader who was also secretary in various school clubs.

They had been friendly and, although Charlie had never summoned up the courage to ask her out, he had once, before a major exam in the spring, offered to swap tests when it became clear that another low grade would lead to her flunking the class. She had agreed, and he had taken her sloppily typed page as his. Consequently, she had passed the course with a rockbottom C and Charlie's grade had dropped from an A to a B. After graduation and the army, he had never seen her again until now.

"Have you been in Saratoga all this time?" Charlie asked.

She shook her head. "We just came back about three years ago. I married Neal right out of high school. He'd been working at the track and was only up here for August. After we married, we moved down to Long Island. Neal had a job as a groom for a trainer at Belmont. We were down there nearly twenty years."

"Why'd you come back?"

"My dad was sick. Then when he died, he left me a couple of cottages out on Hedges Lake near Cambridge and we've been trying to sell them." As she spoke, she kept pushing her fingers through her gray hair, as if making herself more presentable now that she knew that Charlie wasn't a stranger.

"Is that where Neal is?" asked Charlie.

She didn't say anything at first, then said: "He wouldn't tell me what was wrong. I knew he was scared though. After he left, I heard about Mr. Ackerman. Neal liked Ackerman. I mean, he wasn't mixed up with his murder, if that's what you're thinking."

"I wasn't thinking anything," said Charlie, "I just want to talk to him." He kept searching Janet's face for the young face burned beneath the age and sharp lines. He wondered what she saw in his own face. She looked like she'd had a difficult time. If her husband had worked around race tracks for twenty years, he guessed she probably had.

"You have any kids?" Charlie asked.

Janet looked surprised. "A daughter. She's grown up now. Last I heard she was living in Omaha."

"How do I get to this cottage?"

She stood by the sink, rubbing her left arm with her right hand as if she were cold. "Don't let him know I told you, don't even let him know you've seen me." She paused again, raised her shoulders, then let them drop. "Go north on Route 22 from Cambridge, then turn left just before Dead Lake, then take your first right. After about a mile, you'll come to a bunch of cottages on the water side of the lake. Neal will be in the seventh one. It's red with a screened-in porch. You can't miss it."

"What kind of car is he driving?"

"He's got a motorcycle: a red Honda 750."

"What's he been doing out there?"

"He said he was going to do some painting." She paused and walked over to a yellow Formica table. She wore fluffy blue slippers that made a scratching noise on the linoleum floor. "He said he was going to call me, but he hasn't. I don't know, just don't tell him I said a word."

"Is there a phone out there?"

"No."

"Does he drink?"

"Not any more."

"Why do you think something was bothering him?"

"He was jumpy, that's all. Maybe he'd been working too hard."

"That's not enough of a reason."

The woman shrugged. She had narrow, pointy shoulders and Charlie couldn't imagine anyone embracing them or, as he once had, desiring to embrace them. "He had a gun in his bureau drawer. It's not there now. He must have taken it with him."

6

▼▼▼

"SO THIS GUY, see, he was a druggist and one Sunday I popped by his house to see how he was doin. We were friends, right? So I get there and troop up the steps like some little bimbo sellin Girl Scout cookies and just as I'm raising my hand to hammer away at his door I catch a glimpse through a gap in the curtains as to what's going on inside. Charlie, I tell you, it changed my life."

"What was it?" asked Charlie. He had asked Victor to come with him out to Hedges Lake. Charlie was driving his yellow Volkswagen and they had just passed through the small town of Greenwich. It was noon and hot and after they saw Claremon, Charlie had promised he would buy Victor lunch at the hotel in Cambridge which claimed to have invented pie a la mode. Victor liked pie a la mode.

"There was my buddy," Victor continued, "sittin in the middle of the living room floor wearin nothing but a huge diaper and holdin a baby bottle with one of those rubber nipples. Standin above him is a frau I take to be his wife. She's dressed up like a nurse with a little peaked white cap and she's shaking a finger at him, you know, scoldin him. Well, he drops his bottle and begins to bawl. This guy, he's fifty if he's a day and while he doesn't have much more hair than a baby, neither does a baby have a walrus moustache."

"What'd you do?" asked Charlie.

"Like an Arab, I packed up my tents and tiptoed away. Never told him I'd come visitin and never went again. Now and then we'd meet for a beer, but it wasn't the same. That diaper was always on the table between us, so to speak. Anyway, maybe it was like that with Ackerman."

"I don't follow you," said Charlie. Sometimes he felt destined to be dragged along after Victor's monologues like a cat on a leash. Looking ahead, he saw the Green Mountains rising over the green fields and white Victorian farmhouses. Charlie downshifted at a sharp left curve. In front of the Easton Volunteer Fire Department, a small collie dog prepared to dash out at the Volkswagen, then fell to scratching itself.

"Jesus, Charlie, what I been sayin is that maybe Ackerman led some secret life that nobody knew about and maybe whoever bumped him off was tied into that life. I mean, I can't picture Ackerman in diapers, but it could of been, you know, anything. Like where did he go Tuesday night after he ditched Krause? You gotta admit that's suspicious. Think of all the people that go loopy over rubber raincoats. Maybe there's a connection. You're the hotshot investigator, get crackin."

"I'm not investigating anything."

"Yeah, well, what're you doin drivin thirty miles out to some lake? Just soakin up the summer sun?"

Charlie had to admit Victor had a point. "I want to find out why Claremon hasn't come to work."

Even as he said this, Charlie felt vaguely hypocritical since he had never told Victor that Claremon felt it necessary to take a gun out to the cottage.

"Well, maybe I'm just a dumb, old ex-haberdasher and ex-New York super, but if I was investigatin who knocked off Mr. Ackerman, who was the only man of breeding I've come across up here in this two-bit horse hole, present company excepted, I'd try to find out what he did that Tuesday night." Victor leaned back, linked his hands behind his head, and stretched. He wore a gray sweat shirt that matched his gray fluffy hair, and a pair of gray work pants. He often dressed like this and Charlie thought it made him look like a small rain cloud. Victor looked out the window and began to whistle a phrase from "Camptown Races."

"Nice country around here," he said. "By the way, you scored yet with that waitress from the Backstretch?"

With slight irritation, Charlie wondered if there was something particularly interesting about his life which attracted people's attention or if all people had to put up with such scrutiny. As a shy man, Charlie often asked questions because he couldn't think of anything else to say; but while Victor might have problems, Charlie felt that shyness wasn't one of them.

"We've gone out to dinner once," he said. "She says she doesn't want to get involved with anyone until her divorce is settled."

"You meet her in the Backstretch? Is that why you hang out in that dump?"

"No, I met her before that. I mean, I didn't actually meet her, but I saw her."

Charlie didn't feel like explaining this so he shut up. He had first seen Doris Bailes walking through Congress Park near the

Canfield Casino. Not that he had really seen that much of her. It had been late November and snowing and Doris had been wearing a heavy green down jacket with a hood. It was fresh snow and theirs were the first tracks. Charlie had gone out to see what had happened to the ducks in the pond surrounding the bandstand. For several weeks, their swimming space had been decreasing as each day the pond froze a little more. The previous day the five ducks had been limited to an area six feet across. This particular morning the pond had been completely frozen and the ducks were gone, whether caught beneath the surface or rescued Charlie never knew. In their place, as it were, had been this woman walking along the perimeter of the pond. As she passed Charlie, she had said, "Good morning," in a businesslike way and continued on without slowing. If she had slowed, Charlie would have asked her about the ducks; but since she didn't, he only stared after her departing figure. As he watched, the woman stopped and lay down in the snow. At first Charlie thought she might be sick, then he saw she was making a snow angel. After a moment, she got up, looked at the indentation and walked on just as businesslike. Charlie had started to follow her, but halted at the snow angel, which he had studied for a long time. Some days later he discovered she worked at the Backstretch.

Victor shook his head and made a clucking noise with his tongue. "Look, Charlie, you won't get anywhere bein a nice guy. The truth is broads don't even like nice guys. You've got to give her a line that makes you entirely different from any dumbo in her past. You know that woman you saw me hassling last week at the Triple Crown? The one that walked out?"

Charlie remembered an attractive woman in her early forties. "What about her?"

"Just that she finally saw things my way, but believe me, I couldn't just shimmer all over like a good soldier until she decided to sleep with me for the pure virtue of the act, no, I had to make myself verbally enticing."

"What'd you say?" Charlie didn't believe that he himself could ever be verbally enticing.

"Told her that I had cancer, that I had maybe two months to live."

"You serious?"

"God's truth."

"What's going to happen when she sees you still walking around?"

"I don't know," said Victor, scratching his chin, "but whatever I say, it should be good for another date."

Cambridge, like Greenwich, was another heavily treed town of white Victorian and Colonial houses, but while the stores in Greenwich suffered economically from being too close to Saratoga, Cambridge seemed to be thriving. Charlie turned north on Route 22 and in five more minutes had reached the turnoff before Dead Lake.

The cottages bordering Hedges Lake were small and packed together. Victor counted them off in his Lawrence Welk voice and at the seventh one, Charlie pulled over and cut the engine.

Neal Claremon's cottage appeared deserted, windows closed, curtains drawn. It seemed to have about three rooms while attached to the front was a large screened porch which ran the width of the cottage. About ten feet of sand separated it from its neighbors. The cottage had been painted bright red and attached to the roof of the porch was a white sign with the words: "Home At Last." Charlie knocked on the porch door. There was no answer

"Nobody home there," shouted a voice. Charlie turned to see a man half leaning out of a gable window of the cottage to his right. "Nobody been there since Saturday."

Charlie nodded, opened the screen door, walked across the porch to the front door and knocked again. There was no answer. On the porch was an old brown sofa and two overstuffed chairs, as well as some aluminum lawn chairs. Charlie tried the door. It was locked. The window in its center was covered with a blue curtain and he couldn't see around it.

"I just told you, there's nobody home," called the man next door. "You ever hear of criminal trespass?" The head disappeared and Charlie assumed the man was coming downstairs.

The small lake was ringed with cottages. Out on the water, at least a dozen motorboats were towing water skiers. Charlie went around the left side of the cottage and began trying to look through windows. Victor followed him.

"You'd think that furniture on the porch would get wet," Victor said.

Through a crack beneath the shade of a kitchen window, Charlie saw a box of Ritz Crackers and a wedge of moldy cheese. The rest of the windows seemed to be completely covered by curtains, but then, on the right side of the house, Charlie found a living room window where the curtain had been folded back against the sill, leaving an opening about the size of his thumb. Charlie knelt down beside it, but even with this small peephole, the room was still too dark to see anything.

"Victor, get my flashlight from the car."

"Shonuff, bossman."

A door slammed next door and a portly man of about fifty in tartan plaid Bermuda shorts and a yellow and green striped shirt came bustling toward them. "I told you and told you," he said, "there's nobody home. You gonna leave or am I gonna call the cops?"

As Charlie straightened up, his attention was caught by the man's sneakers which were white with the word "disco" printed all over them in different kinds of lettering. "Neal Claremon works for me," he said, "and I want to know where he is."

"Could of fooled me. You don't look like Ackerman, you don't look like a dead man. You think I'm dumb or something?"

Charlie took a business card from his wallet. "I'm Charles Bradshaw, chief of security, Lorelei Stables. This is my assistant, Victor Plotz."

Victor clicked his heels together as he handed Charlie the flashlight.

"You want to call the police," said Charlie, "then go ahead. When was the last time you saw Claremon?" Charlie knelt down to the space between the curtain and windowsill, trying

to keep his eye to the hole and shine the light in the room at
the same time.

"Claremon was around on Saturday, said he had some painting to do. Why you peeking through that window?"

But Charlie didn't answer. He had seen a tiny portion of the
wheel of a motorcycle and something else that made him get
up and walk rapidly around the corner of the cottage and
across the screened porch to the front door. It never occurred
to him that he ought to call the police. For a moment, he
forgot he wasn't a policeman himself. Turning slightly and balancing on his left foot, he kicked the door a little below the
knob. The glass rattled, but the door stayed shut.

"Here now," shouted the man with disco sneakers, "that's
private property."

Charlie ignored him and kicked again harder. This time the
door sprung open, swung around and hit the wall with a crash.
Through the door, almost leaping through it Charlie thought
later, came the sweet, heavy smell of decomposing flesh. Charlie caught his breath, then groped around the corner for a light
switch, found one, and flicked it on. What he saw, he had seen
many times in his twenty years as a policeman, but even after
this long he couldn't see a corpse without wanting to throw
up. He turned back to the man from next door.

"You want the police? Then call them. Make sure you also
call Chief Peterson in Saratoga. Give him my name and tell
him he should get out here."

Without waiting for the man's response, Charlie turned back
to the open doorway. Victor started to walk across the porch,
then sniffed, then stopped.

"I know what's in there," he said, "but if you think I'm
going to take a look, you're wackola."

There was no furniture in the room and the walls had recently been painted white. Mixed with the smell of rotting flesh
was the smell of fresh paint. A man whom Charlie assumed to
be Neal Claremon lay on his stomach near the opening to the
kitchen. He wore only a dark blue bathing suit with white trim
and in his back were six red holes. He was a small man and
very thin and lay sprawled on the floor as if he had been

dropped there. Nearly the entire floor was covered with a partially dried layer of his blood. It had been the blood which Charlie had caught a glimpse of through the window. With his left arm flung forward and his right arm reaching back, Claremon appeared to be swimming through it. Parked in the middle of this red lake was a bright red motorcycle.

7

▼▼▼

"I STILL DON'T SEE what reason you had kicking open the door, Charlie. I mean, any way you cut it that amounts to interfering with police business."

Charlie stuck his hands in his pockets and glanced out at the lake where it seemed even more people were now water-skiing. As he looked, an attractive woman in a yellow bikini shot by Claremon's small dock and waved at the policemen. "There was no way of knowing Claremon was dead," Charlie said lamely.

"After five days what the hell you figure he's doing there on the floor? Humping a board?" Peterson put his hands on his hips and grinned at Charlie. It wasn't a pleasant grin. He was a tall man, about three or four inches over six feet, who liked to accentuate his height by bouncing on his toes. As usual, he wore a three-piece blue suit with a silver chain across his large stomach. Peterson was about forty-five, had thick, black hair, and a hoarse voice. People said he looked more like a senator than a police chief. Actually, his title was Director of Public Safety, but to most people he was simply Chief.

"It seemed best to find out," said Charlie.

"Why'd you come out here in the first place?"

"I told you, we're shorthanded at the stable. Claremon had called in sick. I thought he was out here drinking."

There were a dozen police cars from the State Police, Cambridge police, sheriff's department, Salem and Greenwich police, plus two cars from Saratoga. Four or five of the policemen

were holding back a crowd of gawkers dressed mostly in bathing suits, who were hoping to see the body removed. The rest
of the police wandered around the outside of the cottage waiting for the arrival of the State Police lab crew. Charlie guessed
the case would be handled by the State Police and the Washington County sheriff's department. In any event, Peterson was
basically a visitor.

Charlie and Peterson stood near the right-hand corner of the
porch. Through the front door of the cottage, Charlie could
see Claremon's blood in the bright living room light as if the
blood itself were a beacon which had drawn together policemen and gawkers alike. The only person who appeared uninter-
ested was Victor Plotz who had taken off his shoes and was
sitting at the end of Claremon's dock dabbling his feet in the
water.

Although the various policemen were certainly serious and
even somber, Charlie detected that element of vindication
which he had observed before on similar occasions, as if the
police felt energized by this fresh example of foul behavior:
behavior which once more proved their importance to the community. It made him again grateful that he had quit his job
with the Saratoga police department.

"How're you coming with the Ackerman investigation?"
asked Charlie, trying to keep his voice toneless but polite.

Peterson clasped his hands behind his back and nodded to
a deputy from Salem. "It's moving along. You know how it
is: Bit by bit you find all the pieces. Lots of elbow grease and
good luck. Had a piece of good luck last night as a matter of
fact. Some kid turned up the white raincoat, rain hat, and an
old nylon stocking in a garage about two blocks from the
YMCA."

"Can you trace it?" asked Charlie.

"Nah, it's old stuff. Came from Sears. I gotta man on it,
but it looks like a dead end."

"What did ballistics say about the gun?"

"Seems to have been a European jobby, a .9mm." Peterson
looked disapprovingly at Charlie. He had thick black eyebrows
which Charlie suspected he brushed down to make him look

more foreboding. "Just what's your interest in the matter?" he asked.

"Lew was my friend and I worked for him."

"Well, you know, we're following up a number of leads. I can't say we've got anything definite yet, but on the other hand I think we've covered a lot of ground."

Charlie, who had heard Peterson deliver speeches like this hundreds of times, found himself clenching his teeth. Glancing away, he caught the eye of Claremon's chubby neighbor, whose name had turned out to be Patrick Truesdale. The man wore an expression of superior gloating and it occurred to Charlie that Truesdale thought he was being arrested.

"Do you plan to arrest Field?" asked Charlie abruptly.

Peterson raised himself on tiptoe and balanced there a second before dropping back down. "Charlie, I can't possibly discuss such matters, I mean, how can you think . . ."

"Do you have evidence against him?"

"How can you think I would reveal . . ."

"What do you plan to do about Claremon?"

"As far as I can tell, it's not my case."

Looking away, Charlie tried to define his mood to himself. He felt frustrated and angry, but he wasn't sure why. He hoped it simply wasn't a matter of having his feelings hurt because Peterson wouldn't confide in him. Glancing toward the lake, he saw Victor skimming stones into the water.

"Claremon worked for Ackerman five days," Charlie said. "He was a loner who Ackerman hired himself. A groom described Claremon to me as nervous and jumpy. Anyway, the minute he learns that Ackerman was shot he comes here to hide out. Not only that, he brings a gun. Later that day, somebody comes and shoots him with a silenced revolver. Not only that, but I bet ballistics will show you it was the same gun that killed Ackerman, your .9mm European jobby."

"How do you know the gun had a silencer?"

"He was shot six times. You think one of these neighbors wouldn't have telephoned? Talk to that guy over there in the striped shirt and see if he heard anything or if Claremon had any visitors."

"You know, Charlie, you're taking a lot of liberties for a private citizen."

There was a stirring in the crowd as the ambulance arrived followed by the State Police lab crew in a blue van. Charlie watched them walk toward the cottage, cross the screened porch, then stop at the door as they realized they couldn't walk into the room without walking through Claremon's blood. One of the ambulance attendants ran to the blue van, took five pair of black rubbers from the back and ran back to the other men on the porch. The five men pulled on the rubbers, then delicately entered the cottage on tiptoe.

"I'm not taking liberties," said Charlie. "I'm just pointing out some information that you might find useful. I'll be telling exactly the same stuff to the State Police and I thought you might like to get the jump on them before they come and start telling you your job."

An hour later Charlie was driving back to Saratoga with Victor. Although it was nearly four o'clock and he hadn't eaten, he didn't feel hungry. Both had decided against pie a la mode at the Cambridge hotel: Charlie because his stomach didn't feel like it and Victor out of sympathy. Later Charlie wanted to go swimming, put in his half mile, but he doubted he would get the time. He found himself on edge as if there were crumbs in his bed or his shoes were too tight. He kept thinking of Claremon's living room as he had last seen it, filled with high-power lights, while lab men tiptoed around dusting for fingerprints. He had watched the ambulance attendants roll Claremon clumsily onto a stretcher. His eyes had been open and his expression was one of faint surprise, as if he'd just understood the punch line of a joke. Then they had covered him with a red blanket and carried him out to the satisfaction of the waiting crowd. Several people in bathing suits had taken photographs, while one woman carefully pointed out what was happening to twin girls in a stroller.

Afterward, Charlie talked to a State Police lieutenant he had known for about fifteen years, as well as a Washington County deputy with whom he occasionally went trout fishing in the

Battenkill. Both had been friendlier than Peterson, but Charlie felt ill at ease and cut off. After describing Claremon's connection with Ackerman, Charlie wanted to give some suggestions as to what they might look for, but the lieutenant politely made it clear they neither wanted nor sought his advice. Basically, Charlie was a private citizen, an outsider.

Out at the lake, Victor had mostly stayed out of the way, except for posing for some photographs as the-man-who-found-the-body. As they rode back to Saratoga, he whistled bits of songs to himself and looked out the window. Charlie couldn't tell if he was thinking or just letting his mind ride empty.

"So whatcha going to do now?" said Victor at last.

"What do you mean?"

"Are you going to investigate or not investigate?"

"I can't do anything, Victor. . . ."

"Vic."

"Sure, sure, but look, I'm a stable guard. I just can't go barging around."

"You're chief of security at Lorelei Stables."

Charlie glanced at Victor to see if he was serious, then looked back barely in time to avoid a tractor which was pulling out onto the road. Victor gave the finger to the kid driving the tractor.

"Vic, that means nothing. It's like saying I'm king of the moon."

"You got five guards workin under you. Make 'em help."

"It's not my business. Let the cops do it."

"So what do you feel like doin right now? I mean, you want to get a few beers and cruise the drive-ins?"

"No thanks, I've got to break the news to Claremon's wife. Peterson would make a mess of it."

"You going to ask her any questions about her husband?"

"I might."

"I see," said Victor. He pulled the collar of his gray sweat shirt out past his chin, blew down the opening several times, then began fanning his face with his hand. "So perhaps it could be said," he continued, "that while you're not exactly investigating, you are investigating more than you were this morning. Right?"

Charlie looked out across the rolling pastures spotted with dairy cows. Many of the hills were topped with trees and in the distance he could see the hazy beginnings of the Adirondacks. He told himself he liked this countryside better than any other and he knew that Ackerman had felt the same way.

"That's right," he said at last.

8

▼▼▼

C HARLIE STOPPED HIS VOLKSWAGEN in front of Claremon's house on Maple Avenue and cut the engine, but instead of getting out he sat with his hands on the wheel. He had dropped Victor off uptown, saying he might meet him that evening at the Backstretch.

Looking up Maple Avenue, Charlie could see a small white house which his mother had rented about ten years before; see another house where a girl had lived whom he had once had a crush on, a girl later killed when she was thrown by a horse; see a house where six brothers lived whom Charlie had coached in Little League baseball. It often seemed to Charlie that his memories were realer than the flickering present that appeared to surround him. As he sat in his car on this Wednesday afternoon in late July, he felt the presence of those past days like seeing different colored threads in a piece of fabric.

Ackerman too had been interested in the past and, partly because of Charlie's encouragement, had begun reading about Saratoga history the same time Charlie had begun to swim at the Y. Most recently Ackerman had begun to study Richard Canfield, the prince of Saratoga gamblers who had closed his casino in 1907 to concentrate on his art collection. Ackerman had been drawn to Canfield, because both men had freed themselves from the poverty of their youth by running poker games in their teens and early twenties. But while Canfield had gone on to build greater and greater casinos, Ackerman had turned to horses, giving up all other types of gambling which he claimed were close to robbery. Canfield had always been honest in telling people that if they gambled they would lose; but he argued against the intermittent closing of the casinos by reformers by saying, "They gambled in the Garden of Eden and they will again if there's another one."

Ackerman had quoted this to Charlie several weeks before, and had added, "That may be true of Eden, but it won't happen here. Gambling ruins a town."

They had been sitting in Ackerman's office at the stable and Frank Warner had chosen that moment to come in to discuss a nervous horse that required a goat tethered in its stall to keep it calm. Charlie wanted to ask Ackerman if he thought there was any chance of a resumption of gambling in Saratoga, but he had never been able to get back to it. Sitting in his Volkswagen in front of Neil Claremon's house, he wondered if he ought to have gotten back to it. But there were dozens of half-completed conversations with Ackerman which he had thought they would have plenty of time to finish. This in fact became another aspect of his grief: that he hadn't had time to ask Ackerman about some horse or book or ask his advice about some problem with his swimming or tell him of a crooked gambler he had been reading about: John North who had been lynched by vigilantes in Vicksburg and whose roulette wheel had been "tied up to his dangling body" as a caution to other gamblers.

One of the pains of Ackerman being dead was that Charlie kept vividly remembering him in all the situations he had ever known him, making it seem as if he were haunted by dozens of Ackermans. As Charlie got out of his car, he realized he had a similar problem with Mrs. Claremon.

It was difficult to think of the woman inside the small renovated garage as the middle-aged wife of the man whose body he had discovered at Hedges Lake and also as the girl who had sat next to him in typing class. Yet his memory of seeing Mrs. Claremon that morning was no more vivid than his memories of Janet Macomb in typing class, and now Charlie had to go in and tell little Janet Macomb that her husband had been shot six times in the back. Well, better him than that fool Peterson.

Charlie crossed the sidewalk, stepping over and around the kiddy debris—tipped-over tricycle, pots and kitchen utensils, tin pail and shovel—to the front door, and knocked. Janet Macomb or Mrs. Claremon, both names registered equally in Charlie's mind, must have been watching because she opened the door immediately.

Looking at her, Charlie searched her narrow face for traces of the younger girl and although he found them in her eyes and cheekbones, it still seemed as if Janet Macomb were wearing a mask like those Japanese theater masks he had once seen on television.

"I'd like to talk to you," he said.

Janet stood back and Charlie walked past her to the kitchen which was bright and sunny and didn't have the living room's cheap pine panelling which Charlie hated. Janet followed but stopped in the doorway with her hand on the frame as Charlie turned and looked at her. He knew she could tell something was wrong.

"I'm sorry to have to do this to you," Charlie said, "but your husband's been killed." As soon as he had uttered the words, Charlie judged himself for saying the wrong ones; but he had broken this sort of news to the survivors many many times and each time he judged himself for not doing it carefully enough, although he didn't know how he could ever say it to make it all right.

Janet Claremon didn't appear to react. She looked down at the floor. Then, for a moment, she seemed smaller to Charlie. Even her blue checked gingham dress now seemed too big for her, as if she were trying to draw in her body, reduce it to the smallest possible size. The sun came in through the window over the kitchen sink, making the yellow Formica table sparkle.

"Was it the motorcycle?" she said at last.

"He was shot. The police will come and tell you about it, but I wanted to tell you first."

"Why would anyone shoot him?"

"The police don't know."

She looked at him briefly with large brown eyes, then looked away again. "What happened?"

"I don't know either. I found him in the cottage. He'd been shot several times in the back. Apparently he's been dead for a few days."

"You mean he's just been lying out there?"

Charlie nodded.

Janet walked slowly to a wooden chair by the table and sat down. She noticed a spot on the yellow Formica and began to pick at it. Her fingernails were long and red, and Charlie remembered that years before she had worried that typing would damage them.

"Do you mind if I ask you some questions about your husband?" said Charlie. He went to the sink, filled a glass with water, and handed it to Janet, who took the glass and set it down without drinking.

"I guess not."

"Do you know why he was frightened?"

She dipped her fingers in the glass of water and touched them to her eyes. As if she were giving herself tears, thought Charlie.

"No, I asked him what was wrong, but he wouldn't say. He could be awfully touchy."

"How long had he seemed frightened?"

"I don't know, maybe I noticed it about ten days ago. But he wasn't really frightened, just that something was bothering him. When he heard Mr. Ackerman had been killed, that's when he really seemed frightened."

Charlie leaned against the sink and looked over at the small woman sitting at the table. It was almost with surprise that he realized he was asking her questions which were basically none of his business. "Had your husband known Ackerman a long time?" he asked.

"I don't think so, at least he never mentioned him before. He must of known who he was though. I mean you couldn't spend twenty years working at race tracks and not know who he was."

"Who did your husband work for before Ackerman?"

"Mr. Dwyer. First down on Long Island for ten years, then up here."

"Why did he leave?"

"I don't know. I mean, I don't know if he quit or was fired. Sometimes he just wouldn't talk, but I know he was upset when he left and I know he liked Mr. Dwyer."

"When did he leave Dwyer?"

"A little over two weeks ago."

Robert Dwyer had been at the track for as long as Charlie could remember. He had a stable on the west side of Saratoga, across the highway from the Saratoga Spa State Park. He also had property on Long Island and a farm in Kentucky. Although Charlie knew who he was, he'd never actually spoken to him. He knew, however, that he'd been friends with Ackerman and that Dwyer had given Ackerman a lot of help when the younger man began to buy and train horses. From what Charlie had heard, Dwyer had turned over much of the control of his stable to his son-in-law, Wayne Curry. Dwyer had had a stroke some years before and was still confined to a wheelchair. Whenever Charlie saw him in public—at a concert at the Performing Arts Center or at a restaurant—he was always being wheeled by Curry. It was the son-in-law, Charlie remembered, who pushed Dwyer forward when he delivered the eulogy at Ackerman's funeral, and had then stood the whole time as if at attention.

"And your husband said nothing that would give you any idea why he left Dwyer's stable?" said Charlie.

"No, I asked him, but he ignored me. Sometimes, when things were bothering him, he'd go out on his motorcycle. He did that a lot after he left Dwyer."

Charlie watched her sit with her hands in her lap. She was so thin that he could see the sharp points where her bones pressed against the fabric of her dress. Although he guessed she hadn't had much of a marriage, he was sorry her husband had been killed and wished her pain was like a cloak so he could lift it from her. That he had once had a slight crush on her didn't matter. Charlie had always been prone to useless crushes and sometimes it seemed that half the women in Saratoga had at one time or other unwittingly received his attention.

Along with Charlie's sorrow at the death of Janet's husband, he felt angry that there was somebody around who thought he could just erase people as if they were no more than a smudge on a blackboard. And although he didn't, like Jack Krause, wish he could destroy this person himself, he wished that Peterson could somehow blossom into the perfect policeman he had never shown himself to be in the past.

"Is there anything I can do for you?" asked Charlie.

"No, you've been very kind. I just need some time by myself, I guess."

"You have enough money?"

She nodded but didn't speak.

Charlie considered asking her not to tell Peterson that he had been there, instead he said, "Will you call me if you remember anything your husband might have said about why he was frightened or why he left Dwyer's stable?" He gave her his card and wrote his home phone number on it.

She nodded again, then said, "Are you working with the police?"

"No," said Charlie, "I've nothing to do with the police."

9
▼▼▼

"NOW LOOK ME IN THE EYE," said Victor leaning over the bar, "the reason you won't be Charlie's girl is that you're stuck on me. Is that right?" Then he laughed and scratched his head.

Doris Bailes set his drink down before him. "I just can't resist men with hair like dirty cotton candy," she said.

"Dirty hair, clean heart," said Victor. He was sitting on a stool at the Backstretch waiting for Charlie. It was just past six and Victor was beginning on his third vodka collins. Doris had come to work a few minutes before and now Victor was trying to get her going, as he expressed it to himself. At the end of the bar, the young blond stripper was waiting for the Chinese restaurant to close so she could begin work.

"See here," said Victor, "you come over to my place and I'll show you my tattoo."

"Why can't you show me here?" Doris had begun washing glasses, and the steam from the hot water tap made her cheeks turn red. She wore a white blouse and jeans. Around her neck was a thin gold chain.

"Not private enough."

"Is it dirty?"

"No, but I'm the only guy you'll ever meet with a picture of President Nixon tattooed on his ass. What the hell, it was cheaper than the butterfly. You like cats? You could come over and see my cat. He's only got one eye. Or I could show you my swatch collection."

"Your what?"

"Swatches. You know, samples of fabric. Started collecting them when I sold men's clothing, then stopped when I got fired. Must have over a thousand. Seemed a shame to throw them out. Would you like them?"

"What would I do with them?"

Victor shrugged. Although he took pleasure in cracking wise, as he called it, he knew he was becoming a little maniacal. But the discovery of Claremon's body that afternoon had unnerved him; and whenever he thought of it, he could see that awful red cottage; and even though he had refrained from looking at the body, his imagination was doing its best to invent its own grisly picture. In any case, he enjoyed talking to Doris Bailes. Not that he would actually make a pass at her, but he liked how she seemed to be her own person. Victor, who knew he had a tendency to act up a little—he wouldn't go so far as to call it showing off—felt that Doris would always be consistent, behaving the same way before a crowd of people or by herself.

"Tell me the truth," asked Victor, "are you sweet on some third party?"

Doris pushed her brown hair out of her eyes with the back of one hand. "I'm not sweet on anyone at the moment. Why can't I just be happy by myself? It's cheaper that way, safer too."

"You're too pretty for that. Maybe you're holdin the torch for some guy in prison or some guy in the army who right now is slogging his way through the Georgia swamps. You know what they say, lovin keeps you young."

"Is that what keeps you so young?"

"You better believe it. I got skin like a baby. But seriously, why won't you let Charlie fall to one knee and pop the question: decent guy, steady habits, reads books, doesn't snore. If I wasn't committed to broads, I'd take up with him myself."

Doris raised her eyebrows. "You'd look cute on a dance floor." Then she paused and asked: "You think Charlie will investigate Ackerman's murder?"

"Where'd you hear that?"

"A groom from Ackerman's stable was in here talking about it."

Victor drank some of his drink. "News gets around, right? Charlie don't know it yet, but he's hot on the scent. That Peterson, he's on the case nearly a week and nothin happens. Charlie takes over and right the first day he finds another murder. Now that's what I call investigatin." Victor described driving out to Hedges Lake and finding Claremon's body. He also wanted to say how he felt when he saw the ambulance attendants hurry out with the body on the stretcher covered with a red blanket, but he couldn't find the right words.

"It must have been terrible."

"Yeah, I been feeling queasy all day. Give me another one of those vodka collinses, will you?"

As she made his drink, Victor looked at the photographs of boxers: Billy Conn, Gorilla Jones, Fritzie Zivic. He didn't recognize the names, but figured Charlie must know who they were. Actually, Victor had never been much of a boxing fan. It was too clean. Wrestling was what he liked, Australian tag teams. But mostly he didn't like sports, didn't like just watching things, although years before he had enjoyed bird watching, but that had been when his kid was little and things were easier. Victor still had on his gray sweat shirt. Continuing to look at the boxers on the wall, he reached his right hand down through his collar and scratched his chest.

Doris handed him his drink. "Does Charlie have any ideas about who might have killed Ackerman?"

"Yeah, he must have. You know Charlie though, he stays pretty quiet about what he's thinking. But I'll tell you something: last Tuesday night Ackerman ditched his bodyguard and went off by himself. Now I'm not sure if that's a clue or evidence or suspicious or what the fuck you want to call it, but I find it interesting."

"What if I told you he was in here?"

"You're kidding."

"I'm sure it was Tuesday," said Doris, "because I had a trotter that won that night and I bought everyone at the bar a drink. Ackerman had a straight tomato juice."

Doris stood with her hands on the bar facing Victor. The way she squinted her eyes as she remembered reminded Victor of a cashier who had worked with him at the men's clothing store on Madison. In those days, Victor had been firmly married and never drank. He had never even fantasized about this woman until years later, long after she had quit and he'd been fired.

"You mean Ackerman ditched his bodyguard," said Victor, "just so he could come here and drink tomato juice? He must of been sweet on you too."

Doris shook her head. "No, he must have been someplace else as well, because he came in around ten o'clock and stayed about fifteen minutes."

"Did he come here often?"

"Maybe every couple of months. I've never really talked to him, although I recognized him of course. He was a handsome man."

"What'd he act like? Think he'd been seein a broad?"

"I don't think so. He seemed angry. I said a few words to him and although he wasn't exactly unfriendly, he seemed preoccupied."

"How d'you mean? Did he act funny in some way?"

"No, I mean, he was usually pretty friendly and that night,

I don't know, he seemed quiet and angry. He didn't talk to anyone. Just sat at the bar and drank his tomato juice."

"I'd feel better if you'd seen him kick a cat. Did he say anything about what he was doing over here?"

Another customer had come in and Doris paused to draw him a beer. Victor watched her figure as she walked away and decided it was time to call up one of his girlfriends. The sooner the better. When Doris came back, he said, "You still joggin? Say, I wasn't jokin about showin you that tattoo. It shows Nixon with that little dog of his. The dog's a real knockout. Okay, okay, tell me about Ackerman."

"It wasn't much. I asked him what he was doing over here and he said he had some stuff to take care of."

"Stuff?"

"That's what he said."

"You know how he was getting around since Krause wasn't there to drive him?"

"I don't know how he got here, but one of the regulars gave him a ride home."

"Yeah, who's that?"

"A stooper by the name of Wally Berrigan."

"A what?"

"A stooper, you know, someone that picks up tickets at the track, hoping to find a winning one that someone's dropped."

"Seems like a great way to earn a living. Have any idea where he lives?"

"In a rooming house on Phila, just past Lena's." Lena's was a coffee shop that had folk music on the weekends. "I've seen him sitting on the front porch."

"Maybe I'll have a word with him," said Victor. "Do me a favor, will you, don't tell Charlie about this."

"Why not?" She tilted her head slightly as she looked at him. Victor thought it made her look like an intelligent bird. Nothing like an owl. Maybe some kind of partridge or grouse. Anyway, it was a bird he liked.

"I want to surprise him," he said.

10

▼▼▼

A S HE DROVE DOWN the northeastern shore of Saratoga Lake, Charlie thought it must have been along here that Old Smoke Morrissey had built the grandstands from which people could watch the boat races he had introduced during the Civil War. Thousands had come to see the international amateur races and then, later on, the intercollegiate regattas. In the evening, sportsmen could continue their quest for action in Old Smoke's casino: an activity from which women and the male residents of Saratoga Springs had been barred.

Charlie wondered if it had been common to exclude town residents from the casinos. He knew that Richard Canfield had kept townspeople out of his casino in the nineties and had been closed Sundays as well in an effort to placate the reformists. Presumably residents, including women, could bet in at least some of the other twenty gambling houses. Charlie recalled that the owner of the track at the time, Gottfried Walbaum, had had a special room where women and children could bet and lose their money in private.

Charlie was sorry that the popularity of boat racing had declined. This evening the lake was spotted with speedboats and sailboats, and Charlie regretted he knew nothing of the professional scullers of the past. He sighed and turned his attention back to the road.

He had decided it was time to see Ackerman's partner, Harvey Field; and instead of meeting Victor at the Backstretch, Charlie was driving out to Field's house on Saratoga Lake. He felt nervous about this, because Field himself made Charlie nervous. He had a sepulchral presence: the sort of man you didn't hear enter a room or see leaving it. He was a small man with light gray eyes and looking at you it seemed he didn't really see you but was looking through to some other place. Charlie had no idea what Field thought of him, no idea if he even knew who Charlie was. Field was the man who handled the money, and among Ackerman's diverse friends and acquaintances, Charlie thought Field one of the strangest.

Charlie also felt nervous, because he knew he had no business to see Field. So far he didn't think of himself as investigating Ackerman's death as much as stumbling into situations which gave him information about that death. But seeing Field was a definite act in his stumbling investigation.

Field lived on a cliff above the lake and the house was approached by a winding, tree-lined driveway marked with signs saying, Private Drive, No Trespassing. Charlie turned left, shifting his Volkswagen into second as he began to climb the hill. He told himself that he also wanted to settle in his mind once and for all whether Field was mixed up with Ackerman's death. If Charlie decided he wasn't involved, then he wanted to ask Field if he would back him in his own investigation. That too made him nervous.

Reaching the top of the hill, Charlie parked by the triple garage door. It was a long, single-story white house with picture windows. In the backyard was a dog run surrounded by a high chain link fence. The dog run seemed almost as long as the house itself. In the front, a sloping yard ran down about one hundred yards to the first trees, giving a panoramic view of the lake. Charlie walked around to the front door. Finding no bell, he knocked. It was a large red door with a small bronze plate with the name "Field" engraved on it. Charlie could hear cars passing down on the road, birds fluttering and chirping among the bushes, and from inside a noise which sounded like growling. It was a warm evening, but the air was so clear he could pick out individual trees on the other side of the lake. Charlie had on his tan suit, and as he waited he tugged at his cuffs and smoothed down his tie.

The door was opened abruptly by a short, round Oriental with black hair cut like a helmet. The man might have been fifty or ninety. "You want?" he said.

"I'd like to see Mr. Field," said Charlie. He gave the man one of the cards that said he was chief of security at Lorelei Stables. The man was about five feet tall and, while not actually as wide as he was high, he gave that impression. He wore a dark suit and steel rim glasses.

"Wait, please." The man shut the door.

When he returned ten minutes later, Charlie had decided he must have interrupted Field's dinner. This made him even more uncomfortable.

"Follow, please."

The small Oriental stood aside to let Charlie enter, then closed and locked the door. The house was dark and much cooler than it had been outside. Charlie followed the man down a long, carpeted hallway with brightly colored prints on the walls. He didn't know any of the artists and some of the pictures appeared no more than squiggles. As he paused to look at a squiggle, he felt something wet touch his left hand. Glancing down, he saw a white Doberman pinscher practically enveloping his hand in its mouth. Charlie gasped and jerked away, trying to pull his hand free. The dog braced itself and tightened its grip, not breaking the skin. It looked up at him calmly with pink eyes.

The man stopped when he heard Charlie make a noise. "Dog won't hurt," he said.

Charlie wanted to say, "But what about me?" Instead he only nodded, not wanting to do anything to upset the white Doberman. His hand tingled and felt wet and clammy. He imagined the Doberman burying it in the backyard. Charlie had never liked the breed, feeling they looked like a sort of sexual weapon, and the albino was probably the least attractive Doberman he had seen. Slowly, he again began to follow the Oriental. The Doberman moved at his side, keeping his hand firmly in its mouth. Because of the dimness of the hall, the white dog was like a light flickering at the corner of his eye.

The man led him to a tiny room at the back of the house furnished only with a desk, two straight chairs and a file cabinet. One window was set high in a light green wall. There were no pictures, but on the floor was a maroon rug.

"Wait here."

Charlie sat down and the dog sat down beside him, still gripping his hand. The man left without glancing at Charlie or the dog. Charlie kept looking at the dog, which looked back at him with its pink eyes. It seemed very alert and ready. Charlie knew that someone like John Wesley Hardin or one of the Dalton boys would have just hauled off and shot the dog.

Field appeared five minutes later. He seemed even thinner and smaller than Charlie remembered. He didn't look at Charlie but went to the chair behind the desk and sat down. A pair of shiny black shoes poked through from underneath.

"I don't have much time," he said. "I told Warner if there was any trouble at the stable he should handle it himself. That being the case, I don't see what you are doing here." He folded his hands in front of him on the blotter. He had on a white shirt, gray pants, and suspenders. His face was a perfect almond shape and just as wrinkled: a gray almond.

"First of all," said Charlie, "maybe you can tell your dog to let go of my hand." Charlie hadn't meant to speak so abruptly, but he was beginning to feel ill-used.

Field, who until that moment had appeared determined and businesslike, sighed and looked uncertainly at the dog. "I'll see what I can do," he said.

Reaching into his pocket, he took out a chrome-plated whistle, which Charlie recognized as an Acme Thunderer. Field raised it to his lips and blew it twice. The noise occupied the room like broken glass in a paper bag. Charlie winced and the dog winced as well but continued to keep a firm grip on Charlie's hand. Field blew the whistle several more times with no more effect than to cause a growing pain in Charlie's ears.

Field put away the whistle and stared at the dog. Then he stood up and walked around the desk. "Swaps," he said, "drop the hand. Swaps!" The dog continued to sit with Charlie's hand in its mouth, looking, Charlie thought, basically contented. Field approached the dog, dropped to one knee and tried to pry open the dog's jaws. For a few moments, Charlie's hand was wrenched this way and that until Field was at last able to force open the jaws and Charlie pulled his hand free.

Field got to his feet. "Now lie down!" The dog lay down in the center of the maroon rug and stared at Field as he returned to his chair behind the desk. When he had sat down and began to breathe more slowly, Field said, "Lew Ackerman gave me that dog. He's named after the first horse that Lew ever won money on." Field hesitated and again there was that uncertain look. "I don't know why he gave it to me. I've never liked dogs."

"Why don't you get rid of it?" asked Charlie.

Field shook his head. "I couldn't do that. Give away Lew's dog? I couldn't do it." He glanced at the dog, which was staring at him attentively with its chin on its crossed front paws. Even its nose was white and its nostrils opened and closed as it breathed. "Anyway," Field continued, "none of this explains what you're doing here."

Charlie looked at the small man, nominally his employer, sitting behind the desk. He had become fragile and comic. As he thought this, Charlie remembered his uncle once furiously pursuing a beagle puppy under the dining room table because he refused to have the dog in the room while he ate dinner. It was difficult to maintain one's dignity while chastising a dog.

"One of the grooms has been murdered," said Charlie. "A man named Neal Claremon who Lew hired about two weeks ago. I found Claremon's body this afternoon." Charlie went on to explain how Warner had thought Claremon was out drinking, how he had gone to Claremon's house and from there to Hedges Lake.

"What I was wondering," said Charlie, "was if you knew anything about Claremon or why Lew hired him?"

As he had told the story, Charlie had seen Field's face close down and become determined and businesslike so that it was impossible to guess what he was thinking. Field had very thin gray hair that was brushed back across his pink scalp. Before he spoke, he smoothed it back with his hands as if brushing cobwebs out of it.

"Certainly, I am shocked," said Field, without showing the least emotion, "but what I don't entirely understand is what this has to do with you. Presumably the police are investigating."

This was just what Charlie didn't want to hear. He stretched in his chair, took a fairly clean handkerchief from his breast pocket, and blew his nose. The white Doberman glanced at him, then looked back at Field.

"I believe," said Charlie, "that Claremon's death is connected to Lew's. I would like to discover what that connection is. Chief Peterson isn't certain there is a connection, although he may change his mind when he gets the ballistics report. Peterson believes that Lew was either murdered by some criminal out of his past or he was murdered by you."

Field sat up as if he had been jabbed. "Are you serious? Why should I kill Lew? He was my best friend."

Charlie shrugged and slowly began to fold his handkerchief. "People told him the two of you had been quarreling. Also you're somewhat mysterious, I mean, the way you live out here by yourself. You're an unknown figure and so people speculate about you."

"Just because I like my privacy . . ." Field hesitated, then continued, "I know nothing about Claremon. Lew and Warner were completely in charge of running the stable."

"I figure," said Charlie, "that Peterson will come out here this evening and ask you some questions about Claremon. Can you prove you didn't know him?"

"How would I know him? I don't even recognize the name. Okay, so Lew and I had a few quarrels, but they didn't mean anything."

"What kind of quarrels?"

"Business quarrels. They don't concern you."

"Why didn't you go to the funeral?"

Field looked away toward the dog. He seemed to Charlie one of those solitary men whose shyness and fear of human contact lead them into sad lives. On top of that, he was also a stubborn man.

"I said my goodbyes at the funeral home the previous evening," said Field, "and I had no desire to have my hand pumped by a lot of fools. Anyway, I don't see why I have to explain myself to you."

"You don't, really. I'm just trying to give you an idea how people are thinking. As I said, people also think Lew might have been killed by some hood, somebody who had known him before and maybe recently got out of prison."

Field shook his head. "Lew knew all kinds of people, but they liked him. He wasn't killed by hoods."

"In that case," said Charlie, "that makes you even more suspect. I mean, if he was either killed by hoods or by you and we take away the hoods, what's left?"

"But I tell you he was my friend," said Field, raising his voice. "I'd known him nearly thirty years."

"How'd you first meet him?" asked Charlie. He had noticed that Field had red splotches of flaky skin on the backs of his hands. Now, as he talked, Field began to pick at them.

"I was an accountant in New York, quite a young man. Lew started talking to me in a restaurant one day at lunchtime. It turned out he had a poker game and supported himself by playing cards. He wasn't even twenty at the time. Finally he asked me if I wanted to invest in him, I don't know, put up a stake of five hundred dollars. We'd been talking about two hours. He was very businesslike and promised me forty percent of what he won. We were sitting at a counter at Schrafft's. I must have been crazy. Anyway, I finally decided it wouldn't be a bad investment. We went to my bank and I gave him five hundred dollars. There was a brightness about him and he seemed to have no doubts about anything. I liked that."

Charlie considered this, trying to imagine the young accountant being basically conned by the even younger Ackerman. "Did you make money?" Charlie asked.

Field laughed. It was a noise like wind in dry leaves. "He nearly lost it, did, in fact, lose most of it. The next morning I thought I'd been a terrible fool. I went to his room before work to demand my money back. He'd lost four hundred dollars the previous night and just smiled at me, said you had to give yourself room to lose. He even asked me for four hundred dollars more, but I thought he was crazy. He was crazy and I was crazy, too. I left and spent the rest of the day kicking myself. The next day, when I was sitting at my desk at work, he walked in. I worked at an insurance company at the time. He walked in past the secretaries, past everybody. I remember he was wearing an immaculate gray tweed suit and he looked like he could have been the son of the president of the company. Anyway, he walked up to my desk and put seven one-hundred-dollar bills down in front of me."

"What'd you do?" asked Charlie.

Field stopped rubbing and picking at his hands and sat staring at them. "I pushed the money back toward him and told him to 'let it ride.' He picked it up, put it back in his pocket, and walked out. After that we won and lost a lot of money together. Won mostly. Anybody who'd think I could kill him, well, that's crazy."

"If I keep looking for Lew's murderer and the police bother me about it, can I tell them that I'm following your instructions?"

"Are you a licensed private detective?"

Charlie had a sinking feeling. "No, I'm just a stable guard, but Lew was one of my best friends, too."

Field thought about this. Then he took a small, black box from his pocket, opened it and removed an ivory toothpick. Tentatively, he explored one of his upper molars.

"No," he said finally, "I can't help you. I don't want to get mixed up with it. Leave it to Peterson." He withdrew the toothpick, replaced it in the box and returned the box to his pocket. The box looked like a miniature coffin. "Anyway," he continued, "I don't think I'll be keeping the stable for long. With Lew dead I don't see much point in living here anymore."

"You'll sell the stable?"

"That's right. Dwyer might buy it."

"Isn't he a little old to be taking on new property?"

"His son-in-law would run it, Wayne Curry. Lew said he was a real hustler. He's been up here to talk to me a couple of times. You know him?"

"I've seen him around." The closest Charlie had ever gotten to Wayne Curry was one night when he and Lew had been having steaks at the Firehouse. Curry had come over to ask a question about some horse that Dwyer had claimed away from Ackerman at Aqueduct a few months before. What struck Charlie was that Curry hadn't bothered to apologize for interrupting and hadn't acknowledged Charlie's presence in any way. He had commented on this to Ackerman a few minutes later. Lew had shrugged and only said, "He's like that." Charlie tried to imagine him running Lorelei Stables.

"Look, Mr. Bradshaw," said Field, "I know you're upset about Lew's death, a lot of people are, but you can't just go racing off hoping to find the killer."

"I was a policeman for twenty years."

"And now you're a stable guard," said Field. "Let it go. Let Peterson do it." Field began rubbing the backs of his hands again. "After all, it's his job."

Five minutes later, Charlie was driving down Field's driveway. It was nearly dark and great rain clouds had begun to build up in the east. Turning onto Route 9p toward town, Charlie saw a blue Chevrolet parked along the side of the road. It was one of the police department's unmarked cars and the man sitting at the wheel, Emmett Van Brunt, was a man Charlie had brought onto the force and worked closely with in the Community and Youth Relations Bureau. Charlie slowed and waved to him. Van Brunt looked the other way.

Charlie had felt disappointed by Field and since leaving his small office he'd been keeping his mind empty, just thinking about where he put his feet and getting into the car and manipulating it down the curving driveway. But then to be ignored by Van Brunt acted as a release for his feelings, and a current of anger swept through him. Almost without thought he slammed on the brake and pulled the Volkswagen over to the side of the road. He walked back to the blue Chevrolet and peered in through the window.

"Didn't you see me, Emmett?" asked Charlie.

Before Van Brunt could answer, a black Buick slowed, then turned into Field's driveway. It was being driven by a Saratoga policeman and Chief Peterson sat in the back seat. At that moment, Peterson was staring at Charlie and Van Brunt.

They watched the car disappear up the driveway, then Van Brunt said, "Shit, Charlie, am I going to get yelled at."

"Did Peterson tell you not to talk to me?"

Van Brunt began to roll up his window. He was a relatively

young man with red curly hair and black horned-rimmed glasses. "Get out of here, Charlie. Go back to your fuckin horses."

A few big drops of rain began hitting the top of the blue Chevrolet. Charlie turned and walked back to his car.

Instead of driving into Saratoga to meet Victor at the Backstretch, Charlie made a U-turn and headed home. It was raining hard by the time he got there. He ran to the cottage and began closing windows. Then he went to the back door and watched the rain make little pockmarks in the gray water until it got too dark to see. He turned back into the kitchen, took some eggs out of the refrigerator, and made a couple of fried egg sandwiches on soft white bread smeared with mayonnaise. As he carried them into the living room along with a beer, he could hear his wife's voice accusing him of eating trashy food, even though he had left her two years before. During the evening, he read about the outlaw empire of John A. Murrel in a book called *The Outlaw Years:* "My mother was of the pure grit: she learnt me and all her children to steal so soon as we could walk. At ten years old I was not a bad hand."

He was just getting into bed when the phone rang. It was Janet Macomb Claremon.

"Charlie? I'm sorry to bother you so late, but I've been thinking about Neal. There was one thing he said about two weeks ago. I don't know if it means anything. He never talked much and when he said this I guess he said it as much to himself as to me."

"What was it?" asked Charlie.

"He said something like, 'There's nothing worse than a stable fire.' "

"Is that all?"

"That's right. He said that and when I asked him what he was talking about, he wouldn't say any more."

11

▼▼▼

"WHAT HE SAID was that Hyde Street was all dug up and you couldn't even walk down the sidewalk in some places. I then said they were fixin the sewer and he said that would do it and then I asked him if he was going to have any big winners this year and he said all his horses was going to be big winners and after that we didn't say much and a little after that I dropped him off. I mean, it wasn't a long ride or anything like that."

"So you figure he'd been over on Hyde Street?" asked Victor. He was talking to Wally Berrigan, the stooper who had driven Ackerman home from the Backstretch a week ago Tuesday. It was Thursday morning and they were sitting in Berrigan's room in a shabby rooming house on Phila. The walls were covered with an ancient yellow wallpaper with pink and violet peonies. A large framed photograph of a severe woman in black hung over the washstand. Berrigan had identified the woman as his mother, saying he took the picture with him to all the tracks in the country. Victor had said that was nice. Berrigan sat on the edge of the unmade bed, while Victor leaned back on a straight chair across the room by the window. It had stopped raining about half an hour before and now Victor could see that the emerging sun was making the sidewalks steam.

"I don't figure anything," said Berrigan. "I'm just telling you what he said." Berrigan was a puffy, sandy-haired man in his late forties and wore an undershirt, khaki pants, and a madras porkpie hat tilted back on his head.

"How far's Hyde Street from the Backstretch?" asked Victor.

"A coupla blocks. No more."

"He talk about anything else?"

"Nah, I mean, maybe he said it was a nice night and I agreed or maybe I was the one that said it was a nice night."

"Jesus," said Victor, "you'd make a pretty useless witness."

Berrigan stirred indignantly on the bed. "How'd I know he was going to go and get himself killed?"

"You gotta be prepared," said Victor. "A policeman or a detective, he's always gotta have his eyes open. Even when he's relaxing." Victor had been talking to Berrigan about ten minutes and felt he was beginning to scrape the bottom of this particular bucket. "What'd he seem like? I mean, neither of you said much and you both sat like lumps. Didn't you wonder what was goin through his head? You know, if they ask you these questions in a court of law, you'll have to be ready."

"I told you, he seemed upset like something was bothering him. And he was pretty, what do you call it, abrupt. Like he asked me for a ride home and I agreed and then he just sat there. I figured he had something on his mind so I pretty much left him alone. Maybe I asked him what he was doin in that neck of the woods and he said he'd some business to take care of."

"Business on Hyde Street?"

"Now that I can't tell you."

A few minutes later, Victor thanked Berrigan for his help, told him to keep his nose clean, and set off down Phila to the Executive to have a cup of coffee and a bagel. The morning had become warm and sunny and around him on the street were about a half dozen young women wearing various styles of shorts and halter tops. When Victor was feeling depressed and in need of a drink, halter tops were one of the things which convinced him that life wasn't so bad after all.

The man behind the counter at the Executive looked enough like Victor to be his son: the same heavy build, jowly face and hair that stood up as if electrically charged, although this man's hair was brown and he had more of it. His name was Dave.

He wiped the counter in front of Victor and gave him a glass of water. "You in here again, you old scoundrel? I better warn the waitress."

Victor sniffed the water, wrinkled his nose, and pushed it away. Then he did a little motion with his hips. "Yeah, well, they don't call me the beef torpedo for nothing," he said.

"Where's your buddy?" Charlie often came to the Executive to discuss the history of Murder Incorporated with this man's father.

"Out chasin crime, I guess. Gimme some coffee and a cinnamon bagel." It seemed to Victor that he too was out chasing crime but he wasn't sure where to begin. He asked himself what Charlie would do and after he thought about that for a while, he decided Charlie would first go over to Hyde Street and start knocking on doors to see if anyone had seen Ackerman that Tuesday night. It didn't seem very exciting, but maybe he'd find a lonely housewife.

Dave put the coffee and toasted bagel in front of Victor. "What kind of crime is Charlie chasing?" he asked.

"He's trying to find out who shot Ackerman."

"Now there's a guy I'd like to see fried," said Dave, pulling an imaginary switch in midair. "I liked Ackerman."

"Didn't we all," said Victor with his mouth half full of bagel. It had occurred to him he would need a photograph of Ackerman. Probably he could get one from the newspaper.

"Is Charlie working with Peterson on this?"

"Nah, Peterson's a dope," said Victor. "He couldn't even solve the kiddy crossword. Charlie's doin it by himself. 'Course I'm givin him some help."

When he had finished eating, Victor walked up Maple to the newspaper to get a photograph. Learning that he'd have to pay three dollars for it, he nearly refused, then changed his mind. The photograph, as well as the bagel, coffee, and maybe lunch, could go on an expense account and Charlie could reimburse him. The photograph showed Ackerman receiving a plaque at the Lions Club awards banquet the previous spring. Ackerman appeared so cheerful and in control of his world that it made Victor sad to look at it. Then he raised his hand and, like Dave at the Executive, pulled an imaginary switch.

Leaving the newspaper, Victor retrieved his car from a lot behind the Algonquin. He had an old rattletrap Dodge Dart that Charlie had found for him which was basically dark blue but also had large spots of gray primer. Actually, Victor was keeping his eyes open for a Volkswagen Beetle.

As he drove down Broadway and looked at the shops and Victorian buildings which seemed to glitter in the morning sun after a night of rain, Victor again congratulated himself for coming to Saratoga in April. Of course he wouldn't tell that to Charlie. No point in puffing him up. But Saratoga had been a helluva smarter choice than Chicago where he had nearly gone and then decided he simply couldn't face it. If what he didn't like was cities, then moving to Chicago wouldn't help, even though Victor's son Matthew lived in Chicago and worked at one of the hospitals as a medical technician, a job which to Victor seemed slightly less interesting than watching an ant cross a sidewalk.

Matthew and his wife owned a small house in Evanston and they had told Victor they'd fixed up the basement rec room for him. Victor could imagine the life, keeping his young granddaughter and grandson from killing each other, while Matthew and Bernice had a high old time. No, Chicago would have been the wrong choice and even though he liked Matthew he'd always thought of him as something of a sissy. As for Bernice, well fuck it, Victor would have had to kiss his girl-chasing days goodbye. Bernice thought two sexes were one too many and the world of hot pursuit was distasteful to her. Victor was all for broads getting a decent wage and being treated with respect, but that was no reason for him to unhook his genitalia and hide them up on th shelf along with the china figurines. Passing the Grand Union supermarket, Victor turned right onto Congress.

So at the last moment when his bags were packed and the ticket bought and Moshe howling in his wicker basket, he had called Charlie in desperation and Charlie had said come up to Saratoga. So he had, even though he hadn't seen Charlie for two years or even been in touch except for a couple of joking postcards asking him if he was keeping his clock clean and stuff like that. And Charlie had put him up on his couch for a couple of weeks even though he was allergic to cats and probably sneezed eighty zillion times a day. Then Charlie found him an apartment at the Algonquin and lent him money for this car and got him a job at the stable and well, shit, if he'd gone to Chicago, right now he'd probably be sitting in some clammy basement watching "Love of Life" while his grandkids tried to suck off his toes.

Hyde Street was two blocks long and lined with maples and oaks. Halfway up the block from Grand Avenue, Victor saw a yellow backhoe and some men in white hard hats working, presumably, on the sewer. Part of the road and sidewalk where he had parked seemed new and Victor guessed the crew was working its way down the entire street. He got out of the car, unlocked the trunk and removed a brown corduroy jacket which he shook several times, then put on over his gray sweat shirt. If he had thought about this earlier, he told himself, he would have neatened up. Well, it didn't matter. They could love him dirty, like it or not. There appeared to be thirty to forty older houses on Hyde Street, ranging from small to large. Taking a deep breath, Victor walked up to the first: a small, white house with white shutters. He knocked on the door.

After Victor knocked several more times, the door was opened by a nearly square man of his own age with a square head and big square hands and black unruly hair. The man wore workman's blue overalls and was holding a hammer. "I'm not buying," he said.

"That's okay," said Victor, "I'm not selling." He took Ackerman's photograph and held it up before the man's face. "You seen this guy around here a week ago Tuesday night?"

"Who wants to know?" said the man, not looking at the picture.

"I want to know. I'm Vic."

"Means nothing to me," said the man, beginning to close the door. From inside the house, Victor could hear laughter and applause from some television quiz show.

"Wait a second, Mac, this is a criminal investigation and if you don't answer with a simple yes or no, you could be in a helluva lot of hot water."

"You a cop?"

"Sorta."

"Where's your ID?"

"The kind of cop I am we don't have ID. I work with horses, you know, in security."

"You a horse cop?"

"No, I'm a stable guard."

The man made a grunting, coughing noise which Victor knew was meant as a humorous response, then he looked at the photograph. "That's Ackerman, isn't it? I recognize it from the paper. What makes you think he was around here?"

"I was just sort of wondering. You see him?"

"Nah, not me."

"Anyone in your house see him?"

"Nah, I live alone."

"That don't surprise me none," said Victor, turning away. Already he felt it was going to be a long day.

12
▼▼▼

IT WAS A TALL, green metal gate with a twelve-foot stone pillar on each side and the name "Dwyer" done in metal letters over the top. It had been there as long as Charlie could remember and he recalled bicycling by it many times as a small boy. A chain link fence stretched away in both directions. Charlie slowed his Volkswagen, then drove through the gate. Before him he saw a parking lot and beyond that some shed rows and a large house. To his left a colt was being cantered around a training track. The colt was gray with two white front feet, and it reminded Charlie of the gray colt on which his mother was basing her fortune.

That morning Charlie had received a card from his mother mailed in Lexington, Kentucky, again urging him to "bury the hatchet" with his cousins and stay out of trouble. She would be home in September. Ever Ready had apparently won again. On the reverse of the card was a picture of the federal hospital for drug addicts in Lexington.

Hazel had purchased Ever Ready with her partner Hank Justice, a free-lance electrician, at a claiming race in Saratoga for five thousand dollars. All four feet had been bandaged and he had limped onto the track. Justice, however, had seen the same horse run in Louisiana two years before and had seen it win. That time too the horse had been bandaged and limped, and later he learned that its trainer had spent a lot of time teaching it to limp to discourage bettors and increase the odds. He would also enter the horse in claiming races beneath its ability. Hazel happened to be with Justice that afternoon and the two claimed Ever Ready almost before he left the gate. Hazel had also bet one hundred dollars and when the horse won at fifteen to one, she believed she could see her dream motel slowly materializing through the fog. Now she and Justice drove around the Midwest in an old United Parcel Service truck with the horse sleeping on one side and them on the other. At sixty-three, she felt her life just beginning.

Charlie had been thinking of his mother a lot as he drove over to Dwyer's stable, since he knew that staying out of trouble was exactly what he wasn't doing. Last night he had almost decided once and for all to forget about Ackerman's death and let Peterson solve it his own way, if he was able. Then Janet Claremon's call had thrown him off again. Why should her husband talk about a fire? Then, that morning, as he watched the first sun break through the rain clouds over the lake, he decided he at least had to see Dwyer and find out why Claremon had quit or been fired or whatever had happened. He told himself he owed that to Lew; and as he went out to drink his coffee on his dock, he remembered mornings when the two of them had had breakfast on that dock and how beautiful it could be there.

Charlie parked his car next to a few others in a small lot and got out. Before him were two lines of green stables with piles of soiled straw at each end. A yellow feed truck had pulled up to the shed row which ran in front of the track. Charlie walked toward it. Nobody was around the truck, but nearby a young man was rubbing down a chestnut colt.

"Where can I find Dwyer?" Charlie asked.

"You got an appointment?"

"That's right. Is he around?"

The young man waved a hand over his shoulder. "He might be in the house. Curry's there at least."

Charlie started to walk in that direction, then paused. "You know a guy that worked here by the name of Neal Claremon?" he asked.

The man stopped rubbing the horse's front leg and glanced up. He wore dark glasses and Charlie couldn't see his eyes. "You'd better talk to Curry about that," he said.

At the end of the shed row was a two-story green house with a mansard roof and a large, screened-in front porch. Beyond it were two more rows of green stables. The four rows of stables nearly surrounded the house and approached to within twenty feet of it. In front of the house, near the track, was a small green barn, while beyond the house was a cluster of birches and a pond with a few ducks. Charlie climbed the front steps and opened the screen door.

"You looking for someone?"

Charlie peered into the relative dimness of the porch and saw a man lying on a chaise longue reading a newspaper. He recognized him as Dwyer's son-in-law, Wayne Curry.

"I'd like to talk to Mr. Dwyer," said Charlie.

"Does he know you're coming?" Curry got to his feet and walked toward Charlie. He wore khaki pants, a khaki shirt, and highly polished, brown jodhpur boots. Although a tall man, he moved quickly and delicately like a dancer. Charlie guessed he was about thirty. Curry carefully folded up the newspaper as he waited for an answer.

Charlie decided to avoid the question. "I'm Charles Bradshaw, chief of security at Lorelei Stables. We have a groom who was murdered this week and we found he had previously worked for Mr. Dwyer. I wanted to ask him some questions." Charlie handed Curry his card. Curry looked at it briefly, folded it in half, drawing his thumb down along the crease, and stuck it in his shirt pocket.

"Who was killed?"

"Neal Claremon."

"Is it certain he was murdered?"

"He was shot in the back. Six times in the back."

Curry tossed his newspaper onto the chaise longue. "That's too bad. You're working with the police?"

"No, Chief Peterson is handling his own investigation."

"I'm not sure I understand what your jurisdiction is."

Before Charlie could make up an answer, the door of the house swung open and banged against the wall. Charlie looked to see Dwyer in his wheelchair at the top of a small ramp which led down to the porch. Slowly, Dwyer eased his chair through the door and down the ramp. Although it was a warm morning, he had a heavy red and blue plaid blanket over his legs and wore a beige Irish fisherman's sweater. Behind Dwyer, Charlie could see a walnut paneled room with photographs and paintings of horses on the wall and a glass bookcase filled with trophies.

"What's this about Claremon?" Dwyer asked.

"He's dead," said Curry.

Charlie was struck by the fact that Curry's face was not so much expressionless as constantly blank, like the face of a manikin. It was a tanned, almost ruddy face, narrow and smooth with a long thin nose and a narrow chin. His copper-colored hair was perfectly groomed: combed back over his ears and just brushing the collar of his khaki shirt.

"What happened to him?" asked Dwyer. His voice was low and breathy, and he spoke with effort.

"I found him yesterday at his cottage on Hedges Lake," said Charlie. "He'd been shot several days before."

"Who shot him?"

"The police don't know."

"How'd you happen to go out there?" asked Dwyer.

"He hadn't shown up for work for about five days and I wanted to find out why."

Dwyer glanced at his son-in-law. "But Claremon works for us."

"He quit about two weeks ago, Dad."

"You never told me that."

"I'm sure I did. I told you that night at the Firehouse. You said you didn't think we needed to hire anyone else."

Dwyer wrinkled his brow, then turned slowly from Curry back to Charlie. "Aren't you Charlie Bradshaw?" he asked.

"That's right."

"And so Claremon was working for Lew?"

"Lew hired him about ten days ago. I wanted to find out why he left here and came to our stable." Both Charlie and Dwyer looked at Curry who was lighting a cigarette.

"All he told me was he wanted to quit," said Curry, shaking out the match and dropping it in a glass ashtray on the table. "I figured he'd had a better offer someplace else."

"But he'd worked for us almost fifteen years," said Dwyer. "Why didn't he come to me? Did you offer him more money?"

Curry drew on the cigarette, then looked at Charlie and shook his head as if to indicate that wasn't how it happened. "I asked him why he was leaving, but he wouldn't say. As a matter of fact, his work had been getting a little sloppy and so when he said he wanted to leave I was just as glad."

Dwyer had seen Curry's gesture to Charlie and was growing red in the face. He had thick silver hair, blue eyes, and a large square jaw. He waited a moment before he spoke, allowing himself to calm down. "How was his work sloppy? He was one of my best grooms."

Curry held up one hand, then dropped it. "People change," he said. Then he turned to Charlie. "Aren't you the guy who used to work for the police department and was fired?"

"I quit," said Charlie.

"Whatever," said Curry, "but I'm still not sure why you've come over here. Presumably the police will be talking to us. I don't see how you come into it."

Charlie had noticed that Curry's fingernails were perfectly groomed and shone slightly as if covered with clear polish. Glancing at Dwyer, he saw the older man was staring out at the training track. Charlie thought about how Curry had shaken his head and how Dwyer, though angered, had appeared to accept it. "We've a lot of expensive property coming into Lorelei," said Charlie, "a lot of new horses. First Lew is murdered, then Claremon. Whoever did it is still wandering around. It's my job to protect the stable so I'm trying to learn what's going on."

"You think the murders were connected?" asked Curry.

"Sure they're connected. Both men were killed with a silenced pistol and at this point nobody knows why."

Curry stubbed out his cigarette. "Isn't Chief Peterson working on it?" he asked.

"Peterson's prime interest is finding the murderer, while mine is to look out for the interests of Lorelei Stables. Perhaps I could talk to some of the other grooms and they could give me an idea why Claremon quit."

Curry folded his arms and glanced at his father-in-law, who was still staring out at the track. "Look, Mr. Bradshaw, I appreciate your concern and understand you have every reason to be worried, but I also feel I shouldn't let you talk to my men until I've talked to Peterson. Whatever your qualifications, he's the policeman and for all I know he may want to talk to my people first."

Charlie appeared to consider this, then said, "I don't see how this would interfere with Peterson's line of inquiry. My concern is the security of Lorelei Stables."

"I appreciate that, but despite your connection with Lorelei you are still basically a private citizen and I can't allow you to wander around Dwyer Stables disrupting work just to satisfy your curiosity. Why don't we wait until Peterson comes here and I'll give you a call afterward. But I can't believe that Claremon's death had anything to do with Dwyer Stables and, although he left here abruptly, he also left on good terms."

Charlie knew he had been outmaneuvered. Looking at Curry's face, he still couldn't identify any expression, not even polite interest. It was like talking to someone who was wearing dark glasses. He began to think he had seen Curry someplace else in Saratoga, but he couldn't remember where. Charlie decided to try a different track. "Do you have any ideas as to why someone might want to kill Ackerman and Claremon?"

Curry shook his head. "Lew Ackerman was a man I had a lot of respect for, but we all know he'd had a checkered past.

I expect the solution to the puzzle will be found in something that happened ten, fifteen, twenty years ago. As for Claremon, if the two murders are really connected then possibly Claremon stumbled onto something and the murderer decided to kill him as well. What do you think, Dad?"

Dwyer, whose attention was still focused on the track, obviously hadn't been listening. He jerked his head toward Curry, looked blank for a moment, then said only, "I guess so." He hesitated, then turned toward Charlie. "I'd known Lew for twenty years and we fought and lied to each other and claimed each other's horses out from under our noses and spied on each other, but if I had one friend . . ." Here he paused again. Up to this point, it had seemed to Charlie that Dwyer intended to give a speech, but now his voice changed and he began to speak more quietly. "I remember one time I sent a kid over to his stable to secretly clock one of his horses. Lew caught him and packed him into an old steamer trunk and shipped him back to me collect, but before he locked up the trunk he stuck in a bottle of Wild Turkey because he knew I liked it." He paused, then said, "You think Claremon's wife could use some money?"

"I expect so," said Charlie.

"I'll take care of it then." Dwyer had large red hands and he kept rubbing them back and forth on the arms of his wheelchair.

"I'll walk you back to your car, Mr. Bradshaw," said Curry.

Charlie was sorry not to talk longer to Dwyer, not necessarily about the murders but about Lew, to sit around and swap stories. He approached the wheelchair and stuck out his hand. "Thanks for your help, Mr. Dwyer."

Dwyer took it briefly and let it go. Charlie thought it was like holding a beanbag. "Good luck," said Dwyer.

Walking back along the shed row, Curry said, "My father-in-law is not a strong man, nor is he a happy man, and so I'm sorry you came and disturbed him."

Charlie didn't say anything. They walked past horses being rubbed down or washed, horses simply sticking their heads over the lower doors of their stalls. The green buildings were in need of paint and could use reshingling in places. Charlie was also struck by the fact that most of the people he saw were young, say, in their early twenties, and that they were all men. At Lorelei Stables at least half of the grooms were women. Curry walked a little ahead of Charlie, as if he were leading him.

When they reached the parking lot, Charlie said, "I like your father-in-law and I've got a lot of respect for him. And I'm also sorry I upset him, if I did. On the other hand, I want to know why Claremon quit."

"As I suggested, perhaps he had a better offer."

Charlie watched a small, thin man lead a boy colt over to the hot-walker. "No," said Charlie, "Claremon went and asked Ackerman for a job. He didn't have one when he left here. Did he seem angry or frightened or bothered by anything?"

"All he said was that he wanted to leave. Maybe he did have some reason I don't know about. When Peterson comes, I'll suggest that he look into it."

"When Peterson comes."

"That's right."

Charlie looked up at Curry's face, trying to find some suggestion of what he was thinking. He guessed the man had spent some time in the service, because his face reminded Charlie of someone listening to a senior officer he didn't like: alert and withheld. Perhaps there was a trace of condescension. Charlie was tempted to tell Curry what Claremon had said about there being nothing worse than a stable fire, but he decided against it. Curry was too much of a question mark. As for Claremon, Charlie began to think more and more that the reason why he had left Dwyer's stable would also explain why he had been shot six times in the back.

13

▼▼▼

C HARLIE PARKED HIS VOLKSWAGEN next to the phone booth and got out. To his left was the main box office of the Saratoga Performing Arts Center. The day had become hot and he paused to take off his tan suit coat and throw it in the back seat. About thirty people were lined up to buy tickets for the Philadelphia Orchestra, which would be giving concerts during the month of August. Beyond the gate was the open-sided, roofed amphitheater where Charlie had once taken his mother to hear Frank Sinatra. Behind him, bordering Route 52, stretched a parking lot which he guessed was about fifty acres. Charlie dug in his pocket for change and dialed Janet Claremon.

She answered on the fifth ring, sounding as if she had been asleep.

"How're you feeling?" asked Charlie.

"Better. Still sort of dazed. The police released the body to the funeral home. I guess he'll be buried this week. His brother's flying in from Salinas."

A groundkeeper on a red tractor mower passed close to where Charlie was standing and he had to strain to hear. "Is there anything I can get you or do for you?" he asked.

"No, I'll be okay in a few days."

"By the way," said Charlie, "do you know the names of any of the guys Neal worked with at Dwyer's?"

"I think so. Why do you want them?"

"I'm trying to get an idea why Neal quit. Maybe they'd know."

"Actually, I only know one man and he's not even working there anymore. He left about a month ago."

"Have any idea where he lives?"

"No, I don't, but last I knew he was working at the Citgo station across from the track. His name's Henry something-or-other and he's got bright red hair. If he's there, you won't miss him."

"Thanks, Janet."

The lawn tractor made another pass and when it had gone by Charlie heard Janet saying, "By the way, Charlie, the police were here again and Chief Peterson asked me not to talk to you. I thought you'd like to know."

Charlie felt touched by her complicity. "What did Peterson want?"

"He asked me if Neal gambled or was mixed up with any gamblers."

"You mean at the track?"

"No, I gather he meant cards and things like that."

Charlie thought about this. It indicated that Peterson was pursuing some line of inquiry which Charlie knew nothing about. He grew aware of Janet's slow breathing in the receiver and could almost visualize her in her bright, tidy kitchen with the photographs of New England villages. "What did you tell him?" he said at last.

"Nothing, I mean Neal never went out and hardly talked to anyone. And he never bet on horses unless he was pretty positive he had a sure thing."

"What did Peterson say to that?"

There was a pause, then with more spirit than she had shown so far, she said, "He said that maybe I was mistaken. Can you believe it?"

A little later, as he drove across Saratoga to see Henry at the Citgo station, Charlie knew he would soon have trouble with Peterson. He wondered if there were any way to placate him. It reminded Charlie of Canada Bill Jones who made several fortunes skinning greenhorns in three-card monte games on the Union Pacific during the 1860s and 1870s. When he became too well known and conductors kept throwing him off the trains, he wrote to the president of the company offering him ten thousand dollars plus an annual percentage of the take if he would grant Bill the sole franchise for three-card monte games on the Union Pacific. Bill further promised to bilk only Methodist ministers and travelers from Chicago, both of whom he hated.

The Citgo station was on a corner across from the main entrance to the track and across from the main stabling area and Oklahoma training track, which had been the original race track built by Old Smoke Morrissey in the 1860s. The elms and maples were particularly lush after last night's rain and as Charlie climbed from his car he paused to look at the bright green wineglass shapes rising above the white Victorian bandstand just inside the grounds. As he looked, it seemed that one delivery truck after another kept passing through the gates of the track from which came the banging of carpenters' hammers. Usually Charlie made a point of going on opening day. Last year he had been in Ackerman's box. This year he figured he would be with Victor standing somewhere along the rail, unless he could convince Doris to go.

Charlie walked toward the garage. In the back of one of the bays, he saw a tall, red-haired man changing a tire. "Are you Henry?" he called to him. The man straightened and dropped a flat metal bar that clanged on the cement.

"Who wants me?" he said. He had a soft Southern voice. Charlie guessed he was about six feet four and doubted he weighed 140 pounds. His red hair stood straight up on his head and Charlie guessed it felt bristly.

"My name's Charlie Bradshaw. I'd like to talk to you about Neal Claremon."

"Damn, weren't that awful," said Henry, "when I heard that on the radio, I figured it had to be the wrong Neal Claremon." He dragged a dirty red rag out of the back pocket of his blue coveralls, wiped his hands on it, and stuck out his right hand toward Charlie. "Henry Dietz," he said. "You a friend of Neal's?"

"I never met him, but he'd started working for Lorelei Stables and that's where I work as a guard." For some reason, Charlie didn't feel like dragging out one of his cards.

"So that's where he went, is it? He was lucky to get himself another stable job. That damn Curry, he fixed me so no other outfit will take me on."

"What do you mean?"

"Fired me for stealing a coupla watches, then refused to give me a reference. Shit, I'd worked for Dwyer eight years. What would I want to go and start stealing things for? You tell me that."

He looked so angry that Charlie wondered if he expected an answer. Dietz took out a pack of nonfilter Camels, offered one to Charlie, and when Charlie refused, lit one for himself with a shiny Zippo lighter that had the picture of a horse's head engraved on the side.

"You mean he accused you of stealing the watch just so he could fire you?"

"That's what I said, in't it? He tried to get me to quit by giving me a hard time, making me take care of the worst horses, but I wouldn't have any of it. Old Man Dwyer always gave me a square deal and I figured I'd stick by him."

"Why would Curry want to get rid of you?"

"He wants his own boys in there. For the past year or so, he's been dumping all the old hands. Me and Claremon was the last. Then, after I got fired at the end of June, I ran into Claremon and said he'd get it too. But he didn't think so. He said he'd talked to Dwyer and Dwyer said he'd keep him on no matter what. You see, it was Claremon that hauled Dwyer in after he'd had his stroke, and the doctor told him if he'd been out any longer, he'd of been a dead man for sure."

"When was this?" asked Charlie. The two men stood next to a white Volkswagen bus. Dietz was leaning against it with his arms folded and his cigarette dangling from his lower lip.

"Five years ago. We was at his farm in Kentucky. He and Claremon had ridden out somewhere checking spring foals. Then I remember I was rubbing down some horse and I looked up and here comes Claremon galloping across the field hollering. Dwyer was lying across his saddle and Claremon was sitting behind him. You know, Claremon was a fella who hardly ever said a word and to see him come galloping and shouting put the fear into you. Anyway, we rushed Dwyer to the hospital and called his daughter and Curry. They was living out in L.A. Then Dwyer has another stroke in the hospital and the doctor says he's not going to make it. He's a tough old bird though. He pulls through and's moving around before anyone figured he would, although he's changed a lot."

"How so?"

"Well, he's quieter, for one thing. He used to be a great shouter. Didn't mean much, like they say his bark was worse'n his bite. Then he was also the kind of fella that liked to do everything himself and once he gets out of the hospital he gets Curry to stay around and bit by bit Curry's doing more'n more stuff until by the time I get fired, Curry's running the whole show."

"Was the daughter around too?"

"Yeah, now and then, but she's got this interior decorating or design place out in L.A. so she never stays long. I guess Curry used to work there too, but he gave it up quick enough. She'd fly out every month or so and everything seemed hunky-dory, but I called it a pretty strange marriage."

"Does Dwyer have any other children?"

"Just that daughter. I heard he had a son that was killed in a car accident about twenty years ago but that was way before my time." Dietz ground the cigarette out on the heel of his boot. A red Fiat Spider with the top down pulled up to the pumps. "Scuse me a minute," said Dietz, walking toward it.

Charlie leaned against the VW bus and looked across East Avenue. Off to his left, he could see several exercise boys cantering horses around the Oklahoma track. He asked himself again why Claremon should quit Dwyer's only a short time after getting assurance that he wouldn't be fired. Maybe he really had been fired and Curry was lying. But Charlie doubted that. Claremon had told several people he quit and there seemed to be no reason to lie about it.

"What was Curry like to work for, as compared to Dwyer?" asked Charlie when Dietz had returned.

"He's a jumpy kinda guy. You never knew what he was going to do next. Also, he don't seem to like horses, like they make him angry or something. Dwyer might be tough on you, but you always figured he knew what he was doing. Not so with Curry. He wouldn't pay attention to feed orders and getting new tack. There was always something going wrong. Then you never knew how he was going to act. One guy who'd been with Dwyer about ten years told him he didn't know what he hell he was doing and Curry hit him in the face. So help me, I was standing right there. Ignoramus, the guy called Curry an ignoramus and Curry hauled off and belted him. The funny thing was you couldn't even see it coming, like Curry didn't give any warning, just smashed the guy in the face and broke his nose. After that everyone gave Curry a lot of room. Then

Curry starts hiring these new guys. For Christ's sake, some of them never even seen a horse before. I had to spend half my time showing them the ropes."

"What was Dwyer's reaction to this?"

"Nothing, he didn't say a word. I mean, I could of sworn he hated it, but he never said a word."

"Can you think of any reason why Claremon might have quit?"

"No reason, unless he'd had enough of Curry. Claremon was a strange guy. Did his work and never spoke. Now and then I'd take him out for a beer. We'd sit in a bar two, three hours and if I got ten words out of him about the weather I figured I was doing well." Dietz paused to light another Camel, then both men were silent as they watched a young woman in extremely tight white shorts and a tight white T-shirt ride by the gas station on a blue ten-speed.

"How'd you get framed for stealing the watch?" asked Charlie.

Dietz scratched his head, making his red hair stand up even more. "Well, there'd been a lot of petty theft going on, you know, watches and rings, maybe a wallet. I figured it was one of those new guys of Curry's. Then one day they had a search and found two watches in my bunk. Shit, I sure know I didn't put 'em there, but what could I do?"

"And you haven't been able to get another job?"

"No, I guess Curry talked to a bunch of other trainers."

"You go to Ackerman's?"

"Yeah, I talked to some guy, Warner his name was. He said they didn't need anyone."

"Would you rather work at a stable than work here?" asked Charlie.

"Mister, I been working with horses for twenty years, since I was sixteen. You think I want to be stuck here in a filling station?"

"Go see Warner again," said Charlie. "I'll talk to him. Mind you, I'm not promising anything because Warner doesn't like me much, but I'll give it a try."

Dietz looked momentarily suspicious. "Why do me the favor?"

Charlie shrugged. "Why not?"

After a second or two, Dietz began to grin. "Damn, I don't mean to be ungrateful. I'll shoot by there this afternoon."

"By the way," said Charlie, "when was the last time you saw Claremon?"

"Last Friday night, as a matter of fact, least I think it was him. I was in this bar around the corner, King's. It was pretty crowded. I saw Claremon and waved to him, but either he didn't see me or he ignored me. Personally I think he ignored me, 'cause by the time I got across the room to talk to him, he was gone. Just ducked out."

14

▼▼▼

VICTOR DASHED UP THE STEPS, spun around, and raised the broken branch he held in his right hand. The chow dog which had chased him halfway down the block paused at the gate, panting. Victor thought its black tongue looked particularly mean-spirited. With a baleful glance, the dog turned and trotted back up the street. Victor threw the branch after it. The branch clattered on the sidewalk and bounced into the street. The dog didn't seem to notice. What the hell, thought Victor, those six houses he had missed because he had run past them as fast as a man could run, well, he could try them later.

Victor turned back to the door and rang the bell. As he waited, he straightened his jacket and checked his sweat shirt. It was almost dry. That had been another tactical error, along with calling the dog Fido. Afterward, Victor had realized that the woman was probably one of those rare creatures who are genuinely friendly to everyone. It had been wrong to assume she was making signals for him alone. And even if there had been such signals, it had been wrong to pinch her cheek while she was holding that pan of water.

Victor rang the bell again. There had been a name on the

light post by the gate, but he had been running too fast to read it. The house was the last one on the block and bigger than the others; a three-story white Victorian house with ginger-bread trim and a two-story carriage house in back.

A thin woman of about fifty in a black dress and white apron opened the door. "Maid," said Victor to himself. He held up a photograph of Ackerman. "Do you know if this man visited this house Tuesday before last," said Victor. "I'm conducting a survey."

"Survey?" asked the maid.

"That's right," said Victor, "I go from house to house asking questions."

Before the woman could respond, a man's voice behind her said, "Who is it, Lettie?"

"Some man with a survey, Mr. Dwyer."

She stood aside and in the hall Victor could see an old man in a wheelchair. He recognized the name Dwyer, knew that it belonged to someone connected with horses. For that matter, everyone he met seemed connected to horses. The man had on a brown suede jacket over a white shirt and his long white hair looked as if it had been just brushed. He had the sort of square jaw that Victor associated with cowboy heroes.

"What kind of survey?" asked Dwyer, rolling his chair up to the door.

Victor showed him the picture of Ackerman. "You know if this man was in the neighborhood a week ago Tuesday?" People in wheelchairs depressed Victor because they reminded him of the years his own wife had been confined to one. Even beyond that, this fellow looked decidedly down in the dumps. Victor hoped to be done here soon so he could return home to change. He had to be at work at five and it was four already.

"That's Lew," said Dwyer, surprised. He took the picture and held it close to his face. "This is from the awards banquet last spring."

"That's right. Got it from the paper. Did you see Ackerman around here?"

"Lew was a friend of mine. Sure he was over here now and then."

"Yeah, but was he over here a week ago Tuesday? That's what I wanna know."

"What's this have to do with a survey?" asked Dwyer. He had a hoarse, gravelly voice which came, thought Victor, from a life of bossing people around.

"Nothin, that's just something I say to people to get their attention. Look, Mac, I'm sorry if Ackerman was a friend of yours. I liked him pretty much myself, but I gotta be at work in hardly any time at all, so maybe you could answer my question."

Dwyer rolled his wheelchair back several feet and looked at Victor in such a way as to make him think he'd been too frank. Then Dwyer looked away and rubbed his check roughly as if he were tired. In one hand, he still held the photograph which he had rolled up into a tube, making Victor afraid that he might damage it. "Why don't you come in and we can talk about this," said Dwyer.

Victor stood on the top step. Inside, next to Dwyer, was a large wooden coatrack and umbrella stand with a full-length mirror in which he could see Dwyer's reflection. "Thanks anyway," said Victor, "but as I say, I'm pretty rushed."

"Are you working with the police?" asked Dwyer.

"No, I'm Charlie Bradshaw's assistant at Lorelei Stables. We're tryin to clear this problem by ourselves. It's Mr. Bradshaw's opinion, and I must say I'm in agreement with him, that the police are pretty much being dopes about the whole thing. You mind givin me back that photograph before you mess it up?"

Dwyer seemed surprised to find he was still holding it. He handed it back to Victor. "Perhaps you could tell me what makes you think Lew was here that Tuesday night," he said.

"Not necessarily here," said Victor. "What my informants tell me is that Mr. Ackerman was someplace *around* here on that Tuesday night. He'd ditched his bodyguard, tellin him he had some business to take care of, then he came over to this street. I don't know, maybe he had some floozie. Now, it's 4:15, you mind tellin me if you saw him that night?"

"No, I didn't see him." Dwyer had a plaid blanket covering his legs and he began to pick at a loose strand of blue yarn. "You mean, you've been going up and down this street asking everyone these same questions?"

"That's right, except I missed a bunch of houses on account of a hostile dog. I hope to catch those tomorrow. You live here alone? I mean, is there anyone else he might of seen?"

"No, I'm sure he didn't come here. What does Bradshaw think Lew was doing that night?"

"He doesn't know. He's just trying to find out, thassall. Does someone live back there in that carriage house?"

"My son-in-law."

"Maybe Ackerman saw him. Is he around?"

Dwyer shook his head. "He's at my stable. Anyway, I'm sure Lew didn't see him."

Victor shrugged. "Maybe I can catch him some other time. You know anyone else around here that Ackerman might of seen?"

"Not offhand. Lew knew a lot of people. What makes you think he was on this street?"

"He mentioned to my informant how it was all dug up. So I figured he'd been along here someplace."

Dwyer rolled the wheelchair back a little. The hall floor was covered with a blue carpet and the movement of the chair was soundless. "Then it could have been the next street," said Dwyer. "It didn't have to be this street at all."

Victor sighed. He hated the thought of knocking on more doors. "I guess that's right," he said. "All I know is he was over in this area."

"Do you have any evidence to show that what he was doing over here had anything to do with his death?"

"Not really," said Victor, beginning to feel uncomfortable. "Just stands to reason, that's all."

"What reason? You mean coincidence?"

It occurred to Victor that he didn't know enough about Dwyer and his family to be able to do any more than antagonize the old man. Not that he minded antagonizing people, but Victor began to wonder if he was getting in over his head.

"Look, Mr. Dwyer," Victor said, "I hate to cut this short, but I've got to get to work. I'll come back some other time to talk to your son."

"Son-in-law."

"That's what I said," said Victor.

15

▼▼▼

BECAUSE OF THE HOSTILITY of his ex-wife and the disapproval of his cousins, and because his ex-wife and two of his three cousins had businesses on Broadway, Saratoga's main street, Charlie rarely went downtown or, if he did, he stuck to Maple, a seedier street that ran parallel to Broadway. But after seeing Henry Dietz and taking care of some other errands, he decided to stop by the Montana Bookstore to see if a book he had ordered on John Dillinger had come in yet. He had to be at work at five and if the book was in and the evening quiet, then he might get some reading done if Victor would let him. Besides, he had about twenty minutes to kill before driving to the stable and he wanted to talk to Liz Hood, owner of the Montana and one of the few non-ex-cons, non-track-affiliated, non-swimmers who didn't feel themselves disgraced to be seen in Charlie's presence.

He had parked his Volkswagen half a block away from the Montana on Caroline and had almost reached the door of the bookstore without seeing anyone he knew, when a voice behind him called his name.

"Bradshaw!"

There was a certain stridency about the voice that made Charlie wince. He turned to see Emmett Van Brunt looking embarrassed.

" 'Lo, Emmett, you decided to be friendly again?"

The plainclothesman scratched the back of his neck and glanced out at passing cars. "This is more official than that, Charlie."

Charlie smiled. "You here to arrest me then?" They stood in the middle of the sidewalk in front of the bookstore. People passed around them as if they formed a rock in a stream. In the front window of the bookstore a gray cat slept.

Van Brunt flushed and began to stutter, "It's like this, Ch-Charlie."

"Jesus, Emmett, you really did come to arrest me."

"No, no, Charlie. Peterson wants to talk to you, that's all. Don't make it so hard on me."

Charlie felt relieved. "Sure, I'll talk to him. I've got to be at work in about ten minutes. Tell him I'll stop by tomorrow morning. What time would be good?"

Again Van Brunt looked embarrassed. "It's gotta be now, Charlie." He had on black and white plaid trousers and a green and yellow plaid shirt, and the mismatched plaids made him difficult to look at, as if he were exemplifying nervousness or emotional tension.

"I've just told you, Emmett, I've got to be at work."

"That don't matter, Charlie."

"So you *are* arresting me. Emmett, why don't you just come out and say it?"

Van Brunt put his hands in his pockets and looked down at the sidewalk. "Not 'arresting,' Charlie, don't say 'arresting.' Peterson said he wanted a few words with you right away. Nobody's going to book you or anything like that."

"Great, that's just great. What if I said I couldn't do it right now, would you use the handcuffs? Would I get charged with resisting arrest?"

"Jesus, Charlie!" Van Brunt looked around, hoping people hadn't heard. "Can't we just do this amicably? Why talk like a troublemaker?"

"Emmett, we worked together five years and now you're treating me like a crook. How friendly you expect me to be? All right, let's go. You won't need the cuffs."

Van Brunt's face brightened. "Thanks, Charlie. You'll see it's nothing. Just a little talk."

"I can imagine."

The police station was only another half block up Broadway,

but in that distance Charlie saw several people he knew. A trainer beeped his horn at him. Jim Connor tooled by on a blue Kawasaki and gave him a thumbs up. He even saw his ex-wife's sister and business partner, who had married his middle cousin, Robert, who sold insurance and real estate. A few months before, Robert had offered Charlie a job in his office in order to get him away from the track, as he said. Charlie had refused. Lucy looked at Charlie from the steps of the Adirondack Trust across the street, looked at Van Brunt, then looked away, ignoring Charlie's wave as he entered the police station.

It had always struck Charlie as perverted that in a town full of racehorses, Chief Peterson should cover the walls of his office with pictures of Irish setters. Peterson raised them and they were the only creatures about which Charlie had ever heard him speak affectionately. He had now bred six champions, plus a good pack of also-rans. Along with colored pictures of his best dogs were framed pieces of parchment citing Peterson for improving the quality of the breed, whatever that meant. To Charlie it implied he had taught them to speak. Peterson leaned back in his black leather armchair and glared at Charlie as he entered.

"You know, Charlie, far as I can see it, you're only makin trouble for one fuckin person."

"How's that, Chief?" Charlie sat down in the smaller black leather armchair on the other side of the half-acre desk. He was irritated at being dragged off the street and saw no reason to be placating. Van Brunt still hovered in the doorway. Peterson snapped his fingers at him and Van Brunt disappeared. It was a gesture, Charlie knew, held over from Peterson's years with the military police, and seeing it Charlie once more patted himself on the back for having brains enough to quit the police department.

"Tell me, Charlie," said Peterson, "why is it that wherever I go, I find you been there first muddying the water?"

"What do you mean, Chief?"

"Don't play dumb with me. Yesterday, out at Claremon's, I believed you when you said you'd gone there to see why he hadn't shown up for work. But then I find you've gone back and been bothering Mrs. Claremon with questions, then you go bother Field. Then I start hearing wherever I go in Saratoga that you're going to solve my case for me, that you don't think I got the brains to do it myself. How you think that's goin to make me feel, Charlie?"

Charlie wasn't sure if Peterson was serious. "I never told people I was going to solve any case."

"Oh, yeah? I go into the Executive for a sandwich and the guy behind the counter tells me how he hears I can retire because Sherlock Holmes Bradshaw is on the trail. Then I hear it from grooms and bartenders, bums in the drunk tank. Look, Charlie, I got fuckin feelings like anyone else. Then I come back here and I find you been bothering old man Dwyer. I don't like that, Charlie. Dwyer's a personal friend of mine. What'd you want to go over there and bother him with questions for? His health's not good and maybe his mind's a little iffy besides."

"Did he call and complain?" asked Charlie.

Peterson raised his thick eyebrows as if to indicate that of all the dummies he knew Charlie took the cake. He got up from his desk, walked around it, and stood in front of Charlie, bouncing on his toes. He wore his three-piece blue suit with a silver chain across his stomach, and as Peterson bounced the silver chain did small leaps.

"Charlie," said Peterson, "can't you get it through your head that you're not a cop? How can I talk to these people when you've already been at them? It's none of your business, can't you see that? What am I going to do, lock you up?"

Charlie leaned back in his chair and tried not to look at Peterson. Not only did he not like the Irish setters, he also disliked their silly robot postures, and he wondered how much you had to pound on a dog's head to make it stand like that.

"Look, Peterson, I know you're doing a job. Well, I'm doing one too. Lew Ackerman hired me to protect Lorelei Stables and that's what I'm doing. I'm not trying to interfere with you, I'm just trying to make sure nothing else happens." As he said this, Charlie wondered if he believed it. He supposed he did, although it didn't indicate his anger at the murderer or his lack of faith in Peterson.

"I asked Field if you were working for him and he said no."

"Field's an accountant. I'm working for Ackerman."

"He's dead."

"I can't help that." It occurred to Charlie that he had never spoken to Peterson so aggressively before.

"Charlie, you can't think we're sitting still on this. We got leads and we're going after them."

"You mean Field?"

"Field schmield, I'm not ruling him out, but right now he's back on the shelf. No, everything we've learned points to bigger fish than Field."

"Tell me about it."

"No can do, Charlie."

"You think it's tied into gambling, right? Lew was pretty dead set against gambling. Is there any connection there?"

Peterson squinted his eyes at Charlie, then stepped back and sat down on the edge of his desk, nearly knocking over a brass nameplate that said, "Harvey L. Peterson—Commissioner of Public Safety." "Maybe the gambling's part of it," he said. "As you know, there's a move on to start gambling again in Saratoga. Some people figure what works in Atlantic City can work twice as well here. As you say, Ackerman was dead set against it. He knew the guys who were pushin to open the casinos and thought they'd bring nothing but trouble. You know, a number of people in Albany would like to see gambling up here. It'd mean a lotta new tax dollars. Ackerman's been down in Albany trying to line up the people who are against any reopening. It made him unpopular and there was some big money on Long Island that wanted him out of the way."

Charlie thought about this. It had been twenty-six years since the casinos had closed following Senator Kefauver's evidence that they were run by a syndicate of racketeers. Governor Dewey had called for a special grand jury and that had been that. The next year the biggest of the great hotels, the Grand Union, had closed its doors for good, putting Charlie's mother out of a job. The first casino had been opened in 1842 by Ben

Scribner and during the next 110 years gambling had been banned several times by reform-minded citizens. Charlie knew there was a movement to reestablish gambling in Saratoga and that Ackerman had been against it. He had also assumed that like it or not gambling would some day be legalized, if only because Saratoga was that kind of town.

"What about Claremon?" asked Charlie.

Peterson got up and walked over to a color photograph on the side wall showing a particularly silly looking Irish setter sniffing the wind in a corn field. With his thumb, Peterson moved the picture to the right, then left. It hadn't seemed to Charlie that the picture had ever been crooked.

"You were right about that," said Peterson. "Ballistics showed they were killed by the same .9mm handgun. What I figure is that Ackerman told Claremon something or Claremon overheard something that made him dangerous to the murderer."

"Maybe it was the other way around."

"What d'you mean?" Peterson walked back to his desk and sat down.

"Maybe Claremon told Ackerman something."

"What could a guy like that tell anybody?"

"Why did he leave Dwyer's stable?"

"Grooms, how can you figure them? He left, that's all. I mean, I think Wayne Curry's doing a heck of a job over there, but you don't need to tell me that his ways are going to be different from the old man's. You go into a place, you gotta have people who are loyal to you. Claremon sounded like quite an eccentric guy. Maybe he and Curry bumped up against each other too much and so finally Claremon quit."

"Is that what Curry told you?"

"I'm telling you, Charlie, Curry's all right."

"Did you talk to any of the people who worked with Claremon?"

"Some of them. They couldn't tell me anything I didn't already know. Jesus, Charlie, I'm trying to explain to you, that's a blind alley."

"What makes you think so?"

Peterson stretched his arms out before him on the desk and clasped his hands. It made him look avuncular and, Charlie thought, somewhat patronizing. "Look at the way Ackerman and Claremon were killed. That wasn't any amateur job. It all points to some racketeer shooting. There're a lotta good men working on this case and all the feedback points to gambling interests. Why'n't you take a rest? I know you're worried about the stable, but there's nothin you can do up here. Bullying old men and telling everyone in town what a great cop you are, believe me, Charlie, that's no way to get your old job back."

16

▼▼▼

V ICTOR'S GRATITUDE to Charlie for hiring him as a guard was tempered by the knowledge that the other four guards were all ex-cons. Stumble bums, Victor called them, although they weren't bums and didn't stumble. He even liked them. That, however, was Victor's own secret, since he believed his fellowman was better off with hostility than friendship. It kept people on their toes.

The guard that Victor liked best was Rico Medioli who had been born and raised in the same part of lower Manhattan as Victor himself. Although only twenty-four, Rico had spent six years in jails and juvenile homes, having been first sent away at age twelve for breaking and entering. The sentencing had come after fifteen or seventeen arrests, Rico couldn't remember for sure. He remembered his first arrest at age eight for shoplifting and his last at twenty-one for breaking into a wealthy Upper West Side New York apartment, but in between was such a confusion of being tossed into and booted out of the slammer, as he called it, that the specific details were lost.

When Rico had been released from Auburn six months before, he decided to go straight—not because of a newly defined sense of right and wrong, but because he decided there was nothing more boring than criminal life as experienced behind bars. When he had gotten out of jail, he told his probation officer he didn't want to return to New York City, a place of many temptations, and the probation officer sent him to Charlie.

What Victor liked about Rico Medioli, apart from the qualities of a personality hardened by prison, was that he obviously had a bowling ball in his recent ancestry. He was short and square with a thick neck, weight lifter's shoulders, and very curly brown hair. He looked, Victor thought, as if he had once been eight feet tall, then had a heavy weight fall on his head, reducing him to about five feet five. He looked as if he had been designed to roll rather than walk.

It always cheered Victor to see him and so when Rico and Jack Krause strolled into Charlie's small office next to the tack room shortly after midnight, Victor felt his lot measurably improved. Not that he found Charlie bad company, but Charlie was being sullen about something and had spent the entire evening reading some book about John Dillinger. To make matters worse, it was raining again and Victor's feet were wet from making his rounds along the shed rows, plus his legs were tired from spending the day wandering up and down Hyde Street.

"Whatcha doin here early, you no account sneak thief, you aren't due for an hour yet?" Victor winked at Krause who shook his head.

"Thought I might catch you poundin your pud or dorkin that she-goat they're keepin with Best-in-the-West."

"I was tempted," said Victor, "but I saw she still had your ring hanging from her scrawny neck. You and Krause keepin company these days? Least you can't knock him up.'

"Nah, I ran into him at the Backstretch and he told me how Charlie is showin the cops what for, so I decided to pop by and find out about it."

Regretfully, Charlie put down his book. He had reached the part where Baby Face Nelson had leaped for his machine gun to polish off Homer Van Meter in Nelson's hotel room in St. Paul. Van Meter had laughed at Nelson's cavalry charge bank holdup tactics and was barely saved by Dillinger who assured Nelson they were "all pals here."

"I'm not showing the police anything," said Charlie. "I've done as much as I can do."

Charlie, Victor, and Rico were all wearing gray guards' uniforms with the name Lorelei stitched in red on the left breast pocket. Krause, in a brown suit, was in the process of shaking out his raincoat and hanging it on a hook behind the door. There had been thunderstorms off and on all evening and Krause and Rico had caught the tail end of one as they ran from the parking lot to the stable.

"He's fuckin scared of them," said Victor. "Fuckin' chief of police yanked him in this afternoon and threatened to throw his ass in jail. When I first met Charlie, he had the whole New York City police department chasing after him. Think that bothered him any? Not fuckin likely. He went down to the Apple to do something and he did it, cops or no cops."

Charlie shook his head. It made him uncomfortable to be the butt of snappy conversation. "I went down there to help somebody and he wound up getting shot and thrown in jail."

"Yeah, but he deserved it," said Victor. "Least the girl got off. What happened to her anyway?"

"Her parents took her to Europe."

"Personally," said Victor, "I'd rather go to jail than go to Europe. Least in jail you can drink the water."

"Is that the girl that cost you your job and made your wife dump you?" asked Rico. He stood in the center of the room and had begun touching his toes, moving quickly and easily, giving the floor a rap with his knuckles each time he bent. He was someone, Charlie thought, who morally disapproved of standing still.

"Don't you believe it," said Victor. "Fuckin Charlie, he's like the driven snow, didn't even lay a finger on her. Chance missed is life lost, that's what I always say."

"Charlie, what do you mean you've done as much as you can do?" asked Krause. He had taken a chair by the door and was wiping splashes of mud off his pants with a paper towel.

"Just what I said. I thought I had some information, but it

turned out to be nothing. Not only that, but I was interfering with Peterson, I mean, interfering to no purpose."

"But even if you did a little bit," said Krause, "that'd be more'n what Peterson's doing."

"That's not true. Peterson's following some pretty good leads. All I'm doing is making things difficult for him."

"Let's just say," said Rico, "that you kept pushing along on your own. What would you do that Peterson's not doing?"

Charlie considered this. He was leaning back in his swivel chair and had his feet up on the desk. Victor sat across the room in a ragged brown armchair. The room was in one corner of a barn and the walls were whitewashed pine boards. On the wall behind Charlie was a poster showing Pancho Villa mounted on a horse over the words "Viva la Revolución."

"I guess," said Charlie, "I'd spend some time looking into Dwyer's stable."

"Lew and Dwyer were pretty close friends," said Krause. "Didn't Dwyer give the eulogy at the cemetery?"

"That's true," said Charlie, "but something doesn't feel right over there. For a stable only four days before a meet, that place looks half empty."

"Dwyer's an old man," said Krause. "Maybe he just wants to slow down a little."

"Yeah, but he ain't the guy runnin the place," said Victor. "He's turned the whole shebang over to his son-in-law, Wayne Curry."

"Never met the man," said Krause. "Seen him of course, but never met him."

"He's been workin down at Dwyer's farm in Kentucky for about four years," said Victor. "Just came up here last September."

Charlie looked at his friend who had paused to put his fingers in his mouth and check on a tooth to see if it wiggled. "How did you know that?" Charlie asked.

"Common knowledge," said Victor.

Krause leaned forward and put his elbows on his knees, letting his big hands hang loosely before him. Although he wore nothing but dark suits, they always looked wrong on him, as if he were in disguise. "I drove Lew to the wedding," he said, "but I waited in the car while he went in. I'm not much of a one for churches. That must of been in '72 or '73."

" '72," said Victor.

"I guess so," said Krause. "Lew said Dwyer was just as glad to see her married. You ever run into her when she was at Skidmore, Charlie? She had that old white Caddie convertible. Had a pretty heavy foot."

Since seeing Dwyer that morning, Charlie had been trying to remember the daughter. With the mention of the white Cadillac convertible, he began to recall a thin girl with long blond hair who drove too fast. He didn't in fact remember much more than that; but there was a period of a few years where it seemed that whenever he was sent to investigate a loud party or kids being rowdy out at the lake, there had been this blond girl in her white Caddy convertible.

"I'd forgotten," said Charlie. "She lost her license and we picked her up a couple of times driving without it. Then about ten years ago she left town."

"Went out to Los Angeles," said Victor. "She's a decorator or designer or somethin out there. Met Curry down at Belmont when she came back on a visit. You know the story, whirl-wind romance."

"Where'd you hear all this?" asked Charlie.

Victor laid one finger along the side of his pear-shaped nose. Each side was decorated with little nets of red capillaries. "I knows what I knows," he said. He got to his feet and took Charlie's yellow slicker from a hook behind the door. "Mind if I wear this? I gotta check the horsies." He pulled on the yellow slicker and stuck the yellow rain hat on the back of his head. "Don't tell any dirty stories without me," he said.

"Check on Red Fox, will you, Vic? He doesn't like thunder."

"Him and me both. Hey, Rico, were there many other cars in the lot when you came in?"

"Just a couple. Why?" Rico had stopped touching his toes but was still standing in the middle of the room looking ready.

"No reason. Lotta the guys went to the movies to see *Snow White*. I wondered if they were back yet." Victor opened the door and Charlie could see it was still raining heavily. "I hate soggy feet," said Victor and disappeared.

Krause took a thick cigar from the inside pocket of his jacket, tore off the cellophane, and sniffed it appreciatively. Charlie hated cigar smoke, but feeling that Krause had been more upset by Lew's murder than anybody and was thus in greater need of comfort, he remained silent through the ritual of snipping off the tip of the cigar with some silver pocket tool, then lighting it with a fat kitchen match.

"I don't like to see you giving up on the investigation, Charlie," said Krause, through a cloud of smoke. "I told you I'd pay you. Any trouble you get into, I'll see you get out."

"I appreciate that, Jack, but it won't work. I asked Field if he'd back me, but like he said, I'm just a stable guard. If I keep going against Peterson, I'll get me and the stable in trouble. Besides, Peterson's got a police department of nearly eighty men and has access to every other department in the country. I can't just poke around."

"Tell him to kiss your ass," said Rico. "You got your own police department. There's Krause and you got five eager guards. What more'n you need than that?"

Charlie laughed. "Like I said, let's give Peterson more of a chance."

"Let's say, just for the sake of argument," said Rico, "that you kept up with your investigation, what would you do next?"

"I told you, I'm not doing any more." Charlie picked up his book on Dillinger.

Rico put his hands on his hips and violently began twisting his torso from left to right. "Yeah, but let's say you did," he asked, "what would you do next? You can answer me that, can't you?"

Charlie put his book back down. He'd be leaving in half an hour and could read at home. "I'd find out more about Wayne Curry," he said.

Victor kept his head bent as he followed the circle of light thrown on the mud and wet grass by the flashlight in his hand.

Even though rain was running down his face and neck, and even though his shoes had become small buckets, he was chuckling to himself. After seeing Dwyer that afternoon, he had stopped by the Backstretch and had gotten a lot of useful information about Dwyer, his daughter, and her husband from Doris and the owner, Berney McQuilkin. He wasn't sure what he'd do with it and he didn't intend to do anything until he had checked the houses he had missed on Hyde Street. But more and more Victor began to suspect that Ackerman had visited Dwyer's house that Tuesday night. Who he had seen or why he had gone, Victor didn't know, but the possibility of Ackerman seeing one of Dwyer's neighbors for something completely unconnected to Dwyer seemed improbable.

But he had enjoyed seeing Charlie's surprise as he had trotted out bits of information about Dwyer's daughter, and as he walked along the shed row he indulged in a fantasy in which he went ahead and solved the case by himself, perhaps concluding with one of those classic scenes where he brought together all suspects and interested parties and bit by bit unfolded to them the story of the crime as the actual murderer grew increasingly nervous and at last made a bolt for the door. How would he stop him? He imagined Moshe, his one-eyed cat, grown huge and carrying the murderer back into the room as he had once seen him carry a rat: almost tenderly between his jaws. And who was the murderer? That, unfortunately, he couldn't tell.

As he approached Red Fox's stall, he was jarred from his thoughts by seeing that instead of being closed, the Dutch door was wide open, bottom and top. Victor hurried toward the door, his flashlight projecting a bobbing circle of light on the muddy ground and white and green stalls. Running into the stall, he saw immediately that Red Fox was gone. Then, just as quickly, he sensed a movement behind him, but as he began to turn someone grabbed him, wrapping his arms around Victor's shoulders, and pinning Victor's arms to his sides. Victor kicked backward and heard a grunt, but before he could do more a second person took hold of his left hand, knocking the flashlight into the straw. There followed a brief struggle as

Victor tried to pull his hand free and the man behind him tightened his bear hug. Victor could hear the man breathing in his ear, but then his attention shifted as in the dim light he saw the man before him raise his hand above his head. Victor threw himself back, trying to yank his arm free. Then the man violently swung down his arm and a length of pipe smashed down onto Victor's left arm between the wrist and elbow.

It seemed to Victor that his whole arm had been jabbed with pieces of glass and he opened his mouth to scream. But before he could do more than suck in his breath, there was another quick movement and something hit him hard in the stomach. Simultaneously, the person behind him let go and shoved him forward. Victor staggered across the straw, retching and holding his stomach with his good hand. The flashlight between his feet made his shoes look big and muddy. Then he sensed another movement and as he tried to stagger away he was hit on the head. Again, the pain was like being stabbed with glass. As he fell, he tried to catch himself with his damaged arm and as the arm buckled beneath him Victor screamed a high scream like a car suddenly braking or wind rushing through a crack in a door. He fell on his side and held his arm to his chest. It felt as if his body was scattered in a dozen pieces around the stall. Trying to focus on his surroundings, he realized he was alone. He told himself he had to get Charlie and the last thing he remembered was crawling toward the door and feeling the rain spatter against his face as he crawled out of the stall.

When he awoke, he was being lifted out the back door of an ambulance. Looking up, he saw Charlie's worried, round face looking down from one side of the stretcher and Krause looking down from the other. The pain in his arm was such that he felt sure he would pass out again.

"Somebody fuckin' whopped me, Charlie. They steal Red Fox?"

"No, he was out on the track. He'll be okay. You see anybody?"

Victor shook his head. He felt he was going to be sick. The ambulance attendants wheeled him through the emergency entrance into a brightly lit hallway. A doctor and two nurses hurried toward him. "Didn't see a fuckin soul," he said.

An hour later, Victor, wearing a blue hospital gown, was settled into a private room where he was to spend the night. For observation, as he had been told. His left arm had been broken and was now in a cast. Charlie and Krause had gone with him up to the room, along with a little orderly who knew Charlie and who brought in extra pillows, magazines, and a triple shot of Jack Daniel's in a paper cup. He was a thin little man, not much taller than five feet, and was one of those unfortunates who don't go bald in a smooth process but in bits and pieces, making his hair look like something that the cats had fought over.

As Victor began to sip the Jack Daniel's, Charlie sat down on a chair next to the bed. He had had no chance to talk to Victor since his friend had been admitted. "So you have no idea who broke your arm?" asked Charlie.

"None. Couldn't see their faces. Couldn't even see what they were wearin except it was dark. Shit, it could of been a coupla broads. What'd I get hit with?"

"I found a length of lead pipe in the straw," said Charlie. "The police must have it by now."

Charlie had seen the police arriving just as he had been leaving in the ambulance. Rico had shown them around and presumably they would soon appear at the hospital. Charlie had telephoned Rico and learned that the police suspected what Charlie had at first suspected himself, that is, that Victor had accidentally interrupted two men who had been trying to do something to Red Fox. That was what Charlie had originally thought, but now he wasn't so sure. There was no evidence they had tried to steal Red Fox and there was no evidence he had been physically tampered with. Of course that couldn't be certain until the horse was examined by the vet, but the groom, Petey Gomez, had checked him over pretty carefully and Red Fox had seemed fine, according to Rico.

Beyond that, what struck Charlie was that Victor's arm had been broken, well, carefully. As if the intruders had come for the sole purpose of breaking the arm. The problem, however, was that Charlie knew no reason why anyone should want to hurt Victor. The only thing he could think of was that since Victor had been wearing Charlie's yellow raincoat, they had attacked him mistakenly. As he thought this, Charlie wondered what reason anyone had for hurting him, and with the question came the realization that it had to have something to do with Ackerman's death. Sitting next to Victor's bed and watching him sip the Jack Daniel's, Charlie tried to guess the odds of convincing Peterson that he himself had been the intended victim. He knew, however, that the police chief would instead believe the simpler interpretation, that is, that Victor had been attacked because he had interrupted somebody tampering with Red Fox.

The small man with the patchwork hair appeared at the foot of Victor's bed. "Is there anything else you would like, Mr. Plotz, a sandwich or maybe a deck of cards? I can get you a *Playboy*."

"Nah, that's all right. Thanks for the drink."

After the man left, Victor asked Charlie, "He a friend of yours?"

"Sort of. He was one of the first guys I ever arrested and I stayed in touch with him in prison. Got him a lot of books about birds, if I remember right."

"What was he in for?"

"Killed someone in a bar."

"How come?" Victor tried to sit up, then winced and stayed where he was.

"I don't know, he said the man had stolen his wife's affections. Something like that. I sort of doubted his wife had ever cared much for him in the first place. Nice guy though, once you got to know him."

Victor drank off his Jack Daniel's and dropped his cup on the floor. "Jesus, Charlie, I should of known that hangin around somebody who only knows criminals and reprobates would land me just where I am right now. I must be the only fuckin respectable friend you have."

"That's probably true," said Charlie.

17

▼▼▼

C HARLIE ALWAYS DID his best thinking underwater. As he negotiated a slow turn at the end of the pool, then started back for his second length, he felt his body beginning to free itself from the cocoon of frustration and social convention which had confined his day. It was about quarter past seven Friday evening and around Charlie in the YMCA pool were seven or eight other swimmers engaged in the slow process of accumulating laps.

Charlie liked that. He liked the comradely anonymity of the pool. He liked that for the most part the people around him knew him primarily as a swimmer: someone who could be counted on to do a certain number of laps and stay in his own lane.

Jim Connor swam on one side of him, much faster and more graceful, but still a friendly presence. On the other side was a young woman in a dark blue Speedo suit. Outside the pool, she was chunky and heavyset, but in the pool she was completely streamlined, like a large beautiful seal. Charlie saw himself a little like that: not beautiful exactly, but streamlined and efficient, moving purposefully in the one place in life where he didn't stumble over his feet.

In the eyes of his family, he knew he had begun to stumble badly. That morning he had received a telephone call from James, his oldest cousin, five years older and the owner of a small construction company. He had said Chief Peterson had dropped by to tell him Charlie was acting foolishly and irresponsibly, interfering with a criminal investigation to the extent the criminals were most likely benefiting from his intrusion. James didn't want to interfere, didn't want to tell Charlie what he should or should not do. Far be it from him to remind his young cousin the family had a position to maintain in the community, but perhaps Charlie wouldn't mind dropping by the office that afternoon and they could have a chat over a cup of coffee.

The call had come at 7:30 that morning, waking Charlie after three hours sleep. It was James's contention that a mentally, emotionally, and physically healthy person only required four hours sleep per night, and he proved this by never sleeping more than four hours himself. It was this feat, he believed, which was also responsible for his business success, his election as president of the Lions Club, and his being a six-time recipient of the Little League Booster Award. He also believed, somewhat inaccurately, that Charlie required vast quantities of time-squandering sleep and that he had inherited this weakness from his father's side of the family. Charlie had expected James to remind him once again how his father had welched on his IOU's to bookies by sending a bullet through his brain, but James had chosen to be subtle. In any case, Charlie had not gone to his office and had no intention of going.

As he swam back and forth, he grew increasingly certain that the attack on Victor had been intended for himself and, further, the attack was an indication that his small investigation was seen by someone as a threat. The veterinarian's report on Red Fox showed the horse had not been tampered with beyond being freed from his stall. Chief Peterson at first argued that Victor had interrupted the tampering, but it now seemed clear Red Fox had escaped to the training track about ten minutes before Victor had appeared on the scene. Beyond this, Charlie was not happy that it had been Victor who was attacked, rather than himself, since it gave Charlie the nagging sense there was information unaccounted for. The fact Victor was wearing Charlie's yellow slicker seemed to explain this, but still Charlie wondered if something wasn't being left out.

In any case, Peterson had finally agreed that the purpose of the intrusion was most likely the attack rather than the horse. Victor hadn't simply been knocked unconscious, his arm had been neatly and carefully broken. But although Peterson had come to this conclusion, the reasons he gave for it were different than Charlie's.

Charlie had stopped by police headquarters that morning to

see if Peterson had any new information about what had happened. Peterson was even more patronizing than usual. "Now, Charlie," he had said, "you know and I know that Plotz has a bad habit of chasing the women. What I figure is that some husband or some boyfriend finally had enough. Who can blame them, an old guy like that?"

"Maybe they were after me," Charlie had said.

"How come? You after the women, too?"

"Perhaps I've upset someone by asking questions about Ackerman."

"Aw, Charlie, give me a break. I already told you what I thought about the case. You know as well as I do that when Plotz likes some female, he just asks them point-blank and when they say no, he just keeps asking them. Some guys don't like that and I can't say I blame them."

Charlie had spent some time arguing with Peterson, but the police chief just shook his head and looked wise. The result was that Charlie, who had sincerely decided to give up investigating Lew Ackerman's death, decided to press his investigation a little further.

The girl in the blue tank suit had left the pool to be replaced by a man in his mid-seventies whose free style stroke was a combination of the dog paddle and drowning. It seemed to Charlie that if even the smallest bird landed on this swimmer's shoulders he would certainly go under. Charlie recognized him as an ex-city councilman whose suspect real estate deals allowed him to make a fortune when the Interstate was put through at the edge of town. Beyond that, Charlie recalled a questionable interest in little girls. In the lane next to Charlie, however, he was just a man doing his laps.

As a consequence of Peterson's dismissal of the attack on Victor, Charlie had returned to the stable around noon to assemble what Rico Medioli called Charlie's Police Force. Besides Victor, who stayed home, and Krause and Rico himself, there were: Phil Tyler, an ex-real estate and confidence swindler who had sold thousands of acres of phony property in Florida, New Mexico, and Arizona and whom Charlie had hired primarily because he looked like the White Knight in *Alice Through the*

Looking Glass; John Wanamaker, slightly younger than Charlie, ex-burglar and drunk and now a born-again Christian and member of A.A. who never did his rounds without his Bible; Eddie Gillespie, a none-too-bright youngster from nearby Ballston Spa who was only happy at speeds over 100-miles-per-hour and was presently on probation for car theft. As these five men gathered in Charlie's office, he realized there were some of the people he liked best in Saratoga.

Charlie explained what he knew about the two murders, said what Peterson's ideas were, and went on to say that he felt they should learn more about Dwyer's stable and Wayne Curry in particular. He didn't necessarily suspect Curry, but there were unanswered questions arising from Neal Claremon's departure and what he had learned from Henry Dietz, the groom Curry had fired for stealing watches. Charlie had talked to Jack Warner the previous day about hiring Dietz, and when Charlie saw the trainer that morning, Warner told him that Dietz would probably start work before the end of the week, although Warner swore he meant to keep a close eye on him to make sure he kept his nose clean. In any case, Krause and the four guards agreed that the starting point of their investigation ought to be Wayne Curry.

Rico agreed to find out where Wayne Curry had come from in Connecticut, then drive down and see if he could dig up any dirt. Tyler said he would see if there was anything to be learned from Curry's years on Dwyer's farm from friends he had on neighboring horse farms in Kentucky. Krause, Wanamaker, and Gillespie agreed to look around Saratoga, talk to people who worked for Curry, trying to find out what sort of person he was.

Having set this part of his investigation in motion, Charlie had then left the stable to seek out various gamblers he used to know in Saratoga in order to verify Chief Peterson's story about a move to reestablish gambling. After several hours, he had run across Max Tubbs, a thin dapper gambler of sixty-five from whom Charlie had once confiscated a dozen slot machines.

Tubbs would sometimes say the Max stood for Maxwell

and sometimes for Maximilian, but generally he was known as Maximum Tubbs. He had begun gambling in Saratoga in 1931 and for the next twenty-one years, before Governor Dewey closed down the tables, he had accumulated enough money to make him rich—would have made him rich if he hadn't lost it just as quickly in other people's games. However, the habit of those years was such that Maximum Tubbs had tried to maintain his role as gambler ever since, which had led to frequent arrests and a friendship with Charlie Bradshaw.

Around three in the afternoon, Charlie found him dealing blackjack in the back of a Texaco station at the edge of town. Tubbs agreed, after some prodding, to find out about Ackerman and the current status of Saratoga gambling, then meet Charlie that evening at the Backstretch.

Charlie finished his thirtieth length and glanced at the clock. It was just 7:30. It took Charlie about twenty-two minutes to swim half a mile: thirty-six lengths. He was satisfied with that, although he knew it was about fifteen minutes longer than the record. Seeing the clock made him realize it was at this time that Ackerman often went swimming. Charlie would look up and there would be Lew spitting into his goggles at the edge of the pool or tightening the string of his green Speedo suit. If he saw Charlie looking, he would wave. If there was a lane free next to Charlie, Lew would take that one.

As he headed back up the pool, Charlie remembered the number "730," which Ackerman had written on his new blotter, and it again struck him as peculiar that Ackerman should have to remind himself when he swam. Then Charlie wondered why he had thought it signified a time. Probably because he had noticed it at about the same moment he came across the goggles in the top drawer of the desk. Actually, the number could be anything. It could even be a date. As this occurred to him, Charlie could feel his mind grow more alert. July 30th would be Sunday, two days away. Again, Charlie had the sense he was forgetting something, and with that was the fear that something as terrible as the murders was swimming toward him out of the future.

Charlie finished his half mile and climbed out of the pool. As he showered and washed his hair, he kept thinking of the number on the blotter and the possibility that it was a date that had some connection with Ackerman's death. He dressed quickly, wanting to get to the Backstretch as soon as possible; but as he was leaving he happened to glance into the weight room, which was empty except for one man on the Universal. Only when he had gone a few steps past the door did Charlie realize that the man was Wayne Curry.

Charlie stopped, then went back to the doorway for a second look. Dressed in gym shoes and purple shorts, Curry was on his back on a bench repeatedly pulling the bar down to his midriff. Charlie knew little about the Universal, but guessed that the weights attached to the pulley weighed certainly more than fifty pounds. As if there were no weights at all, Curry lowered and raised his arms as easily as if he had been swimming. His muscular body was tanned and glistened with sweat. The pulley made a creak, then a rattling crash, over and over, as the weights returned to position.

Charlie continued to watch until he happened to glance further into the room and saw a mirror attached to the far wall. In the center of the mirror was Curry's lean face and Charlie realized the man was staring at him. Charlie started to look away, then didn't. Despite the effort and physical exertion of repeatedly pulling down the bar, Curry's face bore the same manikinlike nonexpression that had struck Charlie the previous day. It was only with difficulty that Charlie could make himself believe Curry was staring at him. Then, when he did, he grew embarrassed and hurried out of the building to find his car.

Five minutes later, Charlie was in his yellow Volkswagen on his way to the Backstretch. As he drove, he kept thinking of Curry staring at him in the weight room mirror, while in his memory the size of the weights increased until it seemed that Curry had been effortlessly pulling two hundred pounds. It gave Charlie the immediate sense that he had no time to spare. Regretfully, he glanced down at the biography of Dillinger on the seat beside him. Just the sight of the half-finished book seemed to soothe him. He liked the fact that the anarchy and uncertainty of Dillinger's life could be arranged in 450 digestible pages.

It had pleased Charlie to discover that Dillinger had been a great second baseman, both for his home team in Martinsville, Indiana, and for the Indiana State Reformatory team in Pendleton. The governor had thought Dillinger good enough to play major league ball and transferred Dillinger to the state prison in Michigan City because it had the best prison team in Indiana.

Dillinger had been a strong White Sox fan and might have played for the White Sox had his life been different. He certainly could have been no worse, Charlie thought, than Shoeless Joe Jackson, Swede Risberg, Buck Weaver, Happy Felsch, and the other four White Sox players who had been paid $70,000 to throw the first two games of the 1919 World Series. Dillinger had been sixteen at the time and his criminal activity up until then had consisted of stealing coal from the Pennsylvania Railroad yards and selling it to neighbors.

Charlie pulled into the parking lot next to the Backstretch and cut the engine. Actually, he thought, it was a famous Saratoga gambler who had been accused, but never convicted, of masterminding the World Series fix. Arnold Rothstein, known in the city as Mr. Big, had once owned the Brook, the most exclusive of the Saratoga casinos after World War I, as well as owning a stable of horses, and being the silent partner in a number of other casinos including the Chicago Club. Rothstein drank milk instead of whiskey, collected Whistler etchings, and employed Legs Diamond as his private killer. He was finally murdered in 1928 in the Park Central Hotel in New York City for refusing to pay the $320,000 he had lost in cards to Nigger Nate Raymond.

Rothstein sometimes reminded Charlie of Lew Ackerman, since both men began their fortunes by running poker games in New York as teenagers. But while Lew enjoyed people and had some sense of ethics, Rothstein had become involved in everything from industrial rackets to selling narcotics. Hours before he was shot, he had been in Lindy's where he wagered

$500,000 that Herbert Hoover would defeat Al Smith in the imminent presidential election. Rothstein's lawyer once described him as like "a mouse standing in a doorway, waiting for his cheese." Nobody could ever have said that about Lew Ackerman.

Doris Bailes was behind the bar and smiled at Charlie as he came in. Seeing her and feeling the responding tension in his chest, Charlie once more regretted having a temperament formed by the romantic movies of the 1940s. He nodded and made his way to the pay phone near the entrance to the back room where the blond stripper was just taking her place on the stage. Charlie got Frank Warner's home phone number from information and dialed. He was hoping the trainer could shed light on the number 730, explain it away as a horse medicine or the best speed on six and a half furlongs. Frank answered as the juke box began blaring out "Boogie-oogie-oogie."

"Frank, this is Charlie, can you think of any reason that Lew would have written the number 730 on his blotter?"

There was a silence, then a suspicious voice which Charlie had to strain to hear: "Why? What's so important about it?"

"I'm not sure," said Charlie. "Lew wrote it down shortly before he was shot. It could be some perfectly innocent thing connected with the stable so I thought I'd ask you."

"I thought the police were handling the investigation."

"They are, but I just ran across this and thought it might be important."

"Doesn't ring any bells with me, Charlie. Where you calling from anyway?"

"A pay phone. What about as a date, you know, this Sunday? Do you know if he had anything planned for then?"

One of the two sailors from the naval base who were watching the stripper began to shout, "Take it all off, baby, take off the fuckin G-string. Let's see a little nookie." Charlie imagined Warner listening carefully so he could report it later to Charlie's cousins. It had only been about a month before that his middle cousin, Robert, had laid his hand on Charlie's shoulder and said, "Charlie, it makes me proud to say that in all my twenty-five years of marriage Lucy has never seen the inside of a saloon."

"No, Charlie," said Warner, "the number doesn't mean anything special. You know as well as I do that Sunday's the day before the track opens. Is that all you wanted? I've still got some work to do."

"Sure, Frank. Thanks."

Charlie made his way back to the bar and ordered a beer from Doris. She had on a white Mexican blouse and a Mexican tin necklace. The top three buttons of her blouse were undone, and her tan skin, the line of her breasts, made Charlie want to reach out and touch her. As he thought this, he wondered if he wasn't the corrupt and disreputable black sheep Warner thought him to be. For his first dozen years as a policeman, Charlie was constantly arresting aged drunks and derelicts who fondly claimed friendship with his father, remembering him as a man who would wager on anything. Recalling this, Charlie also remembered his mother telling him that his father had bet a thousand dollars that Al Smith would defeat Herbert Hoover.

Charlie glanced at his watch. It was just past eight. Maximum Tubbs should be arriving shortly, while Victor had said he would stop by around 9:30. Charlie was worried about Victor. There appeared to be something bothering him apart from the attack of the night before. Charlie had asked him what was wrong, but Victor just brushed it off. He hoped Victor hadn't decided to return to New York or go live with his son in Chicago. Even though Frank Warner felt there was nobody more low class than Victor Plotz, Charlie knew he had no better friend in Saratoga.

Doris came over and wiped off the bar in front of him. "I like it when you've been swimming," she said, "it makes your ears all pink and shiny."

"Is that a good enough reason for you to come home with me tonight?"

"For gin rummy or sex?" Doris looked at Charlie steadily for a moment, then pushed her dark brown hair away from her eyes.

"Sex," said Charlie.

"You lost me there. I might have come for gin rummy."

"All right, gin rummy."

"Ah, Charlie, you've lost me again. You've got to stick to your guns."

Charlie looked down at his beer glass, then looked up again. "What about gin rummy and sex combined? Not only that, but I'll throw in an order of scrambled eggs and bacon."

"I've got enough trouble with my figure without eating all night, but if I had known you were so handy with a skillet I would have stopped by this morning. I jogged by your cottage around 6:30. Would I have been welcome?"

"Without a doubt," said Charlie. "A truly healthy person only requires four hours sleep a night."

"I'll remember that next time," said Doris.

Maximum Tubbs appeared about ten minutes later. He was a small, trim man with a full head of thick, steel gray hair and an immaculate blue seersucker suit. Before he sat down at a booth, he wiped off the seat and back with several napkins.

"Never know who's been sitting someplace," said Tubbs. "Germs are the enemies of old age."

Charlie ordered another beer and Tubbs had a Vichy with a twist of lime. He had clean, pink hands with long fingers that were never still but tapped and snapped and drummed on the table.

"So what did you find out?" asked Charlie once they were settled.

"I don't know where you got your information, Charlie, but that move to legalize gambling doesn't seem much greater than it ever is."

"I heard the state was looking into it."

"Well, they've got some committee, but there's no sign of its even meeting yet. It's true that Ackerman was dead set against gambling. He wanted Saratoga for the symphony and ballet. No more casinos." Tubbs paused to make sure his tie was straight. It was a dark blue tie with dozens of miniature white dice. "Maybe Ackerman would have appeared before this committee, but that would of been some time off."

"So you don't think Lew could have been murdered because of his opposition to gambling?"

"Who's to say," said Tubbs. "Gamblers are funny people. Ackerman was one himself. He ran a pretty big poker game before he quit."

"What about gambling interests on Long Island?"

"That's just the thing, Charlie. There's always gambling interests on Long Island that want to open up casinos in Saratoga and, sure, those people probably aren't too sorry that Ackerman is dead, but that's not to say they killed him. Personally, I think gambling's going to come back. I mean, it's bound to. But it's not going to happen tomorrow."

"What if gambling were legalized, where do you think the casinos would be?"

"That's hard to say," said Tubbs, looking critically at his thumbnail. "Maybe in some of the old mansions, like where the Chicago Club used to be. Maybe in the hotels. The Gideon Putnam could easily put in a casino. And there's a new hotel being planned that will make the Gideon Putnam look like small potatoes. It'd be built so a casino could be put right in and it'll have a big bar and restaurant and a stage show. You know, live acts straight from Las Vegas. They've already begun putting together the financing."

"Where's it going to be?"

"Don't know for sure. They're looking into a couple of sites. They want to have it near the Performing Arts Center. About as near to it as the Gideon Putnam. The whole thing's still pretty secret."

"Is Robert Dwyer involved in this by any chance?"

"That old guy? No, he's not. Funny you should ask though, because his son-in-law's into it pretty heavy. I forget his name."

"Wayne Curry."

"That's right. Curry. He's one of the big investors."

"Wouldn't these guys have to put up a lot of money?" asked Charlie.

"Damn right. A fortune."

18

▼▼▼

"WHAT I BEEN THINKIN," said Victor, "is I wouldn't have to go to Chicago or back to New York. I might go down to Nashville instead. Make my fortune in the country music business."

"So what do you know about country music?" asked Charlie. They were in Charlie's Volkswagen driving along the eastern shore of Saratoga Lake. What he had learned about Curry and the proposed hotel had made Charlie decide to talk to Field one more time. It was past ten o'clock and to Charlie's right he could see a nearly full moon rising over the lake as he drove by darkened cottages and stores.

"Good grief, Charlie, music's my middle name. What do you think of this little number:

> "*I'm not a man for candy,*
> *Don't tempt me with apple pie,*
> *You won't find me drinkin soda pop,*
> *Whiskey is all I try.*
> *I've lost my taste for sweet things*
> *Since you said goodbye.*"

Victor sang in a high, clear falsetto that Charlie would not have guessed possible. The Volkswagen seemed to quiver on the road.

"So you're set on leaving Saratoga?" asked Charlie, keeping his tone of voice conversational.

"No, not set, I wouldn't say set. I just been thinkin about it, that's all. I'll make up my mind once we wrap up this investigation. You think Field will back you up now?"

"Perhaps. If I explain what we've found out about Curry, then maybe. But there's still a lot that doesn't make sense. I can't believe Curry had Ackerman killed or killed him himself just because of his objection to gambling in Saratoga. Also, where's Curry getting the money for the hotel?"

"I read of a guy once who killed his poor old grandmother because he didn't like how she ate, her soup. What're you goin to do after you see Field?"

"I guess I'll try to find out where Lew went that Tuesday night."

Victor didn't respond to this but seemed to be staring out at the lake.

"You told me the other day you thought that was probably important," said Charlie. "Have you changed your mind?"

Victor remained silent. As they drove, the moon path kept up with them across the water, lighting up boats and the choppy waves stirred by a southern wind.

"Well," said Victor at last, "I may have made some trouble for you there."

"What do you mean?"

Victor rapped his knuckles on his cast, which was supported by a sling around his neck. "I mean maybe I know why I got my arm busted and when I tell you, maybe you'll want to bust the other one."

"What are you talking about?"

"I'm trying to say I think I found out where Ackerman went. You see, he turned up at the Backstretch on foot later on that Tuesday night. Then he got one of the regulars to drive him home." Victor continued to explain how he had talked to the man who had given Ackerman a ride, how he had learned about Hyde Street and knocked on doors, how he had talked to Robert Dwyer and how it was only later when he learned more about Dwyer that he realized it might be important.

"I didn't want to say anything about it," said Victor, "until I checked those last six houses, but I checked them this afternoon and they'd seen Ackerman about as much as they'd seen Santa Claus or Rudolph Valentino. What I think is that he really went to Dwyer's, although maybe he didn't see Dwyer himself. Maybe he saw that Curry fellow. He's got the carriage house behind Dwyer's. I been lookin for him, but he wasn't there yesterday and he wasn't there today. Just some horsey guys sittin around and they didn't know nothin."

"You mean you just knocked on all the doors on Hyde Street and asked if Ackerman had been there for some reason that later got him killed?"

"Not exactly like that. I was pretty subtle."

"You're lucky you weren't killed last night," said Charlie. He couldn't believe Victor had ever been subtle in his life. "Then you went back today? You're not even safe to be around."

"Well, that's what I figured when I came to in the ambulance. I mean, I guess I lit a real fire under somebody."

"Jesus, Victor, you're the one who got burned."

"Vic," said Victor.

But Charlie was no longer paying attention. He was thinking about what Neal Claremon's wife had said about her husband's remark that there was nothing worse than a stable fire. Then, almost without transition, it occurred to Charlie that if Dwyer's stable burned and the insurance were paid off, then Curry would have both money and location for the new hotel. And again, almost without transition, there came to him the possible significance of the number 730 on Ackerman's blotter. The 30th was Sunday, only a day before the races, and the stable would be at its fullest and most valuable. Then Charlie asked himself, what if Claremon had found out there was going to be a fire and went to Ackerman with the information?

"You know," said Charlie, "I think I've just figured out what Curry's been doing."

But now it was Victor who wasn't paying attention. "What the hell's wrong with that asshole behind us that he won't dim his lights?"

For a few seconds, Charlie had been vaguely aware that the interior of the Volkswagen had grown quite bright. Glancing into the rearview mirror, he saw the four lights of what he guessed was a pickup truck about ten feet behind his rear bumper. Charlie slowed down and moved a little to the right. Instead of passing, however, the truck moved steadily closer until there was a metallic clang and jolt as it touched the back bumper.

"If that's another one of your asshole criminal friends," said Victor, "you can tell him from me to stop fuckin around. I like my jokes purely verbal."

Charlie didn't say anything but sped up slightly. The truck dropped back a few feet. It made a high roaring noise and Charlie guessed it was a four-speed in third gear. He turned his attention back to the highway, which was empty and dark. The pickup sped up again, hitting the bumper with a louder clang and making the Volkswagen swerve on the road.

"I expect," said Charlie, "that they're the same people who broke your arm."

Charlie accelerated to sixty, but the truck stayed inches behind him. The road along the lake curved one way, then another as it followed the shore. There wasn't enough space between the two vehicles to let Charlie either slow or turn without being rammed from behind. Charlie found himself thinking of a time ten years before when Chief Peterson sent him to Syracuse to attend a State Police training session on avoidance tactics in a high speed chase. Although Charlie knew how to execute a split-second U-turn at 120-miles-per-hour, he could think of nothing to do about an oversize pickup truck less than a foot away from a Volkswagen bumper. The four bright lights in his mirror were blinding. He reached out and tilted the mirror upward so he could see ahead more clearly. They had passed no other cars.

"Take a shot at them," said Victor. "Shoot right back through the back window and I'll pay for the damage."

"I'm not armed."

"You kiddin? I thought you always had a gun."

"I hardly ever carry one."

"Christ, Charlie, you cop types, I thought you'd feel naked unless you went out armed to the teeth. You mean we're stuck with this madman and all I can do is throw the roadmap at him?"

"That's about it."

The truck dropped back a few feet, then surged forward,

smashing the rear of the Volkswagen so hard that it swerved
onto the dirt shoulder, then back across the lane into the left
lane as Charlie struggled to keep the car under control. Just as
he managed to straighten the wheel, the truck again rushed
forward, smashing into his bumper, and again he swerved to
the right, then left. He heard the sound of breaking glass and
bits of metal falling into the road, and irrelevantly he found
himself thinking about the financial damage to the back of his
car. At the same time, he couldn't quite think what the truck
wanted. Then he realized that was foolish. They weren't being
threatened or frightened. This was going to be murder and as
the truck roared ahead and smashed his bumper for yet another
time, Charlie knew there was absolutely nothing he could do
about it. Glancing at Victor, Charlie saw he had his hand flat
against the dash and was pushing himself back in his seat.
Beyond him through the window, Charlie caught sight of a
small darkened grocery where he often stopped to buy Freihofer chocolate chip cookies if he felt thinner than usual and
in need of soothing. The grocery now seemed to be a place in
another country.

Then Charlie saw the trees and cottages drop away as the
road rose slightly above the lake. At that moment he realized
what the truck had been waiting for. There was now nothing
between them and the water. As if his thought were a signal,
the truck dropped back about five feet, then swerved out into
the left lane and surged forward again with a roar. Charlie
slammed on his brakes and tried to pull over, but it was no
use. The truck swung sharply to the right, smashing the rear
left fender of the Volkswagen and sending it rushing off the
road as easily as a Ping-Pong ball.

Charlie was aware of a rising moan coming from Victor as
the Volkswagen plunged and rattled down the bank toward
the lake. Charlie knew the spot where they had gone off the
road. Some distance ahead in the darkness was a small cliff
maybe ten or fifteen feet above the lake where all summer he
had seen teenagers diving into the water. The Volkswagen was
sluing to the left and right as it rushed toward the drop. Charlie
wrestled to straighten the wheel so at least they would go over

the edge nose first. Although he had downshifted and kept pumping the brake, he guessed he was still going about forty. High grass whipped the sides of the car. Charlie tried to think if he was terrified, but he was too busy to feel much of anything. He hated the way everything was bouncing around.

"Get ready to jump!" he shouted to Victor.

"I hate sports," said Victor, still pushing back with his hand on the dash.

Letting go of the wheel with his right hand, Charlie quickly swung out and hit Victor across the face. "Victor, you've got to jump!"

The car plunged over the small cliff and for a moment everything was silent, while ahead of them the lights showed nothing but miles of black water.

"Jump!" shouted Charlie.

He opened the door of the Volkswagen, pulled himself out with his fingers gripping the roof and pushed himself upward. Briefly, his feet caught against the pedals, then against the steering wheel, but by this time his body was above the surface of the car and so when the car hit the water, Charlie was thrown forward and free. He curled his body, tucking his knees under his chin, and for a few seconds skimmed along the surface like a skipped stone. Then he went under.

Unable to help himself, Charlie began to choke and breathe in water as his water-soaked clothes dragged him deeper and deeper beneath the surface. The blackness was like death and for the first time that evening he felt panic and began to kick and thrash his arms. Then he took hold of himself and tried to relax. He told himself that water wasn't strange to him, that he swam several miles each week. He kicked off his shoes, slipped out of his jacket and pants and at last floated up to the surface. Then he began swimming back to the Volkswagen and Victor. His great fear was that Victor was dead or trapped inside unable to get out. He pushed away the thought and swam rapidly through the water to where in the moonlight he saw masses of white bubbles and steam rising from his car. Looking further, he saw flashlights bobbing along the shore.

Charlie guessed the Volkswagen was down about ten feet. Taking a deep breath, he dove into the bubbles. He could see nothing but after a moment he touched the roof of the car. Almost immediately something grabbed him, seemingly tried to drag him deeper. Although he knew it was Victor, the attack was so fierce and violent that Charlie again had to force himself not to panic. Victor was clutching one of his legs, trying to claw his way up Charlie's body. Charlie twisted himself so his feet were on the roof of the car, while with his right hand he reached down and caught hold of Victor's collar, both keeping him from climbing any higher or getting away. It was fortunate, Charlie knew, that Victor only had the use of one arm. With two, he wouldn't be able to control him.

Charlie pushed his feet against the roof of the car, trying to drag Victor up with him, but Victor wouldn't budge. Again he tried to push himself upward, but Victor still wouldn't come free. Charlie guessed he was caught in the door. There was no time to dive down and free him even if he could loosen Victor's grip. Charlie's lungs ached and he was desperate for air. Bending his knees, he let Victor pull him down to the roof of the car as Victor frantically clawed his way upward and at last circled Charlie's head with his arm. Then Charlie pushed with all his strength against the Volkswagen roof. At first nothing happened, but then Victor came free. Charlie began to kick desperately, using his one arm to pull himself through the water. When he broke the surface, he took great gasping breaths. He slipped his head free of Victor's wrestling hold, pushed him away and rolled over on his back.

There was a shout and, glancing toward Victor, Charlie saw him thrashing and slowly sinking beneath the surface. Charlie rolled over, kicked his way toward him, and grabbed Victor's good arm just as it disappeared.

Resurfacing, Victor began clawing his way up Charlie's arm. Charlie drew up his legs and kicked Victor away; then, grabbing his collar, he held him at arm's length as he pedaled his feet to keep his head above water.

"Can't you swim?" shouted Charlie.

Victor shook his head and tried to shout something.

"Try to relax and I'll tow you in. Don't fight me or I'll leave you."

It was only about twenty-five feet to shore. Charlie turned Victor over on his back and, again grabbing his collar, slowly towed him in to where he could see a group of people with flashlights. Victor kept coughing and spitting up water. Charlie thought how beautiful the lake looked with the moonlight shimmering on its surface. Then he thought of his yellow Volkswagen. He had prided himself on the fact it had no dents, scratches, or rust. After that it occurred to him that someone had tried to kill him.

When the water was waist deep, he let go of Victor and stood up. Victor stood beside him. Charlie could hear his teeth chattering.

"You saved my life," said Victor, shivering. "I thought that only happened on the TV."

"I didn't want to take care of your cat."

"Hey, Charlie, you watch out or you'll find yourself with a sense of humor."

"Heaven forbid," said Charlie.

What angered Charlie more than having his car run off the road was the fact the police lieutenant required him to take a blood test.

"I'm not drunk and I haven't been drinking. I already told you what happened. We were bumped off the road by a pickup truck. Somebody tried to kill us."

"Look, Bradshaw, it's part of the routine. If you refuse to take the test, I can only assume you have something to hide."

They had been brought into the police station and stood dripping in front of the desk. Both Victor and Charlie had gray army blankets draped over their shoulders. On the bench behind them, an old woman whose drinking had caused her to be kicked out of bars for the past fifty years kept saying: "Don't take it so hard. Troubles happen to the best of us."

The lieutenant was a sandy-haired, sandy-faced, ex-military policeman named Schultz. Peterson had hired him and advanced him because of his military background. Charlie had never liked him nor liked the way he bullied prisoners.

"Sure I'll take the test, but you better put out an alert for that truck. It'll have yellow paint marks on the right front fender."

"Yeah, yeah, I've called the state boys."

When Peterson arrived at midnight, Charlie and Victor were preparing to leave police headquarters dressed in some old clothes. Peterson made them wait while he talked to Schultz who had become more obliging after receiving proof that Charlie was sober.

"Now, Charlie," said Peterson as he came out to where Charlie and Victor were waiting, "what's all this about your being bumped off the road?"

Charlie could tell by his tone that Peterson was ready to make up and be, if not friendly, at least cordial. Even at this hour, he was dressed in his impeccable blue suit. Charlie on the other hand had little interest in making up. All he cared about was getting home and getting to bed.

"I already told Schultz. It looked like a large three-quarter-ton truck. I couldn't determine the color, but if you drag my car out of the lake you can get paint samples from where the truck hit me."

"Why would anyone want to knock you into the lake?"

"That's what I intend to find out," said Charlie.

"Now, Charlie, you know it's your duty to tell us what you've found out. Does this have anything to do with Ackerman?"

Until this moment, Charlie hadn't realized how he felt betrayed by a police department to which he had given twenty years of his life. Having to take the blood test, instead of Schultz accepting his word, simply galled him.

"Peterson," he said, "I wouldn't tell you a thing."

"Damn right," said Victor, "that's what I like to hear."

19

▼▼▼

"T
HAT'S RIGHT, it was a clear case of hit-and-run. Knocked
the kid off his bike. Lucky it didn't kill him."

"Did he do time for it?" asked Charlie.

"No, his old man's got some money," said Rico. "Must of paid a bundle to keep Curry out of jail."

"And when was all this?"

"Fall of '71," said Rico. "He'd been out of the army about a month."

Rico was calling from Greenwich, Connecticut. It was about four o'clock Saturday afternoon and Charlie was in his office at Lorelei Stables. Outside some of the exercise boys were throwing a Frisbee and Charlie could hear them calling to each other in Spanish.

Rico had learned that Curry had gone to a private boys' school, quit in his junior year to hitchhike out to California, joined the army, and got into the Green Berets, served three tours in Viet Nam, and came out a lieutenant in 1971. The hit-and-run accusation appeared to be the one thing against him and it had never been proved in court.

"It must of been his father that got him the job at Belmont, some kind of public relations thing. He'd only had it a couple of months when he met Dwyer's daughter."

"And they were married fairly quickly?"

"That's right. Two weeks after they met. Curry quit his job."

"What's his relationship with his family now?" asked Charlie.

"Seems pretty nonexistent. Least he's never down here. His mother died in '70 and the father remarried about four years later. You want me to dig around and find out?"

"No, come on back up. We'll need you tonight."

After Charlie hung up, he walked to the door of his office. In the ten yards between his corner of the barn and the training track, about a dozen different colored Frisbees were spinning through the air, while his youngest guard, Eddie Gillespie, was in the act of vaulting the fence to the track to retrieve a red Frisbee that lay in the dirt.

Earlier Gillespie and John Wanamaker had stopped by to tell Charlie what they had learned about Wayne Curry in Saratoga. There hadn't been much. Curry was active in the country club and a number of civic organizations. His friends tended to be wealthy: men who had made their money in real estate speculation, construction, investments. Four times a year, when his wife visited from California, Curry would throw large catered dinner parties. He appeared to have no close friends or cronies.

After telling Gillespie and Wanamaker he would need them that evening, he let them go. It seemed interesting to Charlie that Curry appeared to know no gamblers or race track people, and moved in entirely different social circles than his father-in-law.

For the first time that week, Charlie felt comfortable about the relationship of his actions to the world around him. His earlier sense that something was being overlooked had disappeared when Victor confessed to his own investigation, while getting run off the road was at least proof that his assumptions about Ackerman's death were generally accurate. The previous night Charlie had decided it would be dangerous to go home, so he and Victor had slept on cots at the stable. While there, they had worked out a plan of action for the coming evening which, if it worked, would put Curry behind bars for good.

But even as he stood in the doorway congratulating himself on his grasp of events, Charlie knew there were two points of confusion which indicated there was information still unaccounted for. The first was something which had happened to Dwyer and the second was the fact that Curry was going to great lengths to make people think Charlie was crazy. He had discovered this when he saw Field that morning.

Charlie had borrowed Victor's Dodge Dart and had driven out to Field's to explain his interpretation of the case and to convince Field to give him backing. This time Field received him in his living room which had a wall of glass facing the lake. The view, to Charlie, was nearly overpowering. He could even see the spot where he had been knocked into the water. Earlier Charlie had directed a tow truck and diver to the site, and as Charlie talked to Field he kept glancing northward to where his yellow Volkswagen was being removed from the lake.

"You could have been killed," said Field.

"That was the point."

"I still don't see why you can't turn your information over to the police." Field was sitting in a deep armchair in the darkest corner of the room. The albino Doberman lay at his feet staring at Charlie. Whenever Charlie spoke, the dog would growl very quietly. The noise was like a purr.

"Peterson is pursuing his own investigation and hasn't shown himself interested in what I have to say. Also he's a close friend of Dwyer's and thinks my interest in Dwyer, or rather Curry, is an attempt to make him look bad. If I am right that Curry intends to burn the stable either tonight or tomorrow night, then I would rather catch him myself than let Peterson bungle it."

"Don't you think you're being controlled too much by your feelings?" asked Field. "Why not tell Peterson about the fire?"

"Because I have no evidence it will take place. A comment that a groom makes to his wife, a number on a blotter, Curry's plan to build a hotel and the possible future of gambling in Saratoga—Peterson would just laugh at it."

Field's narrow gray face appeared concerned and uncertain. Looking at the sad gray eyes, Charlie grew irritated with himself for ever thinking the accountant a cold man.

"You know that Curry called this morning to complain about you?" asked Field.

At first Charlie didn't think he had heard correctly. "Called to complain about me?"

"That's right."

"What did he say?"

"That you'd been badgering both him and Dwyer with your

suspicions about Ackerman's death. He said he didn't care himself, but it was upsetting to his father-in-law, who isn't well.
He asked me if I thought you were all right in the head, that
you had gone both to the stable and his house, that he had
talked to the police about it and was preparing to get a court
injunction. He also said he knew I was willing to sell Lorelei
Stables and he was willing to make an offer, but because of
your accusations he didn't want to do anything until the real
murderer was caught. Why do you think he told me all that?"

Charlie wasn't sure. He couldn't imagine why Curry had
decided to draw attention to himself. It was at this point Charlie began to wonder if he was leaving something out. Through
the window to his right, he saw a flash of yellow as the top
of his Volkswagen broke the surface of the water. That at least
was not something he had made up.

"I guess he's trying to make me look bad, maybe get you to
fire me. Did you believe him?"

"He made it sound quite believable. On the other hand, Lew
had a lot of faith in you. Let's say I believe Lew, even though
I've known him to be mistaken. You think Curry shot Lew
himself?"

"I think Lew went to him on that Tuesday night and told
him he had heard he intended to burn Dwyer's stable. He
probably thought that would be enough to keep Curry from
doing it. What Lew may not have known was that Curry had
already committed himself to paying large sums of money that
he could only get if he had a fire. Curry lifts weights at the Y.
He could easily calculate the difficulty of killing someone in
the pool."

"Charlie, go to the police."

"Give me until August first. If there's no fire, then I'll go to
Peterson. Thanks to Victor, Curry thinks I'm a bungler. Well,
maybe I am, but we've got more information about him than
he has any idea of. Hopefully, he'll go ahead with his plans.
If he does, well, I've got six people plus myself and we could
get the police and fire department over there in three or four
minutes."

As Charlie stopped speaking, he again heard the dog growl.

Lying at Field's feet in the dimmest part of the room, it looked more like the ghost of a Doberman.

"And if it goes wrong and you're arrested, then I'm supposed to say you're working for me. Is that right?"

"I'm hoping nothing so extreme will happen."

"Charlie, at this point, I want to sell and get out. Do what you have to, but don't do anything to interfere with that. I don't like it around here without Ackerman."

A few minutes later, as he had driven out of Field's driveway, Charlie saw Emmett Van Brunt parked along the side of the road in an unmarked blue Chevrolet. The policeman ducked down when Charlie pulled out and Charlie pretended not to have seen him.

The road curved right after Field's driveway and the moment the Chevrolet was out of sight, Charlie parked the Dodge Dart and ran back along the shoulder. Van Brunt neither saw nor heard him coming. When Charlie reached the police car, Emmett was talking into the radio.

"Yeah, he just left. You want me to follow him? Jesus, Chief, I don't see why you don't throw his ass in jail. That's a shame about Mr. Dwyer. You think he'll pull through?" There was a pause, then Emmett said, "All right, I'll head over there."

Van Brunt returned the microphone and started the car. Charlie stood right behind him at the open window. "What's this about Dwyer?" he asked.

Van Brunt turned in his seat so quickly that he cracked his elbow against the steering wheel. He began rubbing it furiously. "Jesus, Charlie, people like you should be locked up." Van Brunt kept his head turned away, still concentrating on his elbow. He wore a sport coat of green, yellow, and brown plaid.

"What about Dwyer?" asked Charlie. "Come on, Emmett, tell me what happened?"

"You won't get anything from me, Charlie. I know your tricks." Van Brunt rolled up the window, then put the Chevrolet in gear and drove off, leaving Charlie standing at the side of the road.

Charlie shrugged and walked back to Victor's car. He wondered what sort of tricks he was capable of and if he could make a living at them after someone bought Lorelei Stables and he lost his job.

For the rest of the morning, Charlie had looked for an ex-torch he used to know in order to determine the best way to burn a stable. The man had once burned empty buildings for a group of realtors in Albany. When finally arrested, he had received a light sentence in return for testifying against his former employers. He was a small fat man and after his release he devoted his life to hanging around the sleazier Saratoga bars discussing the intricacies of arson. Charlie went to a half a dozen of these bars trying to find him only to learn he had apparently moved out to the West Coast.

Charlie had also tried to learn what had happened to Dwyer. Without much difficulty, he found out Dwyer had been rushed to the hospital in the middle of the night, but despite a number of phone calls he couldn't discover why, whether it had been another stroke or if he had fallen downstairs. All he could learn was that Dwyer was still in intensive care.

Instead of locating the ex-torch, Charlie himself was found by his cousin Jack only moments after he had gone up onto Broadway to buy a paper. It seemed that whenever he set foot on Broadway he was grabbed by people he wanted to avoid.

Actually, Jack was the cousin Charlie liked best, even though he had made his childhood the greatest misery. Jack was a year older and the owner of a successful hardware store. What made him difficult to be around as a child was that he did everything right, was always good humored, never sick, received letters in three sports, and slept with the window open throughout the winter. He helped Charlie with his homework, gave him clothes he'd grown out of himself, and introduced him to the girls he didn't want. He had been a boy without impure thoughts, and Charlie, for whom impure thoughts seemed a way of life, had felt bullied.

Later Jack married an intelligent and beautiful woman, had three sons who became Little League stars, and twice received civic awards for service to the community. Although Charlie would have been shocked to discover his cousin dealt narcotics or did dirty things to little boys, it would have made him easier to bear.

This morning Jack was concerned because he had spoken to Frank Warner and learned that Field wanted to sell Lorelei Stables.

"I wanted to tell you, Charlie, you've no reason to worry about your future. If you're interested, there'll always be a place for you at the hardware."

"Thanks, Jack, I appreciate that." Despite his words, it was with a sense of relief that Charlie realized the offer meant nothing to him. Not long before such an offer would have made him crawl along the sidewalk in gratitude.

"You know, we have a type of profit-sharing plan so the more willing you are to work, the more you earn."

"That's great, Jack, that really is."

They stood on the sidewalk between city hall and the newsstand. Jack was about five inches taller than Charlie with wavy brown hair and wore khakis and a tattersall shirt from L. L. Bean's. His chin was as square and ruddy as the end of a brick. As he talked to Charlie, he kept pausing to wave to people he knew.

"Another thing, Charlie, you know a man by the name of Wayne Curry? He's Bob Dwyer's son-in-law. Now there's a grand old man for you. Where would Saratoga be without him?"

"Where indeed?" asked Charlie. "What's this about Curry?"

"He was in the store yesterday buying some rope and he asked if I knew any reason you might be holding a grudge against him and his father-in-law. I gathered he thought you'd been bothering them in some way and that old man Dwyer was upset. Is that true, Charlie?"

"Well, you know, Jack, I've been helping Peterson with the Ackerman murder and of course I've had to ask Curry and Dwyer some questions." Charlie said this off the top of his head while wondering what Curry was up to. Even so it sometimes surprised him how easily he could lie.

"Dwyer's got a lot of friends in this town, Charlie. You don't want to get him mad."

"You don't have to worry about me, Jack."

"And how have you been generally, Charlie? Staying out of trouble?"

"You better believe it."

"And your mother? She's a great old lady."

"She's made a bundle on this racehorse. Now she wants to come back in October and open a fancy whorehouse. I might get a job as bouncer."

A shadow flitted across Jack's high forehead as if he were experiencing a pain, then he smiled. "You were always a joker, Charlie."

"That's me," said Charlie.

It wasn't until he had returned to his office in the early afternoon that Charlie learned what happened to Dwyer. Victor had been sitting behind the desk with his feet up on the blotter. Leaning against the wall beside him was a small-bore pump gun. Charlie recognized it as belonging to Ackerman. It had been one of Ackerman's vanities that he was an excellent shot. Consequently, he prided himself on never firing anything heavier than this .410 when he went bird hunting in the fall. And even though he used nothing but 2½-inch shells, he always brought back more birds than his friends armed with .12 or .20 gauge shotguns.

"From now on," said Victor, "I'm not going anyplace without this old equalizer. Who'd give my cat the kind of lovin he deserves if I got killed?"

Charlie sat down on the wooden chair across from Victor. "Can you think of any reason why Dwyer should be in the hospital? He was taken there in the middle of the night and I can't find out why."

"Maybe he was run off the road by a pickup truck."

"I'm serious."

"Why d'you think it's important?"

"I won't know if it's important until I find out why he's there, but it seems too much to believe that it's a coincidence."

Victor tapped a pencil against his cast which was already covered with multicolored hearts and signatures. "Well, maybe

I can find out. Hold on." He leafed through the telephone book until he found a number, then he dialed. After a moment, he said, "Hey, Mac, why's Dwyer in the hospital? Okay, call me back." He read out his number, then hung up.

"Who was that?" asked Charlie.

Victor put one finger to his sealed lips and shook his head. A few minutes later the telephone rang and Victor picked it up. After listening for a moment, he said, "Yeah? You don't say. Jesus, what's the world coming to? Sure, I'll tell him you said hello."

Victor hung up the phone. "Took an overdose of pills. They pumped him out, but he's still in a coma. It's not certain he'll recover."

"A suicide attempt?"

"That's what it looks like."

"How'd you find that out?" asked Charlie.

Victor looked at his fingernails. "I called that orderly, that old murderer of yours. What's the point of knowing hoods if you don't make use of them?"

Charlie stared at Victor for a moment. He felt outmaneuvered in a way he couldn't quite put his finger on. "What did Dwyer seem like the other day?" he asked.

Victor scratched his elbows. "I don't know. Not a lotta laugh lines."

"I bet your visit raised a lot of questions in his mind."

"That's the kind of guy I am," said Victor.

Charlie asked himself what Dwyer would have done if he came to believe that his son-in-law was responsible for Ackerman's death. He remembered how he had been the other day: fragile, slightly wandering, thinking about the old times when he and Ackerman had been friendly competitors. He thought of him delivering the eulogy at Ackerman's funeral with Curry standing behind his wheelchair like a soldier at attention. He imagined the old man coming to the realization that Curry had murdered his old friend and then trying to live with it. On the other hand, perhaps Dwyer had never taken an overdose, perhaps it had been administered to him.

"You know," said Victor, "I once knew a guy that tried to asphyxiate himself with a motorcycle in a garage."

"Did it work?"

"Nah, we found him the next morning reading his way through a stack of old *Collier's* with the motorcycle still chugging away. He said he had a headache, but I figured it was from reading in that bad light."

"Are you ever serious?" asked Charlie.

"Only when I'm bein beat up or drowned."

After he talked to Rico on the phone that afternoon, Charlie drove to the Blacksmith to meet Phil Tyler, the one guard he had not yet heard from. It was a warm and sunny Saturday afternoon and as he drove down Union Avenue past the track, he saw that black metal kettles of red geraniums had been hung around the old white gingerbread grandstand. Sprinklers watered the garden in the center of the track and swans busied themselves on the small lake.

In forty hours the track would open and Charlie and about thirty thousand others would crowd into the grounds. Until the first race, anything was possible, all systems of symbolism and logic pointing to the most improbable winners were full of promise. At that very moment racing addicts all over the East were attuning themselves to receive important messages from the ether: the licenses of cars which nearly hit them, a marred date on a shiny penny—numbers which on Monday would be translated into winners.

Charlie carefully studied the past performances in the *Racing Form,* studied training records, inspected the horses from hock to muzzle, but when he made his decision he knew the part of him which did the choosing was the same part which years before in high school had led him into unfortunate crushes on fast fat girls.

As he passed the paddock and track grounds and drew up to the light at Nelson Avenue, Charlie heard a siren and looked in his mirror in time to see Peterson's black Buick swerve around him. Instead of passing him, however, it swerved across his path and squealed to a halt. Since Charlie was sitting at a stop light and in any case wouldn't have considered making a run for it, he couldn't see the point of Peterson's melodramatics.

Peterson jumped out of the police car and stalked back toward the Dodge Dart. He looked like a man eager to break something. As he bent over to look in Charlie's window, the silver chain across the blue vest of his three-piece suit fell forward and from it dangled a miniature silver revolver.

"You hear about Dwyer?" he demanded.

"Just this afternoon. Is he going to pull through?"

"I doubt it. You know whose fault it is that he's in there?" He paused, but before Charlie could answer, Peterson surged ahead again: "It's yours, Bradshaw. Curry told me how you been hounding the old man, making him suspicious and miserable. You know he's not strong in the head. He was sick and depressed and you had to make it worse. People don't think much of you around here, Bradshaw, and after this you'll be nothing: a fat zero. All I'm hoping is that you give me reason to pull you in. I'd love to turn the key on you."

Before Charlie could reply, Peterson stormed back to his car and squealed away, leaving about ten thousand miles of rubber in the intersection. Charlie wished he had Victor's ability to tell the world to kiss his ass. He found himself thinking of an El Paso cowboy by the name of "Cowboy" Bob Rennick, a little man who was rarely armed and had the reputation for being a dude. On the night in question—April 14, 1885—he had just bought himself a large white cowboy hat, of which he was overly proud, and had gone to the Gem Saloon to show it off. There, unfortunately, he met Bill Raynor, a former lawman and constant troublemaker who was known as "the best dressed bad man in Texas." Raynor proceeded to make fun of Cowboy Bob's hat, pointing out its various comic possibilities and adding that if he didn't like what he was saying, then Cowboy Bob could fight. Raynor had been involved in many gunfights and always won. Too frightened to speak up, Cowboy Bob indicated he was unarmed and with a snort of disgust Raynor wandered into the billiard room.

Cowboy Bob then ordered a couple of drinks, bolted them down, and announced in a loud voice, "I've been imposed upon enough and won't stand for it." Then he snatched a revolver from the faro dealer. Seeing that Cowboy Bob was now armed, Raynor rushed into the bar with his guns blazing—"guns blazing" was a combination of words that always made Charlie breathe a little faster. Cowboy Bob knelt down and fired two shots, hitting Raynor in the stomach and shoulder. Mortally wounded, Raynor urged the bystanders to tell his mother he "died game." As he watched Peterson's black Buick disappear up Union Avenue, Charlie said to himself: "I've been imposed upon enough and won't stand for it."

By the time Charlie reached the Backstretch, it was past six. Phil Tyler was drinking a Jenny and Charlie sat down on the stool beside him.

"How you doin, old buddy?" asked Tyler.

Although Charlie didn't choke up, it was nice to hear someone express affection for him, even though that someone in his unreformed state had bilked dozens of citizens out of their savings by convincing them to buy nonexistent acreage in paradise. Tyler was tall, thin, dressed like a cowboy in jeans and a jean shirt, had long gray hair that touched his shoulders and a gray gunfighter's moustache. He always spoke quietly and delicately.

"You find out anything about Curry in Kentucky?" asked Charlie.

"Little bit, not much. He ran Dwyer's farm for a couple of years and all I could find out was he didn't like it and wasn't very good at it."

"How come Dwyer kept him on?"

"I don't think he heard about it. Curry was good at finding people who knew the business. The guy I talked to said he'd met him at a couple of parties. People down there like horses and Curry didn't, that's all it amounts to."

Charlie ordered a beer from Berney McQuilkin, then turned back to Tyler who was cleaning his nails with a jackknife. "You ready for tonight?" asked Charlie.

"Sure thing. We meet in your office at ten. We going to be armed?"

"Me and Krause are the only ones with licenses. Maybe we'll take a rifle as well." Remembering Peterson's expressed desire to lock him up, Charlie felt uncomfortable about trespassing with six armed men.

"I used to be pretty hot stuff with a rifle," said Tyler. "I bet I could shoot the match right out of Curry's hand."

"I'll remember that," said Charlie.

After Tyler left, Charlie sat drinking another beer. Doris hadn't come in yet and he kept glancing at the front door every time it opened. That night, if nothing went wrong, he and his guards would try to catch Curry burning Dwyer's stable. Part of Charlie kept urging him to turn it over to the police, but even if the police had been friendly and welcoming it's unlikely that he would have gone to them. In these warm days before the opening of the track, Charlie had moved through Saratoga as if the ghost of Ackerman were accompanying him. They were soft days, the sort of days that made Charlie recall the time when Broadway was lined with wineglass elms, when he could walk from one end to the other and count over five hundred men in Panama hats seated in rockers on the piazzas of the old hotels. Whoever had killed Ackerman, Charlie wanted to catch him himself.

His plan was to have two men go into the stable area with radios, while the other five waited outside. If either of the two saw anything suspicious, they would call Charlie, who would contact the police and the fire department on the CB. The other guards would then try to keep Curry and his associates from getting away. It would be a full moon that night and if Curry tried to start a fire, he would certainly be seen. Charlie felt fairly confident about this plan. His only question concerned Curry's reasons for telling people that Charlie was harassing him and was, in part, the cause of Dwyer's suicide attempt. It seemed eventually this could only draw attention to Curry himself.

Charlie was startled by a touch on the shoulder and, turning, he saw Doris sitting down on the stool beside him.

"I've got a few minutes before I start," she said. "Mind if I join you?"

"Not at all. Tell me, would you like me better if I was the manager of a hardware store?"

"No, I wouldn't. Are you planning to become one?"

"Not necessarily. What about an insurance and real estate executive or the foreman of a construction company, would you like me better then?"

"Can't say that I would." Doris was half turned toward Charlie. She wore a red bandanna over her brown hair and had on a white blouse and a blue denim skirt. Her face, framed by the bandanna, looked cheerful and expectant.

"I was afraid of that," said Charlie. "Then tell me this, will you go to the races with me on Monday? Red Fox is running in the fifth."

"Is Red Fox that Jesse James's horse?"

"That's right. Red Fox is the only horse in the world. No horse looks stronger or handsomer. That doesn't mean he'll win, but right now he's a champion."

"Do you think he'll win?"

"Of course I do, but that doesn't mean much. That's the trouble with horse racing. Will you come?"

"I'd be glad to."

Charlie was so startled he hardly thought he had heard her correctly. "You mean it?"

"Would you believe me any more if I put it in writing?"

"No, your word's good enough. I can't tell you how pleased I am that we'll see Red Fox lose together."

As he said this, Charlie was aware of someone else sitting down on the other side of him. Turning, he saw it was Jack Krause.

"What's up?" asked Charlie.

"I been talking to Vic," said Krause, "and I've decided to stick by you until all this gets finished. Sorry for the inconvenience, but I don't want you to get shot as well." Krause flicked a cigarette butt off the bar as if to signify Charlie's getting shot.

Charlie felt both touched and irritated. Turning back to

Doris, he noticed she was halfway around the bar. When she saw him looking, she said, "Don't forget, I'm holding you to Monday."

Not only would Krause be upset if he were shot, thought Charlie, but it would be truly bad luck to be killed just when Doris had agreed to go out with him.

20

▼▼▼

"SURE," SAID CHARLIE, "Owney Madden, Dutch Schultz, Johnny Torrio, Lucky Luciano—they had the syndicate that controlled the casinos. Luciano ran the Chicago Club himself. Took in $250,000 every August. They usually kept Schultz off the floor. In the early thirties, the Chicago Club was the classiest and most expensive club in town and Dutch Schultz held it as a matter of religious faith that it was a crime to pay more than two dollars for a shirt. Then Schultz decided he had to rub out Thomas Dewey who was busting up his rackets in New York, and Luciano knew that would bring a lot of heat down on the syndicate, so he told Anastasia at Murder, Inc., to get rid of Schultz. Actually, it was Charlie 'The Bug' Workman who shot Schultz in the john of the Palace Chophouse in Newark while Schultz was taking a leak."

Krause rubbed his big left fist along the line of his jaw. "How come you know this stuff?" he said.

"I don't know. I read about it, then I like to go over it in my mind," said Charlie. "It's like knitting."

Charlie and Krause were driving out to Charlie's cottage in Victor's Dodge Dart in order to get Charlie's revolver. It was about 9:30 Saturday evening and Charlie wanted to get over to Dwyer's by eleven. Nervously, he kept looking in the rearview mirror, but the road behind him was clear. It was a full moon and so bright that Charlie felt he could drive without lights.

"Nice night," said Charlie.

Krause grunted, then took an immaculate white handkerchief from the breast pocket of his suit coat, delicately blew his nose in three little puffs and refolded the handkerchief. "Victor tells me you think Curry killed Lew, is that right?" asked Krause.

"I'm not so sure," said Charlie.

"When do you think you're going to be sure?"

Charlie knew what was coming and tried to be evasive. "Maybe tonight or tomorrow night, but we won't really be sure until we see him sent up for it."

"Remember what I asked, that's all. If Curry's the guy, then you gotta let me kill him. No sweat, I'll just put a bullet in his head." Krause patted a spot at his waist where Charlie assumed he was carrying his revolver.

"I'm not working for you," said Charlie, "and I can't just let you murder a man."

"You working for Field?"

"I guess I'm working for myself," said Charlie as he slowed for his driveway.

"Bet you don't get paid much," said Krause.

Charlie parked and they got out of the car. As they walked across the gravel to the house, Krause said, "I once fought Joey Maxim right after the war. That was years before he became light heavyweight champion. It was my biggest fight and the farthest I ever got. Because I'd been around a while and'd won my last couple of fights, I was the favorite. Maxim, he got in the ring and he walked all over me. I was out by the fourth round."

Krause paused. His forehead protruded slightly and in the moonlight it shone almost white, while the lower part of his face was dark.

"A writer for some rag in New York said I'd thrown the fight," Krause continued. "Shit, I didn't throw no fight. Maxim was a better fighter, that's all. Well, this writer kept suggesting I'd taken a dive and one night I ran into him in a bar, like I was coming back from the juke box and he was passing in the other direction. He gave me a bad look and I grabbed his shirt.

He just smiled. He knew if I hit him I'd be outta boxing forever. No training camp jobs, no nothing. Besides which, I'd land in jail. So I let him go. He called me something I didn't catch and left. After that, right up till I quit boxing, he always wrote bad about me. I've always regretted not punching him. Just one punch to the head. It would of been worth the jail and no boxing. Just one punch to the head. When someone hurts you, you gotta hurt them back. What I'm saying, Charlie, if Curry's the one, you gotta let me have him. Understand?"

They had been standing at Charlie's front door while Charlie hunted for the key and swatted mosquitoes. At last Charlie unlocked the door and they went inside. "I understand you well enough," he said, "I'm just not going to help you do it. Excuse the mess." Discarded shirts, pants, shoes, and about eight socks were scattered across the living room floor. "I haven't had time to clean up."

Going into the kitchen, Charlie opened the drawer by the sink where he kept his .38 in its holster. The revolver was empty and Charlie loaded it, taking a box of shells from on top of the kitchen cabinet. Then he attached the holster to his belt, put a few extra shells in his coat pocket, and returned to the living room where Krause was staring out at the moonlight on the lake.

"You think you'll use that gun tonight?" asked Krause.

"I hope not," said Charlie. "I'm a rotten shot." He picked up a blue shirt off the floor, laid it across the back of a chair, then shrugged. "Let's go," he said.

As they turned toward the door, however, a pair of headlights swung into Charlie's driveway, drew up behind the Dodge Dart and blinked out.

"You expecting anyone?" asked Krause.

Charlie didn't answer but listened to the sound of a single pair of feet walking across the gravel toward the house. At first Charlie thought it might be Peterson, then he thought it might be Rico who still had not returned from Connecticut. Charlie flicked on the porch light and opened the door. Wayne Curry stood on the steps.

Curry looked at him with his pale blue eyes in a way Charlie was getting used to. "I want to talk to you, Bradshaw."

Charlie stood aside and let Curry enter. Krause stood by the window and watched. He seemed very still. Charlie shut the door and followed Curry into the room. "What do you want to talk about?" he asked.

"I want to know what you have against me."

"What makes you think I've got anything against you?" asked Charlie.

"You've been bothering the people who work for me and you've been bothering Mr. Dwyer. He's a sick man, don't you know that? That friend of yours really upset him. If he dies, then a lot of people are going to think you're responsible. You think I killed Ackerman? Come on, tell it to my face."

Charlie leaned against the doorway to the kitchen. He was uncertain why Curry had come and as he thought about it, he became increasingly uncomfortable. "Why did Lew Ackerman visit you three nights before he was killed?"

"Is that what's worrying you?" Curry paused to light a cigarette, then flicked the match into the fireplace. "I wanted to talk to Ackerman privately to see if he wanted to buy Dwyer's stable and I didn't want Dwyer to know. Lew agreed to stop by."

"Why didn't you tell the police?" asked Charlie. He glanced at Krause who had his hands shoved into the pockets of his brown suit coat and stood almost motionless, as if waiting to be clicked on.

"I still didn't want Dwyer to know and it didn't seem very important."

"Why didn't you want Dwyer to know?"

Curry was wearing jeans and a blue and white gingham shirt with pearl snaps. The shirt fit him tightly, exposing ridges of muscle across his stomach. His short copper-colored hair looked like it had been brushed moments before.

"He's signed the stable over to his daughter, my wife," Curry said. "I'm running the place and legally we're owners. We wouldn't sell it while he was alive, but I thought it would do no harm to see if Lew was interested."

"Why did Dwyer try to kill himself?"

"I told you, he's a sick man. Lew's death upset him, but he's been depressed for a long time now."

"You didn't put anything in his food, did you?" asked Charlie.

Curry drew one last puff on his cigarette and tossed it in the fireplace. "What do you mean by that?" he asked.

Glancing down, Charlie saw that Curry was standing on one of his best white shirts. "Did Dwyer guess you'd killed Ackerman?" he asked. "Is that why he took the pills?"

"Why should I kill Ackerman?"

"Because Neal Claremon told him you were going to burn Dwyer's stable for the insurance money so you could build a big hotel on the property. That's also why you killed Claremon. Somehow he found out you were planning a fire and you wanted him dead. So tell me, what did you and Ackerman really talk about?"

Curry glanced down, saw Charlie's shirt and pushed it aside with the point of his black cowboy boot. He seemed unconcerned by Charlie's accusation. "You really expect me to confess to a murder?" he said.

Charlie didn't answer this but kept staring at Curry as if he were waiting. He was irritated at himself for not picking up his clothes and felt it weakened his credibility.

Curry took a quick look at Krause, then shrugged. "I didn't think I had any choice," he said. "Ackerman told me if there was a fire he'd go to the police."

"And so you shot him?"

Curry lit another cigarette. This time he watched the match burn a little before blowing it out. "I knew when he swam and I knew the layout of the Y. It seemed easy."

Charlie couldn't imagine why Curry had decided to confess. In a way, Charlie was sorry he had, because now he couldn't think what to do with him. He didn't believe Curry would allow him to call Peterson to come and arrest him. Thinking about the next few minutes, he couldn't guess how they would turn out; and as he ran through the possibilities, he became more nervous. Also, in the back of his mind, something else had begun to bother him. It was like an itch beginning to declare itself.

"And you tried to kill me and Victor too, right? You knocked us off the road."

Before Curry could answer, Krause took his hands from his pockets and began walking slowly toward Curry who was about eight feet away. Curry looked at him but did no more than toss away his cigarette.

"Jack," said Charlie, "leave him alone."

As Krause walked, he reached under his coat and Charlie knew he was reaching for his revolver.

"Krause, you can't do it!" Charlie took a few steps toward him and stopped.

Krause paused to glance at Charlie and in that moment Curry moved forward and as easily as a dancer raised his left leg and whipped it toward Krause's stomach, burying his boot, it seemed, in the fat. Krause was thrown back, grabbing at his stomach and retching. He tripped over a chair and sprawled backward across the dining room table, which creaked, then one of its legs buckled under and Krause was sent crashing to the floor.

Fumbling at his waist, Charlie drew his revolver and pointed it at Curry. "Stand right where you are."

Curry looked as if nothing had happened. Krause rolled over on his stomach, then pushed himself up on his hands and knees and knelt there gagging and coughing.

Then Charlie heard a noise behind him. As he began to turn, he realized that what had been bothering him was whether the kitchen door had been locked or if only the screen had been latched. Before he could even complete this thought, an arm wrapped itself around his throat and he was yanked backward. Then a damp cloth was pressed against his mouth. The cloth reeked of chloroform and Charlie told himself he had to act quickly. It was the last thing he remembered.

21

▼▼▼

WHEN CHARLIE RETURNED from New York City after his ill-fated search for the missing son of a high school sweetheart and told his wife he wanted a divorce, her response was one of fierce indignation. As a no-nonsense business woman, she had always seen herself as the long-suffering member of the Charlie Bradshaw and Marge Odel Bradshaw team, while Charlie, with his passion for criminal history, Little League baseball, and the aquatic films of Esther Williams, accounted, she thought, for a lot of nonsense. Still, by being his wife she had located herself in the same family as her older sister who had married Charlie's middle cousin, Robert; and although Charlie, unlike Robert, was no pillar of society, he was at least a sergeant in the police department and people, for no reason she could imagine, appeared to respect him.

Marge found it difficult to believe that Charlie was leaving her for what she called no reason. There was no other woman and while they hadn't been doing much talking, neither had they been quarreling. They had been sitting in Lou's Luncheonette on Broadway across from the Montana Bookstore and Charlie had told her, "I just don't feel like being married anymore."

"Feel like," Marge had said, "what do you think I've felt like being married fifteen years to a simpleton?"

Charlie had never thought of himself as a simpleton and so was surprised rather than hurt. He imagined simpletons as being clownish and ineffectual. People whose shoes were always untied and had wisps of straw caught in their hair. But since that time whenever he did something that turned out unhappily, the word would reoccur to him and he would ask himself if Marge hadn't been right.

It was the word "simpleton" which kept repeating itself in Charlie's brain when he woke to find himself lying uncomfortably on his stomach on a floor covered with dirty straw. As he tried to get up, he realized a thick rope was wound loosely around and around his body. His head felt heavy, as if it were several sizes larger; and beyond aching miserably, it pulsed like a blinking light. He shut his eyes and thought of Marge. When he opened them again and glanced around he saw Krause, wound as he was with a thick rope, lying unconscious a few feet away. Noticing the wooden walls, Dutch door, the one bare light bulb dangling from a wire, mounds of soiled straw, Charlie realized they were in a horse stall, but how they got there he had no idea. Mixed with the smell of horse and manure was another smell which he at first couldn't place. Then he recognized it as gasoline. As he began to think about this, he heard a noise behind him.

Kicking his feet and flopping onto his side, Charlie turned himself enough to see Wayne Curry standing near the door of the stall. Around Curry were ten five-gallon gasoline cans. Curry looked at him as if he weren't there at all, as if he were just so much more dirty straw. It was at that point Charlie realized that Curry not only intended to burn the stable, he meant to burn him and Krause along with it. The shock of this stirred him into speech.

"You really think you can get away with it?" A residue of chloroform made his tongue feel heavy and he spoke sleepily.

Curry didn't answer. The mixture of gasoline and manure smelled so strong that Charlie was afraid he was going to be sick and he found himself concentrating on the silver horsehead buckle of Curry's belt in order to control his increasing nausea.

"Won't they be suspicious when they find our bodies?" he asked. Charlie tried to keep his voice steady and conversational, as if he found nothing unusual about the present situation. Part of this was pride, part was the concern that if he acknowledged his fear it would overwhelm him.

Curry lifted two of the five-gallon cans, began to leave, then looked back at Charlie. "You went to a number of bars the other day looking for a man who is generally known as a professional torch. That wasn't very smart of you, Bradshaw. You get found here, what do you guess people will think?"

Curry turned back toward the door, kicked it open with his boot and left.

As Charlie lay on the straw testing the ropes, he tried to answer Curry's question. Even though witnesses could be found to testify he had been looking for the torch, he couldn't believe Peterson would accept this as sufficient evidence of his guilt. But as he thought that, he realized why Curry had talked to Field, Peterson, his cousin, and presumably others to complain about Charlie's supposed harassment. If Curry could make people think Charlie had a grudge against him, then perhaps he could also make them think he had set the stable on fire.

Immediately, Charlie pushed the thought away. People would never believe it. But what was his reputation in Saratoga? Unstable and undependable. It was known that he and Krause had been badly disturbed by Ackerman's death, that Charlie had tried to investigate the murder himself and had come to believe that Dwyer and/or Curry were responsible. The people who would know him to be innocent were not people of power. Again Charlie thought of the word "simpleton."

In any case, Charlie knew, his body would be found along with Krause's. A little more chloroform, remove the ropes, and blow them up. In his years as a policeman, Charlie had come across would-be arsonists who had blown themselves up by lighting a cigarette or even striking a nail with the heal of a shoe at the wrong moment. Certainly, people would think it improbable he had burned down Dwyer's stable, but then, to contradict it, here was his body in evidence.

Charlie began to pull frantically at the ropes, then he forced himself to relax. His fear kept rising up as a palpable object and he had to keep clenching himself to push it away. All the intellectualizing and analyzing wouldn't change the fact that he was tied up on the floor of a horse stall which would soon be on fire. Charlie looked at Krause, saw he was still unconscious, and decided that one way or another he had to get over to him.

The door opened and Curry reappeared and picked up two more gas cans. Charlie tried to heave himself into a sitting position but couldn't and flopped back down. As Curry started to leave, Charlie said, "Peterson won't believe it."

Curry stopped with his back to Charlie and turned his head slightly. "Peterson's my friend. We're supposed to play golf tomorrow afternoon. He'll believe what I want him to believe."

The door opened and a young man whom Charlie recognized as a groom he had seen several days before came in and picked up two more gas cans.

"You got those rags in place?"

"Frank's hooking them up to the house." The man looked at Charlie, then looked away. He had curly black hair and wore jeans and a black T-shirt with the name "Santana" printed across the front in red lettering.

"And the shed rows?"

"Just finished. I'm going to douse 'em again now. You going to leave these last four cans in here?"

"That's right," said Curry. "Bradshaw needs help burning. He's too green."

"Maybe I should pour some over his clothes?"

"That's okay. This twenty gallons should do it. Right, Bradshaw?"

When Charlie didn't answer, Curry shrugged, then he and the groom left the stall. In the long run, Charlie knew it wouldn't work. Curry didn't realize how much Charlie had found out, how he had involved all his guards, had discovered a motive for burning the stable and a personality reckless enough to try it. Eventually Curry might go to trial, but Charlie wouldn't be alive to testify.

He thought again of Claremon's statement that there was nothing worse than a stable fire. Here, one day before the opening of the meet, the stable was at its fullest and most valuable. Grooms were probably away at the movies or a bar or the clubhouse. Perhaps there weren't even any grooms staying here. Curry's guard would be found knocked out. Charlie had seen fifty gallons of gasoline and there was probably more. With all that wood and straw, it would take only a couple of minutes for the building to be totally engulfed in fire, while the trailers of gasoline-soaked rags would carry the fire to the other buildings. He thought of the horses crazy with fear and his own death which would at least, he thought, be fairly quick.

Again Charlie tried to switch off that part of his mind which was trying to distance himself from his present predicament by turning it into an analytical problem. The ropes were loose and he guessed that had been done so they wouldn't leave marks on their bodies. He looked around the stall for any sharp object, any nail sticking out of the wall or even a rusty pipe, but the stall was empty. His revolver was gone, as was his small Swiss army knife.

Looking toward Krause, Charlie saw he had begun to stir. Still on his stomach, Charlie began to half push and half wriggle his way toward him. As he inched his way along, he could feel damp straw being pushed down the collar of his shirt.

Krause raised his head, looked around, then let his head fall back on the straw. Pushing himself forward another foot, Charlie bumped his head against Krause's shoulder, stirring him awake again.

"Krause, come on, we've got to get out of here."

"I can't move, Charlie."

Like Charlie's, Krause's hands were tied behind him. Charlie pushed himself forward, then heaved himself over until his back was facing Krause. "Can you reach any of these knots?" he asked.

After a pause, Krause said, "Maybe with my teeth. Try and get closer."

Charlie heaved himself back a little further. "Now?"

"A bit more."

Again Charlie heaved himself back. This time he felt his hands bump against Krause. There was a tug, then another as Krause's teeth pulled against the knots.

The door opened and Curry came back in. Seeing what Charlie and Krause were doing, he took a step forward, then stopped. He watched the two of them as if they were some slightly interesting experiment. Then Krause grew aware of his presence and lifted his head.

"Just like something out of an old movie," said Curry. He walked quickly toward Charlie, drew back a boot and kicked him hard in the stomach so he was thrown back against Krause. Charlie gagged and tried to curl himself into a ball.

Curry reached down, grabbed hold of the ropes, and dragged Charlie back across the stall so his face scraped on the floor. Then he dropped him. As Charlie rolled away and tried to catch his breath, Curry kicked him again.

"It's going to give me pleasure to see you burn, Bradshaw. You been getting in my way all week. The world's full of jerks like you: no class, no money, and no brains. Well, I'm going to roast you."

As Curry turned toward the door, he stumbled against one of the four remaining gas cans, knocking it over. The top was loose and popped off and immediately gasoline began to gurgle onto the straw several feet away from where Charlie was lying.

Curry looked at it but left it where it was. Then he glanced toward Charlie and began to smile, showing his teeth. Charlie stared back at him, trying to keep his face from showing fear. After a moment, Curry turned and left the stall.

"You all right, Charlie?" asked Krause.

"Yeah, let's try it again." Rolling over on his stomach, Charlie began to wriggle and push and heave his way toward Krause. The pain in his stomach and side where Curry had kicked him was almost a distraction from his fear. He wondered if Curry had cracked a rib and what the coroner would think when he discovered the broken rib at the inquest. Then he wondered if it was brave of him to be thinking of his own inquest, instead of dissolving into terror. Then he again thought of the word "simpleton."

When Charlie had pushed himself about five feet toward Krause, he heard the door open behind him. He let his head drop forward on the straw. He felt futile and wished everything were over.

For a moment the stall was quiet, then a voice said, "Whatcha doin down there, playing caterpillar?"

Charlie yanked his head around to see Victor standing in the doorway with Ackerman's small-bore pump gun in the crook of his right arm. His left arm, still in its cast, was supported by a sling made from two blue bandannas.

"Hurry," said Charlie, "get us out of these ropes. No jokes, Victor."

"Vic." Victor laid the shotgun down on the straw, took a small penknife from the pocket of his jeans, and began sawing through the ropes which bound Charlie's hands.

"You bring the police?" asked Charlie. He could hardly believe Victor was really there and he kept turning his head to make sure.

"Nah, I just came over with Rico and Phil. When you didn't come back, we decided to go over to your house. It reeked of chloroform so after I called the Backstretch and some other places we decided to take a peek over here. What's going on?"

Charlie scrambled to his feet and grabbed the shotgun. "Curry wants to burn us up with the stable. Are Rico and Phil armed?"

"Nope, I decided to bring along the shotgun at the last minute." He began to cut the ropes from Krause.

"You ever fired one?" asked Charlie, keeping the gun pointed toward the door.

"Never had the opportunity. Rico wanted to carry it, but he's still on pro so I figured I better carry it myself being the oldest and most responsible. He put some bullets in it for me."

"Shells," said Krause.

"That's what I said," said Victor.

"How're you going to shoot it with only one arm?"

"All's I need is one finger," said Victor.

Krause looked at him, started to speak, then embraced him instead, lifting Victor's feet off the floor and squeezing him until he made a squeaking noise. "Thanks," said Krause, setting him back down.

Victor straightened his gray sweat shirt. "Nada, like the Ricans say," he said.

"You seen Curry?" asked Charlie.

"Yeah, I seen him and a coupla his buddies prowling around with gasoline cans."

"Where's Rico and Phil?"

"Dunno, we split up. They were goin to check the other buildings."

Charlie hefted the shotgun in his hands. He guessed it held five shells. He had used a .410 several times as a kid and had never hit anything except a squirrel which he'd wounded and then had to nurse back to health. He seemed to recall that its effective range was under twenty-five yards. He wondered if he had time to get to a telephone. Then he heard a gunshot. After a moment, he heard another. Charlie took a deep breath, then let it out slowly so it made a whistling noise. Whatever was happening, they would have to deal with it themselves.

"Let's go," said Charlie. He flicked off the light and opened the door.

Charlie didn't know what kind of scene he expected to find on the other side of the door, but he at least assumed it would be violent. Instead it was bucolic: a full moon lighting up the elms and the shed rows, outlining the mansard roof of the two-story house at the center of the stable complex. There was no one in sight and no sound except for an occasional whinny. They had been in a small equipment barn between the training track and the house. On either side the four shed rows stretched away in the moonlight. Linking the barn to the house and stables were ghostly trails of white rags and sheets smelling of gasoline. One passed near Charlie. He hurried over and began to kick it apart.

There was a third shot and Charlie dropped to his knees. Then he saw someone running from the shed row at the far-thest left toward the house. The man must have seen them at the same time, because he stopped and pointed his arm at them. There was a spark of light, then a gunshot.

"Get down," shouted Charlie.

He was aware of Krause and Victor crouching down behind him. Charlie flopped onto his stomach in the grass, aimed the shotgun at the man near the house, and fired. At that range he didn't expect the birdshot to have any effect, but it would at least make the man keep his distance.

The man backed toward the house and fired again. Charlie heard a thunk as the bullet hit the wall of the barn behind him. Since he was still in a direct line with the barn, he was afraid that a ricochet off one of the metal gas cans might cause a spark which could ignite the gasoline-soaked straw. He crawled toward the house and fired again. Then, from the shed row to his left, came more gunshots and he knew someone was attempting to ignite the barn.

Turning, Charlie saw Victor and Krause crawling on their bellies toward several elm trees to their right. Charlie knew he should be breaking up the other trailers of rags. Instead he tried to make himself as flat as possible. He felt powerless with the small shotgun. He fired at the shed row to his left, then he saw what he had been most afraid of: a snaking quick movement of flame racing along the rope of sheets and rags toward the small barn. If the barn went up, the other trailers would be ignited.

Charlie jumped to his feet. "Get those trailers," he shouted. "Krause, Victor, break up those lines of rags."

There were more gunshots and Charlie heard the bullets hit the wall of the barn. The flame on the line of rags dashed along the ground like a small angry animal. Then it rushed into the barn. For a moment, there was silence, then the barn exploded, sending a flash of orange flame through the doorway with a great whoosh.

Even as the barn became engulfed in fire and burning debris shot into the air around them, Charlie was running toward the two trailers extending to the shed rows to his right. Glancing over his shoulder, he saw both trailers burning, seeming to rush along the ground faster than he could hope to run. He reached the first line of rags and hurriedly kicked it apart. Then he ran toward the second about five yards away. As the flame snaked along the ground, Charlie knew he wouldn't be able to reach it in time. Raising the shotgun, he fired and the birdshot struck the string of rags, scattering them. The rushing flame flickered to a stop. Even though he had only been about two yards away and the shot had been simple, Charlie immediately wanted to tell someone about it.

"The house," shouted Victor. "Get the one to the house!"

Turning, Charlie saw Krause running toward the house while in a converging line was a white length of sheets and rags with an orange flame skittering along it. Charlie also began to run toward it, although he was farther away. The burning barn behind them lit up the yard and the air was thick with smoke.

About ten yards away to his right, Charlie saw the form of
Phil Tyler lying motionless in the dirt with one arm thrown up
above his head. Then there were more gunshots: these coming
from the house. Krause had nearly reached the string of sheets,
but as the gun started firing from the front window he dove
to the ground and the fire on the trailer sputtered past him,
sputtered up the front walk, sputtered up the steps and into
the house. Charlie, who had also ducked down, jumped to his
feet and ran toward Phil Tyler. There were the sounds of cracking, burning wood and horses whinnying in terror. Then, added
to that, was another great whoosh and the sound of glass
breaking as the house exploded in fire and orange flames
smashed through the downstairs front windows.

Seconds later a man came rushing out of the house with his
clothing on fire. He half fell, half jumped from the steps and
stumbled into the yard. He still had his gun and was firing as
he ran, but randomly, up in the air, wherever the gun happened
to be pointing as if the act of firing could drive away the fire
that engulfed him.

He was about twenty yards away and Charlie left Tyler and
ran toward him. Flames were shooting up the side of the house
and now he could see them upstairs as well. There was another
whoosh and the second-floor windows blew out, sending pieces
of glass spraying across the yard. Victor shouted something,
but the noise of the fire and terrified screaming of the horses
was so great that his words were lost in the roar. Both Victor
and Krause were running toward the burning man, while beyond him toward the further shed rows Charlie saw Rico also
running. Rico ran with one hand held out and Charlie realized
he was holding a gun.

The burning man slowed to a stop and stood swaying back
and forth still wrapped in flame. He stood beneath one of the
large elms, and the flames threw light and shadow on the trunk,
while the leaves above him flickered as if in a wind. The man
raised his arms high above his head and began to cry out in a
wailing voice that seemed to rise above the sound of the fire. It
was at that moment that Krause reached him. Without pausing,
Krause tackled him, knocking the man to the ground and roll-

ing him over in the dirt. Victor followed, tossing dirt on the flames, patting out the small fires that sprang up on Krause's clothing.

"It's not Curry," said Rico as he ran up to where Charlie stood. "I took care of one of the others with a bit of two-by-four."

"Find a phone," said Charlie. "There should be one in the shed rows. Get an ambulance and the fire department if they're not already on their way." Then, remembering Phil Tyler, he left Rico and ran back to him.

Tyler was sprawled on his stomach with his feet wide apart. Bending over him, Charlie gently pushed his legs together, then turned him over. Tyler made a moaning noise. He had been shot in the shoulder and leg and was losing a lot of blood. The front of his white shirt was soaked red. Tyler slowly shook his head and opened his eyes.

"No more night duty, Charlie," he said. "I don't want to do no more night duty." Then he closed his eyes again.

Charlie heard sirens or thought he did. Looking up, he saw Victor standing beside him. His face seemed to flicker in the light from the burning house. He looked at Tyler and shook his head.

"I think that guy who was on fire is dead," said Victor. "Probably just as well. Anyway, I got his gun." He raised a .38 revolver and showed it to Charlie.

Charlie got to his feet. The gun looked like his own. He felt tired and his only gratification was that the horses were safe. "Is it loaded?" he asked.

"How can you tell?"

Charlie took it and flicked open the chamber. "It's empty." He checked his pockets for the extra shells but they were gone. Handing the revolver back to Victor, he knelt down to see if he could stop Tyler's bleeding."

Victor spun the revolver on his finger. "First a deadly weapon," he said. "Now a paperweight."

Rico ran up, then knelt beside Charlie. "Ambulance is on its way." He tore open the fabric surrounding the bullet wound in Tyler's leg, then pressed his thumbs on a spot a little above the wound. "Doncha know any first aid?" he said. "Let me take care of this."

"What the fuck's Krause doin?" asked Victor, pointing to the parking lot about fifty yards away.

Charlie looked to see Krause yank open a car door, half disappear inside, then draw back and run to another car. In the middle of the lot was a large mercury vapor light on a telephone pole and surrounding it were about eight cars and several pickup trucks. Krause yanked open another car door, half disappeared, then left the car and ran to another.

"Wacko," said Victor, shoving the empty revolver in his back pocket. "Always happens to boxers sooner or later."

Krause was now at the door of a red pickup truck. This time he climbed in entirely. There was the sound of the starter, then the motor caught and the lights went on. Almost without thinking, Charlie found himself running toward the lot. Victor was only a little behind him.

"Where's your car?" Charlie shouted.

"We came in Rico's. It's parked on the road. I got the keys."

The pickup bumped out of the parking lot, swung toward the front gates about two hundred yards away, and accelerated. Caught in the headlights halfway up the metal gate was the figure of a man. The person reached the top of the gate, then disappeared.

"It's Curry," shouted Victor. "There was another car parked further up the road."

When the red pickup reached the gate, it barely paused as it smashed through the tall metal panels, sending them flying back. Charlie ran faster. He was still holding the pump gun in his right hand.

22
▼▼▼

PPARENTLY THE BLUE Plymouth Fury had missed the curve on the Avenue of Pines, bumped over the curb, and slid sideways into the big spruce in the center of the grass triangle. In any case, the car was a mess.

The Avenue of Pines ran between Dwyer's stable and downtown Saratoga, bordering the Saratoga Spa State Park and the Performing Arts Center. Charlie usually avoided it in the summer because it was crowded with tourists, but this night—or rather morning, since it was nearly 2:00 A.M.—the road was deserted.

The blue Fury seemed halfway up the spruce and what had been an expensively sculptured front end now appeared to be mimicking a concertina. The front and rear windows had been smashed while the back end with its elaborate stabilizer had been turned into so much scrap metal, presumably where Krause's pickup truck had rammed into it. Then there were additional gouge marks in the grass where the pickup had backed up and taken off toward the rear gates of the Performing Arts Center less than a quarter of a mile away.

Victor got back into Rico's tan Ford. "Nobody's there and there's no blood. Either he's okay or he's a vampire."

Charlie backed up, turned, then bumped the Ford over the curb as he followed the tracks of the pickup toward the theater.

"Why would he go in there?" asked Victor. He had one hand pressed against the dashboard and was pushing himself back in his seat.

"He's probably cutting through to the other side. If he can get to Route 50, then he can stop a car at the light. Except for the fences, this is the shortest way across."

"And what's Krause doin, if you're so smart?"

"Krause wants to kill him."

The large metal gates onto the grounds of the amphitheater

had been smashed open and ripped from their hinges. Charlie drove through the gates and stopped near a pair of green trash cans that lay on their sides dented like beer cans. Ten feet further on the red pickup was caught up on a stone bench and tilted so far to the right that it seemed ready to topple over. Its lights were on and shone up into the leaves of the elms. There were three bullet holes in the smashed front window, but no sign of blood. As Victor and Charlie stood by the truck, they heard sirens. A moment later, there was a gunshot from the direction of the theater. It was a small noise like a distant backfire. Charlie turned toward it. The theater was a huge fan-shaped building which could seat more than five thousand persons and provided space for another seven thousand on the sloping lawns. Although roofed, the sides were open and on very windy, rainy nights only the large balcony would stay completely dry. There was another gunshot followed immediately by its echo. Charlie was certain it came from the theater.

"Let's go," he said. Still holding the shotgun, he began running toward the side of the theater, aiming down toward the stage which in a few days would be ready for the Philadelphia Orchestra now that the New York City Ballet had completed its season.

The full moon was bright enough, Charlie thought, to allow him to read a book, and he and Victor had no trouble making their way between the small trees and bushes along the side of the theater. The theater itself, however, was dark except for the red exit signs. Charlie and Victor ducked down between the first row and the orchestra pit as they peered back into the massive black space looking for some sign of Curry or Krause. Some birds in the theater had been disturbed and were twittering wildly. The sirens seemed much nearer and Charlie guessed that the police had found Curry's wrecked Plymouth Fury.

There was a metallic noise as of something hitting the back of one of the seats. This was followed by a spark and a gunshot, then the whine of a ricochet. The spark seemed to occur high up in the air and Charlie guessed that Curry was standing near the railing of the balcony. More birds began to twitter frantically and the air seemed full of the whirr of wings. Charlie raised the shotgun, pointed it toward the balcony, and fired. The explosion was immense as it echoed through the black space. Then there was a rattling noise as the birdshot fell among the seats, far short of where Curry presumably was standing. Seconds later, there were three more gunshots which pinged and ricocheted off the seats around them and sent Charlie and Victor diving to the floor.

"Give me some more shells," said Charlie.

"I didn't bring any more. How'd I know you'd turn into a shootin fool?"

There were two more gunshots and the bullets clanged into the metal chairs and music stands in the orchestra pit. It would give, Charlie thought, some oboist something interesting to talk about.

"What'd you want to shoot at him for in the first place?" asked Victor. "You only made him mad."

"I want to distract him from Krause."

"He's probably already killed Krause."

Charlie crawled along the concrete floor with the empty shotgun balanced across his arms until he found the gap of an aisle. From where he lay, he could see straight back to a red exit sign at the rear of the theater. The birds were still chirping and fluttering through the dark. Charlie guessed Krause was also on the balcony and felt the best he could do was to keep Curry's attention on himself and so give Krause his chance. Getting to his feet, he ran about twenty yards up the aisle, then ducked down again.

"Curry," he shouted. "Throw down your gun. I'm going to take you to jail." Even as he said this, Charlie knew he was using nearly the same words Wyatt Earp had used when he arrested Ben Thompson for shooting down the sheriff of Ellsworth, Kansas.

Before his words had stopped echoing, there were two more gunshots, both of which hit the seat just above him. Charlie lay on his back and looked up into the dark. As if it were a film being shown on the roof of the theater, he pictured the burning house and the man wrapped in flame leaping from the front steps. Then Charlie took a deep breath, rolled over, and got to his feet. Through the back of the theater he could see car lights bumping across the grass: three sets of lights with a blue flashing gumball on the top of each car.

Charlie took the shotgun by the barrel, swung it around and around his head, then let go. There was a silence, then a crash, followed by another as the shotgun bounced across the seats in front of him. Immediately, there were two more gunshots.

Charlie heard a noise behind him and turned to see Victor sitting in the aisle. "If he ever gets a look at you," said Victor, "he's goin to turn you into a fuckin sieve. I don't see whatcha want to drive him crazy for. I'm sick of stayin down here under the chewing gum."

Just as he stopped speaking, the lights went on in the theater. Charlie ducked behind the seats. Looking up, he saw Curry standing as if frozen by the railing near the middle of the balcony. He held his pistol with both hands and was pointing it down into the theater. To his left at a side entrance, Charlie saw Chief Peterson standing with about six policemen. One of them pointed up at the balcony.

"Jesus," said Victor, "look at Krause."

The ex-boxer was crouched down about ten feet behind Curry. As Charlie looked, Krause jumped to his feet and began to run down the aisle toward Curry.

Peterson stepped forward into the theater. He was holding a revolver. "Krause," he shouted, "stop or I'll shoot."

The only person to respond was Curry, who spun around and saw Krause only several feet away. Dodging to his right, Curry raised his gun and fired twice. Krause staggered, but then reached Curry, knocked aside his gun and, grabbing him by his belt and arm, lifted him up until he held him at shoulder height nearly forty feet above the main floor.

"Put him down," shouted Peterson. "Krause, I'm . . ."

Krause stood swaying at the railing. His brown suit was torn and flecked with straw. He tried to raise Curry even higher above his head, lift him until his arms were stretched straight up, but Curry kept kicking and clawing at his face.

Slowly, Krause tilted against the railing, tilted more until almost gently his body tilted over the side and his feet kicked upward as he fell off the balcony. Charlie was already running toward the spot where they would hit. As the two men fell, Krause pushed Curry away. Curry began to scream, a sharp staccato scream which he repeated over and over. Then there was a thud and crash as they hit the floor. Krause fell into the aisle, Curry among the seats.

Charlie was the first one to reach them. Curry lay folded up between the two back rows. His head was twisted nearly all the way around and it was clear that his neck must have hit the back of a seat, snapping it, and killing him instantly. His eyes were open and his face had the same blank expression it had had in life. Charlie turned away to where Krause lay on his back. His eyes were also open, but he was alive and staring at the ceiling. Blood was trickling from the corners of his mouth. Charlie knelt down beside him.

Krause lifted one of his big hands and slowly began brushing bits of straw from the lapels of his suit coat. "Charlie," he asked, "is Curry dead?"

Charlie nodded and began stroking his friend's forehead.

"Never killed a man before," said Krause. He spoke quietly as if he were forcing the words to come a long distance. "Makes me feel good," he said.

"Don't talk any more," said Charlie. He was aware of Victor standing beside him. Various Saratoga policemen were rushing around. Peterson had been looking at Curry. Now he joined Charlie and Victor.

"Everything's all right now, isn't it, Charlie?" asked Krause. "I mean, I did the right thing."

"You did fine," said Charlie.

"I think I'll rest a little," said Krause.

As Charlie got to his feet, Peterson grabbed his arm and pulled him toward him, digging his fingers into Charlie's muscle. Then he jabbed a revolver in Charlie's stomach.

"If he lives," said Peterson, "I'm going to see he's sent away forever. You too, Bradshaw. You'll be away from Saratoga for a long time."

Charlie looked down at the revolver pressing against his

stomach. Peterson's face was bright red. Slowly, Charlie raised his hand until it touched Peterson's cheek. For a moment, he thought of Krause's story about the sportswriter he had always regretted not hitting. Then Charlie patted the police chief's face.

"Peterson," he said, "you were always a stupid man."

23

▼▼▼

NORMALLY, DOWNTOWN SARATOGA at 7:30 Sunday morning was a pretty dull place. But this morning, July 30, just a day before the opening of the track there were horse trailers, campers, Winnebagos, grooms in souped-up Fords; exercise boys, trainers, jockeys and their agents, bug boys going in and out of Lou's Luncheonette or the 24-hour Star Market, and enough general activity that the mere sight of it was enough to tire Victor out.

It was a blue, cloudless morning and the breeze blowing down Broadway carried bits of paper, styrofoam cups, paper bags so that even the street seemed in a hurry. Victor braked slightly as the front page of the *Racing Form* blew across the windshield of his Dodge Dart. He and Charlie were driving along Broadway toward the Spa City Diner where they intended to have breakfast. In his mind, Victor was debating between poached eggs, French toast, or both. He was most inclined to both. He hadn't slept, his eyes felt scratchy and his last meal was a distant memory: a vague cheeseburger and maybe a small slice of apple pie. They had only just left police headquarters after spending hours talking and waiting around, talking and waiting around. At the same time, Victor was surprised to be at liberty at all. Back at the Performing Arts Center, he had decided he was in for a ten-year jail term and he'd worried how to break the news to his son in Chicago.

It was Charlie who got them out of that. After he had patted Peterson's cheek, he suggested the police chief examine Curry's fancy European pistol—a 15-shot Beretta Model 92S–1—to see if it wasn't the same gun which killed Ackerman and Claremon. Then he suggested that Peterson check the front fender of the red pickup from Dwyer's stable for traces of yellow paint from Charlie's Volkswagen. After that he suggested they return to Dwyer's stable to question the man whom Rico had captured. Despite this, Peterson still insisted on arresting them, although even his own men were apologetic.

Curry was dead, as was the other man who had been burned: Victor never learned his name. Peterson had found the second accomplice—Harry Something—bound hand and foot in Dwyer's parking lot with Rico standing nearby with a length of two-by-four. Rico had already convinced Harry that the world would be a happier place if he told all. Driving down Broadway, Victor took pleasure in remembering Peterson's face as Harry explained how Curry intended to burn the stable, where he bought the gasoline, how he meant to frame Charlie and Krause and have them killed in the fire.

After that Peterson grudgingly admitted he must have been mistaken and they drove to police headquarters, where much of the night was spent with Charlie and Victor giving their statements. They had sat in Peterson's large office and Victor went so far as to smoke one of Peterson's expensive cigars, even though he didn't like cigars. Peterson had listened and at least had the decency not to interrupt. Subdued was how Victor described him. Then, around seven, the State Police called to say that Curry's Beretta was indeed the same gun that killed Ackerman and Claremon, while the red pickup was the one that bumped Charlie into the lake.

Phil Tyler was in critical condition but would recover. With Krause it wasn't so certain. Not only had bones been broken in his fall from the balcony, but he had been shot once in the abdomen. When Victor and Charlie left the police station for the Spa City Diner, the doctors were pessimistic. Charlie wanted to drive to the hospital after they had eaten and, although he would have preferred a dozen hours sleep in his own nice bed, Victor had agreed.

The car windows were open and as Victor drove he tapped

his cast lightly against the steering wheel in time to the punk rock being broadcast by the Skidmore radio station. Charlie looked at him with mild irritation. He was worried about Tyler and Krause and kept telling himself if he had seen Peterson earlier both men would be all right. Even as he thought that, however, he doubted Peterson would have acted in time to save the stable.

Looking out at the bright summer morning, Charlie told himself he should feel glad it was nearly August, his favorite time of year. He told himself tomorrow he would take Doris Bailes to the track, and he would put some money on Red Fox in the fifth and maybe a whole new life would begin. Charlie kept repeating these things and after a while he told himself he felt a little better.

As they drove past the YMCA, Victor said, "What I don't see is why Curry shot Ackerman there instead of someplace else."

"Probably no place would have been easier," said Charlie. "He knew the Y and knew Krause usually stayed in the locker room."

"But what if Krause hadn't?" said Victor. "I mean, what if he had gone in with Ackerman?"

"I expect Curry was watching," said Charlie. "The weight room is right by the locker room. He could have made sure Krause was in the locker room, then gone out the back and around to the side door of the pool."

"So if Krause had gone into the pool area, Curry would just of shot Ackerman some other time?"

Charlie yawned and covered his mouth. "I guess so," he said, "except he wanted to make it dramatic enough to look like a slick, cynical, professional killing."

"How come?"

"He wanted the murder blamed on organized crime, on racketeers who were angry at Ackerman for interfering with their gambling interests."

"And that's what Peterson did, right?"

"That's what he did at first," said Charlie. "I keep thinking he would have caught on eventually."

"Sure," said Victor, as he pulled into the lot of the Spa City Diner, "after you'd got burned up at the stable and I came pounding on his door. Dopes like Peterson can't figure anything unless it's written on a billboard. . . . By the way, you hear anything new about Dwyer?"

"No, he's still in a coma. The doctor said they'd just have to wait and see."

"You think Curry slipped him something?"

"I doubt it. I mean, I wouldn't put it past him, but more likely once Dwyer realized what was happening he decided to bow out. He didn't have the strength to fight Curry, much less stop him, and he couldn't have stood the publicity if Curry were arrested."

"Sounds like he was caught between the frying pan and the deep blue sea," said Victor, getting out of the car.

"That's about it," said Charlie.

The diner was attached to the bus station and despite the early hour large buses from New York and Montreal were disgorging tourists who hoped to make their fortune at the track. All over people were quarreling about cabs, buying tip sheets, being paranoid about their suitcases, and greeting old friends.

As Charlie made his way through the crowd and entered the restaurant, he thought it fortunate that his mother had quit her job as waitress to pursue her career as a racehorse owner. Charlie was dirty, his clothes were torn from being dragged around the stall, plus being spotted with soot and ash from the fire. Attempts to clean himself up at the police station had done little more than smear the dirt around. His mother would think such dishevelment indicated a night of carousing and she would remind him the family had a position to maintain, that it was Charlie's duty to look what she called his picture-pleasing best.

They took a table in the new part of the diner and the waitress brought them coffee. It was a large room filled with clattering plates, harried waitresses, and customers who all wanted something more. Charlie glanced around, then picked up his menu.

"You know," said Victor, "I partly came to Saratoga because I no longer felt safe in the city, but in the past week my arm's been broke, I was nearly drowned, and I've been shot at, I don't know how many times, a lot. If in the city I'd gone out on First Avenue and shouted, 'Ricans, take me, I'm yours,' I couldn't have had it any worse."

Charlie closed his menu and sipped his coffee. He didn't want Victor to leave. "So you're going back?" he asked.

Victor shrugged. "Like I say, it beats watchin the TV. Maybe I'll stay a bit longer." Taking a handful of napkins, Victor blew his nose. Then he scratched under his arm, leaned back in his chair, and glanced around the room looking for cute girls. After a moment, he said, "By the way, you know those three guys at that table over there? They keep starin at you."

Charlie glanced in the direction Victor indicated and saw his three cousins just finishing breakfast. They were clean, prosperous, and obviously respectable. All the dirt on Charlie's body suddenly felt heavy. He gave a half-hearted wave, then watched as the three men ignored it and returned to their meal.

"They're my cousins," said Charlie. "I was pretty much brought up with them."

"Guess they don't like the straw in your hair," said Victor.

Charlie again picked up his menu and tried to decide if he really wanted blueberry pancakes. Then he gave it up. He wondered what new round of gossip he would have to contend with. In the long run, it would be easier to go bad. But as he thought this, Charlie grew irritated at himself for being so easily cowed. Hadn't he outwitted the police? Hadn't he solved Ackerman's murder? Charlie pushed away his menu. He would force his cousins to acknowledge him. No more would he stand for their moral bullying.

"There," said Victor, "that got them."

Charlie looked up to see his three cousins making their way between the crowded tables toward the exit. They seemed to wobble with indignation.

"What'd you do?" asked Charlie.

"Blew 'em a kiss," said Victor.

SARATOGA
HEADHUNTER

▼▼▼

Gambling is in the atmosphere. Formerly men of wealth and social position, statesmen and philosophers, students and artists gathered here to drink the waters that nature forces through a hundred fissures and enjoy the crisp, invigorating air and picturesque scenery which have united in making Saratoga America's most famous summer resort. They came to ride, to drive, to dress and to secure that freedom from business and domestic care that gives perfect rest and brings back bodily health and vigor.

Now the great summer population of Saratoga is largely composed of those gathered here to gamble or to live off those who do gamble. From one of the most reputable and most exclusive of American watering places, it has been transformed into the wickedest and wildest.

Nellie Bly
New York World
August, 1894

1

▼▼▼

BLACK JACK KETCHUM, the member of the Wild Bunch who turned train robber out of unrequited love, used to hammer himself on the head with a gun butt whenever he made a serious mistake. When Black Jack attempted to stop the train near Folsom, New Mexico, and had his arm shot up by the express agent, what he seemed to regret most was that the subsequent amputation robbed him of the power to punish himself for getting caught.

All through one October, Charlie Bradshaw felt he had Black Jack Ketchum's example of self-abuse ever before his eyes. "I could have kicked myself," he would tell his friend Victor Plotz, "or worse."

Charlie's problems began on a rainy Sunday evening at the beginning of the month. It was the sort of autumn rain that makes the leaves turn color, and even tastes of winter though the days remain warm. So far, the leaves around Saratoga Springs had only begun to turn, but Charlie knew that in the morning bright scarlet patches would show in the maples around his small house on the lake.

Charlie had spent the early part of the evening attempting to fix the stopper on the toilet, with the result that he now had to wiggle the handle for five minutes instead of one in order to make the water stop running. He had just decided to give up and go to bed when there was a knock at the door. This too was an irritation. He had to be up at four thirty and it was already approaching ten. On the other hand, he had heard no car and so was curious.

The man at the door was several inches shorter than Charlie, about five feet five or six, and at first Charlie didn't recognize him because he was fat.

"Hey, Bradshaw," said the man, "how you been?"

Charlie stood back to let him enter. He was wearing a tan raincoat and rain hat and when he took off the hat, Charlie realized that the man was the suspended jockey Jimmy McClatchy. In his left hand was a blue canvas suitcase.

McClatchy was so much the last person that Charlie expected to see that he looked at him dumbly as if the jockey were some creature just sprung from a rock.

McClatchy seemed to enjoy Charlie's surprise. "Long time no see," he said, grinning.

"I thought you were hiding out," said Charlie.

McClatchy tossed his wet hat and coat onto a chair. "I am. You got anything to drink?" McClatchy had short mahogany-colored hair, a flabby, moon-shaped face and lips as thin as a pair of fifty-cent pieces. He wore a blue blazer and a blue-and-white polka-dot bow tie. The blazer had shiny gold buttons embossed with good-luck horseshoes.

"A few bottles of beer," said Charlie.

"Beer's fine. And bring some crackers if you have any."

Charlie went into the kitchen to look. He hadn't seen McClatchy since he had last raced in Saratoga over a year ago. During that time, McClatchy had gained about forty pounds. He was tall for a jockey and was known as a puker—that is, a jockey who ate a lot, then threw it up afterward. But since he had stopped racing, he clearly had been keeping his food in his stomach.

Charlie got a bottle of Pabst from the refrigerator, then located a chunk of cheddar cheese. From the cupboard over the sink he took down a box of Ritz crackers.

All he knew about McClatchy during the past year had come from newspapers. But this was quite a lot. McClatchy was something of a celebrity, if that was the right word for a man who had become famous by testifying against old friends and associates.

McClatchy's notoriety had begun a year ago September when he had been subpoenaed by a New Jersey grand jury and later indicted for race fixing in Atlantic City. The indictment was subsequently dropped and during the trial McClatchy had appeared as an unindicted co-conspirator testifying for the prosecution. His testimony helped send a dozen men to jail.

The race-fixing charges had concerned themselves with about fifteen races over a two-year period—all were exacta and trifecta races, where people wager on the first two or three horses to cross the finish line. By slowing certain horses it was possible to greatly increase the odds as to which two or three horses would finish first, while the money to be won in such a fix could be in the hundreds of thousands.

But the more people who got involved, the greater was the chance of discovery. The New Jersey investigation had begun in response to a drunken groom's accusations in a bar. McClatchy, to his credit or discredit, had been able to exchange his prison cell for a secret address and salary paid for by the Federal Witness Program. Nor did his testimony stop with Atlantic City. The grand jury in New Jersey led to a grand jury in Delaware, and again McClatchy was the star witness. This time ten people had gone to jail. Now there was talk of additional grand juries in Massachusetts and Pennsylvania, while a New York grand jury was just beginning to hear testimony in Brooklyn. Only that afternoon Charlie had read that McClatchy was scheduled to appear before the Brooklyn grand jury, again as an unindicted co-conspirator.

Charlie returned to the living room with the beer, crackers and cheese and set them on the coffee table. "Aren't you supposed to be testifying in Brooklyn?" he asked.

McClatchy lay stretched out on the couch in front of the fireplace where a couple of birch logs were burning. "Yeah," he said, "I gotta be there in a week or so."

"Then what are you doing here?" Charlie sat down on the rocker next to the couch.

"To tell you the truth, I didn't feel safe."

McClatchy sat up, drank several mouthfuls of beer, then methodically began cutting small squares of cheese and putting them on crackers. Charlie thought that McClatchy's fingers looked like little cocktail sausages.

"The Feds were keeping me hidden in Allentown. All day I was cooped up in a tiny apartment with nothin' to do except watch the TV or play gin rummy with a coupla assholes. Anyway, there's lots of guys who'd like to make sure I don't show up in Brooklyn and I couldn't trust some cop not to talk, so I lit out."

McClatchy's mouth was full and as he spoke he spat tiny bits of crackers onto the rug. He sat forward with his elbows on his knees, drank some more beer and belched.

"You got any salami or anything like that?"

"No," said Charlie. "How'd you get up here anyway? I didn't hear a car."

"First, I took a bus, then I hitched rides. How about another beer?"

Charlie went back to the kitchen. He had no doubt there were people who wanted McClatchy dead. He had told the papers that he had helped fix races in more than a dozen states and all those states had begun to investigate his charges. In many cases, McClatchy had been the moneyman, paying off jockeys to slow their horses. The payoffs had ranged from five hundred to a thousand dollars. Charlie had been surprised that jockeys would risk their careers for so little.

Charlie returned from the kitchen, handed McClatchy the beer and sat down. It was still raining and he could hear the drops hitting the roof. "But what I don't understand," said Charlie, "is what you are doing in Saratoga."

McClatchy drank some more beer, then wiped his mouth on the back of his hand. "I needed a place to hole up for a week. Saratoga seemed the best bet. I mean, I can shoot right down to New York with no trouble."

"Where are you staying?" asked Charlie. He thought it would be difficult for McClatchy to find a place. The jockey had always been a loner and now that he had been testifying to various grand juries, it would be hard to find people to help him. In fact, Charlie doubted there was anyone who would stick out his neck for someone as questionable as Jimmy McClatchy.

"That's what I wanted to talk to you about," said McClatchy.

Charlie experienced a substantial attack of dismay. "You mean you want to stay here, with me?"

"That's about it," said McClatchy.

"But there isn't room."

McClatchy glanced around the cottage, which consisted of three rooms, including the kitchen. "It's pretty small but what choice do I have? Maybe you could sleep on the couch and I could have the bedroom."

"Why can't you go to a motel?"

"Think about it, Charlie. Think about what would happen if I showed my face in Saratoga. If you kick me outta here, I'll be a dead man for sure."

"But why me?"

"You always treated me right. Anyway, who else could I ask? Some trainer or jock? The way things are going I wouldn't trust my own mother. Some guys would pay a lotta money to know where I am. Okay, so we were never what you'd call pals but I figured I could trust you and besides, this is the last place anyone would look."

"So you picked me as your sucker." Charlie began to feel angry.

"Not sucker, Charlie, don't say that. I needed a place to stay and you were the only person I could think of. All right, I took a chance, but right now it's either you or nothing."

Charlie got up and put another birch log on the fire. The loose white bark caught right away, sending a rush of flame up the chimney.

For several years, Charlie had been head of security for Lew Ackerman's Lorelei Stables just outside Saratoga. Then, fifteen months ago, Ackerman had been shot dead in the swimming pool of the Saratoga YMCA. Not long afterward his partner had sold the stable. McClatchy had ridden for him perhaps twenty times, but Ackerman had often accused McClatchy of laziness and stopped using him about two months before the murder.

Charlie himself had never liked McClatchy, primarily because he once heard the jockey making fun of Ackerman for being too scrupulous. Charlie, however, was one of those unfortunate human beings who try to be particularly nice to people they dislike, and so, besides being friendly with McClatchy, he had occasionally lent him cab fare from the stables into Saratoga—money that McClatchy had never returned.

McClatchy finished his beer and set the bottle back on the table. "I'll tell you what," he said, "I'll give you fifty bucks a night to let me stay here."

For some reason it seemed worse to have McClatchy pay. Although it was October and the racing season was long past, Charlie guessed there were hundreds of people who would recognize the jockey, even with all that extra weight. And Charlie felt certain that if it became known that McClatchy was in Saratoga, then someone would try to make sure that this particular federal witness kept his lip buttoned forever. Presumably, McClatchy found this distressing, for despite his apparent calm he appeared wary and seemed to be listening for far-off noises. Charlie knew that if he were in McClatchy's shoes, he would have already moved to Zanzibar or Nepal.

"That's all right," said Charlie, "maybe you can help with the food. You think it will be for a week?"

"That's okay. The grand jury begins tomorrow and I'm supposed to show up on Monday."

Charlie stood in front of the fireplace. He had been poking the fire with a pair of metal tongs and now he put them back in the rack. It had just occurred to him that while McClatchy was using his house as a hideout, he couldn't let anyone else pay a visit. Unfortunately, Charlie had the sort of friends who never called before they came over. Apart from his friends, however, he was also half-expecting a visit from his mother. At the moment she was in Atlantic City gambling with money she had made from the sale of her half of a racehorse. Possibly she could stay with one of his cousins, but that would mean disappointment and harsh words.

But the worst thing about McClatchy's visit was that it meant he would have to break a date with Doris Bailes, whom he had invited to dinner for tomorrow night. Mentally, he kicked himself even as he thought about it. Charlie had planned an elaborate meal. He knew that Doris sometimes went out with other men and he had hoped to show her the seriousness of his intentions. In his random imaginings, he had even seen himself proposing. Now he would have to give her some excuse and he wasn't sure how to do it since his face always turned dull pink when he lied.

"You got any more beer?" asked McClatchy.

Charlie started to move toward the kitchen. "I think so."

McClatchy waved him back and got to his feet. "I can get it all right." The jockey walked with a sort of rolling waddle. He paused at the bedroom door and looked in. "That bed pretty comfortable? The couch feels hard."

"Forget it," said Charlie, "if you're going to stay here, you'll sleep on the couch. Not only that but you'll wash your own dishes and keep your muddy feet off the furniture. How'd you manage to hitch a ride right to my front door?"

McClatchy returned to the living room with a beer and a piece of cold chicken. "Guess I was lucky," he said. "You still working for Lorelei Stables?" When McClatchy asked a question, he tended to leave his mouth open as if waiting for the answer to fill it.

"No, Lew's partner sold it. The land was bought by developers. They were planning a subdivision called Lorelei Acres but ran out of money."

Actually, a model home had been completed and ten other houses begun before the company went bankrupt. Charlie often drove by it. Where there were once wineglass elms and neat green and white shed rows, there was now an expanse of mud, the skeletons of houses and one ugly yellow bungalow.

"So how d'you make your money?"

"I do this and that." The idea of putting up with McClatchy for a week was hardly tolerable. "As a matter of fact, I've got a small private detective agency." Charlie wondered if it was too late to tell McClatchy to leave. Yet he knew that to order him out would be almost like putting a bullet in his head.

"You're pulling my leg," said McClatchy.

"No, I started it almost a year ago." It occurred to Charlie that perhaps he could check into a motel and let McClatchy have the cottage to himself.

"You do a lotta divorce work?"

"I stay away from that if I can. It gets a little shady."

"Isn't that where the money is?" McClatchy had unclipped his bow tie and it lay among the remnants of cheese, crackers and chicken bones like a polka-dot butterfly.

"Sure, I'd probably make more that way." Charlie started to continue, then stopped. Why tell McClatchy that the agency hardly paid the rent for the downtown office? Now and then he'd look for someone's missing husband or wife, maybe a runaway teenager. Occasionally, he would get a shoplifting job. "To tell the truth," he said, "I've applied for a job with the Pinkertons."

McClatchy laughed. "I can just see you out there directing traffic at the track. Why bother? I mean, if I needed the money I'd line up some cute girls and make them work for me. Just bust some college girl for coke, do something to give you a little leverage, then you got it made."

Charlie thought again about checking into a motel. "I'm not too keen on the Pinkertons, but I need a job."

The real reason Charlie didn't like the Pinkertons was that they had been responsible for the infamous Night of Blood when their operators had attempted to trap Frank and Jesse James in the Jameses' house in Clay County, Missouri. An explosion had killed Frank and Jesse's eight-year-old half-brother, Archie, and their mother had had her right arm blown off. Frank and Jesse had been miles away at the time.

"Why don't you become a cop again?" asked McClatchy.

"Because I don't want to be a cop."

"How long you do it, twenty-five years? You should have hung in there for your retirement."

"I worked for twenty years, that was all I wanted." Charlie glanced at his watch. It was past eleven. "This is enough talk for tonight. I've got to be up at four-thirty."

"You goin' fishing?"

Charlie had not wanted to explain. "I've got to be over in Schuylerville at five thirty to deliver milk."

McClatchy gave Charlie an uncomprehending stare. "You're a milkman?"

"No, no, nothing like that. You remember John Wanamaker? He was one of my guards out at Lorelei. Well, he's the milkman. But his mother's sick. She lives in Santa Fe and he flew out to be with her. I guess she's dying. He asked me to take over his milk route until he got back."

McClatchy had begun to grin. Far back in his mouth Charlie could see gold teeth. "Why'n't you just tell him to shove it?"

"John's got a pretty long record. If he lost his job, it'd be hard to get another." Listening to himself, Charlie thought how reasonable it sounded. As a matter of fact, he was furious with Wanamaker.

"So how long you been peddling milk?"

"Three weeks."

McClatchy laughed. It seemed to Charlie that he never laughed at anything funny. "Hey, Charlie," said McClatchy, "that's a pretty long time."

Charlie poked the fire, sending up a shower of sparks. "He was supposed to be back in a week, but then his mother got worse. I don't mind telling you I don't like it much. It's six hours a day, six days a week. That's why I want to get to bed. Wanamaker says his mother could die anytime, that the doctors are amazed she's lived so long. I mean, I'd be perfectly happy if she recovered. What can I say, 'Die, die, so I don't have to get up at four thirty anymore?' That's pretty hard."

McClatchy yawned, then bent over and began to untie his shoes. "Tell him to get lost," he said. "So what if he can't get a job?"

"That's all right. I talked to Wanamaker this morning. He figures he'll be back in a couple of days one way or the other."

"Least delivering milk is pretty safe," said McClatchy.

Charlie stretched, then rubbed the back of his neck. He could hear nothing from outside and guessed it had stopped raining. "Not as safe as you might think. One day I was bit by a dog."

"So who's running the detective agency while you're driving the milk truck?"

"An old friend of mine, Victor Plotz."

2

▼▼▼

WHEN CHARLIE WAS A KID in Saratoga before the war, there used to be a dairy that delivered milk by horse-drawn wagon. Charlie remembered many Saturday mornings when he would hitch a ride on the back, sitting on a shelf where metal racks were stored. Sometimes he'd get a wedge of clear ice from inside and, as the wagon clip-clopped its way through Saratoga, Charlie would suck on the ice and look at the houses and wonder who lived in them. At that time, Saratoga was full of huge elms and the hotels were still turning a profit.

As he drove John Wanamaker's milk truck through Schuyler-ville that Monday morning, Charlie tried to recapture the sense of peacefulness he had experienced forty years before. But even though he liked riding on milk trucks, he had never wanted to be a milkman. The idea would have struck him as preposter-ous. His plan was to be a major-league third baseman.

Charlie had left McClatchy snoring on the couch at five o'clock that morning. McClatchy had snored all night. Charlie knew this for certain because he had spent most of the night telling himself: You *must* go to sleep. When he left, Charlie had been surprised by how peaceful McClatchy looked, as if his dreaming mind was completely untroubled by the prospect of testifying against his former friends.

Charlie drew up in front of a two-story house with green asbestos siding, and hurried up the walk with four quarts of skim milk and a container of low-fat cottage cheese. He wore khaki pants and a khaki shirt, a dark blue tie and a rather military-looking khaki hat with a black plastic visor. Embroi-dered in red on the front of the hat and on his left breast pocket were the words WHOLESOME DAIRY.

Charlie picked up four empties and returned to the truck, which was also khaki colored with the name WHOLESOME

DAIRY written in red lettering on the side. It was what Charlie thought of as a typical milk truck, an old Ford that rattled even when empty.

It seemed to Charlie, as he turned left at the corner and headed back to the barn, that his life had reached a new low. The arrival of McClatchy only gave further proof of this. It was nearly eleven o'clock and he imagined McClatchy rummaging through his cabinets and refrigerator for a light snack. Charlie had forgotten to tell him about the broken toilet and he had no doubt that it was running at that very moment. Very likely it would overflow.

Even if Charlie survived this week and was able to send McClatchy off to his grand jury in Brooklyn, he was still faced with the imminent arrival of his mother. For two years she had been traveling the country, following the fortunes of her racehorse. Indisputably, her return would make Charlie's life more difficult. If she had money and was able to open the motel that she had dreamed about for thirty years, she would expect Charlie to help her. If she was broke and had to return to waitressing, she would also expect Charlie to help her. As it was, she called him every week to make sure he was doing nothing to embarrass his wealthy and thoroughly respectable cousins: three men who had been the bane of Charlie's life since the age of two, when Charlie had realized that his various clumsinesses were being compared to their successes.

At the moment, his cousins seemed to think there was a smidgen of hope for Charlie after all. This, however, was because they mistakenly assumed that his job as a milkman was permanent. Several times during the past week Charlie had received calls from his cousin Jack, congratulating him and even threatening to drop in on the Wholesome Dairy to "see how he was adjusting." Charlie knew he ought to tell his cousins that his career as a milkman would be as brief as possible, but he was so unaccustomed to their praise that he had remained silent.

As it happened, Jack was the cousin Charlie liked best, even though he felt bullied by his many successes. Jack was a year older than Charlie and, as they grew up, it had seemed that

Jack had no faults, was surrounded by friends and had never experienced an unhappy day in his life. Now he owned a successful hardware store in downtown Saratoga, was happily married to a beautiful wife and had three sons, all doing well in college.

Long ago Charlie had decided that Jack passed through life in much the same way that Moses had passed through the Red Sea, while his own method he likened to the Egyptians'. Certainly, this would seem no reason to love his cousin, but Jack's easy passage was done with such innocence and good humor that Charlie hardly minded his triumphs. Even so, he did not gladly anticipate a visit from his cousin to the Wholesome Dairy. Consequently, when he drove the milk truck into the yard and saw Jack standing by the barn idly tossing pebbles against a circle drawn onto the wall with white chalk, Charlie felt a vague displeasure.

Jack was five inches taller than Charlie, had wavy brown hair and a chin as ruddy and square as the end of a brick. Although he never seemed to exercise, he was in tremendous shape. When Charlie climbed from the truck, Jack grabbed his hand and squeezed it so hard that Charlie had a mental image of the bones being transformed into a sort of protoplasmic mush.

"Charlie," Jack said, "you can't imagine how glad it makes us to know that you've gone and gotten yourself a decent job. I wish my father were alive to see it."

Charlie extricated his hand and started removing the racks of empties from the back of the truck. Jack grabbed half a dozen racks and began to help, somehow giving the impression that he had done this all his life. Charlie considered telling his cousin that being a milkman was only temporary, that Wanamaker would soon return from Santa Fe and free him from this ordeal. Instead he said, "Your father was a great man, Jack."

Jack made a sad, clucking noise in the back of his throat. The sun twinkled on the gold Masonic pin in his lapel. "You know, Charlie," he said, "it pained us to see you floundering. I think when it becomes known that you're working again, you'll see a big difference in people's attitudes."

It was clear that Jack didn't consider the detective agency to be work. They finished stacking the empty milk crates and Charlie began leading Jack in the direction of his car. "That's great, Jack. I'm glad you're happy. How'd you find out I was delivering milk?"

"Chief Peterson told me. You know, Charlie, he really has your best interests at heart. I wouldn't be surprised that if you give a good showing as a milkman, he might someday find a place for you again in the department."

Charlie's car was a 1974 red Renault station wagon that often wouldn't start. As he opened the door, he hoped this wouldn't be one of those days. Of all the people who disliked Charlie in Saratoga, Chief Peterson disliked him most.

"I appreciate that, Jack," he said, "but as you know I left the department by my own choice and I can't imagine going back. As for Peterson having my best interests at heart, that's"—Charlie again thought of his mother—"perhaps an exaggeration."

Charlie got into the Renault and turned the key. There was a fateful silence, then the engine turned over. He glanced up at his cousin beaming down at him. Soon Jack would learn that Charlie's life as a milkman was short-lived and Charlie would have to deal with his cousin's disappointment.

"Well, Jack, I'm glad for the chance of this little talk but I've got to rush now."

"Still swimming, Charlie?" There seemed just of hint of mockery in Jack's voice.

"That's right, still swimming." Charlie gave a wave of his hand and drove out of the yard. If he hurried, he could reach the YMCA in Saratoga at noon. For several years, Charlie had been coping with his expanding waistline by swimming laps. Now he swam a mile a day, four days a week. Although thinner than he had been as a policeman, Charlie was more or less resolved to the fact that he was someone who would always be about twenty pounds overweight.

Quickly, Charlie drove the twelve miles into Saratoga. The morning was warm and cloudless. Patches of orange and red showed in the trees on either side of the road. Reaching the Y at noon, Charlie spent the next forty minutes laboriously collecting the seventy-two lengths that made up a mile, concentrating on keeping his legs straight and trying to ignore the faster swimmers. One Skidmore girl seemed to zoom by every other lap, her black tank suit passing within inches of his nose. If he bit her, it would only mean trouble. Deep down, Charlie hated to be passed. As he hopelessly tried to increase his speed, he thought his cousin might have been right to mock him.

By one o'clock Charlie was drying himself off with his big blue towel in front of his locker. His arms ached and despite his shower he was sweating slightly. As Charlie began pulling on his shirt, George Marotta came out of the shower and nodded to him.

"Say, Charlie, wait for me outside, will you? I want to talk to you."

"Sure. What's it about?"

"Just wait."

Marotta turned away and began dialing the combination of his lock. He was a thin man of about Charlie's height, with curly gray hair, which at the moment was dripping with water. His face was narrow and bony with a long thin nose that had once been broken and badly set. The swelling in its center looked like a fat knuckle. Charlie guessed that Marotta was in his mid-fifties. He had never liked swimming next to him because although Marotta was nearly ten years older, he passed Charlie constantly.

Charlie finished tying his shoes, then walked to the mirror to comb his hair. About a dozen other men were in the locker room: Saratoga businessmen, students, some officers from the naval base. A few Charlie knew only from swimming, others he had known all his life. Some puddles dotted the blue and gray tiles near the row of sinks, and a small boy, late for tadpole swim, was stamping in them. Several men nodded to Charlie or smiled. Although they weren't exactly friends, they were close acquaintances and Charlie knew enough about them to follow their lives with affection and concern.

Charlie combed his hair straight back over his scalp. There seemed less of it each day, while the bald spot was definitely growing. Once the color had been what he called dog-brown, but since he had started swimming, it had been bleached by the chlorine and was turning gray besides. It was strange to think he could no longer clearly remember what his hair color had been for over forty years: that what had been a commonplace was now a mystery.

Charlie had a round, pink face with few wrinkles, and large blue eyes. His nose, he thought, was too short and puggy: more like a big toe than a nose. At least his teeth were good. He thought of his face as serviceable, like a plain suitcase, and he prided himself that it never showed any expression. This was perhaps not as true as he hoped. He had changed from his milkman's uniform and wore a light blue shirt and dark blue pants. It occurred to Charlie that even after three years of not being a policeman, he continued to dress like one.

As Charlie walked outside to wait for Marotta, he began to wonder what the other man wanted. Marotta owned a large restaurant out in the country, west of Saratoga. Some people swore that his bills were paid by New York racketeers who used the restaurant to launder money. Charlie had no knowledge of that one way or the other, but he knew that outside of August the restaurant was nearly empty and there was no indication of how it stayed in business.

Marotta appeared a few minutes later dressed in an immaculate light gray suit. "Let's get a sandwich at the Executive," he said.

They turned right down Broadway, then crossed Congress Park. A cool wind sent a few fallen leaves chasing one another over the grass, and riffled the surface of the duck pond.

"Your stroke's looking better," said Marotta.

Charlie shrugged. Since Marotta had lapped him a dozen times, he wasn't feeling like any Johnny Weissmuller. They walked by the three-story, red brick Canfield Casino, which was currently a museum. It had once been the center of Saratoga gambling and as they passed the game room, Charlie liked to think he could hear the click of roulette wheels.

The Executive was a bar and delicatessen a block away on Phila Street. The front of the building was covered with dark-stained pine boards interrupted by large windows. Behind the bar were two very heavy young men standing side by side with their elbows on the counter. They had black curly hair and wore T-shirts that said, "I ate it all at the Executive."

Marotta led the way to a booth toward the back of the bar. Charlie followed, nodding to several people he knew. The room smelled of fried food. Marotta sat down, then seemed disinclined to speak. He appeared embarrassed. For a moment, Charlie worried he might know something about Jimmy McClatchy, but that seemed impossible. When the waitress arrived, Marotta ordered a sandwich and a beer, then contented himself with shredding his red paper napkin. From the back room came the click of pool balls.

Charlie waited. The girl brought their sandwiches. Marotta took several bites of his hot pastrami, then pushed away his plate and sat back.

"You know, Charlie," he said, "we've never talked much, but over the years I've heard a number of good things about you, mostly from Lew Ackerman. He said you were pretty smart. I guess that's why I decided to talk to you."

Marotta paused. Two patrolmen came in to pick up a take-out order. One waved to Charlie, the other pretended not to see him.

Marotta put his hands on the edge of the table and leaned forward, wrinkling his brow and looking suddenly angry. "What I want to know, Charlie, is if you're having me followed."

"Are you serious?"

"Never been more. I know you're working as a detective and that you gotta take jobs where you find them, but some things I don't like and taking advantage of a foolish woman is one of them."

Charlie liked to think he was difficult to surprise, yet this was the last thing he expected to hear. Marotta continued to look furious. The swelling in the center of his nose was like a small knot and all his anger seemed to radiate out from it.

"Maybe you should tell me what you're talking about," said

Charlie. He spoke quietly, half-afraid of making Marotta even angrier.

Marotta picked up his sandwich, then set it down again and shook his head. On the wall to Charlie's left were photographs of folk singers who had appeared at Caffe-Lena up the street.

"My wife likes to imagine things," explained Marotta, "and one of the things she likes to imagine is that I fool around with a lot of women. I'm not saying that I'm the world's most moral guy, but in that particular department I been pretty good. I tell her that but she won't listen and every now and then she gets the bright idea to hire some private detective and have me followed. That's what's happening right now and there are a lot of reasons why I don't like it."

Charlie began to feel relieved. "I don't do that kind of work," he said, "and even if I did, I wouldn't accept business from your wife. The town's too small to have you as an enemy."

Marotta leaned forward again, staring at Charlie, then his face relaxed. It had been dark red, as if he were attempting to lift something heavy, now it grew lighter. He started to look embarrassed.

"You sure it's not you, Charlie? I guess it could be someone up from Albany. It's a big guy, maybe a few years older'n me with gray hair that sticks out in all directions. Leastways, he started it. Now there's some punky kid watching me, a lot of black, greasy hair and a leather jacket. I mean, all he does is sit out in the parking lot outside the restaurant and read skin magazines."

As Marotta spoke, Charlie felt his skin begin to prickle. The description of the older man matched his friend Victor Plotz, while the kid could easily be Eddie Gillespie, an ex-car thief who had worked for Charlie as a guard at Lorelei Stables.

"To tell you the truth," said Charlie, somewhat uncertainly, "I've been doing some other work for the past three weeks and have a friend running the office. Possibly, he took the job. You say he had gray hair?"

Marotta started to look angry again. "Yeah, and sort of a fat face and big nose. He was wearing a gray sweat shirt."

Charlie had no doubt it was Victor. He wondered if lots of people had close friends who constantly embarrassed them. "Well, I don't think it's anyone I know," he said, "but I'll check with my partner and if he took the job, then I'll make him quit."

Marotta narrowed his eyes and looked suspiciously at Charlie. "If you can remove this guy, I'd appreciate it. If you can't, then I'll remove him myself. I don't like people talking about me and something like this makes talk. If there's any problem about money, I'll make it up to you."

"Forget it," said Charlie, although he guessed the money from Marotta's wife was all that was paying the rent on the office.

Marotta wiped his mouth and tossed a ten-dollar bill on the table. "At least let me pay for lunch." He stood up, then leaned over the table. "And Charlie," he said, "I'd appreciate it if you didn't tell anybody about our conversation. I like my wife and wouldn't want this to get around."

Five minutes later, Charlie was trotting up Phila Street toward his office, which was on the third floor of a brick building between Broadway and Putnam. As he hurried along, he alternately swore at Victor and felt guilty for upsetting Marotta. The door to the stairs was next to a used-book store. Charlie pulled it open and began to climb. When he reached the top, he paused to catch his breath. Before him was a narrow hall with faded blue walls, while at the far end was a door with Charlie's name painted in large black letters: Charles F. Bradshaw. "Simple, but classy," Victor had said. The door was locked and Charlie unlocked it. Beyond was a small anteroom separated from the main office by a wall of frosted glass. Victor wasn't there. The office was furnished with an old wooden desk, several straight chairs, a file cabinet and a safe. Two windows with green shades looked out on Phila. Tacked to the wall behind the desk was a nude Playboy calendar that had not been there the previous day. Charlie considered removing it, then figured it didn't matter. Why should he worry about offending clients when he didn't have any? He turned and left the office.

He still had to break his date that evening with Doris Bailes. It was terrible to think of trading her for McClatchy. As Charlie walked toward his car, he imagined McClatchy's dirty feet on his couch and his refrigerator ransacked. He was also certain that his toilet was running and that McClatchy was spitefully letting it run. The thought sprang into his mind that if he had told Marotta that the jockey was hiding out in his house, then McClatchy would be gone in a couple of hours. Marotta would call his friends in New York and in no time a big black car would arrive at Charlie's house and take McClatchy away. Guiltily, Charlie started his Renault and drove toward the Backstretch, the bar on the west side of Saratoga where Doris worked.

The Backstretch occupied a one-story, yellowish building on a residential street. Although its name suggested a bar dedicated to horse racing, its walls were covered with the photographs of prizefighters. Each picture bore an inscription to the owner of the Backstretch, Berney McQuilkin. Charlie had once studied these inscriptions only to discover that the handwriting on each was the same. The bar was a long, narrow room; a larger room in the back served as a Chinese restaurant by day, and at night was the province of a topless dancer.

Entering, Charlie waved to several men that he knew, then reached across the bar to shake hands with Berney McQuilkin. A retired policeman bought Charlie a beer, and before he could make his way to Doris he had to discuss the merits of a trotter named Whiskey Breath that had been going great guns at the harness track. Doris was sitting at a table near the jukebox reading a paperback. She had short, dark hair and a smooth, oval face. The book lay open on the table and she leaned over it, wrinkling her forehead. Although about forty, Doris had an eager quality that made her seem younger. She was wearing a white Mexican blouse and an ornate tin necklace. When she heard Charlie approach, she looked up and smiled.

"I thought I wasn't going to see you until this evening," she said.

Charlie felt himself starting to blush. He sat down and put his beer mug on the table. "That's why I stopped by," he said.

"I've got to cancel our date. An old acquaintance has blown into town and will be staying at my place for a while."

"Who is it?"

"I'll tell you some other time."

Doris raised her eyebrows. "Is this person male or female?"

"Male."

"How long is this secret male supposed to stay?"

"About a week."

Charlie said this so sadly that Doris looked sympathetic. "We could have dinner at a restaurant instead, or even at my house."

"That'd be great but I don't trust this guy and I'd like to keep an eye on him, at least for a couple of nights."

"You've got nice friends."

"He's not really a friend. It's just that he had no place else to go."

Doris put a napkin on the page to mark her place, then closed the book. Charlie saw that it was a travel book about Spain. "And you promise to tell me about it sometime?"

"Sure."

"What about your mother? Isn't she coming soon?"

"Yes, but I'm hoping I can keep her away from my house for a bit. Maybe she can stay with one of my cousins or maybe I can sic her on Victor. In fact, I've got to find Victor right now. Then I've got to buy groceries. My guest turns out to be a big eater."

"Did you talk to John Wanamaker? Is he coming back?"

"Not yet. His mother's still hanging by a thread."

Doris had continued to look sympathetic. "Have dinner with me anyway," she said.

"I can't," said Charlie, getting to his feet, "my life has suddenly gotten too complicated for normal pleasures."

It was as Charlie was driving back to his office that he first began to think about Black Jack Ketchum. He found it oddly soothing. Perhaps it was hammering himself on the head with a gun butt that taught Black Jack to face life with a certain humor. Black Jack was the only member of the Wild Bunch to die on the gallows. On the day of his hanging, he seemed cheerful and joked with the sheriff, saying he was glad to be hanged early in the afternoon so he could "get to hell in time for dinner." Maybe self-abuse could accustom a person to the abuse of the world, thought Charlie. Maybe that was the secret.

Parking the Renault on Phila, Charlie again climbed the stairs to the third floor. This time the door was open. As he passed through the anteroom, Charlie heard a prolonged belch followed by a fit of coughing. Victor was sitting with his feet up on the desk, cleaning his nails with a paper knife. He wore a gray sweat shirt that exactly matched the color of his hair.

"Hey, hey, hey," he said, "if it's not Mr. Wholesome Dairy himself."

Charlie slowly lowered himself into the straight chair next to the desk. "Are you following George Marotta?" he asked.

"Darn right. That's the best money we've made all month."

"I want you to stop. He's a friend of mine."

"I thought he was a Mafia contact. You travel in bad company." Victor reached under his sweat shirt and scratched his chest. Outside, a motorcycle accelerated down the street.

"We swim together. He asked me if we were following him and I said no. Then he described you. Let's just drop the case."

"Charlie, his old lady popped in here with a thousand smackers. So maybe she's a little irrational. Who am I to judge the clientele? That's a thousand smackers just to trail this guy around. One hundred bucks a day just to sit on your fanny. For chrissake, he don't do anything except hang out at that restaurant or go to the Y. So I got Eddie Gillespie dogging him for forty. That other sixty a day—hey, Charlie, that's pure gravy."

Charlie glanced up at the Playboy calendar, which showed an attractive platinum blond rubbing her naked belly against a fur rug. "I told you, Victor . . ."

"Vic."

"I told you I don't want to do divorce work. You have anything else like this?"

"Nothing you'd disapprove of. Look, Charlie, you can't start thinking I don't have scruples. Just the other day a woman came by to see if I'd arrest her neighbor for beaming cancer waves at her with a broken TV. Then the ex-wife of my veterinarian tried to hire me to dig up some dirt on him. Did I take these jobs? No way. A good vet is hard to come by and I got my principles like anybody else."

"Just do me a favor and pull Gillespie off the case." Charlie had an impulse to tell Victor about Jimmy McClatchy but knew he couldn't say anything until the jockey had left Saratoga. It made him feel lonely.

Victor pressed a finger to his temple and made an exploding noise with his tongue. "Okay, you're the great white hunter. I'll chase down Gillespie this afternoon."

"What are you doing tonight?" asked Charlie.

"Got a hot date, but I'll drop it if you need me."

"No, no," said Charlie, "I was just wondering." He had been trying to think of a way to tell Victor not to stop by, but could think of nothing that wouldn't make him suspicious. At last he decided to keep silent.

By five thirty, Charlie was on his way home with fifty dollars' worth of groceries in the back of the Renault. Presumably McClatchy would reimburse him. He also had a new tank ball, lift wires and ball-cock assembly for his toilet, and what he hoped was a clear idea how to install them. The sun was low in the sky and the trees along Saratoga Lake seemed to blaze in the sun's last light.

Charlie pulled the Renault into his driveway and parked. His cottage was dark blue with yellow trim around the windows and doors. Although most cottages along the lake were bunched together, Charlie had been able to buy one that was set off by itself and away from the road. Maples and evergreens bordered it on either side. Clumsily, he lifted two bags of groceries from the rear seat, then made his way to the door.

Through the glass, he could see McClatchy sitting with his back to him at the dining-room table. He was leaning forward as if sleeping. The windows on the lake side of the cottage faced west and the setting sun shone on Charlie's face, making it difficult to see into the room. Charlie kicked at the door, hoping to rouse McClatchy so he wouldn't have to set down the groceries. McClatchy didn't move. Through the windows the sun almost seemed to balance on McClatchy's shoulders. Charlie kicked the door several more times, then angrily set the groceries down on the grass.

He opened the door and picked up one of the bags. If McClatchy was going to stay, he'd have to do his share of the work. "Why didn't you get the door?" said Charlie.

McClatchy remained motionless. From the bathroom Charlie heard the gurgling of the running toilet. Staring at McClatchy's back, Charlie knew something was wrong even before he saw the blood: a great pool of it on the floor surrounding the table.

"McClatchy?" said Charlie. Then he saw what had happened. It wasn't that McClatchy was leaning forward with his head on the table. The head was gone completely. It had been sliced off, while the light from the setting sun glistened on the bloody stump of neck. As for the head itself, it appeared to be missing.

3

▼ ▼ ▼

CHIEF PETERSON RAISED THE THICK, pink index finger of his right hand, looked at it with fatherly affection, then leaned over and used it to poke Charlie in the chest.

"What I'm saying, Charlie," he said, "is that the Feds were chasing their tails all over the country looking for this gumball and here he was getting his head sliced off in your house in Saratoga. I mean, they're going to be none too pleased and I can't say I blame them."

"I didn't invite McClatchy here," said Charlie. "I didn't want him here and I'm sorry he got killed here."

"That doesn't change the fact that it got done here," said Peterson.

Charlie and Peterson were standing in Charlie's driveway next to the red Renault. It was seven o'clock and nearly dark. The small house had been taken over by a mob of Saratoga policemen, state troopers and sheriff's deputies. At least a dozen cruisers with flashing lights were parked along the road and a crowd had gathered at the edge of Charlie's driveway. It was a scene Charlie had witnessed a hundred times as a policeman but the fact that it was his own house made it all new.

Inside, men from the state police lab were measuring, photographing, dusting for fingerprints and gathering up smidgens of dirt and lint, which they carefully tucked away in little plastic bags. McClatchy's head had been sliced off clean and when the body was removed there turned out to be a deep cut in the wood of the table.

"Like a samurai sword," said Peterson. "I used to have one that I brought back from the service. I was always cutting myself with the damn thing. Or maybe a meat cleaver. Or those French things—what do you call them?—guillotines." Peterson rose up on his toes, put a hand on the roof of the Renault to steady himself and looked around the driveway. He was a big man, several inches over six feet, with thick black hair and a gravelly voice that Charlie thought he exaggerated on purpose. He wore a three-piece blue suit with a thin chain across his stomach from which dangled a tiny silver revolver.

"What I don't understand," said Peterson, "is why he came to your house in the first place."

"He said he felt safe here."

Peterson cleared his throat and spat into the dirt. "Guess you fooled him," he said. "Wasn't he supposed to testify in New York pretty soon?"

"Next Monday. How do you think anyone knew he was here?"

"Maybe they followed him. You tell anyone?"

"No one."

"Was the door forced?"

"No. Whoever did it, I guess McClatchy let him in."

"Jesus, Charlie, that's the one thing I hate about this horse racing—it attracts a lot of low people." Peterson tugged one of his ears. They were large and soft looking and resembled the sort of toys a child plays with in his tub.

Charlie had called Peterson immediately after finding the

body. Then he had stood back as his house was invaded by the police. That, however, was a minor invasion compared with the death itself. Although Charlie was sorry that McClatchy had been murdered, he was mostly sorry that McClatchy had died in his house, on his table, that McClatchy's blood was all over his floor and rug, had seeped between the floorboards to the dirt below, where, Charlie told himself, it would stay forever.

This was a permanent invasion and Charlie wondered how long it would take to get used to it. He had never liked McClatchy and so he had no great grief for the man, but now McClatchy's murder was part of his home, and the indifference Charlie had felt for his life would be replaced with a kind of intimacy with his death.

For Peterson the most disturbing detail was the missing head. It made him indignant and at first it seemed that the actual murder hardly mattered, that if only the head were found, then these other problems of mortality would quickly clear themselves up.

"Maybe the head was tossed in the lake," said Peterson.

Charlie thought that was unlikely but saw no reason to disagree.

"They sure did a pretty neat job," said Peterson. "Why would anyone want to cut off a head?"

"Maybe to frighten someone."

"You know, Charlie, these guys from New York, these hoods, they're like animals. I wouldn't be surprised if whoever did this had a whole collection of heads. Some shelf in the basement, maybe two shelves, just full of heads."

"What makes you think the murderer was from the City?" asked Charlie.

"Just a guess," said Peterson. "If you want to know the truth, I bet his head got cut off because of that grand jury. You know, to make people keep their mouths shut. Anyway, the FBI should be here soon. McClatchy was their baby and with any luck they'll take over the whole business. I've got enough on my mind with these car thieves."

In the past two months about twenty cars had been stolen

in Saratoga; nearly all were expensive foreign cars owned by Skidmore students. Only one had been recovered. A state trooper in Georgia had pulled over a speeding Porsche belonging to a Skidmore freshman. The driver had been hired in New York City and claimed never to have set foot in Saratoga. All he knew was that he had been paid to leave the car in a parking garage in Miami. It was Peterson's theory that the cars were being shipped to and resold in South America.

"I'm already spending eighty hours a week telling these Skiddies to lock up their cars," said Peterson. "If the Feds don't take McClatchy, I might as well quit sleeping for good. By any rights, they should assign a man to this car snatching. After all, crossing state lines, that's their bailiwick."

Around eight o'clock, Peterson let Charlie go back to Saratoga to get something to eat. Not that he had much of an appetite. Mostly he wanted to find Victor and see about sleeping on his couch. The only trouble was with Victor's one-eyed cat, Moshe. Charlie was allergic to cats. Even if Moshe spent the time locked up in the bathroom, the presence of little bits of fur would keep Charlie sneezing all night.

Charlie had called Victor earlier and Victor grudgingly agreed to cancel his hot date and meet Charlie at Lillian's, a bar and restaurant on Broadway that offered bowls of free peanuts. Victor liked stuffing his pockets with them.

When Charlie reached the bar, he found Victor sitting at a table almost completely covered with peanut shells. Charlie sat down and ordered a beer and a cheeseburger, then he told Victor about the murder. Although Victor was surprised about the murder, what surprised him most was that Charlie hadn't told him about McClatchy's arrival.

"No joke, Charlie, I feel pretty hurt. Like I thought I was your best friend. If I'd known he was there, maybe I could have gone out and kept my eyes peeled."

"How'd I know he'd get killed? Anyway, I thought it best not to talk about it." The waitress brought Charlie's cheeseburger. He took a small bite and put it back on the plate. He thought it tasted funny but guessed it was just him.

"You didn't mention it to Marotta?"

"Of course not."

Victor helped himself to some of Charlie's steak fries. He was drinking Jack Daniel's straight up, and was leaning forward with his elbows on the table and his chin resting thoughtfully on the rim of his glass. "Marotta is supposed to be pretty tight with some bad boys in the City," said Victor. "I bet he'd of been real pleased to know where McClatchy was staying."

Charlie shifted uncomfortably in his chair. "That may be so, but he didn't learn anything from me."

"Okay, so they killed him. Why'd they cut off his head?"

"Peterson thinks it was done as a warning. McClatchy's testimony was making a lot of trouble. Killing him like that, well, Peterson says it would keep other people from talking."

"What do you think about all that happening in your house? I betcha feel pretty lousy."

Charlie speared a chunk of cheeseburger with his fork and looked at it. "Sure," he said, "I feel pretty lousy."

"Was McClatchy a friend of yours?"

"No, I never liked him but I certainly didn't wish him harm. It's terrible he was killed but it's also terrible he was killed on my dining-room table."

Victor sat up, yawned and began scratching a place under his arm. His sweat shirt was several sizes too big for him and flecked with white paint. "So Peterson thinks he was killed by those same people who fixed the races?"

"I guess so. McClatchy's sent about thirty people to jail."

"Anyone see you talking to Marotta?"

"Sure, all sorts of people. We had lunch at the Executive. Why?"

Victor tilted back in his chair and looked around the bar. "Marotta's supposedly pretty good friends with these guys that are in trouble at Belmont. I figure that if Peterson doesn't book someone *muy pronto,* as the Ricans say, then you're going to get some funny looks."

Charlie didn't answer. He was thinking of the wreckage of his house, that his toilet needed fixing and that despite McClatchy's death he still had to deliver milk the next morning. After that he wondered what would have happened if he had been out Sunday night or said no to McClatchy. And after that he found himself thinking once again of Black Jack Ketchum.

When Black Jack was led out to the gallows, he had been upset to discover that a high fence had been built to keep away the crowd. "Why don't you rip down that stockade," he had said, "so the folks can see a man swing who never hurt anybody."

It seemed to Charlie that Black Jack Ketchum was a man who had been forced to endure too much. He was just about to tell Victor about Black Jack when Victor glanced toward the door, then ducked his head. "Oh, oh, here comes trouble."

Turning in his chair, Charlie saw Emmett Van Brunt bearing down upon them. Van Brunt was a plainclothesman whom Charlie had originally hired and worked with for years in the Community and Youth Relations Bureau. But ever since Charlie had left the department, Van Brunt seemed to think him responsible for most of the crime in Saratoga. Van Brunt was a youngish man with curly red hair, black horn-rimmed glasses and the thick, rectangular body of a wrestler.

"Peterson wants to see you, Charlie," said Van Brunt. He was sweating slightly and gave off a smell like burning tires.

"Okay, I'll be over in about twenty minutes."

"He said he wanted you right away." Van Brunt stood next to his chair so that Charlie had to twist his neck to look up at him.

Charlie poked at the cold cheeseburger on his plate. He imagined telling Emmett that he was eating and Emmett saying it didn't matter and he beginning to protest. Charlie pushed back his chair and stood up. "Take care of the bill, will you, Victor?"

"Shonuff."

As they walked toward police headquarters, Charlie asked, partly joking, "Has Peterson solved the case?"

"You could say that," answered Van Brunt. He didn't look at Charlie or even walk next to him but stayed about six feet away.

Peterson was waiting in the police lounge. It was a dank basement room and its walls were covered with posters warning about the dangers of smoking, accidents, stress and high blood pressure, detailing the five danger signals of cancer and explaining what to do if someone choked on his food. Glancing at his watch, Charlie saw that it was nearly ten. He reminded himself that he had to be up at four thirty.

Peterson had been sitting on a tattered couch looking through some papers. When Charlie entered, he got to his feet, raised himself up on tiptoe and looked disgusted.

"So how much did Marotta pay you?"

"What are you talking about?"

"You had lunch with Marotta. He's pals with these guys who are under suspicion for race fixing. I mean, you figure it out—first you talk to Marotta, then McClatchy winds up dead. Seems pretty simple, doesn't it?"

On the right side of the room was a Ping-Pong table and on the table were five smashed Ping-Pong balls. Charlie started to wonder who had smashed them, then stopped himself. Peterson depressed him. "I swear to you," said Charlie, "I never told anyone about McClatchy."

"Then what were you talking to Marotta about?"

"Business."

"You mean you won't tell me?"

What irritated Charlie was Peterson's certainty that he had at last got something on him that made him look small. "If you want to know so much, why don't you ask him."

"Jesus, Charlie, you must think I'm a dope. The Feds will be here in about two minutes and if they don't slap your ass in jail, I'll really be surprised."

Charlie stuck his hands in his pockets and stared down at the floor. "I didn't tell anyone about McClatchy," he repeated.

"Then why were you talking to Marotta?"

For the next half hour, Peterson kept asking about Marotta and Charlie kept repeating that he had said nothing to anybody. He kept looking at the smashed Ping-Pong balls and at last decided that Peterson had probably smashed them himself. They were interrupted around a quarter to eleven by the arrival of an FBI man from New York City.

The door opened and there was a man in a dark gray suit,

calmly surveying the room. His eyes settled on Peterson. "You're the police chief, right?" he asked. "I talked to you on the phone. I'm Hank Caldwell."

He entered, leaving the door open, then looked at Charlie. "And you must be Bradshaw, the guy with the mouth." He turned back to Peterson. "You going to lock him up?"

"He says he never said anything to Marotta."

"And you believe him?" Not waiting for an answer, Caldwell walked over to Charlie. He was about thirty-five and had a narrow face and short brown hair. His nose ended in a sharp point and he seemed to use it like a knife to cut through the air in front of him. He stopped so close to Charlie that their shoes bumped. "So what's your little story?" he said.

"I told nobody about McClatchy. He showed up Sunday night needing a place to stay and I gave him one. I didn't want him there, but I didn't sell the information to get him out. Now, if you don't mind, I'd like to go home. I have to be up at four thirty and it's been a long day."

Caldwell reached out and put a hand on Charlie's shoulder, then he squeezed, digging his thumb into the nerve. His breath smelled of mint. Charlie pulled away.

"This is my case," said Caldwell, "and I don't want you fucking with it. As far as I'm concerned, you're an accessory before the fact and the moment I get the tiniest shred of evidence against you, you're going straight to the slammer."

The dog that had once bitten Charlie and had several times come pretty close was a fat yellow Labrador with a lot of gray around the muzzle. Now when Charlie delivered the two quarts of homogenized and a half-pint of cream to the dog's owners, he took along an empty wire milk crate just for swinging. To Charlie it seemed the height of folly to be fighting off dogs at six in the morning.

But Tuesday morning, after successfully dodging the yellow Labrador and clipping it with the milk crate besides, Charlie realized that the height of folly had been to let Jimmy McClatchy ever see the inside of his house. And briefly he considered allowing the dog to bite him just to punish himself.

The sun was barely cresting the Green Mountains and Charlie could tell it would be another clear day. This morning, however, he could see his breath and there was the sense that winter was waiting someplace nearby. Even though he loved the pyrotechnics of the trees, Charlie hated the approach of cold weather. When he was younger, fall had been his favorite season, but now that he was forty-six, he found he preferred spring.

He had slept badly on Victor's couch and spent much of the night sneezing and blowing his nose. But apart from his allergy to cats, there was the question of McClatchy's head. Who had taken it and why? Although Charlie knew he had said nothing to Marotta, it still seemed possible that the restaurant owner was involved. Perhaps he had asked Charlie to lunch simply to keep him away from his house while the murder was being committed. Consequently, as he was leaving Victor's apartment at four thirty that morning, he had roused Victor to tell him to put Eddie Gillespie back on the job.

"That's what I like to hear," Victor said sleepily.

Charlie's other worry was that his mother might arrive and go out to his cottage. McClatchy's blood was still on the floor and at some point Charlie would have to clean it up. He imagined his mother letting herself in with her key and finding the dried pools of blood. Certainly she would call his cousins in hysterics. Charlie felt guilty that he hadn't posted a warning note and even wondered if he wasn't trying to upset his mother on purpose as she often accused him of doing.

Charlie had almost finished his deliveries and was making his way back to the barn when a white Chevrolet drew alongside him and honked its horn. Assuming it was a friend, Charlie waved and kept going, at which point the Chevrolet abruptly swerved in front of the truck and stopped. Charlie had to slam on the brakes. Milk crates slid to the front and he heard the unpleasant sound of breaking glass.

Turning back to the Chevrolet, Charlie saw the FBI man, Hank Caldwell, walking toward him.

"For chrissakes, Bradshaw, when Peterson told me you were a milkman, I thought he was joking."

Charlie got down out of the truck, pushed his hat farther back on his head and decided that Caldwell's remark didn't need an answer. He was struck by how happy Caldwell looked.

"You know, Bradshaw, I been having trouble with the guy who delivers my yogurt. Maybe you could help out."

"You want anything in particular or you just want to make jokes?"

"I want to know if you're ready to tell me about Marotta." Caldwell wore a brown sport coat and tan slacks. His short brown hair seemed the color and texture of a new doormat.

"I've already told you."

"What did you say to him about McClatchy?"

"Nothing," said Charlie. Caldwell had stopped him on a residential street in front of a white house with black shutters. In the driveway, three teenage boys had been looking under the hood of an old Chevrolet. Now they stood watching Caldwell.

"You should be more cooperative," said Caldwell. "I figure we can also get you on a conspiracy charge. And those race-fixing charges against McClatchy? This could make you an accessory after the fact."

"Is this what you nearly wrecked my milk truck to tell me?"

Caldwell was exactly Charlie's height. He stood with his hands in his back pockets and his head tilted to one side. "I don't want you to leave the area. If I have any trouble finding you, I'll lock you up for sure."

Charlie climbed back into the truck, then turned. "Can I clean up my house or d'you still need it?"

"It's all yours."

"Have you found McClatchy's head?"

"Forget the questions, Bradshaw. It's none of your business."

When Charlie arrived at the YMCA at noon to go swimming, he noticed that although people looked at him with some curiosity, no one would speak to him. Marotta wasn't there and Charlie couldn't remember when he had last missed a day. In his hurry to put on his suit and get in the water, he didn't pay much attention to Marotta's absence or link it to the collective cold shoulder of his fellow swimmers. Once in the pool, however, he realized that the cold shoulder was due to McClatchy's death.

Afterward, as Charlie showered, the only other person in the locker room was a friend of his cousin Jack's: a local realtor whom he had known since high school. Charlie made some comment about the weather but the man didn't reply. Perhaps he hadn't heard. Sure he heard, thought Charlie.

Leaving the Y, Charlie considered going home and cleaning up the blood but decided to go to the Backstretch for lunch. There seemed to be something he didn't know and the Backstretch was a place where he might to find out what it was. McClatchy's blood could wait.

The bar was nearly empty. Usually, the owner, Berney McQuilkin, would stroll over and say a few words, but this afternoon he only glanced at Charlie and looked away.

Charlie sat down at the bar where Doris was washing glasses. "You want a beer?" she asked. She wore a full red skirt and a dark blue leotard that accentuated the curve of her breasts.

"No, thanks. Give me a cup of coffee and a ham and cheese. No mustard." Charlie looked into her face and even with her he thought he saw a change. It wasn't as if she were cold or suspicious; rather, she seemed to be watching him in a slightly altered manner, as if waiting for him to show himself to be the old Charlie or somebody new.

"McClatchy?" he asked.

She stopped washing the glasses and dried her hands on a blue towel. "It's been on the radio and television. I guess the paper will have something this afternoon. A reporter was in here asking about you."

"About me?" Charlie was amazed.

"Wasn't McClatchy staying with you?"

"What have they been saying?"

"Just that McClatchy was hiding out at your place and that someone found him there. Peterson told reporters there was a chance you told someone. There's also a lot of talk about how you had lunch yesterday with George Marotta."

"Do you think I would have told Marotta?"

Doris was silent a moment. Her brown hair was parted in the center of her scalp and fell across her forehead in two symmetrical curves like drapery. Occasionally, one of the curves would half-cover one of her eyes and she would shake her head, flicking it aside. She had dark brown eyes with gold flecks, and looking into them it sometimes seemed to Charlie that he was looking into deep water or night sky.

Doris took the blue towel and wiped off the bar in front of Charlie. "No," she said, "I don't believe you would have said anything."

"I didn't tell anyone about McClatchy," said Charlie, "not Marotta or anyone."

Doris nodded as if the matter were settled. "I'll get your sandwich," she said.

As Charlie waited, he thought about the fact that people seemed so quick to accuse him of selling the information about McClatchy to George Marotta. Then he remembered that he also had thought of telling Marotta, not for money, of course, but just to get McClatchy out of his hair. Didn't that make him as guilty as people thought he was?

Charlie was just trying to determine what sort of punishment would suit him best when he noticed someone in the parking lot approach the door and peer through the glass, linking his hands as a kind of visor over his eyes. The man wore a tattered gray hat with wisps of white hair sticking out from under the brim. He had to bend down to see through the glass, and he looked so peculiar with his hands shielding his eyes and his scrunched-up face that it was with a slight shock that Charlie realized it was someone he had known all his life. At the same instant, the man saw Charlie, waved and gave a nervous smile. It was clear that Charlie was who he was looking for. He opened the door and approached with a sort of sideways gait, constantly glancing around the empty bar as if suspicious that the furniture might leap at him.

The man's name was Rodger Pease and he was a big, bulky fellow who resembled a sack of potatoes. He had a pale, soft-looking face and a small white mustache, which was precisely rectangular and seemed the only element of exactness and precision in the otherwise rumpled landscape of his body. Charlie thought he must be at least seventy-five.

Rodger Pease had been a good friend of Charlie's father, and when Charlie was younger he had often sought out Pease to ask what his father was like. Charlie's father had committed suicide when Charlie was four. He had locked himself in an upstairs bedroom with a bottle of whiskey and a Colt .45 automatic; then, with the whiskey gone and the police hammering at the door, he had blown out his brains. People said he shot himself because he was into the bookmakers for $25,000, but Rodger Pease claimed that Charlie's father had shot himself because he no longer believed in winners.

Pease stopped in front of Charlie and stood uncomfortably shifting his weight from one foot to the other. "I wanted to talk to you, Charlie," he said. "Your friend Victor said you might be here."

"What's on your mind?"

"First of all, I want to say I don't want you to take offense."

"We've known each other a long time, Rodger." It occurred to Charlie that Pease looked frightened.

"I heard about McClatchy," Pease said. He plucked at his white mustache, then looked down at the floor. "I also heard the radio and what people've been saying about you. Charlie, I've got to know for certain if you said anything to Marotta."

"Why do you care?"

"Because I need to know."

"I swear I never told anyone about McClatchy."

Pease winced and shook his head. "That fixes it, then," he said.

"You think I should have told what I knew?" With anyone else Charlie would have been angry, but Pease was so obviously upset that Charlie's curiosity outweighed his indignation.

"No, no, it would have made things easier, that's all."

"What things?"

Pease looked up at Charlie. His lower eyelids were red and droopy like a hound's. "I can't tell you yet. I got some thinking to do."

"Maybe I can help," suggested Charlie.

Pease backed up a few steps. Then he took off his hat, stared into it and hit it several times against his leg. He was mostly bald and his scalp had a pinkness that was almost delicate. "I got to learn some stuff first," said Pease, "then maybe I'll talk to you again."

"Tell me now," said Charlie.

But Pease just shook his head and kept backing toward the door. After he had gone about ten feet, he made a kind of joking salute and hurried out.

As Charlie ate his sandwich, he considered Pease's behavior. Pease had always been eccentric. As long as Charlie had known him, he had barely earned his living by doing odd jobs at the track. Charlie had no idea what he did now. At last Charlie stopped thinking about it. If it was anything important, Pease would contact him again.

When he finished eating, Charlie drove home to clean up his house. He dreaded this but felt it was his obligation, that he couldn't just hire a stranger. As he passed through the doorway, he heard the running of the toilet. He hurried into the bathroom and rattled the flush handle until the tank ball settled into the valve seat. For a moment, he thought of fixing the toilet right away. Then he thought, No, the blood comes first.

The blood on the floor around the table roughly approximated the shape of an elephant. It had dried and didn't seem so much like blood as cheap paint. It was smeared with footprints and those same feet had tracked blood all over the living room.

Charlie had been in the house about five minutes when the phone rang. It was a reporter from Albany. Charlie said he didn't want to talk, then unplugged the phone.

For several hours, Charlie scrubbed the floor. When he finished, he began on the table. He used a wire brush to scrape the blood from the cut made by whatever implement had removed McClatchy's head—meat cleaver or samurai sword. The cut was an inch deep and about a foot long. In order to find a round oak table that he liked, Charlie had driven to nearly every used-furniture and antique store in Saratoga and Washington Counties. The cut was very white, while the rest of the surface was dark brown. Charlie considered filling it with plastic wood. Then he wondered if he would ever be able to look at the table without remembering how McClatchy's corpse had been sprawled across it.

The police had taken McClatchy's belongings. The only trace of him besides the cut on the table was a lot of missing food and a ring of black bristles in the sink where he had shaved. Charlie stared at the bristles, thinking that the face that grew them was now off on an adventure of its own, God knew where.

At five o'clock Charlie decided to deal with his other major problem and called John Wanamaker in Santa Fe. Wanamaker was staying in a boardinghouse and Charlie had to wait several minutes until he was brought to the phone.

"Sorry to take so long, Charlie. I was asleep."

Charlie immediately felt guilty. "You having a hard time?"

"Not so bad, but I had to sit up with mother last night. The doctors say she's sinking fast."

There was static on the line. Charlie had never been to Santa Fe and wanted to ask Wanamaker what he could see from his window. He imagined miles of sand spotted with cactuses and maybe armadillos. "I guess you have no idea when you're coming back," he said.

"No, the doctors say it could be at any time. I mean, I can't hurry her up, Charlie." Wanamaker's voice sounded muffled, as if it came from under a pile of blankets.

"I'm sorry, John, I didn't mean to imply that."

"That's okay. I guess I'm a little on edge. How are things in Saratoga?"

"Great, John, they couldn't be better." Even as he said it, Charlie asked himself why he was lying.

After hanging up, Charlie walked out onto the dock in front of his house, looked at the lake and thought about Black Jack Ketchum. All around the border of the lake he saw flashes of fall color. For most of his life, or at least since the age of twelve, Charlie had read about outlaws, robbers, bandits, kidnappers, gamblers, murderers and the history of the West. He found it comforting. Here was a world where the sequences of cause and effect were clearly understood. A man robbed a bank. He was pursued. He was either caught or got away. If he got away, then he robbed another bank. And in times of stress or whenever he felt anxious, Charlie would consider these bad fellows of the past and think of their stories. It was like knitting. As Charlie thought of how this one was hung or how that one had escaped to rob again, his own anxiety seemed to slip away. He grew calm and ready once again to shoulder the burdens of his life.

When Black Jack Ketchum stood on the scaffold waiting to be hanged, a priest had asked if he could do him any little favor. "Go get a fiddle, padre," Black Jack had said, "and we'll all dance. I want to die as I lived."

Not that Black Jack had done much dancing. The eight-and-a-half-foot drop ripped off his head and it had to be sewn back on for the funeral. Charlie wondered what would happen to McClatchy's head if it showed up after he was buried, whether it would get a separate little grave. Then he wondered at the preposterousness of cutting off the head in the first place.

4

▼▼▼

THE FRONT-PAGE ARTICLE in the *Daily Saratogian* said that Charlie and McClatchy had been good friends ever since they had both been employed by Lew Ackerman's Lorelei Stables some years earlier. Then it went on to recount how Charlie had been seen talking to underworld figures shortly before McClatchy's death. The insinuation was that not only had Charlie known about the race fixing all along but that he had betrayed his friend to the very people he was to testify against. Charlie had driven into Saratoga around six o'clock Tuesday evening just to see what the paper had to say.

Peterson had not specifically accused Charlie of disclosing

McClatchy's whereabouts. What he said was: "Either the murderers followed him to Bradshaw's or Bradshaw possibly told someone. A lot of people would have paid good money to know where McClatchy was hiding. It'd be a temptation."

A further paragraph said that while the New York grand jury was scheduled to continue, McClatchy's death would definitely hamper the prosecution. The head itself was still missing. The article concluded with a brief biography of McClatchy, which revealed that the last time he had raced was in Saratoga fourteen months before.

Charlie read the article sitting in his Renault, which was parked in front of the Grand Union supermarket. When he finished, he walked over to his office to find Victor. All along the street he felt people were staring at him.

Victor was sitting behind the desk looking through a pile of eight-by-ten photographs. When he saw Charlie, he shook his head. "Charlie, here I am trying to set up a decent business and you got to wreck it by getting your name spread all over the newspapers."

"No jokes, Victor."

"Vic."

"All right, all right."

Charlie picked up one of the photographs. It showed a fat man of about sixty and a girl about seventeen crouching on a rumpled bed. Both were naked and appeared very startled. Charlie couldn't imagine what the picture was for and continued looking through the others. All showed the man and girl with different expressions of surprise and attempting to cover themselves.

"What are these?" he asked.

Victor grinned. "Aren't they beauties? Jesus, Charlie, I was so fucking pleased. I mean, you work and work and when it pays off you feel like a million bucks."

"What are these pictures?"

"Me and Rico got them."

Rico Medioli was another ex-stable guard and friend of Charlie's, a man in his mid-twenties who had spent about half his life in jail.

"That still doesn't explain what they are. Who's the old man?"

"That's Ryan Mitchell. You know him, he's got a shoe store out at the mall. His wife thought he was fooling around so she paid us to find out. I don't know who the girl is, some Skidmore bimbo. Kinda cute, hunh?" Victor looked at her appreciatively, then began sucking his teeth.

"You mean you photographed these yourself?"

"Sure. They were cooped up in a motel on the road to Glens Falls. I borrowed this camera with a motor drive from a guy at the paper. Rico and I waited outside till we heard heavy breathing, then he kicked open the door. Fucking eeks all over the place. We were gone in about five seconds."

At first Charlie didn't think he had understood, then he thought he understood too much. He didn't feel so much angry as exasperated. Slowly he picked up the top picture and tore it into four pieces. Then he began tearing up the rest.

"You ever hear of blackmail?" he asked. "You're lucky he didn't shoot you. What other cases are you working on?"

Victor looked unhappily at the torn pictures. "Are you really pissed?" he asked. "Maybe you're just upset because of McClatchy."

"I told you I didn't want to do work like this. It's humiliating."

"I wasn't going to blackmail the guy. His old lady wanted some dirt so I found it."

"Just tell me about your other cases."

"Well, there's a high-school girl who's run away from home. Probably she's shacking up with a boyfriend. Then there's a lady who wants some letters back from a guy, a local lawyer."

"What kind of letters?"

"You know, the kind that say, 'I kiss your feet,' only she don't feel like that any more so she asked me to try and get 'em back, even offer money if I have to. So far the lawyer says no. Most likely he wants her to raise the ante. Then there's a clerk out at the mall who's maybe lifting a little merchandise and I get to stand around and watch him. And there's an insurance company that wants some arson investigation on a guy whose bar got torched. That one's a little tricky. I mean it's all cinders to me. But the night before the fire the guy removed the color TV so I figure that's a bad sign. And then there's Marotta. He's the last, not counting the old fart and the Skiddy."

It occurred to Charlie that since Victor had taken over the detective agency, business had picked up by more than two hundred percent. "You tell Eddie Gillespie to follow Marotta again?" he asked.

"Yeah, except Marotta hasn't left the house all day."

Charlie tried to decide if that meant anything. Maybe Marotta had the flu or had slipped on a cake of soap in the bathtub and had broken his leg. On the other hand, Peterson and Hank Caldwell had presumably interrogated him, so Charlie guessed he was just lying low.

"By the way," said Victor, "there was an old geezer in here looking for you. He stopped by twice. I tried to call you but your phone was busy all afternoon. You running a bookie joint or something?"

"I unplugged it because of reporters. Was he a big man, almost bald, maybe seventy-five?"

"That's him. Pretty jumpy." Victor had retrieved a few fragments of the photographs and on the desk's green blotter he had lined up four little breasts.

"What did he want?"

"Beats me. Maybe he was peddling Girl Scout cookies. The last time he stopped by was around six. He said he was going to drive out to your house."

"I must have passed him on the road. Hand me the phone book, will you?"

Rodger Pease appeared not to have a telephone. It was now past seven. Charlie thought again of Rodger's various eccentricities and hoped his business could wait until tomorrow. He and Victor had intended to have fried chicken at Hattie's Chicken Shack, but as Victor locked up the office, Charlie suggested they have dinner at his house instead. After the article in the *Saratogian,* he wanted to avoid public places.

"You clean up McClatchy's blood?" asked Victor as they walked back to Charlie's car.

"Of course. What do you think I did all afternoon?"

"And you're sure there's not a drop left, not a single drop?"

"Positive."

"What about a smell, is there any kind of funny smell?"

"Of course not."

"What d'you have to eat?"

"Steaks."

"You really know how to take advantage of a guy, don't you?"

As they drove back along Broadway to Lake Avenue, Charlie saw his cousin Robert standing in front of the boutique owned by Charlie's ex-wife and her sister Lucy. Robert, who sold insurance and real estate, was married to Lucy; Charlie often suspected that his ex-wife had agreed to marry him only because she wanted to be related to his respectable cousins. Wearing a tweed jacket and smoking a pipe, Robert stood with his arms folded, looking as if he owned half of Saratoga. If he saw Charlie in the Renault, he gave no sign of it.

Charlie pointed him out to Victor. "You know what would happen if my cousins found out about those pictures?" he asked.

Victor slouched down in his seat and put his feet up on the dashboard. "The trouble with guys like your cousins," he said, "is that they're the ones, when they were teenagers, that got scared off about masturbating."

"What do you mean?" asked Charlie.

"Like maybe they were scared about getting warts on their palms or black hair, you know, that black hair you're supposed to get all over your hands? They were scared that people would look at their hands and say, 'Hey, I know what you've been doing.' So they withheld themselves. Well, it does a lot of damage."

"What sort of damage?" asked Charlie, turning onto Lake Avenue.

"I mean all that sperm accumulates. It doesn't just go away. There gets to be a coupla quarts of it. And after a while it leaks into the brain. Sperm brain. It's a known fact. It rots out the white cells or whatever. I mean you take a smart kid with lots of promise and the whole world before him, then you let him develop a terror of furry palms and before you know it sperm brain sets in and he's no good for anything. You can see them on the street as adults. Their lives over, their senses dulled."

"How can you recognize them?" asked Charlie.

"They're the ones saying, 'Quack, quack,' " said Victor. "Just like your cousins."

It was completely dark by the time they reached Charlie's house. A cold wind blew across the lake and the leaves in the driveway seemed to scurry around their feet. Victor hung back by the car. "I tell you, Charlie, if I stumble over that head, I'll never forgive you."

Charlie started to reply, then noticed a piece of paper fluttering from a nail on his front door. Removing it, he went inside and flicked on the lights. It was a note from Pease: "Charlie, I must see you right away. I'll be at home." There was an address on Ward Street near the harness track, Saratoga Raceway.

"What's up?" asked Victor. He stood in the doorway, looking suspiciously around the room and sniffing.

"It's a note from Pease. I think I should go over to his house."

"What about the steaks?"

"Maybe we can eat them later."

Victor groaned. "Let me get something from the refrigerator. You don't want me to die on you, do you?"

Five minutes later, they were driving back to Saratoga. Victor was trying to balance a chunk of salami, some crackers, a piece of cheese and a beer. "I feel I been had," he said. "Just don't hit any bumps, this is my best sweat shirt. Who is this guy Pease?"

The road along the lake was empty and Charlie drove fast. "A friend of my father's. You know how I told you that my father was a crazy bettor? A lot of those stories came from Pease."

"If he was such a good friend, why didn't he keep your old man from putting a pill in his noggin?"

"Guess he wasn't able to."

Pease had a very small white house about half a block from the main stabling area of the harness track. All the lights were on at the track, making a white glow in the sky; and as Charlie drove up Ward Street, he heard a gathering human roar as the first race came to a close. Charlie only went to the harness track once or twice a year. He told himself it was because the front runners always won, that the sulkies blocked the trailing horses. But actually he felt that an interest in the harness track was somehow disloyal to his love of Thoroughbred racing.

Charlie pulled into Pease's driveway. Parked near the house was a rusty Dodge Dart with a bent hanger for a radio antenna. The house was dark, but through a downstairs window they saw a flickering candle.

"Isn't that touching," said Victor, getting out of the car.

Charlie and Victor stood on either side of the Renault, looking at the small light surrounded by the black of the window.

"What's that smell?" asked Victor.

Suddenly the candle seemed to expand a millionfold, filling the window with light, then flame, blowing out the glass and frame itself with a whoosh that expanded into a roar as the house exploded. Charlie raised an arm to cover his face. Immediately, it was as if a great hand was lifting him and throwing him back. He landed on his side in the street and rolled. The air was filled with light and noise. Charlie kept thinking something had gone wrong with the candle. He tried to stand up, stumbled, then crouched at the curb as glass and bits of debris rained down on top of him. In the glare of the flaming house, he saw Victor sprawled on his stomach behind the Renault.

Painfully, Charlie got to his feet. "Victor!" he shouted. His voice was overwhelmed by the roar of the fire. Shielding his face, Charlie made his way across the street to where Victor was just getting to his hands and knees. Charlie saw that Victor's face was bleeding. The house was full of orange and red flame that pushed out of the windows, licked up the walls and swept over the roof. Billowing skyward was a cloud of black smoke. Little fires kept springing up on the grass.

Charlie pulled Victor to his feet. "You all right?"

"I been better. Why don't you move your car before you lose it."

Charlie ran around to the driver's side, yanked open the door and got in. The windshield was smashed and a layer of debris covered the hood. The Dodge Dart was already burning. Charlie backed his car across the street. In the distance, he heard sirens. Victor joined him, wiping the blood from his face with a dirty handkerchief. The small house was completely wrapped in flames. Charlie rubbed his shoulder. His face burned in the heat. He knew that if Rodger Pease was in the house, he was already dead.

Three hours later, Charlie and Victor were in Peterson's office in police headquarters. Charlie sat in a straight chair next to the desk, slouched down on the tip of his spine with his legs straight out in front of him. Although his predominant feeling was grief for Rodger Pease, he was also bored and out of sorts. Victor was studying some photographs of Irish setters on the side wall. His face was spotted with half a dozen small bandages. Both men had gone from the fire to the hospital and it was from there that Peterson had collected them two hours before.

"Charlie," said Peterson, "if this guy, Pease, had something to say about McClatchy, I don't know why you didn't come to me right this afternoon."

"I didn't think it was important until I got the note."

"Did the note say anything about McClatchy?"

"No, but Pease had asked about him earlier."

"So it's possible," said Peterson, fiddling with the silver revolver on his watch chain, "that the reason he wanted to see you might have had nothing to do with McClatchy."

"It's possible," said Charlie.

"Hey, Peterson," said Victor, "what do you do with all these dogs?"

If the police chief had a single passion, it was for the Irish setters that he had raised and trained during the fifteen years Charlie had known him. On the walls of Peterson's office were color photographs of his eight champions, plus pictures of other winners, citations, letters of commendation from the American Kennel Club and dozens of different colored ribbons. Peterson looked at Victor as if he couldn't remember what he was doing in his office.

Victor had picked up a sort of inverted golden flowerpot topped by a little golden dog. He was swinging it idly.

"Put that down before you break it," said Peterson.

Victor drew back his arm as if to pass the trophy to Charlie like a football. Then he shrugged and put the trophy back on top of a bookcase with a thump. "If you don't want me here," he said, "then why don't you let me go home?"

Peterson ignored him and turned back to Charlie. "What did Pease want when you saw him at the Backstretch?"

"I told you, he wanted to know if I'd said anything to Marotta about Jimmy McClatchy."

"And what did you say?"

"I told him I had never mentioned McClatchy to anyone."

Peterson stood up, then raised himself onto his toes. "You know, Charlie, Caldwell wants you locked up. I tell him we don't have the evidence but he says, what the hell, we could keep you in the slammer for a coupla of days. By any rights I should do it. I should probably lock you up until your lawyer can get you out. You and your bozo buddy. But your cousins are good friends of mine, Charlie. They're men I both admire and respect. . . ."

"Where is Caldwell?" interrupted Charlie. He had no wish to hear about his cousins.

"Down in New York," said Peterson.

"Is he running this case or are you?"

"Well, Charlie, you know how it is. These things become a kind of joint effort."

"What about your stolen cars?"

Peterson looked at Charlie as if trying to decide whether Charlie were having a joke on him. Peterson disliked jokes. He was saved from having to make up his mind by the ringing of the telephone.

As Peterson answered the phone, Charlie got to his feet and wandered over to the window. It had started to rain and the streets were black and shiny. Peterson repeated the word Yeah into the mouthpiece half a dozen times. Victor continued to study the photographs of the Irish setters.

"You know," said Victor thoughtfully, "some people have sex with dogs. I never could see it myself. Dog lovers, they call them. It must take a special kind of personality."

Peterson hung up the phone and began writing something on a note pad. After a minute, he said, "It seems the explosion was caused by gas. All four burners and the oven were left on. Pease's body was found next to the stove. There was a dog there too, I don't know what kind. The gas built up and when it reached the candle in the other room, bingo, an explosion. The point is that it looks like suicide."

"Then why was he looking for me?"

"Don't be so innocent, Charlie. You're an old hand at this. How many suicides have you known who left word someplace, hoping that some good samaritan would come along and rescue them?"

The fact of the phone call made Rodger Pease's death real in a way that not even the fire had done. Charlie told himself that Pease was his friend, that he had known him all his life. He knew that Peterson was partly bullying him with his suicide theory. Peterson could argue that if Charlie had been faster and more responsible, then Pease might have been saved.

Unfortunately, Charlie felt pretty much the same way. He knew that if he had sought out Pease right after Victor had mentioned that Pease was looking for him, then he might have reached the old man in time. Not that Charlie believed the suicide theory. He had little doubt that Pease had been murdered and that the murder was connected to McClatchy. It struck him that Pease was almost the last person in Saratoga, apart from his family, who had known his father.

"What if he was already dead when the explosion occurred?" asked Charlie.

"You mean murdered? Who'd bother to kill an old geezer like that?"

"Maybe he knew something about McClatchy?"

"Charlie, I'm not going to be bullheaded about this. If

there's a link between Pease and McClatchy, I'll find it. But right at this moment Pease looks like a suicide. He's an old guy, no friends, no money, no job, nothing but his old dog. Who can blame him?"

"Hey, Peterson," said Victor, "you ever hear of sperm brain?"

"Be quiet, Victor," said Charlie.

"What's sperm brain?" asked Peterson, puzzled.

"Never mind," said Charlie. He realized that because of McClatchy and because he had been seen talking to Marotta, he had no credibility. True, he and Peterson had been disagreeing for over fifteen years, but occasionally the police chief had believed him, even respected him. Now it seemed that the very fact that Charlie was saying that Pease had been murdered was reason enough for Peterson to believe something different.

"Are you going to do an autopsy?" asked Charlie.

"I guess so, why?"

"Let me know if you find any gas in his lungs."

Charlie walked to the door. He half-expected Peterson to call him back, but when he looked at him he saw that Peterson was rearranging the dog trophies that Victor had disturbed. Charlie opened the door and went out.

"Hey," said Victor, "wait for me."

As Charlie went downstairs, he thought that the suicide theory was especially convenient for Peterson because it allowed him to separate Pease's death from McClatchy's. If Pease was a suicide, then Peterson could continue to concentrate on his stolen cars, leaving McClatchy to Hank Caldwell, who presumably thought the murderers were someplace downstate.

"Wait up," said Victor.

Charlie paused on the sidewalk. The rain had mostly stopped and the air smelled of wet brick.

"What did you mean, gas in his lungs?" asked Victor.

"If there's no gas, it means he was already dead."

They stood in front of city hall at the corner of Broadway and Lake. "You think Pease killed himself?"

"No, I don't," said Charlie, "but maybe I believe that because I don't want to believe he committed suicide."

"That's pretty complicated," said Victor. "What do you plan to do about it?"

Charlie watched a souped-up '36 Ford rumble past on Broadway. He decided it had been built from a fiberglass kit and for some reason that depressed him.

"I guess I'm going to poke around a little," he said.

5

▼▼▼

THE BALL-COCK ASSEMBLY, new tank ball and lift wires took Charlie over two hours to install. Even so he had to give a slight flick of the wrist and several wiggles of the flush handle before it would work properly. He knew that he would be the only one who could operate it, that he would spend a huge amount of time telling guests just how to flick their wrists in order to keep the lift wires from getting entangled. But for the moment, it was done and he could turn his attention to the death of Rodger Pease.

He had brooded about Pease ever since he left Peterson's office the night before. He had brooded about him all morning as he delivered milk. Then, while repairing the toilet, Charlie told himself he had to drive over to Pease's house and look around. What "look around" meant he had not yet decided.

Taking an apple from a bushel basket near the back door, Charlie put on his blue windbreaker and left the house. He had borrowed Victor's yellow Volkswagen until the windshield could be replaced on the Renault. For years it had been Charlie's Volkswagen and he had sold it to Victor after his friend had convinced him that he would be happier with the red Renault, which was newer, more comfortable and which should have been a better car. Maybe it would have been a better car if it started one hundred percent of the time. As it was, it started ninety-five percent of the time and Charlie felt he had been duped.

It was nearly two o'clock when Charlie reached Pease's

house. Not that there was much house left. Instead, there was half a wall, some pipes, charred timbers, mounds of soggy débris and a brick chimney rising up like a single finger. The Dodge Dart had also burned and stood black and dismal on four flat tires. Charlie got out of the Volkswagen, trying to visualize the tidy house he had seen on the previous evening and thinking what a difference it might have made had he arrived five minutes earlier.

Pease's house had been situated between a vacant corner lot and a three-story brown house with a long front porch and rusty screens. Its paint was blistered from the fire and if the wind had been stronger, the brown house might have burned.

Charlie climbed the steps of the front porch and knocked on the door. The floor of the porch was littered with toys and the bottom part of a broken broom. A middle-aged woman in a pink bathrobe answered the door. Her hair was in curlers and she had some sort of white cream on her face.

"I'm all done talking to the police," she said.

Charlie gave her one of his cards, which identified him as Charles F. Bradshaw of the Bradshaw Detective Agency. "I just have a couple of questions," he said. From inside the house came the whistle of a teakettle.

"Like what?"

"Did you know Mr. Pease next door?"

"Never spoke to him. Old men like that, they never wash."

"What about visitors," asked Charlie. "Did he have any visitors yesterday afternoon?"

"I was out all day yesterday." She made it sound as if she had been unconscious. The teakettle continued to whistle.

"Did you ever notice anyone over there? Did he have any friends, anyone who came to see him?"

"No, I never saw anyone. I'll say this for him," the woman added, "he was no trouble. Sometimes his dog barked but in general I never heard any noise. The only time I saw him was when he took that dog for a walk. Twice a day, morning and evening, like clockwork."

After asking the woman to call him if she remembered anything else, Charlie crossed the street. It was another warm fall

day. From the shed rows by the harness track came the smell
of horses and manure. A string of clouds like small white box-
cars trailed across the sky to the east. Charlie climbed the steps
of a small gray house and rang the bell. A dog started yapping,
then a man about Charlie's age opened the door. He was wearing an undershirt, baggy green pants, and had a cigarette stuck
in the corner of his mouth.

"Yeah?" he said.

Charlie gave him one of his cards. "You see anyone across
the street yesterday, maybe late in the day or early in the
evening?"

"Not me, Jack, I didn't see anything." The man started to
close the door. Charlie noticed that he was wearing bright
red slippers.

"How about friends?" asked Charlie. "Did the man across
the street have any visitors?"

"Not that I ever saw."

"Rudy," called a woman's voice from inside, "Rudy, who're
you talking to?"

"Some private dick," shouted the man. "You got any more
questions?" he asked Charlie.

"You ever talk to Pease?"

"Never. Didn't even know that was his name till the cops
told me."

A woman in a blue bathrobe appeared behind Rudy's shoulder. She too had curlers in her hair and Charlie wondered if
anyone on Ward Street ever bothered getting dressed.

"What's he want?" asked the woman, looking suspiciously
at Charlie.

"He's asking about the guy across the street."

Charlie guessed the woman had thought he was after Rudy.
Once she realized that Rudy was safe, she cheered up. "Wasn't
that a shame," she said. "Why'd a nice old man like that want
to go and blow himself up?"

"You ever see any people over there?" asked Charlie. "Or
know if he had any friends?"

"Never saw a soul," said the woman. She kept patting at
her curlers, which contained little pinwheels of black hair. "But

one time we saw him in a bar with an old woman. You remember that, Rudy? They seemed pretty friendly."

"How long ago was that?" asked Charlie.

" 'Bout a month ago. You know the Towne Bar over on the next street? It was over there. They might know something."

The waitress at the Towne Bar hadn't heard about the fire, didn't recognize Pease's description and seemed to think Charlie was making it all up. She was an attractive young woman with thick brown hair that fell to the middle of her thighs. Its weight pulled back her head, making her keep her chin slightly raised so that she looked regal or conceited. Charlie couldn't decide which. He wanted to ask her how heavy it was but instead he concentrated on convincing her that he had to find out about Pease. After he had told her this for the tenth time, she called the owner out of the kitchen. He was a man of about fifty who wore aviator glasses and a baby-blue cowboy shirt with pearl snaps.

"An old guy, you say?"

"Tall," said Charlie, "and big like, well, a sack of potatoes. He was supposed to have been in here with an old woman."

Two girls were playing pool. Neither of them looked eighteen. One had no teeth. She kept laughing, showing her pink gums.

"Yeah, I remember a guy like that," said the man. He glanced down at his cowboy shirt and unsnapped the top two snaps, exposing curls of black hair. "Funny old geezer. Used to come in here with this old woman who was even taller than he was. I tell you, they were quite the couple. Even saw them dancing once. I figured it was his wife but then I said something and the woman said they weren't married. After that I didn't see them again. Her name was Flo something, I don't know her last name. Maybe Maggie does. Hey, Maggie, come out here a minute."

A heavyset woman with damp-looking pink cheeks came out of the kitchen wiping her hands on a white apron.

"What was that woman's name," asked the man. "Flo something, that used to come in here with the old guy?"

"You mean the one you insulted?"

"Who insulted? I never said a thing."

Maggie looked at Charlie, then curled her lips scornfully. "This old fool told them he thought it was swell to see an old married couple who still liked each other. He made a big deal out of it, kept buying them drinks. After that they never came back. I don't know her name, just Flo, like the old fool says, but she told me once that she lived in a rooming house over on Ludlow, because that was the time I was thinking of moving out, and she said it was clean but cheap. Don't ask me if she lives there now. I was so mad at the old fool when they stopped coming back. I knew he had upset them. They'd sit over there in that corner booth, talking with their heads close together and sometimes holding hands. It was a pleasure to see them."

Charlie had left the Volkswagen over on Ward Street and he walked back to retrieve it. Then he drove to Ludlow, which was behind the Fassig-Tipton stables where the yearlings were auctioned each August. There were three rooming houses on Ludlow and the old woman, whose name turned out to be Flo Abernathy, lived in the third. It was a large Victorian house with a sort of turret running up one corner. Flo Abernathy had the turret room on the second floor and the turret itself was full of flowering plants.

Flo Abernathy was at least three inches over six feet, with long white hair done up in a French roll and pinned to the back of her head. She had a long, narrow face and wore a floor-length blue dress with a string of pearls. At first she had not wanted to let Charlie in, but then she seemed to recognize his name. She asked if he would like a cup of coffee and went off to prepare it before he could answer. Her whole body was narrow, like the spine of a book, and she held herself very straight when she walked.

Charlie sat uncomfortably on an antique chair with a wicker seat. In his lifetime, he had broken nearly a dozen chairs like this one by leaning back or stretching or sitting down too abruptly. The blue walls of the room were covered with photographs. Some were of people—Charlie recognized several of Rodger Pease—but there were others of houses, a lake, a couple of racehorses and an elaborate rose garden with Greek pillars and statues.

Flo Abernathy returned with a tray on which were two cups of coffee, a silver cream pitcher and sugar bowl and a little silver plate of chocolate-chip cookies. The room was crowded with furniture, as if the furniture of a dozen rooms were being stored here. Covering the floor were a number of overlapping carpets of the kind that Charlie's mother called Turkey carpets. The windows had red curtains and the afternoon sun filled the room with pinkish light.

Flo Abernathy handed Charlie a cup of coffee and sat down. "Rodger and I were to meet last night. When he didn't appear, I walked by his house. Then I called the hospital and a nurse told me he was dead."

"Had you known him long?" Charlie sipped the coffee, then put his cup and saucer on a little round table. He always felt inadequate in the face of other people's grief. It made him dislike himself.

"We had been friends for forty-five years. I heard on the radio that the police suspect it might have been suicide. It wasn't, of course. But the police are apparently looking for his next of kin. He had a wife who moved to Miami in 1953. I don't know if she's still alive. I suppose after this much time it doesn't much matter, although she would be pleased to hear that he was dead and I was left by myself." Miss Abernathy sat with her cup and saucer in her lap. Charlie doubted that her back was touching the back of her chair. She stared into her cup as she spoke. Then she looked up at Charlie. She had dark blue eyes that matched the blue of her dress.

"What makes you think he didn't commit suicide?" asked Charlie.

"We had talked about suicide in the past. We both had. But after discussing it, we decided it would be wrong for one of us to abandon the other. Until recently we had been very happy. Then something happened to upset him. I don't know what. But he seemed frightened. I considered going to the police. Do you think I should? I would much rather they didn't know of my existence. I would hate to have my name appear in the papers."

Charlie remembered a wealthy family in Glens Falls by the name of Abernathy and he wondered if this woman was related. Then he tried to imagine her involvement with Pease over a period of forty-five years. In the corner, partly hidden by a painted screen, was a brass bed. Charlie tried to think of Pease with his sack-of-potatoes body making love to the tall, delicate woman who sat beside him.

"You have no idea why he was frightened?" asked Charlie.

"No, we rarely discussed our difficulties. It's foolish perhaps but we had a sort of game. We would never talk about the outside world, or at least very little, but would try only to talk about each other. And memories, of course."

"How did he earn his money?" Charlie considered taking a cookie, worried that it would make him seem frivolous, then took two.

"He received a small amount from Social Security, very small, and he supplemented this by being what they call a ten-percenter."

Charlie had almost guessed as much. Ten-percenters were people who cashed in tickets for bettors who wanted to avoid paying taxes on their winnings. Anyone who won over six hundred dollars had to fill out a tax form, and sometimes a person would turn to a ten-percenter instead of filling out the form and putting himself in a higher tax bracket. The tax system, however, was in the process of being changed and next season the taxes would be deducted directly at the window. In the past, ten-percenters had been made up of the unemployed and the elderly—people like Rodger Pease whose taxes would be little affected by a winning ticket. For their services they charged ten percent, although Charlie knew it was often less.

"How long had he been doing this?"

"About fifteen years, ever since he had found it difficult to obtain other work. He also worked at the harness track, but it was with the Thoroughbreds in August that he had the best luck. Once he even tried it down at Belmont but he found it too hard to break in. Here at least he was well known."

"You have any idea who he cashed tickets for?"

"No. As I say, we rarely talked about that part of his life. I knew that he did it and that was all." Miss Abernathy paused and looked away. During their whole conversation, her eyes had been brimming with tears. Now she reached into her pocket, took out a white handkerchief and pressed it first to one eye, then the other. "Excuse me," she said.

Charlie nodded and concentrated on the flowers in the turret. He was what he thought of as an emotional joiner: at the sight of someone else's tears, his own eyes would invariably moisten. He hoped he wouldn't do anything foolish.

"I wonder, Mr. Bradshaw," said Miss Abernathy after a moment, "if you could find out about the funeral. I don't think I should go but I would like to send a wreath. I'd also like to pay to have him buried in Saratoga and pay for a headstone as well. I'm sorry to trouble you with this but you've been very kind. What I want is for you to buy two adjoining plots in the cemetery. Could you possibly do that for me?"

Charlie started to ask why she needed two, then stopped himself. "Certainly," he said.

"It's a shame about the dog. He was such a smelly old thing. I would never let him come up here but now I'd be happy to have him. The terrible thing about a fire is that it's so complete. I have nothing but a few pictures."

Charlie finished his coffee and stood up. Her grief made him feel claustrophobic. He wanted to get away, yet at the same time he condemned himself for his cowardice. "Don't worry about the funeral stuff," he told her. He tried to nod reassuringly but guessed he was just dumbly bobbing his head.

Half an hour later Charlie was back at the wreckage of Pease's house digging through the debris with a borrowed shovel. So far he had found a couple of badly scorched books and a heavy blue mug. A few cars slowed as their drivers stared at him curiously. Charlie dug at the ashes, heaved charred boards out of the way and grew increasingly filthy. It was the murder that made him angry: the fact that someone felt that he or she could erase Rodger Pease as if he were no more than a stick figure on a blackboard.

Charlie guessed that the link between McClatchy and Pease had to do with Pease being a ten-percenter. It made him want to know more about that August more than a year ago, which had been the last time McClatchy had raced.

The shovel clanged against something metallic and Charlie bent over to see what it was. Brushing away the ashes, he found a metal horse about fifteen inches high. He wiped it off on his pants and saw that it was made of brass—a brass horse with a racing saddle. He put it on the grass next to the books and blue cup. He decided he had to go over to the *Daily Saratogian* to look through the newspapers for that last August. Then he realized the paper was the worst place to go unless he wanted to deal with a lot of questions about how he had betrayed Jimmy McClatchy to the Mafia. After a moment, he thought of someplace else.

At six o'clock, Charlie was banging on the screen door of a rundown Victorian house on the west side of Saratoga. Most of the screening had long since rusted away, but the frame made a loud noise when Charlie hammered on it and after a couple of minutes he began shouting as well. "Felix, I know you're in there. It's Charlie Bradshaw. Open up before I kick down the door!" Cradled in his left arm, Charlie carried a bag containing twenty-five pounds of dry cat food and a dozen cans of soup.

It was a square, two-story house with a high attic. Once it had been painted a cream color but most of the paint had peeled. Some of the windows had brown shutters. Other shutters had fallen off and were scattered across the lawn. The grass around the house was knee deep and Charlie doubted it had been cut for years. All the windows were covered with tattered green shades.

"I'm counting to three, Felix, then I'm kicking down the door. One . . . Two . . ."

The door flew open and five cats rushed past Charlie, raced down the steps and across the yard.

"Now look what you made me do!" shouted an angry voice.

Charlie hurried through the door and slammed it behind him.

"Back, kitties, back!" shouted the voice.

The room, a kitchen, was almost dark and Charlie could barely see about twenty cats nervously prowling back and forth in front of the door. Immediately, Charlie felt he was about to sneeze. Then he did: a loud, wet, two-shout sneeze that sent the cats scurrying into the darkness.

"You've scared them," said the voice petulantly.

"They'll get over it. Can we have a little light, Felix?"

"There's some in the other room." Felix had a high, querulous voice that seemed accustomed to complaining. "Would you have really kicked in the door?"

"I expect so. I did it once before, remember?"

"But you're not a policeman now. If you'd kicked down my door, then all my cats would have gotten out."

"Maybe they don't like it here," suggested Charlie. He had followed Felix through a dark hall to a front room, which was dimly lit by light coming around the edges of the green shades.

"Of course they like it here. You frightened them, that's all."

Felix was a small, wizened man with patches of straggly white hair and a pair of knobbly hands that looked like claws. He wore a constantly startled expression as if someone had just shouted, "Hey you!" or "Watch out!" Charlie thought Felix had the whitest skin he had ever seen and he doubted that it was ever touched by sunlight. He wore blue dungarees and a wrinkled white shirt that appeared ten sizes too big for him. His neck stuck up through the collar like a pencil through a doughnut hole.

The room smelled of cats and a hundred different kinds of dirt. The cats kept rubbing themselves against Charlie's ankles. He sneezed again and a dozen cats fled the room. One time, as a policeman, Charlie had been able to keep the authorities from locking up Felix and condemning his house as a health hazard; but whenever he saw the filth and the fifty or sixty cats, Charlie worried that he might not have done the right thing.

Charlie handed the bag of groceries to Felix. "Here's some food," he said.

Felix put the bag on the table, then took out the cat food and soup. "It looks like a bribe. What do you want?"

"I want to look through your *Racing Forms*."

"No, Charlie, they're brand new." Felix's voice rose about an octave. "It's not fair. Ask for something else instead."

"It won't do any good, Felix. I need to look at the *Racing Forms* for August of last year. I promise to be careful."

Felix walked to the other side of the room, muttering to himself. Charlie pressed his finger under his nose so he wouldn't sneeze, then sneezed away. Against two of the walls piles of newspaper were stacked to the ceiling. A tunnel through one pile led to another room. The floor was covered with tin cans, pieces of torn fabric and spilled kitty litter.

Felix came back, still muttering. "I need more cat food, Charlie. They won't stay if I don't feed them."

"I'll bring another bag this evening."

"Are your hands clean?"

"Yes."

"If you tear any newspaper, do you promise to replace it?"

"I promise."

"Come with me," said Felix.

Charlie followed Felix through the tunnel of newspapers and up the stairs. Everywhere stacks of newspapers were piled to the ceiling. Looking through a doorway, Charlie saw a room heaped with bits of paper that he realized were losing tickets from the track. Another room was filled with magazines. Felix led the way to the attic. He walked with a sort of sideways stoop and kept glancing back to make sure Charlie wasn't touching anything. The cats were everywhere and all seemed intent on getting entangled between Charlie's legs. By the time they reached the right room, Charlie guessed he had sneezed fifty times.

The yellow attic room was filled with stacks of *Racing Forms*. Light from the setting sun streamed in around a torn shade that half-covered the gable window.

"This is my favorite room, Charlie. I'd be upset if you disturbed it."

"It's a very nice room," said Charlie.

"Don't humor me, Charlie. You just think I'm crazy."

Felix lifted a stack of papers, put them on the floor, then continued poking through more papers and muttering to himself. After several minutes, he turned back to Charlie. "All right, here is last August and the months before. Don't forget, they're all in order. Make sure you put them back where you found them. I'll leave you here. It would make me too unhappy to watch."

"You mind if I open the window?"

"I wish you wouldn't."

"I'm allergic to cats."

When Charlie was certain that Felix had gone downstairs, he opened the window, leaned out and breathed deeply. Down below, he saw two small boys pointing up at him. They seemed astonished. Charlie waved, then went back to the papers.

Charlie wasn't sure what he was looking for. Primarily, he wanted to see what sort of horses McClatchy had ridden that past August. Although McClatchy was not one of the popular jockeys, he had ridden once or twice a day for the entire month. Charlie first sought out the *Racing Form* for the last day of the Saratoga meet, then worked his way back. Toward the end of the meet, McClatchy had had a big win on a three-year-old colt by the name of Sweet Dreams in a $20,000 claiming race. The horse had had odds of 30 to 1 and paid fifty-six dollars. According to the Past Performance charts, Sweet Dreams had lost badly in his previous three starts, all of which had been $20,000 claiming races. Nor was there anything in his workout times that indicated any speed. A short article on Sweet Dreams the day after the win quoted the owner and trainer as saying that the horse was nervous in the gate but that he hoped the problem had cleared itself up. The article referred to another big win at the beginning of the month at odds of 25 to 1 with the horse paying forty-eight dollars on a two-dollar ticket. That had been in a $12,500 claiming race. But what interested Charlie most was that the owner and trainer of the horse, Willis Stitt, lived in Hoosick Falls, a town about thirty miles from Saratoga.

When he could no longer read by the light from the window,

Charlie turned on a light hanging from a cord in the middle of the ceiling. It appeared to be a fifteen-watt bulb. Cats kept trying to snoop into the room and he shooed them away. After reading through the *Racing Form* for another two hours, Charlie learned that Sweet Dreams had run eleven times between April third and August twenty-sixth, losing badly in nine races and winning twice. McClatchy had been the jockey all eleven times: six races in Belmont, five in Saratoga. What also interested Charlie was that although he looked forward in the September and October issues, he found no further mention of the horse. It seemed that Sweet Dreams had quit racing at the same time as McClatchy.

Sweet Dreams appeared to be an average loser: Sweet Dreams out of Indian Maid and Buckdancer—neither parent rang any bells. Yet he had won two races at great odds. At that time it was not generally known that McClatchy pulled horses, while Willis Stitt's explanation about Sweet Dreams being nervous in the gate seemed sufficient reason for his uneven record.

But now, with Pease and McClatchy dead and Sweet Dreams's owner living only thirty miles away, Charlie decided he wanted to learn more about Sweet Dreams and Willis Stitt. McClatchy had had two other wins that August, plus several second- and third-place horses. But none of the horses had run at great odds or made a lot of money.

It was completely dark by the time Charlie left Felix's house. He first went to Star Market, bought four twenty-five-pound bags of cat food and took them back to Felix. The cats smelled the food and swarmed around Charlie's feet. Felix was moderately pleased but didn't think the cat food was worth the disturbance of his papers. He thanked Charlie but asked him not to come again.

Afterward Charlie drove over to see Flo Abernathy and to give her the books, blue mug and brass horse. The books were two novels about Horatio Hornblower. Flo stood in the doorway and held them, looking down at them for a long time. Charlie was afraid she might cry but she didn't. She just slowly nodded her head.

"I wanted to ask one more question," he said. "Did Rodger Pease do particularly well as a ten-percenter a year ago last August?"

The old woman thought a moment, then turned away and put down the mug, brass horse and books on a small table. "He did quite well that August. That's the last time he had much money. I remember he said his luck had changed. He was even planning to go back down to Belmont but then he didn't. I don't know why."

"Did he ever mention the jockey Jimmy McClatchy?"

"No, never. He never mentioned anybody's name. But that August was a good time for us. One night we even had champagne."

After leaving Miss Abernathy, Charlie spent about an hour searching the seedier Saratoga bars for an old acquaintance by the name of Maximum Tubbs. He finally located him in the Turf Bar on Caroline Street listening to scratchy Al Jolson records on the jukebox. When Tubbs saw Charlie, he slowly shut his eyes and looked away.

Maximum Tubbs was a small, dapper man who, Charlie thought, always looked ready, as if he were constantly calculating odds, doing sums in his head and preparing to place a bet. During August he seemed to live at the track. Otherwise, he was someplace shooting craps, playing poker or on a brief trip to Belmont or Aqueduct. He had soft little white hands that looked as if their only function was to handle dice, playing cards and money. He too had known Charlie's father. As a policeman, Charlie had arrested Tubbs for gambling about twenty times and each time he had felt embarrassed.

Charlie sat down on the stool next to Maximum Tubbs and inquired about his health and his fortunes. Tubbs grunted noncommittally, still not looking at Charlie. Undiscouraged, Charlie asked about Willis Stitt, Sweet Dreams and the sire and dam, Buckdancer and Indian Maid. Tubbs sipped his dry vermouth, then glanced at Charlie quickly. "Are you on a case?" he asked.

"I haven't decided. Do you remember Sweet Dreams?"

"It would be hard to forget him. He was a memorable horse.

I was sorry not to have a little bundle on him. Since then, I've wondered if McClatchy hadn't been strangling him all along. As for Stitt, he runs a small claiming stable. Barely gets by." Tubbs glanced at Charlie again, growing more interested. "The other horses I don't recognize. What were their names again?"

"Buckdancer and Indian Maid." Charlie had bought several bags of peanuts and was wolfing them down. He had eaten nothing else since Flo Abernathy's cookies.

"They don't sound like winners to me. You want me to check?"

Charlie nodded.

"Any other little errands?"

"I guess not. What would happen if it could be proved that Stitt had McClatchy constantly pull that horse?"

"He'd lose his license and be charged with interfering with a sporting event. Also the IRS would probably take an interest in him."

"Would it mean a jail term?"

"It would depend on how good a lawyer he had."

Charlie couldn't imagine killing two men over what was essentially a nickel-and-dime issue, no matter how much money had been won. "Don't tell anyone I've been asking, okay?"

Tubbs lifted his chin and looked at Charlie over the tip of his nose: half-scornful, half-amused. "You're not very popular right now, Charlie. I doubt I'll brag about knowing you. In fact, I probably shouldn't even be seen talking to you. I take it you don't think McClatchy was killed by his New York buddies?"

"I'm not sure what I think."

"You know, Charlie," said Maximum Tubbs, suddenly looking embarrassed, "I'm not one of those people who think you said anything to Marotta."

Charlie started to speak, then found that he couldn't. Instead, he roughly patted Maximum Tubbs's shoulder and hurried out of the bar.

By now it was nine o'clock and Charlie decided to walk over to Victor's apartment to see if his friend would give him a sandwich. After Felix's house, one more cat wouldn't hurt.

But as Charlie crossed Lake Avenue by the police station, he saw that the lights were on in Peterson's office. He remembered that he still had to find out about the funeral arrangements for Pease's body, and as he entered the police station he half-decided to tell Peterson what he had learned about Pease, Willis Stitt and the horse, Sweet Dreams.

Peterson was in his office with the FBI agent, Hank Caldwell. The door was open and when the two men saw Charlie they looked at him with a mixture of curiosity and indignation. Peterson sat at his desk, which was bare except for a brass nameplate that said he was Director of Public Safety. "You got something you want to tell us?" he asked.

"I wanted to find out about the funeral arrangements for Rodger Pease."

Caldwell sat in a straight chair next to Peterson's desk. After having looked once at Charlie, he had turned to an inspection of his fingernails. He wore a gray suit and his thin face and pointy nose seemed as smooth as polished stone.

"Charity case as far as I can see," said Peterson. "We'll probably send him over to Mitchell and Sons in a day or so. He had no bank account and the house was rented."

"Will it be a public funeral?"

"Who'd want to go?" asked Peterson.

"There's a wife in Miami," said Charlie.

Peterson looked at him for a moment. "She died two years ago," he said.

"You going to try and fool around with this case, Bradshaw?" asked Caldwell.

Charlie ignored him. "Have you found out anything else about Pease?"

"Like what?" asked Peterson.

"Like how he died."

"He died in the fire. But since you're so eager to know, I guess there's no harm in saying that he'd taken a pretty strong sedative. We think he didn't want to stay awake waiting for the gas to take effect."

"You still don't think he was murdered?"

Caldwell got to his feet and slowly walked over to Charlie.

Then he reached out and took hold of one of the buttons on his shirt right above his chest. He tugged it slightly. "You ever hear of interfering with a police investigation?" he asked. "We don't need much evidence to lock you up for that one."

Charlie thought about the horse Sweet Dreams, thought about how McClatchy must have held him back for all but two races, then he thought about how Pease must have cashed a whole handful of winning tickets and that whoever had gotten the money had probably killed him. There were little white marks around Caldwell's nostrils. His face looked so rigid that Charlie wanted to reach out and touch it, just to see if the skin was really as hard as it looked. Then he thought better of it and, with a quick backward movement, he pulled himself free and left the room.

6
▼▼▼

THURSDAY MORNING CHARLIE LOST a filling while eating a doughnut. He had been delivering milk and had stopped at the Schuylerville bakery. It was a large doughnut, maple flavored, packed with cream and when the filling popped out of an upper left-side molar, Charlie had considered it a judgment. When he touched it with his tongue, the hole felt as deep as a one-quart bottle. He called his dentist in Glens Falls, but the earliest he could see him was Monday afternoon.

It was late by the time Charlie got back to the barn and he would have to rush if he wanted to go swimming. Consequently, it was with a sinking heart that he saw his cousin James's big white Oldsmobile, with his cousin patiently waiting in the front seat, parked next to the yellow Volkswagen. For a moment, Charlie considered driving straight to Saratoga in the milk truck. Then he decided against it. His tooth had begun to hurt and he wished his life were simpler.

James was five years older than Charlie. During the years he had been a carpenter, people called him Jim or Jimmy; but now that he had his own construction company, everyone called him James. He was president of the local Lions Club, a leading Rotarian and a seven-time recipient of the Little League Booster Award. Additionally, he held it as a matter of religious faith that a mentally healthy person needed no more than four hours sleep a night. James often seemed to worry that Charlie might be making life difficult for Chief Peterson, whom he described as a "personal friend," with the result that Charlie would spend some moments trying to define "impersonal friend."

James remained in his car while Charlie unloaded the milk truck. He appeared to have a small microcassette recorder and was talking into it, presumably dictating material that would later be transcribed by his secretary. James wrote weekly letters to a wide number of Congressmen and imagined himself a political watchdog.

When Charlie finished, he walked over to James's car. His cousin got out to greet him. James was several inches over six feet, athletic, and his almost rosy face was accentuated by thick silver hair. He stuck out his hand. "Charlie, I've driven out here so that we might have lunch."

Charlie shook his hand. "This is really a treat," he said.

The dairy ran a restaurant around the corner and they strolled over in that direction. James walked with one hand resting lightly on Charlie's shoulder. "Tell me," he said, "what have you heard from your mother?"

"I got a card yesterday. She plans to stay in Atlantic City for a few more days."

"She's a great woman, Charlie, but I'm afraid she requires a little looking after."

They took a booth by the door and the waitress brought them menus. James ordered a fruit salad with cottage cheese. Out of perversity Charlie ordered a hot-fudge sundae. The ice cream was extremely painful on his tooth, forcing him to eat only with the right side of his mouth. This required him to tip his head a little to the right in order to chew and some ice cream dribbled out onto his chin. James kept looking at him.

"Charlie, I wanted to talk because I've been hearing things

that have made me unhappy. Astonishing as it might seem, I've heard you had some involvement with the deaths of two men. Charlie, at the age of forty-eight aren't you too old to be playing cops and robbers?"

"Forty-six."

"Pardon me?"

"Forty-six, I'm only forty-six." Charlie wiped some fudge sauce from his lower lip.

His cousin looked at him skeptically. "Charlie, I think it's time to give up this crazy detective agency. I've talked to the people at Wholesome Dairy and they're prepared to offer you a permanent position."

"I don't want to be a milkman," said Charlie. What irritated him most was that no matter how hard he tried, he always seemed to revert to his childhood relationship with James: that of an eight-year-old being corrected by a thirteen-year-old.

"It's a respectable job and it would mean a lot of security. Your mother may need taking care of. She might be coming back to Saratoga completely penniless. She's in her mid-sixties, Charlie, you can't let her go on being a waitress forever."

"I don't like being a milkman," said Charlie. He watched his cousin eating and disliked how he took small bites and chewed very carefully. He suspected that his cousin's teeth were perfect.

"You know, Charlie, Chief Peterson is a personal friend of mine and he told me you might even face criminal charges. Already your name has appeared in the paper several times. Charlie, I don't suppose you remember your father as well as I do, but I remember the kind of chances he took and how people talked about him. He was not a man who commanded a lot of respect. I even remember one time when he spent five hundred dollars in order to smuggle whiskey into the old county jail."

Charlie pushed away the last of his hot-fudge sundae. He wondered why he allowed himself to be so bullied by his family. Practically on the spur of the moment he decided he had to talk to Willis Stitt. He got to his feet and tossed a five-dollar bill on the table.

"James," said Charlie, "I'm glad my father bought whiskey for the jail. It makes me proud."

"That's not a very grown-up way to feel, Charlie," said James.

Charlie tried to think of some crushing response, but he didn't particularly dislike his cousin. He just felt suffocated by him. "Thanks for your concern," he said at last. Then he left the restaurant.

But as Charlie drove the yellow Volkswagen over to Willis Stitt's stable in Hoosick Falls, he continued to worry about his mother, his cousins, his tooth, his semirepaired toilet and even the smashed windshield on the Renault, which was supposed to have been fixed the day before but still wasn't ready. All he really wanted was to coach Little League baseball, go to horse races and spend a lot of time with Doris Bailes. But the Little League Association saw him as a corrupter of the young, racing season was over and he had no chance to court Doris in ways he felt appropriate. Besides, since McClatchy's murder, Charlie wasn't even welcome in the Backstretch anymore.

The sky was lumpy gray, like a tumble of gray blankets heaped on a bed. Leaves gusted down from the trees and the fields of cornstalks on either side of the road looked dismal. Then Charlie thought of his father smuggling whiskey into the jail. James had criticized his father as a man who took chances, but any gambler took chances as long as he thought he might win.

One of Charlie's Saratoga heroes was Bet-A-Million Gates, the turn-of-the-century gambler and stock-market tycoon who had made his first fortune selling barbed wire to Texas cattle ranchers. Bet-A-Million would spend whole nights playing faro at the Canfield Casino, wagering up to $10,000 on each turn of the card.

"That's the way I bet," he would say. "For me there's no fun in betting just a few thousand. I want to lay down enough to hurt the other fellow if he loses, and enough to hurt me if I lose myself."

Charlie liked someone who took chances, who believed in winners. He wanted to be that way himself. But it was hard to take chances when the toilet needed fixing, your fillings fell out and your relatives kept urging you to become a milkman.

Willis Stitt's stable in Hoosick Falls was about a mile from the farm where the painter Grandma Moses had lived. Her grandson ran the farm now and had a vegetable stand where Charlie bought tomatoes whenever he drove over to Bennington or took long summer drives through the country. It made him vaguely feel as if he were patronizing the arts.

The stable consisted of two red barns in need of paint and reshingling, a long red shed row and a shabby-looking Cape Cod house. Even the surrounding elms and maples seemed in disrepair, with a lot of dead branches and their leaves half gone. Leading to the house was a long gravel driveway and as Charlie turned up it, he saw a small circus tent behind one of the barns. It had alternate green and white stripes and seemed so out of place that he couldn't imagine its purpose. Between the barns was a corral with a wooden fence surrounding half a dozen horses.

Charlie parked the Volkswagen and got out. From the direction of the circus tent came the sound of a Strauss waltz played by a circus band. He heard a door slam. Charlie looked to see a young man in jeans and a blue sweat shirt coming toward him from the house.

"You Willis Stitt?" asked Charlie.

The man shook his head. "Nah, he's inside." He turned and shouted toward the house. "Hey, Will, somebody's here!"

"Thanks," said Charlie. "By the way, what's in the tent?"

The young man glanced toward the tent as if looking at something unpleasant. "That's Artemis. She's wacko." Without bothering to explain, he jogged off toward the corral.

The house door banged again and a rather pudgy man of about thirty-five came trotting down the steps. "You Mr. Emerson?" called the man. He had thick black hair, a wide owl-like face and a goatee.

"No, my name's Charlie Bradshaw." Charlie gave him a card. "You're Willis Stitt?"

"That's right," said the man, looking at the card. He seemed disappointed.

"I wonder if I could ask you some questions?" asked Charlie.

"I guess so," said Stitt. "What's it about?" Stitt wore jeans and a red-and-blue-plaid Western shirt that was too tight, so that the fabric around the pearl snaps was all stretched. Although he wasn't particularly cordial, neither did he seem suspicious.

"I wanted to ask you about a horse of yours named Sweet Dreams," said Charlie. As he pronounced the horse's name, it seemed to Charlie that Stitt stiffened slightly.

"What about him?"

"Did he run at all after that Saratoga meet over a year ago?"

"No. He injured his leg a few weeks later and I haven't raced him since." Stitt looked into Charlie's face as if trying to see behind it. After a moment, he took out a pack of cigarettes and offered one to Charlie. When Charlie refused, Stitt took a cigarette for himself and lit it with a kitchen match which he struck on his thumbnail.

"How'd he injure his leg?" asked Charlie.

"He hit his right foreleg on the door of his stall, breaking the pastern joint."

"Can it heal?"

Stitt shrugged. "He won't race again."

"The horse had an interesting record," said Charlie. "He raced only eleven times, is that right?"

"Yeah."

"And he won two races at great odds, how do you explain that?"

"I don't know how much you know about horses, Mr. Bradshaw, but there's a lot of chance involved. Sweet Dreams hated the gate and then a couple of times it didn't seem to bother him. If I'd kept racing him, maybe he would have turned into a good horse."

"You make a lot of money on those two races?"

Stitt shook his head. "No, nothing on the first race, maybe I had ten dollars on the second."

"How come you didn't race him as a two-year old?"

"I didn't think he was ready."

The Strauss waltzes were still coming from the circus tent. Beyond the tent to the east, the Green Mountains were covered in cloud.

"You know a man named Rodger Pease?" asked Charlie.

"Never heard of him."

Charlie felt he was lying. It wasn't that Stitt seemed tense; rather, he seemed to be forcing himself to appear relaxed. Stitt ground out his cigarette on the heel of his boot, then glanced over toward the man in the corral.

"Pease was a ten-percenter who worked at the track," said Charlie. "He was murdered on Tuesday. His house blew up and he was inside it. What about Jimmy McClatchy, you know him?"

"Sure I knew McClatchy. He used to ride for me." Stitt paused, then looked at Charlie more carefully. "You're the guy he was staying with, aren't you? I knew I'd heard your name before. Charlie Bradshaw. People say you sold him out. How come you're over here bothering me?"

Charlie didn't feel like answering that at the moment. "You have any idea why someone would want to cut off his head?"

"No, no idea. You still haven't said why you came over here."

"McClatchy was the only jockey you used on Sweet Dreams. How come?"

"I used him a lot over the years. He didn't charge as much as some of the others."

"You know he strangled horses?"

"I heard rumors, but you hear that about everyone. When the news broke about the Atlantic City scandal I was as surprised as anybody." Stitt took out another cigarette and lit it. "You still haven't answered my question."

Stitt seemed genuinely uncertain as to why Charlie was trying to connect him to the dead jockey. He took a large puff of his cigarette and blew smoke from his nose. Charlie decided that Stitt had begun to seem frightened, but of what he couldn't determine.

"Isn't it coincidental that Sweet Dreams and McClatchy stopped racing at the same time?" asked Charlie. "Maybe

McClatchy also held back Sweet Dreams for all but those two races. Maybe you made a killing on those races and maybe Pease cashed the tickets."

Stitt pushed his face toward Charlie's. "Are you suggesting I might have murdered them?" He seemed both puzzled and angry. "You better get out of her, Mr. Bradshaw. If you have any charges to make, why don't you go to the police?"

"What about Monday," insisted Charlie. "Can you tell me what you were doing during the time McClatchy was murdered?"

Stitt ground his cigarette out on the gravel. "Get out of here, Bradshaw."

The music had stopped in the circus tent. A drop of rain fell on Charlie's wrist, then another on his bald spot. "Okay, Mr. Stitt, I just wanted you to know the kind of questions you could expect from the police."

"I've been here all week," said Stitt, "and I can prove it if I have to. Why should the police want to talk to me anyway?"

Charlie smiled and shook his head, as if to indicate that they both knew very well why the police should want to talk to him. It seemed to Charlie that Stitt's fear came partly from confusion, as if he wasn't sure what exactly had happened. He appeared to be indifferent to the deaths of McClatchy and Pease, yet nervous about Charlie's questions concerning Sweet Dreams. Stitt's black hair was long, brushed back over his head and Charlie guessed it was one of his little vanities.

"Where's Sweet Dreams now?" asked Charlie. "I wonder if I could look at him." He knew he was pushing his luck but he wanted to see what would happen.

"Bradshaw, you've got no legal right to ask me anything. Why don't you get out of here?"

"Just let me see the horse," said Charlie.

Stitt turned quickly toward the corral where the young man was doing something to the watering trough. "Hey, Tony, come here and help me with a problem!"

"Forget it," said Charlie. "I was just leaving." As he drove out of the driveway, he saw Stitt still staring after him.

*   *   *

At three o'clock Charlie arrived at Mitchell and Sons Funeral Home to arrange Rodger Pease's funeral. Ten minutes later he was walking back to his car, unhappy with himself for not finding out how much Flo Abernathy wished to spend. Did she want Pease buried or cremated? If buried, did she want the seven-hundred-dollar or seven-thousand-dollar casket? Then there was the headstone and the double cemetery plot. Charlie left saying he would return the next day.

He drove to the Backstretch, where he was supposed to meet Victor at three-thirty. As he crossed Broadway it began to rain. Only the left-hand wiper seemed to work and it didn't wipe so much as bat fretfully at the raindrops. Charlie parked next to the Backstretch, then got soaked as he ran to the door.

Besides Doris, there were four people in the bar and again Charlie sensed that they looked at him with suspicion and dislike. Although he was used to the disapproval of his cousins' friends, the dislike of people whom he had considered good acquaintances was unpleasant and made him feel lonely.

"Want a beer?" asked Doris. She smiled and when Charlie reached out his hand, she took it and pressed it. She wore a red blouse and a string of yellow beads. Charlie was struck by the whiteness of her teeth. They made his own damaged molar begin to ache. Taking a couple of napkins from the container on the bar, he wiped the rain from his face and hair.

"No, let me have a cup of coffee. Has Victor been in?"

"I haven't seen him."

"Will you have dinner with me Saturday night?" asked Charlie.

When Doris smiled, the top part of her cheeks bunched up in a way that reminded Charlie of half a plum or peach. It was a physical characteristic that he had admired in his favorite actresses of the 1940s.

"Sure, I'd be glad to go to dinner."

"Maybe we'll drive down to Albany. I don't seem too popular around here."

Doris put a mug of coffee on the bar in front of Charlie. "That's true enough," she said. "I just heard about that other man this morning. Did he really commit suicide?"

"I think he was murdered," said Charlie. "You know, when McClatchy showed up at my house he said he had hitchhiked, but it seemed unlikely that he could catch a ride along the lake on a Sunday night. Also, I never heard a car. It seems possible that he went to Pease's house first and then Pease drove him to my place. Maybe he meant to stay with Pease and Pease refused. I don't know, but Pease clearly knew something about McClatchy that no one else did and I'll bet he knew what McClatchy intended to do in Saratoga."

"And what was that?" asked Doris.

But before Charlie could reply, Victor hurried into the Backstretch. His brown sport coat was dripping wet and his hair was plastered down over his forehead. Glancing at the other men in the bar, he wiped the rain from his face with his hand, then gave Charlie a military salute.

"Well, there he is," said Victor, "Saratoga's own pariah and black sheep, Mr. Charlie Fucked-Up Bradshaw himself. Take a bow, Mr. Bradshaw, and say hello to the folks."

"Lay off, Victor."

"Vic. 'Lo, Doris, aren't you afraid of blowing your reputation being seen with this guy? Jesus, Charlie, everywhere I go I hear a bunch of assholes saying what a bad hat you are. Wasn't your fuckin' fault that the old man's house blew up."

Charlie saw that Victor had a large purple bruise under his left eye. "What happened to your face?" he asked.

"Someone punched me. Can you believe it? Laid his whole fuckin' fist on the sacred flesh."

"Why'd he punch you?" It occurred to Charlie that he himself had been the reason. Perhaps someone had insulted him and Victor had protested. Charlie prepared himself to be deeply touched.

"He caught me lookin' through his desk," said Victor.

Charlie stopped feeling touched. "You're lucky he didn't call a cop," he said.

Victor shoved his thumbs through his belt loops and gave his pants an upward tug. "He told me to wait in his office. Is it my fault I can't be trusted? It was that lawyer. Leakey. I offered five hundred dollars for those letters and he turned me down. Hell, for five hundred dollars I was tempted to write them myself. Anyway, he went out for a second, so I took a gander at his desk. Nothin' there but some pencils and a pistola. Guess I'm lucky he didn't shoot me. By the way, some guy by the name of Maximum Tubbs called you. Says you should call him at the Turf Bar. You sure got queer friends."

Charlie called Maximum Tubbs from the pay phone at the back of the bar just where the smell of stale beer met the smell of soy sauce from the Chinese restaurant. As Charlie waited for Tubbs to come to the phone, he could just make out the scratchy voice of Al Jolson singing, "How I love ya, how I love ya."

"Say, Charlie, I found out about those nags. Neither was worth a cheap cigar, if you ask me. The mare, Indian Maid, wasn't so bad but Buckdancer was a real loser. Not a drop of blood in him. Can't see why anyone would want to use him for stud. As a teaser, sure, but not for stud."

A teaser was a stallion used to excite the mare to see if she was ready to breed.

"Hell," said Tubbs, "I'm surprised that Sweet Dreams could find his way around the track. Half-dog, that's what he looks like to me."

7

▼▼▼

THE DRIVER'S SEAT on the milk truck—actually it was a sort of perch—had a broken spring and whenever Charlie hit a particularly bad bump, the spring would jab him. Saturday morning, Charlie hit a lot of bad bumps.

The previous night he had again talked to John Wanamaker, who said there was nothing new to report except that his mother's endurance was making a kind of medical history. Charlie said he was glad to hear it, that maybe she would get better.

Wanamaker said no, she was already nine-tenths dead. All that was left, he said, was the bright spark of intelligence that makes the difference between human beings and animals.

"So when will you be coming back, John?" Charlie had asked.

"As soon as I can, Charlie. You know, this afternoon, I was sitting by my mother's bedside listening to her faint breathing and I thought, It would be so simple, all I would have to do would be to cover her face with a pillow and my mother would sleep in peace."

Charlie was shocked. "Don't do anything rash, John."

"I'm glad you understand, Charlie."

As he drove back to the barn, Charlie asked himself what had been his criteria for ever hiring John Wanamaker as a guard at Lorelei Stables. He had hired him solely because an earlier Wanamaker had once been owner of the Grand Union Hotel, the largest of Saratoga's grand hotels, which had rooms for 1,500 guests, over a mile of broad piazzas, and had its own church and opera house on the grounds. Charlie's mother once worked there as a maid.

John Wanamaker was not related to his famous predecessor, nor had he heard of him. Wanamaker himself was an ex-burglar and alcoholic who had become a born-again Christian in prison and was subsequently paroled into Charlie's care. Although in the beginning he had always carried his Bible on his rounds as a stable guard, he soon gave it up, becoming a lapsed-again Christian. Charlie imagined Wanamaker's mother living on year after year, as articles about her were published in popular-science magazines and Wanamaker himself appeared as a featured guest on the nightly talk shows: the man with the immortal mother.

By eleven o'clock Charlie had returned the milk truck to the barn and a half hour later he was ready to drive back to Saratoga, where he hoped to go swimming. He still had the yellow Volkswagen, much to Victor's dislike. The man responsible for fixing the windshield of the Renault had come down with the flu. Come hell or high water, Charlie had been told, he would have the Renault Monday afternoon, exactly at the time he was supposed to see the dentist in Glens Falls.

Charlie's tooth had settled down to a dull ache. As he took the back road out of Schuylerville, he told himself that what he disliked most was his inability to keep his tongue out of the hole. He constantly fiddled with it. His dentist was an old resident of Glens Falls and, besides fixing his tooth, Charlie hoped he could tell him whether Flo Abernathy was related to the wealthy Glens Falls family of the same name.

Charlie had spent much of Friday taking care of Pease's funeral, which had required a dozen trips between the funeral home and Miss Abernathy's turret room on Ludlow. Miss Abernathy had wanted everything just right and as Charlie drove back and forth he decided she must have a little money. Although the final funeral arrangements were modest, the bill had come to nearly five thousand dollars. The funeral itself would be Tuesday morning, out of the Episcopal Church, and as far as Charlie could figure, he and Flo Abernathy would be the only mourners.

Charlie had also spent some time on Friday learning about Willis Stitt. He discovered that Stitt had moved to Hoosick Falls eight years ago from Long Island, where he had worked as an assistant trainer. It seemed that in 1972 Stitt's wife had died in a car crash and he had become the beneficiary of her small inheritance. He had used the money to open the stable, but although he had had several winning horses, he appeared to be losing money and had probably gone through most of his wife's estate.

Stitt appeared to have few friends, rarely came to Saratoga and hadn't remarried. He also bred horses in a small way and the most interesting fact Charlie had learned was that Stitt was using Sweet Dreams for stud. Given Sweet Dreams's lineage, it seemed unlikely that the foals were worth much.

Charlie parked in front of the Y, checked his wallet and watch at the desk, then went into the locker room. Several men glanced at him but no one spoke. Quickly, he changed into his suit, then showered and went into the pool area. There was no sign of George Marotta and Charlie wondered if he had given up swimming for good. Eddie Gillespie was still watching Marotta's house and had seen Marotta walking from room to room. He left his house only to go to the restaurant, and then only late at night. Charlie assumed that Marotta's actions were governed by fear, but of what he couldn't determine. Certainly it was something more than the disapproving looks of his fellow swimmers.

Charlie smeared saliva into his goggles, then dove into the medium lane. Kicking his way back to the surface, he began to swim almost automatically, following the black line from one end of the pool to the other. As he swam, he thought about Willis Stitt. It occurred to Charlie that since McClatchy had been granted immunity by the grand jury, he had been in a perfect position to commit blackmail. If he had really held back Sweet Dreams, he could confess that fact without fear of prosecution. How simple then to come to Saratoga, contact Stitt and demand money. Charlie had read in the paper that McClatchy was receiving eight hundred dollars a month from the Federal Witness Program. McClatchy had expensive tastes and Charlie doubted that eight hundred dollars would go far.

The problem was that Stitt didn't seem like a murderer. Even if he had engaged in pulling Sweet Dreams, the criminal charges were rather trifling. He might be finished as a trainer but given his lack of success such a reversal might be all for the best. Furthermore, even though Stitt had known that McClatchy was staying with Charlie, it hadn't been McClatchy's name that made him nervous, but Sweet Dreams's.

Charlie continued to slog through the water, trying to kick his feet hard enough to keep his legs at the surface. Every so often a faster swimmer passed him and briefly the water filled with turquoise bubbles. When he had finished his seventy-two lengths, Charlie rested a minute, then climbed out of the pool, feeling clean and virtuous.

He showered, then in the locker room he tried to start up a conversation about the World Series with a fellow who was assistant coach of a local Little League team. The man appeared not to hear him. His name was Raymond Sharp and each year he tried to get the kids to call him Razor Sharp.

"What do you think about Philadelphia?" Charlie asked.

Raymond Sharp stood at the mirror tying his tie, which was blue with the initials RS repeated over and over in an overlapping pattern. The three other men in the locker room tried not to look at them. Forget it, said Charlie to himself, just forget it.

That Saturday afternoon Charlie staked out a house for Victor, who was trying to locate a sixteen-year-old runaway expected to visit her boyfriend. It was the sort of work Charlie was worst at and after two hours of fiddling with his bad tooth and musing about the whereabouts of McClatchy's head, he fell asleep. An old car accelerating down the street woke him at five o'clock. His neck was stiff and he had a stomachache. The house—a cheap, two-story house covered with brown shingles—looked deserted, although Charlie knew that in the time he had been asleep several elephants could have tripped in and out. Instead of being upset, he found himself wondering why Willis Stitt was using Sweet Dreams for stud.

Charlie started the Volkswagen and drove back to the office. That evening he would take Doris out to dinner. They would drive down to Albany, maybe even see a movie. He would be constantly aware of her presence, would keep touching her, holding her coat, touching her arm or hand. He would forget about Rodger Pease and his funeral, the milk truck, the imminent arrival of his mother, his bad tooth and McClatchy's missing head. The sky had grown dark and it began to rain. With every leaf that swirled down from a tree, Charlie felt a wrench. He parked on Phila and hurried up to the third floor.

Victor was sitting with his feet on the desk. "Did she show up?" he asked.

"I didn't see her."

"You look like you been asleep. Your eyes are all baggy." Victor leaned forward and stared at Charlie.

"That's true," said Charlie. "I fell asleep."

"Hey, look," said Victor, "I'm the last guy to complain. Forty winks is forty winks."

"It was half the afternoon," said Charlie. "I'm sorry."

Victor linked his hands behind his head, leaned back in the swivel chair and raised his eyebrows. "As long as her old man didn't see you, what's the diff? But I should say, Charlie, that old eagle-eye Gillespie never but never falls asleep. He might smoke a little reefer or take a nip now and then but he's always wide-eyed. By the way, you better keep your coat on. Some guy wants to see you."

"Who?" asked Charlie.

"Some guy named Willis Stitt. He's over at the Roosevelt Baths. Room 14. He said he'd be there until about five thirty. I was going to come over and get you if you didn't show up. Good thing I didn't catch you napping."

"Why does he want to meet there?" asked Charlie, half to himself.

"That he didn't divulge," said Victor. "Maybe he wants to keep it quiet or maybe he's a regular. You know, soaking in that funny water and having some ex-wrestler beat up his decrepit flesh. Is he mixed up with this McClatchy business?"

"McClatchy rode for him." Charlie stood by the desk, feeling undecided about what he should do.

"I don't want to tell you your business, Charlie, but don't go riling up Peterson again, will you? He could make it hard for us to keep working."

"Did Stitt say what he wanted?"

"Nah, hardly said anything at all. Just that it was important. What's his voice sound like anyway?"

Charlie had put his blue jacket back on and was zipping it up. "I don't know, a regular voice, neither high or low, no discernible accent. Why?"

"The guy's voice on the phone was sort of low and muffled, like he was talking through a damp rag."

"Are you telling me he was trying to disguise his voice?" asked Charlie.

Victor took a dirty red handkerchief from his back pocket, blew into it and speculatively eyed the results. "I wouldn't go so far as to say that," he said, "but if he *was* trying to disguise his voice, that's how it would sound. What do I know, maybe he was just scared."

Charlie stood for a moment, then went to a small safe in the corner, knelt down, spun the dial several times and opened the door. The safe was empty except for a snub-nosed .38 revolver. Charlie took the revolver and stuck it in his belt.

"Want me to come along?" asked Victor.

"No, I don't think there'll be any trouble."

"Just packing the pistola to feel like a big guy, right?"

Charlie didn't answer.

It was raining even harder when he hurried across Phila to the yellow Volkswagen. Accelerating up Putnam, he circled around the block to Broadway. The street lights were all coming on, even though it was only five fifteen.

The Roosevelt was the last of the baths that remained open year round. Two others had closed down permanently and the Lincoln Baths were only open in the summer. For nearly two hundred years the springs had been the main reason that people came to Saratoga, but now they were mostly an oddity. The baths were run by the state and Charlie guessed that they operated at a loss.

Charlie drove up Broadway to the Avenue of Pines. The wind had blown a few small branches across the road and the Volkswagen bumped across them. In the glare of his headlights, the trees looked shiny and new. Charlie drove around by the theater and tennis courts. The park with its semi-Georgian buildings was deserted. Charlie drew up in front of one of the four Greek columns supporting the portico of the baths. Built in the 1930s, the Roosevelt baths occupied a U-shaped, red brick building with a gray slate roof. Each wing had about twenty rooms where a visitor could bathe in a tub of carbonated water heated exactly to body temperature, receive a massage, then doze while wrapped in warm sheets on a narrow cot. Charlie had gone once. It made him feel tubercular.

Charlie passed through the tall glass doors to the lobby. A young woman in a glass reception booth glanced up, yawned, then went back to her book. He turned right past her desk to the men's wing, then turned left down the long green hall, which was partly blocked by large laundry hampers overflowing with white towels. The air felt damp. A fat man wearing white trousers and a white T-shirt sat on a bench fanning his face with a copy of *Racing Form*. He belched faintly as Charlie passed. Some doors were open and Charlie saw white-haired men lying on metal cots. Through one door he saw a naked one-legged man lying on a massage table. The stump of the man's leg pointed toward the door like a cannon. A faint humming noise came from the phosphorescent lights. They made the air itself seem green, as if the hall were under water. At the far end of the hall was another door that led out across the lawn to the performing-arts center. The door was open and through it Charlie could see the dim shapes of trees blowing in the wind.

The doors along the hall were numbered and Room 14 was on the left near the back. Charlie knocked but there was no answer. He waited a moment. From another room someone began whistling *The Streets of Laredo*. Charlie tried the knob and the door opened.

The room was about ten feet by ten feet with white tiles going halfway up the wall, then peach-colored paint after that. Along the left wall was a low white bathtub filled with what looked like seltzer water. Against the wall opposite the door was a hospital cot with a rumpled gray blanket, as if someone had just been sitting on it. Above the cot was a window looking out onto the darkened and rain-soaked lawn. It was slightly open. The room was lit by a single light set into the ceiling. On a coat tree in the corner hung a man's leather jacket.

The room was empty. Charlie glanced around, shutting the door behind him. It was very quiet and his rubber-soled shoes made a squeaking noise on the tiles. Some water and wet towels on the floor showed that the tub had been recently used. Past the tub was another door. Charlie walked over and opened it.

It was a bathroom. Willis Stitt sat on the floor, leaning back against the toilet. His black hair hung in damp strands across his forehead. Hearing the door, he slowly looked up. His cow-

boy shirt was unbuttoned and there were two red holes in his
chest. Blood was seeping from both in a pair of upside-down
Ys. A revolver lay on the floor next to his leg.

Stitt tried to focus on Charlie. His mouth was open and a
little blood trickled over his lip and into his goatee. He appeared to be listening to something far away. Slowly he raised
his right arm, propping his elbow in his lap so that the forearm
stood straight up and his fingers pointed to the ceiling. He
relaxed his wrist and his hand fell to the left. Once more he
raised his hand, pointing his fingers at the ceiling, then again
he let it fall to the left. He did it a third time. It was as if he
were waving. Charlie stared at his face but there was only that
listening expression and a look of surprise. Stitt began lifting
his hand a fourth time.

Suddenly Charlie leaped sideways, pulling his revolver from
his belt. An instant later the room seemed to explode behind
him and Charlie felt a hot tug at his left arm. Falling to his
knees, he twisted and fired twice at the open window. One of
the ricochets whined around the room. Charlie reached up and
flicked out the light. The room smelled of gunpowder. Holding
his revolver with both hands, he kept it pointed toward the
window as he got to his feet. The window formed a gray rect-
angle in the darkness. Charlie moved toward it until he could
see trees and the women's wing across the lawn. Poking his
gun through the torn screen, Charlie looked out. At first he
saw nothing. Then he saw someone in a light-colored raincoat
running across the grass toward the performing-arts center.

Shoving the gun back in his belt, Charlie ran to the door.
His arm was beginning to hurt but he ignored it. He yanked
open the door and ran out into the hall. Half-sliding on the
tiles, he turned toward the door at the end of the hall leading
out to the lawn. He guessed that the person was running toward the parking lot at the performing-arts center and he
thought he had half a chance to catch him.

At that moment, something hit him from behind, sending
him flying to the floor and crashing into a hamper of towels.
There was the smell of sweat and the soft feel of damp flesh.
Before Charlie could think what to do, his good arm was

wrenched behind him into a hammerlock. He wanted to tell whoever it was to stop. Then the person grabbed a fistful of his hair and began pounding his forehead against the floor. The last thing he remembered was the way his teeth banged together each time his head smacked the tiles.

The bars of the Saratoga jail were painted medium green and the cots were covered with brown blankets. As Charlie sat on the edge of a cot three hours later, he tried to calculate how many people he had put into these cells. Maybe a thousand, maybe more. He had never expected to be here himself. On the wall above the toilet, someone had written, "What train's going to come to carry me across so wide a town?"

Stitt was dead and Charlie was accused of his murder. Of the person in the raincoat, there was no sign. Charlie kept trying to tell various policemen about him, but his words were met with skepticism and silence. Although Charlie felt generally unhappy, his major distress had come from being unable to pick up Doris Bailes at seven o'clock.

He had yet to see Peterson and had been booked by his old friend Emmett Van Brunt, who had refused to speak except to ask his name, address and occupation. When Charlie said he was a private detective, Emmett had made a sort of choking noise, which Charlie realized was meant to be laughter. He even had to give Emmett his belt and shoe laces, and it was only grudgingly that Emmett had let him keep the new sling that supported his left arm.

Charlie had first been taken in handcuffs from the Roosevelt Baths to the hospital where his arm had been bandaged. The bullet wound in the fleshy part of his upper arm was a clean hole and would heal in a couple of weeks. It hardly even hurt. What hurt was his forehead where the fat masseur had hammered it against the floor. The bruise was covered with a thick pink piece of adhesive and Charlie kept picking at it. The bandage felt as large as a pillow and there was a loud ringing in Charlie's ears.

Around nine o'clock, Emmett returned to take Charlie upstairs. His black horn-rim glasses had slipped down his nose, making him appear professional. "The chief wants to see you," he said. He unlocked the cell door, then stood back as if expecting Charlie to jump at him.

Charlie remained seated on the edge of the cot. "I want to make a phone call," he said.

"You can make it after you see the chief."

"Emmett, I get to make it right now."

"You calling a lawyer?"

"What's it to you?"

Emmett led him to a small office and pointed to the phone. "No more than two minutes," he said.

Doris answered right away and when Charlie said hello she made a growling noise. "Where are you?" she asked. "I've already chewed off my lipstick twice."

"In jail. Peterson thinks I killed someone."

"Did you?"

"Of course not."

"So we'll have dinner some other night?"

"I hope so. By the way, could you call Victor and tell him that if he doesn't hear from me tonight, then he should have a lawyer over here the first thing Monday morning."

"You mean you'll be there all weekend?"

"Possibly. If I'm charged, they won't set bail until Monday."

"What about the milk?"

Charlie had forgotten about the milk. He found himself imagining a giant milk bottle about ten stories tall. "Tell Victor that if he doesn't hear from me tonight, then he should call the dairy tomorrow." Charlie was sure it would mean the loss of that job, which meant Wanamaker would be fired.

"Anything else?"

"No, I guess not." Charlie could just make out the sound of her breathing. It was a steady, comforting noise. He wanted to tell her how much he regretted missing their dinner but Emmett Van Brunt was standing about two feet away and looking at his watch.

"I'm sorry about tonight, Charlie. I was looking forward to it."

"So was I," said Charlie. "I can't tell you how much."

After Charlie hung up the phone, Van Brunt led him upstairs to Peterson's office. Actually, he walked several feet behind him and kept his hand on his revolver. Charlie wanted to tell him that he was behaving foolishly, that they had known each other for years. But he knew it would do no good. He had the fleeting sense that perhaps he was wrong after all, perhaps he really *was* a criminal or at least a sort of social failure. Then he decided there was no future in that kind of thinking. Even if he was as bad as people thought, he still had to stick by himself.

When Charlie entered Peterson's office, he found the police chief staring at him from behind his desk. His bushy eyebrows looked bushier than ever. Peterson shook his head. "Looks bad, Charlie, really looks bad."

"I didn't shoot him, if that's what you think." Charlie was amazed that he was actually being accused of murder.

"Now, Charlie, let's not get off on the wrong track. This isn't an interrogation. Stitt was a friend of McClatchy's. So maybe he thought you were responsible for his buddy getting killed. All right, so he decides to get even. He gets you over to the baths and draws a gun. Too bad for Stitt you got a gun yourself, right? Hey, Charlie, who's going to blame you? Someone sticks a rod in your face and you blast him. Let's call it second degree."

Charlie sat down in the straight chair in front of Peterson's desk. On the edge of the red blotter was a rosewood box with the profile of an Irish setter carved on the lid. The box contained cigars. Charlie took out a cigar and sniffed it. His head hurt and the ringing in his ears seemed worse. He returned the cigar to the box. "Where's Caldwell?" he asked.

"Somewhere downstate. I been trying to reach him on the phone."

"You doing ballistics tests?" asked Charlie.

Peterson stood up and shoved his hands into the side pockets of his suit coat. "It's all part of the routine," he said.

"Stitt was shot by somebody standing outside the window," said Charlie. "Did you look for footprints? The ground was pretty wet. There's bound to be some."

"I haven't got a full report yet."

"No? Then send me back downstairs until you do. Either that or let me go home."

"I can't send you home, Charlie, this is serious."

"Then put me back in a cell so I don't have to listen to you."

Peterson leaned above Charlie like a great blue tree. Charlie guessed he was meant to feel intimidated. But he had known Peterson too long for that. Instead, he straightened the sling supporting his left arm. It would probably make driving the milk truck even more difficult.

"Hey, Emmett," Peterson shouted, "put Bradshaw back in his cell."

"You got a magazine or something I can read?" asked Charlie.

"What do you think this is," said Peterson, "a lending library?"

As Charlie was led back downstairs, he passed several cells occupied by drunks and petty thieves. Charlie knew four of them and they greeted him warmly. "That's Charlie Bradshaw," said one drunk, "he's as good as gold."

Once in his cell, Charlie asked himself what would have happened if he hadn't taken his .38 to the Roosevelt Baths. Presumably the person at the window would have shot him, then tossed the gun inside. There already had been a revolver next to Stitt and the presence of the two corpses and two guns would make it appear that Charlie and Stitt had shot each other. Of course, fingerprint and paraffin tests would show that neither man had fired a gun but perhaps Peterson wouldn't have bothered with the tests. Charlie, however, doubted that. Peterson sometimes might be mistaken but he wasn't a total incompetent. Charlie asked himself if he believed that one hundred percent. Not quite, he decided. It depended how eager Peterson was to solve the crime.

Then Charlie wondered what his cousins would say when they learned he was in jail. He was sure they wouldn't be surprised. It was as if they already knew there was a jail cell in his future and the only question was precisely when it would appear. He could hear his cousins saying how he had been offered the path of virtue and had turned it down.

Charlie gingerly touched the bandage on his forehead. He tried to forget his difficulties and soon found himself thinking about Butch Cassidy, one of the leaders of the Wild Bunch, who at one time had tried to set aside the fast life and seek a pardon from the Governor of Utah. He had grown tired of being chased all over simply for robbing a few trains. He wanted to settle down. It seemed to Charlie that he understood just how Cassidy felt. Cassidy had even agreed to take a job as express guard on the Union Pacific in order to scare off those same outlaws who had been his partners a few weeks before. Unfortunately, the plan fell through when Cassidy, in need of spending money, robbed the train in Tipton, Wyoming. Once more Cassidy was hounded all over the West. In search of a little peace and quiet, he hid out for three months in Fanny Porter's Sporting House in San Antonio, Texas, where the only violence he engaged in came from learning how to ride a bicycle. But then he became the greatest cyclist in San Antonio and the whores leaned from their windows and cheered when Butch Cassidy rode by waving his derby hat.

Shortly after eleven p.m., Charlie was taken back upstairs to see Peterson. He had been asleep and would have preferred to stay asleep.

Peterson stood next to his trophy case with one hand resting on the marble statue of a dog. "Charlie," he asked, "what made you so interested in Stitt in the first place?"

Charlie remained by the doorway. "You get the test results?"

"Ballistics show your gun didn't kill Stitt. It was the other gun, but there were no prints on it. We also found footprints, and a masseuse in the women's wing says she noticed a man out on the lawn, although it was pretty dark and she couldn't give much of a description, just that he was wearing a tan raincoat."

"So that means I can go?"

"Tell me what made you interested in Stitt?"

But Charlie was tired of being helpful. "Maybe I wanted to sell him some milk," he said.

Peterson cleared his throat and looked disappointed. Then he carefully put the statue of the dog back in the trophy case and locked the door. "This is no joking matter, Charlie. Who-ever killed McClatchy and cut off his head has been sending out photographs. I mean, photographs of the head by itself, just sitting on a table. The Jockey Guild got one, so did the *New York Post* and the federal prosecutor in Brooklyn."

"Is that what Caldwell's dealing with?"

"I talked to him half an hour ago. He said the pictures were mailed from the City. You shouldn't be so hard on him, Char-lie. It's not as if he was just some FBI agent up from Albany. He was in charge of McClatchy. That was his big case. Cald-well thinks I should keep you for the weekend, but I don't know. I mean, you're clearly meddling, but I've got no real grounds. You know that two Mercedes were stolen last night, two big fuckin' Mercedes? You got to stop fiddling with this case, Charlie. I know you were upset about McClatchy. Maybe you didn't say anything to Marotta, I don't know. Caldwell swears you did. I bet I been on the phone to your cousin James half a dozen times. You got two choices, Charlie, either you drop the whole thing and Caldwell lets you go, or you keep messing around and Caldwell puts an interference charge on you."

Peterson stood behind his desk, leaning forward with his hands on the blotter. Charlie felt almost sorry for him. Then he remembered how Stitt, dying on the bathroom floor, had tried to warn him. And there was also Rodger Pease, who had come looking for him and whom Charlie hadn't found in time.

"I appreciate your concern," said Charlie, "and if I was just working to clear my own name, then maybe I'd forget it, but I've got a client."

Peterson eyed him suspiciously. "Who is it?"

"I'm not at liberty to say, but I'll talk to the client and if the client gives me permission, then I'll tell you."

"I think you're lying," said Peterson.

8
▼▼▼

"**B**Y A STRING, CHARLIE, my poor mother's hanging by a string. You expect me to desert her, to leave her in some strange hospital surrounded by people who don't care if she lives or dies?"

"No, John," said Charlie, "I was simply wondering if you had any better idea when you might be coming back to Saratoga." It was ten o'clock Sunday morning and Charlie's sole pleasure came from knowing he had waked Wanamaker up.

"I told you, Charlie, I'll come back as soon as I can. The doctors say they never seen anything like it. I know you want her dead but it's really a miracle, a God-given miracle."

"I don't want her dead, John, I only want to know how much longer I've got to deliver milk."

"That's up to the Lord, Charlie. But just believe me when I say I'll be back as soon as I can."

Ten minutes later Charlie was driving the yellow Volkswagen over to Ballston Spa to see Eddie Gillespie, the ex-car thief and stable guard who had been following Marotta. It was difficult to drive with his left arm in a sling and he kept having to steer with his knees. Charlie told himself he truly didn't want Wanamaker's mother to die. If she recovered, he would be delighted, but he had taken the milk route for four days and here it was already four weeks.

The morning was so bright and sunlit that it appeared to have been specially polished by the previous day's rain. Charlie estimated that the colors were at their peak—the maples had turned a startling red, the birches were a dozen shades of orange. The entire Hudson River valley between the Green Mountains and the Adirondacks seemed to flicker with color. As for Charlie, his appreciation was tempered by his injuries and preoccupations. Tilting the rearview mirror to the left, he again inspected the bandage on his forehead. The intense pink of the previous evening was slightly soiled and spotted with drops from the grapefruit he had eaten for breakfast. The bandage, he thought, occupied his forehead in the way an oven door occupies the front of a stove. As for his preoccupations, two truths had become obvious: one, he had fully committed himself to the investigation; two, he appeared to be losing. That, however, would have to change, which was why he wanted to see Eddie Gillespie.

Ballston Spa was a small town about six miles to the southwest, which had once attempted to compete with Saratoga as a place of pleasure. But although Ballston Spa was nice enough, it had failed as a fashionable resort. Charlie tended to think of it as the town that had lost, which made it, he felt, a suitable home for Eddie Gillespie, another loser.

It wasn't that Eddie Gillespie was bad. Charlie could point to no one who was kinder or more generous. The problem was that Eddie Gillespie seemed unable to resist temptation, and since the age of fifteen his prime temptation had been driving stolen cars at speeds in excess of 120 miles per hour.

Recently, however, Eddie had been able to balance his desire to race stolen cars against his disinclination to go to jail. As a result, he had turned his attention to milder temptations: girls, alcohol, drugs and sleeping late in the morning. It was to that last temptation that Eddie Gillespie was submitting himself when Charlie found him at his mother's house at eleven o'clock Sunday morning.

Eddie was twenty-five, had tousled black hair and appeared to be naked under the covering of a none too clean white sheet. Charlie sat on a chair covered with a substantial mound of Eddie's clothes—mostly T-shirts advertising rock-and-roll bands. On the wall above his bed was a poster from a Rolling Stones concert, showing a red mouth and a long protruding tongue.

"I guess you caught me at a bad moment, Charlie. What happened to your forehead?"

Eddie sat up in bed and pulled the sheet up to his middle. He took a Lucky Strike from the pack on the bedside table and lit it. Some sparks fell onto the sheet and he patted them out. He had a round, open face with a wide nose and a constant wondering expression.

"I ran into a door. Are you still following Marotta?"

"Finished last night. Vic said we'd used up all the money." Eddie's chest was covered with curly black hair. He began scratching it. From downstairs came the sound of a vacuum cleaner.

"I want you to keep following him for a while. You don't have to do it all the time. Just make sure he knows you're there."

"Did his old lady cough up some more dough?"

"You'll be paid okay."

"He still hasn't left the house except to go to his restaurant."

"Doesn't matter."

Eddie blew a series of smoke rings toward the ceiling. "That's fine by me, Charlie. It's just the kinda work I like, sittin' in a car listenin' to the radio. Like I'm your friendly and dependable private eye."

"There's some other work I'd like you to do for me as well," said Charlie, "which is a little more complicated."

"Is it dangerous?" asked Eddie.

"Not really. Have you ever delivered milk?"

"Milk?"

"That white stuff that comes in bottles that you put on your cereal each morning."

"I don't eat cereal. What's it got to do with milk?"

"Let me tell you more about it," said Charlie.

It had taken a great deal of persuading before Eddie Gillespie had agreed to deliver Wanamaker's milk. Charlie had had to suggest it was a special undercover job for the detective agency. Beyond that he had been forced to offer Eddie six dollars an hour, which was two dollars an hour more than Charlie was making himself. However, it would be worth the extra twelve dollars a day not to get up at four thirty in the morning. He gave Eddie a map of his route and various warnings about dogs and bad bumps, and after Eddie had sworn to do his best, Charlie left, thinking it might be a perfect match. After all, Eddie liked driving around in vehicles that didn't belong to him.

From Ballston Spa, Charlie drove over to Doris's apartment in Saratoga Springs. She lived on the third floor of a yellow Victorian mansion on Circular Street. She wasn't home. Charlie imagined that she had gone out with another man the previous evening and had been seduced. Maybe she had fallen in love, maybe she was already engaged. From Doris's, he drove over to Ludlow to see Flo Abernathy.

As Charlie climbed out of the Volkswagen, he heard the sound of someone playing the clarinet. He paused for a moment on the sidewalk. The music was quiet, almost melancholic. The Sunday-afternoon street was very still, while the sunlight through the multicolored leaves made the air shimmer and dance. Charlie entered the rooming house and went upstairs. It turned out to be Miss Abernathy playing the clarinet. She sat in the turret with her back to Charlie, surrounded by flowering plants. She hadn't heard him knock and when he touched the door it had opened. The music, she told him later, was part of a clarinet sonata by Brahms. Miss Abernathy wore a black dress and the sunlight streamed over her shoulders. Charlie realized she was wearing mourning. He didn't find it strange that she was playing the clarinet but the music made him sad. He stood in the doorway as she sat perfectly straight in her chair and when she had finished, he said, "Excuse me."

She turned but didn't seem surprised. Perhaps she had heard him knock after all. She came over and shook his hand and again her superior height made him feel timid. Above her left breast she wore a cameo in a gold setting, showing a woman's profile.

"Would you like some coffee?" she asked.

"That'd be fine," said Charlie.

She left him to go over to the kitchenette, which was half-concealed behind another screen. Both this screen and the one by the brass bed were Oriental and had pictures of mountains, golden clouds and cranes flying. Up the side of one mountain wound a procession of men with triangular hats. At least fifteen small tables stood around the room and all were covered with various objects. On the table nearest Charlie was a ship in a bottle with tiny black cannons and gossamer rigging. Behind it were two glass snowstorms: one showed a polar bear on its hind legs, the other had a miniature Christ on the cross.

Flo Abernathy returned with the silver tray, silver cream pitcher and sugar bowl, coffee and a small plate of chocolate-chip cookies.

"Is this a social visit?" she asked.

"I'm afraid not. I need a favor."

"And what's that?" She poured him a cup of coffee.

"I need you to hire me as a private detective."

She paused, mildly surprised, then poured a cup of coffee for herself. "And why do I need a private detective?"

"To prove that Rodger Pease didn't commit suicide."

"But I already know he didn't commit suicide."

"Then to find out who killed him."

"I don't particularly care about that. He's already dead and the details surrounding that death can only be depressing."

Charlie sipped his coffee and burned his tongue. "I'm going about this in the wrong way. What I mean is that I've been trying to find out who killed McClatchy and Pease and a third man you don't even know about. Unfortunately, the police aren't happy that I'm doing it on my own. I have to have a client. Therefore, I'm asking you to hire me."

"Why not let the police take care of this business by themselves?" asked Miss Abernathy.

"Because they've got it all mixed up. They think that Rodger Pease killed himself and that McClatchy was killed by gangsters after I told them he was staying at my place. Partly I want to clear my own name. I mean, people will only be convinced I didn't betray McClatchy if I find out who actually killed him. Beyond that, I guess I just think it's untidy to have a bunch of unsolved murders."

Flo Abernathy glanced at the bandage on Charlie's forehead but didn't say anything. Then she glanced at his arm in its sling. She sipped her coffee and set the saucer on a table. "How much do you cost?" she asked.

"You can have my services for a five-dollar retainer."

"That doesn't seem like much."

"It'll do. All I need is a signed receipt."

"I think I can afford that," she said. "I've never hired a private detective before. And you promise to keep my name out of the papers?"

"I promise, but I might have to tell Chief Peterson if that's all right with you."

Twenty minutes later Charlie was driving out to Willis Stitt's stable in Hoosick Falls. He drove slowly, looking at the trees. Although the day was bright, it was also chilly and he kept his windows rolled up. Between the towns of Greenwich and Cambridge was a high ridge from which he could see panoramas to the east and west. Charlie pulled over to the side of the road. The yellow cornfields, cows in their green pastures, clusters of trees and the greater masses of woods with their leaves shading from green through all the gradations of yellow and orange, an occasional rise of smoke, red barns and white houses, winding roads and rolling hills—it occurred to Charlie that this had been his home for forty-six years. It seemed significant that it was fall, that the year was ending. In his ears he still heard the reedy sound of the clarinet as if the notes and swirls of the Brahms sonata were directing his attention across the landscape. Charlie thought of all the deaths—those of the season and those he kept stumbling upon. He asked himself if he truly expected to slow down the process of entropy. Perhaps only its unnatural forms. High to his left Charlie saw a ragged V of Canadian geese. They appeared to be flying north. His impulse was to urge them to correct themselves, to tidy up their pattern. Then he grinned at himself and started the Volkswagen.

Several cars were parked in front of Stitt's run-down Cape Cod when Charlie arrived. As he got out of the Volkswagen, two men walked up the driveway to meet him. One was the young man he had spoken to the other day. The other was older: a short, fat man wearing a Yankees baseball cap. As a Red Sox fan, Charlie felt an irrational wave of antipathy. From the circus tent, there again came the blare of a Strauss waltz played by a brass band. A black Saab was parked near the tent.

"What's on your mind?" asked the young man. He wore jeans, a brown sweat shirt and a jean jacket. On the front of the sweat shirt was a picture of a tyrannosaur.

"I wanted to ask some questions about your boss, Willis Stitt."

The fat man stuck his hands in his back pocket and stared up at Charlie. "We already spent a long time talking to the cops. Who are you?"

Charlie gave the man one of his cards. "I'd like to know who Stitt's friends were."

"We were his friends," said the fat man.

"Nah, Freddie," said his companion, "this is Charlie Bradshaw, he's the one who blew the whistle on McClatchy. Seems to me, Mr. Bradshaw, that if you'd stayed out of this, Willis would still be alive." In the corral a gray horse whinnied, then reared up and began pawing the air.

"I came here the other day to ask about McClatchy. I had nothing to do with his death, any death." Charlie wondered if either of these men could have been the figure outside the window at the Roosevelt Baths.

"Who're you working for?" asked the young man. He picked up a couple of pebbles from the driveway and began rattling them in his palm.

"A friend of Rodger Pease's."

"And who's that?"

"He got blown up in his house last week. Don't you remember him? He's the one who got paid to cash in the winning tickets on Sweet Dreams."

The young man stared at Charlie, then tossed the pebbles into the grass. "Like my friend said, we already told the cops all we know. You want to hear about it, then go to them. As far as I can see, you've been causing a lot of trouble. I didn't care two cents about McClatchy but if he was staying with you and you ratted on him, well, I don't like that. Then you came out here to see Willis and he got killed. I don't like that either. Now you're talking about some guy who got blown up in his house. Seems to me that you carry around a lot of bad luck. I don't like bad luck so why don't you get lost."

Charlie straightened the sling supporting his arm. It was light blue and he thought of how he would have to wear it for several weeks. "You mind if I talk to the person in the tent?" he asked.

"You mean Artemis? Why?"

"Maybe I like circus music."

"Look, buddy," said the fat man, "just beat it, okay?"

"I want to talk to Artemis," Charlie insisted. He had no idea who Artemis was. Presumably it was a woman's name and the worst she could do was to ask him to leave. On the other hand, maybe she could tell him a little about Stitt.

The young man glanced over at the tent, then looked back at Charlie. "Sure, talk to Artemis," he said. "You deserve each other. But when you're done, then get out. I don't want you hanging around."

Charlie walked toward the circus tent. Its precise green and white panels rippled in the wind. As he got closer, he heard the sound of horse's hooves galloping along in time to the music. Charlie passed through the opening of the tent, then immediately leaped out of the way as a huge, pinkish horse thundered by him.

Stumbling forward, he fell, then sat in the dirt and watched the horse continue its leisurely gallop around the tent. Standing on the horse's back was a small slender woman in a black leotard. She was staring at him. Her arms were folded, her feet were slightly apart and it seemed to Charlie she could have been standing on any street corner. She had what he thought of as finely chiseled features: a long, narrow nose; flat cheekbones; a high, clear brow. Her hair was the color of dark leather and fell in a wave across her forehead.

As the horse again bore down upon him, Charlie jumped to his feet and hurried into the center of the ring. The woman slowly bent over backward until both hands touched the horse's withers so that she was bent like a croquet hoop. Then she kicked up her feet and stood on her hands.

"You nearly bumped into Phillip," she said.

"Phillip?"

"This is Phillip." The woman patted the horse's rump, then somersaulted onto her feet again.

"Phillip nearly bumped into me," said Charlie. "Are you Artemis?" Charlie stood in the center of the ring, turning slowly in a circle, as the pink horse galloped around the tent. It was a big, thick, rectangular horse like a large loaf of bread with legs. Charlie considered how close Phillip had come to trampling him.

"Yes, I'm Artemis, although on the Continent I'm known as Lucette Bonchance. Have you come to book me?"

"Book?" asked Charlie, for whom the word meant to charge with a criminal offense.

"To offer me employment as an equestrienne."

"I don't think I need one," said Charlie.

Artemis did another somersault so that she was again balancing on her hands on the horse's back. "Regrettably, I hear that more and more often," she said.

Charlie wasn't sure what they were talking about. He decided to abandon that line of conversation and try another. "I'm here because I wanted to ask you some questions about Willis Stitt."

Artemis flipped herself over onto her feet and again crossed her arms. She was so slender that Charlie guessed he could count her ribs. She fixed her eyes on him, widening them slightly, then said, "Poor Willis never had this much attention when he was alive. It's a pity he couldn't be brought back for an hour to enjoy it. I'm sorry I can't offer you a place to sit. Perhaps you would like to sit up here with me."

"No, thanks," said Charlie. The tent was empty except for a large blue and red ball, half a dozen red Indian clubs and a small cassette recorder that was still playing the Strauss waltzes. "Did you know Stitt very well?" he asked.

"We had a brief affair some years ago but I grew bored with it. Willis had no sense of humor, no depth of character, and he snored. Therefore my contact with him became limited to my use of his stable, although occasionally we would go out to dinner. I'm only in the States two or three months each year. My actual home is in Vienna, although I also have a small house in Bennington. Too small for dear Phillip." As she talked, Artemis did a series of stationary cartwheels. The horse moved along as smoothly as a locomotive.

"The police were here to ask about Willis. Are you connected with them? I must say they were a trifle rude. The man in charge actually had the nerve to ask me to get down from my horse. I never get down from Phillip—well, hardly ever. When I'm in the States, we're inseparable. Poor Phillip has passed the age where he feels comfortable with circus life. The smell of the crowd upsets him. Whenever you pass through Vienna," said Artemis, "you must come and see me perform."

She kept widening her eyes and raising her eyebrows so that her face was constantly busy. It seemed to Charlie that he could almost see her think and it reminded him of a clear plastic model he had once seen of an internal combustion engine.

"I'd like to come to Vienna," he said, "but I'm not connected to the police. I'm a private detective."

"How romantic," said Artemis. "Is that where you received all your injuries?"

Charlie touched the pink bandage on his forehead. "I suppose so," he said.

"Are they a sign that you're winning or losing, or are you just very earnest?" As she had been talking, the waltz came to an end. Artemis gestured toward the cassette player. "Would you mind flipping that over? Phillip hates silence. My sense of private detectives derives strictly from low reading. Aren't you supposed to smoke a cigar?"

"They give me stomachaches," said Charlie as he turned over the cassette. "So you were still friends with Stitt?"

"After a fashion. I had come to regard Willis as a little brother: the sort of little brother that one loves and regrets, embarrassed to find him making mud pies. Poor Willis was always putting his hands in dirty places."

Charlie continued to turn slowly, following Phillip in his stately gallop around the ring. It made him dizzy. He found Artemis beautiful and compact, entirely without excess. Although he guessed that what she was doing was dangerous, his main impression was one of grace. Her features were sharp, almost strict, but she had a nice humanizing smile. Charlie imagined it charming the Viennese crowds. He expected that beneath her calm, she was something of a fanatic: the kind of person who in another life would have been a martyr or poet. He wondered if she ate and slept on Phillip's back. He imagined sandwiches and pizzas being delivered to the circus tent. Probably Artemis didn't eat pizzas. Probably she only ate croissants.

"Tell me more about Stitt," asked Charlie.

Artemis was standing on her hands again, then she arched her back and slowly raised her left arm so that she was balancing on just the right. "When they throw me roses," she said, "this is how I catch them." She lowered her legs, bending herself into another croquet hoop. "I was very fond of Willis but he was a man too easily satisfied with the second rate. He had no sense of personal dignity. You know how water seeks its lowest level? That's what Willis was like. He would often put on great airs, discuss art and literature, but basically he had no ideas that were not borrowed. His appeal was in a certain childlike quality. Often he reminded me of a boy about five."

"Could he fix races?"

"Do you mean cheat or repair?"

"Cheat."

"Certainly, if he could be sure not to be caught."

"Could he commit murder?"

"No, he had no passions or convictions. Essentially, there was nothing mean about him, nothing sadistic, and although he could be cruel, it was only out of selfishness or fear. Was he involved in a murder?" Artemis was now sitting cross-legged on Phillip's back with her elbows on her knees and her chin in her hands.

"I don't know," said Charlie. "He had employed a jockey by the name of Jimmy McClatchy and I think he paid McClatchy to hold back a horse. This McClatchy was murdered in my house about a week ago."

"I have always felt," said Artemis, "that if one hangs around with dubious types, then dubious things will happen to one.

Do you think Willis killed this McClatchy? I can't believe he would."

"No, he didn't, but I think he knew who did and that's what got him killed. Another man was murdered as well, a ten-percenter by the name of Rodger Pease." Charlie went on to explain about McClatchy and the Brooklyn grand jury, what he had learned about Pease and Sweet Dreams, and how he had found Stitt dying in the Roosevelt Baths and had been shot at himself.

You seem to have been having an exciting time," said Artemis. "The only one with whom I am personally acquainted is Sweet Dreams, who occupies the stall next to dear Phillip. A handsome horse but with little to say for himself."

"Is he lame?" asked Charlie.

"Not so one would notice."

"Do you know who Stitt's friends were?"

"Some. Occasionally Willis would take me to parties if I promised to behave. There was Ralph Conrad. I believe he was a businessman in New York. Then there was a doctor by the name of Jespersen, or perhaps he was a veterinarian. And Paul or Peter Reinhardt. He built houses. Let me see, there was a lawyer by the name of Leakey and another horse owner by the name of Perez."

Charlie wrote them down. The only name he recognized was Leakey but he wasn't sure where he had heard it. "Any others?" he asked.

"Yes, I expect there were quite a few. Willis trained horses for about half a dozen people and rented stable space to some others. He was a man who wanted to be liked. That seems such a simple desire, don't you think? Personally, I would rather be envied for something no one else could do."

Charlie thought about that for a moment. He wasn't sure he understood it. "Why does that young man outside dislike you?" he asked.

"He thinks it is my duty to go to bed with him, and I encouraged dear Phillip to run him down. Fortunately, the young man hopped out of the way. I've never cared for unmerited vanity. That was another of Willis's shortcomings. He believed that certain things were owed him simply because he was Willis Stitt."

They talked for a little longer about what Stitt did and who he knew, and at the end of it Charlie asked her to call him if she remembered any more names. He took out one of his cards and held it up for her as she rode by. Artemis did a backward flip, neatly picked the card from Charlie's fingers and tucked it down the front of her leotard.

As Charlie drove back to Saratoga, he thought that under different circumstances he could have easily developed a crush on Artemis. The results would have been disastrous. It would have been like a little pink pig becoming infatuated with a dove.

9

▼▼▼

"I KEEP TELLING YOU," said Victor, "how do I know this joker was disguising his voice unless I know what his voice sounded like in the first place? Maybe he was born hoarse."

"You said he was disguising his voice," said Charlie.

"I said he might have been. Anyway, maybe it was Stitt who called after all. Maybe he wanted to talk to you in private, then got himself killed first. Who's to say?"

"But if it was someone disguising his voice," said Charlie as patiently as possible, "the reason would seem to be that he was afraid you might recognize his real voice, which would imply that person is a person you know or at least have talked to." Charlie leaned back in his chair and looked at Victor in what he hoped was a kindly manner. It was late Sunday afternoon. Charlie had returned from seeing Artemis half an hour before and had found Victor in the office. On top of the file cabinet was a stuffed parrot, which had not been there yesterday. Charlie was certain that Victor was waiting for him to ask where the parrot had come from but he refused to rise to the bait.

Victor locked his hands behind his head and eyed Charlie with displeasure. "For Pete's sake, Charlie, you don't have to talk to me like I was a moron. Either it was Stitt or somebody else. If it was somebody else, then that person might or might not have been disguising his voice. If he was disguising his voice, then either he was somebody I know and was afraid I'd recognize his real voice, or he was a lunatic. Personally, I think he was a lunatic but, hey, flip a coin and I'll go with the crowd."

"So it could have been Leakey since he's someone you've talked to before."

It had turned out that Roy Leakey, the lawyer named by Artemis, was the same lawyer whom Victor had been bothering about some old love letters and who had punched Victor for poking through his desk.

"If Leakey turns out to be the murderer," said Victor, "nobody will be happier than me. I'll even write to my Congressman and ask him to bring back the chair. But if it was Leakey who called, then I didn't recognize his voice."

"But if he was disguising it," suggested Charlie, "then how could you recognize it?"

Victor threw up his hands and slapped them down on the desk. "You got me. I've fallen prey to your spider logic once again. Okay, so it might have been Leakey, but I've also talked to Marotta. So maybe it was him that called."

"Fine," said Charlie, "but the point is you never talked to the others. You never talked to this Ralph Conrad or Reinhardt or Jespersen or Perez . . ."

"Hold it," said Victor.

"What?"

"I talked to Jespersen."

"How come?"

"He's Moshe's vet. Jesus, Charlie, don't you remember anything? Remember I said his old lady wanted me to get some dirt on him and I said I couldn't. I mean, a good vet is more important than a client."

"What did she want you to do?"

"We never got that far, but I think she wanted me to dig

around and see how much money he has. I figured she suspected she was getting stiffed out of a little alimony. I sympathized but my hands were tied."

"Well," said Charlie, "I'll talk to Leakey, Marotta and Jespersen tomorrow. I've got a dentist's appointment in the afternoon but I might be able to see them first. After that we'll decide about those others. By the way, I talked to Eddie Gillespie this morning and told him to keep following Marotta."

"What for? We used up all his old lady's bread. Who's paying for it?"

"We will. There's a chance he had lunch with me in order to keep me away from my house, so if he's guilty, then maybe we can startle him into doing something drastic."

"No freebee tail jobs, Charlie. How we supposed to make an honest buck? Anyway, if he really killed three people, then it seems a little iffy to try and make him mad."

"Eddie won't be doing it for long." Charlie decided not to mention that he had hired Eddie Gillespie to deliver milk as well. He glanced again at the parrot on the file cabinet. It had blue and red feathers and looked as if something had been chewing on its tail. Maybe it was a cockatoo. He imagined asking Victor about it and then being hit with some punch line. Charlie disliked being the butt of Victor's practical jokes.

"I also have some good news," said Charlie. "We now have a client for the McClatchy stuff. She's a friend of Rodger Pease's and she's hired us to investigate his death. Put this in the safe, will you?" He handed Victor the check he had gotten from Flo Abernathy.

Victor looked at it. "Five fucking dollars. Is this what you call good news?"

"It might keep us out of jail."

"Hey, Charlie, if it comes to a showdown between working for five dollars or going to jail, I'd rather go to jail."

The next morning Charlie was roused at eight o'clock by a night letter from his mother. She was on a winning streak and wouldn't arrive until Wednesday. She asked if he knew anyplace in Saratoga where she could buy a roulette wheel. Charlie didn't. He thought of her cutting a swath through Atlantic City: a sixty-six-year-old lady with $40,000 looking for trouble. She sent Charlie her best and asked him to touch rabbit fur.

Charlie wandered into the bathroom and looked at himself in the mirror. The pink bandage was turning gray. Carefully, he peeled it off. Underneath, the skin was shiny red and developing a scab about two inches across. It looked like he had had a third eye which he had chosen to have surgically removed. He decided not to replace the bandage. Both his forehead and arm would keep him from swimming for at least two weeks. The arm had settled down to a dull ache and what Charlie minded most was the nuisance of the sling.

Charlie went into the kitchen and made himself some coffee and two pieces of toast with apricot jam. The previous evening he had taken Doris over to Skidmore College to see a double feature with Fred Astaire and Ginger Rogers. He had found the movies very restful. Nobody had been hurt. Nobody had died. During the 1940s, Charlie had seen a movie every week. Maybe five hundred movies and at least a quarter had been musical comedies. Even before wanting to be a third baseman, Charlie had wanted to be a tap dancer. Sometimes he still found himself in that musical-comedy world, as if his expectations about life had been shaped by Judy Garland, Gene Kelly and Ray Bolger. It meant believing that bills would be paid, that pretty girls would love you back, that the guns would be loaded with blanks.

Charlie took his toast and cup of coffee and walked out to the end of the dock that extended about ten feet into the lake. The water sloshed peacefully at the wooden pilings. Although cool, it was another sunny morning. A little mist rose off the water and obscured the far end of the lake near Kaydeross Park. Some mornings Charlie could see herons. He saw none today. The lake was ringed with trees at the height of color, but already a border of brown leaves littered the shore.

Charlie shivered and went back inside. He worried that Eddie Gillespie wouldn't make much of a milkman. Better get dressed and find Roy Leakey so that he wouldn't be wasting the morning. His dentist's appointment was at three and would probably take the rest of the afternoon. Then, tomorrow morning at nine, was Rodger Pease's funeral.

His meager bank account worried him, and Charlie was afraid he would have to take a mortgage on the cottage. With any luck, the Pinkertons would offer him a job, but even as he thought it, Charlie hoped they wouldn't.

After the Pinkertons had blown up the house of Jesse James's mother in Clay County, Missouri, Jesse had gone to Chicago to get revenge. Later he said he had trailed Allen Pinkerton, head of the agency, for four months, intending to shoot him. Then he gave it up and went home.

"I wanted him to know who did it," Jesse said. "It wouldn't do me no good if I couldn't tell him about it before he died. I had a dozen chances to kill him when he didn't know it. I wanted to give him a fair chance but the opportunity never came."

Roy Leakey's law office was on the second floor of a building directly behind the Adirondack Trust and across from the post office. The walls of the waiting room were walnut paneled and hung with pictures of racehorses and ballet dancers. Charlie had plenty of time to study them in the forty-five minutes he waited. Even though Victor had described Leakey as "a mean son-of-a-bitch," all Charlie knew was that he was a lawyer who had some love letters sent to him by a woman who had hired Victor to get them back.

Shortly after ten, Leakey opened the door to the waiting room and stood glaring at Charlie. He was a slender, muscular man of about thirty-five with short dark hair and a dark, tanned face. He wore a rust-colored suit that looked expensive, and he had light gray eyes that Charlie thought of as cold. At least they were looking coldly at him at that particular moment.

Leakey cocked a finger and pointed it in Charlie's direction. "I want you to tell your bozo friend that if he doesn't stop bothering me, I'm going to get an injunction and slap his ass in jail. Is that clear?"

Charlie had been sitting in a chair by the window reading

Sports Illustrated. Slowly, he got to his feet. "Do you mean Victor?" he asked.

"I mean that fat, frog-faced guy I caught rifling my desk."

Charlie glanced at the young secretary, who was reading a movie magazine. She didn't seem to notice her employer. Perhaps he was often like this.

"I'm not here on Victor's business," said Charlie. "I wanted to ask you some questions about Willis Stitt." He wondered again if Leakey could have been the figure outside the window at the Roosevelt Baths.

"Stitt?"

"Yes, I found him right after he'd been shot."

"You're *that* Charlie Bradshaw?"

Charlie wondered how many Charlie Bradshaws Leakey expected to find in Saratoga.

"You must be even more of a crook than your asshole friend," said Leakey.

The secretary continued to read her magazine. It seemed to Charlie that her refusal to look up was a commendable form of patience. He turned back to Leakey. "Have the police talked to you about Stitt?" he asked.

"No, why should they?"

"You knew him, he was a friend of yours. Now he's been murdered. Were you involved in any track business with Stitt? Looks like you like racehorses." Charlie nodded toward a photograph on the wall showing a horse and jockey in the winner's circle.

Leakey took a few steps into the waiting room and stood by the desk. His hands hung loosely at his sides as if he didn't know what to do with them. "Bradshaw, I don't want you here. If the police want to question me, that's fine, but you, you're nobody, nobody at all. And for your information, I wasn't a close friend of Stitt's. I did some tax work for him and maybe we had dinner a couple of times."

It didn't seem to Charlie that Artemis would have mentioned Leakey's name if he was only a slight acquaintance. "What about Sweet Dreams?" asked Charlie. "Weren't you involved with Stitt over a horse named Sweet Dreams?"

"Never heard of him," said Leakey. "Or maybe I heard something, I don't remember. Stitt was always talking about horses. In any case, I wasn't 'involved' with him as you call it."

"I guess I've been told different," said Charlie. "Stitt and McClatchy were involved in racing Sweet Dreams and holding him back. They won twice at pretty hefty odds. An old ten-percenter by the name of Rodger Pease cashed in their tickets. Now all three are dead. I think there was a silent partner mixed up in this, someone who had a lot to lose if McClatchy mentioned his name to the grand jury."

"What would he have to lose?" asked Leakey. He had moved a few feet closer to Charlie and stood with his thumbs tucked under his belt.

"He could be disbarred for one thing."

Even as he said it, Charlie knew he had gone too far. He had been irritated with Leakey and wanted to give him a little verbal poke. Leakey immediately lunged at him, spinning him around and pushing him up against the wall.

"That's slander, Bradshaw." Leakey's mouth was about an inch from Charlie's ear. "If you ever come back here again, I'll throw you down the stairs. I hate little toads like you."

Using his bad arm, Charlie shoved himself away from the wall with enough force to send them both staggering across the office. He tried to pull his arm free of its sling but only managed to get it more entangled. He kicked backward at Leakey's shin. The secretary had stood up and was watching them impassively. When Leakey crashed against the opposite wall, Charlie was able to break free. He spun around and swung a fist at Leakey, who blocked it easily and gave him a little push toward the door.

"Get out of here, Bradshaw. I'm not going to fight a cripple."

Without glancing at Leakey, Charlie pulled open the door and went down the stairs, leaving the door open behind him. When he reached the bottom, he heard the door slam. The yellow Volkswagen was parked behind the post office. Charlie was breathing heavily and trying to make himself relax to the point where he no longer hated Leakey, where he could tell himself he was just doing a job. He got into the car and started it up. The Volkswagen needed a new muffler and roared. When he had sold the car to Victor, it had been on the condition that Victor would take care of it. But not only did it need a new muffler, the tires and the emergency brake were shot. There was also a funny clicking noise in the engine that didn't sound right. Victor was simply wrecking the car and Charlie meant to tell him when he picked up his Renault and returned the Volkswagen later that afternoon. Then Charlie stopped himself. The car didn't matter. Leakey didn't matter either. It was October, the leaves were beautiful and on Thursday he had been invited to have dinner with Doris in her apartment and who knew what might happen.

David Jespersen's office was on Clark Street near Five Points, an intersection on the south side of Saratoga where five streets came together. The building was a long, brick ranch house with white shutters and a chain-link fence in the back. Charlie heard dogs barking, the kind of barking that dogs at vets make when they think they recognize the sound of their masters' cars: I'm here, I'm here! A U-shaped driveway led up to the front door.

Charlie gave his card to the receptionist in the waiting room, then took a seat. His arm hurt and he hoped he hadn't broken open the wound by tussling with Leakey. Across from Charlie a middle-aged woman was rocking a small Boston terrier and whispering to it soothingly. Now and then the dog would lift its head and lick her nose. Next to her sat another woman with a cat-carrying case between her feet. From inside the case came the sound of mewing. Charlie felt his nose beginning to run. The walls were covered with pictures of dogs, cats, horses and health tips for keeping your pet happy. Above the receptionist's desk were Jespersen's credentials and diploma from Cornell.

After about ten minutes, Charlie was shown into Jespersen's office: a comfortable room with bookcases and soft leather chairs. Jespersen had been sitting at a desk and stood up to greet him. He was a tall, slender man with a long face and a small, round chin like half a golf ball. His sandy blond hair was turning gray. He wore glasses with gold wire frames, which Charlie thought made him look grandfatherly. On the wall behind the desk were several pictures of men practicing karate in what appeared to be white pajamas. One of the men, photographed in the act of crashing the edge of his hand down on another man's shoulder, was Jespersen.

"I don't have much time, Mr. Bradshaw, perhaps you could tell me the nature of your visit."

His voice was cool but cordial. In the background, Charlie still heard dogs barking. He sniffed, then sneezed. Taking a tissue from a box on the desk, he blew his nose. "Allergy," he said. Jespersen waited.

"I'm the one who discovered Willis Stitt's body over at the Roosevelt Baths," said Charlie, "and I'm trying to find out some additional information about him."

"Are you working with the police?"

"In conjunction with them, yes. You were friends with Stitt?"

Jespersen crossed his arms and sat down on the corner of his desk. He wore a white laboratory coat, and sticking up from his breast pocket were about a dozen pens. "I took care of his horses, had dinner with him several times and perhaps invited him to a party or two. Did you know him?"

"I met him only briefly."

"He was a difficult man to be friends with, primarily because he wanted to be friends so badly. When he talked to you, it seemed his interest was caused more by his great need to be liked than by any true feeling. Unfortunately, this created a sort of barrier. I liked him, felt sorry for him, but he was really no more than a good acquaintance."

"What's the difference between an acquaintance and a friend?" asked Charlie.

"Let's put it this way," said Jespersen. "I would never have confided in Willis Stitt. When we were together, most of the time was spent discussing his concerns. In a true friendship, there must be more of a balance."

"Did you know Jimmy McClatchy?"

"The jockey? I've seen him ride, of course, but I never met him. Once or twice I saw him with Willis."

"What about Rodger Pease?"

"I don't recognize the name." Jespersen took a pack of Kents from under his laboratory coat, shook out a cigarette and lit it with a large brass lighter in the shape of a Model-T Ford. Instead of setting the lighter back on the desk, he glanced down at the flame, then ran it back and forth under his fingers very briefly before snuffing it out with his thumb.

"He was a tall, bulky-looking, balding man of about seventy-five. He hung around the track a lot."

"No, it doesn't ring any bells. Was he a friend of Willis's?"

"I believe they were business associates," said Charlie.

"Willis led a complicated life," said Jespersen. "He knew a lot of people, was involved in a lot of deals. Because of the horses, I saw him fairly often, but I never had the sense that I knew him."

"You think he could have held back horses in a race?"

"If he did, I knew nothing about it."

"Have you had any thoughts about his death?" Charlie looked again at the photographs of Jespersen practicing karate, and wondered why the veterinarian had chosen to hang them in his office.

"You mean who killed him? The newspaper suggested that his death was connected with McClatchy's death, whose death, according to the newspaper, was related to racketeering and race fixing. There was also some talk about organized crime. For all of Willis's desire to be liked, he was essentially a very private man. He could easily have known racketeers without my knowing about it. I was surprised, of course, but it didn't seem wholly improbable."

"What about the horse, Sweet Dreams? What can you tell me about him?"

"What's there to tell? He's a healthy four-year-old that broke the pastern joint of his right foreleg in his stall. A not-uncommon injury."

"How come Stitt was using him for stud if he was a mediocre horse?"

"He had a little speed. I gather his main problem was a nervousness in the gate. In any case, there're many racetracks in this country, Mr. Bradshaw. Sweet Dreams's progeny would be handsome, strong and fast enough to win at a few state fairs. Any more questions? I believe I have patients waiting."

"Do you know Victor Plotz?"

Jespersen shook his head, then pushed his glasses up onto his nose with his left forefinger. "I don't recognize the name," he said.

"He's a big man in his late fifties. He brings his cat to you. A one-eyed cat named Moshe. He works for me."

Jespersen laughed. The sound reminded Charlie of paper being crinkled. "I remember the cat. I even remember the man. Something of a joker, isn't he? I had no idea he worked for you. He spent a lot of time trying to convince my receptionist to go out with him. She finally had to ask me to intervene."

"That's Victor," said Charlie.

10
▼▼▼

PEERING INTO THE MIRROR, Victor Plotz leaned over his bathroom sink and placed a round Band-Aid in the center of his right cheek. It covered a small cut—the last of several needing bandages—which he had received when Pease's house had blown up a week earlier. Victor then turned his attention to the bruise under his left eye where Leakey had punched him. He touched it gently. It was still tender but the purple was fading.

Victor liked his face. It reminded him of potato sculptures he had made years ago in grade school. All the individual features were oversized: lips, nose, ears, mouth, baggy eyes. Even his pores were deep and cavernous. Consequently, he regretted this sudden collection of cuts and bruises, and their presence made him doubt the wisdom of his recent choices. After all, there were only so many bruises a single face could tolerate without a drop in aesthetic appeal. It seemed that his first loyalty was to his own appearance, and that being the case, then maybe he should stay in bed.

Victor felt torn. As a matter of professional pride, he thought he ought to put enough pressure on Roy Leakey to persuade him to return those love letters. On the other hand, Leakey had already punched him once and, if he had actually killed three men, there seemed no limit to the damage he could inflict. Perhaps he should forget about Leakey and buzz over to the Pyramid Mall and stake out the suspicious salesclerk. That, however, was dreary work. He stood and stared at the salesclerk; the salesclerk stood and stared at him. After eight hours, Victor would have nothing to show for it but sore feet.

It was nine o'clock Tuesday morning and, glancing out the window, Victor decided it was going to rain. He went to the closet, took out a rather dirty tan raincoat, then headed for the door. Victor had a third-floor apartment in the Algonquin, an ornate redstone building on Broadway in downtown Saratoga. He hurried down the stairs and by the time he reached the sidewalk, he had decided to see Leakey one more time. First, however, he would visit his client. Her name was Ruth MacDermott and every time Victor saw her, he became short of breath. She was a tall woman with a mass of red hair and great long legs. Maybe she was forty. Her best feature, Victor was convinced, was a large bosom and a fondness for low-cut dresses that exposed milky-smooth breasts dotted with a few freckles.

The yellow Volkswagen was parked around the corner on Grove Street. Victor had retrieved it from Charlie the previous evening and had spent an inordinate amount of time listening to how he should treat it better. Charlie had been in a bad mood, having just spent two hours at the dentist.

Grove Street was a steep hill that dead-ended at Maple, the next street. The Volkswagen was the only car on the block, and pointed downhill. It was a tidy car, Victor thought, and he had agreed with Charlie that he should give it special attention.

The sky was dark gray and the wind was tugging leaves from the trees. It was a dreary morning and Victor was glad he hadn't gone with Charlie to Rodger Pease's funeral. As he reached the Volkswagen, Victor happened to notice that his right shoe was untied. Pausing, he put his foot up on the back bumper. Victor was wearing blue basketball shoes with high tops. He tied the shoe, then, as he straightened up again, he saw that the Volkswagen had begun to roll forward.

"Hey," he shouted.

The Volkswagen rolled into the middle of Grove Street and began coasting down the hill. Running after it, Victor managed to grab the back bumper. For a moment it seemed he might be able to stop the car, but then he was pulled forward onto his knees and forced to let go. He jumped to his feet and began to run. He never bothered to lock the Volkswagen and he thought if he could just reach the door, then perhaps he could jump inside.

"Stop!" shouted Victor.

There was no one else on the street. For a few seconds, Victor gained on the Volkswagen, but then it picked up speed and steadily drew away from him. Victor was running as fast as he could down the center of the street, with the tails of his raincoat flapping behind him. He disliked running, disliked all forms of physical exercise, and he began to worry about how he would stop. Beyond the intersection at Maple was a vacant lot and the car rushed toward it.

"Watch out!" shouted Victor.

The Volkswagen rushed across the intersection, hit the curb, bounced, rose in the air and then, inexplicably, continued to rise as a great orange ball of flame erupted from underneath its front end. Immediately, the car began to fly apart as the orange flame swept over it. Both doors sailed off. Bumpers, tires, fenders and hundreds of unidentifiable parts separated from the flaming mass of the body and rose up in high arcs above the vacant lot.

Victor, still running, forgot he was running, until he collided with the force and noise of the explosion, which stood like an invisible wall across the street. He smashed against it and was hurled back into the gutter. Landing on his side, he rolled head over heels across the pavement, as dirt and chunks of debris pelted down upon him. Then, for a moment, he lay still, making a silent inventory of all his moving parts. The wind had been knocked out of him, his face had scraped against the pavement and there were dozens of small pains that might become serious. He was about to try to get to his feet when his attention was distracted by the squeal of brakes.

Lifting his head, Victor saw a large blue car at the bottom of the hill fishtailing toward the burning back half of the Volkswagen. As the blue car swung to the left, its right rear fender smashed against the wreckage. Then it bounced over the curb, ran down a stop sign and came to a halt halfway across Grove Street about ten feet from where Victor lay sprawled. Victor realized it was a police car. Then he saw Chief Peterson climb from the front. Victor put his head back down on the pavement. He didn't feel ready to talk to policemen. The remnants of the Volkswagen were burning fiercely, sending a great cloud of black smoke into the gray sky.

Victor squinted through half-closed lids and saw Peterson hurrying toward him. At first he thought the police chief intended to help him. Then Peterson began to shout.

"You crazy fool, you nearly killed me!"

Victor dragged himself to his feet. His raincoat was ripped up the back to the collar. His hands and wrists were scraped from where he had hit the pavement. Bits of gravel were embedded in the cuts on his face. There was a tear in his trousers, and blood was coming from a cut on his left leg. His anger, however, temporarily allowed him to forget his bruises.

"Why should I waste a perfectly good car on an asshole like you?" he said.

Peterson stopped a few feet away and stood breathing heavily. His moment of terror had left him looking rumpled, as if his blue suit was too large or he had slept in his clothes. "Then why did it nearly hit me?" he said.

"That's kismet, bad karma, tough luck. How should I know? But you only got a dented fender and I lost my whole fuckin' car. If you had any decency, you'd stop your paranoid blowin' and call an ambulance. Then you'd find the homicidal lunatic who tried to kill me."

*   *   *

Victor had a hatred of hospitals dating from those last years that his wife had been sick. He hated the smells, the hushed voices, the urgent requests for doctors over the PA system. On the other hand, he liked the nurses. He liked teasing them about their starched white dresses to get them going, as he called it. But this morning, he felt so shaken by the narrowness of his escape that he didn't even try to get any telephone numbers.

Thirty minutes after Victor's arrival by ambulance, Chief Peterson appeared and began badgering him about the explosion. It turned out that some sort of device had been attached to the underside of the car. Peterson insisted that Victor must know who had put it there.

"I'm a man with a million friends," said Victor. "Wherever I go, I set little children's hearts a-singing. Believe me, if I knew who blew up my car, I'd be happy to tell you."

"But it must be connected to something you're working on."

"That seems like a safe bet. I been watching a clerk over at the Pyramid Mall who snitches ties. Maybe it was him."

Peterson and Victor were in a small room attached to the emergency ward of Saratoga Hospital. A young blond nurse was putting a bandage on Victor's forehead. Her starched bosom was so close to his face that it made his teeth ache. Peterson stood by the door.

"I don't want to joke with you, Plotz. Was it connected to something Charlie's doing?"

Victor glanced down at the bandages on his wrists and another on his leg. His left shoulder was sore and his face burned. "Hey, Peterson, I know nothing about it. I walked to the car, it started to roll, then it hit the curb and blew up. That's all I know. Okay, somebody stuck a bomb underneath. Don't bother me with dumb questions, go find him."

"Where's Charlie?"

"He went to Pease's funeral."

But at that moment, the door was pulled open and Charlie hurried into the room. Pushing past Peterson, he went to where Victor was sitting on the edge of the bed. "Are you all right?"

he asked. "I just heard about it. Did the Volkswagen really blow up? Are you okay?"

"I may have some dimples I didn't have when I woke up this morning," said Victor, "but otherwise I'm pretty perky."

"What happened?"

"Like you say, the Volkswagen blew up. Fortunately, I wasn't in it." Charlie wore a brown suit, a narrow brown tie, and Victor thought he looked like a high school teacher.

"Why'd it blow up?"

"Peterson says there was a bomb in it. I don't know, maybe the tires were overinflated."

Charlie turned back to Peterson. "What about you? I heard you cracked up your car."

Peterson rubbed his chin. He seemed unsettled and lacked his normal self-assurance. "I'm okay," he said, "but your friend here nearly killed me."

"Peterson thinks it's a plot," said Victor. "Can you believe it? He thinks I wrecked the Volkswagen just to needle him."

"All right, all right," said Peterson, "I was upset."

It seemed to Charlie that Peterson was still upset, but because of Victor's joking he couldn't determine the seriousness of what had happened. "What about the car," he asked, "can it be fixed?"

"Not unless you're a whiz at putting ten million tiny pieces back together again," said Victor. "At one moment, it was a self-respecting Volkswagen. In the next, it was two thousands pounds of confetti."

"Can't you shut this guy up?" asked Peterson. "I mean, a car explodes right in the middle of Saratoga and all your buddy can do is laugh. It's my job to find out who did it. Am I going to get any cooperation? Charlie, is it something you're working on? Is it Stitt?"

"I don't know," said Charlie. He didn't want to tell anything to Peterson. "Where's Caldwell? Still downstate?"

"Yeah, he's in New York. He's supposed to come back today. Charlie, stop fooling around. Who blew up the car?"

"How should I know? I wasn't even there." Charlie picked up Victor's raincoat. When he saw how it was torn and ripped up the back, he looked at Victor's bandages more closely. After a moment, he turned back to Peterson. "Have you learned anything new about McClatchy and Stitt?"

Peterson seemed unhappy. "You know how these things go, Charlie. We've been talking to a lot of people, collecting a lot of information. Caldwell insists it's tied up with Marotta."

"And you've got your stolen cars."

"You know what the FBI's like. It's Caldwell's show. Are you going to tell me about the Volkswagen?"

The nurse had left. Victor sat on the edge of the bed, holding his head in his hands. When he shut his eyes he could see little flashing lights, like on the screen of a video game.

"I know nothing about it," said Charlie. "But I'm the one who's been driving that car all week, so I guess the bomb was meant for me. Caldwell says I told Marotta about McClatchy, then some racketeers killed McClatchy and cut off his head. Maybe those same racketeers are trying to blow me up."

"You don't believe that," said Peterson.

Charlie undid the top button of his shirt and loosened his tie. "So what? That's what Caldwell will believe and, as you said yourself, it's his show."

"Don't joke with me, Charlie. I mean, I might like to see you move away from Saratoga but I don't want you dead."

Charlie was almost touched. "That's nice of you, Chief, but you know me—I just deliver milk, and Victor here investigates suspicious salesclerks and runaway schoolgirls."

Peterson made a disgruntled noise, then opened the door. "Even when you worked for me, you were a smooth liar. By the way, you're going to be in some trouble about that milk route of yours. I was just coming to find you when that damn car blew up."

"What do you mean?"

Peterson sucked his teeth, then took a pocket watch from his vest pocket and checked its time against the clock on the wall. "The Schuylerville police called me," he said. "Your apprentice milkman was clocked driving his milk truck at 68 miles per hour through downtown Schuylerville at eight o'clock this morning. The chief also said he was drunk and disorderly."

* * *

That Eddie Gillespie might not make a top-notch milkman, Charlie had expected. Still, he hoped for a few days relief from the milk truck and, who knows, perhaps during that time, Wanamaker's mother would die and Charlie could lay down this particular burden forever. These hopes had proved ill-founded.

By eleven o'clock Tuesday morning, Charlie and Victor were driving in the Renault over to Schuylerville. It was drizzling slightly and Charlie wished he could check into a motel and sleep for a week.

"You know," said Charlie, "I'd like to turn this car around and drive all the way to Key Largo. I bet you could get some rest there."

"Forget it," said Victor. "You got to find the fellow who tried to blow me up. What kind of hotshot detective are you anyway?"

Charlie looked over at his friend. Victor had a large bandage on his left cheek and another on his forehead. Charlie's own forehead was still sore and his wounded arm ached and felt stiff. Together they looked like a Band-Aid commercial. As for being a hotshot detective, Charlie wondered if he shouldn't remain a milkman after all.

"You know what I did last night?" asked Charlie. "I spent some time finding out about Roy Leakey. I learned that he's been a lawyer here for five years, that he passed his bar exam in 1974, that he spent six years in the Army and four of those years in Vietnam as a demolitions expert."

"So you figure he knows about bombs?" said Victor.

"That's right."

"You think he did it?"

"Maybe. On the other hand, maybe it was meant to look like he did it or maybe it was meant to look like Marotta did it."

"Why Marotta?"

"Racketeers are supposed to like bombs. Anyway, Leakey could easily have seen me driving the Volkswagen. And that's also true of Jespersen."

"What're we going to do about another car?" asked Victor.

It began to rain harder. Half the road was covered with brown leaves. Charlie thought of how much he had liked the yellow Volkswagen. "I'll borrow the milk truck," he said.

"Won't you feel foolish driving around Saratoga in a Wholesome Dairy milk truck?"

Charlie grinned. "If whoever is committing these murders thinks he's dealing with idiots, then maybe he'll take more chances."

This didn't please Victor. "Hey, Charlie, your murderer took a pretty big chance in blowing up the Volkswagen. If he starts taking even bigger chances, then I'm going to be spending a fortune on cotton gauze and Mercurochrome. Why rile him up?"

"Because I want to catch him," said Charlie.

Victor yawned, then scratched his scalp. "You know, I've learned several things in this detective business. Like I've learned you can approach a problem like Sherlock Holmes and crush the enemy with superior brain power or you can try using your method."

"And what method is that?" asked Charlie.

"It's like the clown in the carnival that sits up on a perch over a tub of water. He keeps insulting people and making them really mad until they throw the ball at the target and send him splashing into the water. That's what you do, you rile up Leakey or Jespersen or Marotta or whoever until they come after you. But, well, there's only one trouble with that."

"What do you mean?"

"The consequences are a lot more serious than a tub of cold water." Victor glanced out the window at the gray fields, then shifted painfully in his seat. Maybe it was better to watch the crooked salesclerk after all. "So how was the funeral this morning?" he asked.

"Sad."

"Were you and that old lady the only ones?"

"No, there were about a dozen people. All elderly and living in rooms somewhere, all full of stories about Saratoga in the '20s and '30s. Several of them knew Flo Abernathy. You know,

I asked my dentist about her yesterday. She's the daughter of a guy who used to own a big chunk of Glens Falls. She'd been a student at Skidmore in the '30s and then quit. She wanted to be a singer. Her family just wrote her off."

"What happened to her singing?" asked Victor.

Charlie shrugged. "She sang in some local clubs, but I guess she wasn't good enough. Luckily she inherited some money from her mother, but it seems she's been out of contact with her family ever since. There's a brother that's living, also some cousins."

"If she's got money," said Victor, "maybe she can pay us more than five dollars."

"I want to find out who killed Pease for my own reasons," said Charlie. "The money's not important."

"Not me," said Victor, "if I can't do it for money, then let me do it for revenge. I didn't like that car blowing up in my face and if the lunatic who did it turns out to be Leakey, then I'll be one cheerful fella. Did I ever tell you about my happiest moment of revenge?"

"No, but I take it you're going to tell me now," said Charlie. He pulled out to pass a slower car. Victor waited until the Renault was back in the right-hand lane.

"This concerns a girlfriend I once had that some greaser stole away from me," Victor said. "It was a sad time and I was very unhappy but the lady said how she really liked the greaser, and that I should let bygones be bygones and bite the bullet or some shit like that. Well, this was back in the days when I was a young guy selling men's clothing and I was fool enough to say okay.

"But then one night I'm sitting in a local bar and in comes this greaser and he sits down beside me and says, Hey, I feel pretty bad about this myself, but what the hell, love is love. I'd had a couple of drinks and was ready to forgive and forget so, like a dumbo, I say, You know, Agnes—that was the young lady's name—Agnes likes little treats like flowers and candy, and if you're going to steal her from me, then you got to treat her right. And the greaser says, I appreciate you telling me and I'll try to do the proper things. He's very polite. I think he worked for a funeral home or something. Then he says, Is there anything else she likes? And I say, She likes sleeping late on Sunday mornings and she likes a good back rub when she just gets home from work. Wow, says the greaser, I really appreciate your telling me this, what else?

"But then I stop and say to myself, Hold up, what are you doing giving this tub of lard such a load of information? Hasn't he robbed you of your heart's desire? All this time the greaser keeps saying, What else, what else? So I say, You know, our Agnes, she's got some pretty queer tastes. And the greaser, he leans over and says, Ohhh? and I say, Nah, I can't tell you this, it's too intimate. The greaser is leaning over so far that he's practically in my lap. Tell me, he says. And I say, I can't, it was a secret shared between Agnes and me. And the greaser says, You can trust me not to abuse your confidence, or some shit like that. So I say, You know how excited our Agnes can get when it comes down to actual lovemaking? Yeah? says the greaser. Well, I say, I made this little discovery that drove her absolutely crazy with passion. Tell me, begs the greaser.

"But I wasn't ready, so I tell him it's like a sacred pact, a trust, something that had happened during a holy moment and in no time at all he's panting like a dog. Okay, I say, right when we were making love, right when I could tell she was ready, really ready, right when she was trembling like a spring leaf, I reached over to a cup that I was keeping next to the bed and at the last possible moment, I took an ice cube and I slipped it into her ass."

"Jesus, Victor," said Charlie.

"That's right," said Victor, "that's what I told him."

"What happened?"

"Well, two days later I heard this guy was in the hospital with some kind of strain."

"Strain?"

"That's what I said. When he tried that little number with the ice cube, our Agnes leaped sideways about as fast as a cat touched by a hot match. That's what did it. Yanked his root half fuckin' off."

11

▼▼▼

J ESSE JAMES HAD NOT BEEN the only outlaw tormented by the
Pinkertons. They had hounded poor Butch Cassidy over
the entire United States when all he wanted was to settle
down and raise a few cows. Worse, they had forced Cassidy,
along with the Sundance Kid and Etta Place, to flee the country
and try to make a life for themselves in Argentina, where the
government had given them four square leagues in Cholilo,
Province of Chubut, District 16 de Octubre. They bought thirteen hundred sheep, five hundred head of cattle, thirty-five
horses and tried to make a go of it.

But even in Argentina they weren't safe. Two years later, in
March 1903, Pinkerton operative Frank Dimaio arrived in Bue-
nos Aires and began plastering the country with Wanted posters. Cassidy and Sundance were forced to sell their ranch to a
Chilean beef syndicate and start robbing banks, beginning with
el Banco de la Nación in Mercedes where they got $20,000,
but killed the bank manager. Butch was nearly forty. He'd had
only five years of living without fear and constant worry. Once
again, Charlie asked himself, how could he work for the
Pinkertons?

It was Tuesday night and Charlie was trying to pay some
bills and balance his checkbook. If he didn't work for the Pinkertons, then maybe he could get a job as a guard in a supermarket. He couldn't think of anybody famous who had ever
held up a supermarket. On the other hand, considering the
state of his finances, maybe he should just remain a milkman.

Eddie Gillespie was still in jail and Charlie had had to deliver
the milk that Gillespie hadn't bothered to deliver himself. On
Monday it turned out that Gillespie had skipped about half
the houses. He also hadn't emptied the truck and instead of
delivering fresh milk Tuesday morning, he had simply used the
milk left over from the previous day, which had gone sour.

Charlie knew he could get the money to bail Gillespie out of jail, but he didn't feel like it. Maybe tomorrow or the next day.

For much of the evening, Charlie had been trying to call John Wanamaker in Santa Fe, but without success. Somewhat guiltily, he wondered if this was a sign that Wanamaker's mother had died.

Charlie got to his feet and began to gather up his papers. He had been working at the dining-room table and as he stood next to it, he let his finger trace the groove in the wood caused by whatever instrument had cut off McClatchy's head. And where was the head? Why was someone sending photographs of it to the Jockey Guild and various newspapers? Surely that was more interesting than delivering milk or guarding eggs in a supermarket.

It was eleven o'clock. Charlie decided to make himself a cup of peppermint tea with honey, then go to bed. But as he was putting his old checks and bank statements into an envelope, there came a loud knock at the door. This made him jump because he hadn't heard a car. It reminded him of the night that McClatchy had appeared. Again the person knocked. Quickly, Charlie went into the kitchen, opened a drawer full of dish towels and took out a revolver. Then he returned to the living room.

Opening the door, Charlie found a middle-aged man in a gray overcoat and black cap who looked vaguely familiar. He had just been raising his hand to knock again. Charlie held the revolver out of sight against his leg. The man had a big smear of a nose that looked as if lots of people had taken swings at it.

"What's up?" asked Charlie.

"Someone wants to see you," said the man. "I'm the chauffeur."

"What if I don't want to go?" said Charlie.

This seemed to please the chauffeur, who smiled. "Mr. Marotta said I wasn't supposed to take no for an answer."

Charlie considered showing the man his gun, then changed his mind. "Let me get my coat," he said.

Charlie followed the man out to an old black Cadillac parked along the road. The man held open the back door. "I was hoping you'd make trouble," he said. "Jimmy McClatchy was an especial favorite of mine."

"He must have lost you a lot of money," said Charlie, getting into the car.

The chauffeur settled himself in the front seat and started the engine. Then he turned around in Charlie's driveway and headed back toward Saratoga. "I don't mean I ever bet McClatchy to win," said the chauffeur. "It's just that it's good to know who the losers are."

"I never thought of it that way," said Charlie.

"That's the trouble with you punks," said the chauffeur. "You never think."

Marotta's restaurant was five miles west of Saratoga on a country road with several dairy farms. It was a long yellow building and on either side of the front door were two Roman pillars made from a combination of plywood and plaster. The Roman decor was continued inside with more pillars, reproductions of statues like the Discus Thrower and a wall mural of the Coliseum. Red tablecloths covered the tables and bunches of red plastic grapes dangled from the archways. Although the restaurant could have easily seated three hundred people, on this evening it was practically empty. Three waiters in black suits with white napkins over their arms stifled yawns as they watched the color television in the bar, where one cowboy was jumping up and down on another cowboy's hat. The bartender gave Charlie a small wave. Before quitting the police department, Charlie had arrested this man about five times for cashing bad checks.

The chauffeur led Charlie to a table next to the empty dance floor and said that Marotta would be out in a minute. A black piano player in a tuxedo was playing Cole Porter songs.

As Charlie removed his blue jacket, the maître d' approached almost on tiptoe. "Mr. Marotta says you may order whatever you like." The man was dignified and expectant.

"Just a beer, I guess."

"We have fresh oysters."

"That's okay, a beer's fine."

"Domestic or imported?"

"Domestic's okay with me."

As the man disappeared, Charlie wondered if he had turned off the stove before leaving the house. He had been intending to make tea and couldn't remember if he had actually put the kettle on to boil.

Marotta appeared five minutes later. He wore an immaculate gray silk suit with the tip of a red handkerchief poking out of the breast pocket. On the little finger of his left hand was a large gold ring with a blue stone. He nodded to Charlie but didn't offer to shake hands. As he sat down, a waiter brought over a tray with a glass, a small bottle of Saratoga Vichy and a little silver bowl with several wedges of lemon. Marotta poured himself some Vichy and added a few drops of lemon. His fingernails were perfectly groomed and Charlie imagined him spending an hour every day with a beautiful manicurist. Marotta sipped the Vichy.

"I realize," he began, "that Chief Peterson and half of Saratoga believe you told me about Jimmy McClatchy and that this led to his death. I also realize that you and I are the only two people who know for certain that this is not true. We talked, if I remember right, only about my wife and the fact she was paying you to have me followed. I asked you not to discuss the subject with anyone and it seems you haven't. I appreciate that. I also asked you to stop having me followed. This you have failed to do. Although I haven't noticed anyone today, there was a young man sleeping in a car in my parking lot for much of last night."

"He's in jail," said Charlie. He finished his beer and wondered if he should ask for another.

"Jail?"

"That's right, he was pulled over in Schuylerville for doing 68 miles per hour in a milk truck."

Marotta pressed the bump on his nose between his thumb and index finger. He seemed on the verge of asking what Gillespie had been doing in a milk truck. "So he won't be following me?" he asked.

"I don't know about that," said Charlie. "I might bail him

out tomorrow." It seemed that Marotta was frightened and Charlie couldn't imagine why.

"Haven't you run through the money my wife gave you?"

"I'm paying him myself." The maître d' drifted near their table and Charlie signaled to him. "Get me another beer, will you?"

"Why are you paying him to follow me?" asked Marotta. He had started to lift his glass of Vichy and now held it frozen between the table and his mouth.

"We both know I told you nothing about McClatchy," said Charlie. "But there's still the chance you already knew that McClatchy was staying at my place. Maybe somebody told you to keep me occupied while they went out there and cut off his head."

Marotta put down his glass and began to look angry. "You know the trouble I'm in because of that damn lunch with you? I've had the FBI and Peterson out here a dozen times and I've had that dope sleeping in my parking lot. Everybody knows he's working for you and everybody knows that you're investigating these murders. Consequently, they think I'm involved."

He took another sip of Vichy and looked over at the piano player, who had begun to play "Moonlight in Vermont." The maître d' brought Charlie's beer. By now all the other tables were empty.

"Let me tell you my problem," said Marotta. He paused, then leaned slightly over the table. "Over the years I've heard rumors that I am in some way connected with organized crime. This is greatly exaggerated but it's what people like to talk about. Recently, however, people have begun to say that you are having me followed precisely because of this connection. This upsets me. Perhaps I do have a few friends who got in a little trouble a long time ago. One of the main reasons I'm their friend is because I have no bad marks. And maybe I'm useful to them in various ways. They're not going to like my being followed. That punk kid and your friend Victor Plotz have no subtlety. In no time at all my friends will hear about them. I can't afford that. Plotz and that kid could make my friends drop me like a hot brick. If that happens, I lose the restaurant and go broke."

Marotta seemed to expect Charlie to say something, but Charlie drank a little beer instead. He felt foolish for having brought the revolver. Certainly Marotta was more afraid of him than he had been of Marotta.

"Okay, so this afternoon I hear about Plotz's car getting blown up," said Marotta. "People are already saying it's the Mafia and that the reason the car was blown up was because Plotz was messing with me. This could ruin me, Charlie."

Off to the side of the restaurant, Charlie could see five waiters watching them. It occurred to him they were worried about their jobs. "So what do you want?" he asked.

"How much did my wife pay you to have me followed?"

"One thousand."

Marotta took a billfold from his breast pocket, counted out ten one-hundred-dollar bills and tossed them on the red tablecloth.

Charlie looked at the money. "Keep it," he said. "Neither Victor or Eddie Gillespie will bother you, but I don't want the money."

"I want you to have it," said Marotta.

Charlie shook his head. He wished Marotta would put the money back in his pocket. "No, I appreciate the offer but it's not necessary."

Marotta retrieved the money and stuck it in his side pocket. Then he again massaged the bump on his nose. He had dark brown eyes that rarely seemed to move. He looked at Charlie for several moments, as if trying to decide something about him. "For your information," he said at last, "I want to tell you that racketeers or gangsters or whatever you call them were in no way connected with McClatchy's death. Maybe if you told me what you've found out, I could give you some help."

Charlie hesitated. He knew that just because Marotta claimed not to be involved didn't mean it was true. "Do you know a Saratoga lawyer by the name of Roy Leakey?" he asked.

"Not very well. I know he likes horses and women and has

a temper. The one time he was out here he got so drunk I had to ask him to leave."

"What about a veterinarian by the name of David Jespersen?"

Marotta thought a moment. "He also likes horses. A lot of people do in Saratoga. I've heard he's involved with a young woman who owns a boutique downtown. Her name's Kathy Marshall and the store's called something like the Blue Lion."

Charlie knew the store. It was next door to the store owned by his ex-wife and her sister. Since Charlie tried to avoid those two women whenever possible, he rarely walked around on that part of Broadway. "Wasn't Jespersen recently divorced?" asked Charlie.

"About two years ago, I gather. He started up with Kathy Marshall about a year before that. She's got a lot of money from someplace. They got together when he ran for city commissioner."

"I didn't know about that."

"He nearly won and I've heard he wants to run again. Kathy Marshall also likes horses. She's even bought a few. Maybe Jespersen was involved with that since he can't race horses himself."

"What do you mean?"

"It's illegal for vets to own Thoroughbreds and race them at tracks where they do any work. That's a New York State law. It's considered a conflict of interest. Jespersen works for about half a dozen trainers every August. And he does some work at Belmont as well."

"What about a horse named Sweet Dreams?" asked Charlie. "You ever heard of him?"

"Never. Should I have?"

Charlie told Marotta about Sweet Dreams's eleven races, and that McClatchy had ridden him each time. "He was owned by Willis Stitt," said Charlie. "That's the guy who was murdered at the Roosevelt Baths on Saturday."

"I'd met Stitt a couple of times," said Marotta, "but didn't have any sense of him as a person. What kind of breeding does Sweet Dreams have?"

"Not so hot. A mare named Indian Maid and the stallion was Buckdancer. Neither horse ever did anything."

"You have a blood test done?"

"No." It had never occurred to Charlie.

"There's a fair chance that Sweet Dreams was a mediocre horse that McClatchy strangled. On the other hand, maybe he's a ringer. There's been a lot of trouble because of that horse. I'd guess there's more involved than just holding him back. If he was a much better horse than his breeding indicated, then he'd stand a better chance of winning. What's he doing now?"

"They're using him for stud."

Marotta finished his Vichy, then poked at the wedge of lemon with a black swizzle stick with the name MAROTTA printed on it with gold lettering. "If I were you, I'd see about a blood test. Maybe Buckdancer's not the sire after all."

"How would I find out about that?"

"Get the Bureau involved."

"The FBI?"

"No, the Thoroughbred Racing Protective Bureau. It's part of the Thoroughbred Racing Association. They police about sixty tracks. Their offices are in Lake Success near Belmont on Long Island."

12

▼▼▼

CHARLIE HELD THE HANDSET of the telephone a short distance from his head and squinted at it in irritation. "What do you mean you can't investigate without grounds. I'm giving you grounds."

There was a mild belch, then a voice answered, "That's not good enough. You tell me this horse is a ringer and we should take a blood test. We can't just rush in because you say so."

The man on the other end of the line was Lenny Ravitz at the Racing Protective Bureau. Charlie had been arguing with him for about fifteen minutes. It was early Wednesday afternoon and Charlie was in his office. On the other side of the desk, Victor was cutting out a string of paper dolls. Charlie kept staring at them. He'd never seen buxom paper dolls before.

Charlie gripped the handset a little tighter. "Look at the horse's record," he said. "McClatchy was strangling it."

"Maybe he was, but that doesn't prove he's a ringer. Don't you remember Carry Back?"

"Who?"

"Carry Back, by Saggy out of Joppy, a horse with no breeding and no style that won the Derby and the Preakness in 1961. What I'm saying is that blood mostly counts but sometimes it doesn't. Possibly Sweet Dreams is like that: a fluke."

Ravitz had a very slow, raspy voice and Charlie kept losing patience with it. On the file cabinet, the beady black eye of the stuffed parrot seemed to be mocking him. He still hadn't asked Victor where it had come from and didn't plan to.

"You ever hear of Roy Leakey, a Saratoga lawyer?" Charlie asked.

"No, should I?"

"I'm not sure," Charlie said. "Doesn't it mean anything that Stitt was using the horse for stud?"

"Not necessarily. Anyway, we can't go in there without grounds. Look, don't think we don't have a strong interest. If we had a blood sample and checked it against Buckdancer and it turned up wrong, then that would give us the edge to go in and demand an official sample."

"So how would you get a blood sample?"

"That's for you to figure out," said Lenny Ravitz.

"Why do you have a strong interest?"

Ravitz made a snorting noise into the phone. "We've received two snapshots of McClatchy's head. Just the head, by itself, on some kind of table with a hole in the forehead and the eyes a little open and stupid looking."

After Charlie hung up, he sat staring out the window, trying to decide what he should do. Across the street was a dentist's office and Charlie could see some poor fellow sitting in the dentist's chair with his mouth open. It made his jaw ache. His own dentist had found three cavities on Monday afternoon and Charlie's mouth still felt stretched and tampered with.

"So what did he say?" asked Victor, wadding up his chain of paper dolls.

"He wants me to send him a blood sample."

"Let me and the boys do it."

"He wants a sample, not a bucket."

"Charlie," said Victor, "you got to learn to trust me. I've your best interests at heart." Victor stood up and put on his ripped tan raincoat, which had been restitched up the back with black thread. The two bandages on his face and the others on his wrists made him look particularly fragile. His gray hair stood out about three inches from his head in all directions, making his head look like a gray dandelion clock.

"Where're you going?" asked Charlie.

"That MacDermott lady called me. She says she's got some information about those love letters she sent Leakey."

"Be careful with Leakey," said Charlie.

"Believe me, the picture of that Volkswagen blowing up will be forever stamped on my brain. Did Peterson tell you anything new?"

"No, nobody saw anyone tampering with the car. Caldwell isn't convinced the explosion was connected with McClatchy. He asked Peterson if you'd ever been mixed up with organized crime."

"Sure," said Victor, "I used to sell them little girls. Maybe I slipped them a goat by accident. What's with this Caldwell anyway?"

Charlie straightened the sling supporting his left arm. The arm felt stiff and itched under its bandages. "He's got one idea in his head and can't get rid of it. I think even Peterson's beginning to disagree with him."

Victor paused in the doorway, then gave a little salute. "Wish me luck with this MacDermott lady," he said, "I think she likes me."

Shortly after Victor left, Charlie decided to drive over to the Backstretch and talk to Doris. He remembered her mentioning

Jespersen's girlfriend, Kathy Marshall, and he wanted to learn more.

The milk truck was parked in a lot on the corner of Putnam. That morning in Schuylerville, Charlie had had to apologize to about twenty irate customers. Now they were only mildly angry. Gillespie must have driven the truck through a field because it was spattered with mud, and weeds dangled from the bumpers. Charlie was sorry that he hadn't washed it before driving to Saratoga. As he climbed into the truck, he glanced around to see if anyone was looking.

After work that morning he had bailed out Eddie Gillespie, who had seemed contrite and subdued. His only explanation for drunkenly racing the truck through Schuylerville had been that he wasn't born to be a milkman. Charlie didn't feel he was born to be a milkman either, but he had been tactful enough not to say this. He had offered to drive Eddie home in the milk truck, but Eddie said he would rather hitchhike.

As Charlie drove over to the Backstretch, he kept wondering how he could obtain a blood sample. He knew that if he just broke into the stable and jabbed the horse, there would be trouble. Possibly he could ask someone.

Charlie had been correct about Doris knowing Kathy Marshall. "I worked for her for a couple of weeks after she opened the Blue Lion," she told him. "I liked her well enough but she was too bossy."

Charlie and Doris sat across from each other in a booth at the back of the bar. His shoes were on either side of hers and he enjoyed the illusion that he was containing her. The afternoon sun through the window gave a reddish tinge to her hair.

"Do you know Jespersen?" asked Charlie.

"I never met him. When I knew Kathy she was dating a lawyer."

"You know his name?"

"No, it was a few years ago."

"Was it Roy Leakey?"

Doris squinched up her eyes as she tried to remember. "Maybe that was it but I'm not sure. I never met him either. I know Jespersen's ex-wife a little. In fact, I told her to hire you."

"Me, what for?" Charlie had been drinking coffee and he set the white mug back on the table.

"She was trying to get additional alimony from her husband and he said he had much less money than she thought he had. Something like that. I remember she told me he was secretive with his money. She thought a private detective might help and I gave her your name. Did she call?"

"She called Victor once but never called back. Victor in the meantime decided he couldn't take the case because of a conflict of interest."

"What conflict of interest?"

"Jespersen takes care of Victor's cat. What's Jespersen's ex-wife like?"

Charlie's right hand was resting flat on the table. Doris reached over and slowly outlined his fingers with one of her own. "I like her. She married Jespersen when she was eighteen. I gather he gave her a hard time. We were both in the same exercise class at the Y. That was last year. I haven't seen much of her since except on the street or in a store."

"What about Kathy Marshall?" asked Charlie. "What's she like?"

"Ambitious and hard-boiled, but nice under all that. I guess her family has some money. She graduated from Skidmore about five years ago and opened the Blue Lion a year later. The last time I talked to her, which was last spring, she was busy buying a racehorse. I don't know if she did or not." Doris paused, noticed a speck of something on the front of her purple blouse and brushed it off. "But I'm certainly positive she wouldn't be involved in killing someone," she added.

"Stitt had a secret partner," said Charlie. "It might have been Leakey or Jespersen or it might have been someone else. Whoever it was had a lot to lose if McClatchy testified against him. What's interesting about all three murders and even the car being blown up is they were designed to point the blame at presumably innocent parties. Pease supposedly committed suicide. I supposedly killed Stitt. And racketeers supposedly killed McClatchy and blew up the car."

Some construction workers with yellow hard hats came into

the Backstretch and Doris stood up. "I have to get back to work," she said. "Are you still coming to dinner tomorrow night?"

"What are you having?" Charlie couldn't imagine why she should think he would change his mind.

"Baked snake," said Doris. "I thought since you were delivering milk again you might not want to." She stood next to the table smoothing her dark gray skirt down over her thighs.

"I have to have something nice in my life," said Charlie. "If I'm really lucky, maybe Wanamaker will come back from Santa Fe."

A few minutes later Charlie left the Backstretch to drive over to the Star Market to pick up some groceries. Again he began to brood about the blood sample. It was embarrassing. Here he knew the histories of a thousand desperadoes who had stolen everything from a Union Pacific locomotive to the Mona Lisa and he couldn't think how to swipe a teaspoon of blood.

The market was crowded and Charlie saw several people he knew. By their expressions, he realized he should have come at a less public time. The papers had reported Charlie's connection with Stitt's murder and the explosion of the Volkswagen. One had even printed his picture, showing him in a plaid winter hat with ear flaps. Charlie was certain he had never seen the hat before and couldn't think when the picture had been taken.

After wheeling his cart down several aisles, Charlie saw a rather small and familiar-looking woman staring at him fixedly. He looked away. He needed beer, bread, cereal, and Freihofer's fruit cookies. He hurried to get them. At the cereal shelf, he again noticed the small woman. She was attractive, in her thirties, and after a moment Charlie realized it wasn't that she was small, but that he was seeing her without her horse. Also she was wearing a skirt and brown sweater instead of a leotard. Charlie pulled his cart to a stop and clumsily said hello.

"I was wondering how many times I would have to wheel my Post Toasties past you before you realized who I was," said Artemis.

Charlie felt his face grow hot. "I didn't recognize you without your horse," he said.

"I left him in the car. He hates public places without his makeup."

Charlie was about to speak again when he felt a sharp pain in his left ankle caused by someone bumping into him with a cart. He turned to discover his ex-wife's sister, Lucy, who had married his cousin Robert. She was a tall, severe woman who always wore dresses and whose blond hair was sculpted weekly into extravagant designs by a local beautician named Big Ruby. Charlie was almost glad to see her since she owned the store next to Kathy Marshall's Blue Lion, and he wanted to ask her several questions. One look at Lucy's face, however, and he knew he could expect no help.

"I'm surprised to see you in Saratoga, Charlie," she said, "considering what's being said about you."

Charlie started to make some apology when he was interrupted by Artemis: "That's all right, dearie, I gave him ten cents to push my cart."

Lucy stared at Artemis in surprise, then, without answering, she continued down the aisle. Charlie realized that Lucy must have bumped into him on purpose.

"You have nice friends," said Artemis.

"She's sort of an ex-relative." Charlie looked at Artemis. She was perhaps five inches shorter than he was. Again, she struck him as very compact. Then an idea occurred to him about the horse Sweet Dreams. It seemed to leap into his head. "I don't suppose I could interest you in a little petty crime," he asked.

Artemis smiled and rose up on her toes like a ballerina. "On the contrary," she said, "petty crime is my middle name."

At eleven thirty that night, when Charlie ought to have been sound asleep if he hoped to face the next day with any enthusiasm, he stood whispering with Artemis near the closed flap of her circus tent. She wore a black turtleneck and black pants. Charlie guessed that her choice of clothing had been determined by movies she had seen about commando operations.

"From what I've read," said Artemis, "I think we should dig a tunnel. The best prisoners always escape through tunnels."

"Sweet Dreams is not a prisoner, nor are we going to rescue him," said Charlie. "Do you know where he's kept?"

"He was in the stall next to Phillip but they moved him the other day. Now he's in that little barn and I believe the door is locked. Shall we go see?"

Artemis led the way out of the tent. The air was cold and Charlie zipped up his jacket. High over the house shone a half moon but it scarcely gave enough light to keep him from stumbling over his feet. He had left the milk truck in front of the hotel in Cambridge where Artemis picked him up. She had offered to supply the syringe and even do the blood test. This pleased Charlie, who had no idea where to look for blood on a horse. Artemis said the jugular vein was the best bet.

"You know," said Artemis in a whisper, "if those two men in the house catch you, they are likely to do you damage."

"That had already occurred to me," said Charlie.

The door to the barn was locked by a large padlock and a shiny new hasp. Artemis flicked off her small pencil flashlight. "That was put on quite recently," she said.

Charlie took hold of the padlock and tried to twist it. Although it created a problem, Charlie felt encouraged since the lock indicated that Sweet Dreams was more valuable than he seemed.

"Do you have a crowbar?" he asked.

"I have even better," said Artemis. "Wait here."

Charlie waited. From the shed row came the occasional snort of a horse. Far away he heard a dog barking. The night was cloudless. Charlie found the Big Dipper and Cassiopeia, then began looking for Orion. He had left his .38 at home, not wanting to become dependent on it. He began to wish he had brought it.

After a few minutes, Charlie saw a black shape as big as a house lumbering toward him. It was the horse, Phillip, with Artemis on his back. She hopped off when she was next to Charlie.

"Here, you hold the light on the lock," she said.

Charlie did as he was told. Artemis took a length of rope, passed it through the padlock, then tied the rope around Phillip's neck. She moved briskly, like someone tidying a room. Making certain the rope was secure, she produced a carrot and gave it to Phillip who chewed it contentedly with a steady and peaceful slurping. When he was quite finished, she patted his forehead and said, "Up, Phillip!" in a kindly but commanding voice.

The huge horse heaved himself onto his hind legs. There was a loud cracking and breaking as the door to the small barn was torn from its hinges.

"Do you see how convenient a properly trained horse can be?" asked Artemis. "Down, Phillip!"

Phillip plummeted back down to four legs and the door crashed to the ground. Artemis quickly unfastened the rope. "Now we must hurry. I'm sure those two men heard the noise. Sweet Dreams is in here." She led Charlie into the barn. "You listen for those men and I'll get the blood. Do you think I'd make a capable criminal? Perhaps my talents are wasted in show business."

It was only minutes later that Charlie saw the yellow beam of a flashlight. "It came from over here," said a man's voice.

Charlie hurried into the barn. "Artemis, they're coming."

Artemis emerged from the stall. "Here's the syringe," she said. "Presumably this is enough blood. There's a hayloft upstairs. You go and hide and I'll deal with the enemy."

"What if they hurt you?" asked Charlie, uncertain whether hiding in the hayloft was the right thing to do.

"I should like to see them try," said Artemis. "Hurry, I hear their catlike tread."

Charlie put the syringe in his breast pocket, removed his arm from its sling and began climbing the ladder to the hayloft. As he reached the top, he heard Artemis say: "Gentlemen, come see what my bad horse has done."

"Is that you, Artemis? What the hell's going on?"

"Jesus, Freddie, look at this fuckin' door. You do this, Artemis?"

"I'm afraid to confess it was Phillip. He bounced into it." Artemis spoke energetically.

"Bounced?"

"Sort of jitterbugged. Up, Phillip!"

"Jesus, Freddie, watch out!"

There was a loud whinnying noise from Phillip. From where Charlie lay, he could see the flicker of flashlights underneath the door of the hayloft. The floor was covered with several feet of loose straw. Already Charlie had straw down the back of his neck and up the legs of his trousers.

"Down, Phillip! I was taking Phillip for a short walk and we became separated in the dark. This always makes him anxious. I was standing by this door when we had our little reunion and the excitement was too much for him."

"You mean this horse just knocked the door down?"

"He was so pleased to see me," said Artemis.

'Let's look inside, Freddie."

Charlie began to burrow under the straw. He heard the men downstairs, then one of them climbed the ladder to the loft. Charlie held his breath as he saw the light flicker above his head. Then the light disappeared.

"Nothing up here."

"Hey, Freddie, what're we going to do about this goddamn door?"

"Nail it shut for now. We'll fix it tomorrow. There's a hammer and nails in the storeroom."

Charlie heard the men bumping around. Then the door to the barn was heaved back into place. This was followed by the sound of a hammer. Charlie counted seven or eight nails being driven into the door, he wasn't sure which.

"You want something else, Artemis?" asked Freddie.

"The sight of physical labor invigorates me."

"Why don't you take your damn horse back to your tent, Artemis?"

"Why don't you take your hand off my arm, pal, before Phillip steps on you?"

"Hey, Artemis," said Freddie, "let's go back to the house for a drink."

"You boys have a drink without me. Phillip and I still have work to do."

"Come on, Freddie, she's a looney."

"Well, good night, Artemis. Keep your horse under control from now on, will you?"

"I certainly shall. Goodnight, gentlemen."

As Charlie listened to the sound of departing footsteps, he climbed out of the straw and stood up, pressing one finger under his nose to keep from sneezing. Then he brushed himself off. It was completely dark in the hayloft. After a moment, he waded through the straw to where he had seen a door. It was a small door, no more than four feet high and fastened by a hook. He undid the hook and pushed the door open. As he did so, he saw a great black shadow as Phillip returned through the dark.

Charlie sneezed.

"Was I spectacular?" asked Artemis. She was standing on Phillip's back.

"Very good. If there was any money to be made as a private detective, I'd offer you a job. How do I get down from here?"

"You can lower yourself onto Phillip's back." Artemis and the horse were directly below Charlie. She briefly flicked her penlight on and off to show him.

"I'd rather not," said Charlie.

"Then you'll have to jump or learn to love that hayloft."

"Okay, okay, tell me what to do."

"Take off your shoes and hang them around your neck. Phillip dislikes the feel of shoes. Then slide out on your stomach and onto his back. Just be careful of the syringe. I don't have another."

Charlie sat down, took off his shoes, tied the laces together and hung them around his neck. The horse's back was about five feet below the door. Again taking his arm out of its sling, he turned around and eased his legs through the doorframe. As he lowered himself, Artemis guided his feet. At first he went bit by bit, but then he slipped and slid on his belly until his feet came down hard on Phillip's back. The horse shivered, but remained still. It felt to Charlie that he was standing on a warm and prickly sofa. Artemis took his arm so he wouldn't fall. Charlie stood for a second, then lowered himself to a sitting position. It still seemed like a long distance to the ground.

Artemis made a clicking noise and the horse slowly walked forward. Charlie found himself wishing that Chief Peterson could see him. Then he started to slide off and squeezed his legs tightly against Phillip's ribs.

"I would have made a rotten cowboy," Charlie said.

"I don't like sitting so much myself," said Artemis. "That's why I stand."

13

▼▼▼

VICTOR LEANED BACK in the swivel chair, gingerly lifted the .38 and looked down the barrel. Its interior was dark and gloomy. He decided to leave it in the safe. Leakey was presumably still at the movies at Pyramid Mall and even if he left early, he was unlikely to drive out to his cottage.

It was the cottage, really a cabin, that Victor had heard about from Ruth MacDermott the previous day: a two-room cabin on a pond in Greenfield a few miles north of Saratoga. Leakey seemed to use it exclusively for amorous adventures, and Ruth MacDermott said that was where Leakey was hiding her love letters.

Victor had already driven out to the cabin just to look at it—an actual log cabin set back from the road with a large fieldstone chimney and a screened-in porch. It was now nine o'clock Thursday evening and in about half an hour Victor meant to do some burglary.

Of course he hadn't told Charlie, who, unfortunately, believed that honesty was the best policy. Victor too thought honesty was a pretty good policy, but it wasn't the only policy. Far from it, there were lots of other policies almost as good.

Victor stood up and returned the .38 to the safe. He still limped from being hurled to the street when the Volkswagen had blown up. In the dark window, he happened to see his reflection and he paused to study it. Although his large bandages had been replaced by smaller ones, his injuries reminded him that Leakey had threatened to do him physical harm. Victor had no wish for further scars. On the other hand, he wanted those letters. It rankled that Charlie had not taken him to get that tablespoon of Sweet Dreams's blood. It seemed to indicate a lack of trust. Victor hoped to regain that trust, or at least some respect, this evening.

As for the blood, Charlie had sent it off to New York by an express bus. Lenny Ravitz at the Thoroughbred Racing Protective Bureau had said that Buckdancer's blood was on file, so it would be an easy matter to compare it with the sample taken from Sweet Dreams. All blood testing for the Jockey Club was done at a lab at the University of California at Davis. Most mares were already blood typed, as were about seven thousand stallions.

Victor took his raincoat from the hook behind the door and left the office. The red Renault was parked up on Broadway in public view where, he hoped, nobody would shove a stick of dynamite under its hood. Charlie had wanted to use it this evening but Victor insisted he needed it for work. This was true, but beyond this truth was Victor's determination never to be seen driving the milk truck. It was okay for Charlie. People already expected the worst of him. But what if one of Victor's girlfriends saw him tooling around town in a Wholesome Dairy milk truck? How could he keep up his reputation as a Casanova if the ladies thought he was peddling skim milk and yogurt?

Charlie had said he had a big date and didn't want to go courting in a milk truck. Victor had suggested he could put a mattress in the back.

"Come on, Victor," Charlie had complained, "this is an important relationship."

"They all are," Victor had told him.

It wasn't as if Charlie was taking Doris to dinner or to a movie. He intended to be at her apartment for the entire evening and had told Victor several times that he was not to be disturbed. Victor was only sorry that he hadn't had the chance to short-sheet her bed. Starting the Renault, Victor discovered that the headlights didn't work. He banged on the dashboard until they came on. Then he made a screeching U-turn and accelerated rapidly up Broadway.

Victor sympathized with Charlie's various problems. It depressed Charlie that his cousins thought him no better than a bandit and that people believed he had betrayed McClatchy to racketeers. It seemed to Victor that the farther you kept away from the dopes, then the better off you were. What was the good of having a fat ass if you couldn't tell the dopes to kiss it? And of course Charlie was sick of being a milkman. Who wouldn't be? But it was his own fault for taking the job in the first place. Ditto with McClatchy. Charlie wouldn't be in his present trouble if he had told McClatchy to hit the bricks. And now this afternoon Charlie had got a telegram from his mother asking if he could raise some money, which she might need in a hurry. Charlie had practically cried.

Victor drove first to Leakey's house on Underwood in northwest Saratoga. The house was a white split-level with green shutters. It was dark and there was no sign of a car. Then Victor drove over to the movie theater at Pyramid Mall to see if Leakey's BMW was still in the lot. It was. Victor decided there was no help for it but to break into the cabin. If he got arrested, Charlie would bail him out.

The cabin was on an unlit dirt road. Victor thought there were too many trees and not enough houses. Trees were all right in their place, in parks, for instance, but Victor disliked how they pushed their way all over the countryside. Furniture on the loose, that's how he saw them. Escaped pulp products, runaway picket fences. Here the trees pressed up against the road, forming a deep arch.

Victor drove past the turnoff to Leakey's cabin, then turned around. Parking the Renault some distance up the road, he took a flashlight from the glove box and walked back. Between the leaves, he could see a few stars. Victor heard an owl but for the most part he thought it was too dark and too quiet. His footsteps in the gravel seemed noisy and he was afraid they would attract attention. He imagined the woods full of animals and remembered stories he had heard about bears wandering down from the Adirondacks. Perhaps he should have brought the .38 after all. He kept the light off and flicked it on only occasionally to keep from falling into a ditch.

Victor reached the driveway to Leakey's cabin. He simply couldn't imagine anyone living out in the woods unless he had something to hide. Victor doubted he had ever spent more than a day of his life not surrounded by concrete and the bustle of a city.

The front door of the cabin was locked. Victor had expected that. After all, Leakey was no fool. Victor walked around the cabin trying all the windows. They too were locked. The cabin was a plain, rectangular building—the kind of log cabin that arrives in a thousand pieces on the back of a flatbed truck. Victor massaged the back of his neck and decided he would have to break a window.

After seeking out a fist-sized rock, he returned to the back of the cabin. First he tapped the glass with the rock. Nothing happened. Then he took out his handkerchief, held it against the window and hit the handkerchief. Still nothing happened. So much for being careful, he thought. Pulling back his arm, he threw the rock at the window, smashing a pane of glass above the latch. The noise seemed huge. He imagined all the bears perking up their ears. Quickly, he opened the window and crawled over the sill.

Once inside, Victor got to his feet and shone his flashlight over the room. Against the far wall to the right stood a large brass bed covered with what appeared to be a polar-bear rug. Near it was a pine bureau and vanity. The bedroom area was several feet above the rest of the room. On the lower level was a brown couch in front of the fireplace, then some stuffed chairs, several bookcases full of books and a rolltop desk. Hanging from the ceiling was a chandelier made from a wagon wheel.

Victor tried the desk first. It was full of little cubbyholes containing letters but none were the right letters. He looked through the drawers, even behind and under the drawers. Then he searched the bureau, the vanity and the drawers of a table in the living room where he found a deck of cards showing fifty-two different naked ladies, which Victor put in his pocket.

Then he searched the closets and the pockets of all the jackets and coats. The floors were covered with thick rugs that felt soft and spongy under Victor's feet. Victor tried to stack all the clothes in a neat mound but then he fell against them, knocking them over.

When he had finished with the closets, he began on the bookcases, first looking behind the books, then opening and leafing through each volume. He piled all the books on the floor. Victor had seen small safes disguised to look like books but all of Leakey's books were authentic. The problem, as he saw it, was that Leakey had no reason to hide the letters. If they were really in the cabin, they would be in a fairly obvious place.

The kitchen was separated from the living room by a wooden counter about waist high. Victor shone the light over the cabinets and shelves, over the cans and boxes of food, Saltine crackers and pea soup. He took everything out of the cupboards to make sure nothing was behind them, then he looked in the stove. When he had searched every possible place, he opened the refrigerator. Its interior light seemed particularly bright after the dimness of the flashlight. On the top shelf was McClatchy's head.

Victor leaped back, stumbling over a metal kitchen chair and falling against the counter. The head was lying on its side and McClatchy appeared to be drowsing. His thin lips were slightly parted and his eyes were half shut. Victor saw a glimmer of teeth, a glimmer of eye, as if McClatchy was studying the room through half-closed lids. Occupying the center of his forehead was a bullet hole. The neck ended in a precise cut, revealing the bone and windpipe. McClatchy's brown hair was ruffled as if by a breeze. His fat cheeks were paper-white. The light from the refrigerator and the darkness of the room made the head seem as if it stood on a small stage. Just beneath the head was a grapefruit and two cans of Budweiser.

Victor scrambled to his feet and half-scrambled, half-tumbled backward toward the front door, keeping his entire attention on the head, as if without that attention McClatchy might wink one eye or open his mouth. Victor knocked over a lamp and another chair. Reaching the door, he unfastened the latch, backed hurriedly across the porch and stumbled down the steps. As he ran up the driveway to the dirt road, he glanced behind him and saw the light of the refrigerator and, he was certain, the round shape of McClatchy's head.

Victor ran up the road and at first couldn't find the Renault. For a terrible moment he thought someone had stolen it. But then he found it, yanked open the door and in his rush badly banged his knee on the steering wheel. He could hardly fit the key into the slot. Starting the car with a roar, he spat stones and gravel for twenty feet as he accelerated toward Saratoga.

As Victor drove, he realized he would have to tell Charlie. Never mind Doris and Victor's promise not to bother them, he still had to tell Charlie about the head. He tried to think of an alternative but there was none. It was just ten thirty. Perhaps Charlie and Doris were finishing dinner or watching the TV. But Victor doubted it.

The milk truck was parked several doors down from Doris's building on Circular Street. Pulling up to the front, Victor jumped out of the car and ran across the lawn. Doris lived on the third floor in an apartment that ran the length of the house. Victor hurried up the back stairs and knocked at the door. After a couple of minutes, Doris opened it. Her hair was rumpled and Victor knew they hadn't been watching TV. When she saw Victor, she raised her eyebrows.

"Is something wrong?" she asked.

"I've got to see Charlie."

"Wait here."

A minute Charlie appeared buttoning his shirt. He looked at Victor but didn't say anything.

"I've found McClatchy's head," said Victor. "It was out at Leakey's cabin. I wanted to know what I should do."

"What were you doing at Leakey's cabin?"

"Looking for those love letters."

'You broke in?"

"No, he sent me an invitation. Jesus, Charlie, don't you care about McClatchy's head? I found it. It was in the refrigerator with a bullet hole right smack in the middle of the forehead."

Charlie finished tucking in his shirt. He looked, thought Victor, as if he didn't care two hoots about McClatchy's head.

"You're not playing a joke on me, are you, Victor?"

"Charlie, for Pete's sake, I'm your friend!"

"I guess we better drive out there."

They drove without speaking. Victor became a trifle irritated. After all, he had risked his sanity, his very ability to sleep at night, just for Charlie's detective agency.

"Charlie, I wouldn't have bothered you if I hadn't thought it was important. I thought you'd want to know."

"That's okay," said Charlie, "you did the right thing."

"Were you in the sack?" asked Victor.

"I don't want to talk about it."

"Jesus, Charlie, how many times do I have to say I'm sorry?"

"Never mind. I'm glad you came. Did you find the letters?"

"Not a single one."

"How'd you get inside?"

"Busted a window."

Charlie made a groaning noise.

"Hey, it was a little window in back. You want I should leave him a couple of bucks?"

When they reached Leakey's cabin, Victor thought something was wrong but he couldn't quite put his finger on what it was. Charlie pulled up to the front, leaving on the headlights. The lights made the bare wood of the cabin look golden. When they got out of the car, Victor saw that the front door was shut. He started to say something about it, then changed his mind. He tried the front door. It was locked.

"The broken window's around back," he said.

Victor led the way with the flashlight. He almost expected to find it fixed and was relieved when he saw the glass smashed and the window open.

"See what a little window it is," he said.

"The size is not important," said Charlie.

Victor climbed through the window and Charlie climbed after him, bumping his head on the frame, then falling forward, hitting his knee on the floor.

"You okay?" said Victor.

Charlie didn't answer. He got to his feet and looked around. "Where's the refrigerator?" he asked.

Victor flashed the light toward the kitchen. "In there. You do it. I don't want to see it again. Makes me want to puke."

Charlie kept looking around the cabin. Drawers were pulled out, books and papers were scattered across the floor, cushions were thrown around. "You sure made a mess of this place," he said.

"I'm an eager searcher. Just look at the head. Want me to find a paper bag for it?"

Charlie walked to the refrigerator. Victor remained about five feet behind him, trying not to look but looking all the same. Charlie opened the refrigerator door.

"What is it?" said Victor, who had turned away.

Charlie didn't answer.

"Come on, tell me," said Victor.

"The head's not there."

"You're fuckin' kiddin' me." Victor looked around Charlie's shoulder. The head was gone. He nearly pushed Charlie out of the way in order to make certain.

"I swear to you," said Victor, "the head was there on the top shelf."

Charlie knelt down and ran a finger over the shelf. "Well, there's no sign of it now."

"Hey, really, I wouldn't have dragged you out of the sack for a joke. Charlie, you're my buddy. The head was right there like I said. Somebody was here. And when I left, the front door was open. Leakey's gone and swiped the head on us. Charlie, tell me you believe me."

Charlie shut the refrigerator door. "I believe you all right. Let's get out of here."

They drove back to Saratoga. Victor kept talking about the head, swearing he had seen it until at last Charlie told him to shut up. Charlie drove over to Leakey's house, which was still dark. Then he drove over to the Pyramid Mall, even though the movie had let out half an hour earlier. Leakey's car was gone.

"How'd you know he went to the movies?" asked Charlie.

"I followed him."

"Was he by himself?"

"Nah, he had a date. Hot little number in tight red pants."

"Did you bother to see if anyone was following you?"

"Why should anyone follow me?"

Charlie drove back to Doris's apartment. Looking up at her windows, he saw they were dark. He decided to go home.

"The way I see it," said Victor, "Leakey left the movie early, drove out to the cabin with this floozy and discovered someone had been there. So what does he do? He moves the head. Who could blame him?"

"Why'd he keep the head in the refrigerator in the first place?" asked Charlie.

"He had to keep it cool. I mean, a head once it's cut off is just so much hamburger. Probably he wants to take more pictures."

"So where's the head now?"

"Probably in his truck or maybe in his back seat or something."

"You've got all the answers, don't you?"

"Hey, Charlie, I'm a private detective. I gotta be on the ball."

14

▼▼▼

THE VOICE ON THE TELEPHONE coughed, cleared his throat with a long, gargling noise, then said. "Yeah, it's definitely not Buckdancer. No telling who it is but we've tipped off the Jockey Club. They're going to launch an official investigation." Lenny Ravitz began to cough again and Charlie pulled the phone away from his ear.

It was early Friday afternoon. Charlie had called the Thoroughbred Racing Protective Bureau from the office right after arriving from Schuylerville and the Wholesome Dairy. Because of his arm, he hadn't gone swimming. In fact, he hadn't gone swimming for over a week. This made him dislike himself. He imagined becoming so fat that no chair would fit him, that doorways would have to be specially widened.

"So the Jockey Club was interested?" asked Charlie.

"You bet. They're going to kick that horse right out of the Stud Book. And they'll also put a quick stop to he sale of his foals. Which reminds me, you know that guy Leakey you asked about? He's down as buying two of them."

"And now he can't race them?"

"Not on any Thoroughbred track he can't. They got no blood."

"You learn anything about Stitt?" asked Charlie. Victor sat across the desk listening and gently cleaning his ears with the eraser of a pencil. On top of the file cabinet, the stuffed cockatoo or toucan or parrot stared down at them. Charlie couldn't imagine why Victor had thought the office needed a stuffed parrot.

"Not much to learn. We thought there might be an angle on the inheritance, but his heir turns out to be a brother in Ohio. Teaches biology at some community college. Anything else?"

"Not right now. Let me know if you turn up anything new."

"Sure thing, and thanks again for the help."

As Charlie hung up the phone, Victor asked: "Who can't race where?"

"Your lawyer friend, Leakey. He bought two of Sweet Dreams's foals."

"You going to tell Peterson?"

Charlie looked out the window. It was raining and all his clothes felt damp. "I think I'll talk to Leakey first."

"Better take a gun," said Victor.

Charlie started to put on his jacket. "By the way," he asked, where'd that bird come from?" He decided he had to find out one way or the other, even if it made him the butt of one of Victor's jokes. The bird was missing a lot of feathers and looked moth-eaten.

"What bird?" Victor glanced toward the ceiling.

"That parrot on the file cabinet."

"Oh, yeah, that showed up the other day. Didn't you get my note?"

"What note?"

Victor began rummaging through the papers on the desk. "Here it is. Your mother sent it from Atlantic City. You owe me fifteen bucks."

"Why?"

"She shipped it collect."

Charlie took three five-dollar bills from his wallet and tossed them on the desk. "Any idea why she sent it?" he asked.

"Not me. Maybe we can boil it down for soup."

Charlie descended the stairs, then paused at the street door and watched the raindrops hit and bounce off the pavement. He thought how his curiosity had just cost him fifteen dollars and that he still had no better idea what the parrot was doing in his office. Why should his mother send him a stuffed parrot? Didn't he have enough to worry about already? It seemed to be raining a little harder. Charlie's umbrella was in the milk truck about a hundred yards away. Liquid winter—Charlie flung open the door and rushed down the hill. He was drenched before he had gone twenty feet.

The engine of the truck refused to start. Charlie flooded it, then had to wait. He felt undecided about Leakey, and made up his mind to see Jespersen first. He was almost sorry that he was on such bad terms with Peterson, because he wished he had someone to talk to. He needed to attach all the facts to little pieces of wood and see if they built anything. The starter on the truck made a growling, whirring noise. Just as Charlie thought the battery was about to die, the engine turned over and caught. He shoved it into first and it lurched forward.

It was clear to Charlie that if Victor had not come rushing up Doris's back stairs, then he, Charlie, would have spent the night in Doris's bed. That single fact shoved into the forefront of his brain was enough to leave him shortwinded. A door had been opened. There had been a vision of bright light. The door had been slammed shut, leaving Charlie in the dark.

Even if the head had been in the refrigerator, its discovery would not have been worth Victor's interruption. Charlie would have delivered the head to Peterson. There would have been a certain amount of hoopla. Doris would have slept alone.

Peterson, presumably, would have arrested Leakey, who was either guilty or being framed. If he was being framed, then it implied that some unknown party was keeping a fairly close eye on their activities. It meant Victor had been followed.

Who had followed him? Charlie tried to concentrate but nibbling away at his ability to think rationally were his accumulated frustrations. When would Wanamaker return from Santa Fe? Why had his mother sent him a stuffed parrot? He again thought of Butch Cassidy and the Sundance Kid searching for peace and quiet in Argentina. What did it get them? In one version, they had been surprised by soldiers while attempting to rob a bank in Mercedes, Uruguay. An American salesman named Steele had seen the bodies of Cassidy, the Sundance Kid and Etta Place half-covered with a tarpaulin in the dirt of the town square.

"The woman was outside with the horses and was shot down first," Steele had said. "The two men rushed out and were killed in the street." It was December 1911. Butch Cassidy was forty-four.

Charlie drove the milk truck along the edge of Congress Park. The windshield wipers made a violent whap-whap noise. Had any bandits managed to die of old age? The most famous was probably Frank James, but his thirty-three years of life after the murder of Jesse was a lonely and frustrated time. He had sold shoes and men's clothing. He had tended horses. He had even appeared in Saratoga in the summer of 1894 to work as a bookie.

Jesse too must have known Saratoga. Twenty years earlier he and Frank had hid out in a hotel in Chatfield's Corners, just north of Saratoga, where they had distant cousins. At that time the neighboring town of Middle Grove was named Jamesville, while the local bank, the James Bank, had been founded by an industrial tycoon, also named Jesse James, who lived on a mountain.

Charlie tried to imagine the outlaw Jesse James in Saratoga in the 1870s. Jesse had raced horses in Memphis and was said to know more about horses than any other man in Missouri. He too had been a kind of tycoon: a tycoon of disorder. Certainly he had gone to the track. Charlie was only sorry that he hadn't robbed the Adirondack Trust.

But Frank hadn't done well in Saratoga. At the end of the 1894 season, he packed up and moved to St. Louis, where he had taken a job as a "greeter" in a burlesque house. It amazed Charlie that Frank and Jesse James had probably ridden their horses along these very streets that he was now driving to Jespersen's office.

This time Jespersen's waiting room was empty except for a boy with a Great Dane whose right front paw was wrapped with about a mile of white adhesive. The Great Dane took no interest in his surroundings but stared at the bandage with his head tilted first to one side, then the other as if he were on the very brink of having his first thought.

"Put his foot in a rat trap," said the boy. "I told him not to."

After another minute, an elderly woman with a parakeet came out of a consultation room and the receptionist told Charlie to go in. From someplace in back, a dog was whimpering. Jespersen stood reading a piece of paper attached to a clipboard. He glanced up and nodded to Charlie. He was a tall man, probably six feet two or three. As before, he wore a white laboratory coat. He took off his glasses and put them in his breast pocket. Without them, his blue eyes looked watery and insubstantial.

"What's on your mind, Mr. Bradshaw?"

"Just a couple of questions. Stitt was also a breeder, wasn't he?"

"In a small way, yes."

"Did you give him a hand with that?"

Jespersen leaned back against a white Formica counter, picked up a small rubber mallet and tapped it against his palm. "About a dozen times or so. I believe there's also a vet in Bennington who he called upon, Dr. Herman Schmidt."

"What about the mare, Indian Maid? Do you remember that horse?"

"I remember her, yes. What about her?"

"She was bred with Buckdancer and the result was the colt, Sweet Dreams. Did you assist in that?"

"No, I didn't. In fact, I had very little to do with Sweet Dreams. When he injured his leg last year, I happened to see him. Maybe two or three other times as well. Actually, I've been thinking about that horse since our talk earlier this week. It struck me that the fact that I had little to do with him might be somewhat suspicious—that Willis was trying to keep me away from him. As I say, I was involved with all of his horses, but that one probably the least."

"Did you and Stitt ever breed horses by artificial insemination?"

Jespersen looked at Charlie uncertainly. "I don't know whether you are aware of this, Mr. Bradshaw, but it's illegal to breed Thoroughbreds by artificial insemination. Sometimes artificial insemination may be used as a little extra insurance, but only after the mare has already been covered by the stallion."

"So you think this Schmidt from Bennington took care of Sweet Dreams?"

"Possibly, but I don't really know."

"Was anyone else involved with that horse?" Charlie stood by a pair of tall cabinets. Nearly everything in the room was white. Suspended from a wire above him like sheets from a clothesline were five X-rays of hips.

"Not that I know of." Jespersen paused and put the rubber mallet back on the counter. "As a matter of fact, there was a local lawyer who had an interest in Sweet Dreams. He was afraid that the horse might have to be put down after his accident."

"Was his name Leakey, by any chance?"

"That's right. Roy or Ray Leakey, I'm not sure which."

"Have you ever wanted to own a racehorse?"

Jespersen laughed and again Charlie was reminded of paper being crinkled, perhaps wax paper. "Too much trouble. I advise my girlfriend sometimes. She's got a couple of horses. But that's as close as I want to get."

A few minutes later, Charlie left Jespersen's clinic. As he drove back across Saratoga toward Leakey's office, he tried to think about what Jespersen had told him. The veterinarian's calm self-assurance made it difficult to get past his words, to see what propped them up. But instead of thinking about Jespersen, Charlie again began worrying about his mother and her question as to whether he could raise any money. The answer was definitely no. If she wanted to lose a fortune in Atlantic City, that was her business, but Charlie didn't want to put a mortgage on his house just so she could lose even more. Again he imagined her sleeping on his couch. No, thought Charlie, I'd be the one stuck with the couch; she'd get the bed.

Cole Younger had been another bandit who survived to old age. Arrested with eleven bullet wounds after the Northfield Raid in 1876, he had remained in prison for twenty-five years and then joined Frank James in the James-Younger Wild West Show. Both men were about sixty. The conditions of Younger's parole kept him from actually performing, but he sat in a special section of the theater and chatted with the audience. Later he would say a few words at a reception. These were so well received that he decided to go on the lecture circuit. His topic was "What Life Has Taught Me." Since he still had seventeen bullets lodged in his body, it could be guessed that life had taught him a great deal.

Before seeing Leakey, Charlie telephoned the veterinarian Herman Schmidt in Bennington to see if he had helped Stitt take care of Sweet Dreams. Schmidt was friendly but denied having heard of the horse. He said that in the past five years he had only visited Stitt's stable five or six times.

Charlie drove on to Leakey's office, then parked in the lot behind the Adirondack Trust. It was still pouring. Running to the lawyer's front door, he paused in the hall to wipe his face with a handkerchief before going upstairs. Leakey was in the reception room talking to his secretary. When he saw Charlie, he half turned away.

"I don't have any time for you, Bradshaw."

Charlie ignored him and busied himself with taking off his jacket and shaking it. Then he hung it on the coatrack.

"Maybe we should talk in your office," said Charlie, "unless you don't mind your secretary listening."

Leakey was about Charlie's height but at least twenty-five

pounds lighter. Charlie saw a muscle in his jaw moving up and down, up and down. Like a flashing light, he thought.

"Are you deaf, Bradshaw?" he asked. "I want you out of here."

"You told me you had never heard of the horse Sweet Dreams," said Charlie. "This morning I learned you bought two of his foals. The Jockey Club has asked the Protective Bureau to investigate that horse. It seems he's a ringer."

Leakey stared at Charlie, then went to the door of his office, opened it and motioned Charlie to enter. Taking his time, Charlie brushed past him into the adjoining room. The office had a shiny leather chesterfield and two windows looking out on Church Street. Charlie could see people running through the rain to the post office.

"How much did you pay for those foals?" he asked. "Hell, they'll be good saddle horses. You like riding? Or maybe you could find a state fair someplace that won't mind seeing them run."

"Who says that Sweet Dreams is a ringer?" asked Leakey.

"The Protective Bureau. He was supposed to have been sired by Buckdancer but the blood doesn't match. Apparently the mare was artificially inseminated. The trouble is you knew there was something wrong. That's why you told me you'd never heard of Sweet Dreams. What else have you been lying about? Did McClatchy call you when he came up here?"

Leakey didn't say anything, but looked angrily at Charlie. The muscle in his jaw continued to pulsate. Charlie thought it seemed to be counting out the seconds, like a stopwatch or a kitchen timer.

"Maybe you were Stitt's silent partner after all," said Charlie. "What kind of case could be made against you? You were friends with Stitt and knew about Sweet Dreams. You bought two of his foals. Also you were a demolitions expert in Vietnam, so you'd know how to blow up a car, right?"

"You don't have a case, Bradshaw." Leakey stood by the door. Although the lawyer was clearly tense, Charlie had no feeling of personal threat.

"Last night my friend Victor broke into your cabin," said Charlie.

The muscle in Leakey's jaw grew stiff. "Say that again?"

"Victor was searching for some letters that a client of his wants to get from you. I guess you know about those letters."

Leakey unfolded his arms. He seemed hesitant, as if he couldn't understand why Charlie was telling him about the cabin. "Are you serious? He could go to jail for that."

"You have no evidence and I'll deny it if I'm asked. It's pretty much of a mess but nothing's been broken except a back window. The main thing is that inside the refrigerator Victor found McClatchy's head."

If Charlie had expected Leakey to be surprised, he was mistaken. Mostly he looked suspicious. He stared at Charlie as if trying to make up his mind about something. "Did you see the head?" he asked.

"No, someone had taken it away by the time I got there."

"Then your friend's lying."

"No again. Victor has his faults but he wouldn't lie to me. If he says the head was there, it was there. We can draw two possible conclusions from this. Either you put it there or someone else put it there. If it was someone else, then that someone is trying to frame you for murder. You know that somebody's been sending around pictures of McClatchy's head?"

"Bradshaw, if you think you've got a case, then go to the cops. There's no reason I should talk to you. I get nothing from it and you just make me angry."

Charlie stood his ground. "I asked if you knew about the pictures?"

"Pictures? Yeah, I got a whole bunch of them." Leakey walked to his desk, opened a drawer and took out a large white envelope. He handed it to Charlie.

Opening it, Charlie found a dozen Polaroid snapshots of McClatchy's head. The eyes were half-closed and looked sleepy. In the middle of the forehead was a bullet hole, just as Victor had described. The head stood up on its severed neck on a table. Holding the head in place was a pair of bookends in the shape of rearing silver horses.

"Where'd you get these?" asked Charlie.

"They'd been slipped under my door. I found them when I came in."

"When was this?"

"This morning."

"You know what it looks like, don't you?"

"What?" The muscle in Leakey's jaw had begun to pulsate again.

"That you're the guy taking the pictures. I bet those are even your bookends, am I right?"

"Yes, they're out at the cabin."

"Why haven't you given these pictures to Peterson?"

"I haven't made up my mind yet."

It occurred to Charlie that Leakey knew something else he wasn't telling about. "You know, both Stitt and Pease were killed because they had some information that they had decided not to tell Peterson. As I say, there are two possibilities. Either you killed these people or somebody else is trying to set you up for it. Where were you last night? Where'd you go after the movie?"

"Forget it, Bradshaw, no more questions."

"What about late Saturday afternoon when Stitt was killed? Do you have an alibi for that time?"

"Get out."

"Does that mean you don't?"

"Get out!"

15

▼ ▼ ▼

CHARLIE TOOK A SWIZZLE STICK and jabbed at the bubbles in his beer. Then he glanced across the bar at an eight-by-ten glossy of Jersey Joe Wolcott crouched down in a fighting stance ready to do somebody damage. To be a boxer, a man had to accept the possibility of getting punched in the head. Maybe the same was true of being a private detective, thought Charlie. Maybe that was why he kept going to see Roy Leakey: simply in the hope that Leakey might punch him.

Charlie was waiting for a phone call from Lenny Ravitz at the Protective Bureau, whom he had unsuccessfully tried to telephone right after seeing Leakey. It was six o'clock Friday evening. Doris was at the other end of the bar serving beers to two off-duty policemen. All three were laughing. Although the bar was crowded, Charlie had a vacant stool one either side of him. He had almost stopped noticing such details of his unpopularity.

Doris wore a blue denim dress and a string of yellow beads. Her profile was to Charlie and he kept staring at the small of her back. She was a strong woman and one time during a softball game, Charlie had watched her hit the first pitch over the centerfield fence. He sometimes wondered if that was why he loved her. Charlie also played for the Backstretch team but was lucky if he managed a single during the entire day, which was why he'd been nicknamed Grounded-Out-To-Short Bradshaw.

The phone rang and Berney McQuilkin picked up the receiver. He glanced around the bar and when he saw Charlie he nodded. Charlie walked to the pay phone at the back of the room. It was Lenny Ravitz.

"I wanted to ask you," said Charlie, "who bought those other foals." There was a lot of noise in the bar and Charlie had to cover one ear.

"Three people bought them. I got their names right here on my desk. Bob Wilks, Michael Forbes and Kathy Marshall. That make any sense to you?"

"Only the last name. She's got a store in Saratoga. Do you know the others?"

"Just Wilks. He's a trainer on Long Island. By the way, the Jockey Club's pretty grateful for your help with Sweet Dreams. I guess there'd been some suspicion about his two wins. They're contacting the FBI. Interfering with the outcome of a sporting event, that's a federal crime. Anyway, if I can ever do you a favor, you got it."

"Thanks," said Charlie, "maybe you can give me a recommendation to the Pinkertons."

Ravitz assumed he was joking and laughed.

When Charlie finished his beer, he decided to drive home. It was still raining and the windshield wipers on the milk truck were ponderously slow. Gusts of wind pushed at the truck. In the morning, many trees would be bare.

The first thing he did when he got home was to call Wanamaker in Santa Fe. There was no answer. Then he made himself a ham and Swiss cheese on rye and opened a Labatts. He felt jumpy and kept his .38 tucked in his belt. Twice he drew it when he heard branches rattle against the side of the house. Then he locked the windows and pulled all the shades. As he was cleaning up, a washer broke on the cold-water tap so that no matter how tightly he turned the handle there was still a gush of water. There were no extra washers in his toolbox. He settled the problem by turning off the main shut-off valve.

Charlie went to bed early, the lay awake listening to the sound of rain splashing through the remaining leaves and hitting the roof. He kept thinking about the old age of Frank James. When faced with a bank robbery, Frank James had been bold, resolute and acted without hesitation. But when faced with living out his life, he had seemed ineffectual and clumsy. His role in the James-Younger Wild West Show had been even smaller than Cole Younger's. He rode his horse in the grand finale and, in one of the dramatic pieces, he was a passenger on a stage coach held up by desperadoes. These successes later led him to take a job with a traveling stock company. He had bit parts in two plays: *Across the Desert* and *The Fatal Scar*.

For years Frank James had hoped to be named doorkeeper for the Missouri Legislature. Some Democrats had lobbied for him but in the end it was considered politically dangerous. There had always been the suggestion that his acquittal twenty years before had less to do with evidence and more to do with the fact that the Republicans wanted him in jail and the Democrats didn't.

This rejection soured Frank James and led him to support Teddy Roosevelt and the Bull Moose Party in the 1904 election. He saw Teddy as a man of action like himself. Unfortunately, he announced his support at a reunion of Quantrill's guerrillas in Independence. The aging ex-guerrillas were fierce Democrats to a man and nearly shot Frank James. Having thrown over his old friends, James left Missouri and took up farming in Oklahoma. At the time of his death in 1915, he was so certain that unscrupulous showmen would steal his body that he had his wife deposit his ashes in a savings bank where they remained for thirty years.

It had always amazed Charlie that Frank James, who, with his brother Jesse, had led the very first bank robbery in the United States committed by an organized gang (Clay County Savings Bank, February 13, 1866—a date engraved on Charlie's heart), should have spent so much of his death in a safe-deposit vault. When Frank James's wife died in 1944, she and her husband were buried in a Kansas City cemetery. This too amazed Charlie: that he had been a pudgy fourth-grader when Frank James was at last put in the ground.

Saturday morning, after he had finished delivering milk, Charlie drove into Saratoga to see Kathy Marshall. It was a cool morning and absolutely clear. Most of the leaves had blown down in the rain and those that were left were pale yellow. The distant line of the Adirondacks was as sharp as if drawn with a pen. Charlie kept sneezing. The side door of the milk truck didn't close completely and a cold wind tugged at his pants leg.

Charlie parked the truck by the office, then walked up Broadway to Kathy Marshall's store, the Blue Lion. When he passed the store belonging to his ex-wife he sort of crept sideways, keeping his back to the glass and his head ducked down. A young mother wheeling her child in a stroller steered a wide path around him. When he reached the Blue Lion, he straightened up and sighed. It was a large store with two large windows displaying women's clothes, cookware and expensive children's toys from Sweden. Charlie hurried inside.

Kathy Marshall was a trim woman in her mid-twenties. She had the perfect features of a movie star and when she stood, she seemed to push her face slightly forward as if for inspection. She wore a tan dress with a blue border, and a thin gold chain around her neck with a single pearl.

"Yes, I bought the foal," she said. "I like horses. Willis told me it was particularly promising, so I thought why not?" She was only a few inches over five feet and looked up at Charlie with her head to one side.

"Did Jespersen give you any advice about it?" asked Charlie. They stood at the front of the shop near the cash register. Behind Charlie was a rack of white Mexican blouses.

"Not really, although he's helped me with other horses. He just looked at the foal and said it was perfectly healthy. What do you mean, that it's no good?"

"Sweet Dreams is a ringer. His blood doesn't match up with the stallion that was supposed to have sired him. It means that none of his foals can run on a Thoroughbred track."

Although Kathy Marshall must have been disappointed, she gave no sign of it. Charlie wondered if she already knew. He found it impossible to get past her beauty and guess intelligently about her thoughts. Her blond hair was short and cut close to her head. On her left wrist, she wore a large digital watch with a gold band. She held a yellow pencil and tapped it against her front teeth as she looked back at Charlie.

"Did you come here just to tell me that my foal was no good?" she asked.

"No, I wanted to know how well you knew Willis Stitt."

"Not very well. I bought a horse from him, that's all."

"What about Roy Leakey?"

"I know him better, but I haven't seen him to talk to for about a year."

"And Jespersen, how well do you know him?"

Kathy Marshall squinted her eyes at Charlie, then shook her head. "Mr. Bradshaw, who are you?"

"I gave you my card."

"Yes, but what right do you have to ask these questions, any questions? Why should I talk to you? You see these people waiting? They want my assistance. My lawyer is Toby Brown. Why don't you see him."

"Has Chief Peterson asked you about any of these murders?" asked Charlie.

"No, he hasn't and I can't imagine why he would."

Kathy Marshall turned to a woman customer waiting nearby and smiled with what appeared to be affection and good cheer. It was like seeing a light being flicked on and the charm of it made Charlie feel doubly excluded. He hated being a sucker for pretty girls.

After leaving the Blue Lion, Charlie drove across Saratoga to visit Jespersen's ex-wife, who had an address on Diamond Street. The truck rattled terribly and the empty milk racks banged against one another. Occasionally the truck backfired, making people on the street jump and stare after him.

Mrs. Jespersen lived in a white Colonial house with two big maples in the front yard. A teenage boy was raking leaves and stuffing them into green garbage bags. Charlie parked the truck several houses away, then walked back.

Mrs. Jespersen answered the door and, when Charlie gave her his card, she invited him in. She was about forty-five, slender and very attractive. She looked like a kind of racehorse: muscular and athletic and she even had a chestnut coloring with long chestnut-colored hair that reached past her shoulders. She wore jeans and a white blouse.

Charlie followed her through the front hall. Although he assumed he was interrupting her, she seemed perfectly content to talk. She offered him coffee, then went off to make it.

"You're Doris's friend," she said from the kitchen. "She speaks very highly of you." There was the sound of cupboards being opened and closed. "All I have is instant but there's cream if you want it."

"Black's fine," said Charlie. He sat on a sunporch at the back of the house. In the backyard were flowers and a small vegetable garden in which there were still some tomatoes and one large, yellow pumpkin. After several minutes, Mrs. Jespersen came out carrying two mugs.

She sat down on a chaise longue next to Charlie. A strand of hair fell across her face and she brushed it back. "Just what did you want to talk about?" she asked.

"I was curious about how well you knew Willis Stitt," said Charlie. He sipped the coffee, then set the mug down on a glass-topped table.

"When I was still married, he was over here to dinner several times. And once after that he asked me out, but I refused. I didn't dislike him but neither was I attracted to him. He was involved in various business deals with my husband but they didn't seem to be close friends."

"Do you think your husband could have owned horses with Stitt?"

"Possibly. My husband confided in me very little."

"Doris told me you'd been thinking of hiring a private detective and that she had recommended me. Do you mind telling me why you wanted a private detective?"

Mrs. Jespersen hesitated. She had long, thin fingers with long, narrow nails. She touched one hand to her throat. "I'm not sure I want to talk about that," she said. "The reason I wanted a private detective had to do with my settlement with my husband. We finally came to a compromise. Is it important?"

"I think it is," said Charlie. "At this point, anything I can learn is important."

Mrs. Jespersen sipped her coffee. "My husband's the sort of man who reveals very little about himself. I used to think he was just modest but really I think he hates to let anything go or to have anything known about him. He offered very little in the settlement and I felt he had more. David is very fond of Krugerrands—you know, those South African gold coins. He buys them, then tucks them away. He grew up very poor and part of him expects to be poor again. I once found twenty of them in a jar, way at the back of the closet. He also owns a fair amount of property in the country. I told him I thought he was being unfair about the settlement and that unless he offered more I would hire a private detective. When we married, I had a little money and David used it to pay for veterinarian school. I didn't feel I was robbing him."

"And he agreed to give you more money?"

"Yes. He hated the idea of a private detective. Three years

ago he ran for city commissioner and I'm sure he'll run again. He was afraid that a private detective would attract bad publicity."

The sunporch was furnished with white metal furniture with green cushions. A variety of green plants hung from the ceiling. Charlie recognized a begonia but that was the only plant he knew. "Did you ever happen to meet the jockey Jimmy McClatchy or hear your husband speak of him?"

"No. I never heard of him until I read he'd been killed at your house."

"What about Rodger Pease?"

"I don't recognize the name."

"What about Roy Leakey?"

"Isn't he a lawyer? I've never met him but I remember hearing that he was once involved with Kathy Marshall. If that's true, then David must dislike him. He can be very jealous."

"What kinds of things is Jespersen interested in?" asked Charlie. "You think he likes horses?"

"I suppose he must but I don't really know. You'd think after twenty-five years of marriage I'd know him like the back of my hand, but that's not true. After the first few years we didn't spend much time together. We had a child who died." Mrs. Jespersen drank a little coffee. She held the blue mug with both hands as if to warm them. "We were never close after that. This is a big house and we each had our own life."

"But there must be things he really likes."

"He likes women. He likes to be thought of as important. He likes money. He's also quite keen on karate. It frightened me sometimes how he could just smash things with his hands."

"Could he commit murder?"

Mrs. Jespersen looked out at the backyard. The leaves had been raked into several piles and a gray squirrel ran back and forth from one pile to another. 'I don't know," she said.

Charlie left Mrs. Jespersen around three, and went to his cousin's hardware store where he bought washers to fix his broken faucet. As always the clerk gave him a ten percent discount but treated him like a poor relation, which is true enough, thought Charlie.

Then, for the remainder of the day, Charlie learned what he could about Jespersen. He had been a veterinarian in Saratoga for ten years. Before that he had a practice in White Plains, where he also looked after horses at Belmont and Aqueduct. He'd spent three years in the Army and six years at Cornell. Jespersen had always been involved with horses but never seemed to own any. He played golf, was a member of the Rotary Club and also the Lions.

Early in the evening Charlie spent some time trying to locate Bob Wilks, the trainer on Long Island who had bought one of Sweet Dreams's foals. He finally reached him having dinner at a Deer Park country club.

Wilks said he bought the foal because Stitt had assured him it was a hot prospect. He and Stitt had trained horses together on Long Island in the early 1970s. No, he had never heard of Leakey or Jespersen. Yes, it was a shame about Stitt's death. Wilks said he had meant to fly into Saratoga for the funeral but at the last moment something big had come up.

Charlie left his office around eight and drove home. He took the stuffed parrot with him, then stopped at the first trash can and tossed the parrot inside. So much for bad jokes, he thought. He had the sense that he was beginning to cope with the chaos around him. When he got home, he made himself a bowl of tomato soup and a couple of toasted cheese sandwiches. During the evening he called John Wanamaker three times without success. A man at Wanamaker's rooming house said he hadn't seen him all week. Charlie fixed the washer in the cold-water tap, worked a little at adjusting the lift wires in the bathroom toilet, then went to bed early but had trouble sleeping. His .38 was under his pillow and each time he touched it he woke up frightened.

The next morning Charlie opened his eyes at six with the knowledge that he had to see Flo Abernathy. It was as if the idea itself had waked him. Having registered the idea, he tried to go back to sleep but couldn't. Outside it was still dark. The water was loud against the shore. He could hear the wind blowing through the trees and the branches seemed to be whipping and lashing each other. At last Charlie got up. As he made breakfast, he put on a Benny Goodman record just to drown out the noise of the weather.

At eight thirty, he drove into Saratoga by way of Route 29 so he could stop at a greenhouse and buy some flowers. He got a dozen long-stemmed roses wrapped in green paper. It seemed like a good idea at the time, but when he arrived at Flo Abernathy's door with a dozen roses under his good arm, he began to feel foolish.

He hadn't seen Miss Abernathy since Tuesday at Rodger Pease's funeral. When she opened the door, she smiled, then stepped back to let Charlie enter. She wore a long, blue silk dressing gown with cloth-covered buttons. Her white hair hung loose down her back. She seemed paler somehow, more transparent. At first Charlie thought she was sick, then he realized it was grief.

"I brought you some flowers," he said.

She took the roses as if uncertain what to do with them. In contrast to the red of the flowers, her skin was the color of a cloud. "I'll put them in water," she said. "Have you come to give me a progress report? At least you seem to have no more bruises. How's your arm?"

"Still stiff, but I hope to go swimming with it next week."

The air in the room smelled stale and there seemed to be more general clutter. Charlie guessed there were at least twenty chairs. He picked up an ivory carving of a mountain with a little hut near the top and two men outside the door smoking their pipes. A zigzagging trail led up to the hut. He put the carving back on top of a bookcase filled with leatherbound books.

"Would you like some coffee?" asked Flo. "I'm afraid I have no chocolate-chip cookies but I could make some cinnamon toast."

"Just coffee would be fine." Charlie threaded his way between the furniture to the turret, which was half-filled with plants. Each of the four narrow windows looking out on Ludlow had a window seat with a red leather cushion. Down on the street three boys on bikes attempted synchronized wheelies as a beagle puppy ran around them barking.

Flo Abernathy found a tall blue vase for the roses but there seemed to be no unoccupied surface on which to put it. She removed several photograph albums from a table and set them on the floor. The teakettle began to whistle.

Shortly, she joined Charlie in the turret with the coffee and a plate of cinnamon toast. Each piece of toast was cut into three long sections. She offered the plate to Charlie. "When I was a child," she said, "we called these Trotwoods, I'm not sure why. It had something to do with *David Copperfield*."

Across the room, Charlie saw the brass horse that he had dug out of the ruins of Rodger Pease's house, all polished and standing on a white doily in the middle of a small round table. It reminded him of the two silver horses that had been used to prop up McClatchy's head. "You grew up in Glens Falls?" he said.

"That's right." Flo Abernathy sat down on a window seat across from Charlie.

"Do you still have family there?"

"A brother. I haven't seen him since my mother's funeral in 1950." She gestured vaguely toward the rest of the room. "It was my mother who left me this furniture. Sometimes I read about my brother in the paper. He and the rest of my family, they all disapproved of my quitting college and remaining in Saratoga, and disapproved of Rodger too, of course."

"Why don't you get in touch with your brother?" asked Charlie.

"It's been too long."

"It's only a telephone call, or I could even drive you up there." He had a momentary picture of Flo Abernathy in the milk truck.

"He wouldn't care to see me."

"Why don't you find out? Aren't you curious about him?"

Miss Abernathy looked at Charlie, then smiled. "I'll consider it," she said. "You know, after I last saw you, I realized I had known your father. He was one of the first people I met after I decided to remain in Saratoga and become a singer."

"Did he borrow money from you?" asked Charlie.

"No, nothing like that. I had been auditioning at the Chicago Club. It was in the middle of the afternoon. A rainy September day. I was waiting for Rodger to pick me up but he thought I'd be longer. I didn't get the job. Your father was the only other person in the lounge. The whole town seemed empty. He came over and sat down and began to talk. He had heard me singing and told me how much he liked it. He wasn't being fresh or trying to flirt. I remember I liked his face. It was bright and energetic. His shiny black hair was slicked back and not a strand was out of place. It turned out that he knew Rodger. I'm not sure how it happened but soon we were betting pennies on the raindrops that were rolling down the big window. We did this for at least an hour. I remember I won fifteen cents. The Rodger arrived and your father took us both out to dinner. I expect I saw him another half dozen times before I heard he had committed suicide."

Charlie didn't say anything. He had hardly any memory of his father: a vague recollection of being tossed in the air, of falling and being caught at the last moment. He remembered the suicide only because the house had been full of policemen who were kind to him.

"By the way," said Charlie, "I wanted to ask you if you know what happened to Rodger's dog. I'd forgotten about it."

"I have no idea. I assume it was buried."

"Did Rodger ever have to take it to a vet?"

"Certainly, it was quite old and had all sorts of complicated problems."

"What vet did he go to?"

Miss Abernathy smiled as if remembering a joke. "Rodger used to boast that he got free service from the best vet in Saratoga."

"Who was that?"

"I don't recall his name but he once ran for city commissioner."

Not long afterward, Charlie left Miss Abernathy and drove over to see Victor, who turned out to be sleeping. Charlie had to hammer on his door for several minutes. From the other side he heard various grumbles and groans and at last the door was opened. Victor was naked but held a dirty sweat shirt to his waist.

"Don't you realize this is Sunday?" he asked.

Charlie pushed past him. Moshe, the one-eyed cat, stared at Charlie, then ran into the kitchen.

"Where were you last night?" asked Charlie.

Victor scratched the gray hairs on his chest and began pulling on some tattered underwear. "Storming the heights of sexual transport. Have you ever known a woman who could walk on her hands?"

Victor's clothes were scattered around the room. Charlie removed a pair of pants from a rocking chair and sat down. On the wall above him was a poster of the Three Stooges.

"I wanted to ask you," said Charlie, "about the woman who hired you to get back those letters."

"Ruth MacDermott, what about her?" Victor continued to get dressed, putting on blue jeans and a black sweat shirt. He looked in the mirror over the mantel, bared his teeth, picked at the front ones with one fingernail, then grinned at himself.

"Why did she think the letters were at Leakey's cabin?"

"Beats me. I figured she'd been out there."

"Where does she live?"

Victor gave him an address on Seward. "You going to bother her?"

"Just a couple of questions. What's she like?"

"Helluva bosom. Nice big eyes. You might do worse." Victor began picking his clothes off the floor. When he had an armful, he went to the closet and threw them in.

"One other thing," said Charlie, standing up, "I want you to keep a close watch on Roy Leakey. Forget everything else but that."

Victor paused in the middle of the room. "Why? You want him to beat my head with a stick, maybe kick me in the balls?"

"I think he's in danger."

"Couldn't happen to a nicer guy."

"I want you to stay near him. If you see Jespersen hanging around, then call me right away."

"Why Jespersen?"

"I think he killed McClatchy."

"You going to tell Peterson?"

"Not yet."

Ruth MacDermott's bosom gave the appearance of having been made from a feather bolster. It was large, cream colored and dotted with freckles. She wore a dark red dressing gown, which exposed a sizable V of flesh. Charlie looked away to the wallpaper, which was red with paisley designs in black velvet. It was like the wallpaper in a whorehouse, thought Charlie, who had never been in a whorehouse. Some fellow soldiers had attempted to take him to one in Germany but at the last moment he had got cold feet.

It seemed to Charlie that the whole room was like a room in a whorehouse, a Western whorehouse like Fanny Porter's Sporting House in San Antonio: overstuffed furniture covered with red velvet, thick red drapery, a Persian carpet, dark mahogany tables and sideboards, oval portraits of big-bosomed women with dreamy eyes. On one of the overstuffed chairs, a white Persian cat lay washing itself.

"I hadn't thought of the cabin until I talked to Kathy Marshall at a cocktail party. She used to be intimate with Roy. She told me that he kept all his letters up there. That's why I told Vic. Isn't he sweet?"

"Who?" asked Charlie.

"Why, Victor. He's so eager."

Charlie glanced at Ruth MacDermott, who sat perched on the edge of a chair with her hands in her lap. She was a large woman, almost heavy. Charlie had never thought of Victor as sweet. "He's a good friend," said Charlie, not knowing what else to say.

"I adore roguish men," said Mrs. MacDermott.

"Just when did Kathy Marshall tell you about the cabin?" asked Charlie.

"Last Tuesday evening at the Warnkes'. There was a small party."

"Was she with Jespersen?"

"No, he was busy."

"Do Jespersen and Leakey know each other?"

"Slightly, but Jespersen dislikes Roy for having been involved with Kathy Marshall. He prefers his women unused."

Mrs. MacDermott had masses of dark red hair piled on top of her head. She took a purple cigarette from a box on the table and lit it with a small silver lighter. Charlie glanced at her again, then looked back at the wallpaper. "Were you ever involved with Jespersen?" he asked.

"Good heavens, no. He's too fond of the tomboy type."

"And when did you tell Victor about the letters?"

"Wednesday, the very next day. I'm sorry he didn't find them. Sometimes a woman in love can be indiscreet. I would hate to think of someone reading those letters and misunderstanding." She kept the purple cigarette in one corner of her mouth and it waggled up and down as she spoke.

Charlie wished he could take a look at those letters. "I expect to see Leakey in a day or so," he said. "I'll tell him again that you want them back."

Mrs. MacDermott turned the force of her brown eyes in Charlie's direction. "Then I would be completely in your power," she said.

Sunday evening Charlie spent several hours typing up what he knew about the three murders and his reasons for suspecting Jespersen. He had continued to be on mildly agreeable terms with a lawyer in the prosecutor's office, and on Monday he meant to pay him a visit and present his charges. Presumably the lawyer would call in Peterson. Although Charlie had no real proof of Jespersen's guilt, he knew Peterson well enough to believe that the police chief would open an investigation. If once the police actually questioned Jespersen, then kept plaguing him in an official sort of way, it might be too much for him to stand. After all, Jespersen had political ambitions. Even the slightest legal attention would be damaging.

But Charlie felt dissatisfied. He wanted to arrest Jespersen himself, to confront Peterson and Caldwell with the established fact of Jespersen's guilt. That, however, seemed impossible and Charlie tried to dismiss his desire as no more than vanity. Still, he hated to hand all his work over to Peterson, then scurry back to his cottage on the lake.

Twice that evening Charlie tried calling John Wanamaker. The manager of the rooming house told him that although Wanamaker's belongings were still in his room, Wanamaker himself had apparently disappeared. Charlie imagined him hit by a car and lying unconscious in some hospital.

Apart from Wanamaker, Charlie also worried that he hadn't heard from his mother. He expected her to call and beg him to get her out of trouble. Maybe he would have to rush down to Atlantic City. As a result, Charlie felt jumpy and alert. All day he had carried his revolver and was constantly aware of its pressure against his stomach where he kept it tucked beneath his waistband. He knew Jespersen must be desperate. Again he sought out Victor to make sure he was watching Roy Leakey. He had even gone so far as to ask Victor to hire Eddie Gillespie if he needed help.

Charlie went to bed around ten. The wind was still roaring in the trees and he thought how the noise would keep him from hearing anyone sneaking up on the cottage. Just as he began to get scared, he fell asleep. At midnight he was awakened by the ringing of the phone. It was Victor.

"Hey, Charlie, I know this is a bad time to call but I just saw someone slipping out of the back of Leakey's house and if I was a betting man I'd give you even odds it was Jespersen. Is that worth waking you up for?"

"I'll be right over."

Charlie dressed, grabbed his revolver and hurried out to the milk truck. All the way into town, he kept the pedal flat to the floor. The empty milk crates banged and rattled against each other over the roar of the motor. There was no other traffic.

Charlie turned down Leakey's street and saw Victor leaning against the red Renault. All the houses were dark. As Charlie drew to a stop, the brakes of the milk truck made a screeching noise.

"Madcap Bradshaw and his Milkmobile," said Victor.

Charlie was tired of jokes about the milk truck. "What

makes you think it was Jespersen?" he asked. He looked over at Leakey's house, a white split-level. It too was dark.

Victor stood scratching his elbows. "It was a tall, thin guy sneaking away from the back of the house. Maybe it wasn't Jespersen. Maybe it was only a sneak thief."

"How long have you been here?"

"I followed Leakey home around eleven. He went in. All the drapes were shut so I couldn't see anything. After about forty-five minutes the lights went out and about five minutes later I see this guy in the backyard."

"Did you follow him?"

"Heck no, I get paid for watchin', not tacklin'."

Charlie and Victor stood whispering between the Renault and the truck. The air was cold and Charlie wished he had brought a heavier coat. There would be frost tonight for sure. In the air was the lingering smell of burning leaves.

"Hand me the flashlight in the glove compartment and let's go," said Charlie.

"Where we going?"

"We're going to poke around."

Victor looked unhappy. "Charlie, I don't want to get shot and I don't want to spend the night in jail. Tell me those things won't happen."

"Come on," said Charlie.

Charlie cut across Leakey's lawn to the front steps and rang the bell. It chimed like Big Ben—eight long notes. Charlie waited a minute, then rang again. The porch had a black metal railing. Victor waited on the grass, flapping his arms to keep warm.

"Let's go around back," said Charlie.

Without waiting for Victor, he hurried around the side of the house and immediately stumbled over a barbecue grill, which clanged noisily as it collapsed on the stone patio.

Victor helped Charlie to his feet. "I should have called the local drum and bugle corps," he said.

Reaching the back door, Charlie tried the knob but it was locked. Between the house and grass was a border of stones and small shrubs. Charlie picked up a stone, hit it against a pane of glass, then hit it harder. The glass shattered.

"When I think of the grief you gave me about breaking that tiny window at the cabin," said Victor.

"Don't you ever stop joking?"

"You think I'd be joking if I wasn't terrified? Leakey's probably listening to rock-and-roll music through the stereo headphones. Won't he be surprised when we come rushing into his bedroom holding a .38 and a chunk of granite. That's how people get strokes."

Charlie opened the back door, felt around for a light switch, then flicked it on. The presence of light was comforting. They were in a back hall leading to the kitchen. The house was silent except for the hum of the refrigerator.

"I'll check upstairs," said Charlie. "You look around down here."

"What're we looking for?" They stood in the kitchen next to a large butcher block with a place for knives and meat cleavers. Victor removed a meat cleaver and ran his thumb along the blade.

"We're looking for Leakey," said Charlie.

"Wouldn't it be better to stick together?"

"No, it wouldn't. You want the gun? Take it."

Victor replaced the meat cleaver. "I'd only hurt myself," he said.

The stairs were by the front door. Whenever Charlie came to a light switch, he turned it on. At the top of the stairs was a long hall hung with reproductions of Impressionist paintings. All the floors were carpeted. Charlie looked through one bedroom, then another. He could hear Victor banging around downstairs and whistling. At the end of the hall was the master bedroom. On the door was a large white plaque that said CAPTAIN. Charlie found Roy Leakey lying on his back across the double bed. He wore a dark brown suit. His tie was undone and his shoes lay on the carpet. Next to him on the white bedspread was a small syringe.

Bending down, Charlie put his fingers against Leakey's

throat to feel a pulse. It was very slow. Leakey's skin looked gray, like dust or cardboard. He dragged Leakey into a sitting position and shook him. The lawyer had been so carefully groomed when Charlie saw him before that to see him all rumpled made him look like another person. Leakey made a faint groaning noise. Charlie slapped his cheek and shook him again but couldn't bring him around. Standing up, he slipped his arm out of its sling, then grabbed Leakey's wrist and pulled him off the bed and onto his shoulder. Briefly, in the mirror, he saw his reflection with Leakey on his back. It looked as if they were wrestling. Charlie put the syringe in his pocket and headed for the door.

Victor met him at the bottom of the stairs. He was holding a sheet of paper. "Is he dead?"

"Not yet. I'm taking him to the hospital."

"Guess what I found," said Victor, holding up the paper. "Leakey confessed to all three murders."

"Is it signed?"

"No, but it was in his typewriter."

"Go look in the refrigerator, then meet me at the car."

"You think it's there?"

"Just check."

"I don't want to see it again."

"Check!"

16

▼▼▼

THE RED PLASTIC CARRYING CASE between Charlie's feet was designed to look like a barn. A pair of brass hooks held together the two halves of the green gambrel roof. It was nine thirty Monday morning and Charlie was sitting on a hard wooden chair in the waiting room of Jespersen's clinic. The carrying case belonged to Victor's cat, Moshe. Charlie wore his khaki milkman's uniform and the starched collar chafed his neck.

Across from Charlie sat an old woman with a white German shepherd that lay on its stomach sniffing and whining. Charlie's .38 was in his back pocket and gouged him uncomfortably. He would have shifted it but the old woman kept staring at him.

"What's wrong with your poor cat?" she asked. She wore a trench coat and had bright circles of pink makeup on her cheeks.

"He won't eat."

"Ralphie usually likes cats," said the woman.

Charlie smiled. He hoped he wouldn't have to discuss the complexities of pets. He half-regretted coming to Jespersen's office and again told himself he was only being motivated by vanity. Better to leave the whole business to Peterson. Well, Peterson was supposed to arrive soon enough.

The door to the examination room opened and Jespersen began to pass through it. When he saw Charlie, he stopped.

Charlie took hold of the case and stood up. "Victor's cat is sick," he said. "He wasn't able to come so I brought him."

Jespersen gave Charlie a long look. He held a clipboard in his arm as if to shield himself. "What seems to be the matter?" he asked.

"He won't eat."

Jespersen glanced out the window. The Wholesome Dairy milk truck was parked behind his white Buick in the U-shaped driveway. "Come on in," he said, reaching for the case.

Charlie handed it to him. The case slipped from his fingers and would have fallen if Jespersen hadn't grabbed for it.

"This cat usually makes a lot of noise," Jespersen said.

"He's very sick."

Charlie followed Jespersen into the examination room, then went over and leaned against the far door. He found himself remembering how Victor had described his method as a detective: the clown over the barrel of water at the carnival, as if Charlie proceeded solely by means of aggravation. Perhaps that was true, thought Charlie.

Jespersen put the case on the stainless-steel table. He wore his white laboratory coat with the row of pens in the breast pocket. Charlie couldn't imagine why anybody needed a dozen pens. All of Jespersen's movements were cautious and deliberate. From the kennel in the back it seemed that about fifty dogs were barking.

Jespersen undid the hook securing the top of the case. On the wall behind him was a poster showing the canine family tree. "For how long hasn't he eaten?" he asked.

Charlie didn't answer.

Jespersen folded back the lid. Inside was McClatchy's head. All of Jespersen's muscles seemed to become rigid at the same moment. He took a quick breath, then glanced at Charlie. "What's this supposed to mean?"

"You left it in Roy Leakey's refrigerator and I'm returning it."

Jespersen stared at the head, which lay facing upward. From where Charlie stood, he could see the tip of McClatchy's nose sticking above the sides of the case: a small, white stub of a nose like a stub of chalk.

"You have any proof?" asked Jespersen.

Charlie nodded toward the door of the waiting room. Jespersen turned to look. For a moment nothing happened except that sweat broke out on Charlie's forehead. Jespersen looked back at Charlie, questioningly, and as he turned again the door opened to reveal Roy Leakey leaning against the doorframe. He appeared ill and very weak.

Leakey pushed himself up straight. "I'm still here, Jespersen," he said. "It didn't work."

Jespersen remained by the table, his hands resting on the edges of the cat-carrying case. Then he removed his glasses and put them in a pocket under his laboratory coat. Taking out a cigarette, he lit it and blew a stream of smoke through his nose. Near him was a tray of scalpels. He no longer appeared tense. Indeed, Charlie thought, his long, angular face seemed almost peaceful. Jespersen stared down at his cigarette, then tapped some ashes onto McClatchy's forehead. The case looked like a miniature barn in the middle of the stainless-steel table.

Charlie and Roy Leakey stood blocking the two doors. Charlie removed his left arm from its sling and felt for his revolver

in his hip pocket. Then he paused to look at his watch. Peterson was late.

"You killed Jimmy McClatchy," said Charlie. He glanced
past Leakey for any sign of the police. "You want to say anything about that?"

Jespersen dropped the cigarette on the floor and stepped on
it. Then he reached into the cat-carrying case. Slowly he lifted
out McClatchy's head, raising it until it was level with his own.
It was a fat, doughy face with fat cheeks and a fat little chin.
The mouth had fallen open and Charlie could see a glitter of
gold teeth. The eyes looked unfocused and stupid. The brown
hair looked as if it had never been combed. The face was the
color of snow. Jespersen held it, Charlie thought, as one might
hold the face of a lover.

"He tried to blackmail me." Jespersen had long fingers and
he clasped the head by the jawbone, pressing his thumbs over
the corners of McClatchy's mouth. "He called me from your
house. He said he was going to tell the grand jury about Sweet
Dreams. I couldn't let that happen."

"Put down the head," said Charlie. He again began to reach
for his revolver. As Charlie moved, Jespersen wheeled and
tossed the head at him so that it spun over and over through
the air. Then he snatched up a scalpel and ran toward Leakey.
Charlie started to duck but at the last moment he caught the
head with both hands.

Leakey attempted to block Jespersen, who knocked him
aside and slashed at him with the scalpel. Leakey raised an
arm to protect himself, then yelped as the scalpel cut through
his shirt. Jespersen shoved him out of the way and ran through
the door.

Hurriedly, Charlie stuck the head back into the case. There
was shouting from the waiting room, as well as the barking of
a dog. Charlie's hands felt filthy. Roy Leakey knelt on the floor
holding his arm. Running to him, Charlie crouched down and
saw blood soaking through his shirt over his left shoulder.

"Go after him," Leakey said. "I'll be okay."

Charlie jumped to his feet just as Victor came barreling

through the door and bumped into him, knocking him back toward the table.

"He cut my coat," said Victor. He pointed indignantly to a rip in the front of his tan raincoat. "First the back, now the front—my whole coat is a wreck."

Charlie pushed past him and ran into the waiting room. The receptionist and the old woman stood by the door looking frightened. The white German shepherd began barking and lunging at Charlie as the old woman tried to hold the leash. Jespersen's white laboratory coat lay on the rug. Charlie kicked the coat toward the dog as he tried to dodge around it toward the door. Just at that moment, he bumped into someone's arms. He turned to see Peterson's face about six inches above him. Charlie looked out at the street but there was no sign of Jespersen. Peterson lightly shook Charlie's shoulder as one might shake the shoulder of a troublesome schoolboy.

"Now Charlie," he said, "what's all the fuss?"

"Where's Jespersen?" Charlie felt so frustrated that he could have wept.

"He just hurried by me. You been bothering him?"

"Where the hell have you been?" Charlie asked. The German shepherd again began barking and whining.

"I had an important long-distance call."

"If you had got here when I said, you could have arrested Jespersen for the murders of McClatchy, Pease and Stitt."

Peterson stood in the middle of the waiting room with his hands in his back pockets. "Those are pretty serious charges, Charlie. I hope you got proof."

"I'll get you some," said Charlie, and walked past Leakey into the examination room. Victor stood by the table poking one finger through the tear in his raincoat. Fastening the lid of the cat carrying case, Charlie returned with it to Peterson.

"Here," said Charlie. "Anything else you want to know, you can ask Leakey. Let's go, Victor." Charlie gave the case to the police chief who looked at it curiously.

"What's this?" he asked.

Charlie went outside. Leakey had parked his BMW in front of Jespersen's white Buick, boxing it in. Wherever Jespersen had gone, he had gone on foot. As Charlie walked toward the milk truck, he heard Peterson make a peculiar strangulated cry. It reminded Charlie of the sound of a bagpipe played by a beginner with no musical talent. He climbed into the truck, turned the key and began pumping the gas.

Victor jumped in the other side. "You think that was necessary?" he asked.

Charlie backed out the driveway onto Clark Street. "There are moments that are destined to happen," he said.

"You gotta watch out, Charlie, it's no fun being known as a practical joker. What are we gonna do now, wait for our reward?"

"No, everything's been messed up. If we don't find Jespersen after all that foolishness, we'll look pretty stupid. Since Peterson passed him, then maybe he was going downtown. We'll try Kathy Marshall's store." It was a warm, Indian-summer day, even though the trees were mostly bare. Charlie shifted into third and gunned the motor.

"I don't mind looking stupid," said Victor. "Why don't we just let Peterson get him?"

"Because I want to do it myself. I don't like heads being thrown at me."

"Why'd you catch it?"

"Because I couldn't stand the idea of watching it bounce."

"What'd it feel like?"

"Sort of hard and cold and soft all at the same time."

Victor braced himself between the front window and a stack of milk racks. "I don't see why you brought it in the first place."

"I thought it would create an effect."

"It did," said Victor.

With only a partial load of milk in the back, the truck was at its noisiest. Charlie held onto the wheel with both hands, ignoring his bad arm as he tried to coax more speed out of the engine. Glancing at Victor, he saw that his friend was again investigating the cut in his raincoat. Charlie found himself worrying about the housewives who were beginning to look down the street, waiting for their eggs, milk and cream. He had only done a third of his route that morning before coming into Saratoga.

"What do you think Jespersen's up to?" shouted Victor over the noise.

"I expect he'll try to get out of town."

Charlie pumped the brakes, downshifted, turned right onto Broadway, then accelerated. The light at Circular Street turned yellow. Charlie leaned on the horn and kept going, yanking the wheel to the left to pass a car that had stopped. There was a crash from the back as some milk racks tipped over. As Charlie again hit the brakes, a white wave of milk spilled into the cab.

"His wife told me that he likes to hide money," continued Charlie. "Maybe he'll try to retrieve some." Charlie saw three of his fellow swimmers talking together in front of the Y. They turned and stared as he roared past.

"You ever been to the milk-truck races in Oneonta?" asked Victor.

Charlie didn't answer. He roared down Broadway, riding the middle line and swerving around slower cars. There seemed to be a lot of traffic. The truck's horn sounded old and feeble, more like a joke than a horn. Milk from the broken bottles spilled out of the truck from the back and side doors, leaving a white trail down the center of the street.

Charlie pulled up to the fire hydrant in front of his ex-wife's boutique. Drawing the .38 from his back pocket, he jumped down from the truck. About a dozen people on the sidewalk stopped to stare at him. In his khaki milkman's uniform, he felt almost official, almost like a policeman. He ran into Kathy Marshall's store. An attractive brunette in a tight red T-shirt glanced up from behind the cash register. There was no sign of Jespersen or Kathy Marshall.

"Was Jespersen here?" asked Charlie.

"He left just a minute ago," said the girl.

"Did Kathy go with him?"

"No, she's in Albany. He wanted her car."

"What did he do?" asked Charlie.

The girl shut the drawer of the cash register. "I don't know," she said. "He went into Kathy's office." She kept looking at the gun in Charlie's hand.

"Do you know why?" he asked.

The girl hesitated.

"He's wanted for murder," said Charlie.

"Kathy kept a pistol in her desk," said the girl. "David took it. I saw it in his hand when he ran out of the store."

"Which way did he go?"

"He turned left."

Charlie ran back to the truck. Victor stood beside it. Little waterfalls of milk flowed from beneath the doors. As Charlie climbed back into the cab, he heard his name being called. Even four years after his divorce, his ex-wife's voice made him jump. He decided not to turn around. Pressing down on the horn, Charlie swerved out onto Broadway, cutting off a blue pickup and making a U-turn. Victor barely managed to jump back inside. Glancing over his shoulder, Charlie saw his ex-wife and his cousin Jack standing on the sidewalk.

"He picked up a gun," said Charlie.

"Great," said Victor, "just what we need."

"You want to get out?"

"Hey, what's a coupla bullets between friends?"

Two blocks up Broadway in front of the newsstand, Charlie noticed a retired bookie that he used to arrest each August. Charlie slowed down and called to him across the street. "Louie, have you seen the vet, David Jespersen?"

"He ran into Congress Park a few minutes ago."

"Thanks."

Charlie again leaned on the horn and pulled into traffic. The horn made a noise like *tootle-tootle*. He turned left on Spring Street adjoining the park. Jespersen was nowhere to be seen. Driving all the way around the park, Charlie passed the YMCA for a second time. His fellow swimmers were still talking out in front. Again they stopped and stared after him.

Charlie turned into the park, drove past the red brick Canfield Casino, then turned around at the duck pond and drove back to Broadway. Pausing at the light, he turned right, then turned right again at the library. Two police cars with lights flashing and sirens wide open shot past him down Broadway toward Jespersen's office. After another minute, Charlie drew to a stop at the corner of Circular and Union Avenues. There was no sign of Jespersen. He felt stumped.

"Why should he come in this direction?" asked Charlie. "His house, office, girlfriend and even his ex-wife are all on the other side of the park."

"Maybe he wanted to visit the site of past glories," suggested Victor.

"What's that?"

"The track." The Saratoga racetrack lay four blocks up Union Avenue.

"We'll try it. If we can't find him, we'll try the Northway. He might be trying to hitch a ride south. If he's not there, you can help me deliver the rest of my milk. It was stupid to play that game at Jespersen's office, especially if he gets away. Peterson can really make trouble for us."

He continued to drive slowly down Union Avenue. The day was becoming hot. In front of the Victorian mansions, people were raking leaves or putting up storm windows. Some students near a Skidmore dorm were throwing a Frisbee. Nearly half the big houses were closed up for the winter with shutters over the windows—homes for summer residents from New York or Boston or Montreal. Charlie coasted through the light at Nelson Avenue. To their right were the grounds of the track. The tall elms and maples were entirely stripped of their leaves. To the left were the four white columns of the National Museum of Racing.

The main gate of the racetrack stood open. Inside, a small army of carpenters, painters and maintenance men were making the track ready for the winter, covering the clocks with sheets of plastic, stacking the hundreds of wooden red chairs, taking down the red-and-white striped awnings. The trees around the outside buildings and jockeys' quarters were evergreens and looked as they did in August. All that was missing were the thousands of people.

Charlie drove around to the left of the grandstand on a gravel path that led the short distance to the track. The old white grandstand with its red trim and gray slate roof was empty except for some men painting and piling up chairs. A yellow grater was plowing the dirt in front of the tote board.

"There's someone running on the track," said Victor.

Charlie looked. A thin figure was running along the far turn of the track by the three-eights pole. "It's Jespersen," he said. He was running along the rail past one of the several towers used for filming the races. They looked like guard towers in a prison or concentration camp.

Charlie drove the milk truck onto the track through the gate by the chute. The surface was soft and spongy.

"But what's he doing?" asked Victor.

"He's heading for the shed rows along the backstretch. That's where Sweet Dreams was stabled."

"Yeah, but why now?"

Charlie pushed his foot down on the accelerator. "I'm not sure, maybe he hid something there."

"Like what, Sherlock?"

"Like maybe some money."

As Charlie accelerated through the soft dirt, the rear end of the truck began to slew back and forth. The remaining milk bottles rattled together and the metal milk racks banged against the sides of the truck. The floor was swamped with milk, and Charlie's shoes were soaked with it. He could feel his socks squishing between his toes. In order to keep the truck roaring ahead in a reasonably forward direction, Charlie had to hunch over the steering wheel and hold it with both arms. Crossing the track every fifteen feet was a ridge of dirt like an oversized mole's tunnel and whenever the truck bounced over one, all the milk racks rose up a foot, then crashed back down. This is what cacophony means, thought Charlie. The truck screamed along at the very top of third gear but Charlie was afraid to take his hands from the wheel in order to shift into fourth.

Victor tried to brace himself against the door. "What're you going to do?" he shouted.

"Arrest him."

"But you're not a cop."

"So what?"

The truck zigzagged forward. Jespersen glanced over his shoulder, then stumbled, scrambled to his feet and tried to run faster. A metal fence kept him from crossing over the far side of the track, but about twenty yards ahead, the horse ambulance gate out of the backstretch stood open. He stumbled again. Then, by the three-and-a-half furlong pole, he stopped and turned to face the truck. Charlie could see a gun in his hand.

"Oh-oh," said Victor.

There was the faint crack of a pistol shot and a hole appeared in the middle of the windshield. The bullet ricocheted through the metal milk racks as the truck swerved from left to right.

"Get down," shouted Charlie.

"That much I can figure out for myself. Where the hell's your gun?"

"In my back pocket."

"Why don't you shoot him, for cryin' out loud?"

"I can't let go of the wheel."

Victor began to tug at the .38 in Charlie's back pocket. The spur of the hammer caught on the fabric and Victor pulled harder. Charlie imagined the gun accidentally discharging.

"Leave it alone!"

There was another gunshot and the glass on Victor's side of the truck disintegrated. Victor crouched back down on the floor. His pants were soaked with milk and bits of glass were caught in his hair.

To his right, Charlie saw the small lake in the middle of the track, a few naked elms and the last of the red flowers. There was a third gunshot and Charlie's half of the windshield blew apart, covering him with pellets of glass. Without the windshield, everything was noisier and the wind blew in their faces, making Charlie's eyes water.

"They're going to love you at Wholesome Dairy," shouted Victor.

Jespersen stood in the center of the track with his legs apart. He held the pistol in both hands, stretching his arms straight out in front of him. He wore a blue jacket and white shirt.

His tie had blown back over his shoulder and his hair fluttered in the wind, flicking long yellow strands across his forehead.

Charlie had crouched down so that he was just barely peering over the edge of the windshield. His arms half-surrounded the wheel and each time he let go to reach for the revolver, the truck swerved toward the rail.

Jespersen kept firing, aiming into the truck. The bullets ricocheted and crashed into the milk crates. Steam began pouring through a hole in the radiator. Charlie was no more than twenty feet from Jespersen. He could see his face, furious and concentrated. Jespersen lowered the pistol and shot at the front tire. There was an explosion as the tire blew up, making the truck veer sharply to the right.

Charlie spun the wheel but without effect. The truck began to skid in a circle, throwing Charlie against the door. He had no idea where Jespersen was. Through the empty windshield he saw a swirl of clouds, trees, blue sky and trees again as the truck spun around. Crash followed crash as the remaining milk crates tipped over. There was a thump against the side of the truck. Attempting to stand, Charlie stumbled against Victor and splashed to the floor. The truck smashed sideways against the rail. There was a long tearing sound, then the truck came to a halt. All the noises stopped except for the dripping and splashing of milk.

Charlie yanked the .38 from his back pocket, jumped from the side door and fell forward onto his stomach in the soft dirt. Five feet away Jespersen lay face down. The truck had slid into him, knocking him into the rail. His gun was still in his hand. Charlie scrambled to his feet, hurried over and kicked the gun into the grass. Then he bent down beside him.

"Is he dead?" asked Victor.

"No, just unconscious."

"We going to wait for the cops?" asked Victor. "I think some of these horse people are going to be pretty pissed." A group of men were hurrying toward them across the center of the track.

"We're going to deliver him," said Charlie.

Charlie retrieved Jespersen's pistol. It was some sort of foreign make that he didn't recognize. Then Charlie tied Jespersen's hands with his necktie.

"Help me carry him," he asked.

Victor lifted Jespersen's feet and Charlie lifted his shoulders. Together they put him on the floor of the truck, lying on his back in the milk. Then Charlie took his place behind the wheel and pushed the starter, listened to it grind and grind until the engine turned over. The truck backfired. It seemed that only four cylinders were working. Revving the engine, Charlie made a U-turn and accelerated down the track toward the stands. A zigzagging trail of milk showed the way they had come. The men in the center of the track began shouting at them. Charlie drove faster. He had to press his whole weight down on the wheel to keep from veering to the right. The truck was spattered with mud and its windshield was gone. Its front was pockmarked with bullet holes and it was still spewing steam. Along the right side was a deep crease and tear in the metal where it had hit the rail. Loose milk crates jangled together and there was the sound of broken glass sliding back and forth on the metal floor. The right front tire went flappety-flap, flappety-flap.

Charlie drove out of the chute and onto the gravel path leading to the front gate. A group of about fifteen workmen watched silently. Continuing out of the grounds onto Union Avenue, Charlie turned left toward town, lurching forward at no more than 10 miles per hour. The floor of the milk truck was an inch deep with milk, which swirled and lapped around Jespersen as if around a large island. He made a groaning noise, tried to sit up, then fell back with a splash. Three police cars roared past on the way to the track. Charlie felt tremendously pleased. He glanced at Victor, who stood leaning forward with his head half through the empty windshield. His fluffy gray hair blew in the wind and he was grinning.

Charlie turned onto Circular, drove past Doris's apartment, then turned left onto Lake Avenue. All along the street, people stared at the truck. Victor waved to them. When they reached the police station, Charlie drew to a stop and leaned on the horn. He no longer cared that it went tootle-tootle. He kept leaning on it until a policeman hurried out. It was Emmett Van Brunt.

"Get that truck outta here, Charlie. Are you fuckin' off your rocker?"

"I want Peterson," said Charlie.

"He's organizing a statewide search."

"Tell him not to bother," said Charlie.

17
▼▼▼

W HAT UPSET CHARLIE MOST was the long-distance call that had delayed Peterson's arrival at Jespersen's office. The call had come from the police chief of Santa Fe, New Mexico. John Wanamaker had been arrested in the middle of a burglary. The police had found him hiding in a closet. Neither closet nor house belonged to him. When the police went back to Wanamaker's room, they found odds and ends from about fifteen earlier burglaries. There had been a rash of break-ins in Santa Fe during the past month by an unknown person whom the newspaper had labeled The Cat. Now The Cat had been captured.

"He never even *had* a mother," said Charlie. "The whole thing was a lie."

Victor wiped up a last piece of French toast from his plate. "I never trust those religious types," he said.

They were having a late breakfast at the Spa City Diner and waiting for the bus from New York. Charlie's mother had called at seven o'clock that Tuesday morning asking him to pick her up. Although he thought of himself as happy to see her, he was also uneasy and even suspicious. He had made a date that evening with Doris and he wanted nothing, but nothing to get in the way.

"Not only didn't he have a mother," said Charlie, "but the only reason he went to Santa Fe was to rob houses. Jesus, when you think how I worried."

"You're too soft," said Victor.

But Charlie wasn't listening. Someone was waving to him across the restaurant and he gave a brief nod in reply. In the half hour in which they had been eating, about a dozen people had spoken to Charlie and more had simply stared. This was owing to the publicity.

The offices of the *Daily Saratogian* lay catty-corner across the street from the police station and while Charlie had been honking the horn of the milk truck for Peterson, an enterprising photographer had hurried over to record these moments on film. As a result, Charlie had been all over the front page of the afternoon edition, plus being featured on the six o'clock news of the Albany television stations. This had had various consequences.

For instance, when Charlie returned to the Wholesome Dairy late Monday afternoon, he had been immediately fired. The truck was a wreck, the milk was ruined and angry customers had been calling all day. But after the paper and TV stations began showing pictures of Charlie standing next to the Wholesome Dairy truck wearing his Wholesome Dairy uniform as Jespersen was being handcuffed, the owner of the dairy had personally telephoned Charlie to offer him a permanent position.

Charlie had refused. He refused despite the fact that the Pinkertons had turned him down for a job, saying that he appeared to lack the stable personality required of a first-class Pinkerton operative. He refused even though it appeared he would have to support his mother, as well as pay for the damage to the milk truck.

Another result of the publicity was that people who had been treating Charlie like a piece of gum stuck to the sole of a shoe now half fell over themselves to be friendly. Five people had offered him jobs: drugstore clerk, used-car salesman, assistant realtor, insurance salesman, bartender. Charlie again refused, suspecting their motivations and even their purity of heart.

"Think of it this way," Victor had said, "they'll always lend you money."

"I don't want their money," said Charlie.

David Jespersen had been charged with the three murders but refused to talk. From Kathy Marshall, however, the police learned that Jespersen had indeed been Willis Stitt's silent partner. She had agreed to testify in return for not being charged with anything herself. In any case, in Jespersen's home police found the revolver used in two of the murders, as well as a Polaroid camera of the kind that had taken the pictures of McClatchy's head. Throughout Charlie's interviews with the police, the press and the district attorney's office, Chief Peterson had played the role of Charlie's dearest friend. Charlie had been polite but not warm. During these proceedings, he had expected to see Hank Caldwell, but the FBI man had apparently disappeared.

Victor signaled to the waitress for more coffee, then turned back to Charlie. "Let's say that when I found McClatchy's head at the cabin, I'd taken it to the police. What would Jespersen have done then?"

"He would have had to fake Leakey's suicide a lot sooner."

"How did he know I'd find the head?"

"He had Kathy Marshall tell Ruth MacDermott that was where Leakey kept his love letters, then he followed you. I expect he should have left the head in the cabin and killed Leakey right then, but Leakey had gone off with the woman in the red pants and Jespersen had to delay. That was probably a mistake. When he finally acted on Sunday, it was too late."

Victor poured several tablespoons of sugar into his coffee. "Was that his biggest mistake?"

"Maybe. But it was also a mistake not to tell me he knew Pease. When Flo Abernathy said that Pease took his dog to Jespersen, then it was clear he was lying."

"And what's going to happen to the head?" asked Victor.

"Peterson wanted to give it to the Racing Museum but McClatchy's family objected. He was buried in Philadelphia. They plan to dig him up and put the head back in place."

"It's better that way," said Victor, "otherwise I'd always worry that I might run into it."

Mabel Bradshaw's bus arrived at the Spa City Diner shortly

after eleven. Charlie and Victor were waiting outside to meet it. It was a cool morning and the sky was clear with the sort of deep blue that made Charlie think of forgetfulness or loss. On the roof of the Spa City Diner stood a statue of a small chestnut filly.

The first person off the bus was a miniature old lady in a black dress and a blue straw hat.

"Is that her?" asked Victor. For the occasion he had exchanged his gray sweat shirt for a bright red turtleneck.

"Wait," said Charlie.

The second person off the bus was a large, rather blowzy woman with blond hair, a tight purple dress and purple gloves that reached her elbows. Draped over one shoulder was a silver fox, while around her neck were several strands of pearls. She hesitated on the bottom step, glanced around and when she saw Charlie, she waved.

"You're kidding," said Victor.

Mabel Bradshaw tottered toward them on spindly high heels. Although sixty-six, she looked fifty. She half fell into Charlie's arms and began to weep. Since Charlie had last seen her, she had dyed her hair and put on thirty pounds. He patted her back. Then, just as abruptly, she stopped weeping, pulled away and said, "Help me with my boxes. There's a dear."

Charlie introduced his mother to Victor.

Mabel held out a hand. Several large rings twinkled from her gloved fingers. "You're cute," she said.

From under the bus, the driver was stacking box after box of Mabel's possessions.

"Is all that stuff yours?" asked Charlie.

"Just a few odds and ends. Where's your car?"

Charlie pointed to the Renault. He was greatly relieved that it wasn't the milk truck. "Did you lose very much in Atlantic City?" he asked.

"Lose? Are you pulling my leg? I won. I won over fifty thousand dollars. Play big, win big—that's my motto. Tomorrow I'm going to see about buying a hotel: a big hotel with lots of red satin and soft things to sit on."

"Fifty thousand dollars?" said Charlie.

"That's right," said his mother. "Didn't you get my lucky parrot? That's how I did it. I never made a bet without that parrot right beside me and when I had my bundle, I sent it to you for safekeeping. That parrot saved my life."

"Aha," said Charlie, not knowing what else to say. He wondered if Doris would mind spending the evening searching through the Saratoga city dump.

Mabel took their arms and led them toward the Renault. "How would you boys like to work for me?" she said. "Charlie, you can be night manager. And you, cutie . . ." She paused to give Victor an affectionate poke, "I'll keep you for room service."

Victor waggled his hips. "Room service is my middle name," he said.

FOR THE BEST IN PAPERBACKS, LOOK FOR THE

In every corner of the world, on every subject under the sun, Penguin represents quality and variety—the very best in publishing today.

For complete information about books available from Penguin—including Puffins, Penguin Classics, and Arkana—and how to order them, write to us at the appropriate address below. Please note that for copyright reasons the selection of books varies from country to country.

In the United Kingdom: Please write to *Dept. JC, Penguin Books Ltd, FREEPOST, West Drayton, Middlesex UB7 0BR.*

If you have any difficulty in obtaining a title, please send your order with the correct money, plus ten percent for postage and packaging, to *P.O. Box No. 11, West Drayton, Middlesex UB7 0BR*

In the United States: Please write to *Consumer Sales, Penguin USA, P.O. Box 999, Dept. 17109, Bergenfield, New Jersey 07621-0120.* VISA and MasterCard holders call 1-800-253-6476 to order all Penguin titles

In Canada: Please write to *Penguin Books Canada Ltd, 10 Alcorn Avenue, Suite 300, Toronto, Ontario M4V 3B2*

In Australia: Please write to *Penguin Books Australia Ltd, P.O. Box 257, Ringwood, Victoria 3134*

In New Zealand: Please write to *Penguin Books (NZ) Ltd, Private Bag 102902, North Shore Mail Centre, Auckland 10*

In India: Please write to *Penguin Books India Pvt Ltd, 706 Eros Apartments, 56 Nehru Place, New Delhi 110 019*

In the Netherlands: Please write to *Penguin Books Netherlands bv, Postbus 3507, NL-1001 AH Amsterdam*

In Germany: Please write to *Penguin Books Deutschland GmbH, Metzlerstrasse 26, 60594 Frankfurt am Main*

In Spain: Please write to *Penguin Books S. A., Bravo Murillo 19, 1° B, 28015 Madrid*

In Italy: Please write to *Penguin Italia s.r.l., Via Felice Casati 20, I-20124 Milano*

In France: Please write to *Penguin France S. A., 17 rue Lejeune, F−31000 Toulouse*

In Japan: Please write to *Penguin Books Japan, Ishikiribashi Building, 2–5–4, Suido, Bunkyo-ku, Tokyo 112*

In Greece: Please write to *Penguin Hellas Ltd, Dimocritou 3, GR−106 71 Athens*

In South Africa: Please write to *Longman Penguin Southern Africa (Pty) Ltd, Private Bag X08, Bertsham 2013*